MAGGIE SHAYNE

WINGS IN THE NIGHT

Published by Silhouette Books
America's Publisher of Contemporary Romance

SILHOUETTE BOOKS

ISBN 0-373-65208-9

WINGS IN THE NIGHT

Copyright © 1999 by Harlequin Books S.A.

The publisher acknowledges the copyright holder
of the individual works as follows:

TWILIGHT PHANTASIES
Copyright © 1993 by Margaret Benson

TWILIGHT MEMORIES
Copyright © 1994 by Margaret Benson

TWILIGHT ILLUSIONS
Copyright © 1994 by Margaret Benson

CONTENTS

MAGGIE SHAYNE

is a national bestselling author whom *Romantic Times Magazine* calls "brilliantly inventive." The author of more than twenty novels for Silhouette Books and a mainstream audience, she loves to imbue her characters with *extra*-special qualities.

For Silhouette Books, she has been included in numerous continuity series, and will launch THE FORTUNES OF TEXAS continuity in September 1999. Readers also rave about THE TEXAS BRAND, her very popular miniseries for Silhouette Intimate Moments. And WINGS IN THE NIGHT, her most requested vampire series for the Silhouette Shadows line, was spun off into a single title called *Born in Twilight*.

Maggie's mainstream novels can be described as "contemporary fantasy."

Maggie has won numerous awards, including a *Romantic Times Magazine* Career Achievement Award. She is also a three-time finalist for the Romance Writers of America's prestigious RITA Award.

In her spare time, Maggie loves collecting gemstones, reading tarot cards, hanging out on the Genie computer network and spending time with her family. They live in a rural community in central New York.

TWILIGHT PHANTASIES

To the real "hearts" of New York, the members
of CNYRW.

And to the young blond man on the balcony high
above Rue Royale.

PROLOGUE

Desires and Adorations,
Wingèd Persuasions and veiled Destinies,
Splendours, and Glooms, and glimmering Incarnations
Of hopes and fears, and twilight Phantasies;
And Sorrow, with her family of Sighs,
And Pleasure, blind with tears, led by the gleam
Of her own dying smile instead of eyes,
Came in slow pomp.

—Percy Bysshe Shelley

March 20, 1793

The stub of a tallow candle balanced on a ledge of cold stone, its flame casting odd, lively shadows. The smell of burning tallow wasn't a pleasant one, but far more pleasant than the other aromas hanging heavily all around him. Damp, musty air. Thick green fungus growing over rough-hewn stone walls. Rat droppings. Filthy human bodies. Until tonight, Eric had been careful to conserve the tallow, well aware he'd be allowed no more. Tonight there was no need. At dawn he'd face the guillotine.

Eric closed his eyes against the dancing shadows that seemed to mock him, and drew his knees closer to his chest. At the far end of the cell a man coughed in awful spasms. Closer, someone moaned and turned in his sleep. Only Eric sat awake this night. The others would face death, as well, but not tomorrow. He wondered again whether his father had suffered this way in the hours before his appointed time. He wondered whether his mother and younger sister, Jaqueline, had made it across the Channel to safety. He'd held the bloodthirsty peasants off as long as he'd been able. If the women were safe he'd consider it well worth the sacrifice of his own pathetic life. He'd never been quite like other people, anyway. Always considered odd. In his own estimation he would not be greatly missed. His thirty-five years had been spent, for the most part, alone.

His stomach convulsed and he bent lower, suppressing a groan. Neither food nor drink had passed his lips in three days. The swill they provided here would kill him more quickly than starvation. Perhaps he'd die before they could behead him. The thought of depriving the bastards of their barbaric entertainment brought a painful upward curve to his parched lips.

The cell door opened with a great groan, but Eric did not look up. He'd learned better than to draw attention to himself when the guards came looking for a bit of sport. But it wasn't a familiar voice he heard, and it was far too civilized to belong to one of those illiterate pigs.

"Leave us! I'll call when I've finished here." The tone held authority that commanded obedience. The door closed with a bang, and still Eric didn't move.

Footsteps came nearer and stopped. "Come, Marquand, I haven't all night."

He tried to swallow, but felt only dry sand in his throat. He lifted his face slowly. The man before him smiled, absently stroking the elaborately knotted silk cravat at his throat. The candlelight made his black hair gleam like a raven's wing, but his eyes glowed even darker. "Who are you?" Eric managed. Speaking hurt his throat after so many days without uttering a word, or downing a drop.

"I am Roland. I've come to help you, Eric. Get to your feet. There isn't much time."

"Monsieur, if this is a prank—"

"I assure you, it is no prank." He reached to grasp Eric's upper arm, and with a tug that seemed to cost him minimal effort at best, he jerked Eric to his feet.

"You—you don't even know me. Why would a stranger wish

to help me now? 'Twould be a risk to your own freedom. Besides, there is naught to be done. My sentence is passed. I die on the morrow. Keep your head, friend. Leave here now."

The man called Roland listened to Eric's hoarse speech, then nodded slowly. "Yes, you are a worthy one, aren't you? Speak to me no more, lad. I can see it pains you. You'd do better to listen. I do know you. I've known you from the time you drew your first breath."

Eric gasped and took a step away from the man. A sense of familiarity niggled at his brain. He fumbled for the candle without taking his eyes from Roland, and when he gripped it, he held it up. "What you say is quite impossible, monsieur. Surely you have mistaken me for someone else." He blinked in the flickering light, still unable to place the man in his memory.

Roland sighed as if in frustration, and blocked the candlelight from his face with one hand. "Get that thing out of my face, man. I tell you I know you. I tell you I've come to help and yet you argue. Can it be you are eager to have your head in a basket?" Eric moved the candle away, and Roland lowered the hand and faced him again. "In your fourth year you fell into the Channel. Nearly drowned, Eric. Have you no memory of the man who pulled you, dripping, from the cold water? The eve of your tenth birthday celebration you were nearly flattened by a runaway carriage. Do you not recall the man who yanked you from the path of those hooves?"

The truth of the man's words hit Eric like a blow, and he flinched. The face so white it appeared chalked, the eyes so black one couldn't see where the iris ended and the pupil began—it was the face of the man who'd been there at both those times, he realized, though he wished to deny it. Something about the man struck him afraid.

"You mustn't fear me, Eric Marquand. I am your friend. You must believe that."

The dark gaze bored into Eric as the man spoke in a tone that was oddly hypnotic. Eric felt himself relax. "I believe, and I am grateful. But a friend is of little use to me now. I know not even the number of hours left me. Is it full dark yet?"

"It is, lad, else I could not be here. But time is short, dawn comes soon. It took longer than I anticipated to bribe the guards to allow me this visit. If you want to live, you must trust me and do as I say without question." He paused, arching his brows and awaiting a response.

Eric only nodded, unable to think for the confusion in his brain.

"Good, then," Roland said. "Now, remove the cravat."

Eric worked at the ragged, dirty linen with leaden fingers. "Tell me what you plan, monsieur."

"I plan to see to it that you do not die," he said simply, as if it were already done.

"I fear no one can prevent tomorrow's fate." Eric finally loosed the knot and slid the cravat from his neck.

"You will not die, Eric. Tomorrow, or any other day. Come here."

Eric's feet seemed to become one with the floor. He couldn't have stepped forward had he wanted to. His eyes widened and he felt his throat tighten.

"I know your fear, man, but think! Am I more fearsome than the guillotine!" He shouted it, and Eric stiffened and looked around him, but not one body stirred.

"Why—why don't they wake?" Roland came forward then, gripping his shoulders. "I don't understand. Why don't they wake?" Eric asked again.

The guard pounded on the door. "Time's up!"

"Five minutes more!" Roland's voice boomed, nearly, Eric thought, rattling the walls. "I'll make it worth your while, man! Now go!"

Eric heard the guard grumble, and then his footsteps shuffle away from the door as he called, "Two minutes, then. No more."

"Blast it, lad. It has to be done. Forgive me for not finding a way to make it less frightening!'' With those words Roland pulled Eric to him with unnatural strength. He pressed Eric's head back with the flat of one hand, and even as Eric struggled to free himself Roland's teeth sank into his throat.

When he opened his mouth to release a scream of unbridled horror, something wet sealed his lips. It sickened him when he understood that it was a wrist, gashed open and pulsing blood. Roland forced the severed vein to him and Eric had no choice but to swallow the vile fluid that filled his mouth.

Vile? No. But warm and salty. With the first swallow came the shocking realization that he wanted more. What was happening to him? Had he lost his sanity? Yes! He must have, for here he was, allowing another man's blood to assuage his painful hunger, his endless thirst. He didn't even cower when the word rushed through his brain like a chilling breeze. *Vampire.* Fear filled his heart even as Roland's blood filled his body. He felt himself weakening, sinking into a dark abyss from which he wanted no escape. It was a far better death than the one the dawn would bring. The blood drugged him, and Roland stepped away.

Eric couldn't stand upright. He felt emptied of everything in him, and he sank to the floor. He didn't feel the impact. His head floated somewhere above him and his skin pricked with a million invisible needles. ''Wh-what have you d-done to me?'' He had to force the words out, and they slurred together as if he were drunk. He couldn't feel his tongue anymore.

''Sleep, my son. When next you wake you will be free of this cell. I promise you that. Sleep.''

Eric fought to keep his eyes from closing, but they did. Vaguely he felt cold hands replacing his soiled cravat. Then he heard Roland pound on the door and call for the guard.

''He'll not live long enough for his execution, I fear.'' Roland's voice seemed to come from far away.

''The hell, you say! He was fine—''

''Look for yourself, man. See how he lies there? Dead before the dawn, I'll wager. I'll send a coach for the body. See to it, will you?''

"For a price, sir.''

"Here, then. And there will be more to follow, if you do it precisely as I say."

"Well, now, if he dies, like you say, I'll see he gets in your coach. But if not, I'll be here to see he keeps his other appointment. Either way he ends up the same. In the ground, eh, mister?'' Harsh laughter filled the cell and the door slammed.

CHAPTER ONE

In the dream she was running. From something, toward something. *Someone.* She plunged through dense forest woven with vines and brambles that clawed at her legs, snared her, pulled her back. Swirls of smoky mist writhed, serpentlike, around her calves. She couldn't even see where her feet touched the ground. All the while she kept calling for him, but, as always, when she woke she couldn't remember his name.

Jet hair stuck to her face, glued there by tears and perspiration. Her lungs swelled like those of a marathon runner after a race. She dragged in breath after ragged breath. Her heart felt ready to explode. Her head spun in ever-tightening circles and she had to close her eyes tightly against the horrible dizziness. She sat up quickly, pushing the damp hair from her forehead, and glanced at the clock beside the bed and then at the fading light beyond the window.

She needn't have done so. The dream assaulted her at the same time each day, just one part of her increasingly irregular sleep patterns. Nighttime insomnia, daytime lethargy and vivid nightmares that were always the same had become a predictable part of her existence. She'd made a habit of rushing to her room for a nap the second she got home from work, knowing it would be the only sleep she was likely to get. She'd sleep like the dead until just before dusk, only to be wakened by that frightening, lingering dream.

The effects slowly faded, and Tamara got to her feet, pulled on her satin robe and padded to the adjoining bathroom, leaving tracks in the deep, silvery pile of the carpet. She twisted the knob on the oversize tub and sprinkled a handful of bath oil beads into the rising water. As the stream of water bubbled and spurted she heard an urgent knock, and she went to the door.

Daniel's silver brows bunched together over pale blue, concern-filled eyes. "Tam? Are you all right?"

She closed her eyes slowly and sighed. She must have cried out again. It was bad enough to be certain her own sanity was slipping steadily out of her grasp, but to worry the man who'd been like a father to her for the past twenty years was too much. "Of course, I'm fine. Why?"

"I...thought I heard you call." His eyes narrowed to study her face. She hoped the circles beneath her eyes didn't show. "Are you sure you're—"

"Fine. I'm fine. I stubbed my toe on the bedpost, that's all." Still he looked doubtful. "You look tired."

"I was about to take a nice hot bath and then I'm down for the night." She smiled to ease his worry, but it turned to a frown when she noted the coat over his arm. "You're going out? Daniel, it's been snowing all day. The roads—"

"I'm not driving, Tam. Curtis is coming to pick me up."

She felt her spine stiffen. Her breath escaped her in a rush. "You're going to spy on that man again, aren't you? Honestly, Daniel, this obsession you have—"

"Spying! It's surveillance. And don't call it obsession, Tamara. It's pure scientific study. You should understand that."

Her brows rose. "It's folklore, that's what it is. And if you keep dogging the poor man's every step he's going to end up dragging you into court. Daniel, you've followed him for months. You have yet to come up with a shred of evidence that he's—"

"Daniel." Curt's voice cut her off, and in a moment he'd hurried up the stairs to join Daniel outside her bedroom door. "Are you ready?"

"And you!" Tamara rushed on as if he'd been privy to the entire conversation. "I can't believe you're encouraging this witch-hunt. For God's sake, the three of us spend every day in a high-tech, brass-and-glass-filled office building in White

Plains. We're living in the nineties, guys. Byram, Connecticut, not fifteenth-century Transylvania!''

Curt stared at her for a moment. Then he tilted his head to one side and opened his arms. She sighed and allowed his embrace. ''Still not sleeping nights?'' His voice came smoothly, softly.

She shook her head against the damp fabric of his coat.

''I'm worried about leaving her alone,'' Daniel said, as if she were not there.

''I have experiments to finish in the basement lab,'' Curt offered. ''I could hang around here, if you want to do the surveillance alone.''

''I don't need a baby-sitter,'' she snapped.

Daniel ignored her. ''I think that's a good idea,'' he said. He leaned over to plant a dry peck on her cheek. ''I'll be back around dawn.''

She pulled from Curt's arms and shook her head in frustration. ''Daniel and I know what we're doing, Tam,'' Curt told her, his tone placating. ''We've been in this business a lot longer than you have. DPI has reams on Marquand. It's not legend.''

''I want to see the files.'' She sniffed and met his gaze.

His lips tightened at the corners. ''Your security clearance isn't high enough.''

It was the answer she'd expected, the same one she got every time she asked to see the data that the Division of Paranormal Investigations had on the alleged vampire, Marquand. She lowered her head and turned from him. His hand on her shoulder stopped her. ''Tamara, don't be angry. It's for your own—''

''I know. For my own good. My tub is going to run over.'' She stepped away from him and closed the door. Curtis would sequester himself in the basement lab and not give her a second thought, she was sure of it. He didn't worry about her the way Daniel did. He did seem to feel he had the right to boss her around more than usual lately. She shrugged, vowing not to worry anymore about Curt's proprietary attitude toward her. She stopped the water in the bathtub and stared down into it for long moments. No hot bath was going to help her sleep. She'd tried everything from warm milk to double doses of a prescription sleep aid she'd pressured her doctor into giving her. Nothing worked. Why go through the motions?

With a frustrated sigh she padded to the French doors. On a whim, she flung them open and stepped out onto the balcony. A purple-black sky, lightening to silvery blue in the west, dropped snowflakes in chaotic choreography. The sun had set fully while she'd been arguing with her insane guardian and his stubborn cohort. She stared, entranced by the simple grace of the dancing snow. All at once she felt she had to be a part of it. Why waste all this nervous energy lying in bed, staring up at the underside of the white canopy? Especially when she knew sleep wouldn't come for hours. Maybe she could exhaust herself into oblivion. How long had it been since she'd been able to put aside her gnawing worry and enjoy some simple pleasure?

She hurried back inside, eager now that the decision was made. She yanked on tight black leggings and a bulky knit sweater, two pairs of socks and furry pink earmuffs. She grabbed her coat and her skates from the closet, dropped them into her duffel bag, shoved her purse in beside them and opened her bedroom door.

For a moment she just listened. The hollow dinosaur of a house was silent. She tiptoed through the hall and down the stairs. She paused at the front door just long enough to stuff her feet into her boots, and then she slipped silently through it.

Crisp air stung her cheeks and her breath made little steam clouds in the falling snow. Twenty minutes of walking and snow-dance watching brought her to the outskirts of Byram. Childish delight warmed her when her destination came into view.

The rink sparkled from its nest amid the town park's shrubbery and carefully pruned elms. Meandering, snow-dusted sidewalks, wrought-iron benches with redwood slatted seats, and trash cans painted a festive green made a wreath around the ice. Tamara hastened to the nearest bench to change into her skates.

When he woke, Eric felt as if his head were stuffed with wet cotton. He'd swung his legs to the floor, landing with unusual clumsiness. He hadn't needed a window to sense the pale blush that still hung in the western sky. It hadn't been the coming of night that had wakened him. Hadn't been that for weeks. Always her cries echoed in his head until he could no longer rest. Fear and confusion were palpable in her wrenching pleas. He felt her need like a barbed hook, snagged through his heart and pulling him. Yet he hesitated. Some preternatural instinct warned him not to act hastily. No sense of imminent danger laced her nightly summons. No physical weakness or life-threatening accident seemed to be the cause. What, then?

That she was able to summon him at all was incredible. No human could summon a vampire. That anything other than mortal danger could rouse him from his deathlike slumber astounded him. He longed to go to her, to ask the questions that burned in his mind. Yet he hesitated. Long ago he'd left this place, vowing to stay clear of the girl for her own sake. He'd hoped the incredible psychic link between them would fade with time and distance. Apparently it had not.

He relaxed for an hour in the comfort of his lair. With the final setting of the sun came the familiar rush of energy. His senses sharpened to the deadly keenness of a freshly whetted blade. His body tingled with a million needles of sensation.

He dressed, then released the multitude of locks on the heavy door. He moved in silence through the pitch-black hall and pushed against a heavy slab of stone at the end. It swung inward easily, without a creak of protest, and he stepped through the opening into what appeared to be an ordinary basement. The door, from this side, looked like a well-stocked wine rack. He pushed it gently closed again and mounted the stairway that led to the main house.

He had to see her. He'd known it for some time, and avoided the knowledge. Her pull was too strong to resist. When her sweet, tormented voice came to him in the velvet folds of his rest, he felt her anguish. He had to know what troubled her so. He moved into the parlor, to the tall window, and parted the drape.

The DPI van sat across from the front gate, as it had every night for two months now. Another reason he needed to exercise caution. The division had begun with a group of pious imbeciles, intent on the destruction of any and everything they did not understand, over a century ago. Rumor had it they were now under the auspices of the CIA, making them a threat not to be taken lightly. They occupied an entire office building in White Plains, according to Eric's information. It was said they had operatives in place all over the United States, and even in Europe. The one outside seemed to have made Eric his personal obsession. As if the front gate were the only way out, he parked there at dark every night and remained until dawn. He was as bothersome to Eric as a noisy fly.

He shrugged into a dark-colored overcoat and left through the French doors off the living room, facing opposite the front gate. He crossed the back lawn, stretching from the house to the sheer, rocky cliff above Long Island Sound. He went to the tall iron fence that completely surrounded his property, and vaulted it without much effort. He moved through the trees, gaining the road several yards behind the intense man who thought he was watching so well.

He walked only a short distance before he stopped, cleared his mind and closed his eyes. He opened himself to the cacophony of sensations that were usually denied access. He winced inwardly at the bombardment. Voices of every tone, inflection and decibel level echoed in his mind. Emotions from terrible fear to delirious joy swept through him. Physical sensations, both pleasure and pain, twisted within him, and he braced himself against the mental assault. He couldn't target an individual's mind any other way, unless that person was deliberately sending him a message—the way she'd been doing.

Gradually he gained mastery over the barrage. He sifted it, searching for her voice, her thoughts. In moments he felt her, and he turned in the direction he knew her to be.

He nearly choked when he drew near the ice rink and caught sight of her. She twirled in the center of the rink, bathed in moonglow, her face turned up as if in supplication—as if she were in love with the night. She stopped, extended her arms with the grace of a ballerina and skated slowly, then faster, carving a figure eight into the ice. She turned then, glided backward over the ice, then turned again, crossing skate over skate, slowing her pace gradually.

Eric felt an odd burning in his throat as he watched her. It had been twenty years since he'd left the innocent, raven-haired child's hospital bed after saving her life. How vividly he recalled that night—the way she'd opened her eyes and clutched his hand. She'd called him by name, and asked him not to go. Called him by name, even though she'd never seen him before that night! It was then he'd realized the strength of the bond between them, and made the decision to leave.

Did she remember? Would she recognize him, if she saw him again? Of course, he had no intention of allowing that. He only wanted to look at her, to scan her mind and learn what caused her nightly anguish.

She skated to a bench near the edge of the ice, pulled off the earmuffs she wore and tossed them down. She shook her head and her hair flew wildly, like a black satin cloak of curls. She shrugged off the jacket and dropped it on the bench. She seemed unconcerned that it slid over the side to land in the snow. She drew a breath, turned and skated off.

Eric opened his mind and locked in on hers, honed his every sense to her. It took only seconds, and once again he marveled at the strength of the mental link between them. He heard her thoughts as clearly as she did.

What he heard was music—the music she imagined as she swooped and swirled around the ice. It faded slightly, and she spoke inwardly to herself. *Axel, Tam, old girl. A little more speed...now!*

He caught his breath when she leapt from the ice to spin one and a half times. She landed almost perfectly, with one leg extended behind her, then wobbled and went down hard. Eric almost rushed out to her. Some nearly unheard instinct whispered a warning and he stopped himself. Slowly he realized she was laughing, and the sound was like crystal water bubbling over stones.

She stood, rubbed her backside and skated away as his gaze followed her. She looped around the far end of the rink. That's when Eric spotted the van, parked in the darkness just across the street. Daniel St. Claire!

He quickly corrected himself. It couldn't be St. Claire. He'd have heard the man's arrival. He would have had to arrive after Eric himself. He looked more closely at the white van, noticing minute differences—that scratch along the side, the tires. It wasn't St. Claire's vehicle, but it was DPI. Someone was watching—not him, but Tamara.

He would have moved nearer, pierced the dark interior with his eyes and identified the watcher, but his foot caught on something and he glanced down. A bag. Her bag. He looked toward Tamara again. She was completely engrossed in her skating. Apparently the one watching her was, as well. Eric bent, snatched up the bag and melted into the shadows. Besides her boots the only thing inside was a small handbag. Supple kid leather beneath his fingers. He took it out.

An invasion of her privacy, yes. He knew it. If the same people were watching her as were watching him, though, he had to know why. If St. Claire had somehow learned of his connection to the girl, this could be some elaborate trap. He removed each item from the bag, methodically examining each one before replacing it. Inside the small billfold he found a plastic DPI keycard with Tamara's name emblazoned so boldly across the front that it hurt his eyes.

"No," he whispered. His gaze moved back to her as he mindlessly dropped the card into the bag, the bag into the duffel, and tossed the lot back toward the place where he'd found it. His heart convulsed as he watched her. So beautiful, so delicate, with diamondlike droplets glistening as if they'd been magically woven into that mane of hair while she twirled beneath the full moon. Could she be his Judas? A betrayer in the guise of an angel?

He attuned his mind to hers with every ounce of power he possessed, but the only sensations he found there were joy and exuberance. All he heard was the music, playing ever more loudly in her mind. Overture to *The Impresario*. She skated in perfect harmony with the urgent piece, until the music stopped all at once.

She skidded to a halt and stood poised on the ice, head cocked slightly, as if she'd heard a sound she couldn't identify. She turned very slowly, making a full circle as her gaze swept the rink. She stopped moving when she faced him, though he knew she couldn't possibly see him there, dressed in black, swathed in shadow. Still, she frowned and skated toward him.

My God, could the connection between them be so strong that she actually sensed his presence? Had she felt him probing her mind? He turned and would have left but for the quickened strokes of her blades over the ice, and the scrape as she skidded to a stop so close to him he felt the spray of ice fragments her skates threw at his legs. He felt the heat emanating from her exertion-warmed body. She'd seen him now. Her gaze burned a path over his back and for the life of him he couldn't walk away from her. Foolish it might have been, but Eric turned and faced her.

She stared for a long moment, her expression puzzled. Her cheeks glowed with warmth and life. The tip of her nose was red. Small white puffs escaped her parted lips and lower, a pulse throbbed at her throat. Even when he forced his gaze away from the tiny beat he felt it pound through him the way Beethoven must have felt the physical impact of his music. He found himself unable to look away from her eyes. They held his captive, as if she possessed the same power of command he did. He felt lost in huge, bottomless orbs, so black they appeared to have no pupils. My God, he thought. She already looks like one of us.

She frowned, and shook her head as if trying to shake the snowflakes from her hair. "I'm sorry. I thought you were..." The explanation died on her lips, but Eric knew. She thought he was someone she knew, someone she was close to. He was.

"Someone else," he finished for her. "Happens all the time. I have one of those faces." He scanned her mind, seeking signs of recognition on her part. There was no memory there, only a powerful longing—a craving she hadn't yet identified. "Good night." He nodded once and forced himself to turn from her.

Even as he took the first step he heard her unspoken plea as if she'd shouted it. *Please, don't go!*

He faced her again, unable to do otherwise. His practical mind kept reminding him of the DPI card in her bag. His heart wanted her cradled in his arms. She'd truly grown into a beauty. A glimpse of her would be enough to take away the breath of any man. The glint of unshed tears in her eyes shocked him.

"I'm sure I know you," she said. Her voice trembled when she spoke. "Tell me who you are."

Her need tore at him, and he sensed no lie or evil intent. Yet if she worked for DPI she could only mean him harm. He sensed the attention of the man in the van. He must wonder why she lingered here.

"You must be mistaken." It tore at his soul to utter the lie. "I'm certain we've never met." Again he turned, but this time she came toward him, one hand reaching out to him. She stumbled, and only Eric's preternatural speed enabled him to whirl in time. He caught her as she plunged forward. His arms encircled her slender frame and he pulled her to his chest.

He couldn't make himself let go. He held her to him and she didn't resist. Her face lay upon his chest, above his pounding heart. Her scent enslaved him. When her arms came to his shoulders, as if to steady herself, only to slide around his neck, he felt he'd die a thousand deaths before he'd let her go.

She lifted her head, tipped it back and gazed into his eyes. "I do know you, don't I?"

CHAPTER TWO

Tamara tried to blink away the drugged daze into which she seemed to have slipped. She stood so close to this stranger that every part of her body pressed against his from her thighs to her chest. Her arms encircled his corded neck. His iron ones clasped tight around her waist. She'd tipped her head back to look into his eyes, and she felt as if she were trapped in them.

He's so familiar!

They shone, those eyes, like perfectly round bits of jet amid sooty sable lashes. His dark brows, just as sooty and thick, made a slash above each eye, and she had the oddest certainty that he would cock one when puzzled or amused in a way that would make her heart stop.

But I don't know him.

His full lips parted, as if he'd say something, then closed once more. How soft his lips! How smooth, and how wonderful when he smiled. Oh, how she'd missed his smile.

What am I saying? I've never met this man before in my life.

His chest was a broad and solid wall beneath hers. She felt his heart thudding powerfully inside it. His shoulders were so wide they invited a weary head to drop upon them. His hair gleamed in the moonlight, as black as her own, but without the riotous curls. It fell instead in long, satin waves over his shoulders, when it wasn't tied back with the small velvet ribbon in what he called a queue. She fingered the ribbon at his nape, having known it was there before she'd touched it. She felt an irrational urge to tug it free and run her fingers through his glorious hair—to pull great masses of it to her face and rub them over her cheeks.

She felt her brows draw together, and she forced her lips to part. "Who *are* you?"

"You don't know?" His voice sent another surge of recognition coursing through her.

"I...feel as if I do, but..." She frowned harder and shook her head in frustration. Her gaze fell to his lips again and she forced it away. The sensation that bubbled in her felt like joyous relief. She felt as if some great void in her heart had suddenly been filled simply by seeing this familiar man. The words that swirled and eddied in her mind, and which she only barely restrained herself from blurting, were absurd. *Thank God you've come back...I've missed you so...please, don't leave me again...I'll die if you leave me again.*

She felt tears filling her eyes, and she wanted to turn away so he wouldn't see them. The pain in his flickered and then vanished, so she wondered if she'd truly seen it there. He stared so intensely, and the peculiar feeling that he somehow saw inside her mind hit her with ridiculous certainty.

She wanted to turn and run away. She wanted him to hold her forever. *I'm losing my mind.*

"No, sweet. You are perfectly sane, never doubt that." His voice caressed her.

She drew a breath. She hadn't spoken the thought aloud, had she? He'd...my God, he'd read her mind.

Impossible! He couldn't have. She stared at his sensual mouth again, licked her lips. Had he read her mind? *I want you to kiss me,* she thought, deliberately.

A silent voice whispered a reply inside her brain—his voice. *A test? I couldn't think of a more pleasant one.*

She watched, mesmerized, as his head came down. His mouth relaxed over hers, and she allowed her lips to part at his gentle nudging. At the instant his moist, warm tongue slipped into her mouth to stroke hers, a jolt went through her. Not a sudden rush of physical desire. No, this felt like an actual electric current, hammering from the point of contact, through her body to exit through the soles of her feet. It rocked her and left her weak.

His hands moved up, over her back. His fingertips danced

along her nape and higher, until he'd buried them in her hair. With his hands at the back of her head he pressed her nearer, tilting her to the angle that best fit him, and preventing her pulling away as his tongue stroked deeper, kindling fires in her belly.

Finally his lips slid away from hers, and she thought the kiss had ended. Instead it only changed form. He trailed his moist lips along the line of her jaw. He flicked his tongue over the sensitized skin just below her ear. He moved his lips caressingly to her throat, and her head fell back on its own. Her hands cupped his head, and pressed him closer. Her eyes fluttered closed and she felt so light-headed she was sure she must be about to faint.

He sucked the tender skin between his teeth. She felt sharp incisors skim the soft flesh as he suckled her there like a babe at its mother's breast. She felt him shudder, heard him groan as if tortured. He lifted his head from her, and his hands straightened hers so he could gaze into her eyes. For an instant there seemed to be light in them—an unnatural glow shining from somewhere beyond the ebony.

His voice, when he spoke, sounded rough and shaky. It was no longer the soothing honey that had coated her ears earlier. "What is it you want of me? And take care not to ask too much, Tamara. I fear I can refuse you nothing."

She frowned. "I don't want—" She sucked air through her teeth, stepping out of his arms. "How do you know my name?"

Slowly the spell faded. She breathed deeply, evenly. What had she done? Since when did she go around kissing strangers in the middle of the night?

"The same way you know mine," he said, his voice regaining some of its former strength and tone.

"I don't know yours! And how could you—why did you…" She shook her head angrily and couldn't finish the sentence. After all, she'd kissed him as much as he'd kissed her.

"Come, Tamara, we both know you summoned me here, so stop this pretense. I only want to know what troubles you."

"Summoned you—I most certainly did not summon you. How could I? I don't even know you!"

One brow shot upward. Tamara's hand flew to her mouth because she'd pictured him with just such an expression. She had no time to consider it, though, since his next odd question came so quickly. "And do you know *him?*"

He glanced toward the street and she followed his gaze, catching her breath when she saw Curt's DPI van parked there. She knew it was his by the rust spot just beneath the side mirror on the driver's door. She could barely believe he had the audacity to spy on her. On an indignant sigh she whispered, "He followed me. Why, that heavy-handed son of a—"

"Very good, although I suspect his reason for being posted there is known to you full well. This was a trap, was it not? Lure me here, and then your attentive friend over there—"

"Lure you here? Why on earth would I lure you here, and how, for God's sake? I told you I've never seen you before."

"You call to me nightly, Tamara. You've begged me to come to you until you've nearly driven me insane."

"I don't think it would be a long trip. I told you, I haven't called you. I don't even know your name."

Again his gaze searched her face and she felt her mind being searched. He sighed, frowning until his brows met. "Suppose you tell me why you think that gent would follow you, then?"

"Knowing Curt, he probably thinks it's for my own good. God knows he tosses that phrase around enough lately." Her anger softened a bit, as she thought it through more thoroughly. "He might be a little worried about me. I know Daniel is…my guardian, that is. Frankly, I'm worried myself. I don't sleep at night anymore—not ever. The only time I feel even slightly like sleeping is during the day. In fact, I've fallen asleep at my desk twice now. I take to my bed the second I get home and sleep like a rock, but only until dusk. Just at nightfall I have terrible nightmares and usually cry out loud enough to convince them both I'm losing my mind, and then I'm up and restless all night lo—'' She broke off, realizing she was blurting her life story to a perfect stranger.

"Please don't stop," he said at once. He seemed keenly interested in hearing more. "Tell me about these nightmares." He must've seen her wariness. He reached out to her, touched her cheek with the tips of his long, narrow fingers. "I only want to help you. I mean you no harm."

She shook her head. "You'll only agree with me that I'm slipping around the bend." He frowned. "Cracking up," she explained. She pointed one finger at her ear and made little circles. "Wacko."

"You most certainly are not...wacko, as you put it." His hand slipped around to the back of her head and he drew her nearer. She didn't resist. She hadn't felt so perfectly at peace in months as she felt in his arms. He held her gently against him, as if she were a small child, and one hand stroked her hair. "Tell me, Tamara."

She sighed, unable to resist the smooth allure of his voice, or of his touch, though she knew it made no sense. "It's dark, and there is a jungle of sorts, and a lot of fog and mist covering the ground so I can't see my feet. I trip a lot as I run. I don't know if I'm running toward something or away from something. I know I'm looking for someone, and in the dream I know that person can help me find my way. But I call and call and he doesn't answer."

He stopped stroking her hair all at once, and she thought he tensed. "To whom do you call?"

"I think that might be what's driving me crazy. I can never remember. I wake as breathless and exhausted as if I really had been running through that forest, sometimes halfway through shouting his name—but I just can't remember."

His breath escaped in a rush. "Tamara, how does the dream make you feel?"

She stepped away from him and studied his face. "Are you a psychologist?"

"No."

"Then I shouldn't be telling you any of this." She tried to pull her gaze from his familiar face. "Because I really don't know you."

She stiffened as her name was shouted from across the ice. "Tammy!"

She grimaced. "I hate when he calls me that." She searched the eyes of her stranger again, and again she felt as if she'd just had a long-awaited reunion with someone she adored. "Are you real, or a part of my insanity?" *No, don't tell me,* she thought suddenly. *I don't want to know.* "I'd better go before Curt worries himself into a stroke."

"Does he have the right to worry?"

She paused, frowning. "If you mean is he my husband, the answer is no. We're close, but not in a romantic way. He's more like a...bossy older brother."

She turned and skated away across the ice toward Curt, but she felt his gaze on her back all the way there. She tried to glance over her shoulder to see if he was still there, but she caught no sight of him. Then she approached Curt and slowed her pace. He'd been hurrying across the ice, toward her.

He gripped her upper arm hard, and marched her off the edge of the ice. On the snowy ground she stumbled on her skates, but he continued propelling her at the same pace until they reached the nearest bench, and then he shoved her down onto the seat.

"Who the hell was that man?"

She shrugged, relieved that Curtis had seen him, too. "Just a stranger I met."

"I want his name!"

She frowned at the authority and anger in his voice. Curt had always been bossy but this was going too far. "We didn't get around to exchanging names, and what business is it of yours, anyway?"

"You're telling me you don't know who that was?" She nodded. "The hell you don't," he exploded. He gripped her shoulders, pulled her to her feet and held her hard. He glared at her and would have frightened her if she hadn't known him so well. "What did you think you were doing sneaking out alone at night like that? Well?"

"Skating! Ouch." His fingers bit into her shoulders. "I was only skating, Curt. You know I can't sleep. I thought some exercise—"

"Bull. You came out here to meet *him*, didn't you?"

"Who? That nice man I was talking to? For God's sake, Curtis, I—"

"Talking to? That's a nice name for it. I saw you, Tammy. You were in his arms."

Anger flared. "I don't care if I had sex with the man in the middle of the rink, Curtis Rogers. I'm a grown woman and what I do is my business. You followed me here! I don't care how worried Daniel gets, I will not put up with you spying on me, and I won't defend my actions to you. Who do you think you are?"

His grip tightened and he shook her once—then again. "The truth, Tammy. Dammit, you'll tell me the truth!" He shook her until her head wobbled on her shoulders. "You know who he was, don't you? You came here to meet him, didn't you? Didn't you!"

"L-let me go...Curt-tis you're-rr...hurt-ting..."

Her vision had blurred from the shaking and the fear that she didn't know Curt as well as she thought she did—but not so much that she couldn't see the dark form silhouetted beyond Curtis. She knew who stood there. She'd felt his presence... maybe even before she'd seen him. She felt something else, too. His blinding anger.

"Take your hands off her," the stranger growled, his voice quivering with barely contained rage.

Curt went rigid. His hands fell to his sides and his eyes widened. Tamara took a step back, her hand moving to massage one tender, bruised shoulder. The heat of the stranger's gaze on her made her look up. Those black eyes had followed the movement of her hand and his anger heated still more.

But how can I know that?

Curtis turned to face him, and took a step backward...away from the man's imposing form. Well, at least she now knew he was real. She couldn't take her gaze from him, nor he from her, it seemed. Her lips throbbed with the memory of his moving over them. She felt as if he knew it. She should say something, she thought vaguely. Sensible or not, she knew the man was about to throttle Curtis.

Before she could think of a suitable deterrent, though, Curtis croaked, "M-Marquand!" She'd never heard his voice sound the way it did.

Tamara felt the shock like a physical blow. Her gaze shot back to the stranger's face again. He regarded Curtis now. A small, humorless smile appeared on his lips, and he nodded to Curt. A sudden move caught her eye, and she glimpsed Curt thrusting a hand inside his jacket, as the bad guys did on television when reaching for a hidden gun. She stiffened in panic, but relaxed when he pulled out only a small gold crucifix, which he held toward Marquand straight-armed, in a white-knuckled grip.

For a moment the stranger didn't move. He stared fixedly at the golden symbol as if frozen. She watched him intently, shivering as her fingers involuntarily touched the spot on her throat, and she recalled the feel of those skimming incisors. Could he truly be a vampire?

The smile returned, sarcastic and bitter. He even chuckled, a sound like distant thunder rumbling from deep in his chest. He reached out to pluck the cross from Curt's hand, and he turned it several times, inspecting it closely. "Impressive," he said, and handed it back. Curt let it fall to the ground and Tamara sighed in relief, but only briefly.

She understood now what the little encounter between her and

Marquand had been all about. She resented it. "You're really Marquand?"

He sketched an exaggerated bow in her direction.

She couldn't hold his gaze, embarrassed at her earlier responses to what, for him, had been only a game. "I can appreciate why you're so angry with my guardian. After all, he's been hounding you to death. However, it might interest you to know that I had no part in it. I've argued on your behalf until I'm hoarse with it. I won't bother to do so anymore. I truly appreciate that you chose not to haul Daniel into court, but I would not suggest you attempt to use me to deliver your messages in future."

She saw his brow cock up again, and she caught her breath. "Your guardian? You said so once before, but I—" His eyes widened. "St. Claire?"

"As if you weren't aware of it before your little performance over there." She shook her head, her fingers once again trailing over the tender spot on her throat. "I might even be able to see the humor in it, if I wasn't already on the brink of—" She broke off and shook her head as her eyes filled, and her airways seemed suddenly blocked.

"Tamara, that isn't what I—"

She stopped him by shaking her head violently. "I'll see he gets your message. He may be an ass, Marquand, but I love him dearly. I don't want him to bear the brunt of a lawsuit."

She turned on her heel. "Tamara, wait! What happened to your parents? How did he—Tamara!" She ignored him, mounting the ice and speeding to the opposite side, where she'd left her duffel bag. She stumbled over the snow to snatch it up, and sat hard on the nearest bench, bending to unlace her skates. Her fingers shook. She could barely see for the tears clouding her vision.

Why was she reacting so strongly to the man's insensitive ploy? Why did she feel such an acute sense of betrayal?

Because I'm losing my mind, that's why.

Anger made her look up. She felt it as if it were a palpable thing. She yanked one skate off, stomped her foot into a boot and unlaced the other without looking. Her gaze was on Marquand, who had Curtis by the lapels now, and was shaking him the way Curt had shaken her a few moments ago. When he stopped he released Curt, shoving him away in the same motion. Curt landed on his backside in the snow. Marquand's back was all she could see, but she heard his words clearly, though not with her ears. *If I ever see you lay hands on her again, Rogers, you will pay for it with your life. Do I make myself sufficiently clear?*

Sufficiently clear to me, Tamara thought. Curt seemed to be in no danger of being murdered at the moment. She put her skates in her bag and slipped away while they were still arguing.

Pain like a skewer running the length of his breastbone, Eric stroked the pink fur of the earmuffs she'd abandoned in her rush to get away from him. She'd left her coat, too. He carried it slung over one arm as he followed the two. Rogers had caught up to Tamara only a few minutes after she'd left. He kept pace with her angry strides, talking constantly in his efforts to end her anger.

"I'm sorry, Tammy. I swear to you, I didn't mean to hurt you. Can't you understand I was scared half out of my mind when I saw you in his arms? My God, don't you know what could've happened?"

He scanned the bastard's mind with his own, and found no indication that Tamara was in danger from him. He did the same after they'd entered Daniel St. Claire's gloomy Victorian mansion, unwilling to leave her in their hands until he could be certain. And even then he couldn't leave.

How the hell had St. Claire managed to become her guardian? When Eric had left her all those years ago she'd had two adoring parents who'd nearly lost their minds when they'd thought they might lose her. He could still see them—the small Miranda, a frail-looking woman with mouse brown hair and pretty green eyes brimming with love whenever she glanced at her adorable child. She'd been in hysterics that night at the hospital. Eric had seen her clutching the doctor's white coat, shaking her head fast at what he was telling her as tears poured unchecked over her face. Her husband's quiet devastation had been even more painful to witness. Kenneth had seemed deflated, sinking into a chair as if he'd never rise again, his blond hair falling over one eye.

What in hell had happened to them? He sank to a rotted, snow-dusted stump outside the mansion, his head in his hands. "I never should have left her," he whispered into the night. "My God, I never should have left her."

He remained there in anguish until the sky began to pale in the east. She now thought he'd only used her to make a point to St. Claire. She obviously had no conscious memory of him, nor knowledge of the connection between them. She called to him while in the throes of her subconscious mind—in a dream. She couldn't even recall his name.

She paused outside Daniel's office door to brace herself, her hand on the knob. Last night she'd avoided further confrontation with Curt by pleading exhaustion, a lie he'd believed since he knew how little sleep she'd been getting. This morning she'd deliberately remained in her room, feigning sleep when Daniel called from the doorway. She'd known he wouldn't wake her if he thought she was finally sleeping. She'd waited until he left for DPI headquarters in White Plains, then had got herself ready and driven in late, in her battered VW Bug. Her day had been packed solid with the trivial work they gave her there. Her measly security clearance wasn't high enough to allow her to work on anything important. Except for Jamey Bryant. He was important—to her, at least. He was only a class three clairvoyant in DPI's book, but he was class one in hers. Besides, she loved the kid.

She sighed, smiling as she thought of him, then stiffened her spine for the coming encounter. She gripped the knob more tightly, then paused as Curt's voice came through the wood.

"Look at her! I'm telling you, something is happening and you're a fool if you don't see it."

"She's confused," Daniel said, sounding pained. "I admit, the proximity is having an unexpected effect on her, but she can't be blamed for that. She has no idea what's happening to her."

"*You* think. *I* think she ought to be under constant observation."

She grew angry fast, and threw the door open. "Do you have any idea how tired I am of being talked about like one of your cases?"

Both men looked up, startled. They exchanged uneasy glances and Daniel came out of his chair so fast it scraped over the tiled floor. "Now, Tam, what makes you think we were discussing you? Actually, we were talking about a case. One we obviously disagree about."

She smirked, crossing her arms over her chest. "Oh, really? Which case?"

"Sorry, Tammy," Curt snapped. "Your security clearance isn't high enough."

"When has it ever been high enough?"

"Tam, please." Daniel came toward her, folded her in a gentle embrace and kissed her cheek. He stood back and searched her face. "Are you all right?"

"Why on earth wouldn't I be?" His concern softened her somewhat, but she was still sick and tired of his coddling.

"Curt told me you met Marquand last night." He shook his head. "I want you to tell me everything that happened. Everything he said to you, did to you. Did..." Daniel paled right before her eyes. "Did he touch you?"

"Had her crushed against him like he'd never let go," Curt exploded. "I told you, Daniel—"

"I'd like to hear her tell me." His pale blue eyes sought hers again. They dropped to the collar of her turquoise turtleneck, under the baggy white pullover sweater. She thought he would collapse.

Curtis seemed to notice her choice of attire at the same instant, and he caught his breath. "Tammy, my God, did he—"

"He most certainly did not! Do you two have any idea how insane you both sound?"

"Show me," Daniel said softly.

She shook her head and expelled a rush of air. "All right, but first I want to explain something. Marquand seems to be very well aware of what you two think he is. This meeting at the rink last night, I think, was his way of sending you a message, and the message is lay off. I don't think he was kidding." She hooked her first two fingers beneath the neck of the shirt and pulled it down to show them the blue-and-violet bruise he'd left on her neck.

Daniel gasped. "Look closely, you two. There are no fang marks, just a...well, let's be frank about it, a hickey. I let a perfect stranger give me a hickey, which should illustrate to you both just how much stress I've been under lately. Between this sleep disorder and your overprotectiveness, I feel like I'm in a pressure cooker." Daniel was leaning closer, breathing down her neck as he inspected the bruise.

He satisfied himself and put a hand on her shoulder. "Did he hurt you, sweetheart?"

She couldn't stop the little smile that question evoked, even though she erased it immediately. "Hurt her?" Curtis slapped one hand on the surface of the desk. "She was loving every minute of it." He glared at her. "Don't you realize what could've happened out there?"

"Of course I do, Curtis. He could've ripped my jugular open and sucked all my blood out and left me dying there on the ice with two holes in my throat!"

"If I hadn't scared him off," Curt began.

"Keep your story straight, Curt. It was he who scared you

off. You were shaking me until my teeth rattled, if you remember correctly. If he hadn't come to my defense I might have come into work wearing a neck brace today.''

Curt clamped his jaw shut under Daniel's withering gaze. Daniel shifted his glance to Tamara again. "He came to your defense, you say?'' She nodded. "Hmm.''

"And,'' Tamara went on, almost as an afterthought, "he took the crucifix right out of Curt's hand. It did not even burn a brand in his palm, or whatever it's supposed to do. Doesn't that prove anything?''

"Yeah.'' Curt wore a sulking-child look on his face. "Proves vampires are not affected by religious symbols.''

Tamara rolled her eyes, then heard Daniel mutter, "Interesting.'' She felt as if she, even with her strange symptoms, was the only sane person in the room.

"I know you think we're overreacting to this, Tam,'' Daniel told her. "But I don't want you leaving the house after dark anymore.''

She bristled. "I will go where I want, when I want. I am twenty-six years old, Daniel, and if this nonsense doesn't stop, then I'm…'' She paused long enough to get his full attention before she blurted, "Moving out.''

"Tam, you wouldn't—''

"Not unless you force me, Daniel. And if I find either you or Curt following me again, I'll consider myself forced.'' She felt a lump in her throat at the pained look on Daniel's face. She made her tone gentler when she said, "I'm going home now. Good night.''

CHAPTER THREE

Her mental cries woke him earlier tonight than last. Eric stood less than erect and squeezed his eyes shut tight, as if doing so might clear his mind. Rising before sunset produced an effect in him not unlike what humans feel after a night of heavy drinking. Bracing one hand upon the smooth mahogany, his fingertips brushing the satin lining within, he focused on Tamara. He wanted only to comfort her. If he could ease the torment of her subconscious mind, though she might not be fully aware of it, she'd feel better. She might even be more able to sleep. He couldn't be sure, though. Her situation was unique, after all.

He focused on her mind, still hearing her whispered pleas. *Where are you, Eric? Why won't you come to me? I'm lost. I need you.*

He swallowed once, and concentrated every ounce of his power into a single invisible beam of thought, shooting through time and space, directed at her. *I am here, Tamara.*

I can't see you!

The immediate response shocked him. He hadn't been certain he could make her aware of his thoughts. Again he focused. *I am near. I will come to you soon, love. Now you must rest. You needn't call to me in your dreams anymore. I have heard—I will come.*

He awaited a response, but felt none. The emotions that reached him, though, were tense, uncertain. He wanted to ease her mind, but he'd done all he could for the moment. The sun far above, though unseen by him, was not unfelt. It sapped his strength. He took a moment to be certain of his balance and crossed slowly to the hearth, bending to rekindle the sparks of this morning's fire. That done, he used a long wooden match to ignite the three oil lamps posted around the room. With fragrant cherry logs emitting aromatic warmth, and the golden lamplight, the Oriental rugs over the concrete floor and the paintings he'd hung, the place seemed a bit less like a tomb in the bowels of the earth. He sat himself carefully in the oversize antique oak rocking chair, and allowed his muscles to relax. His head fell heavily back against the cushion, and he reached, without looking, for the remote control on the pedestal table beside him. He thumbed a button. His heavy lids fell closed as music surrounded him.

A smile touched his lips as the bittersweet notes brought a memory. He'd seen young Amadeus perform in Paris. 1775, had it been? So many years. He'd been enthralled—an ordinary boy of seventeen, awestruck by the gift of another, only two years older. The sublime feeling had remained with him for days after that performance, he recalled. He'd talked about it until his poor mother's ears were sore. He'd had Jaqueline on the brink of declaring she'd fallen in love with a man she'd never met, and she'd teased and cajoled until he'd managed to get her a seat at his side for the next night's performance. His sister had failed to see what caused him to be so impressed. "He is good," she'd declared, fanning herself in the hot, crowded hall. "But I've seen better." He smiled at the memory. She hadn't been referring to the young man's talents, but to his appearance. He'd caught her peering over her fan's lacy edge at a skinny dandy she considered "better."

He sighed. He'd thought it tragic that a man of such genius had died at thirty-five. Lately he'd wondered if it was so tragic, after all. Eric, too, had died at thirty-five, but in a far different manner. His was a living death. All things considered, he hadn't convinced himself that Mozart had suffered the less desirable fate. Of the two of them, Mozart must be the most serene. He couldn't possibly be the most alone. There were times when he wished the guillotine had got to him before Roland had.

Such maudlin thoughts on such a delightfully snowy night? I

*don't recall you were all that eager to meet the blade, at the
time.*

Roland! Eric's head snapped up, buzzing with energy now
that the sun had set. He rose and hurriedly released the locks,
to run through the hall and take the stairs two at a time. He
yanked the front door open just as his dearest friend mounted
the front steps. The two embraced violently, and Eric drew Roland inside.

Roland paused in the center of the room, cocking his head
and listening to Mozart's music. "What's this? Not a recording,
surely! It sounds as if the orchestra were right here, in this very
room!"

Eric shook his head, having forgotten that the last time he'd
seen Roland he hadn't yet installed the state-of-the-art stereo
system, with speakers in every room. "Come, I'll show you."
He drew his friend toward the equipment, stacked near the far
wall, and withdrew a CD from its case. Roland turned the disc
in his hand, watching the light dance in vivid rainbows of green,
blue and yellow.

"They had no such inventions where I have been." He returned the disc to its case, and replaced it on the shelf.

"Where *have* you been, you recluse? It's been twenty years."
Roland had not aged a day. He still had the swarthy good looks
he'd had as a thirty-two year old mortal and the build of an
athlete.

"Ahh, paradise. A tiny island in the South Pacific, Eric. No
meddling humans to contend with. Just simple villagers who
accept what they see instead of feeling the need to explain it. I
tell you, Eric, it's a haven for our kind. The palms, the sweet
smell of the night—"

"How did you live?" Eric knew he sounded doubtful. He'd
always despised the loneliness of this existence. Roland embraced it. "Don't tell me you've taken to tapping the veins of
innocent natives."

Roland's brows drew together. "You know better. The animals there keep me in good stead. The wild boar are particularly—"

"Pigs' blood!" Eric shouted. "I think the sun must have penetrated your coffin! Pigs' blood! Ach!"

"Wild boars, not pigs."

"Great difference, I'll wager." Eric urged Roland toward the velvet-covered antique settee. "Sit. I'll get refreshment to restore your senses."

Roland watched suspiciously as Eric moved behind the bar, to the small built-in refrigerator. "What have you, a half dozen freshly killed virgins stored in that thing?"

Eric threw back his head and laughed, realizing just how long it had been since he'd done so. He withdrew a plastic bag from the refrigerator, and rummaged beneath the bar for glasses. When he handed the drink to Roland, he felt himself thoroughly perused.

"Is it the girl's nightly cries that trouble you so?"

Eric blinked. "You've heard her, too?"

"I hear her cries when I look inside your mind, Eric. They are what brought me to you. Tell me what this is about."

Eric sighed, and took a seat in a claw-footed, brocade cushioned chair near the fireplace. Few coals glowed in this hearth. He really ought to kindle it. Should some nosy human manage to scale the gate and breach the security systems, they might well notice that smoke spiraled from the chimney, but no fire warmed the grate.

Reading his thoughts, Roland set his glass aside. "I'll do that. You simply talk."

Eric sighed again. Where to begin? "I came to know of a child, right after you left last time. A beautiful girl, with raven curls and cherub's cheeks and eyes like glossy bits of coal."

"One of the Chosen?" Roland sat forward.

"Yes. She was one of those rare humans with a slight psychic connection to the undead, although, like most, she was completely unaware of it. I've found that there are ways of detecting the Chosen, aside from our natural awareness of them, you know.''

Roland looked around from where he'd hunkered before the hearth. "Really?''

Eric nodded. "All those humans who can be transformed, those we call Chosen, share a common ancestor. Prince Vlad the Impaler.'' He glanced sharply at Roland. "Was he the first?''

Roland shook his head. "I know your love of science, Eric, but some things are better left alone. Go on with your story.''

Eric felt a ripple of exasperation at Roland's tight-lipped stance on the subject. He swallowed his irritation and continued. "They also share a rare blood antigen. We all had it, as humans. It's known as Belladonna. Only those with both these unlikely traits can become vampires. They are the Chosen.''

"Doesn't seem like an earth-shattering discovery to me, Eric. We've always been able to sense the Chosen ones, instinctively.''

"But other humans haven't. Some of them have now discovered the same things I have. DPI knows about it. They can pinpoint Chosen humans, and then watch them, and wait for one of us to approach. I believe that is precisely what has happened with Tamara.''

"Perhaps you need to back up a bit, old friend,'' Roland said gently.

Eric pushed one hand through his black hair, lifting it from his shoulders and clenching a fist in the tangles. "I couldn't stay away from her, Roland. God help me, I tried, but I couldn't. Something in her tugged at me. I used to look in on her as she slept. You should've seen her then. Sooty lashes on her rosy cheeks, lips like a small pink bow.'' He looked up, feeling absurdly defensive. "I never meant her harm, you know. How could I? I adored the child.''

Roland frowned. "This should not trouble you. It happens all the time, this unseen bond between our kind and the Chosen. Many was the night I peered in upon you as a boy. Rarely to find you asleep, though. Usually, you were awake and teasing your poor sister.''

Eric absorbed that information with dawning understanding. ''You never told me. I'd thought you only came to me when I was in danger.''

''I'm sorry we haven't discussed this matter before, Eric. It simply never came up. You only *saw* me those times you were in danger. There was little time for discretion when a coach was about to flatten you, or when I pulled you spluttering from the Channel.''

''Then you felt the same connection to me that I felt for her?''

''I felt a connection, yes. An urge to protect. I can't say it's the same because I haven't experienced what you felt for the child. But, Eric, many young ones over the centuries have had a vampire as a guardian and never even known it. After all, we don't go to them to harm, or transform, or even make contact. Only to watch over, and protect.''

Eric's shoulders slumped forward, so great was his relief. He shook his head once and resumed his story. ''I woke one night to sense her spirit fading. She was slipping away so steadily I was barely able to get to her in time.'' The same pain he'd felt then swept over him now, and his voice went lower. ''I found her in hospital, her tiny face whiter than the sheets tucked around her. Her lips...they were blue. I overheard a doctor telling her parents that she'd lost too much blood to survive, and that her type was so rare no donors had been located. He told them to prepare themselves. She was dying, Roland.''

Roland swore softly.

''So you see my dilemma. A child I'd come to love lay dying, and I knew I alone had the power to save her.''

''You didn't transform her! Not a small child, Eric. She'd be better dead than to exist as we must. Her young mind could never grasp—''

''I didn't transform her. I probably couldn't if I'd tried. She hadn't enough blood left to mingle with mine. I saw another option, though. I simply opened my vein and—''

"She drank from you?''

Eric closed his eyes. "As if she were dying of thirst. I suppose, in a manner, she was. Her vitality began to return at once. I was ecstatic.''

"You had right to be.'' Roland grinned now. "You saved the child. I've never heard of anything like this happening before, Eric, but apparently, it worked.'' He paused, regarding Eric intensely. "It did work, did it not? The child lives?''

Eric nodded. "Before I left her bedside, Roland, she opened her eyes and looked at me, and I swear to you, I felt her probing my mind. When I turned to go she gripped my hand in her doll-sized one and she whispered my name. 'Eric,' she said. 'Don't go just yet. Don't leave me.'''

"My God.'' Roland sank back onto the settee, blinking as if he were thunderstruck. "Did you stay?''

"I couldn't refuse her. I stayed the night at her bedside, though I had to hide on the window ledge every time someone entered the room. When they discovered the improvement in her, the place was a madhouse for a time. But they soon saw that she would be fine, and decided to let the poor child rest.''

"And then?''

Eric smiled softly. "I held her on my lap. She stayed awake, though she needed to rest, and insisted I invent story upon story to tell her. She made me sing to her, Roland. I'd never sung to anyone in my existence. Yet the whole time she was inside my mind, reading my every thought. I couldn't believe the strength of the connection between us. It was stronger even than the one between you and me.''

Roland nodded. "Our blood only mixed. Yours was nearly pure in her small body. It's no wonder... What happened?''

"Toward dawn she fell asleep, and I left her. I felt it would only confuse the sweet child to have contact with one of us. I took myself as far away as I could, severed all contact with her.

I refused even to think of seeing her again, until now. I thought the mental bond would weaken with time and distance. But it hasn't. I've only been back in the western hemisphere a few months, and she calls to me every night. Something happened to her parents after I'd left her, Roland. I don't know what, but she ended up in the custody of Daniel St. Claire."

"He's DPI!" Roland shot to his feet, stunned.

"So is she," Eric muttered, dropping his forehead into his hand.

"You cannot go to her, Eric. You mustn't trust her, it could be your end."

"I *don't* trust her. As for going to her…I have no choice about that."

Even while Tamara was arguing with Daniel and Curtis, he'd been on her mind. All day she had been unable to get that mysterious stranger—who didn't seem a stranger at all—out of her thoughts. She'd only managed to cram him far to the back, to allow herself to concentrate on her work. Now that she was home, in the secure haven of her room, and now that she'd wakened from her after-work nap, she felt refreshed, energized and free to turn last night's adventure over in her mind.

She paused and frowned. Since when did she wake refreshed? She usually woke trembling, breathless and afraid. Why was tonight different? She glanced out at the snow-spotted sky, and realized it was fully dark. She normally woke from her nightmare just at dusk. She struggled to remember. It seemed to her she *had* had the dream—or she'd begun to. She remembered the forest and the mists, the brambles and darkness. She remembered calling that elusive name….

And hearing an answer. Yes. From very far away she'd heard an answer; a calm, deep voice, full of comfort and strength, had promised to come to her. He'd told her to rest. She'd felt uncertain, until the music came. Soft strains she thought to be Mozart—something from *Elvira Madigan*—soothed her taut nerves.

She allowed a small smile. Maybe she was getting past this thing, whatever it was. The smile died when she wondered if that was true, or whether she was only exchanging one problem for another. The man from the ice rink filled her mind again. Marquand—the one Daniel insisted was a vampire. He'd kissed her and, much as she hated to admit it, she'd responded to that kiss with every cell in her body.

She rose slowly from her bed and tightened the single sash that held the red satin robe around her. She leaned over her dressing table and examined the bruised skin of her neck in the mirror. Her fingers touched the spot. She recalled the odd, swooning sensation she'd experienced when he'd sucked the skin between his teeth, and wondered at it.

Lack of sleep, and too much stress.

But he knew my name....

Simple enough to answer that one. He'd done a little research on the man who'd been harassing him. Daniel was her legal guardian. It was a matter of public record.

Then why did he seem so surprised when I told him that?

Good acting. He must have known. He just assumed I'd be the easiest, most effective way to get his point across.

She frowned at her reflection, not liking the look of disappointment she saw there. She tried to erase it. "He only wanted to scare Daniel into laying off, so he followed me to the rink for that little performance. Imagine him going so far as to actually..."

She pressed her palm to the mark on her throat, and turned from the mirror. She'd failed to convince herself that was all there had been to it. So many things about the man defied explanation. Why did he seem so familiar to her? How had he made her feel as if he were reading her thoughts? What about the way she'd seemed to hear what he said, when he hadn't even spoken? And what about this...this *longing.*

Blood flooded her cheeks and a fist poked into her stomach. Desire. She recognized the feeling for what it was. Foolish

though it was, Tamara was lusting after a man she didn't know—
a man she felt as if she'd known forever. She had to admit, at
least to herself, that the man they called Marquand stirred reactions in her as no other man ever had.

As she stood she slowly became aware of a peculiar light-
headedness stealing over her. Not dizziness, but rather a floating
sensation, though her bare feet still connected her to the floor.
A warm whirlwind stirred around her ankles, twisting up her
legs, swishing the hem of the robe so the satin brushed over her
calves.

She blinked slowly, pressing her palm to her forehead, waiting
for the feeling to pass. The French doors blew open all at once,
as if from a great gust, and the wind that surged through felt
warm, heady.... It smelled faintly of bay rum.

Impossible. It's twenty degrees out there.

Yet it lingered; the warmth and the scent. She felt a pull—a
mental magnet she was powerless to resist. She faced the heated
blast, even as it picked up force. The scarlet satin sailed behind
her. It twisted around her legs like a twining serpent.

Like the mist in my dream.

Her hair billowed around her face. The robe's sash snapped
against her thighs. She moved toward the doors even as she told
herself not to. She resisted, but the pull was stronger than her
own will. Her feet scuffed over the soft carpet, then scraped over
the cold, wet wood floor of the balcony. The whirlwind surrounded her, propelled her to the rail. She heard the doors slam
behind her, and didn't even turn. Her eyes probed the darkness
below. Would this unseen hand pull her right over? She didn't
think she'd be able to stop it if it wanted to.

God, what is happening to me?

She resisted and the wind stiffened. The sash whipped loose
and the robe blew back. No part of her went untouched by this
tempest. Like invisible hands it swirled around her thighs, between them. Her breasts quivered. Her nipples stood erect and
pulsing. She throbbed with heightened awareness, her flesh hy-

persensitive to the touch of the wind as it mercilessly stroked her body. Her heart raced, and before she could stop herself she'd let her head fall back, closed her eyes and moaned softly at the intensity of the sensations.

All at once it simply stopped. The warmth and the essence of bay rum lingered, but that intimate whirlwind died slowly, giving her control of her body once more. She didn't know what it had been. A near breakdown? A mental lapse of some sort? Whatever, it was over.

Shaken, she pushed her hands through her hair, uncaring that her robe still hung gaping, having been driven down, baring one shoulder. She turned to go back inside.

He stood so close she nearly bumped into his massive chest. Her head came up fast and her breath caught in her throat. His black eyes seemed molten as they raked her. The mystery wind stirred gently. She could see silver glints behind those onyx eyes, and she felt their heat touch her as the wind had when his gaze moved slowly upward from her bare feet. She felt it scorching her as it lifted, over her legs. The hot gaze paused at the mound of black curls at the apex of her thighs and she thought she'd go up in flames. Finally it moved again, with deliberate slowness over her stomach. She commanded her arms to come to life— to pull her robe together. They did not respond. His eyes seemed to devour her breasts, and she knew her nipples stiffened under that heated stare. The man licked his lips and she very nearly groaned aloud. She closed her eyes, but they refused to stay that way. They opened again, against her will. They focused on his, though she didn't want to see the lust in his eyes. Finally he looked at her throat. The bruise he'd put on her there seemed to come alive with his gaze. It tingled, and she felt the muscle beneath the skin twitch spasmodically. She saw his Adam's apple move as he swallowed. He closed his eyes briefly, and when they opened again they locked with hers, refusing to allow her to look away.

Her arms regained feeling and she jerked the robe together in a move that showed her anger. "You," she whispered. She felt fear and confusion. More than that, she felt sheer joy to see him again. She refused to let him see it. "What are you doing here?"

CHAPTER FOUR

"Waiting for you," he said slowly, watching her.

Her mind rebelled against what that implied. "That's ridiculous. How could you have known I'd come out here?"

The intensity of his gaze boring into her eyes was staggering. "I summoned you here, Tamara…just as you've summoned me nightly with your cries."

Her brows drew together so far it hurt. She shook her head in denial as she searched his face. "You said that before. I still don't know what you mean."

"Tamara…" He lifted one hand in slow motion. He turned it gracefully at the wrist, and trailed the backs of his long fingers downward, over her face. She closed her eyes involuntarily at the pure rapture his touch evoked, but quickly forced them open again and took a step back. "Listen to your heart. It wants to tell you—"

"Then I *do* know you!" She felt as if there were a bird trapped in her stomach, flapping its wings desperately. Her eyes tugged at his as she tried to pull the answer from their endless depths. "I thought so before. Tell me when we met, Marquand. You seem so…familiar to me." *Familiar* wasn't the word that had been on her lips. He seemed precious to her—like someone she'd cherished once, someone she'd lost.

She saw the indecision in his eyes, and a glimmer that might have been pain, before he closed them and shook his head. "You will remember in time. I cannot force it on you—your mind is not yet ready. For now, though, I would ask that you simply trust me. I will not harm you, Tamara."

His eyes opened again, and danced over her face. The way he looked at her made her feel as if he couldn't do so enough to appease him, as if he were trying to absorb her through his eyes. She stilled her responses to the feeling, and reminded herself of the game he'd played with her last night. Her shoulders squared. Her chin lifted.

"Your message was delivered, Marquand. Daniel knows about our meeting and your little...performance. I made sure he understood." As she spoke her fingers touched the still-tender skin at her throat. "It probably won't change anything, though. He doesn't listen to me where you're concerned, so you can see how ineffective this conversation will be. Leave me alone. If you have something to say to Daniel, say it to him in person."

He listened...so well it seemed he heard her thoughts as well as her words. When she finished he tilted his head very slightly to one side. "You believe I kissed you only to make a point with St. Claire," he stated, his words slow, carefully enunciated and laced with the barest hint of an accent that she had yet to place. "And the thought causes you pain."

She released a clipped sigh and shook her head. "Why would it cause me pain? I don't know you. I don't care—"

"You felt drugged when I kissed you, sweet Tamara. You felt the ground tilt beneath you, and the sky above begin to spin. Your heart raced, your pulse roared in your temples. Your skin came to life with sensation. In those moments, as I held you, nothing else existed. No," he said when she shook her head fast, and parted her lips to blurt angry denials. "No, don't. I know what you felt, because I felt it, too. The touch of your hands, the taste of your mouth, the feel of your body pressed to mine sent me to the very edge of my control."

She felt the blood rush into her face. Her cheeks burned hotter with his every word, and yet the familiar knot of longing formed in the pit of her stomach. She wanted to tell him he was crazy to believe that, but she couldn't seem to form the words.

Again his hand rose to her face, and she didn't pull away this time. She couldn't say why, but she felt like crying. "Tamara, I swear to you, I did not know you were even acquainted with

St. Claire until you said the words. I came to you because you begged me to do so. In your dreams you begged me to come.''

Her eyes had begun to drift closed as his hand stroked her cheek, but they flew wide now. She searched her brain frantically. How could he know about the dreams? She shook her head quickly. ''No, that isn't true.''

''What isn't true? That you dream each night before dusk? That the dreams are testing your sanity, Tamara? That you cry out to someone in your sleep and cannot recall the name when you wake? Do not forget, you confided all of these things to me last night.''

Relief nearly made her limp. ''That's right, I did.'' She had told him about her nightmares. That explained why he knew.

''The dream was different tonight, though,'' he said softly.

Again her eyes widened. It had been different. He couldn't know that. She hadn't told him that. She swallowed the lump in her throat. ''The name I call, I can't remember what it is, but I know it isn't Marquand. Why do you want to play with my mind?''

''I want only to ease your mind. It is true, you have never cried my surname. It is my first name you call in your sleep.'' His hand had fallen from her face, to gently stroke her hair.

Breathlessly she whispered, ''I don't even know your first name. So it can't be—''

''Yes, you do, Tamara.'' His gaze took on a new dimension as he stared into her eyes. ''You know my name. Say it.''

And she did. Just like that, she knew the name she'd cried over and over again in her recurring dream. She knew it as well as she knew her own. The shroud had been lifted from her memory, and she knew. But it couldn't be him. She shook her head. ''You aren't—''

''I am.'' Both his hands rested on her shoulders now, and he squeezed gently. She winced inwardly because he'd put pressure on the spots where Curt had held her last night, and the skin there had bruised. He immediately readjusted his grip on her, as if he'd sensed her discomfort at the instant she'd felt it. "Say it, Tamara."

Choking on unshed tears, she croaked, "Eric?"

He nodded, his face relaxing in an approving half smile. "Yes. Eric. If you require confirmation, I'm certain your St. Claire can provide it."

She looked at the floor, her relief so great the muscles of her neck relaxed. She didn't need confirmation. She knew he told the truth. Why this intense relief, though? And why had she dreamed of him in the first place?

"You've begged me to come to you, Tamara, and I am here." He caught her chin in gentle fingers, and lifted her face to him. "I'm here."

She wanted to fling herself into his arms. She wanted to hold him desperately and beg him not to leave her ever again. But that was crazy. It was insane. *She* was insane. As tears spilled over and rolled slowly down her face, she shook her head. "This isn't happening. It isn't real. I'm hallucinating, or it's just another dream. That's all. It isn't real."

He pulled her against him suddenly, his arms going around her, his hands stroking her back and shoulders, lifting her hair, caressing her nape. "It is real, Tamara. I am real, and what you feel for me is real...more real, I think, than anything else in your life." His head turned and she felt his lips pressed to her hair just above her temple...lower, to her cheekbone...lower, to the hollow of her cheek. His voice uneven, he spoke near her ear. "How did St. Claire manage to get custody of you? What happened to your family?"

She found herself relaxing against him, allowing his embrace to warm and comfort her. "I was six when I fell through a plate glass window," she told him, her voice barely audible to her own ears. "I severed the arteries in both wrists and nearly bled to death. They called it a miracle when I pulled through, because they hadn't been able to locate any donors with my blood type. Everyone expected me to die." She drew a shuddering breath.

In truth, she remembered very little about the accident, or her life to that point. Daniel had always insisted it was probably best for her not to try to remember. What was blocked out was blocked out for a reason, he'd said. If her mind didn't think she could handle it, she probably couldn't. After all, near-death experiences were traumatic, especially for a six-year-old child.

She released the air she'd taken in, drew a steadier breath and continued. "I was still hospitalized when my parents were taken with an extremely rare virulent infection. By the time the virus was isolated and identified, they...they'd both succumbed."

"I am more sorry for that than I can tell you," he said softly, his breath caressing her skin as he spoke. "I wish I had been there for you."

"So do I," she blurted before she had a chance to consider the words. She cleared her throat. "But Daniel was there. He worked part-time in the research lab at the hospital then. As soon as he heard about the miracle girl upstairs, he came to see me. After that he was there every day. He brought presents with every visit, and constantly went on about how he'd always wanted a little girl like me. By the time my parents got sick, Daniel and I were best friends. When they died he petitioned the courts for custody, and got it. I had no other close relatives. If it hadn't been for Daniel, I would've been alone."

She felt his swift inhalation, and the slight stiffening of his body. "I'm sorry." The words were almost a moan, so much pain came through in them. His arms tightened around her and he rocked her slowly.

God, why did his touch feel like heaven? Why did the wide, hard chest beneath her head and the steel arms around her feel like the safest cocoon in all the world?

His voice only slightly more normal, he said, "It was Daniel who arranged for your employment at DPI, then." She only nodded, moving her head minimally against his chest. "And what do you do there, Tamara? Do you work with St. Claire?"

"No," she mumbled into the fabric of his coat. "My security

clearance isn't—'' She broke off, stiffening, and jerked away from him. My God, he'd played her well! "DPI is a government agency, a subdivision of the CIA, for God's sake. And you are the subject of one of their most long-running investigations. I certainly don't intend to discuss what I do there with you." She broke eye contact, and shook her head in self-deprecation. "God, you're good. I was actually buying all of this. You just wanted to milk information from me."

"You know better." His deep voice held anger now, and for the first time Tamara felt afraid of him. She backed up another step and felt the iron rail press into the small of her back. Eric Marquand stood between her and the doors. "I only want to discern whether I can trust you. St. Claire is out to destroy me. I cannot dismiss the possibility that you are a part of that plan."

"Daniel wouldn't hurt a fly!" She bristled at the suggestion that her beloved Daniel was anything less than the sweet, loving man she knew him to be.

"I know that to be false. I do not need proof of his intent. I already have it. It is you I need to be sure of, Tamara. Tell me what your duties entail."

He took a step nearer and there was nowhere for her to go. "I won't," she told him. "I can't betray the division...or Daniel."

"You would rather betray me?"

She shook her head fast, confusion muddling her brain. "I couldn't betray you. I know nothing about you."

"You could easily be the instrument of my destruction."

"But I wouldn't—"

"Then tell me. Answer whatever I ask, it is vital—" She shook her head again. He sighed and pushed one hand back through his hair, loosening several black silk strands from the queue in the back. When he looked into her eyes again the intensity had returned. "I can force you, you know."

Fear tiptoed over her spine. "If you touch me, I'll scream."

"I don't need to touch you. I can make you obey my will just as I made you come out here tonight...with my mind."

"I think you need help, Marquand. You're more screwed up than I am, and that's saying something."

One raven brow rose inquiringly. "You doubt what I know to be true?" He stared at her, and she saw an iridescent shimmer, as if the jet irises were suddenly translucent and the swirling light behind them came through. She felt her mind turn to water, and the hot whirlwind began to stir around her ankles, gaining force as it rose until it surrounded her like a twister. Her hair whipped her face. The satin robe flagellated her legs from calf to thigh. The wind moved, forcing her forward until only millimeters separated her from him.

He put his hands on her throat, his thumbs caressing the hollows above her clavicle. His fingers slipped beneath the material of the robe at her shoulders. The wind whipped the sash free, seemingly at his command. Slowly he pushed the scarlet satin from her shoulders, and it fell, to her horror, in a shimmering cascade at her feet. Yet she was incapable of lifting her arms to prevent it. She tried to tell her body to move. He wasn't holding her to him by force. Her arms hadn't been pinioned to her sides by his iron grip. They only hung limply there, abnormally heavy, unable to move. Her feet seemed to have the same mysterious malady. She could not make them take her a single step away from him.

Her eyes had followed the soft red cloth as it fell, but he caught her chin now and lifted it. He stared down into her eyes, but his gaze shifted every few seconds to her throat.

Part of her mind screamed in protest. Another, primal part screamed for his touch. He lowered his head and caught her earlobe between his lips. He nibbled it so lightly his touch was almost imperceptible, yet desire shot through her in fiery jolts. His lips trailed a path around her face and stopped only when they reached hers. They lingered there, barely touching. His hands touched the backs of her thighs and rose slowly, cupping her buttocks, squeezing, parting. One slipped around her hips, to cup her most intimate place, while the other remained behind her, to hold her immobile. She felt his fingers touch lightly, part her, probe her, and she heard a stifled whimper that must have been hers. Fire coursed through her veins, heating her blood until it boiled. She wanted this...damn him, he was making her want it!

Both hands flattened against her stomach and inched slowly upward. She trembled violently, knowing what was next. Awaiting it with a burning need that came against her will. Still his lips worked hers, sucking at them, first upper, then lower. Biting them softly, licking them with quick tiny flicks of his tongue, followed by slow, languorous laps that traced their shape. His fingers finally reached her breasts. He positioned a thumb and forefinger at each nipple, barely touching. She moaned low and hoarsely in supplication, and he closed them, pinching, rolling the erect nubs between his fingers until they pulsed like the rest of her.

She realized she'd regained use of her arms when she found them linking behind his head and pulling him closer. Her mouth opened wide to him, and his tongue plunged into it, stroking hers, twining with hers, tugging at it. He pulled it into his own silken moistness, and suckled the way she wished he would suckle her breasts. They throbbed for his mouth.

Before she'd completed the thought his hands were at her back, between her shoulder blades. His lips burned a path of liquid heat down over her chin, over her throat, along her chest. She arched backward, supported by his hands behind her, one at her back, one at her buttocks. He bent over her and unerringly found one swollen crest with his mouth. Mercilessly he worried it, licking until she whimpered, sucking until she cried out and biting until her hands tangled in his hair, holding him to her.

She couldn't catch her breath. She wanted him so badly it was out of control. Her center throbbed with hot moisture, and longed to be filled...with him.

He lifted his head and eased her upward until she had her balance. At some point during the rapacious seduction he had released her mind. She was unsure when, exactly, but at some time she had been free to object, to pull away, to slap him. She hadn't. Instead she'd responded like an animal. She was angry, with herself, with him and with her mind for refusing to give her the memory she needed to make sense of all of this.

He bent down, retrieved her robe and straightened again, slipping it over her shoulders. "You see?" He said it very softly.

"Why are you doing this to me?" Her voice cracked as she asked the question. She tugged her robe together, yanking the sash tight. She couldn't look him in the eyes.

"Not *to* you, Tamara. I came tonight *for* you. To help you, if you'll permit it."

"Was what you just did to me supposed to help me, too?"

When he didn't answer right away she looked at him. To her surprise his gaze fell before hers. "No," he finally whispered. "I meant to demonstrate.... I did not intend to go so far."

She frowned, looking at him—*really looking* at him—for the first time since he'd peeled his body from hers. His eyes fairly glowed with passion and were still hooded. His breaths came in short, shallow gasps, just as hers did. My God, he'd been as swept away by what had happened between them as she had! He moved past her, his hands trembling as he gripped the iron rail and looked down over it into the blue-black night, and the illuminating snow-covered ground below. His back was presented to her, its broad strength slightly bowed. Nothing prevented her going back inside.

"I am afraid I've handled this badly," he said slowly and carefully, though his voice was still hoarse. "It is not my wish to frighten you, or to make you loathe me. I care for you, Tamara. I have for a very long time."

She allowed his words to penetrate the confusion in her mind. "I think I believe that."

He turned, faced her and seemed to search for the correct

words. "I truly came to you because I heard your cries. I had no other motive. Can you believe that, as well?"

She drew a slow breath. "I work with a young boy who has, on occasion, demonstrated some psychic ability. Several operatives have had sessions with him, besides me. But his powers, however slight, are always a good deal more evident when he is with me. I suppose there's a chance I might have some latent clairvoyant tendency that's been enhancing his. Maybe you *did* somehow hear my dreams. I won't say it's impossible."

She was trying to give him the benefit of the doubt, no matter how outrageous his claims seemed to be. Besides, how else could she explain what had been happening?

Encouraged, it seemed, he went on. "I came to you only because of the desperation in your cries. I swear this to you. I had no idea St. Claire was your guardian." He took a step forward, one hand lifting, palm up, a gesture of entreaty. "Try to imagine how I felt when I discovered it, Tamara. The woman who'd been calling me to her, living under the same roof as the man who has doggedly pursued me for months. How could I not suspect a conspiracy to entrap me?"

She listened as he presented his case. She supposed he had a point. She would have thought the same if she'd been in his place. "I suppose you had cause to be suspicious." She looked at the floor, bit her lip. She could reassure him without revealing any sensitive information. The truth was, she knew very little that was classified. "I have a low security clearance. Sometimes I think they invented a new one, just for me, it's so low." She smiled slightly when she said that, and she faced him. "I can't count the number of times I've tried to argue Daniel out of this crazy idea that you're…" Why couldn't she finish the sentence? She swallowed and went on. "He always counters my rationale with the claim that he has loads of evidence to prove his theories. And I always respond by asking to see the files. The answer never changes. My clearance isn't high enough." She studied his face, but it gave no evidence of whether he believed her. He listened attentively. "I never told him about the dreams. I didn't want to worry him."

He nodded. "Is there a chance he might've found out in another way?"

"How could he, short of reading my mind?" She blinked and looked away suddenly. "Unless…" He waited expectantly. She made up her mind. What she had to say couldn't hurt Daniel. If anything, it might help him avoid a lawsuit if she could stay on good terms with Marquand. She tried to avoid the burning knowledge of her own powerful feelings for a man she barely knew. "There were times when I cried out loud, loud enough to alert Daniel and bring him to my room. He always told me he hadn't heard clearly enough to guess what I'd said in my sleep, but I suppose there's a chance he might not have told me if he thought it would add to the problem."

"Or if he knew I would come to you, and planned to lie in wait."

Until that point she'd done her best to see his side of things. Now her head came up fast and she bristled. "You need to get that idea out of your mind. I admit, Daniel follows you, lurks outside your house and watches everything you do. But why on earth would he want to trap you, as you say? What do you suppose he'd do with you when he got you?"

"He specializes in research, Tamara, not surveillance. What do you suppose he'd do with a live specimen of what he considers an unstudied species?"

Tamara's stomach lurched. Her hand flew to her mouth, and she closed her eyes. "That's ludicrous! Daniel would never… He's the most gentle man I've ever known." She shook her head so hard her hair flew around her. "No. No, Daniel couldn't even entertain the thought."

"You don't know him so well as you believe to." He spoke gently, but his words were brutal. "Has it occurred to you that he might have known of the connection between us all along, that it might have been what drove him to take you in from the start?''

Eyes wide, she stared at him, shaking her head in disbelief. ''It would never occur to me to think that. Daniel loves me. I love him! He's the only family I have. How can you suggest—'' She stopped and tried to catch her breath. Suddenly her head throbbed. The lack of sleep seemed to catch up to her all at once. Every limb of her body ached with exhaustion.

''You have to at least consider the possibility. He knew about me, even then. I can prove it to you, if—''

''Stop it!'' She pressed her palms flat to the sides of her head.

''Tamara—''

''Please, Eric,'' she whispered, suddenly too tired to shout or to argue any longer. ''Please don't do this, don't say these things to me. I feel so close to losing my mind I don't trust my own senses anymore. I'm not sure what's real and what's delusion. I can't deal with all of this.''

Her head bowed, her eyes tear filled, she didn't see him come closer. He gathered her into his arms and held her. His arms offered only comfort this time. There was no lust in his touch. ''Forgive me, Tamara. My thoughtless words cause you pain. Forgive me. I don't wish to hurt you. My concern for you overwhelmed my common sense.'' He sighed, long and low. ''God, but I've bungled this.''

She found too much comfort in his arms. She felt too warm and safe and cherished there. It made no sense. She needed to be away from him. She couldn't think when he was so close. She straightened, stepping out of his embrace. ''I think...I think you ought to leave.''

The pain that flashed in his onyx eyes was almost more than she could bear to see. He dipped his head. ''If you wish.'' He met her gaze again, his own shuttered now. ''Please do not forget the things I've said to you tonight. If ever you need me, you have only to call to me. I will come.''

She blinked, not bothering to argue that his claim was impossible. Perhaps he had picked up on her dreams, but they had been exceptionally powerful dreams. He couldn't possibly think this odd mental link of theirs extended beyond the one isolated incident. He didn't give her time to ask. His hand at the small of her back, he urged her toward the French doors. He opened them for her and gently pushed her through. She stepped inside and stopped, suddenly aware of the cold. Goose bumps rose on her arms and an involuntary shiver raced through her. She stood there a moment, then whirled to ask him how he'd gotten onto her balcony in the first place, a question she'd stupidly not thought of sooner—but he was gone. She shook her head hard and looked around her. It was as if he'd never been there.

CHAPTER FIVE

Jamey Bryant squirmed in his chair, his eyes focused more often on the falling snow beyond the window than on Tamara or the box in the center of the table.

"Come on, Jamey. Concentrate." She felt guilty ordering the boy to do what she found impossible. All day she'd been unable to get Eric Marquand out of her mind. His face appeared before her each time she closed her eyes. The memory of his touch, the way his lips had felt on hers, the security of being rocked in his arms haunted her without letup. The pain she'd seen in his eyes before he'd vanished haunted her more than anything else.

Then again, she still had a tiny doubt he'd been real. He could have been a figment of her imagination, a delusion, a dream. How else could he have vanished from her balcony so quickly? He couldn't have jumped. At the very least he'd have broken a leg. So maybe he hadn't been real....

But he had. She knew he had, and the way he made her feel had been real, as well. Nothing so intense could be imaginary.

Jamey sighed and fixed his gaze on the cube of cardboard between them. He screwed up his face until it puckered and the furrow between his fine, dark brows became three. He leaned forward and his freckle-smattered face reddened until Tamara thought he was holding his breath. Her suspicion was confirmed a moment later when he released it in a loud whoosh and sank back into his chair. "I can't," he said. "Can I go now?"

Tamara tried to summon an encouraging smile. "You really hate this, don't you?"

He shrugged, glanced toward the window, then back to the box again. "I wish I could be like other kids. I feel weird when I know things. Then when I don't know something I think I should, I feel stupid. And then there are times when I get things that don't make any sense at all. It's like I know something, but I don't know what it means, you know?''

She nodded. "I think so.''

"So what good is it to be able to know something if you can't make sense out of it?''

"Jamey, you aren't weird and you know you aren't stupid. Everyone has some quality that sets them apart. Some people can sing notes that seem impossible to the rest of us. Some athletes do things that seem supernatural to those who can't do the same. That's exactly what extrasensory perception is, something you do a lot better than most people. It's just not as understood as those other things.''

She studied his face, thinking he didn't look much comforted by her pep talk. "Maybe you should tell me what it is that's bothering you.''

He blew air through his lips, and shook his head. "You know I'm lousy at this. It's probably nothing. I—I don't want to scare you for no reason.''

She frowned. "Scare me? This is about me, Jamey?''

He nodded, avoiding her eyes.

She rose from her seat, walked around the table and dropped to one knee in front of him. Since she'd begun working with Jamey six months ago, they'd formed a tight bond. She couldn't have loved him more if he were her own son. She hated that he was agonizing so much over something involving her. Always, he'd been incredibly sensitive to her feelings. He always knew if she felt upset, or under the weather. He'd known about the nightmares and insomnia, too.

"You are not lousy at this. At least, not where I'm concerned. If you've picked up on something, just tell me. Maybe I can explain it.''

His mouth twisted at one side. He looked at her seriously. His intense expression made him look like a miniature adult. "I keep feeling like something's going to happen to you...like someone is going to—to hurt you.'' He shook his head. "But I don't know who and I don't know what, so what good is it to know any-thing?''

She smiled softly. ''There's been a lot going on with me lately, Jamey. Personal stuff. Stuff that's upset me quite a lot. I think you might be picking up on that.''

''You think so?'' His dark eyes met hers hopefully, then dark-ened again with worry. ''Is everything okay?''

She nodded hard. ''I think so. And, yes, everything is working itself out. The nightmares I'd been having are gone now.''

''Good.'' His frown didn't vanish, though. ''But I still get the feeling there are people out to get you.'' He chewed his lip. ''Do you know anyone named Eric?''

Something hard, like a brick, lodged in the center of her chest. She gasped audibly, and rose so fast she nearly lost her balance. ''Eric?'' she repeated dumbly. ''Why? Is there something about him—''

''I dunno. I just keep getting that name floating in at the odd-est times. I always feel really sad, or else really worried, when it comes. I think maybe that's what he's feeling like, but like I said, I'm lousy at this. I could be reading it all wrong.''

She let the moment of panic recede. She'd thought he might say Eric was the one out to hurt her. She still wondered if it might not be the case, but didn't want to let Jamey sense it. She drew several calming breaths and tried to compose her face be-fore she looked at him again.

''Thanks for the warning, Jamey, but I think you're overre-acting to this danger thing. Look, why don't you open the box? At this point I don't even remember what was inside.''

After a last cursory glance, as if assuring himself he hadn't frightened her, he leaned forward, swung one arm out and caught the box, drawing it to him on the follow-through. When he looked inside his eyes widened, and he pulled the video game cartridge out. ''Dungeon Warriors! Mom's been looking all over for this—where'd you find it?''

"Your mom didn't look as hard as you thought. I told her not to."

He examined the colorful package eagerly. "Thanks, Tam." He stood, obviously in a hurry to get home and try out the new game.

"Go ahead, Jamey. Your mom's waiting right downstairs." He nodded and started for the door. "Jamey," she called after him. When he glanced back at her she said, "If you get any more of these weird vibes about me, and if they bother you, just call. You have my number. Okay?"

"Sure, Tam." He gave her a broad, dimpled grin that told her his mind had been eased for the moment, and hustled through the door, leaving Tamara alone to contemplate his warning.

She worked late that evening, trying to use her mundane duties to fill her mind. It didn't work. She finally went home to find the house looking abandoned. Of course, it was past dusk, so Daniel and Curtis had already left on their nightly spying mission. Despite his unfounded accusations against Daniel, Tamara felt a little sorry for Eric Marquand. It must get tiresome looking out his window night after night to see them there.

She bounced in her VW Bug over the curving, rutted driveway. Snowflakes pirouetted over the rambling Victorian mansion, caught in the glow of her headlights. Their pristine whiteness emphasized the age-yellowed paint. Tall, narrow windows stood like sad eyes. Rusty water stains like teardrops beneath each one enhanced that fanciful image. Tamara set the brake and got out to wrench open the stubborn overhead garage door, muttering under her breath. She'd argued for an automatic one every winter for the past three, all without success. Daniel wouldn't budge an inch. What he couldn't do to the old house himself simply wouldn't get done. He didn't want a crew of strangers snooping around and that was final.

She drove her car inside, noting the absence of Daniel's Cadillac. A finger of worry traced a path along her spine. She hoped he wasn't driving tonight. The roads were slippery and, dammit all, she'd never replaced the spare after he'd had that flat two months ago. She imagined Curt was with him, and comforted herself with the thought.

She flicked on lights as she moved through the foyer. The phone began ringing before she'd even sat down to remove her boots. She tracked across the faded carpet to pick it up.

"Tammy, it's about time you got home. Where've you been?"

She bit back the sharp retort that sprang to her lips. "Curtis, are you with Daniel?"

"Yeah, but that doesn't answer the question."

"I came straight home from the office, if you must know. I worked a bit late and the roads are slick. I don't want him driving."

"I'll take care of him. Look, Tam, are you in for the night?"

She frowned hard. "Why?"

He hesitated, started to speak, stopped and started again. "It's just, after that incident with Marquand the other night, Daniel and I both feel it would be best if you, uh, try to stick close to home after sundown. I know how much you resent being told what to do, but it would be for your own—"

"My own good, I know." She sighed and shook her head. "Look, I don't have any plans to leave the house tonight. Besides, I thought you guys were watching Marquand's every move."

"We are, but—"

"Then you don't have anything to worry about, do you? I'm heading for a long soak in a scalding bath, and then straight to bed, if that makes you feel any better."

"It does." He was quiet for a moment. "It's only because we're worried, Tammy."

"Yeah, I know it is. Good night." She replaced the receiver before he could make her any angrier, and headed upstairs to follow her own advice about the hot bath. As for straight to bed, she knew better. At work she'd been on the verge of falling asleep on her feet all day. Now that she was home she felt wide awake and brimming with energy.

She toweled herself dry after a soothing, if not a relaxing, soak, and pulled on a pair of comfortable jeans and a baggy sweater. She wriggled her feet into her heaviest socks and half-heartedly dried her hair, before padding downstairs to hunt for something to fill her empty stomach. She'd just settled on the sofa in the huge living room with a thick bacon, lettuce and tomato sandwich sliced diagonally on a paper plate, and a can of cola, when the doorbell chimed.

Tamara rolled her eyes, lowered the sandwich she'd just brought to her lips and went to open the door. Her irritation disappeared when Eric Marquand stepped over the threshold into the foyer. She slammed the door after giving a fear-filled glance down the driveway, and looked at him agape. "You shouldn't be here, Eric. My God, if Daniel saw you here, he'd have a stroke!"

"He won't. He and Rogers will remain on sentry duty outside my front gate until dawn, as they do every night, I promise you. They did not see me leave. I took great pains to assure that."

She stood still, fighting the bubbling sense of joy she felt at seeing him, arguing inwardly that it made no sense to feel so about a stranger. It was there, all the same.

"After my behavior last night, I half expected you to throw me out. Will you, Tamara?"

She tried to tug her gaze free of his, but was unsuccessful. "I...no. No, I'm not going to throw you out. Come in. I was about to have a sandwich. Can I make one for you?"

He shook his head. "I've already dined. If I'm interrupting your dinner..."

She shook her head quickly. "No, I mean, you can hardly call a sandwich and a cola dinner." He followed her into the living room and sat beside her on the sofa, despite the fact that she'd waved her arm toward a chair nearby. She reached for the dewy can. "I could get you one."

"Thank you, no." He cleared his throat. "I've come because..." He shook his head. "Actually, there is no other reason, except that I couldn't stay away. Tamara, will you come out with me tonight? I give you my word, I will say nothing against your St. Claire. I'll ask you no questions about DPI. I only want your companionship."

She smiled, then stopped herself. Did she dare go out with him? After all the warnings Daniel had given her about him?

Eric took her hand in his, his thumb slowly stroking the tops of her fingers. "If you cannot believe my charges against him, Tamara, you should equally doubt his against me. It is only fair."

She nodded slowly. "I guess you're right. Okay. I'll come with you." She stood quickly, more eager than she wanted him to see. "Should I change? Where are we going?"

"You are beautiful as you are, sweet. Would you mind if we simply went driving until something better occurs to us? I don't wish to share you with a crowd just yet."

"Okay. I'll grab my coat and... Driving? I didn't see a car. How will we—"

"Finish your sandwich, Tamara. It is a surprise."

She couldn't stop herself from smiling fully at that, and for a moment he seemed almost staggered by it. "I'm not hungry, anyway," she told him, rushing past him to the foyer and the closet near the front door. "I was only eating to fill the loneliness."

She tugged on her heaviest coat, a long houndstooth check, with a black woolly scarf around the collar and matching mittens in the pocket. She stomped into her boots. When she looked up again he was staring at her. "Have you been lonely, then?" he asked softly.

She blinked back the instant moisture that sprang to her eyes at the question. It never occurred to her to lie to him. "I often think I'm the loneliest person I know. Oh, I've got Daniel, and a few friends at work, but..." She looked into his eyes and knew he'd understand. "I'm not like them. I feel set apart, like there's an invisible barrier between us." She frowned. "I don't feel that way with you."

His eyes closed slowly, and opened again. Flustered more than a little bit, she hurried through the room and took the telephone off the hook. Without an explanation she trotted upstairs to her room and spent a few minutes stuffing spare blankets underneath her comforter, to make it look as if she were asleep there. She shut off her bedroom light and closed the door.

When she turned, Eric stood there. One brow lifted as he looked down at her. "For St. Claire's benefit?"

"This way I can relax and enjoy our evening," she said softly, her gaze lingering on his lips for a long moment. She saw his Adam's apple move as he swallowed. When she lifted her gaze to his eyes, she saw they were focused on her lips, and her tongue darted out involuntarily to moisten them.

"I promised myself I wouldn't touch you tonight," he told her in a voice softer than a whisper. "But I don't believe I can prevent myself kissing you."

"You're bound to, sooner or later," she told him, striving to keep her own voice level. "Maybe we ought to get it out of the way now." He stood perfectly still, not a single muscle moving. She stepped forward, tilted her head back and touched his lips with hers. She felt him tremble when she settled her hands on his rock-solid shoulders. She let her eyes fall closed, parted her lips against his and tentatively slid the tip of her tongue over them.

He sighed into her mouth as his arms came around her waist to crush her against him. The pressure of his lips forced hers to part for him, and he tasted every bit of her mouth, even reaching his tongue to the back of her throat in a forceful, thrusting motion that hinted at far greater pleasures to come. His hands moved over her body, one holding her to him while the other tangled in her hair, pulling her head back farther to accommodate that probing tongue more deeply. She felt his hot arousal pressing into her belly, telling her how much he wanted her. She moved her hips against him, to let him know she felt the same mindless need.

When the fire in her blood raged out of control he pulled away, panting. "This is not the way, Tamara. With everything in me, I want to take you right here. I want to lift you to the wall, or take you on the floor, dammit. But it is not the way. You might hate me tomorrow, when the fire no longer burns in your eyes." He stroked the hair away from her face. He pressed his lips to each eye in turn. "Agree with me, before I lose control."

Tamara's body was screaming that she wanted him to lose control. Her mind knew he was right. She didn't know him. She had once, she was certain of it now. But she couldn't remember that. It would be like making love to a stranger, and that would make her feel cheap and ashamed. She stepped away from him. "You're right. I—I'm sorry."

"Never apologize for kissing me, for touching me, Tamara. Your caress is a gift worthy of any king...one I will be grateful for whenever you choose to bestow it."

Eric could barely bring himself to stop what she'd started in St. Claire's corridor. He'd only just restrained himself in time. The desire she stirred in him was a beast he could hardly subdue. He had to, though. The blood lust in him intertwined with sexual desire. The two were so closely linked among his kind that there was no separating them. If he took her, he'd take her blood as well as her body. She'd know the truth then, and she'd despise him forever.

Or worse...

No. he refused to believe she could be party to Daniel St. Claire's machinations.

Refusing to believe it does not make it impossible.

If she was plotting his destruction, he'd know, he reminded himself as he descended the stairs beside her. He'd see it in her mind.

Vampires can learn to guard their thoughts. Why not her?

She is no vampire, he thought angrily. I've never known a human to be capable of such a thing.

You've never known a human like Tamara.

At the bottom of the stairway Eric glimpsed a light glowing beyond a doorway at the far side. She'd flicked off every other glaring electric light she'd come to, so he touched her shoulder now, and pointed. "Do you wish to shut that light off, as well?"

She shook her head quickly, opened her mouth to explain, then seemed to think better of it. Not before Eric heard what was in her mind, however. To go through that door was forbidden to her. St. Claire's basement lab lay at the bottom of the staircase there, and he'd deemed it off-limits. Eric would have liked to go down there now, to examine the ruthless scientist's files and equipment. But he'd given Tamara his word that he'd come here only to be with her. How could she believe him if he betrayed her trust in such a way?

He'd spoken the truth when he'd spoken those words, yet he could've told her more. He wanted to be with her because he feared for her safety. That St. Claire had known of the connection between them from the start was obvious. He'd orchestrated events to gain custody of the child, Eric felt certain of it. Whether to brainwash her into helping him in his plots or to use her as unwitting bait remained to be seen. Either way, though, Tamara was no more to St. Claire than a pawn in a high-stakes game. She could not be safe with him. That Eric had to leave her side by day had him at his wits' end, but what choice did he have? He would stay by her side when he could, and he'd try to learn exactly what St. Claire had on his mind. He'd protect Tamara if he had to kill the bastard himself. In the three times Eric had seen her since returning from his travels, he'd learned one thing he hadn't fully realized before. He still adored her.

The emotions had changed, radically. She was no longer the small child in need of bedtime stories and lullabies. She was a woman grown, a woman of incomparable beauty and incredible passion...a woman capable of setting his pulse throbbing in his temples, and his blood to boiling for want of her. He knew what he felt for her. He understood it. Constantly he needed to remind himself that she did not. She couldn't, nor could she fathom her own feelings for him. To her, he was a stranger...at least until her memory returned, and until she became aware that she could know anything about him simply by searching his mind. Now, though, at this moment, he was a stranger.

He hoped to remedy that to some extent tonight.

She locked the door, pocketed the key and turned toward him. Eric allowed himself the pleasure of encircling her shoulders with his arm. No matter how good his intentions, it seemed he couldn't prevent himself from touching her, holding her close whenever possible. Her coat was too thick for his liking. He could scarcely feel the shape of her beneath it. He urged her down the curving driveway, and felt her start in surprise when she caught sight of the vehicle that awaited her there. One horse's ears pricked forward and his head came up at the sound of their approach.

Tamara stopped walking to turn wide eyes toward Eric. He smiled at the delight he saw in them. "I thought a sleigh would be more enjoyable than any other mode of transportation," he said.

Her smile took his breath away, and she hurried forward, sending a powdery blizzard ahead of her as she plowed through the five inches of new snow on the ground. She stood in front of the black, speaking softly, for the horse's ears only, and stroking his muzzle. He blew in appreciation. Eric joined her there a second later. "This is Max. He's a gelding, and I think he's as enchanted by his first glimpse of you as I was."

She glanced up, meeting his eyes, her own acknowledging the compliment, before Eric continued. "And this—" he moved toward the golden palomino beside Max "—is Melinda, his partner."

Tamara stepped to the side and stroked Melinda's sleek neck. "She's beautiful—they both are. Are they yours, Eric?"

"Unfortunately, no. I was able to rent them for the night." He watched the emotions in her face and felt those in her mind as she touched and caressed one horse, then the other. "I'm thinking of buying them, though," he added. It was true. The moment he'd seen her joy at the sight of the animals, he'd wanted to own them.

"Oh?" Her attention was, at last, on him again. "Do you have a stable?"

"I'll have one built," he announced. She laughed as he took her arm and led her around the horses, to help her into the sleigh. Eric climbed in beside her and picked up the reins.

"I've always loved horses. When I was a little girl I wanted to own a ranch, where I could raise them by the hundreds."

Eric nodded. He remembered her love of horses. He'd hoped it still existed. He snapped the reins lightly and clicked his tongue. The sleigh jerked into motion, and Tamara settled back against the cushioned seat. He took them off the paved road as soon as possible, onto a snow-coated side road that was barely more than a path. He watched her more often than the road ahead. She remarked on everything with little sighs of pleasure—the full moon glistening on the snow, making it sparkle as if it held tiny diamonds just beneath the surface, the ice-coated branches that made ugly, bare limbs turn into sculpted crystal. The crisp, clean air that touched her face, and the scent of the horses' warm bodies.

Eric nodded in agreement, but in truth he was aware of none of it. It was her scent that enveloped him. It was seeing the way the chill breeze played with her hair and reddened her cheeks and the tip of her nose that entranced him. He felt only the warmth of her body, pressed alongside his own, and saw the moonlight glistening in her eyes, rather than upon the snow.

Beyond the rhythmic thudding of the horses' hooves he heard the music in her voice.

Her arm was wrapped around his, and her head rested upon his shoulder. "This is wonderful, Eric. It's the most fun I've had in…" She blinked and considered a moment. "I can't remember when I've enjoyed a night this much."

"Nor I," he whispered, certain it was true. "But you must tell me if you grow tired, or I'll likely keep you out all night."

"I don't get tired at night. Not ever. I haven't slept a night through in over a month…closer to two. So if you want to keep me out all night, I'll be more than willing."

She seemed so exuberant and happy. Yet he worried about this sleeplessness. She'd mentioned it before. "Are you able to sleep by day, then?"

"No, I have to work. I usually catch a few hours in the afternoon, though." She tipped her head up and saw his frown. "Do I look like I'm suffering from exhaustion to you?"

"Quite the opposite," he admitted.

She settled against him again, then straightened, snapping her fingers. "It's French, isn't it?"

"What?"

"Your accent."

"I wasn't aware I had one." God, she was beautiful. Her eyes in the moonlight seemed luminous, and he noticed again the thickness of the lashes surrounding them.

"It's very slight. I barely notice it myself. I've been trying to place it. Am I right?"

He nodded. "I was born in France."

"Where?"

He smiled down at her, amazed that she even cared to ask. "Paris. I haven't been back there in…years."

"You sound as if you'd like to go, though," she said, studying his face. "Why haven't you?"

"Bad memories, I suppose. My father was murdered there. I nearly suffered the same fate, save for the intervention of a good friend." He saw her eyes widen. He'd vowed to be as honest with her as he could without giving away the secret. He wanted her to feel she knew him.

Her hand clutched his upper arm more tightly. "That's horrible."

He nodded. "But a long time past, Tamara. I'm recovered."

"Are you sure?" He met her intense scrutiny. "Have you talked it out with someone, Eric? These things have a way of festering."

He tilted his head, considering his words. "It was… political…and utterly senseless. It left me without any family at all, and if not for Roland, I'd have been without a friend, as well." He looked down to see her listening raptly. "I never had many to begin with, you see. I always felt separate—set apart from my peers."

"You didn't fit in. I know exactly what you mean."

He looked deeply into her eyes. "Yes, I imagine you do."

"Tell me about your friend. Do you still keep in touch?"

He chuckled. "It is sometimes a long time between letters, or visits. But Roland happens to be staying with me at the moment."

Her head came up, eyes eager. "Could I meet him?"

He frowned. "Why would you want to?"

She had to give her answer a long moment's thought before speaking it. "You…said he saved your life. I…" Her gaze fell to her hand, resting on her knee. "I'd like to thank him."

Eric closed his eyes at the warmth her words sent through his heart. "He's a recluse. Perhaps I can arrange it, though. Unlike me, he still has a residence in France, though he rarely lives there. He owns a sprawling medieval castle in the Loire Valley. He hid me there for a time after we fled Paris."

When he glanced at her again it was to find her gaze affixed to his face as it had been through most of the ride. "You are a fascinating man," she whispered.

"I am a simple man, with simple tastes."

"I'd love to see your home."

"Another time, perhaps. If I took you there while my reclusive friend was in residence, he'd likely throttle me." He slipped his arm around the back of the seat, and squeezed her to his side. "It is furnished almost exclusively in antiques. Electric lighting is there, of course, but I seldom use it. I prefer the muted glow of oil lamps to the harsh glare of those white bulbs, except in my laboratory."

"You're a scientist?"

"I dabble in a few projects that interest me."

Her lovely eyes narrowed. "You are being modest, I think."

He shrugged, gave a tug on the reins to stop their progress and reached beneath the seat for the thermos he'd brought along. "You told me once, a very long time ago, that your favorite beverage was hot chocolate. Is it still the case?"

For the first time in years Tamara felt completely at ease with another person. The hours of the night flew past almost without her knowledge. They talked incessantly, touching on every subject imaginable, from music and art to politics. He fascinated her, and the more she learned about him the more she wanted to know.

Through it all she was constantly aware of the physical attraction that zapped between them. She'd deliberately sat close to him, so her body touched his. She liked touching him, so much so that she felt cold and alone when they hit a rough spot in the road and she was jarred away from his side. Without hesitation she resumed her former position. He seemed to share her need to feel her close. He touched her often. He kept his hard arm around her, managing the reins with one hand. When they passed beneath an overhanging branch and a handful of snow dusted her, he stopped the sleigh and turned to brush it away from her shoulders and her hair. Their eyes met, and she felt the irresistible pull of him. He leaned forward and pressed his lips to hers with infinite tenderness. He held himself in check, though. She sensed his forced restraint and knew he was determined to go slowly with her...to give her time to adjust to what was happening between them.

She wondered exactly *what was* happening between them. She knew that it was intense, and that it was real. She knew that she'd never felt this way toward another human being in her life. And she knew that whatever it was, she didn't want it to end. She wanted to tell him so, but didn't quite know how.

He left the sleigh in the same spot near the end of the driveway when they returned to the house. He walked her to the door, and stopped as she fit her key into the lock. Her heart twisted painfully at the thought of leaving him. The lock released, but she didn't open the door. She turned and gazed up at him, wondering if he knew.

"I'd like to see you again," she said, suddenly shy and awkward with him, which seemed strange considering all that had passed between them before.

"I think it would be impossible for me to go a night without seeing you, Tamara," he told her. "I will come to you again... do not doubt it."

She bit her lower lip, searching his face. "I'm a grown woman. It's silly to have to sneak around this way. You know you could end this foolish notion Daniel has about you, if you wanted to. Just come to the house during the day. He'd have to realize then—"

"He would only assume I had some protection against the daylight, sweet. Nothing can change his opinion of me." He looked away from her briefly. "I have my own schedule—one that is vital to me. Should I alter that to accommodate the whims of a man determined to persecute me?"

"No, I didn't mean it like that!" She sighed, feeling deflated. "It's just that I hate deceiving him."

"If you tell him you're seeing me, Tamara, he'll find a way to prevent it." She met his gaze again, and saw the hint of impatience vanish as he regarded her. "Let me amend that. He would try to find a way. He would not succeed."

She believed that he meant it. "I'm glad you said that," she admitted.

She knew he would kiss her. She saw the heat come into his luminous eyes in the instant before his arms imprisoned her waist. Her lips parted as his descended. The restraint he'd shown earlier dissolved the instant her arms encircled his corded neck and her body pressed to his. His lips quivered as they covered hers, and she accepted his probing tongue enthusiastically. Even with her heavy coat between them she was aware of the heat of him touching her, as if his hands touched her naked skin. He explored her mouth, and his fingers moved lightly over her nape, sending exquisite shivers down her spine.

She'd experimented with sex. In college, though she'd lived at home at Daniel's insistence, there had been plenty of opportunities and no shortage of eager tutors. Her times with men had been few, though, and inspired more by curiosity than passion. Tonight, with Eric, she wanted it. A hunger like nothing she'd known existed made a cavern inside her—a vast emptiness that only he could fill. It gnawed at her mercilessly, and the longing made her groan deep in her throat.

He straightened, and she knew he saw the need in her eyes. His own closed as if he were in pain, and his arms fell away from her. "I must go," he rasped. He reached past her and threw the door wide. There was no tenderness in his touch when he pushed her through it.

She felt tears stinging her eyes when he turned and walked away.

CHAPTER SIX

At 7:00 a.m. she sat across the table from Daniel, nursing a strong cup of coffee and a pounding headache. "It's probably just a bug," she repeated. "I'm tired and achy. I'll spend the day in bed and be myself again by tomorrow morning."

His lips thinned and he shook his head. "I'll call in, make arrangements to work at home today. That way—"

"I don't need a baby-sitter."

"I didn't say you did. I only think I should be here, in case—"

Tamara slammed the half-filled cup onto the table, sloshing coffee over the rim, and got to her feet. "Daniel, this has to stop."

"What? Tam, I'm only concerned about you."

"I know." She pushed a hand through her hair, wishing she could ease the throbbing in her temples. She felt like a wrung-out rag this morning, and in no shape for a confrontation. "I know it's love that motivates you, Daniel—I know you care. But for God's sake, look at me. I'm not an orphaned little girl anymore." She kept her voice level, and moved around the table to press her hands to his shoulders. "You and Curtis are smothering me with all this *concern.* You hover over me as if I'm Little Red Riding Hood and there are wolves behind every tree."

Daniel looked at the floor. "Have we been that bad?"

"Worse." She squeezed his shoulders gently. "But I love you, anyway."

He met her gaze, and slowly shook his head. "I'm sorry, Tam. It's not that I think you need watching, like a child. It's…it's this thing with Marquand, dammit. I'm terrified he'll try to see you again."

She let her hands fall away from him, and straightened. Eric had said he believed Daniel knew of the connection between them. Could he have been right? "Why would you think that?"

He sighed as if she were stupid. "Tamara, you're a beautiful woman! Curtis said the man was obviously attracted that night at the rink. He'd have to have been blind not to be. These creatures have a sex drive like rutting animals. Even one as old as he is."

She turned away from him, trying not to laugh. Eric was not a "creature," nor was he old. The skin of his face was smooth and tight. He moved with a grace beyond anything she'd seen before, and yet his strength was obvious. His body rippled with hard muscles and kinetic energy.

Shaking her head, she reached for her coffee. "Just how old is he?"

"Two hundred and thirty something. I've traced him to the French Revolution, when he was imprisoned and should have been beheaded in Paris. His father was, you know."

Tamara had lifted her cup to her lips, but now she choked on the sip she'd taken. Eric had told her his father was murdered in Paris! He'd said it was "political." My God, could Daniel possibly be right—no. No, that was utterly ridiculous.

But I've never seen Eric during the day.

She shoved the doubts aside. This was nonsense. Absolute nonsense.

"He's dangerous, Tam. Clever as a wizard, too. I wouldn't put it past him to use you to get to me.

And he says you're using me to get to him, she thought. Aloud, she only said, "I'd never let that happen."

"I know, Tam. But promise you'll tell me if he tries to make contact. We have to be careful. He's evil—"

"Yes, you've told me. He's the devil himself. Okay, I'll let you know. Happy?" He studied her face before he nodded. "Go to work," she told him playfully. "He can't bother me during the day, right?"

She tried not to let his words replay in her mind, over and

over again all morning. She only wanted to go back to bed and get some much-needed rest. That was impossible to do, though. She supposed she wouldn't act so impulsively if she'd had a decent amount of sleep in the past several weeks. If she'd been in a normal, relatively sane frame of mind, nothing could have convinced her to do what she suddenly decided she must do. Unfortunately, her sanity was in question, and she thought if she didn't answer the questions in her mind once and for all, it would slip away from her completely.

She had to prove to herself that Eric Marquand was not a vampire. She thought that made about as much sense as trying to prove the earth was not flat, or that the moon was not made of green cheese. Yet several hours later she sat in her pathetic excuse for a car alongside the road in front of Eric Marquand's estate.

She glanced at her watch. Only an hour or so left before sunset. Part of her wanted to put this off until tomorrow. Part of her wanted to put it off permanently. Still, she was here, and she knew if she didn't go through with this now, she never would.

Getting the address hadn't been easy. She couldn't possibly have asked Daniel or Curt without sending them both into hysterics. She couldn't show up at work and tap the DPI computers. Her security clearance wasn't high enough to get her the correct access codes. She'd spent most of the day at the county seat, scouring the records deemed "public domain." She'd struck out on birth certificates. He didn't seem to have a driver's license, or a car registered in his name. He did, however, have a deed to his home. She found the information she needed in the property tax files. His address was there, and she frowned to note it was only a few miles southeast of Daniel's house, on the northern shore of the sound.

She'd spent the entire drive back arguing with herself. Was she about to shore up her sanity, or had it already been buried in an avalanche? Would any sane person visit a man's home during the day to prove he wasn't a vampire?

Too late now, she thought, pulling her car around a bend in the road and easing it close to the woodlot on the opposite side. I'm here and I'm going in. She left the keys in the switch, and walked back to the towering wrought-iron gate. She peered between the bars and the crisscrossing pattern of vines and leaves writhing between them, all made of flattened metal. The pattern was the same as far as she could see in either direction. Beyond the fence a cobblestone driveway twisted its way toward the house. Huge trees lined the driveway, so she had to move around a bit to get a glimpse of the building beyond them.

When she did she caught her breath. The house towered at least three stories high. It was built of rough-hewn stone blocks, each one too big for three men to lift. The windows—at least, the ones she could see—were arched at the tops, and deep set. They reminded her of hooded eyes, watching but not wishing to be seen. She touched the gate and at the same instant noticed the small metal box affixed to a post just inside. A tiny red light flashed in sync with her pulse. This was no antique fence, but a high-tech security device. She drew her hand away fast, wondering how many alarms she'd set off simply by touching it. She waited and watched. No sound or movement came from within.

When she could breathe again she glanced up. The spikes at the top of each of the fence's bars looked real, and sharp. Climbing over would be impossible. But there had to be another way inside. She squared her shoulders and began walking the perimeter.

It seemed like a mile as she pressed through tangles of brush and a miniature forest, but it couldn't have been that much. The fence bowed out, and curved back toward the house in the rear. She didn't find a single flaw in it, and she bit her lip in dismay when she reached the end. The last spiked bar of black iron sank into the ground at the edge of a rocky cliff. Below, the sound roiled in whitecapped chaos. The wind picked up and Tamara shivered. She had to do something. Go back? After all this?

She eyed the final spear of the fence. The ground near its base didn't look too solid. Still, she thought, if she gripped the fence tightly she might be able to swing her body around to the other side. Right?

She gripped a filigree vine with her right hand, the right side of her body touching the fence. She faced the sound and the biting wind that came off it. She had to lean out, over, and twist her body in order to grip the same vine on the other side of the fence with her left hand.

Bent in this awkward, painful pose, she glanced down. Points of slick, black rock jutted sporadically from water of the same color. They appeared and disappeared with each swell. They winked at her, like supernatural, unspeakably evil eyes. Her hair whipped around her face. Her nose and cheeks burned with cold, and her eyes watered. She edged forward until her toes hung over, then drew a breath and swung her left leg out and around, slamming it down again on firm, solid earth.

She couldn't stop her gaze from slanting downward once more as she straddled the iron fence, one arm and one leg on either side while her rear end jutted into space. A wave of dizziness, almost exactly corresponding to the waves of seawater moving below, temporarily swamped her brain. She had to close her eyes to battle it. She swallowed three times in quick succession before she dared open them again.

Grunting with the effort, she released her right hand from the outside of the fence and brought it around to cling to a bar on the inside. She clung for all she was worth. All that remained was to move her right leg around to this side now. She lifted it, drew it backward, out over the water, and jerked it in again, slamming her foot down on the ground near the edge. But the ground she stood on dissolved like sugar in hot coffee. *Too near the edge,* she had time to think. Her right foot scraped down over the sheer face of the cliff until the entire leg, to the thigh, made an arrow pointing to certain death on the rocks below. Her left leg lay flat, heel down, on the ground so she was almost doing a split. She still clung to the fence with her left hand. Her right had been torn free when she'd slipped so hard and so fast.

The filigree vine she gripped began slowly to cut into her fingers. They burned, and in moments they throbbed incessantly. She knew she couldn't hold on another second with each second that she held on. The muscle in the back of the thigh that lay flat to the ground felt stretched to violin-string proportions.

Frantically she dug at the stone face with her toe, knowing as she did that it was useless. She was going to die on those rocks beneath the angry black water…and all for the chance to prove to herself that Eric Marquand was not a vampire.

Her fingers slipped. Her thigh throbbed with pain. She slid a couple more inches. Then her toe struck a small protrusion in the cliff face. She pressed onto it, praying it would hold. It did, and she was able to lever herself higher, and get a grip on the fence with her free hand. She pulled, scraping her foot along the sheer stone, wriggling her body up until she was completely supported by the solid, snow-dusted ground. For a long moment she remained there, hands still gripping the cold iron bars, face pressed to them, as well. Her body trembled and she wished to God she'd never embarked on this crazy mission.

Fine time to change my mind, she thought. I'm certainly not leaving here the same way I came. She sighed, lifted her head and pulled herself to her feet. She'd just have to go inside, confess her lunacy to Eric and hope he wouldn't laugh her off the planet. Then she sobered. He might not find her intrusion funny at all. He might resent her snooping as much as he resented Daniel's.

She brushed snow and damp earth from her jeans, wincing and drawing her hand away. A thin smear of blood stained the denim and she turned her palm up to see spiderweb strands of scarlet trickling from the creases of her fingers. She fought the tiny shiver that raced along her spine, balled her hand into a fist and shoved it into her pocket, then strode over the snowy ground toward the rear of Eric's house. She knocked at a set of French doors similar to her own. When no response came she thumped a little harder. Still no one answered.

He wasn't home. And she was stuck in his backyard until he *got* home, she thought miserably.

The wind howled off the sound, battering the house and Tamara with it. Her jeans were dampened from the snow and the wet ground. Her hand was throbbing. She had no idea when he'd return, or even if he would tonight. She couldn't stand here much longer or she thought she'd suffer frostbite. No, she had to get inside. Eric could be as angry as he wanted, but she'd left herself with few options. She wasn't about to tempt the sound again by trying to leave as she'd arrived. The French doors seemed like an omen. If they'd been any other type, she would have had *no* options. But French doors she could open. She'd had to force her own a time or two when she'd misplaced the key.

She dipped into her coat pocket hoping to find—yes! A small silver nail file presented itself when she withdrew her fist and opened it. She turned toward the doors, and hesitated. Another gust exploded from the sound, and suddenly wet snow slanted across the sky, slicing her face like tiny shards of glass. She huddled into her coat and moved more quickly. She slipped the file between the two panels, nimbly flicked the latch and opened them.

She stepped inside and pulled the doors together behind her. She thought it wasn't much warmer here than outside, then saw the huge marble fireplace facing her, glowing with coals of a forgotten fire. She tugged off her boots, shrugged free of the coat and hurried to the promise of warmth. A stack of wood beside the hearth offered hope, and she bent to toss several chunks onto the grate, then stretched her nearly numb hands toward the heat. She stood for just a moment, absorbing the warmth as the chills stopped racing around her body. Tongues of flame lapped hungrily at the logs, snapping loudly and sending tiny showers of sparks up the chimney.

After a time she lowered her hands and glanced around her. She had the urge to rub her eyes and look again. It seemed she'd been transported backward in time. The chair behind her was a profusion of needlepoint genius. Every scrap of material on the thing had been embroidered with birds, flowers, leaves. The wooden arms and legs had scroll-like shapes at their ends. A footstool of the same design sat before it, and Tamara bent to run one fingertip reverently over the cushion. All of the furniture was of the same period. She was no expert, but she guessed it was Louis XV, and she knew it was in mint condition. Marble-topped, gilded tables with angels carved into their legs were placed at intervals. Other chairs similar to the first were scattered about. The sofa…no, it was more like a settee, was small by today's standards. Its velvet upholstery of deep green contrasted with the intricately carved wooden arms and legs.

She examined the room itself, noting a chandelier of brass and crystal suspended high overhead. Yet at one end of the room shelves had been built to hold thousands of dollars worth of stereo equipment, and rows of CDs, LPs, and cassettes. Nearby, a rather ordinary-looking bar seemed out of place in the antique-filled room, with the parquet floors. She saw oil lamps on every stand, yet a light switch on the wall. The sun sank lower, and she walked toward the bar, snapped on the light and licked her lips. She could use a drink. She was still shivering intermittently, despite the warmth filling the room. If Eric could forgive her for breaking into his home, she reasoned, he ought to be able to forgive her for stealing a small glass of—of whatever he had on hand.

She went behind the bar and ducked down to look at the nearly-empty shelves underneath. Not a single bottle rested there. Glasses, yes. A couple of expensive cut-crystal decanters. She stood, frowning, turning only when she heard the almost silent hum of the small refrigerator, built in to the wall behind her.

Smiling at her own oversight, Tamara gripped the handle and tugged....

A tiny chunk of ice placed itself in the center of her chest, and slowly grew until it enveloped her entire body.

Her jaw fell. She took a step back, blinking, unable to believe what she was seeing. Blood. Plastic bags filled with blood in two neat stacks. She felt as if she'd been dropped into the fury of a cyclone. She saw nothing all at once, except a thin red haze, heard nothing but a deafening roar. Mindlessly she shoved at the small door. It swung, but didn't quite close, and slowly it slipped back to its wide-open position. Tamara didn't notice. She turned away, face buried in her hands, fingertips pressing into her eyelids as if she could erase what she'd seen.

"It wasn't real. It couldn't have been real. I'll turn around. If I turn around and look again it won't be there because it wasn't real."

She didn't turn around, though. She lifted her head, focused on the French doors and hurried toward them. She wanted to run, but couldn't. Just walking in her socks seemed absurdly loud on the parquet floor. She felt eyes on her, seemingly from everywhere. Her own gaze darted about, like a bird flitting from branch to branch on a tree, in constant motion. She couldn't shake the feeling that someone was right behind her, no matter which way she turned. She moved forward, then whirled and walked backward a few steps. Only a yard to go. She'd grab up her boots. She'd snatch her coat as she ran outside. She wouldn't wait to put them on first. Another step. An invisible finger of ice traced a path up her backbone.

"Too crazy," she whispered, turning fast and walking backward again. "It's all too crazy—this place—me. *I'm* too crazy." Her mind cartwheeled out of control and she pivoted once more, ready to make a lunge for the door. Her path was blocked by a broad, hard chest covered in crisp white cotton.

She automatically drew back, but Eric's hands clamped down on her shoulders before she'd moved a half step. Frozen in place, she only stared up at him as her breaths began coming too quickly and too shallowly. Her head swam. Against her will she studied his face. His eyes glistened, and she knew more than just bald terror of this man. She felt a sickening sense of loss and of betrayal. Daniel had been right all along.

"What are you doing here, Tamara?"

She tried to swallow, but her throat was like a sandy desert. She pulled against his hands, surprised when he let them fall from her shoulders. A strange voice behind her made her whirl between heartbeats. "Snooping, of course. I told you not to trust her, Eric. She's DPI." The man standing near the bar waved a hand toward the opened refrigerator. That first glimpse of him nearly extinguished the small spark of reason she had left. He was dressed all in black, with a satin cloak that reached to the floor all but blanketing him. He moved like a panther, with inconceivable grace and latent power. He exuded a sexual magnetism that was palpable. His dark good looks were belied by the ageless wisdom in the depths of his smoldering jet eyes. As she watched he lifted a decanter to the bar, and then a matching glass. He reached into the open fridge and took out a bag.

Tamara had never fainted in her life, but she came very close then. Her head floated three feet above her shoulders and her knees dissolved. For just an instant black velvet engulfed her. She didn't feel herself sink toward the floor. Eric moved even before she knew what was happening. He scooped her up as soon as she faltered, carried her to the settee and lowered her carefully. "That was unnecessary, Roland!" She heard his angry shout, but knew he hadn't moved his lips. Her sanity slipped another notch.

She sat with her back against one hard wooden arm. Eric sat beside her, his arms making walls around her. His right hand braced against the back of the settee, his left against the arm on which she leaned. She cringed into the warm green velvet. "Get away from me." Her words tripped over each other on the way past her lips. "Let me go home."

"You will go home, Tamara. As soon as you tell me what you are doing here. Is Roland correct? Have you been sent by your employers? Perhaps by St. Claire himself?"

CHAPTER SEVEN

Deny it, Eric thought desperately. *Deny it, Tamara, and I'll believe you. If it costs my existence, I'll believe you.* He watched her chalky face go even paler. He honed his senses to hers and felt a shock of paralyzing fear. Fear...of *him.* It hit him painfully.

"Tamara, you needn't be afraid. I'd sooner harm myself than you." He glanced toward Roland. "Leave us for a time." He spoke aloud to be certain Tamara understood.

He had no doubt Roland did so for the same reason. Slanting a derogatory gaze in her direction, he said, "And if she would lead a regiment of DPI forces to the back door?" He stepped out from behind the bar and came nearer. "Well, girl? Speak up. Have you come alone? How did you get in?"

Eric shot to his feet, his anger flaring hot. "I am warning you, Roland, let me take care of this matter. You are only frightening her."

"*I?* Frightening *her?* You think I felt secure when I woke and sensed a human presence in this house? For God's sake, Eric, for all I knew I was about to be skewered on a stake!"

"Th-then it's true." Tamara's voice, shaking and sounding as if every word were forced, brought Eric's gaze back to her. "You're—you both are, are—"

"Vampires," Roland spat. "It isn't a dirty word, at least, not among us."

She groaned and put her head in her hands. Roland shook his head in exasperation and turned away. Eric took his seat beside her once more. He wanted to comfort her, but wasn't certain he knew how. He pulled one of her hands into his own, and stroked her palm with his thumb. "Tamara, look at me, please." She lifted her head, but couldn't seem to meet his gaze. "Try to see beyond your fear, and the shock of this revelation. Just see me.

I am the same man I was last night, and the night before. I am the same man who held you in my arms...who kissed you. Did I frighten you then? Did I give you any reason to fear me?''

Her eyes focused on his, and he thought they cleared a bit. She shook her head. More confident, he pressed on. ''I am not a monster, Tamara. I'd never harm you. I'd kill anyone who tried. Listen with your heart and you'll know it to be true.'' He reached one hand tentatively, and when she didn't flinch or draw away he flattened one palm to her silken cheek. ''Believe that.''

Her brows drew together slightly, and he thought she might be thinking it over. Roland cleared his throat, her head snapped around and the fear returned to her eyes. ''If it is me you fear, you need not. I do not choose to trust you as my dear friend does, but neither would I lift a finger to harm you. My anger at finding you here is directly related to my wish to continue existing.'' The last was said with a meaningful glance at Eric.

''Tamara.'' When he had her attention again, he continued. ''There are those who would like nothing better than to murder us in our sleep. We both thought my security system infallible. Please, tell me how you breached it.''

She swallowed. Her throat convulsed. ''Where the fence ends,'' she said hoarsely. ''At the cliff.'' Her gaze flew to Roland. ''I didn't bring anyone here. I didn't even tell them where I—'' She bit her lips before she could finish the sentence, but Eric had barely heard her words.

''At the cliff?'' he repeated. For the first time he looked at her closely. Her denims were damp and caked with dirt. A streak of mud marred her high cheekbone, and her hair was wild. The scent of blood reached him from the hand he held, and he spread her fingers wider with his own. Drying blood coated her palm. Fresh trickles of it came from narrow slices at the creases of three fingers. It pulsed a bit harder from the fourth. ''How did this happen?''

''I—I fell. I had to cling to the fence, and the vine patterns are sharp. They cut—''

Roland swore softly and whirled to leave the room. Eric could clearly see what she described. He sensed what had happened, her fear, her panic and her pain. The memory embedded itself in his mind as firmly as it had in hers, and it shook him to think of her coming so close to death while he slept, helpless to save her. Roland returned, dropped to his knees beside the settee and deposited a basin of warm water on the table beside it. He squeezed a clean white cloth and handed it to Eric. As Eric gently cleaned her hand, Roland looked on, his face drawn as if he, too, could envision what had happened.

The wounds cleansed, Roland produced a tiny bottle of iodine. He took Tamara's hand from Eric's, and dabbed each cut liberally with the brownish liquid. He recapped the bottle, and took another strip of white cloth from some hidden pocket beneath his cloak. Carefully he began to wrap her four fingers at the knuckle.

"It—it's only a couple of scratches," Tamara croaked, watching his movements in something like astonishment.

Roland stopped, seeming to consider for a moment. He grinned then, a bit sheepishly. "I sometimes forget what century this is. You've likely been vaccinated against tetanus. There was a time when even minor scratches like these could have cost the entire hand, if not treated." He shrugged and finished the wrapping with a neat little knot. He glanced up at Tamara, caught her amazement and frowned. "You assumed we would go into a frenzy at the scent of your blood, like a pack of hungry wolves, did you not?"

"Enough, Roland," Eric cut in. "You cannot blame her for misconceptions about us. She's been reared by a man who loathes our kind. She only needs to see for herself we are not the monsters he would have her believe." He studied Tamara, but found she wasn't looking at either of them. She was staring at the white bandage on her hand, turning it this way and that, frowning as if she didn't quite know what it was, or how it had got there.

His stomach clenched. She'd had a scare out there at the cliff, and now another shock, in learning the truth about him. She was shaken. He'd have to go gently. "Tamara," he said softly. When she looked up, he went on. "Will you tell me why you came here?"

"I...had to know. I had to know."

He closed his eyes and made himself continue. "Then St. Claire doesn't know you've come to me?"

Some of the fear returned to her wide, dark eyes, but to her credit she answered honestly. "No one knows I'm here."

He swallowed, and squared his shoulders. He had to ask the next question, no matter how distasteful. "Did you come to discover my secrets, and take them back to your guardian, Tamara?"

She shook her head emphatically, straightening up in her corner of the settee. "I wouldn't do that!" When she met his gaze again, her eyes narrowed. The fear seemed to be shoved aside to make room for another emotion. "I was honest with you, Eric. I found myself telling you things I had never told anyone, and every one of them was the truth. I trusted you." Her voice broke, and she had to draw a shaky breath before she could continue. In that instant Roland nodded toward Eric, indicating he was satisfied that she posed no threat, and would leave them alone now. Roland vanished through a darkened doorway. Tamara found her voice and rushed on.

"I told you about the nightmares, about how I thought I might be going insane. I bared my soul to you, and the whole time you were deceiving me. Daniel was right. You were only using me to get closer to him!"

Eric felt a shaft of white-hot iron pierce his heart. All she wanted at this moment was to get away from him. He swallowed his pain. "I never deceived you, Tamara."

"You deceived me by omission," she countered.

"And I would have told you the rest of it, in time. I didn't think you were ready to hear the truth."

"The truth? You mean that you've been plotting to rid yourself of an old man's harassment, and you were using me to do it?"

"That I am not like other men. I had no idea you were under St. Claire's hand until you told me yourself, and after that my only goal was to protect you from the bastard!"

"Protect me? From *Daniel?*"

Eric let his chin drop to his chest. "If I was lying to you, you would know it," he told her slowly, carefully, enunciating each word and giving each time to penetrate her mind. She was angry now. He didn't suppose that should surprise him. He met her probing, questing eyes. "We have a psychic link, Tamara. You cannot deny that. You've felt its power. When you called to me in your dreams, when I summoned you out onto the balcony. Have you realized yet that you can cry out to me, across the miles, using nothing but your mind, and that I will hear you?"

She shook her head fast. "The dream was a fluke, and beyond my control. I couldn't do it at will."

"You could. Put it to the test, if you doubt me."

"No, thank you. I just want to go home...and—"

"Do not say it, Tamara. You know it is untrue," Eric cut in, sensing her declaration before she uttered it.

She met his gaze, her own unwavering. "I don't want to see you again. I want you to leave me alone. I can't let myself be used to betray Daniel, or DPI."

"I would never ask you to do either one. I haven't yet, have I?" He grabbed her shoulders when she would have stood, and held her where she was. "As for the rest, now you are the one lying, Tamara—to yourself and to me. You do not wish for me to leave you alone. Quite the opposite, in fact."

She shook her head.

"Shall I prove it to you, yet again? You want me, Tamara. With the same mindless passion I feel for you. It goes far beyond the past we share. It exceeds this mental link. I would feel it even if you were a stranger. Our bond only strengthens it, and vice versa."

She stared into his eyes, and her own dampened. "I can't feel this way for you. *I can't,* dammit."

"Because I'm a vampire?"

She closed her eyes against the glycerin like tears that pooled there. "I don't even know what that means. I only know you despise the man I hold more dear to me than anything in the world."

"I despise no one. It is true that I distrust the man. But I wish him no harm, I swear to you." Her eyes opened slowly, and she studied his face. "I could not long for something that would cause you pain, Tamara. To harm St. Claire would also harm you. I can see that clearly. I'm not capable of causing you pain."

She shook her head. "I don't know what to believe. I—I just want to leave. I can't think clearly here."

"I can't let you go in this frame of mind," he said softly. "Stop trying to rationalize, Tamara. Let yourself feel what is between us. You cannot make it disappear." His gaze touched her lips, and before he could stop himself he fastened his hungry mouth over them, enfolding her in his arms and drawing her to his chest.

She remained stiff, but he felt her lips tremble against his. Barely lifting his mouth away, he whispered, "Close your mind and open your heart. Do not think. *Feel.*" His lips closed the hairbreadth of space again, nudging hers apart, feeding on the sweetness behind them. With a shudder that shook her entire body Tamara surrendered. He felt her go soft and pliable, and then her arms twined around his neck and her soft mouth opened farther. When his tongue plunged deeply into the velvet moistness, her fingers clenched in his hair. One hand fumbled with the ribbon that held his customary queue. A moment later the ribbon fell away, and she swept her fingers again and again through his hair, driving him to greater passion.

He pressed her backward until she lay against the settee's

wooden arm and still farther, so her back arched over it. His own arm clutching her to him rested at the small of her back, protecting her from the hard wood. His other arm stretched lengthwise, up her spine so his hand could entangle itself in her hair. His fingers spread open to cradle her head. He moved it this way and that beneath his plundering lips to fit her to him. His chest pressed hard on hers. He drank in the honeyed elixir of her; he tasted every wet recess his tongue could reach. He caressed the roof of her mouth, the backs of her teeth and the sweet well of her throat.

She groaned, a deep, guttural sound that set an inferno blazing through him. She shifted beneath him so that one leg, bent at the knee, pressed into the back of the settee, while the other still hung off the side, onto the floor. He responded instantly and without thought, turning into her, pressing one knee to the cushion and lowering his hips to hers. He brought one hand down, sliding it beneath her firm backside and holding her to him while he ground against her. He throbbed with need, and he knew she could feel his hardness pushing insistently against her most sensitive spot, as his hand kneaded her derriere. He felt her desire racing through her, and the knowledge that she wanted just what he did added fuel to the fire incinerating his mind.

He trailed a burning path over her face with his lips, moving steadily lower, over her defined jawbone, to the soft hollow of her throat. Her jugular swelled its welcome, and her pulse thundered in anticipation. He tasted the salt of her skin on his stroking tongue, and the stream of her blood rushing beneath its surface tingled on his lips. His breathing became rapid and gruff. His own heart hammered and the blood lust twined with the sexual arousal, enhancing it until both roared in his ears as one entity.

Another moment—another of her heated, whimpering breaths bathing his skin, or one more shift of her luscious body against his straining groin—and it would take over completely. He'd lose control. He'd tear her clothing off and he'd take her. He'd take her completely. He'd bury himself inside her so deeply she'd cry out, and he'd drink the nectar from her veins until he was sated.

She arched against him then, pressing her throat hard against his mouth, and her hips tighter to his manhood. She shivered from her toes to her lips. Even her hands on his back and in his hair trembled, and she moaned softly—a plea for something she wasn't even fully aware of craving.

He gathered every ounce of strength in him and tore himself from her so roughly he almost stumbled to the floor. He whirled away from her, bent nearly double, holding the edge of the table for support.

He heard her gasp in surprise, then he heard the strangled sob that broke from her lips, and when he dared look at her, her knees were drawn to her chest, her face pressed to them. "Why—" she began.

"I'm sorry. Tamara, you make me forget common sense. You make me forget everything except how badly I want you."

"Then…" She paused for a long moment and drew a shuddery breath. "Then why did you stop?"

He had to close his eyes. She'd lifted her tearstained face to search his for an answer. When he opened them again, she was dashing her tears away with the backs of her hands. "I came to you to help you, to protect you. You called to me for help. You thought yourself slipping away from sanity. I had to come to you. But not for this—not to satisfy my own unquenchable lust."

She shook her head in obvious confusion. He stepped forward, extended his hands, and she slipped her feet to the floor, took them in her own and rose.

"There are still many things you do not fully understand. No matter how badly I want you—and I do, never doubt that—I cannot let my desire cloud my good judgment. You are not ready."

She glanced up at him, and very slightly her lips turned up. "I don't know anything about you, and yet I feel I know you better than anyone. One thing I do know is that you were right when you said you were different from other men. Any other man wouldn't have stopped himself just now. The hell with what was best for me.'' She sighed and shook her head. ''When I'm with you, even I say the hell with what is best for me. Sensation takes over. It's as if I lose my will. It frightens me.''

His lips thinned and he nodded. He well understood what she was feeling. The powerful feelings seemed beyond her control. Well, they seemed beyond his, as well. But he'd keep himself in check if it killed him.

''Will you tell me yet, how I know you? When did we get so close? Why can't I remember?''

He reached out, unable to resist touching her again. His body screamed for contact with hers. He lifted her hair away from her head, and let it fall through his fingers. ''You have had enough to deal with tonight, Tamara. Your mind will give you the memory when it can accept and understand. It grieves me to refuse anything you ask of me, but, believe me, I feel it is better for you to remember on your own. Ask me anything else, anything at all.''

She tilted her head to one side, seeming to accept what he said. Then, ''You told me your father was murdered in Paris. Was it during the revolution?''

He sighed his relief. He'd thought she would run from him. Even the strength of their passion hadn't frightened her away...yet. He slipped an arm around her shoulders, and she walked beside him easily. He drew her into the corridor, and through it to the library, where he flicked the switch, flooding the room with harsh electric light. Normally he wouldn't have bothered. He'd simply have lit a lamp or two. He waved a hand to the huge portrait of his parents on the wall. It had been commissioned shortly after their marriage, and so had captured them in the bloom of youth and the height of beauty.

''Your parents?'' She caught her breath when he nodded.

"She's so beautiful, such delicate features and skin like porcelain. Her hair is like yours."

At her words Eric felt a rush of memory. He saw again his petite mother, remembered the softness of her hair and the sweet sound of her voice. She'd spurned the trend of leaving the child rearing to the nurse. She'd tucked him into bed each night, and sung to him in that lilting, lulling voice.

He hadn't realized Tamara stared at him, until she suddenly clutched his hand and blinked moisture from her eyes. "You must miss her terribly."

"At least she escaped the bloody terror. Both she and my sister, Jaqueline, lived out their lives to the natural end, in England. My father wasn't so fortunate. He was beheaded in Paris. I would have been, too, if not for Roland."

"That's when you were…changed?" Eric nodded. "And afterward, when you were free, why didn't you join your mother and sister in England?"

"I couldn't go to them then, Tamara. I was no longer the son or the brother they remembered—the awkward, withdrawn outsider who never fit in and lacked confidence enough to try. I was changed, strong, sure of myself, powerful. How could I have explained all of the differences in me, or the fact that I could only see them by night?"

"It might not have mattered to them," she said, placing a hand gently on his arm.

"Or it might have made them despise and fear me. I couldn't have borne that…to see revulsion in the eyes of my own mother. No. It was easier to let them believe me dead and go on with their lives."

The night was a revelation. What at first had frightened and shocked her she soon found only one more unique thing about Eric Marquand. He was a vampire. What did that mean? she wondered. That the sun would kill him, the way inhaling water would kill a human? It meant he needed human blood in order to exist. She'd seen for herself how he acquired it. Not by killing or maiming innocent people, but by stealing it from blood banks.

As the hours of the night raced past he told her of the night he'd helped his mother and sister escape France, and been arrested himself. At her gentle coaxing he'd shared more of his past. He'd related tales of his boyhood that made her laugh, and revealed a love for his long-lost mother that made her cry. He might not be human, but he had human emotions. She sensed a pain within him that would have crippled her had it been her own. How many centuries of a nearly solitary existence could one man bear?

She found herself likening her solitude to his, and feeling another level of kinship with him. By the time he walked her to her car the feeling that she'd known him forever had overwhelmed her confusion over his true nature.

Until she arrived home, after midnight, to find Daniel and Curtis waiting like guard dogs. "Where have you been?" They snapped the question almost in unison.

"Here we go again," she muttered, keeping her bandaged hand thrust into her pocket. "I was out. I had some thinking to do, and you both know how much I enjoy crisp wintry nights. I just lost track of time."

She was shocked speechless when Curtis gripped her upper arm hard and drew her close. His gaze burned over her throat, and she knew what he sought. "You saw Marquand tonight, didn't you, Tammy?"

"You think I'd tell you if I did? You are not my keeper, Curt."

He released her, turned away and pushed a hand through his hair. Daniel took his place. "He's only worried, just as I am, honey. I told you before we suspected he'd try to see you again. Please, you have to tell me if he did. It's for your own good."

If she told Daniel the truth he'd probably have a coronary, she thought. She swallowed against the bile that rose at the thought of telling him the truth. But lying was equally distasteful. "I didn't see anyone tonight, Daniel. I'm confused and frustrated. I needed to be alone, without you two hovering." She'd done it. She'd told an out-and-out lie to the man she loved most in the world. She felt like a Judas.

Curtis faced her again. He took her arm, gently this time, and led her to the sofa, pushing her down. "It's time you heard a few harsh truths, kid. The first one is this. I do have the right to ask. I love you, you little idiot. I always assumed you'd realize that sooner or later, and marry me. Lately, though, you've been acting like I'm a stranger. I'm tired of it. I've had enough. It ends, here and now. I won't let Marquand come between us."

"Come between—Curtis, how can he? There is no *us*."

He sighed in frustration, looking at her as if she were dense. "You see what I mean?" He made his voice gentler, and he sat down beside her. "Tamara, no matter what he's told you, you have to remember what he is. He'll lie so smoothly you'll hang on every word. He'll convince you he cares about you, when the truth is, he only cares about eliminating any threat to his existence. And at the moment the threat in question is Daniel. Don't let his words confuse you, Tammy. We are the ones who love you. We are the ones who've been here for you, who know you inside and out."

She wanted to answer him, but found herself tongue-tied.

"I know what's happening," Curt went on. "They have an incredible psychic ability. He's pulling one of the oldest tricks in the book on you, Tammy. I'd bet money on it. He's planting feelings in your mind, making you think you know him. You feel like you are intimate friends, but you can't remember when you met or where. You trust him instinctively—only it isn't instinctive. It's his damn mind commanding yours to trust him. He can do it, you know. He can fill your head with all these vague feelings for him, and make you ignore the ones that are real."

My God, could he be right?

"You're confused, Tam," Daniel added slowly, carefully.

"He's keeping you awake nights by exerting his power over you. That's why you feel as if you can sleep during the day. He rests then. He can't influence your mind. By using the added susceptibility caused by the lack of sleep, his power over your mind can get stronger and stronger. Believe me, sweetheart, I've seen it happen before."

She stared from one of them to the other, as a sickening feeling grew within her. What they'd said made perfect sense. Yet she felt a certainty in her heart that they were wrong. Or was that in her mind—put there by Eric? How could she tell what she felt from what he was making her feel?

"What reason would I have to lie to you, Tam?" Daniel asked.

She shook her head. She couldn't bring herself to tell the truth. She'd feel as if she were betraying Eric if she did. But she felt she was betraying them by keeping it from them. She had a real sensation of being torn in half. "It doesn't matter, because you're wrong. I haven't seen him since the night at the rink. He hasn't been on my mind at all, except when you two hound me about him. And my insomnia was just from stress. It's gone now. I'm sleeping just fine. In fact, I'd like to be sleeping right now."

She rose and made her way past them, and up the stairs to her room. She collapsed on the bed and pushed her face into the pillows. She wouldn't close her eyes until dawn. Was it because of Eric? Was he trying to take over her mind? Oh, God, how could she ever know for sure? She herself had said that she couldn't think clearly when she was with him. And hadn't he demonstrated how he could take control of her that night on the balcony?

She sat up in bed, eyes flying wide. How could she stop it?

"I can't see him anymore," she whispered. "I have to stay away from him and give myself a chance to see this without his influence. I need to be objective." The decision made, her heart proceeded to crumble as if it were made of crystal and had just been pummeled with a sledgehammer. "I can't see him again," she repeated, and the bits were ground to dust.

CHAPTER EIGHT

"She despises me." Eric drew away from the microscope at the sound of his friend entering the lab where he'd ensconced himself for the third night running.

"She might fear you, Eric, but it's as you pointed out. She's been reared by a man who thinks us monsters. Give her time to adjust to the idea."

"She's repulsed by the idea." Eric pressed four fingertips to the dull ache at the center of his forehead. "There is nothing I can do to change that. The fact remains, though, that she is in trouble."

Roland frowned. "The nightmares have returned?"

"No, and she no longer cries out to me. But she hasn't slept since last I saw her. I feel her exhaustion to the point where it saps my own strength. She cannot continue this way."

"Not since you saw her? Eric, it's been three nights—"

"Tonight will make four. She's on the verge of collapse. I want to go to her. But to force my presence on her if she's not yet able to handle it could do more harm than good, I think. Especially in her present state of mind."

Roland nodded. "I have to agree. But it's killing you to stay away, is it not, Eric?"

Eric sighed, his gaze sweeping the ceiling as his head tilted back. "That it is. What is worse is that I am not certain I can help her when she's ready to accept my assistance. Why does she not sleep? Is it simply the blocked memory of our encounters keeping her from her rest, or something more? Is it possible that my blood changed her in some way—that its effect is felt even now, after all this time? Or is it only when I'm near she suffers this way? Would she be better off if I left the country again?"

"Use a bit of sense, Eric! Would you leave her without aid in the hands of that butcher who calls himself a scientist?"

Eric shook his head. "No. That I could never do. If these things have occurred to me, they must have occurred to him, as well. I'd not be surprised if he decided to use her for his experiments."

"Are you certain he hasn't?"

"I'd know if she were in pain, or distress."

"Perhaps he has her sedated, unconscious," Roland suggested.

"No. She doesn't summon me, but I feel her. I feel the wall she's erected to keep herself from me. She resists the very thought of me." An odd lump formed in his throat, nearly choking him, and an unseen fist squeezed his heart.

The nights were the hardest. She'd taken to staying late at the DPI building in White Plains. Her reasons were multiple. One was that she got a lot more work done after sunset. No matter how physically and emotionally drained she became, the energy surged after dark. She wondered why Eric would want to torture her this way. She couldn't give in to her body's need for rest during the day. She'd convinced Daniel that she was better, and for the moment it seemed he believed her. At least he wasn't hovering over her constantly. Then again, she hadn't left the house except to go to work and come home again, in days.

Curtis was another problem altogether. He checked in on her three or four times every day while she was at work, and it was an effort to appear wide awake and bright eyed at his surprise visits. He hadn't mentioned again his outrageous suggestion that she marry him. She was grateful for that. She knew he didn't love her, and still had enough acumen in her dulled mind to understand what had prompted his words. He wanted to protect her from the alleged threat of Eric Marquand. He wanted her under his thumb twenty-four hours a day, and especially those hours after dark. He saw that she was outgrowing his and

Daniel's ability to control her. As her husband, he assumed he could keep her in line. She couldn't hate him for it. After all, it was only because he cared so much and was so concerned about her that he had spoken at all.

She gathered up the files on her desk and carried them toward the cabinet to put them in their places. The sun had vanished. She felt wide awake. It frightened her. How much longer could she go on without sleep?

Another question lingered in the back of her mind, one more troubling than the first. She avoided it when she could, but at night found it impossible. Why did she feel so empty inside? Why did she miss him so? It was foolish, she barely knew the man. Or did she? She found it difficult to believe that her sense of knowing him in the past had been planted there by some kind of hypnosis. The familiar sense of him didn't seem based in her mind, but in her heart, *her soul.* And so was the aching need to see him again. She longed for him so much it hurt. How could this feeling be false, the result of a spell she was under?

"Tamara?"

She looked up fast, startled at the soft voice intruding on her thoughts. She blinked away the burning moisture that had gathered in her eyes, and rose, forcing a smile for Hilary Garner.

Hilary smiled back, but her chocolate eyes were narrow. "You look like you've been ridden hard and put away wet," she quipped. "And you've been doing a great impression of a recluse lately, Tam. Haven't even been coming outside for lunch. I've missed it."

Tamara sighed, and couldn't meet the other girl's eyes. Hilary was the closest friend she had, besides Daniel and Curtis. They used to do things together. Lately, Tamara realized, she'd had no thought for anyone other than Eric. "It wasn't intentional," she said, and shrugged. "I've had a lot on my mind."

A soft hand, the color of a doe and just as graceful, settled on Tamara's shoulder. "You want to tell me about it?"

Tears sprang anew, and her throat closed painfully. "I can't."

Hilary nodded. "If you can't, you can't. You aren't going home to that mausoleum to brood on it all night, either, unless you're going through me." The mock severity of her voice was comforting.

Tamara met her gaze, grateful that she didn't pry. "What, then?"

"Nothing wild. You don't look up to it. How about a nice quiet dinner someplace? We'll get your mind off whatever's been bugging you."

Tamara nodded as all the air left her lungs. It was a relief that she could put off going home, pacing the hollow house alone while Daniel and Curt either huddled over their latest "breakthrough" in the off-limits basement lab, or took off to spy on Eric for the night.

Daniel appeared in the doorway and Tamara flashed him a smile that was, for once, genuine. "I'm going to dinner with Hilary," she announced. "I'll be home later and if you waste your time worrying about me I'll be very upset with you."

He frowned, but didn't ask her not to go. "Promise me you'll come straight home afterward?"

"Yes, Daniel," she said with exaggerated submissiveness.

He dug in his pocket and brought out a set of keys. "Take the Cadillac. I don't want you stranded in that old car of yours."

"And what if *you* end up stalling the Bug alongside the road somewhere?"

"I'll have Curt follow me home." He held the keys in an outstretched hand and she stepped forward and took them. She dropped them into her purse, extracted her own set and handed them to Daniel. He gave her a long look, seemed to want to say something, but didn't. He left with a sigh that told her he didn't like the idea of her going out at night.

It was worth it, though. For three wonderful hours she and Hilary lingered over every course, from the huge salad and the rich hot soup to the deliciously rare steaks and baked potatoes with buttery baby carrots on the side, and even dessert—cherry cheesecake. Tamara ordered wine with dinner. It was not her habit to imbibe, but she had the glimmering hope that if she had a few drinks tonight, she might be able to sleep when she got home. She allowed the waiter to refill her wineglass three times, and when dinner was over and Hilary ordered an after-dinner seven-seven, Tamara said, "Make it two."

The conversation flowed as it had in the old days, before the nightmares and sleepless nights. For a short time she felt as if she were a normal woman with a strong, healthy mind. The evening ended all too soon, and she said goodbye reluctantly in the parking lot outside and hurried to Daniel's car. She took careful stock of herself before she got behind the wheel. She counted the number of drinks she'd had, and then the number of hours. Four and four. She felt fine. Assured her ability was not impaired, she started the car, pulled on the headlights and backed carefully out of the lot.

She'd take her time driving home, she thought. She'd listen to the radio and not think about the things that were wrong in her life. When she got home, she'd choose a wonderful book from Daniel's shelves and she'd lose herself in reading it. She wouldn't worry about vampires or brainwashing or insane asylums.

The flat tire did not fall in with her plan, however. She thanked her lucky stars she was near an exit ramp, and veered onto it, limping pathetically along the shoulder. She stopped the boat-sized car as soon as she came to a relatively sane spot to do so, and sat for a moment, drumming her fingers on the steering wheel. "I never replaced the spare," she reminded herself.

She looked up and spotted the towering, lighted gas station sign in the distance, not more than three hundred yards from her. With a sigh of resignation she wrenched open the car door, and hooked the strap of her purse over her shoulder with her thumb. She spent one moment hoping the attendant would be a chivalrous type, who'd offer her a ride back to the car...and maybe even change the tire for her.

She almost laughed aloud at that notion. She knew full well that a few minutes from now she'd be heading back to her car, on foot, rolling a new tire and rim along in front of her. Oh, well, she'd changed tires before. She walked along the shoulder, glad of the streetlights in addition to the moon illuminating the pavement ahead of her. Her cheerful demeanor deserted her, though, when a carload of laughing youths passed her, blasting heavy metal from open windows despite the below-freezing temperature, and came to a screeching halt. Two men—boys, really—got out and stood unsteadily. Probably due to whatever had been in the bottles they both gripped.

She turned, deciding it would be better to drive to the station, even if it meant ruining the rim. As soon as she did, the rusted Mustang that seemed to have no muffler lurched into Reverse and roared past her again. It stopped on the shoulder this time and the driver got out. He came slowly toward her. The object in his hand that caught and reflected the light wasn't a bottle. It was a blade.

She stiffened as they closed in on her, two from behind, one dead ahead. No traffic passed in those elongated seconds. She considered darting off to the side, but that would only put her in a scrub lot where they'd be able to catch her, anyway. Better, she decided, to take her chances here. Any second now a car would pass and she'd wave her arms...step in front of it, if necessary.

She glanced over her shoulder at the two youths. One wore tattered jeans and a plaid shirt, unbuttoned and blowing away from his bare, skinny chest in the frigid wind. The other wore sweats and a leather jacket. Both looked sorely in need of a bath and a haircut, but she couldn't believe they'd hurt her. She didn't think either of them was old enough to have legally bought the beer they were swilling down.

She caught her breath when her arm was gripped, and she swung her head forward. The one who held her was no kid. His long, greasy hair hung to his shoulders, but was rooted in a horseshoe shape around a shiny pate. He was shorter than she and a good fifty pounds overweight. He grinned at her. There were gaps in his slimy teeth.

Without a word he took her purse, releasing her arm to do so, but still holding the knife in his other hand. She took a step back and he lifted it fast, pressing the tip just beneath one breast. "Move it and lose it, lady." He tossed her purse over her head, where the two boys now stood close behind her. "Her big Caddy has a flat. You two get it changed, and we'll have ourselves a little joyride."

"There is no spare," she took great pleasure in telling him, thinking it might thwart his plan to steal Daniel's car.

"But you were on your way to buy one, right, honey?" She didn't answer, as the boy in the leather jacket pawed the contents of her purse. "Ninety-five bucks and change in here."

The man with the knife smiled more broadly. "Take it and go to the station. Take the Mustang. Bring the tire back here and get it changed." He traced her breast with the tip of the knife, not hard enough to cut, but she winced in pain and fear. "I'll just keep the lady company while you're gone."

She heard the patter of their feet over the pavement, then they were past her, on their way to the noisy car. They spun the tires as they headed for the gas station. The man turned her around abruptly, twisting one arm behind her back. He shoved her down the slight slope toward the brush lot. "We'll just wait for 'em down here, outta sight."

"The hell we will." She struck backward with one foot, but he caught it with a quick uplift of his own and she wound up facedown in the snow with him on her back.

"You want it right here, that's fine with me," he growled into her ear. She cried out, and immediately felt the icy blade against her throat. Her face was shoved cruelly into the snow, and then his hand was groping beneath her, shoving up inside her blouse, tugging angrily at her bra. When he touched her, her stomach heaved.

My God, she thought, there was no way out of this. Daniel wouldn't worry. He thought her out with Hilary. Even if he did come looking for her, he'd never look here. She'd only used this exit because of the flat. Her normal route home was three exits farther on the highway. His breath fanned her face. With one last vicious pinch he dragged his hot hand away from her breast, and tried to shove it down the front of her jeans, while his hips writhed against her backside.

He's going to do it, she thought. White panic sent her mind whirling, and she fought for control. She couldn't give up. She wouldn't allow herself to feel the hand that violated her. She refused to vomit, because if she did, she'd likely choke to death. She needed help.

Calm descended as Eric's face filled her mind. His words, soothing her with the deep tenor of his voice, rang in her ears. *I'd never harm you. I'd kill anyone who tried.* She closed her eyes. Had he meant what he'd said? *Have you realized yet,* his voice seemed to whisper in her mind, drowning out the frantic panting of the pig on top of her, *that you can cry out to me, across the miles, using nothing but your mind?*

Could she do it? Would he answer if she did?

If you need me, Tamara, call me. I will come to you.

He had managed to unbutton her jeans. The zipper gaped. He rose from her slightly, removing his filthy, vile hand, to fumble with his own fly. She squeezed her eyes tight and tried to make her thoughts coherent. *Help me, Eric. Please, if you meant what you said, help me.* At the sound of his zipper being lowered she felt the oddest sensation that her mind was literally screaming through time and space. It was a frightening feeling, but not unfamiliar. She'd felt it before...in her dreams. The urgency of her thoughts pierced her brain with a high-pitched pain. *I need you, Eric! For God's sake, help me!*

Eric paused in swirling the liquid in the test tube, and his head tilted to one side. He frowned, then shook his head and continued.

"So what's this hocus-pocus?"

He glanced at Roland, one brow raised. "I am trying to isolate the single property in human blood that keeps us alive."

"And what will you do then? Develop it in a tiny pill and expect us to live on them?"

"It would be more convenient than robbing blood banks, my friend." He smiled, but it died almost instantly. His head snapped up and the glass tube fell to the floor and shattered.

Roland jerked in surprise. "What is it, Eric?"

"Tamara." He whipped the latex gloves from his hands as he moved through the room. The white coat followed and then he raced through the corridors of the enormous house, pausing only to snatch his coat from a hook on the way out. By the time he reached the gate he was moving with the preternatural speed that rendered his form no more than a blur to human eyes. He used the speed and momentum to carry him cleanly over the barrier, and sensed Roland at his side. He honed his mind to Tamara's and felt a rush of sickening fear, and icy cold.

Minutes. It took only minutes to reach her, but they seemed like hours to Eric. He stood still for an instant, filling with rage when he saw the bastard wrench her onto her back and attempt to shove her denims down her hips as his mouth covered hers.

Her eyes closed tight, she twisted her face away, and sobbed his name. "Eric...oh, God, Eric, please..."

He gripped the back of the thug's shirt and lifted him away from her, to send him tumbling into the snow. He bent over the stunned man, pulled him slightly upward by his shirtfront and smashed his face with his right fist. He drew back and hit him again, and would have continued doing so had not her soft cry cut through the murderous rage enveloping him. He turned, saw her lying in the snow and let the limp, bloody-faced man fall from his hands.

He went to her, falling to his knees and pulling her trembling body into his arms. He lifted her easily, cradling her, rocking her. "It's over. I'm here. He can't hurt you now." He pressed his face into her hair, and closed his eyes. "He can't hurt you. No one can. I won't allow it."

She drew one shuddering, slow breath, then another, and yet another. Suddenly her arms linked around his neck. She turned her face into the crook of his neck and shoulder and she sobbed—violent, racking sobs that he thought would tear her in two. She clung to him as if to a lifeline, and he held her tightly. For a long while he simply held her and let her cry. He whispered into her hair, words of comfort and reassurance. It was over now. She was safe.

With an involuntary spasmodic sob she lifted her head, searched his face, her eyes brimming with tears and wide with wonder. "You came to me. You really came to me. I called you…"

He blinked against the tears that clouded his vision, and pushed the tangled hair away from her face. "I could not do otherwise. And you should not be so surprised. I told you I would, did I not?"

She nodded.

"I cannot lie to you. I never have, and I swear to you now, I never will." He studied her, knowing she believed him. Her blouse had been torn, and hung from one shoulder in tatters. The fastenings of her denims hung open. She was wet from the snow, and shaking with cold and with reaction, no doubt. He carried her up the slope to the pavement. Roland moved around the automobile. Eric saw that the tire lay on the pavement. Roland had the jack and its handle in his hands and he tossed them into the open trunk.

When he reached the car he glanced down at Tamara once more. She still clung tightly. "Are you injured? Can you stand?"

She lifted her head from his shoulder. "I'm okay. Just a little shaky."

Eric lowered her gently to the pavement, and opened the passenger door of the car. He kept hold of her shoulders as she got in. Roland had just tossed the flat tire into the trunk and slammed it down. Eric called to him. "Where are the others?"

Roland answered mentally, not aloud. *Ran like rabbits, my friend.*

You let them go? Roland, you ought to have thrashed them for this, Eric answered silently, falling into the old habit of speaking that way with his friend.

What of her attacker? Did you kill him?

Not yet. His anger returned when he thought of how close the bastard had come to raping Tamara. *But I intend to, and then those sorry curs that helped him.*

Murder doesn't suit you, Eric. And the other two were mere lads. Leave this as it is. It will be for the best.

Tamara rose from her seat in the car, and Eric realized he hadn't closed the door. Her hand came to his shoulder, and with surprising calm she said, "Roland is right, Eric. They were just kids. When they see the shape you left their friend in, they'll realize how lucky they were tonight. And you know you can't go back there and murder that man in cold blood. It isn't in you."

Both men glanced at her, Roland's gaze astonished. He lifted his brows and spoke aloud. "This will require getting used to. It is odd to think a human can hear my thoughts, although I assume it only occurs when I am conversing with you, Eric. She hears what you hear."

Eric nodded. He slipped his coat from his shoulders, and arranged it over her like a blanket. "She hears what I hear," he repeated. "She can feel what I feel, if she only looks deeply enough. She can read my thoughts and my feelings. I can keep nothing from her." He spoke to Roland but his words were for Tamara's ears. He longed to have her trust. "I'm going to drive her home. Care to ride along?"

Roland took a step away from the auto as if it might bite him. "In that?"

Tamara smiled. Her gaze slid to Eric's and he smiled, as well. She would be all right.

"I am glad you both find my aversion to these machines so highly amusing. I shall manage to travel under my own power, thank you." With a dramatic whirl of his black cloak he vanished into the darkness.

Eric closed Tamara's door, circled the car and got in beside her. For a long moment he simply looked at her, drinking in the familiar beauty of her face. Her eyes moved over his in like manner, as if she, too, had craved the sight of him.

He dragged his gaze away, and searched the car's panel. "It's been a while," he told her, frowning. "But I assume you still need a key."

Her smile sent warmth surging through him. She glanced around, and pointed into the rear seat. "It was in my purse."

He glanced where she pointed and spotted her handbag, spilling over the back seat. He leaned over, located the keys and returned to the correct position. It took him a moment to locate the switch. The last time he'd driven a car the switch had been on the dashboard, not the side of the steering wheel.

He inserted the key, turned it on and jerked at the mechanical hum the car emitted. She laughed aloud, the sound like music to him. He felt some of her tension leaving her with that laughter.

"How long has it been?" she asked him, amusement in her voice.

Smiling, he looked at her. "I don't recall, exactly. But fear not, I am a quick study. Now then..." His feet did a little tap dance on the floorboard. "Where's the clutch?"

"It's automatic." She slid across the seat, closer to him, and pointed to the pedals on the floor. "There is the brake and that's the accelerator. Now hold your foot on the brake."

He slipped an arm around her shoulders and drew her closer to his side. He pressed his foot onto the pedal she indicated. She put her finger on the indicator. "Look. Park, Reverse, Neutral,

Drive. Put it in Drive.'' He did, smelling her hair, then jerking his head around when the car began to move.

He eased it onto the street and moved it slowly until he got a feel for the thing. Soon he maneuvered the car easily, finding the correct ramp and bringing them onto the highway.

''You said you could never lie to me,'' she said softly, settling close to him. ''Is it true?''

''I could attempt to lie to you, but if I did, and you paid attention, you would know.'' He tightened his arms on her shoulders. ''But I'd never have reason to lie to you, Tamara.''

She nodded. ''I don't want to go right home. Could we stop somewhere? Talk for a while?''

CHAPTER NINE

She didn't need to tell him that the first thing she had to do was to wash the memory of the vile man's touch away from her body. It amazed her that he could read her so well, but he did. He took her to his home, parking the Cadillac within the fence, and around a bend in the driveway, so it couldn't be seen from the highway. He then suggested she call Daniel with a plausible explanation for her lateness. She told Daniel that she and Hilary were heading to a nightclub after dinner, and that she didn't know how late she'd be. He grumbled, but didn't throw too much of a fit. She had to give him credit. He was trying.

When she replaced the receiver of the telephone, Eric reentered the living room, carrying a tray with a bottle of brandy and a delicate-looking long-stemmed bubble glass. She eyed it, unconsciously rubbing one palm over her breast where the pig had touched her.

"His filth can't touch you, Tamara. You're too pure to be sullied by one so vile."

She realized what she'd been doing and drew her hand away. "I feel dirty...contaminated."

"I know. It is a normal reaction, from what I understand. Would you feel less so if you bathed?"

She closed her eyes. "God, yes. I want to scrub myself raw every place he—"

"I sensed as much. I drew a bath for you while you spoke to St. Claire."

Her eyes opened then. "You did?"

He lowered the tray, poured the glass half-full of brandy and brought it to her. One arm around her shoulders, he led her down a long, high-ceilinged corridor, and through a door.

The room glowed with amber light from the oil lamps, and

the tall, elegant candles that burned on every inch of available space. A claw-footed, ivory-toned tub brimmed with bubbly, steaming water. He took the brandy from her unresisting hand and set the glass on a stand near the tub. He picked up what looked like a remote control from the same spot, thumbed a button, and soft music wafted into the room, as soothing as the steam that rose from the water, or the halo glows of light around the myriad of tiny flames.

She leaned over the tub, touched an iridescent bubble and felt the spatters on her wrist when it popped. His hand touched her shoulder and she turned, staring up at him in wonder. "I can't believe you did all this."

"I want to comfort you, Tamara. I want to erase the horror that touched you tonight. I want to replace it with tenderness. I cherish you. Do you know that?"

She felt a lump in her throat. His words were so poignant they made her eyes burn.

"I won't lose control. I couldn't unleash my passions on you after what you've experienced tonight. I only want to pamper you, to show you..." He closed his eyes, lifted her hand to his lips. He kissed her knuckles, one by one, then opened his eyes and turned her hand over and pressed his lips to her palm.

She gave her consent, without parting her lips. He heard it, it seemed. He gently removed her tattered blouse, and set it aside. He reached around her, unhooked her bra in the back and then drew the straps down over her shoulders. Her right breast was bruised, and she felt the marks of the other man's fingers would never go away completely.

"The marks are only skin-deep, and they will fade." He pushed her still-damp jeans down, lifted his hands and she held them, to balance while she stepped out of them. She removed the panties herself. She didn't want him to look down at her body. She still felt dirty, despite his words. He kept his gaze magnetized to hers, holding her hands as she lifted one foot, then the other into the bubbly water. She sank slowly down, leaning back against the cool porcelain and closing her eyes.

She felt the touch of the chill glass in her palm and she closed her hand on it. "Sip," Eric instructed. "Relax. Let the tension ebb. Hear Wolfgang's genius."

She tasted the brandy, not opening her eyes. "Mmm. This is wonderful."

"Cognac," he replied. She heard the trickle of water, then felt a warm cloth moving over her throat, and around to the back of her neck.

She frowned, still keeping her eyes closed. "There used to be a legend about vampires and running water...."

She heard his low chuckle. The cloth left her skin to plunge into the water. He squeezed it out, lathered it with soap and returned to his gentle cleansing—of her soul, it seemed. "Completely false." He moved slowly over her chest, washing her breasts as her heartbeat quickened. But he didn't touch her in passion, only in comfort. "And so is the one about the garlic, or wolfsbane. And, as you already know, the crucifix."

"But sunlight..."

"Yes, sunlight is my enemy. It is one of the things I try to work out in my laboratory. The how of it, and the why. What I might do to change it." He sighed, and lathered her stomach and abdomen. "I can't tell you how much I miss the sun." His hand, covered by the wet cloth, moved over her rib cage beneath the water, and down her side.

"The wooden stake?"

"It isn't the stake that would do me in. Any sharp object could, if used properly. A vampire is almost like a sufferer of hemophilia. We could bleed to death quite easily." He ran the cloth between her legs all too briefly, and then moved on to rhythmically massage her thighs.

"Why do we have this mental link?" She took another long, slow drink of the cognac and opened her eyes to watch his face as he answered.

"I will try to begin to explain it to you. You see, not just any human can become a vampire. There are, in fact, very few who could be transformed, all of whom have two common traits." He moved to her calf, kneading the back of it as he soaped it for her. "One is the bloodline. It traces back to a common ancestor, but I suspect it goes back much farther, even, than that."

"Who?"

He captured one of her feet in both his soapy hands and lifted it from the water to rub and caress and massage it until the foot and his hands were invisible beneath a mound of suds. "Prince Vlad the Impaler...better known as—"

"Dracula," she breathed, awestruck.

"Exactly. The other trait—" he rubbed her big toe between his thumb and forefinger "—is in the blood itself. There is an antigen called Belladonna."

She sat up fast. "But I have the Belladonna antigen." He turned his face toward her, his gaze momentarily locking onto her breasts, jiggling with the sudden movement just above the water's surface, bubbles clinging, sliding slowly down.

He licked his lips. "Yes, and you have the ancestor, as well. Such humans with both traits are rare. We call them the Chosen. Always there is a mental link between us and them, though in most cases the humans are unaware of it. We know if they are in danger, and we do our best to protect them. The incident in Paris was not the first time Roland had saved my life, you see." He forced his head to turn away again, she noticed, and he went to work, with his magic hands and fingers, on her other foot. "That is where our link began. It became much stronger, and that part of it you must remember on your own."

She lowered herself into the water again. She believed him. She no longer doubted what he'd told her. The sensation of being able to see what was in his mind was awesome to her, but very real. She knew, for instance, that it would do her no good to insist he tell her more of their past and this link. He wouldn't. For her sake, he wouldn't. And she knew, right now, the effort it was costing him not to jerk her roughly into his arms and to kiss her until her head swam with desire. He held himself in rigid check, knowing the terror she'd felt tonight. For her sake, he held back.

He loved her.

His love was like a soft, warm blanket, enveloping her and protecting her from the world. Nothing could touch her with this feeling around her. It was heaven to be loved so much. Cherished, as he'd told her. The emotions touched her almost physically. Their warmth was palpable.

"Roll over," he said, his voice very deep and soft in the tiny room. She did, folding her arms on the tub's rim to make a pillow for her head. His powerful hands worked the soapy cloth over her back and shoulders. He massaged and caressed and washed her all at once, and his every touch was pure ecstasy. God, she wondered. What would it be like to make love to him?

He shuddered. She felt his hands tremble with it. He heard her thoughts. With her face averted she found the courage to speak them aloud. "Why do you always...hold back?"

His sigh was not quite steady. "This is not the wisest subject to discuss with you naked, wet and plied with brandy."

He kneaded her buttocks with soapy hands, but removed them soon. She rolled over, studying his face in the candlelight. "Do you want me?"

His jaw twitched as he studied her. "More than I want to draw another breath."

"Then why—"

"Hush." The command was bitten out. He rose from his crouching position beside the tub and pulled a blanket-sized towel from a rack. He held it wide open and waited. "It is for your own good, Tamara," he told her.

Tamara got up, stepped out of the bath and onto the thick rug beside the tub. His towel-draped arms closed around her, then moved away, leaving the towel behind. "I'll leave you to dress—"

"You didn't leave me to undress," she snapped. She wasn't certain what made her angrier—the knowledge that she wanted him or the fact that he refused to oblige her.

"Your blouse is ruined." He nodded toward the stand where he'd placed her clothes after she'd discarded them. "There is one of my shirts for you to wear." He turned from her and strode out of the room.

"For my own good," she fumed after he left her. She reached down into the bubbly water and jerked the stopper out. "Why is everything I hate always supposedly for my own good? It's like *I* don't know what's good for me and what isn't."

She roughly adjusted the towel under her arms, and tucked the corners in to hold it there. She knew what was good for her. She was an adult, not a child. She wanted him, whatever he was. And he wanted her, dammit. All of this honorable restraint bull was making her crazy. The only time she felt right anymore was when he held her, when he kissed her.

Tonight...tonight more than ever she needed that feeling of rightness, of belonging. She moved very slowly through the door, down the hallway and back into the living room. Eric's back was to her. He knelt in front of the fireplace, feeding sticks into it. She made no sound as she moved barefoot over the parquet floor, onto the colorful Oriental rug, but he knew she approached. She felt it. She stopped when she stood right behind him, and she placed her damp hands on his shoulders. He'd removed his jacket when they'd arrived here, and rolled his shirt sleeves up when he'd bathed her. His arms, bare to the elbows and taut with tense muscles, stilled at her touch.

Slowly he rose. He turned, and when he looked down at her, his eyes seemed almost pain filled. "You are not making this easy."

His white shirt's top two buttons were open. She touched the expanse of his chest visible there. "Make love to me, Eric."

So hoarsely she wouldn't have known his voice, he answered. "Don't you know that I would if I could?"

"Then tell me why. Make me understand—"

"I'm not human! What more do you need to know?"

"Everything!" She curled her hand around his neck, her fingers moving through the short, curling hairs at his nape, then playing at the queue. "You want to love me, Eric. I feel it every time you look at me. And don't start telling me what's best for me. I'm a grown woman. I know what I want, and I want you."

His eyes moved jerkily over her face. She felt his restraint, and her bravado deserted her. She began to tremble with emotion, and she went all but limp against him. Eric's arms came around her. His hands stroked her shoulders above the towel, and the damp ends of her hair. "Oh, Eric, I was so afraid. I've never been so afraid in my life. He held my face down in the snow—I couldn't breathe—and he—was on me—his—his hands—"

"It's over now," he soothed. "No one will hurt you again."

"But I see him. In my mind I see him, and I can still—smell—God, he stank!"

"Shh."

"Make me forget, Eric. I know you can." She spoke with her face pressed into the crook of his neck. Her hands moved over the back of his head, and she turned her face up. She saw the passion in his black eyes. "I need you tonight, Eric."

His lips met hers lightly, trembling at the fleeting contact. They lifted away. His gaze delved into her eyes, and she saw the fire's glow reflected in his. He moaned her name very softly, before his mouth covered hers again. She tilted her head back, parted her lips to his voracious invasion. His tongue swept within her, as it had done before, as if he would devour her if he were able. It twined around her tongue, and drew it into his mouth to suckle it. She responded by tasting as much of his mouth as he had of hers, as her eager fingers untied the small black ribbon at his nape. She sifted his shining jet hair, pulled a handful around to rub its softness over her cheek. She tugged her lips from his to bury her face in his long hair and let its scent envelop her, drowning out the memory of the other. She turned then, to kiss his neck, and then a warm, wet path down it, to the V of his shirt.

He trembled, his hands tangling in her hair. She brought her own down, to clumsily unbutton and shove aside the cotton that stood between them. She flattened her palms to his hard, hairless chest. She moved them over its broad expanse, her lips following the trail they blazed. She paused at a distended male nipple and flicked her tongue over it, nearly giddy with delight when he sucked his breath through clenched teeth. Her hands moved lower, over the pectorals that rippled beneath taut skin, to his tight, flat belly. Her fingertips touched the waistband of his trousers, and she slid them underneath.

A moment later her hand closed around his hot, bulging shaft. Eric's head fell backward as if his neck muscles had gone limp. He groaned at her touch and she squeezed him and stroked him, encouraged by his response. His head came level again, his eyes fairly blazing when they met hers. He brought one hand around to the front of her and caught the corners of the towel she'd wrapped herself in. With a flick of his fingers the thick terry cloth fell to her feet. His arms slipped around her waist and pulled her body to his, flesh to flesh. The sensation set her pulse racing. His hard, muscled chest and tight, warm skin touching her soft breasts. His strong arms around her, his big hands moving over her bare back, crushing her to him. She clung to his shoulders, further aroused at the sinewy strength she found there.

Attacking her mouth once again, Eric lowered her gently to the floor. She lay on her back, stretched before the fire, and he lay on his side beside her, one arm beneath her, pillowing her head for his plundering mouth. His other hand moved hotly over her body. He cupped and squeezed her breasts, gently pinching her nipples until they throbbed against his fingers. He moved his hand lower, trailing fingertips over her belly, and then burying them in the nest of hair between her thighs.

With a slowness that was torture he parted the soft folds there.

She closed her eyes when he probed her, and felt the growing wetness he evoked from her. She wanted him. She parted her legs and arched toward his exploring fingers, to tell him so. She closed her eyes when he took his mouth from hers and lowered it to nurse at her breast. She felt him tremble when his teeth scraped over her nipple, and she pressed his head to her with one hand and fumbled for the fastenings of his trousers with the other.

He helped her push them down, and then he kicked free of them, lying naked as she was. She opened her eyes to look at him in the firelight. She thought him the most beautiful man she'd ever seen. Every inch of him was tight, hard, corded with muscle. His skin was smooth and taut, elastic and practically hairless. Her gaze moved down his body, up it again, and met his smoldering eyes. *Are you certain?* he seemed to ask, though he never said a word.

In answer she fastened her mouth to his, pulling his body to her. He covered her gently. Instinctively she planted her feet, bent her knees and opened herself to him. Slowly he filled her, and she caught her breath at the feeling. This was more than sex, she thought dimly, as he pushed gently deeper. This was a completion of some cosmic cycle. He belonged here with her, and she with him. This was right. He withdrew, so careful not to hurt her, and began to slide inward again. She gripped his firm buttocks and jerked him into her. The fullness forced the breath from her lungs, but she arched to meet his next powerful thrust.

His pace quickened, and Tamara knew nothing for a time, except for the sensations of her body. His mouth moved over her throat, her jaw, her breasts. He suckled and licked and bit at her, setting her blood to boiling. His hands had moved beneath her to cup her buttocks and lift her to him. They kneaded her, caressed her and rocked her to his rhythm. His rigid shaft stroked to her deepest recesses, no longer hesitant, but hard and fast. She felt a tension twist within her. His movements inside her drew it tighter, and she trembled with the force of it. Tighter, and he caused it. He sensed her body's responses and he played upon them, adjusting his movements to draw out the exquisite torture. She bucked beneath him, seeking a release that hovered just beyond her reach, and she felt a similar need in him.

He moved within her more quickly now, his breaths coming short and fast. His mouth opened, hot and wet against her throat, and she felt her skin being drawn into it. She felt the skim of his incisors and the answering thrum of her pulse. She knew a craving she'd never known before, and she arched her throat to him just as she arched her hips to meet his. She screamed aloud with her mindless need, gripped the back of his head and pressed him harder to her neck.

The tension drew tighter, so tight she thought she'd soon explode with it. He withdrew slowly, and she whimpered her plea. "Please...now, Eric...do it now!" He drove into her, withdrew and drove again, the force of his thrusts beyond control, it seemed. He plunged so violently it would have lifted her body from the floor if he hadn't held her immobile, forcing her to take all of him, with all the strength he could muster. And she wouldn't have drawn away if she'd been able. She wanted this...and more. Another rending thrust and she felt herself reach the precipice. He let her linger there, drawing it out until her cries were like those of a wounded animal. His teeth closed on her throat. She felt the incisors pricking at her skin and she clutched him closer.

They punctured her throat as he plunged into her again, driving her over the edge. The pain was ecstasy in the throes of the climax that rocked her. She convulsed around him, and then harder as she felt him sucking at her throat. Her body milked his, and she trembled all over, violently, with spasms of pleasure she hadn't known could exist. He bucked inside her, and she knew he'd reached the peak, as well. She felt his hot seed spill into her as her own climax went on and on. His mouth open wide at her throat, his tongue moving greedily to taste her, he shook with the force of his own release. He groaned, long and low, and then collapsed on top of her with one last, full body shudder. He carefully withdrew his teeth.

He started to move off her, but she quickly wrapped her arms around him. His head was pillowed on her breasts, and she held him there. "Don't move yet," she whispered. "Just hold me."

He pulled free despite her words, and rolled to the floor beside her. He sat up, gazing down at her, his eyes glistening, mirroring the fire. His fingers touched her throat, and he squeezed his eyes closed. "God, what have I done?" His words were no more than a choked whisper. "What kind of monster am I that I would allow myself—"

"Don't say that!" She started to sit up, but his hands came fast to her shoulders.

"No, you mustn't move. Lie still. Rest." He moved one hand through her hair, over and over again. "I'm so sorry. So very sorry, Tamara."

She frowned, shaking her head. "You didn't hurt me, Eric. My God, it was incredible—"

"I *drank* from you!"

"I know what you did. What I don't know is why you act like you've stabbed me through the heart. I've lost more blood than that when I cut myself shaving!" She made her voice more gentle when the pain didn't leave his eyes. She reached up and stroked his face with her palm. "Eric," she whispered. "What ill effects will there be? Will I become a vampire now?"

"No, that requires mingling of—"

"Will I be sick?"

"No. Perhaps a bit dizzy when you get up, but it will pass."

"Then why are you so remorseful?" She sat up slowly, angled her head and pressed her lips to his. "I loved what you did to me, Eric. I wanted it as badly as you did."

"You couldn't—"

"I did. I feel what you feel, don't forget. I understand now why you held back before. It's a part of the passion for you, isn't it? It's another kind of climax." His eyes searched hers, as if in awe. "You see, I do understand. I felt it too."

He shook his head. "It didn't repulse you?"

"Repulse me? Eric, I love you." She blinked and realized what she'd just said, then looked him in the eyes. "I love you."

CHAPTER TEN

Two in the morning. She lay staring up at the white underside of her canopy, wishing to God she could close her eyes. Eric had insisted on bringing her home after she'd blurted that she loved him. He had seemed shocked speechless for a few moments. Then he was awkward, as if he didn't quite know what to say to her. She was confused. What did he want from her, a physical relationship without emotions? But there already had been emotions between them, deep, soul-stirring emotions she was only beginning to understand. And she'd thought he loved her. He'd implied it. He'd said he had love for her. Was that the same thing?

She turned restlessly onto her side and punched her pillow. Again she glanced at the cognac on the bedside stand. He'd insisted she take it with her, since she'd remarked on how wonderful it was. No wonder, she thought now. The stuff was bottled in 1910. It was probably worth a fortune. And here she was swilling another glassful in hopes of using it as a sleep aid. If she didn't get some sleep soon she was going to collapse at work, in front of everyone, and then what would Daniel do? Probably check her into a rest home.

She wandered into the bathroom, still wide awake a half hour later. What was she going to do about Eric? Daniel would die if he knew the truth. She loved the old coot. She would hate to hurt him. God, her mind was spinning with too much tonight. She opened the medicine cabinet and rummaged until she found the brown plastic prescription bottle. She'd tried the damned sleeping pills before. Single doses, double doses, even once a triple dose. She hadn't even worked up a good yawn. She twisted the cap and poured four tiny white capsule-shaped pills into the palm of her hand. She popped them into her mouth with a cynical glance at her reflection. Who was she kidding? She wouldn't close her eyes until dawn.

A glass of water rinsed the caplets down. She wandered back to bed, realized she still held the worthless bottle of tranquilizers in her fist and dropped it carelessly on the stand.

"Kill him for this."

Daniel? Was that Daniel's voice tickling the fringes of her consciousness? He sounded angry, and strained.

"I tried to tell you." Curtis's voice was louder, more level. "She should have been under constant surveillance. If we'd followed her, we'd have had the bastard."

"If your tranquilizer works. It hasn't been tested, Curtis. You can't be certain it will immobilize him."

"And how the hell do you suggest we test it? Send out a notice asking for volunteers? Look, I've done everything I can think of. All signs are, it will work. There's nothing left to do but try it."

Try what? On whom? And why were they both so angry?

"He raped her, Curtis." Daniel's voice warbled on the words. "It wasn't enough to take her blood, he had to have her body, as well. The son of a bitch raped her…left bruises on her skin. My God, no wonder she couldn't bear to face us in the morning."

"I never thought Tammy would be the kind to try this way out. Pills and brandy!" Curt's voice sounded harsh on her ears. "Why the hell didn't she tell us and let us handle it?"

Raped? Tamara remembered the pig on the highway ramp… his hands on her, his filthy breath on her face. But he hadn't raped her. Eric came and—Eric—my God, they thought Eric had put these bruises on her body. She struggled to open her eyes. Her lips moved but no sound came from them. She had to tell them!

"She's coming around." Daniel's presence lingered closer. She forced her heavy lids to open. Nothing focused and the attempt left her dizzy, with a sharp pain in her head. She felt his hands on her forehead, but it seemed her forehead was not attached to her. Everything seemed distorted.

"Tamara? It's all right, sweetheart. Curtis and I are with you now. Marquand can't hurt you now."

Frantically she tossed her head back and forth on the pillows. Pillows that were too plump and stiff, with cases too starched and white. Not her own pillows. "No...Eric...not...him..." Damn, why couldn't she make her mouth form a coherent sentence?

"*Eric*," Curtis mocked. "I told you she remembered. It's all been an act. I wouldn't be surprised if she went to him willingly, Daniel. We always knew he'd come for her, didn't we? And I always said she'd never be one of us. You brought her right inside DPI. For Christ's sake, I wonder how many secrets she's passed already?"

"She wouldn't betray us to him, Curt," Daniel said, but his voice was laced with doubt.

"Then why did she mix those pills with the booze? It's guilt, I'm telling you! She sold us out and couldn't face it."

"What could she possibly have told him? She doesn't know anything about the research!"

"That we know of," Curtis added, his words meaningful. "He would like nothing better than to murder the both of us, Daniel. We're the leaders in vampire research. He gets rid of us, he sets the entire field back twenty years or more."

"You think I don't know that?"

She struggled against the darkness she felt reaching out to her, but it was a worthless fight. She whispered his name once more before she sank into the warm abyss. The voices of the men she loved grew dimmer.

"He'll come to her...just like before."

"We'll be ready. Get the tranquilizer and meet me back here."

* * *

Eric paced the room yet again, pushing a hand through his hair, adding to its disarray. "Where is she? I attune my mind to hers, and yet I feel nothing!"

"She's probably managed to get some sleep. Do not disturb her."

Eric shook his head. "No. No, something is wrong. I feel it."

Roland's brows creased with worry, despite his feigned sigh of exasperation. "This ingenue of yours is becoming a bit of a bother. What trouble do you suppose she's got herself into this time?"

"Wish to God I knew." He turned, paced away toward the fireplace, spun on his heel and came back. He stopped and met Roland's gaze. "I shouldn't have let it happen. She was already in a fragile state of mind. When she realized what she'd done in the cold light of day she likely felt soiled, infected by my touch, made—"

"Shut up, unless you can say something reasonably intelligent, Eric. If she didn't mind it last eve, she won't mind it now. You think the girl doesn't know her own mind? My interpretation of events is this: your blood, given her so many years ago, altered her to some degree. It sealed the bond between you, and made her feel a natural aversion to sunlight, an abounding exuberance by night. It is a logical guess, then, that she would not be as repulsed by the taking of a few drops in a moment of passion, as a normal human might."

Eric sighed long and loud. "She thinks herself in love with me. Did I tell you that?"

"Only a hundred or so times since we rose a mere hour ago, Eric...not that I'm keeping count. What's so surprising in that? You fancy yourself in love with her, do you not?"

"I don't fancy myself anything. I do love her. With everything in me."

"Who's to say she doesn't feel the same?"

Eric closed his eyes slowly, and left them that way. "I hope to God she doesn't. It is enough that I will have to bear the pain

of our eventual separation. I wouldn't wish such agony on her."
He opened his eyes and met Roland's frown. "It is inevitable."

"It is anything but that. She could be—"

"Do not even think to suggest it." Eric turned away from his
friend, his gaze jumping around the room, settling nowhere.
"This existence has been my curse. I wouldn't wish it to be
hers, as well."

Roland's voice came low, more gruff. "If it is the loneliness
of which you speak, Eric, no one understands better than I."

"Your solitude is self-imposed. It's as you want it. Mine is
an unending sentence of solitary confinement. I don't interact
because I cannot trust in anyone—not with DPI always seeking
a way to destroy me."

"My solitude—" Roland cut himself off, and simultaneously
closed his mind to Eric's curiosity. When he began his voice
was steadier. "Is not the matter we were discussing. Your existence would not be lonely if you had someone with whom to
share it."

Eric closed his eyes and shook his head. "I have already considered this question, Roland. I've made my decision."

"The decision, my friend, is not yours to make."

Anger flared within Eric. His head came up, and he slowly
turned to tell Roland exactly what he thought of that remark,
when the scent slowly twisted around his mind. He gripped it
the way a drowning man would grip a lifeline, and he concentrated, focusing his entire being on that one sensation coming to
him from Tamara. The scent...he frowned harder...clean...
sterile. Sickeningly familiar.

His eyes wide, he faced Roland. "My God, she's hospitalized!"

Eric lunged for the door, but Roland leapt into his path. "A
moment, Eric. You tend to lose all sense of caution where Tamara is concerned." He reached for his satin cloak and flung it
about his shoulders with a long-practiced twist of his arms. "I

dare not imagine what sort of mess you'll end in without me along."

"Fine." Eric paused as he reached for the door. "Roland, you can't wear that to a hospital. You look as if you've stepped out of the pages of that Stoker fellow's book."

"I have no intention of going inside. Can't bear the places, myself."

True to his word, Roland lurked in the shadows outside while Eric followed his sharpening sense of Tamara to the proper floor. He took the stairs, and he sent the probing fingers of his mind out ahead of him, ever on the alert for St. Claire or Rogers. Before long he caught a hint of their presence, very near Tamara's, though he felt it nowhere near as strongly as he felt hers.

He glanced up and down the fourth-floor corridor and quickly spotted the room. He'd have known it without help, but the burly man in the dark gray suit posted outside her door made it obvious. Eric didn't recognize him, but knew at once he was DPI. If he was going to see Tamara he'd need to find another way. Already he felt reassured. Her stamina reached from her mind to his, though he sensed she might still be groggy. She was well. He felt it.

His relief was so great he very nearly didn't notice the hinged metal folder on the counter where nurses milled. A strip of white tape across the front bore the words in black ink. Dey, Tamara. Eric stiffened. He had to see that folder. Only then would he know the extent of her injuries, and exactly what had transpired to land her here. He closed his eyes.

Roland? Are you still out there?

Where else would I be? came the bored reply.

I could use a distraction, Eric told him.

Done.

Eric waited for about thirty seconds, uncomfortably watching both directions, half expecting St. Claire to appear at any second. Then a bloodcurdling scream came from a room in another corridor and every nurse stampeded. A male voice echoed through the halls. "It was *grinning at me*—right through my window! I swear! And it, it had fangs—and its eyes—"

Eric grinned slightly, against his will. He hurried to the desk and flipped open Tamara's folder. He didn't need to scan it long. According to the physician who'd examined her, Tamara had been rushed in early this morning, unconscious and with vital signs that were barely discernible. She'd ingested a large amount of tranquilizers, combined with alcohol. According to the doctor's examination, she had recently had sexual intercourse. He further noted the bruises on her torso, and concluded that she'd been raped sometime the previous night. The pills and alcohol had been, in his opinion, a suicide attempt.

The sheet swam before his eyes. His stomach churned. Had he been alone he'd have roared like a wounded lion. As it was, he had to hold his anguish in check. It wasn't rape that had driven her over the edge, he alone knew that. It was something far more damaging to the soul. She'd made passionate love to a monster. Hadn't he known it would be more than she could face when the fire died down? Nearly blind with pain, he closed the folder and headed back the way he'd come.

Roland had just leapt down from the ledge. "Did you hear that fool bellow?" He laughed hard. "I haven't had such fun in years." He halted his chuckles and cleared his throat. "So, how did you find our girl? Did you see her? Eric—my God, you look like hell. What is it?"

Eric swallowed hard and forced the words to come. It wasn't easy. His throat was so tight he could barely inhale, and when he did it burned. "I...couldn't see her. A guard is posted outside her room. DPI." He spotted a bench nearby and went to it. He needed to sit. It was as if he'd been hit by a train. "She tried to take her own life, Roland."

"What!" Instantly Roland sat beside him, his arm at Eric's back. Eric barely felt it.

"I told you she'd regret what we—what I did to her, when

she could think clearly. But I had no idea it would repulse her so that she couldn't go on living!''

"You are wrong!"

The violence in Roland's voice didn't penetrate the wall of pain around Eric. "Sleeping pills mixed with alcohol. It's all on her charts.''

Roland gripped both of Eric's shoulders and forced him to look him in the eye. "No. She wouldn't do it.''

Eric shook his head. "You barely knew her.''

"True, but I know the despondency it takes to drive one to that extreme! Eric, I've been witness to such, firsthand. I've seen all the signs.'' His voice softened. "I only wish I had known them in time.'' He shook himself then. "Eric, do not accept less than her own words to confirm this theory. I know it to be wrong. See her. Talk to her.''

Eric shook his head for the hundredth time. "I am the last person she would wish to see.''

"If so, she will tell you so and you will have your answer. If not, you'd do her a grave injustice to leave her in that room with a DPI guard preventing her leaving.''

Eric's shoulders stiffened where before they'd been slumping. "I suppose I could go in through the window. But I fear St. Claire and Rogers might be in the room with her.''

"Give me a moment,'' Roland said, dropping his brutal grip from Eric's shoulders and rising to pace away. "I'll think of something.''

She blinked the haziness away slowly, and realized Daniel sat close to her, holding her hand. She wondered why she seemed to be in a hospital room, and bits of the conversation she'd heard earlier began surfacing in her mind.

"You're awake.'' Daniel leaned nearer. "They said you'd be coming around soon. You shouldn't have been out as long as you were, but we all figured the rest would do you good, so we let you be.''

It had done her good, she thought as her mind cleared more and more. She felt the energy surge and longed to toss the covers back and go outside. She licked her parched lips. "It's night, isn't it? My God, how long have I slept?"

"I found you in your bed this morning." He swallowed. "I thought you were asleep at first, but then I saw the pills, and the brandy." He repeatedly pushed one cool palm up over her forehead. "Baby, you should have just told me. I wouldn't have blamed you. It wasn't your fault."

She sat up in bed so fast his hand fell away. Fully now, she recalled the words she'd only dimly been aware of at the time. They all thought she'd tried to kill herself. Moreover, they thought she'd been beaten and raped, by Eric, no less. They'd seen the marks his unbridled passion had left on her throat.

"Daniel, I have to tell you what happened last night."

"Don't torture yourself, sweetheart. I already know. I—" A sob rose in his throat, but he fought it down. "I'll kill him for what he did to you, Tam. I swear to God, I will."

"No!" She came to her feet all at once. "Daniel, you have to listen to me. Just..." A wave of dizziness swamped her, and if Daniel hadn't been there to steady her she'd have sunk to the floor. "Just listen to me, please."

"All right. All right, honey, I'll listen if you feel you need to talk it out. Just get back into the bed first, okay?"

She nodded, clinging to his soft shoulders and easing herself back down. When she was once again settled back against the pillows, she focused on staying calm. "Where is Curtis?"

"Outside. He walks the perimeter once very hour. We're not going to let Marquand get near you again, honey. Don't worry on that score."

She rolled her eyes. "Curt should hear this, too, but it can't wait. You'll tell him everything I tell you. Promise?"

He nodded. She cleared her throat and tried to summon courage enough to be honest with him. She should have been from the start. "I've seen Eric Marquand several times since that night at the rink,'' she blurted at last. Daniel opened his mouth but she held up two hands. "Please, let me get through this before you say anything.'' She licked her lips. "He's taken me on a sleigh ride, and fed me hot cocoa and fine cognac—in fact, the cognac I had last night was a gift from him. I've been to his house, too. We sat before a fire and talked for hours. He's not a monster, Daniel. He's a wonderful, caring man.''

"My God...''

"Last night after I left Hilary I had a flat tire. I had to pull off an exit and was going to walk to a service station. I was—'' she closed her eyes at the memory "—attacked. I fought him, but it was no use. He was very strong. I think he would've killed me when he'd finished. But Eric came just in time.'' Her eyes opened now that she'd gotten past the most horrid memory of last night. "He pulled the man off me, and beat him unconscious. He carried me to the car. He covered me with his own coat, and then he drove. He would have brought me directly home, but I asked him not to. I needed time to calm myself.'' She reached for his hand. "Daniel, Eric saved my life last night.''

Daniel stared at her for a long moment. "But, how could...I don't—''

"He's not the monster you keep telling me he is,'' she told him. "He's more human than a lot of men I know.''

For a moment Daniel appeared uncertain, but then his eyes narrowed. "You can't deny the marks he left on your throat. That's proof of what he is.''

She lowered her eyes. "I won't deny them, but I won't lie about them, either. I'm not going to tell you things that are none of your business, Daniel. But you have to know that everything that happened between Eric and me last night happened because I wanted it to happen. I wanted it, even knowing what he is. He didn't hurt me, and he never will.''

"Tamara, what are you saying? You admit he's a vampire and still you defend him?''

She met his gaze without flinching. She would not be ashamed of her feelings for Eric. But she thought she'd given her guardian enough shocks for one evening. "I'm saying that you don't need to worry about me. No harm will ever come to me with Eric around." She put a hand on his arm and squeezed. "I want you to think about something, Daniel. For a long time you've assumed that because his kind is different, they are inherently evil. You've been wrong. You need to sit down and realize how bigoted that mind-set is."

He shook his head and got to his feet. His eyes on her seemed to hold an unvoiced accusation. "Haven't Curtis and I warned you about the mind control he might exercise over you? Haven't I begged you to tell me if he tried to see you again? Tamara, you cannot believe his lies! He would kill me if he had an opportunity, and you are just the one to give it to him! He's using you to get to me, Tamara. You'd have to be blind not to see that!"

She drew in a sharp breath at the fury in his voice, and in his face. It was as if she'd betrayed him. She'd never seen him so angry. "Daniel, you're wrong—"

She was interrupted by a mechanical beep coming from Daniel's belt. He pushed a button and it stopped instantly. "I have to go. Curtis—" He bit his lip.

"Curtis what?" Tamara felt a chill go up her spine. It had something to do with Eric, she was certain of it. Daniel had said Curtis was out searching the grounds, or something like that. Had he spotted Eric? What would they do to him if they caught him? Daniel didn't answer, but moved quickly through the heavy wooden door. As he did, she saw the guard posted outside it, and her heart raced all the faster. She couldn't get out to try to warn Eric that they were out for blood. My God, what if they got to him?

The door closed and she paced the room, battling the dizziness that tried to return sporadically. She shut her eyes and tried to call out to Eric as she'd done before, with her mind. *Eric, if you're out there, be careful! Daniel and Curt—*

Her thoughts came to a halt as a chill breeze rushed over her

body, and a familiar voice spoke softly. "Are presently being
led a merry chase by Roland, all in order to clear them out of
here." As her eyes flew open, he swung his legs over the windowsill, landing gracefully on the floor. He stood still for a moment, as if waiting for her permission to come any closer.

Tamara raced toward him and threw herself into his arms.
"Eric!" His arms around her seemed hesitant, and then he
pushed her from him and eased her back into the bed. His face,
she now noted, was a study in misery. Lines were etched deep
between his brows and on both sides of his mouth. His eyes
were moist and searching. He dropped to one knee beside the
bed, and his voice thickened with every word he uttered. "Sweet
Tamara, I never meant... My God, I never meant to bring you
to this. I swear it to you. If I'd known—but I should have known,
shouldn't I? I should never have done what I did." He choked
on the words and a single tear slipped slowly down his face.

Her heart wrenched as she reached out to touch it, absorbing
it into her fingertips. "Don't think what you're thinking, Eric.
Not even for a minute. This was an accident, nothing more."
His gaze met hers, and she saw the doubt there. "Look into my
mind, since you're so talented at that sort of thing. Better yet,
look into my heart. How could you think I'd want to leave
you?" She felt him doing just what she'd suggested, and as he
probed her mind she explained what she'd done. "I knew I
wouldn't close my eyes all night, and I had to go to work, or
else Daniel would know something was wrong. I sipped the cognac, but it didn't help. A bit later I tried the sleeping pills that
have been sitting in my cabinet for over a month. I'd taken them
before without any ill effects at all. The problem was that I
wasn't thinking clearly, and didn't stop to consider the consequences of mixing them with alcohol. That's all, Eric. I promise,
that's all."

He gathered her into his arms and she felt the shuddering
breath he released as it bathed her neck. "I thought you'd awakened to regret having given yourself to me. If ever you do, Ta-

mara, you must tell me. I will not be the cause of your despair. I will leave you now, if you tell me to do so.''

Her arms clenched tighter and she whispered, ''No. Don't leave me, Eric. Don't...'' Frowning with a sense of déjà vu so strong it made her light-headed she pulled away from him. ''My God, I've said that to you before. In a hospital bed just like this one. I begged you not to leave me...but you did.''

He nodded, his eyes studying her carefully. ''I honestly thought it best for you. I was wrong. I won't make that mistake again. If you ordered me to stay away from you, I'd never go so far as I did then. You'd have my protection. I'd watch over you, as I should have done before. St. Claire never would have got his hands on you if I'd been wiser then.''

''Then it was when I had the accident. That was when I knew you? All these memories and familiarity stem from the time I was six years old?''

''Yes. It is coming back to you now. Soon the rest will, as well, and you will understand better.''

She nodded, wishing she understood now. She wouldn't press him on it, though. He shouldn't be here. It wasn't safe. ''Eric, I had to tell Daniel it wasn't you who attacked and bruised me, but I couldn't very well hide the marks on my throat.'' His eyes moved to that spot and she felt their heat. An answering warmth spread within her, but she forced herself to ignore it. ''I told him that I went to you willingly, that you forced nothing on me. He still insists you have me under some kind of spell, though. Eric, he's furious. It isn't a good idea for you to be here.''

His lips thinned, and he studied her for a long moment. ''You love this man, and I've tried to restrain myself from speaking against him, for your sake, Tamara. Tonight I cannot. It is better to risk your anger than to allow you to continue in your blind trust of him. It is no more safe for you to remain than it is for me. Especially now that he knows of our intimacy.''

She stroked his face lovingly. ''Old habits die hard. He's so used to thinking the worst of you, he can't do otherwise, and I think you have the same problem. Daniel loves me, Eric.''

He covered her hand with his own, closed his eyes and turned his face to press his lips to her palm. "It kills me to hurt you, Tamara. The traits I explained to you, the ones that make you different from other humans—"

"The Belladonna antigen and the common ancestor?"

He nodded. "St. Claire knew of them even then."

She frowned at him, blinking. "He did? But why hasn't he ever told me?"

Eric held her hand in his own. "Tamara, there is a good possibility that he only took you in because he knew you were one of the Chosen. He knew of your connection to us, and he knew that as long as he had you, one of us might come near enough to be captured."

"Captured?" She searched his face, his mind, as he spoke, but she saw no sign that he was lying to her. "For...what?"

His lips parted, but closed again. He shook his head. "I am afraid for you," he told her. "Believe me that is my only motive for telling you these things."

She shook her head, blinking as hot tears pooled in her eyes. "I know you mean it, you believe all of this...but it's wrong. You're wrong. Daniel loves me like his own daughter." She lowered her gaze and shook her head. "He has to. He's the only family I've had for all these years. If all of that was a lie—no. You're wrong."

Eric sighed, but nodded. "I will not press the matter. But Tamara, he is not the only family you have any longer. You have me. No matter what else might happen, you always will. Do you believe me?"

She nodded in return, but her eyes didn't focus. She was searching her mind, realizing that Daniel must've known Eric had visited her in the hospital all those years ago. It was the only explanation for his overprotective behavior now.

Something niggled at her mind, and she squinted hard, trying to remember. "Eric, when I came around earlier, they were saying something about a...a tranquilizer...." She heard their voices replay in her mind, and had the confirmation she'd dreaded.

He'll come to her, just like before. And then Daniel. *We'll be ready. Get the tranquilizer and meet me back here.* Her stomach clenched.

"No tranquilizer known has any effect on vampires, Tamara."

She shook her head hard. "I got the feeling this was something new, something Curt's been working on." She met his gaze then, her fear for him overcoming her own lingering doubts. "I know I'm safe with them, Eric, but as things stand, you aren't. Please leave before they come back."

"I won't cower in fear of them—"

"But Roland might not be safe, either. If there is some kind of drug, and he lets them get too close..."

He frowned then, and nodded. "I'll go, then—this time." Once again he pulled her upper body to him, and kissed her neck, then the hollow just below her ear, then the ear itself. "I find it unbearable to leave you, though."

She closed her eyes and let her head fall back to give his mouth better access. The sensations he sent through her body would overwhelm her common sense in a few seconds. Her fingers tangled in his hair, and her breath caught in her throat. His lips kissed a path to hers, and then he feasted on her mouth and her tongue as if it were to be his last meal. When he lifted himself from her she clung. She pressed wet lips to his ear. "I wish you could stay. I want you so much it hurts." She felt him tremble in response to her words and her touch.

"It is too soon—you've been through so much." Gently he pushed her until she lay amid the pillows. "I will leave you, but not to go far. If anyone tries to harm you, call to me. You know I will hear you."

"I know."

He left the way he'd come, and Tamara thought it felt as if he'd taken a part of her with him.

CHAPTER ELEVEN

She closed the window, returned to her bed and feigned sleep, though she was wide awake and jittery with restlessness. Daniel returned a few minutes after Eric had left her, and took a seat near the window. Tamara ignored him. She wasn't yet ready for a confrontation, but she knew one had to come. She needed to hear from his own lips that the things Eric suspected were wrong.

Dawn approached and Tamara couldn't avoid sleep's clinging vines. They gradually encircled her and tugged her down into slumber. When her eyes flew wide only a moment later, it was to see the final splash of the sun's orange light slowly receding from the sky. Daniel's chair was empty.

She waited, lying still and lazy as the life seemed to filter back into her body. Amazing that she'd slept all day two days running now, so deeply she hadn't been aware of the time ticking past. Refreshed and energized, she flung the covers back and started opening drawers and closet doors in search of her clothes. She'd had enough of this confinement. The only clothing she found were her nightgown and her long houndstooth-check coat. She sighed relief that her boots rested on the closet floor.

There was no guard now. She guessed Daniel assumed she'd only needed guarding after sundown. She caused quite a stir when she announced to the nurses at the crowded desk in the main corridor that she was checking herself out. Forms needed to be signed and the doctor notified. She couldn't just leave. She coolly requested that whatever forms needed signing be handed over at once. She'd already phoned for a cab, and fully intended to be ready when it arrived.

Less than half an hour later she marched through the imposing front door of the neglected house she'd called home for the past twenty years. Daniel stood just beyond the door, pulling his coat on. He looked up, surprised to see her. His smile died slowly when she didn't return it.

"We need to talk" was all she said in greeting.

His faded cornflower eyes turned away from her probing dark ones. He nodded, and exhaled slowly.

"I left a cabby waiting outside. I'll just go get my purse, and—"

"I'll take care of it." Daniel moved past her and out the door before she could argue the point. She heard the vehicle move away, its tires crunching over the packed snow on the road. Daniel returned a moment later. He removed his coat, draped it on a rather wobbly coat tree and gently helped her out of hers. She'd already toed off her boots.

"You ought to go upstairs and lie down, Tam. We can talk in your room."

She faced him squarely. "Is there a DPI guard outside my door?" His gaze dropped so fast there was no doubting his surge of guilt. "Why was I under guard, Daniel?"

He sighed, his shoulders slumping. "I won't lie to you. I was afraid Marquand would try to get to you there."

"Because he came to me once before in a hospital?"

Daniel's head snapped up, eyes widening. "You—you remember?"

She turned from him, stalking though the foyer and into the huge living room. She knew he followed. Her long, quick stride and stiff spine showed her anger almost as well as her words and tone of voice. She faced him again. "No, Daniel. As a matter of fact, I don't remember. For the past few months I've been slowly, systematically losing my mind because I can't remember. I'm trying..." Her throat threatened to close off, and she bit her lips, swallowed twice and forced herself to go on. "You've known about this—this link between Marquand and me all along, though, haven't you? For God's sake, Daniel, how could you keep something like this from me?"

His brows lifted, creasing his forehead. "Tam, I was only doing what I thought was best for you. Trying to protect you—''

"By watching me go insane? My God, the nightmares, the sleeplessness—you had to know it all revolved around Eric. You knew, and you never said a word."

"You were in a fragile state of mind! I couldn't say anything to make it worse."

"Of course not. You couldn't say anything to ease my fears, either, could you, Daniel? Not the way Eric did. You couldn't simply tell me that it was all right, that I wasn't going crazy—that there was a reason for all I was going through and that I'd understand it as soon as my mind was ready to let me remember. You couldn't comfort me that way, could you?"

Daniel couldn't have looked more shocked if she'd slapped him. "He—"

"But you didn't want me to remember, did you, Daniel? Because you knew. You knew how close Eric and I had become, and you knew he'd come to me some day. All these years you've been waiting, watching."

She waited for a furious denial, but saw only remorse in Daniel's leathery face. She had to press it further. She had to ask the final question, though she dreaded hearing the answer. "Is that why you took me in all those years ago, Daniel? Was I just the perfect bait to lure him to you?"

For a long time he didn't answer. When Tamara turned away from him in disgust, his soft hand shot out to grip her arm and turn her back toward him. "I was blind with ambition twenty years ago, Tam. There was nothing in my life except my work. I'd have done anything to get to Marquand...then. But not now." His hand fell from her arm, and he paced away from her slowly, eyes on his feet, but not seeing. "I grew to love you, sweetheart. How could I not? And it wasn't very long at all until I stopped looking forward to the day he'd come back. I started fearing it. I was terrified he'd come and take you away from me."

She held the tears in check. She wasn't certain where she got the strength to do it. "My entire life has been a lie. From the second you came to my hospital room you were enacting a cold, calculated plot." She shook her head. "What were you going to do with Eric when you caught him?"

There was no remorse in his eyes when he faced her this time. Only the frigid gleam of hatred. "Don't pity him, Tam. He's no better than an animal—a rabid wolf who has to be stopped before he can spread his disease. Oh, I had big plans once. I was going to learn the answers to every question I had about him— his kind. Now all I want is to keep him from hurting you."

"Hurt him, and *you'll* be hurting me, Daniel." He stepped closer to her, slowly shaking his head from side to side as his eyes searched her face. "I love him," she said.

Daniel's eyes closed tight and he released a guttural grunt as if he'd been punched hard in the stomach.

She didn't show mercy. She felt none after what he'd said about Eric. "You say you love me, but I don't think that's true. I think you've used me all along and just can't admit it to me now."

Again he shook his head. "That isn't true. I do love you— couldn't love my own child more than I love you."

"Prove it." He faced her, standing stock-still as if he knew what she would ask of him.

"Tamara, I—"

"Drop the research, Daniel. Give up this plan to capture Eric, or any of them." She took a step toward him, and realized she was willing to beg if it would help. "He isn't what you think. He's kind and sensitive and funny. If you met him on the street you wouldn't know he was different at all. He doesn't want to hurt anyone, only to be left alone. If you want your questions answered, Eric would probably be willing to answer them, once he sees he can trust you."

"That's absurd! If I got within his reach I'd be a dead man. Tamara, you're the one who doesn't know this man. He's cunning and ruthless. You accuse me of using you, but he's the one using you...to get to me, I think.''

She blinked slowly. ''I can see I'm not getting through to you.'' Feeling her heart had been bruised beyond repair, she turned and moved to the curving staircase.

''Where—''

''I'm going to shower and change. Then I'm going out. Tomorrow I'll come back and pick up my things.''

''You can't go to him, Tam! My God, don't do this—''

''I can't stay, not unless you agree to what I've asked. Keep in mind the way you've deceived me all this time, Daniel. How much have I ever asked from you? If you love me, you'll do this for me. If not, then it won't kill you to see me go.''

She moved up the stairs, and did exactly what she'd said she would. Daniel didn't try to stop her. When she left by the front door he was not in sight.

She sank into his arms when he opened his door to her. Eric had sensed her turmoil as she approached, and he felt a burgeoning anger toward those responsible. St. Claire and his protégé, no doubt. He held her, and her tears flowed into his shirt. Beyond her, through the open doorway, he felt eyes upon him, and he kicked the door closed. Rogers, he realized slowly. He'd followed her. Eric felt the man's rage like a blistering desert wind, and not solely directed toward him. The heat of his anger was aimed toward Tamara, as well, and the knowledge shook Eric. He knew when the van moved away. The sense of hatred faded, and Eric put it aside for later consideration. Tamara needed to be the center of his attention now.

He held her tighter, and pulled her with him into the parlor, where a cheerful fire and a pot of hot cocoa awaited her. He settled himself on the settee, pulling her across his lap as he might do a small child. He cradled her head to his shoulder, stroking her hair and feeling the painful throbbing in her temples and the dampness of tears on her skin.

"Oh, Eric, you were right. Daniel knew about us all those years ago. He knew you'd come back some day, and that was the only reason he took me in when my parents died." He felt her shuddering breath.

"He admitted it to you?"

She nodded. "He could—could barely look me in the eye."

Eric released a sigh, wishing he could choke the life out of the heartless bastard for causing Tamara this kind of grief. "I am so sorry, sweet. I wish I had been wrong."

The air kept catching in her throat, making each breath she took like a small spasm. "It hurts to know the truth. I love him so much, Eric."

Love him, not loved him. Eric frowned.

She lifted her head from his shoulder. "I can't stop myself from loving him just because he lied to me. I think...in his own way...he loves me, too."

"I keep forgetting how well you read my thoughts," he told her. "How can you believe he cares for you after—"

"I have to believe it. It hurts too much to think he's been acting the part all these years. He says he came to love me, and that his motives for keeping me with him changed." She blinked away the remaining tears, and gently brushed his white shirt with her fingertips. "I got you all wet."

"I would gladly catch every tear you shed, if you'd permit it, Tamara."

Her lips turned up slightly at the corners, but still they trembled. "I'm giving him one more chance." Eric's brows lifted, one higher than the other, as he was prone to do when puzzled. "I told Daniel that if he truly loves me he'll drop his research, and the investigation of you."

"Sweet, trusting Tamara," he said, lifting a lock of hair with his forefinger and tucking it behind her ear. "Do you believe he'll agree? He's made me his life's work, you know. He was tracing my every movement even before you were born."

"I don't know if he'll agree. But, Eric, if he doesn't I think you should go away from here. I'm terrified of what he has planned.''

He smiled fully. ''I am well aware of what he has planned for me. And no, I will not give you new nightmares by sharing it with you. You needn't fear for me, Tamara. With vampires, age is strength. I am over two hundred years strong. A mere human—or even a pair of them—pose no threat to me.''

''But this tranquilizer I heard them mention—''

''It matters not. I'll not leave you again.''

She gazed into his eyes with so much love Eric nearly winced. ''I wouldn't ask you to. I'd go with you.''

She'd go with him, and he knew she'd stay with him. For the span of her mortal life he would be allowed to cherish her and adore her. And then she would leave him to die of heartbreak. He wouldn't have her for more than a moment in time—a mere twenty more years, at best. For though he hadn't shared the knowledge with her, he was painfully aware that humans with the Belladonna antigen rarely live beyond their forty-fifth year.

Perhaps, he thought, Roland had been right. Perhaps the decision wasn't his to make. But could he sentence her to an eternity of darkness? Would she even want it?

Her hand at his face broke his line of thought, and he looked into her eyes. ''What is it?'' she asked. ''I feel sadness but I couldn't tell what you were thinking.''

''I was thinking that you must leave me in the morning.'' She had enough to deal with tonight. Let the question of her mortality wait for another time. ''I wonder if it is wise, now that St. Claire and Rogers know the nature of our relationship? I do not like to think of you within reach of their wrath.''

''Unless Daniel changes his attitude, tomorrow will be the last time I set foot in that house.'' She looked at him and smiled very softly. ''Unless I'm jumping the gun. You haven't invited me—''

''Shall I come to you on my knees? Shall I beg you to stay with me?''

"You only need to tell me you want me." Her voice came out lower than a whisper, and he saw the glimmer left by the tears turn into a soft glow, put there by passion.

"In my existence I have seen women of such beauty it was said they could drive a man beyond reason. Beside you, they would fade as a candle's flame beside the heart of the sun. Never has a woman stirred me as you have done." He lowered his head, tilting her chin with one hand to settle his lips over hers. Softly he sipped them, suckled them, first upper, then lower. He lifted only enough to speak, and to be able to watch her glorious face as he did. "To say that I want you is not enough. Might as well say that the parched and barren desert wants the kiss of the rain. You are the part of myself that's been missing for more than two centuries."

The shimmer in her eyes now had nothing to do with her earlier pain. "Eric, you make love to me with your words as thoroughly as you do with your body." She pressed her mouth to him, parted her succulent lips and invited his tongue's invasion. He accepted eagerly, and her taste aroused him even more than the last time he'd kissed her. Eventually he lifted his head to breathe. "I can't say it as well as you can," she told him, breathless now. "But I feel the same. My life was so empty. I thought I'd never stop wondering why. Then I found you and I knew. I don't know what went between us before, Eric. I don't know why we are this close, but whatever it was, it bound us together. You are a part of me, as vital to my existence as my own heart. If you leave me again..." She stopped there. The sob that involuntarily blocked her words came without warning, he knew.

He lifted her in his arms as he rose from the settee. "Leave you? *Leave you?* Look into my heart with yours. See what is there, and end your doubts. I would swim naked through a pool of shredded glass for you. I'd crawl on my belly over hot coals— through hell itself—to get to you. You are in me, woman, like a fever in my blood. All I find myself wanting these days is more of you.''

He took her mouth fiercely; plundered it as she'd been longing for him to do. He knew she had. He'd heard her silent begging. Even as he took her mouth he moved with her, to the staircase and up it. By the time he reached the top he was panting, as she was. Her fingers twined and tugged at his hair. Her tongue dipped and tasted him, then wrapped around his and drew it back into her moistness. She suckled it as if it were some rare, prized fruit—something she needed in order to live.

He kicked open the bedroom door, carrying her through it, certain she only vaguely noted the candles and oil lamps that cast their flickering, amber glow over the bed he'd prepared for her. He laid her gently upon the high mattress, then straightened, allowing his gaze to devour her. He'd never thought highly of the denims today's women favored. On her, however, he found them alluring, the way they hugged her form like an outer skin. Then again, on her he thought he'd find a burlap sack alluring.

She blinked and broke eye contact, glancing around the room. The satin coverlet on which she lay was fortunate enough to receive a long, appreciative stroke from her equally soft hand. She regarded the oversize four-poster bed and the hand-tooled hardwood, then the masses of candles and the two lamps burning scented oil. ''You did all of this for me?''

He nodded, watching her face. ''You approve?''

Her smile was her answer. She held his eyes prisoner as her delicate fingers began to release the buttons of her blouse. He took a step toward her. She stopped him with a small shake of her head. Eric swallowed hard, but obeyed her silent request. He stood where he was, as the fire inside him burned out of control.

She shrugged so that the blouse fell from her shoulders, and he saw the creamy-colored silk garment beneath it. She slid from the bed, releasing her button, then her zip. She pushed the denim down over her hips, down her long, bare legs, and daintily stepped out of them. She looked to him like a confection prepared especially for him to savor. Cream-colored lace touched her thighs, and the exposed mounds of her breasts. As he fought to form words she repeated his earlier ones. "You approve?"

A low growl was all he managed before he had her in his arms, crushed against him. When his hands lifted the scanty lace to cup her hips he found them bare to his touch. For him, she'd done this. To please him. To arouse him to the point of madness, he thought. He moved his hips so the aching bulge that strained his own zipper nudged her center. He brought one hand up to push the flimsy strap aside and expose her breast to his rough exploration. As his hand teased her nipple to a taut pebble hardness he spoke, moving his lips upon her throat. "You wish to drive me mad, woman? I hope you're certain you want this. I believe you've pushed me beyond the point of return."

He lifted her, hands on her silk-clad sides, and dropped her onto the bed. She watched him struggle with his shirt. He didn't hesitate, but removed his trousers and shorts, as well. He couldn't wait to be inside her luscious body. He saw her eyes focus on his erection, and he clambered onto the bed beside her, eager to mount her. Then he stopped himself. She was his for the entire night, he reminded himself. He needn't take her in haste. He could love her slowly, drive her as wild as she'd already driven him.

She reached for him, eyes glazed with passion. "Are you in such a hurry, sweet Tamara? Would you deny me the chance to savor you first?"

"You want to drink from me again?" Her words were merely sighs given form. "Do it, Eric. I am your slave tonight. Do what you want."

"What I want is to devour you. Every succulent inch of you. At my leisure. Will you lie still and allow it, I wonder?"

He knelt on the mattress beside her, and reached for her tiny foot. He lifted it, kissing a hot path around her ankle, nipping the bone with gentle teasing scrapes of his teeth, then sliding his tongue over it, tracing its shape. She breathed faster, and he moved his head. His mouth trailed very slowly up the soft flesh of her inner calf. He lifted her leg, flicking his tongue over the sensitive hollow behind her knee. She shook violently, and he glanced up to see that her eyes were closed tight. *Oh, yes, my love. Tonight I'll show you the meaning of pleasure.* His mind spoke to hers, since his mouth was too busy carrying out the promise. He nibbled and tasted and licked at her thigh, moving higher slowly and steadily so she couldn't mistake his intent. By the time he reached the heart of her, her need was so great she whimpered with each breath she released. One flick of his tongue over her, and she cried out. *Open for me, love. Give me your sweet nectar.*

She did. He slipped his hands beneath her quivering buttocks and tilted her up, and then he gave her what she silently begged him for. He ravaged her with his mouth, and his teeth. He plunged into her with his tongue. Her taste intoxicated him. He shook with feeling, for her sensations were his, as well. She gasped for breath, tossing her head back and forth on the pillows, her hips writhing beneath him. He pushed her ruthlessly to the precipice, and then forced her over it. She screamed in ecstasy—and still he persisted. She shuddered uncontrollably and pushed his head away, gasping.

"No, no more—I can't—"

"Oh, but you can. Shall I show you that you can?" He lifted himself and moved until his body fully covered hers. He nudged her opening with his hardness. So wet, and still pulsing with her climax. He drove into her without warning. She shivered beneath him as he withdrew and drove again, and yet again. He gave her no time to recover from the first shattering explosion. He forced her trembling body beyond it, and toward another. He anchored her to him with his arms, forcing her acceptance of his every thrust. He covered her mouth with his, and forced his tongue inside, still coated with the taste of her. He plunged harder, faster, and he knew when her fists clenched and her nails sank into the flesh of his back that she was once again on the brink. He swallowed her cries this time when she went over, and she swallowed his, for he fell with her. His entire body shook with the force of his release. He clung to her, relaxing his body to hers.

Aftershocks of pleasure still rippled through him when he began to move inside her again.

CHAPTER TWELVE

Too soon, she thought, when she knew dawn approached. She studied his profile as he lay beside her, and she thought again she'd never known a man so handsome. No shadow of beard darkened his jawline. In fact, his face was as smooth as it had been earlier. He caught her gaze on him and smiled. "I shall have to leave you soon," he said, giving voice to her thoughts.

She snuggled closer, wishing he didn't. "Where do you go? Do you rest in—in a coffin?"

He nodded, sitting up slightly and reaching for his shirt. "Does the idea repulse you?"

"Nothing about you could ever repulse me, Eric." She sat up, too, as he poked his muscled arms into the white sleeves. She pushed his hands away when he began to button the shirt, and leaned over to button it herself. "I don't think I'd like seeing you in it, though. Why a coffin, anyway? Is it some kind of vampire tradition? Why not a bed, for God's sake?"

He laughed, tipping his head back. Tamara found her gaze glued to the corded muscles in his neck. She leaned nearer and pressed her lips to it. He stroked her hair. "It is for protection. There are more humans who know of our existence than you would believe. Most would like nothing better than to terminate it. We could sleep in vaults, or behind locked doors, I suppose. But nothing offers more protection than a coffin, which locks from the inside and has a trapdoor built beneath it."

"Trapdoor?" She finished with his last button and looked up, interested. "Are you conscious enough to use it?"

"The scent of imminent danger would rouse me even from the deepest slumber. Not much, mind you, but I only need move one finger. The button is placed in the spot where my hand rests. When I touch it the hinged mattress swings down, dumping me into a hidden room below. It springs back into place on its own. The only side effects are a few aches from being dumped bodily."

"You feel pain, then?"

"Not while I'm holding you." As he spoke he pulled her into his arms. "But that is not the answer you wanted, is it? In truth, I feel everything more keenly than a human would. Heat, cold, pain..." His fingers danced over her nape. "Pleasure," he whispered close to her ear. "Pain can incapacitate me, but whatever injuries I might sustain are healed while I rest. It's a regenerative sleep, you see." His lips moved over her temple. He kissed her eyelids, her cheeks and then her mouth, thoroughly and deeply. "I believe I will be in need of it after this night."

She smiled at his little joke, but the smile died when she realized that the sky beyond the window was beginning to lighten. She looked at his heavy-lidded eyes, and she felt his growing lethargy. "You need to rest." She pulled from his embrace, reached for their clothes and handed his to him. "Come on, it'll be light soon."

"Too soon," he told her. But he took the trousers from her, and slid off the bed to put them on. "I still dislike the thought of you going back to St. Claire today."

"I know." She fastened her jeans, and walked around the bed to stand close to him. "I have to, though. And I love you more for not trying to tell me what to do. I know you don't think highly of Daniel, but just like he's wrong about you, you're wrong about him, Eric. He isn't all bad."

In the distance the sky began to turn from gray to pink. Eric's shoulders lost their usual spread. His chin wasn't as high as it had been. She put an arm around his waist, and he draped one over her shoulders. She was beginning to feel tired, as well. They descended the stairs side by side, and all too soon stood locked together in the open doorway as Eric kissed her one last time.

She fought her sleepiness as she drove back home. She thought she might have time to catch an hour or two of sleep before she'd have to force herself awake and head in to work. She'd decided to resign. She couldn't continue working for DPI, knowing how they'd sponsored Eric's constant harassment over the years. Besides, it now was a blatant conflict of interest. She was in love with the subject of their longest-running investigation.

She let herself in, and caught her breath. Daniel, fully dressed, lay sprawled on the sofa, one arm and one leg dangling. A blanket had been tossed over him, but he'd only twisted himself up in it. His hair looked as if he'd been outside in a strong wind. When she drew nearer, the odor of stale alcohol assaulted her, and she saw the empty whiskey bottle on the floor.

"Well, finally made it home, did you?"

She caught her breath and looked up fast. Curtis lounged in the doorway that led into the huge dining room, a cup of coffee in his hand. "What are you doing here, Curt?" She glanced quickly at the clock on the wall. It was only five-forty-five.

"You've been with him all night, haven't you?"

There was something in his eyes, some coldness in his voice, that frightened her. "I'm an adult, Curt. Where I go is my business."

He straightened, came across the room and slammed the cup onto a table. "Can't you see how perverted this is? He's a frigging animal! And you're no better—acting like a bitch in heat. Christ, Tammy, if you'd needed it that bad all you had to do was ask—"

She reached him in two long strides and brought her hand across his face hard enough to rock him back on his feet. "Get out!"

"I don't think so." He stood facing her, and she saw absolute hatred in his eyes. How had she ever thought she had a true friend in this man? He blinked, though, and altered his tone of voice. "You're under some kind of spell, Tammy."

"What went on here last night?" She took a step to the side and went past him, through the dining room, knowing he'd follow. In the kitchen she got a cup of coffee for herself, and added sugar, hoping it would give her an energy boost.

"Daniel drank himself into a coma. What does it look like?" She turned, cup in hand, and frowned at him. "He called me around midnight, babbling about you and Marquand. I couldn't make sense of half of it. By the time I got here he'd drained the bottle. He was slurring something about dropping the research, or losing you forever. Is that the game plan, Tam? You use emotional blackmail on a guy who's been like a father to you? Force him to give up forty years of work, just so you can have your kinky fling?"

She felt no anger at his remarks. Only joy. "He said he was going to drop it?"

Curt's glare was once again filled with loathing. "He was too drunk to know *what* he was saying. But let me tell you something, Tam. I'm not going to drop it. Daniel has taught me everything he knows, so if he's ready to throw in the towel, I'll pick it up. You won't manipulate me the way you do him."

She opened her mouth to hurl a scathing reply, but saw Daniel standing weakly beyond Curt, making his way into the kitchen. "You, Curtis, will do what I tell you. I got you this far in DPI, and I can just as easily have you tossed out."

He made it to a kitchen chair, leaned on the back of it for a moment, head down, then pulled it out and sat down. "Daniel, are you okay?" She turned to pour a cup of coffee, and then set it before him. "Can I get you anything?" He looked at her for a long moment, seemingly searching for something. Finally he shook his head, and stared into the coffee cup.

"I owe her, Curtis. You know it as well as I do. We're dropping it."

"You're falling for her game, hook, line and sinker, aren't you?" Curt paced the room, shaking his head, pushing his hands through his hair. "Can't you see she's sold you out? She's joined the enemy, Daniel. She's the one we should have been studying all this time. I always told you she was more vampire than human!''

''What is that supposed to mean?'' Tamara set her coffee down, spilling half of it.

''You mean to tell me you still don't know?''

''Don't know what?''

Daniel struggled to his feet, one hand massaging his forehead. ''That's enough, Curtis. I think you ought to leave now. Tamara and I need to talk.''

Curtis eyed Tamara narrowly. ''You mark my words, Tammy. You go through with this sick liaison and we'll all end up dead. You'll have my blood on your hands.'' He nodded toward Daniel. ''And his. You just remember that I warned you.'' He turned on his heel and strode away. A second later the front door slammed, rattling the windows.

Daniel returned to his seat, shaking his head. ''He'll get over it, Tam. Give him time.''

She sat across from him and slipped her hand over his. ''He's wrong, Daniel. Eric is the gentlest man I've ever known. I want...'' She drew a steadying breath and plunged on. ''I want you to meet him. Talk to him. I want you to see that he's not what you think.''

He nodded. ''I figured you would, and I suppose I have to. I don't mind telling you, Tam, I'm afraid of him. The scientist in me is excited, though. To be that close...'' He nodded again, and went on. ''The biggest part of me knows this is inevitable. I'll do my best to make my peace with him, Tam. I've been over it a million times, all night long. It boils down to one thing.'' He reached up and cupped her face with one hand. ''I don't want to lose you.'' Slowly he closed his eyes. ''Bringing you into this house, into my life changed everything for me, Tamara. Before that I was...'' He opened his eyes and she was surprised to see tears brimming in them. He shook his head.

''Go on. You were what?''

''A different man. A bastard, Tamara. More of a monster than

Marquand could ever be. And I'm sorry for it...sorrier than you'll ever know."

She shook her head, not certain what to say. She felt this to be the most honest moment they'd ever shared.

She finished her coffee and went to bed, and Daniel didn't wake her. In fact, she was roused by the phone, shocked when she blinked her clock into focus and saw the time. She groped for the phone when it shrilled again, and brought it to her, wondering why Daniel hadn't answered it himself.

"Tam?"

At the familiar voice, her irritation dissolved. "Jamey?" She frowned and checked the clock once more. "Why aren't you in school?"

"I cut out. Tam..." He sighed and it sounded shaky. Tamara sat up in bed. "Something's wrong."

"Are you sick?" Her alarm sent the lethargy skittering to a dark corner of her mind. "Did you get hurt or something? Do you want me to call your mom?"

"No. It's not like that, it's something else." Another shuddering sigh. "I'm not sure what it is."

"Okay, Jamey, calm down. Just tell me where you are, and—"

"I took a cab. I'm at a pay phone in Byram. I didn't want to come to the house."

At least that was normal. The rambling Victorian had always given Jamey a case of the creeps. "I'll be there in ten minutes."

"Hurry, Tam, or we'll be too late."

Fear made her voice soft. "Too late for what, Jamey?"

"I don't know! Just hurry, okay?"

"Okay." She replaced the receiver with shaking hands. Something was terribly wrong. She'd heard the terror in Jamey's voice. Along with her gut-twisting concern was a flare of anger. Whoever was responsible for upsetting him this much would have to answer for it. She yanked on jeans and a sweatshirt. She pulled on socks and sneakers, then a jacket. She took a hairbrush from her purse and jerked it through her hair on the way down the stairs. Daniel was just coming up from the basement.

"What is it, hon?"

"Jamey. He's all out of sorts about something. I'm going to meet him in town, buy him a burger and talk him through it." She hugged Daniel quickly, then shoved the brush back into her bag and pulled out her keys.

Five minutes later she picked Jamey up. He was tugging on the Bug's door before it came to a full stop. He climbed in, looking pale and wide-eyed. "I think I'm goin' crazy," he announced.

Her instinct was to tell him that was nonsense, but she'd felt the same way recently—too often not to take his fear seriously. "I've thought that a time or two myself, pal." She searched his young face. Eleven years old was far too young to have such serious troubles weighing on him. "Tell me about it."

"You know before, when I asked you if you knew someone named Eric?" She stiffened, but nodded. "Well, I hope you know where he lives. We have to go there."

She didn't question Jamey. She put the car in gear and moved quickly down the street. "Do you know why?"

Jamey closed his eyes and rubbed his forehead as if it ached. "I think somebody's trying to kill him."

"My God." She pressed the accelerator to the floor, shifting rapidly.

"It's been coming in my head ever since I hung up the phone. It won't leave me alone until we go there—but it doesn't make sense."

"Why?"

"Because...I get the feeling he's already dead."

She drove the Bug as fast as it would go, and it vibrated with the effort. Even then, it took twenty minutes to reach the tall gate at the end of Eric's driveway. Tamara almost cried out when she saw Curt's car, pulled haphazardly onto the roadside nearby.

She slammed on her brakes, killed the motor, wrenched the door open. She ran to the gate with Jamey on her heels.

It had been battered with something heavy. The pretty filigree vines were bent, some broken. The gate hung open and the electronic box inside was crushed. Pieces of its insides littered the snow. A single set of footprints led over the driveway, toward the house.

"Eric!" Tamara's scream echoed in the stillness as the reality of what was happening bludgeoned her mind. A small, firm hand caught hers and tugged her through the gate.

"C'mon, Tam. Come on, hurry!"

She blinked against the tears but they continued to fall unchecked. She couldn't see where her feet were coming down as she ran headlong, guided only by that strong grip. Eric's castle-like home loomed ahead, a tear-blurred mound of rough-hewn blocks. In a matter of seconds they were at the door, which stood yawning.

She swiped her eyes and hurried through. The living room looked as if a madman had raged through. Maybe that was exactly what had happened. The priceless antique furniture lay toppled. Some had been smashed. One of the needlepoint chairs had a leg missing. Vases lay in bits on the parquet floor. Heavy, marble-topped tables lay like fallen trees.

She stumbled almost blindly onward, through the formal dining room, where a candelabra had been hurled through a window, into the kitchen where cupboard doors had been ripped from their hinges. The sounds of breaking glass reached her and she turned, glimpsing the door she hadn't noticed. It hung open wide with a stairway that could only lead to the cellar. The sounds came from the darkness below, and a hand of ice choked her. She had no idea where Eric's coffin was, but if she'd had to hazard a guess she would have guessed the cellar. She approached the door.

A hand on her shoulder made her jump so suddenly she almost

fell down the stairs. Jamey's other hand steadied her. "I called the police," he told her softly.

"Good. Stay by the front door and wait for them, okay?"

He looked up at her, but didn't agree. He remained at the top, though, as she slowly descended the stairs. Her foot on a different surface told her when she'd reached the bottom. The air was thick with blackness and the strong aroma of spilled wine. Glass shattered and she forced herself to move toward the sounds. "Curtis!" She shouted his name and the noise abruptly stopped. She stood still. "Stop it, Curt. Just stop it—this is crazy."

She waited while her eyes adjusted to the dark. She finally made out his shape. It grew clearer. He stood near a demolished wine rack, and he held a double-bitted ax. Broken bottles littered the floor around him. He stood in puddles of wine. The rack's wood shelves hung in splinters.

"Get the hell out of here, Tammy. This isn't your business. It's between me and Marquand!" He lifted the ax again.

Tamara threw herself at his back, latching onto his shoulders from behind to keep him from doing more damage. He dropped the ax to the floor and reached back, grabbing her by the hair and yanking her from him. She stumbled, hit the wine-soaked floor, but scrambled to her feet again. She faced him, panting less from exertion than fear. "The police are on their way, Curt. You'll wind up in jail if you don't get out of here, right now."

He reached for her so fast she didn't have a chance to duck. He grabbed the front of her coat, bunching the material in his fists. He whirled her around, and slammed her back against what once had been the wine rack. The back of her head hit a broken shelf and red pain lanced her brain. "Where is he, Tammy?"

She blinked, feeling her knees weaken. She pressed her hands to the wall behind her for support, then she froze. She felt a hinge beneath her palm. This was no wine rack. It was a door. What the hell would a vampire want with wine, anyway? Why hadn't she guessed sooner? And when would it hit Curt?

She sucked air through her teeth. "He's not—here."

The back of his hand connected with her jaw, and his knuckles felt like rocks. "I *said,* where is he? You damn well know and you're damn well going to tell me."

Involuntarily a sob escaped. Tears burned over her face. Curtis let go of her coat, but gripped her shoulders. "Christ, Tammy, I don't want to hurt you. You're under his control, dammit. You'll never see him for what he is until he's gone. If I don't do it, he'll kill us all."

She faced him squarely and shook her head. "You're wrong!"

"He's not even human," he told her.

"He's more human than you'll ever be!"

Curt's hand rose again, but it was caught from behind. "Leave her alone," Jamey shouted.

"What the hell?" Curt looked back, shaking Jamey's grip away effortlessly. Then he turned on him. "You little—"

"Curtis, no!" But before he could hit the boy, Jamey lowered his head and plowed into Curt's midsection like a battering ram. Both went down in a tangle of arms and legs and broken bottles. Tamara grabbed Curt's arm and tried to pull him away.

"Hold it right there!" A strong light shone down the stairs, and footsteps hurriedly descended. A police officer took Tamara's arm and pulled her away, while another lifted Curt, none too gently, then bent over Jamey. "You all right, son?"

"Fine. I'm the one who called you." He pointed an accusing finger at Curtis. "He broke in...with that." He angled his finger toward the ax on the floor.

The cop whistled, helping Jamey to his feet, and turned back to Curt. "Izzat right?" He took Curt's arm and urged him up the stairs, while the second officer herded Tamara and Jamey ahead of him. At the top, in the better light, her officer tugged her into the living room and told her his name was Sumner.

"You the owner?"

"No. I...he's out of town and I was keeping an eye on the

place for him," she lied easily. Jamey stood aside, not saying a word.

"I'll need his name and a number to reach him." He'd pulled a stereotypical dog-eared notepad from his pocket.

"He's en route," she said. "But he should be back tonight."

He nodded, took down Tamara's name, address and phone number, then bent his head and frowned, his eyes fixed to her jawline. "Did he do that?"

Tamara's fingers touched the bruised flesh. She nodded, and saw anger flash in the officer's green eyes. "I need to take Jamey home, and...get myself together. I know you need a full statement, but do you think I could come in later and give it to you then?"

He scanned her face, and nodded. "You want to press assault charges?"

"Will it keep him jail overnight?"

He winked. "I can guarantee that."

"Then I guess I do." The officer nodded, took Eric's name down and advised her to have herself looked at by a doctor. Then he went into the dining room and spoke to his partner. Moments later Curtis was led toward the front door with his hands cuffed together behind his back.

"You'll regret this," he repeated again and again. "I'm a federal officer."

"One without a warrant, which in our book makes you just another breaking and entering, vandalism and aggravated assault case." Sumner continued lecturing as they went out the door and along the driveway.

Jamey looked to be in shock. Tamara went to him and ran one hand through his dark, curly hair. "You have guts like I've never seen, kiddo." He looked up but didn't smile. "I hate to admit it, Jamey, but I'm awfully glad you were here with me."

A smile began beneath hollow eyes. "What's going on? Why did Curtis want to kill Eric?"

She looked at him, not blinking. "A lot of reasons. Jealousy might be one, and fear. Curt is definitely afraid of Eric." She wouldn't lie to Jamey. She wasn't certain why, but he was a part of all of this. "Eric is different—not like everyone else. Some people fear what they don't understand. Some would rather destroy anything different, than learn about it." He still looked puzzled. "Do you know about the Salem witch trials?" He nodded. "Same principle is involved here."

Jamey sighed and shook his head, then grew calmer, and got the adult expression on his face that told her he was thinking like one. "Fear what's different, destroy what you fear."

She sighed, awed at the insight of the child. "Sometimes you amaze me." She walked with him out the door, and pulled it closed. She propped the gate with a big rock, so it would at least look like a deterrent. "You think it'll be all right until I get back?"

Jamey frowned at her. "I don't have any more weird feelings jumping in and out of my brain, if that's what you mean." He smiled fully for the first time.

"You know, Jamey, you probably saved my life in there. If you hadn't called the cops..." She shook her head. "And you likely saved Eric's, too, as well as his friend, Roland."

He looked back at the house, with one hand on the car door. "They're in there, aren't they?" He didn't wait for an answer. "They would've helped us, but they couldn't. If Curt had found them, he'd have killed them."

He didn't ask Tamara to confirm or deny any of it. He just slid into the car and rode home in silence.

Tamara told Kathy the bare facts, while trying to gloss over the worst of it. Jamey envisioned a break-in at a friend's house. He and Tamara arrived just in time to prevent it. The suspect was in custody and all was well with the world. Tamara kept the bruised side of her face averted, and made excuses to hurry off without coming inside for a visit. Kathy Bryant, while flustered, took it all in stride.

Tamara arrived back at Eric's front gate a little after 5:00 p.m.

CHAPTER THIRTEEN

Eric opened his eyes and slowly became aware of the smell of dirt surrounding him. He rested in an awkward position, not upon his bed of satin but on the rough wood floor of the secret room beneath it. He frowned, his head still cloudy, and squeezed the bridge of his nose between thumb and forefinger. He recalled the sudden sense of danger that had roused him from the depths of his deathlike slumber to a state hovering near wakefulness. He'd automatically flexed his forefinger on the hidden button, dumping himself into this place. He was safe and the feeling of mortal danger had passed.

Eric stood on the small stool, placed here for just such a purpose, and reached above him to the handle on the underside of his mattress. He pulled downward, then reached higher to release the lock on the lid. A moment later he swung himself over, landing easily on the floor. He attuned his senses, felt no threat and moved across the room to the coffin Roland had set upon a bier. He tapped on the lid, not surprised when Roland emerged from a concealed door in the bier itself, rather than through the polished hardwood lid.

He straightened, brushed at his wrinkled clothing. "What in God's name has been happening?"

"I'm not certain." Eric stood motionless. "Tamara is here."

Roland too, concentrated. "Others have been. Three—no, four others. Gone now."

Nodding, Eric unlocked the door. They moved quickly through the darkened passage, and Eric unlatched and pushed at the wine rack that served as its entrance. It gave a few inches, then jammed. He shoved harder, forcing it open. Both men took pause when they stepped into the cellar.

The electric light bulb above glowed harshly. What had been

a well-stocked wine rack was now a shambles, with only a bottle or two remaining intact. The aroma assaulted Eric, pulling his head around until he saw the plastic pails on the floor, filled to the brim with broken glass and bits of wood. An old push broom and a coal shovel were propped against one pail. The floor beneath his feet was damp with wine. Another scent reached Eric's nostrils and he whirled, immediately spotting the slight stain on the wall near the hidden door, and knew it was blood. Tamara's blood.

He flew up the stairs then, and through the house, skidding to a halt when he entered the parlor.

Tamara lowered the two far legs of a heavy table to the floor. She ran her fingers over the chipped edge, sighed deeply and bent to retrieve an old gilded clock. She brought the piece to her ear, then placed it gently on the marble table. Eric took in the scene around her, realizing she'd already righted much of it. She turned slightly, so he saw the dark purple skin along her jaw, and picked up a toppled chair, setting it in its rightful place.

"Tamara." He moved forward slowly.

She looked up at the sound of his voice, and rushed into his arms. He felt her tears, and the trembling that seemed to come from the center of her body. No part of her was steady. He closed his arms as tightly as he dared around her small waist, and held her hard. Roland had stepped into the room and stood silently surveying the damage.

"Who is responsible for this?" Eric stepped back just enough to tilt her chin in gentle fingers, and examine her bruised face.

"It was...it was Curtis, but Eric, I'm all right. It isn't as bad as it looks."

Eric's anger made the words stick in his throat. "He struck you?" She nodded. He reached around to touch the back of her head gently, and knew when she winced that he'd found the cut. "And what else?"

"He..." She looked into his eyes and he knew she'd considered lying to him, then realized it would be useless. "He shoved me against the wall and I hit my head, but I'm fine."

He sought the truth of that statement, probing her mind, wondering if she was truly all right.

"Must have come through here like a raging bull," Roland remarked.

"I've never seen him so angry," Tamara said.

"Nor will you ever see it again." Eric let his arms fall away from her and took a single step toward the door. Roland blocked his path quickly and elegantly. Eric knew he had little chance of moving his powerful friend aside.

"I believe we should hear the tale before any action is taken, Eric."

Eric met Roland's gaze for a moment, and finally nodded. "Remember, though," he said. "He was warned what would happen if he harmed her." Eric turned to Tamara, and noted that as she came to him her gait was wobbly. He slipped his arms around her and helped her to the settee. Roland left the room, and returned in a moment with one of the remaining bottles. He took it to the bar, poured a glassful and brought it to Tamara.

"Take your time," he said softly. "Tell it from the start." He sat in an undamaged chair, while Eric stood stiffly, waiting, wishing he could reach the bastard's throat in the next few seconds.

Tamara sipped the wine. "I guess the start isn't all that bad. I convinced Daniel to drop the research. He agreed when I told him I'd leave forever if he didn't."

Eric frowned. "He agreed?"

"Yes, and that's not all. I asked him to meet you, talk to you. I want him to see you the way I do, and know you would never hurt me. He agreed to that, too."

Eric sat down hard. "I'll be damned—"

"I'm not at all convinced this is a good idea," Roland said. "But I'll leave that for later. Go on with the story, my dear."

Eric saw Tamara sip again, and her hand on the glass still

wasn't steady. He sat closer to her. "When Daniel told Curtis he was dropping the research, Curt was furious, but defiant. He said he'd continue with or without Daniel's help. Daniel told him to drop it, or lose his job at DPI. Curt left madder than ever…but I still never thought he'd come here."

Eric frowned and shook his head. "How did you know?"

"It was Jamey, the boy I work with. He's something of a clairvoyant, though it's a weak power except where I'm concerned. He knew your name, Eric. He picked up on my nightmares, too. He called me, frantic, and when I picked him up he insisted we come here. He said someone was trying to kill you."

Eric glanced up at Roland, and both men frowned hard. Tamara, not noticing, went on with her story.

"When we got here I heard Curt down below, smashing things. Jamey called the police and I went down to stop Curt. I was terrified your resting place was down there somewhere." She closed her eyes, and Eric knew she had truly been afraid for his life. "I told Jamey to stay by the front door, but he came down, too."

"Stubborn lad," Roland observed.

Tamara's eyes lit then, and her chin came up. "You should have seen him. He charged Curt like a bull, took him right to the floor when Curt tried to hit me again."

"Was the boy injured?" Again it was Roland who spoke. Eric was busy watching the changing expressions on Tamara's face, and reading the emotions behind them. It changed again now, with a silent rage. He felt it rise up within her, and its ferocity amazed him. He hadn't known she was capable of a violent thought.

Her voice oddly low, she said, "If Curt had hurt Jamey, I'd have killed him."

Eric shot a puzzled glance toward Roland, who seemed to be studying her just as intently. Tamara seemed to shake herself. She blinked twice, and the fire in her eyes died slowly. "The police arrived then. I pressed assault charges. He'll be in jail overnight, so you'll have time to regroup." She placed a hand on Eric's arm. "I'm sorry the police got involved. They expect both of us to show up tonight, to give statements."

"I should be angry with you, Tamara, but not for calling the police. For risking your life. You could have been killed."

"If he'd killed you, I'd have died, anyway. Don't you know that yet?" As she spoke she leaned into his embrace, and settled her head on his shoulder. "You have to get this place fixed up. Curt will flash his DPI card around and get himself out by morning."

"Unfortunate for him, should he decide to give up the protection of a jail cell so soon."

"Eric, you can't...do anything to him. It would only give those idiots at DPI more reason to hound your every step."

"You think I care?"

"I care." She sat up and stared into his eyes. "I intend to be with you from now on, Eric, wherever you go. I'd like it if we were free to come and go as we please, and I could visit Daniel from time to time. I want to enjoy our life together. Please, don't let your anger ruin it before it's even begun."

Her words worked like ice water on his rage. The points she made were valid, and while he still thought St. Claire a moral deviate, he knew she loved the man. He glanced helplessly toward Roland.

"I wouldn't want to square off against her in a debate," he said dryly.

Eric sighed. There was no way in God's earth he could allow Curtis Rogers to get away with what he'd done. But he supposed he'd have to plot a fitting retribution later. There was no use arguing with Tamara. She hadn't a vengeful bone in her beautiful body—except where this boy, Jamey, was concerned. And that puzzled him.

"As for the gate and the door," he said, sensing her lingering worry for his safety, "I can make a few calls tonight and have a reliable crew here by first light."

"But he got in once, Eric," Tamara said.

"Dogs!" Roland stood quickly. "That would solve it. We'll acquire ten—no, twelve—of those attack dogs you hear about. Dobermans or some such breed. Tear a man to shreds."

"I think a direct line to the police department will be just as effective." Eric couldn't keep the amusement from his voice. Roland did possess a brutal streak. "An alarm that alerts the police the moment security is breached. I admit, I hate depending on them for security, but it will only be necessary until—" he stopped, and slanted a glance at Tamara "—until I think of something better. Meantime, why don't we visit the police station and get the unpleasantness over with. We may still salvage what remains of the night. I had such plans...."

How he managed to make her laugh after what she'd been through tonight, she couldn't imagine. But he did. By the time they left the police station he was behind the wheel of what he referred to as her "oddly misshapen automobile," and she was splitting a side over his shifting technique.

The house had been restored to order as much as possible. Roland had left a fire blazing brightly, and a vase stood in the room's center, filled with twelve graceful white roses. A card dangling from one stem drew her attention. She lifted it and read, "My thanks for your earlier heroism. Roland."

She shook her head, and turned when she heard strains of music filling the room. Mozart again. "Your friend is certainly chivalrous."

"You inspire that sort of thing in a man," he told her.

She smiled and went into his arms. "What about these *plans* you mentioned earlier?"

"I thought you might like to dance."

She tilted her head back and kissed his chin. "I would."

"Oh, no. I couldn't possibly dance with you dressed like that."

She frowned, stepping away from him and looking down at

her jeans and sweatshirt. "I admit, I'm not exactly elegant to-night, but—"

"I've a surprise for you, Tamara. Come." He turned her toward the stairs and urged her up them. He led her into the bedroom she'd seen before, and left her waiting inside the doorway while he lit two oil lamps. He turned to a wardrobe, gripped its double handles and opened it with a flourish.

Curious, she moved forward as he reached into the dark confines and removed a garment carefully, draping it over his arms. When he turned toward her Tamara's heart skipped a beat. It was something made for Cinderella. The jade-colored fabric shimmered. The neckline was heart shaped, the sleeves puffy and the skirt so fully flared she knew there must be petticoats attached. The green satin was gathered up from the hemline and held with tiny white bows at intervals all along the bottom, to show the frilly white underskirt.

Her mouth opened, but only air escaped. "It belonged to my sister," Eric told her. "She used to cinch her waist with corsets, but she wasn't as petite as you. I suspect it will suit you without them."

She forced her eyes away from the dress and back to him her heart tightening. "Your sister...Jaqueline. And you've kept it all this time."

"I supposed I am a bit sentimental where my little sister is concerned. She wore that gown the night she accompanied me to a performance of young Amadeus, in Paris."

Her eyes had wandered downward to the glittering silk, but snapped up again. "Mozart?"

"The same. She was not overly impressed, as I recall." He smiled down at her. "I should like to see you in the gown, Tamara."

She gasped. "Oh, but I couldn't—it's so precious to you. My God, it must have cost a fortune to keep it so well preserved all this time."

"And no good deal of fuss, as well," he said. "But nothing

is too precious for you, my love. It will make me happy to see you wear it. Do it for me.''

She nodded, and Eric left the room. She was surprised, but didn't question it. She shimmied out of her own clothing, including her bra, since the upper halves of her breasts would be revealed by the daring neckline. She touched the dress reverently, and stepped into it with great care, terrified she'd rip it while putting it on. She slid her hands through the armholes, and adjusted the shoulders. ''Eric!''

At her call he returned, and she presented her back to him. Wordlessly he tightened the laces and tied them in place. He took two steps backward, and she turned slowly to face him. His gaze moved over her, gleaming with emotion. He blinked quickly and shook his head. ''You are a vision, Tamara. Too lovely to be real. I could almost wonder if you would disappear, should I blink.''

''Does it really look all right?'' It felt tight, and her breasts were squished so high they were fairly popping out of the thing.

Eric smiled, took her hand and turned her toward the wardrobe doors, which still stood open. She hadn't noticed the mirrors on the inside of the doors, but she did now. He left her standing there and turned to lift a lamp, better for her to see her reflection.

She caught her breath again. It wasn't Tamara Dey looking back at her. It was a raven-haired eighteenth-century beauty. She couldn't believe the transformation. And the dress! It was more like a work of art than a piece of clothing. She glanced gratefully up at Eric, then froze, and looked back toward the mirror again. ''It's true! You have no reflection!''

''An oddity I still seek to solve, love.'' He closed the doors and took her hand. ''Now, about the dancing...''

He led her back downstairs into the roomy parlor, thumbed a button and the piano sonata stopped abruptly. A moment later a minuet lilted from the speakers. Eric faced her, pointed one toe and bowed formally. Tamara laughed, picking up his thoughts.

She dropped into a deep curtsy, imitating those she'd seen in movies. He took her hand and drew her to her feet.

"Look at me as we turn," he instructed moments later. "The eyes are as important to the dance as the feet."

She fixed her gaze to his, rather than keeping it on her bare toes peeping from beneath the hemline. She tried to imitate his pace as they circled one another.

"That's it." His voice was soft but his gaze intense as the flames in the hearth. "You're a quick study."

"I have an excellent teacher." She met him as he stepped forward, then retreated just as he did. "You must have danced with every beautiful girl in Paris."

His lips quirked upward. "Hardly. I always loathed this type of thing." He lifted her hand in his, high above their heads, placed his other hand on her buttocks and urged her to turn beneath their joined fingers. "Perhaps one needs the right partner."

"I know what you mean. I never liked dancing before, either, even in high school." She stopped abruptly.

"Now you've broken the rhythm. We shall have to begin again."

"No. I think it's my turn to be the teacher." She stepped away from him and hurried to the stereo, fiddling with buttons until she'd stopped the CD, and turned on the FM stereo. She scanned stations until she heard the familiar harmony of The Righteous Brothers on the oldies station. "Perfect." She went back to Eric, slipped her arms around his neck and pressed her body as close to his as the full-skirted dress would allow. "This is the way my generation dances…when they find the right partner. Put your arms around my waist and hold me close." He did, and she settled her head on his shoulder and very slowly began to sway their bodies in time to "Unchained Melody."

"Your method does have its merits. Is this all there is to it? Certainly easily learned."

"Well, there are variations." To demonstrate, she turned her face toward him and nuzzled his neck with her lips. He moved his hands lower, cupping her buttocks and squeezing her to him. He lowered his head and nibbled her ear. "You're a quick study," she told him, repeating his compliment.

"I have an excellent teacher," he replied. He lifted his head slowly, moving his lips to her chin and then capturing her mouth with his. He kissed her deeply, leaving her breathless and warm inside. His hands at the small of her back, he bent over her and moved his tantalizing lips down the front of her throat to kiss her breasts.

She arched backward, her hands tangling in his hair. Her fingers nimbly loosened the ribbon and threaded in the thick jet waves. One of his hands came around her, to scoop a breast out of its satin confines and hold it to his mouth. He flicked his tongue over the nipple, already throbbing and hard, then closed his lips around it and suckled her roughly. She didn't realize he'd moved her until she felt her back pressed to a wall. She opened her eyes, forcing words despite the sighs of pleasure he was evoking. "Eric...what about...Roland..."

"He knows better than to interrupt." He had to stop what he was doing to speak, but he quickly returned to the business of driving her crazy with desire. When she strained against his mouth he responded by closing his teeth on her nipple. She shuddered with pleasure. He anchored her to the wall with his body and used his hands to gather the voluminous skirts upward in the front, no easy task. Nonetheless, he soon had them arranged high enough to allow his hands ample access to her naked thighs and the unclothed moistness between them.

His hand stilled when it found no scrap of nylon barring its way. She'd seen no need for panties, knowing instinctively where the night would lead. His fingers moved over her, opened her and slipped inside, stroking her to a fever pitch. When they finally moved away it was only to release his own barriers, and then his manhood, hot and solid, nudged against her thigh. His hands slipped down the backs of her legs, and he lifted her. He

speared her with a single, unerring thrust, and Tamara's head
fell backward as the air was forced from her lungs. That action
put her breasts once again in reach of his mouth and he took
advantage.

She locked her legs around his body, her arms around his
neck, and she rode him like an untamed stallion. He drove into
her, his hands clutching her buttocks like a vise and pulling her
downward with every upward thrust. In minutes he trembled,
and she hovered near a violent release. His teeth on her breasts
clamped tighter, and rather than pain she felt intense pleasure.
That other kind of climax enticed her nearer. Her entire body
vibrated, her every nerve ending tensed at the two places where
they were joined. Closer and closer he drove her, until she
writhed with need.

Even when the spasms began, she craved more. "Please,"
she moaned, he fingers raking through his hair. It was all the
encouragement he needed. She felt the prick at the tip of her
breast, and then the unbearable tingling as he sucked harder.
With his first greedy swallows she exploded in sensation, both
climaxes rocking her at once. Her entire body shook with pleasure, even as she realized he'd stiffened, plunged himself into
her one last time and groaned long and low against her heated
skin.

As if his knees had weakened he sank slowly to the floor,
taking her with him. He brought her down on top of him, still
not withdrawing from her. He released her breast and cradled
her to his chest, rocking her slowly. "My God, woman," he
whispered into her hair. "You take me higher than I knew was
possible. You thrill me to the marrow. Have I told you how very
much I love you?"

"Yes, silently. But I won't mind if you tell me again."

His lips caressed her skin, just above her temple. "More than
my own existence, Tamara. There is nothing I wouldn't do for
you. I would die for you."

She licked her lips. "Would you meet with Daniel?"

He hesitated, and she felt the tightening of his jaw. "It will not change anything."

"I think it will." She lifted her upper body slightly, and regarded his face. "It would mean so much to me."

He cupped her head to pull her down to him again, buried his face in her hair and inhaled its scent. "If it is so important to you, I will do it. When you return to St. Claire at dawn, tell him I'll come just after nightfall."

She found his hands with hers, and laced her fingers through his. "Thank you, Eric. It will make a difference. You'll see." She lifted her head and pressed her lips to his. "But I'll call him. I don't want to leave at dawn."

She felt his body stiffen and knew he'd argue the point. "Eric, they'll only keep Curtis overnight. What if he comes back here while you rest?"

"No doubt you'd like to meet him at the door with claws extended, my tigress. But I'll not have you in harm's way to protect me. What kind of man do you take me for?"

"You'd be defenseless if he found you during the day."

"Tamara, the workmen will be here at first light, and the repairs completed by noon. They will be under instructions to notify police of any intruders, and to arm the new security system before they leave. No one will disturb my rest."

"I'll leave when they do, then."

His eyes flashed impatience. "You will leave at dawn."

She shook her head from side to side. "I won't go."

"I won't have a woman taking my place in battle."

The harshness in his voice brought burning tears springing to her eyes. "I'm not just a woman. I am the woman who loves you, Eric. I'd sooner peel every inch of flesh from Curt with my nails and teeth than to let him near you during the day." A sob rose in her throat, but she fought it down. "You don't know how I felt when I realized he was in here today…that he might have already murdered you. My God, if I lost you now, I couldn't go on."

The hands that came back to her shoulders and nape were gentle, not angry. "And you do not know, my love, how I felt when I woke to find you had been beaten while I lay only a short distance away, helpless to defend you. How could I bear it if I woke to find you murdered in my own home?"

"But that would never happen. Curt couldn't really hurt me. He only acted so crazy because he cares so much."

Eric's long fingers caught her chin and turned her slightly, so his eyes could scan the bruise. "And I suppose this is a token of his undying esteem."

"He was in a rage. He regretted it as soon as he realized what he'd done."

"No doubt he'd regret killing you the instant the deed was done, as well."

"But he wouldn't—"

"My love, you trust too freely, and too deeply. As much as I hate being forced to do so, I can see I must give you an ultimatum. You will leave here at dawn, or I will not meet with St. Claire. And before you agree, with the intent of stealing back here as I rest, you should be aware that I will sense your presence. I know when you are near, my love." His voice softened, and he touched the skin of her cheek with his fingertips.

She blinked away the stupid urge to cry. One tear spilled over despite her efforts, and he leaned up to catch it with his lips. "Do you truly wish to spend what remains of this night bickering?"

She shook her head, unable to sustain her anger. He only wanted to protect her, just as she wanted to protect him. She understood his motivations all too well. She lowered her head until her pliant lips had settled over his coaxing ones, and she tasted the salt of her own tear.

Eric stood in the doorway long after she'd driven out of sight, heedless of the growing light in the eastern sky.

"Stand gaping like that another five minutes and you will be there permanently, my lovestruck friend.'' Roland came around Eric, shoved the heavy door closed and eyed the broken lock. ''I suppose your men will arrive within the hour to repair that?''

Eric nodded mutely.

''For God's sake, man, snap out of it!''

Eric started, glanced at Roland and grinned foolishly. ''Isn't she something?''

Roland rolled his eyes ceilingward, and shoved a glass into Eric's hand. ''You're whiter than alabaster. You haven't been feeding properly. The few sips you allow yourself are no doubt sweet, Eric, but not enough to sustain you.''

Eric scowled at Roland's rather crude observation, but realized he was right. He felt weak and light-headed. He drained the glass, and moved to the bar to refill it.

''Tell me,'' Roland said slowly. ''Has anything been decided?''

''Such as?'' Eric sipped and waited.

''You know precisely what I refer to, Eric. The decision to be made. Has our lady voiced an opinion?''

''You cannot think I'm considering passing my curse on to her.''

Roland sighed hard. ''When did you begin seeing immortality as a curse?''

''That is what it is.'' Eric slammed the glass down on the polished hardwood surface. ''It's been unending hell for me.''

''And what kind of hell has it been these past days, Eric?'' Eric didn't answer that, knowing Roland had a valid point. ''I thought to save your life two centuries ago in Paris, not curse it. Eric, I live in solitude because it is the only way for me. I had my chance at happiness centuries ago, and lost it. I don't expect another. But you...you are throwing yours away.''

Eric bowed his head and pressed his fingertips to his eyes. ''I don't know if I could do it to her.'' He heard Roland's sigh and raised his head. ''I have made one decision, though. I've agreed to meet with St. Claire.''

"You can't be serious."

"Quite serious. It means a great deal to Tamara that St. Claire be reassured of her safety. She seems to think I can accomplish that by talking with the man. I have my doubts, of course, but—"

"The only thing to be accomplished by such a meeting is your destruction. Think about it, Eric. Wittingly or not, Tamara has lured you into the spider's web, just as St. Claire planned from the start. Once in, there will be no escape."

Eric stood silent, contemplating Roland's words. The idea that the whole meeting scheme might be a trap had niggled at him since Tamara had first broached the subject. Of course, he knew she was no part of it. And if it was a trap, what better way to show Tamara the true nature of those she trusted? Providing, of course, he was able to escape.

Reading his thoughts, Roland bristled. "And suppose you prove this valuable point to the girl, and lose you own life in the process?"

"I won't. I can't, for Tamara's sake. Without me she'd be as she was before. At their mercy."

Roland grimaced. "At the moment, my friend, I fear it is you who are at hers."

Eric smiled. "I can think of no place I'd rather be."

CHAPTER FOURTEEN

As the sky glowed with the rising sun, Tamara peered into Daniel's bedroom. He lay atop the covers, fully dressed, snoring loudly. A half-empty bottle was on its side, on the floor near the bed. The cover wasn't screwed on tightly. Moisture dotted the neck and a few drops of whiskey dampened the worn carpet. A glass lay toppled in an amber puddle on the bedside stand.

She frowned as she moved silently into the room, picked up the bottle and the glass, and retreated again. What was driving him to drink himself in oblivion every night? In all the years she'd known him she'd never seen Daniel drink more than a glass or two at a time. She'd never seen him drunk. She returned with a handful of tissues and mopped up the spills, then dropped a comforter over Daniel and tiptoed away. Something seemed to be eating at Daniel—something more than just the knowledge that she was spending her nights with his lifelong enemy.

She forced the troubling thought out of her mind, determined to concentrate only on the good things to come. Tonight Daniel and Eric would meet. She had no doubt they'd become friends, in time. And Curtis would see reason. He may have lost his head for a time, but he was intelligent. He'd recognize the truth when it was staring him in the face.

The future loomed up before her for a moment as she soaked in a steamy, scented bath. Like a giant black hole, with a question mark at its center, it hovered in her mind. She ignored it. She had all she could deal with at the moment, just trying to keep the present running on an even keel. She'd worry about her future later, when things settled down.

Her plan was to bathe, put on fresh clothes and drive back to Eric's to see if the workers had arrived as he'd promised. With the brilliant sun, glinting blindingly off the snow outside, came physical and emotional exhaustion. She fell asleep in the bath, quite against her will, and for once she didn't sleep soundly. Her dreams were troubled and her sleep fitful. She saw herself old, with white hair and a face deeply lined. Then the dream shifted and she saw a cold stone marker with her name engraved on its face. She saw Eric, bent double with grief, standing beside it, surrounded by bitter cold on a bleak wintry night.

She woke with a start, and realized the now-cold water around her body might have aided in the seeming vividness of the dream. Still, she couldn't shake the lingering images. "It doesn't have to be that way," she said aloud, and firmly. And she knew she was right. Eric had explained to her what it meant to be what he called Chosen. She could be transformed. She could be with him forever. The thought rocked through her, leaving her shaken like a leaf in a storm. She could become what he was....

She pressed a palm to her forehead, and shook herself. Later. She'd consider all of this later. It was more than she could process right now. She toweled herself vigorously, to rub the cold water's chill from her goose-bumped flesh, and dressed quickly. A glance at the clock near her bed chased every other thought from her mind. Noon! By now Curt could have...

She took the stairs two at a time, shocked into immobility when she reached the bottom and saw Curt, comfortable in an overstuffed chair, sipping coffee. Daniel, now awake and sitting with Curt, rose, and she felt his bloodshot gaze move over her still-damp hair and hastily donned clothing.

His gaze stopped at her bruised face, and he spun around to glare at Curtis. "You did that to her?"

He looked at the floor. "You don't know how bad I feel, Tammy. I'm sorry—more sorry for hurting you than I've ever been for anything in my life. I was out of my head yesterday. I— Can you ever forgive me?"

She stepped down from the lowest stair and moved cautiously toward him, scanning his face. She saw nothing but sincere remorse there. He met her gaze and his own seemed to beg for understanding. "I'm still afraid for you," he told her. "I'm afraid for all of us, but—"

"I know you're afraid, Curtis, but there's no reason to be. If Eric had meant to hurt you, he'd have done it by now. Don't you see that? In all the months you two have harassed him, he's never lifted a hand against either of you."

Daniel cleared his throat and came closer to the two of them, forming a circle that seemed intimate. She noticed he'd shaven and taken pains to dress well, in a spotless white shirt and knife-edged trousers, brown leather belt and polished shoes, a dark blue tie held down with a gold clip. Did he want to keep his excessive drinking a secret, then? How could he think she'd not know?

"I have to admit," he began, "it's damn tough for me to consider that I might have been wrong all this time, after the lengths I've gone to." She saw him swallow convulsively and blink fast before he went on. "As scientists, Curtis, we have to consider every possibility. Because of that, and because I love Tamara, I'm going to give the man the benefit of the doubt."

"I can't believe you're going to meet with him, Daniel," Curtis blurted, shaking his head. "But I suppose if you've made up your mind—"

"Has he agreed, Tam?" Daniel interjected.

She nodded, glancing apprehensively toward Curtis.

"Tonight? Here, and not long after dark? He agreed to all of it? I'm not about to meet him anywhere else, even with all your assurances."

"I didn't have to tell him your preference to meet here." She spoke defensively, before she could stop herself. "He suggested that himself."

Daniel nodded, while Curtis let his head fall backward, and stared at the ceiling. Blowing a sigh, he brought his gaze level again. "Okay, if this is unavoidable, then I want to be here."

"No!" Tamara barked the word so loudly both men jumped.

She forced her voice lower. "After yesterday, Curt, I don't want you anywhere near him."

Curt blinked at her, his eyes going round with apparent pain. "You don't trust me?" He searched her face for a long moment, then sighed again. "I don't suppose I can blame you, but..." He let his gaze move toward Daniel, but his words were addressed to Tamara. "I hope to God you're right about Marquand."

"I am," she told him. "I know I am." She glanced toward the door, recalling her hurry to leave. She still wanted to check on the repairs at Eric's even though it now seemed Curt had come to his senses. "I have to go out for a while."

Curt caught her arm as she turned. "You haven't said you forgive me for being such an idiot yesterday." His gaze touched her bruise, then hopped back to her eyes. "I feel sick to my stomach when I think of what I did."

She closed her eyes slowly. She wanted no more anger and hard feelings. She wanted nothing bad to interfere with her happiness. "It's been a tense week, Curt. I knew you didn't mean it. I forgave you almost as soon as it was over."

"You're one in a million, Tam."

She hurried away, glad to be alone behind the wheel of her Bug and headed toward Eric's house.

She found two pickup trucks and a van lining the roadside. Young, muscular men worked in shirt sleeves, despite the snow on the ground. She pulled her car to a stop behind the van, and settled into the seat more comfortably. She wasn't planning to leave here until she knew the place was secure. Despite Eric's threat, she knew he wouldn't stay angry with her.

Twice during her vigil she felt her eyelids drooping, and forced them wider. She got out and walked in the biting winter air to stay awake. The crews didn't pack up to leave until well after four-thirty. In an hour the sun would begin to fade, and Eric would wake. Still she waited until the last man had left, gratified to see him look suspiciously at her car before he drove away. She was certain he'd jotted the plate number. Eric had said they were dependable. He was right. Then she pulled away, too. She wanted to have time to change into something pretty and perhaps do something new with her hair before Eric arrived for his talk with Daniel.

She knew something was wrong with her first glimpse of Daniel's frowning face. "What is it?" She hurried toward him, not even shedding her jacket or stomping the clinging snow from her boots. "Tell me. What's happened?"

"I'm sure it's nothing, Tam. I don't want you to get worried until we know for su—"

"Tell me!"

Daniel looked at the floor. "Kathy Bryant called about an hour ago."

"Kathy B—" Tamara's throat went dry, and her stomach felt as if a fist had been driven into it. "It's Jamey, isn't it?"

Daniel nodded. "The school officials claim he left at the normal time, but...he never made it home."

"Jamey? He's missing?"

Jamey sat very still, because it hurt when he tried to move. His arms were pulled tightly behind him, and tied there. A blindfold covered his eyes and there was some kind of tape over his mouth. It felt like duct tape, but he couldn't be sure.

He'd left school to walk home just as he always did, cutting through the vacant lot behind the drugstore. Someone had grabbed him from behind. A damp cloth had been held over his nose and mouth and Jamey had known it was chloroform. He hadn't recognized the smell or anything, but he'd seen enough movies to know that's what they hold to your nose and mouth when they grab you from behind. Never fails. Chloroform. It stank, too. He'd felt himself falling into a black pit.

Now he was here, although he had no idea where *here* was. He couldn't see, and he could barely move. He assumed he was inside, because of the flat, hard surface he sat on and the one at his back. A floor and a wall, he guessed. He was in an old kind of place, because he could smell the old, musty odors. Inside or not, though, it was cold. Breezes wafted through now and then and he felt no kind of warmth at all. He was glad he'd zipped his coat and pulled on his hat when he'd left school. He sure couldn't have done it now. He couldn't do much of anything now.

Except think. He'd been thinking a lot since he had come around and found himself here. Mostly what he thought about was who had grabbed him. He'd felt a clear sense of recognition flash through his mind the second the guy—and he was sure it had been a guy—had grabbed him. He'd been on the brink of total recall when the chloroform had got to him. If he'd had just a few more seconds...

But maybe it would come to him later. Right now his main concerns were two—his empty stomach, and the dropping temperature.

Tamara listened, numb with worry, as Daniel related the details of Jamey's disappearance. He'd left school to walk home at three-thirty. His mother had been over his route, as had the police, and found nothing. His friends had been questioned, but nothing of any use was learned.

She knew she should remain where she was and wait for Eric. He could meet Daniel when he arrived, and then she'd explain what had happened and ask him to finish the talk another time. He'd help her find Jamey. Rationally she knew that would be the wisest course of action. But her emotions wouldn't allow it. Despite Kathy Bryant's lack of panic when Tamara phoned her, she felt it building within her own mind. Kathy had the assurances of the police, who saw this type of thing all the time, that Jamey would turn up safe and sound within a few hours. But Tamara had her own, sickening intuition that something was terribly wrong. When she closed her eyes and tried to focus on

Jamey she felt nothing but coldness and fear. She had to find him, and she couldn't wait. He was cold, afraid and alone, and...

"I can see you want to go, Tam," Daniel said, placing a gentle hand on her arm.

She shook her head. "I can't. Eric will be here before long, and I know how nervous you are."

He shook his head. "To tell you the truth, I was thinking it might be better for the two of us to have a private talk. You go on, go see to the boy. I'll explain to Marquand when he gets here."

She hesitated. "Are you sure?"

"Go on," he repeated.

She hugged his neck. "Thank you, Daniel." She pressed her trembling lips to his leathery cheek. "I love you, you know."

She whirled from him and rushed to her car, then changed her mind and took his, knowing he wouldn't object. It would be faster.

She got the same story when she talked to Kathy face-to-face. The poor woman seemed to grow more concerned each time she glanced at the clock. Her confidence in the official prediction that Jamey was perfectly all right must be fading, Tamara thought.

Tamara ignored the gathering darkness, knowing Eric would soon meet with Daniel, and probably come looking for her as soon as he was told the reason for her absence. She wasn't worried about his ability to find her. He'd know where she was without thinking twice. She wished her psychic link to Jamey was that strong. If she could just close her eyes and *know*... She shook her head. She couldn't, so why waste time wishing? She spent some time in his bedroom, going through things to see if there was a note or some clue...knowing all the while there wouldn't be. He hadn't left of his own accord. Her link was strong enough to tell her that much.

She had Kathy draw her a map of his usual route home, and she went to the school, parked the car and walked it, all of her

mind honed for a hint of him. The police had been over the path
he would've taken, and found nothing. Kathy had, as well, but
Tamara felt certain she would find something they'd missed...
and she did.

Something made her pause when she began to walk along the
sidewalk past the drugstore. She stopped, lifted her head and
waited. Her gaze turned of its own accord to the lot behind the
store, a weedy, garbage-strewn mess that any parent would forbid her child to cross. Just as Kathy had probably forbidden
Jamey. Yet she detected a meandering path amid the snowy
brown weeds, broken bottles and litter. From her bag she pulled
the flashlight she'd asked Kathy to lend her, and checked the
hand-drawn map. To cross the lot would save several minutes
of his walk home. She folded the map and pocketed it, aimed
the beam and moved along the barely discernible path. Little
snow had managed to accumulate here, and the wind that
whipped through constantly rearranged what there was.

Bits of paper and rubbish swirled across her path as she
moved behind the flashlight's beam. Crumpled newspaper pages
skittered, and a flat sheet of notepaper glided past. She sought
footprints but saw none and knew that if there'd been any the
wind would have obliterated them by now. Pastel bits of tissue
blew past, and then a tumbling bit of white that looked like cloth.
She frowned and followed its progress with the light. Not cloth.
Gauze. A wadded square of gauze.

The breeze stiffened and the scrap tumbled away. She chased
it a few yards, lost sight of it, then spotted it again. She picked
it up, careful to touch only a corner of the material, and that
with her nails. She turned it in the beam of light. It hadn't been
used on an injury. There was no trace of blood anywhere.
Slowly, like a stalking phantom, the odor made its way into her
senses. She wrinkled her nose. Was that...?

"Chloroform," she whispered, but the word was lost in the
wind.

* * *

Eric walked up the front steps of St. Claire's house and pressed the button to announce his arrival. He shuffled his feet as he waited, and frowned when no one answered the door. He'd told himself repeatedly that he could handle whatever kinds of surprises St. Claire might have in store. Still, his mind jangled with warnings. He pressed the button again.

"I tell you, something is amiss!" Roland came from his hiding place among the shrubbery and stood beside Eric at the door.

"And I told you to stay out of sight. If he sees you, he'll be convinced we've come here to murder him."

"Have you not noticed, my astute friend, that no one answers the bell?"

Eric nodded. "Patience, Roland. I'll summon Tamara." His brows drew closer as he honed his senses to hers, but he felt no hint of her presence within the house. The wind shifted then, and the unmistakable scent of blood came heavy to them both. Eric's startled gaze met Roland's, and then both men sprinted around the house, toward the source.

They paused in the rear, near an open window with curtains billowing inward. Without hesitation Eric leapt onto the ledge and then over, dropping lightly to the floor inside. The smell was all-encompassing now, and when he glanced around the room he had to quell the jarring shock. St. Claire lay sprawled on the floor, in a virtual pool of his own blood. It still trickled from a jagged tear in his throat, but from the look, there was little left to flow.

"Decided to join my party, Marquand? You're a little late. Refreshments have already been served, as you can see."

Eric glanced up and saw Curtis Rogers standing in a darkened corner. "You," he growled. He lunged at the man, but Curtis ducked his first attack, flinging something warm and sticky into Eric's face. Blood. And he'd tossed it from a glass. Automatically Eric swiped a sleeve over his face, and an instant later he had the laughing little bastard by the throat. A sharp jab stabbed into his midsection. Not a blade, he thought. It was... *Oh, hell, a hypodermic.*

He flinched at the pain but caught himself, withdrawing one hand from Curtis's throat, clenching it into a fist and smashing it into his face. Rogers went down, toppling a table on the way, breaking a lamp. Eric walked toward him, aware now that Roland had come inside. He felt his friend's hand clasp his shoulder from behind.

"It's a trap, I tell you. We must go, now, before—"

"No!" Eric shook Roland's hand free and took another step toward the man on the floor, who made no move to get away. Suddenly Eric knew why. A wave of dizziness assaulted him. He fell to one knee as Rogers scurried backward like a crab. He felt his mind grow fuzzy, and his head suddenly seemed too heavy to hold upright.

Vaguely he felt Roland gripping him under the arms. He saw Rogers get to his feet and pull another hypodermic from somewhere. He tried to mutter a warning, but couldn't hear his own slurred voice. Roland let him go with only one hand when Rogers approached. He backhanded the bastard almost casually. Curtis sailed through the air, connecting with a bookshelf before slumping to the floor amid an avalanche of literature. Even drugged, Eric marvelled at Roland's strength.

"He's drugged you, Eric!" Roland's voice came from far away. "Fight it, man. Get up."

He tried, but his legs seemed numb and useless. Roland lifted his upper body and half dragged him to the window. Eric knew his thoughts. He suspected Rogers would have an army of DPI agents, possibly all armed with syringes of this new drug, converging on the place at any moment. Yet in his hazy mind all Eric could think of was Tamara. Why wasn't she here? Could she bear the grief of losing St. Claire this way? My God, she adored the man.

But she was here! His mind was suddenly pummeled with her aura. He tried to call out to her, but Roland was already pulling him through the window. "Nnno," he tried to say, unsure if he'd actually made a sound.

As Eric felt himself pulled to the ground he heard her steps, and the opening of a door. He lifted his head and tried to see her. He did. She appeared unfocused, a blurry silhouette, but her eyes found his and connected, just for an instant. Then they moved downward, and he heard her agonized screams.

"Have...to...go...to her."

He slumped into unconsciousness as Roland carried him away.

CHAPTER FIFTEEN

Tamara felt the shock like a physical blow. She'd glanced up automatically when she'd opened the library door. She'd felt Eric's presence like a magnetic force on her gaze. She'd seen him. He'd looked at her briefly, and his face had been smeared with something red. She'd glimpsed scarlet stains on his normally pristine-white shirt cuff, as well, before he'd moved away from the window. She let her puzzled gaze travel downward, drawn there by some inner knowledge she couldn't credit. The scream of unbridled horror rose in her throat of its own volition when she saw the spreading pool beneath Daniel's body...the gaping rent in his throat.

She threw herself to the floor, heedless of the blood, and drew his limp head into her lap, stroking his face as her vision was obscured by tears and her mind went numb, unable to face reality. She mumbled soft words of comfort, unaware of what she said. Her mind slipped slowly, steadily from her grasp.

Curt's hands on her shoulders gripped hard, and shook her. He said something in short, harsh tones, but she refused to hear or acknowledge. "Call an ambulance," she told him with the slurred speech of a drunken person. "He's hurt, he needs help. Go call an ambulance."

"He's dead, Tamara." He released his hold on her, and tried instead to move Daniel's head from her cradling arms. She clung to him more tightly, closing her eyes as her vision cleared. She didn't want to see. "He's dead," Curt repeated loudly.

She kept her eyes closed and shook her head. "He's only hurt. He needs—"

Curt's hands closed on either side of her face, tilting it downward. "Look at him. Open your eyes, dammit!"

The increased pressure made her comply and she found her

gaze focused on deathly gray skin, slitted, already-glazing eyes and the ragged tear in Daniel's jugular. She shook her head, mute, her mind trying to go black. Her body slowly went limp and Curt jerked her to her feet the moment she relaxed her grip on Daniel. She slipped and nearly fell. When she looked down she saw that the floor was wet with blood. Her clothing soaked in it, Daniel's body drenched. Insanity crept closer, its gnarled hands gripping her mind and clenching.

"I told you this was how it would end."

She blinked and looked at him.

"You saw him yourself, Tam. It was Marquand. When I heard Daniel scream I kicked the door in. I couldn't believe what I saw. Marquand was...he was sucking the blood out of him. I jumped on him, but he'd already severed the vein—tore it right open. Daniel bled to death while I fought with Marquand."

Her face blank, she looked again toward the window, recalling her fleeting glimpse of Eric...the blood on his face. No. It wasn't true, it couldn't be. Mentally she cried out to him, closing her eyes and begging him to tell her the truth, to deny Curtis's words. He didn't respond. His silence drove her beyond control, and while she felt curiously detached, she watched as a blood-soaked woman wearing her body gave way to insanity. She tore at her clothing, raking her own face with bloodied nails, tore at her own hair and screamed like a banshee. Curtis had to back-hand the woman twice before she crumpled to a quivering, sobbing heap on the floor. He left the room, but returned in a moment and injected her with something. The proportions of the room became distorted, and voices echoed endlessly. She had to close her eyes or she knew she would be sick.

When she opened them, the unmistakable glint of early-morning sun slanted through her window and across her bed. Her head throbbed, but she was clean and dressed in a soft white nightgown. Her face hurt, and a glimpse in the mirror showed her another deep purple bruise complementing the one on her jaw. This one rode high on her cheekbone. She shook her head, dropped the hand mirror onto the stand and slipped from the bed. The bruise came from Curt's knuckles, landing brutally across her face when she'd lost her mind last night. But none of that had been real, had it? It hadn't really happened....

Silently she moved through her doorway, over the faded carpet in the hallway and down the stairs. All the way she kept thinking it had been a nightmare, or a delusion. She stopped outside the tall double doors to Daniel's library, and paused only a moment before she pushed them open. Her eyes moved directly to the carpet in the room's center. A pungent, metallic odor reached her at the same instant she recognized the bloodstains, and saw the masking-tape outline of Daniel's body.

"Tammy?"

She turned and looked up at Curt, wondering why she was so numb. Why wasn't she wailing with grief? Daniel was dead.

"Honey, I don't want you to let yourself be consumed with guilt. You had no way of knowing he was using you all along. The bastard must have planned this for months. Even Daniel believed him."

That's right, she reminded herself. Eric had never loved her. He'd seduced her. He'd used her to get to Daniel and then he'd brutally murdered a helpless old man. She'd practically caught him in the act. Hadn't she?

No. It isn't possible. I can't believe...I won't believe it.

"This has to be handled delicately and quickly," Curt went on, apparently unaware of her jumbled thoughts. "DPI doesn't want any local cops poking around."

She blinked, searching her brain for rational thought...logic. "But he was murdered."

"It's going down as a heart attack."

She looked back to the bloodstained carpet and shook her head. "A heart attack?"

"Our own forensics team will take care of Daniel. He's being cremated this morning...on the premises, right after Rose Sversky has a look at him. We'll have a memorial service this afternoon."

Tamara frowned at the mention of DPI's top forensic pathologist. Dr. Sversky's patients were kept in cold storage in a sublevel lab. She closed her eyes as she thought of sweet Daniel down there.

"I hate to leave you on your own, Tam, but there's a lot to do. We want to move fast before anyone has a chance to ask any questions. Word of this leaks out, Byram will turn into a circus. Be at St. Bart's at two for the service."

The telephone shrilled as Tamara tried to digest what he was telling her. There would be no burial in a grave she could visit. Daniel would be reduced to ashes within the next few hours. He'd been ripped from her so suddenly, so violently she felt nothing now but shock. As if she'd lost a limb.

Curt turned toward the phone in the living room, ignoring the closer one in the library. "Stay out of there for now, Tam. A cleanup crew will be here this afternoon."

Oh, yeah, she thought. DPI's good old "cleanup crew." When they finished you wouldn't be able to find a blood cell with a microscope. Cleanup would be more aptly named cover-up, but what the hell?

Curt's voice cut through the dark shroud over her heart. "No, Mrs. Bryant, I'm afraid Tamara isn't up to a phone call just now, but I will pass along the—"

She bolted at the sound of "Bryant," and jerked the phone out of Curt's hand before he could finish the sentence. How, even with all that had happened, could she have forgotten about Jamey? "Kathy? I'm right here. Is there any... There isn't?" She sighed in dismay when she learned Jamey still hadn't been found. She listened as the woman poured out the frustrations of a long, sleepless night. When she finally began to run out of steam Tamara cut in. "I'm going to find him, Kathy. I promise you, I will. I'll check in later, okay?"

She closed her eyes and stood still for a long moment after

she hung up. A moment ago she'd wanted nothing more than to crawl into a hole and pull the hole in after her. She'd wanted to sit in a corner and cry until she died. Now she had a purpose to keep her focus. For today, she would do her utmost to find Jamey Bryant. Tonight she would go to Eric and hear what he had to say. She wouldn't believe he'd killed Daniel until she heard it from his own lips. She couldn't believe it...nor could she deny what she'd seen with her own eyes. So she'd give credence to none of it, for now. For now, she'd simply focus on Jamey, and hopefully remain sane long enough to sort out the rest.

Curt was behind her as she moved toward the stairs. "So to anyone who asks, it was a heart attack. Don't forget. The only people who know the truth are Hilary Garner—she came over and helped get you into bed last night—and Milt Kromwell, Daniel's immediate superior. And, of course, Dr. Sversky. Are you sure you'll be all right?"

She nodded, wanting nothing more than to get started doing something that would absorb all her concentration. She was upstairs and in her room dressing before Curt's car left the driveway. She checked her jacket pocket when she pulled it on, and nodded when she felt the bit of gauze still there.

Jamey knew it was morning because he felt the sunlight gradually warming his stiff body. Thank God for the sleeping bag. He'd have frozen to death for sure if it hadn't been for that. The creep had shown up in the middle of the night with the bag, and slipped it up over him. He'd brought a ham sandwich, too, and a cup of chicken soup and some hot chocolate. He'd untied Jamey's hands so he could eat, but the blindfold had stayed put. He had ripped the tape off so roughly it had felt to Jamey as if his lips were still attached to it. Something cold and tubular had been pressed to his temple and a gruff, phony voice had rasped close to his ear, "One sound and I blow your head off. Got that, kid?"

He'd nodded hard. He fully believed Curtis Rogers would do

it. Any guy who'd slug a woman the way Curtis had slugged Tamara wouldn't give a second thought to blowing away a kid. And he knew it was Curtis now. He hadn't seen him, or heard him speak without the phony voice, but he knew. So he'd nodded like a good little hostage and had eaten his soup without seeing it. He had been allowed to relieve himself in a pail before he was tied again, arms behind him just like before, tape back over his mouth.

Damn, he hated that tape. After Curt had left, sometime during the long, cold night, Jamey's nose had started to clog up. He'd felt sickening panic grip him. How would he breathe if his nose clogged up and he had tape over his mouth? One thing was sure, Jamey didn't intend to spend another night here to find out. Curt had rasped that he'd be back in the morning, so Jamey would wait. He had a plan. It wasn't much of a plan, he figured, but it was better than nothing.

He didn't have to wait long. Before the sun had been shining very long, Curtis showed up with another cup of cocoa and a cheese Danish from a fast-food joint. He didn't say much this time, and Jamey didn't have the nerve to ask questions. He ate, did his business and sat calmly while he was retied and taped. But when Curt left this time, Jamey's senses were honed like razors. He listened carefully, memorizing the sounds of Curt's steps across the floor as he left. He waited then, just to be sure Curt wouldn't come back. Then he slid himself across the floor in the direction Curt had gone. He humped and slithered on his rear end. His feet pointed the way. He bent his knees and pulled himself along by digging his heels into the floor. He made good progress, too, until he hit a wall.

He sat there, confused for a moment. Then he realized there must be a doorway. Not a door, since he hadn't heard one open or close. But there must be a doorway. He wriggled around until his back was to the wall so he could run his hands along it as he humped sideways. He figured he'd worn his pants down to the thickness of tissue paper and implanted about a hundred slivers in his backside by the time his hands slipped off the flat wall and into empty space.

The doorway! He'd found it!

He was so excited he didn't even bother turning around again. He just pushed off with his feet and went backward through the opening...and into space.

Not a doorway, you idiot, a stairway. Oh, damn, a stairway....

Rose Sversky was a tiny sprite of a woman with short white hair in a close-to-the-head haircut and Coke-bottle glasses. She looked as if she'd be more at home cutting cookies than corpses. Tamara sat in a hard chair amid the organized chaos of chrome and steel and sheet-draped tables, painfully aware that one of those tables had supported Daniel's body only hours earlier. Maybe only minutes earlier.

Dr. Sversky handed the bit of gauze, now safely encased in a plastic zipper bag, across the desk to Tamara. "You were correct about the chloroform. Unfortunately, gauze is a poor receptacle for fingerprints. I couldn't find a hint of who took him." Tamara sighed hard and swore, but Rose wasn't finished. "There was a small trace of blood. Most likely the boy's though I can't be certain without something to compare it to. Do you know his type?"

Tamara frowned. "No. It's probably in his records, but it'll be easier just to ask his mother. I'll get back to you. It's funny, though, I didn't see any blood."

"I don't think you could have without a microscope. It was just a trace. Probably bit his tongue when he was grabbed." She sat silent behind her huge desk for a long moment, then reached across it to cover Tamara's hand with her own. "I'm sorry you're going through so much at once, dear. Daniel was a good man. I'll miss him."

Tamara blinked. She hadn't wanted to think about Daniel now...here. Still, she couldn't keep her gaze from jumping to the nearest table. "You're doing the death certificate, aren't you?"

"Yes. I've fixed them before, and I imagine, as long as I stay with DPI, I'll fix them again."

"It doesn't bother you, changing a cause of death from something as violent as this to a simple heart attack?"

Rose frowned. "Actually, unless anyone's already heard the rumor, it's going down as an accident." Tamara looked up and Rose hurried on. "It's always better to stick as close to the truth as possible. When I found that blow to the back of the head, I figured we might as well use it as the cause of death."

Tamara stared at her. "I wasn't told about any blow to the head."

Sversky removed her glasses and pinched the bridge of her nose. "I hope it eases your mind to know this. He was hit with a blunt object hard enough to render him unconscious before the laceration to the jugular. He probably never even felt it." She shook her head. "I've never autopsied a victim of—of a vampire attack before. It's nothing like I thought. You always see two neat little puncture marks on victims in the movies. This was—" She broke off and shook her head. "But you don't need to hear about that."

No, Tamara thought. She didn't need to hear it because she'd seen it. She rose slowly, thanked Rose Sversky and left. As she rode up in the elevator her fingers touched the tiny marks on her neck. They were barely noticeable now. She frowned as the doors opened on the ground floor, and she walked out to the Cadillac as if in a daze.

She'd wasted most of the day talking to people who lived along Jamey's route home from school, and more of it waiting while Rose Sversky examined the gauze pad. Mechanically she drove home, showered and changed into a black skirt with a white silk blouse Daniel had bought her one Christmas. As she did, her head pounded and her heart ached. She wanted so badly to find some answer to Daniel's death other than the obvious one. Her mind kept offering hopeful hints as reasons to doubt Eric's guilt, but she had to wonder if she was only seeing what she wanted to see. The fact that Curt claimed to have heard Daniel scream, and kicked the door in to see Eric biting him, was in conflict with what Rose had said about Daniel being unconscious when his jugular was slashed. But Curt might be confused, or might have heard Daniel scream just before he was knocked out. The fact that Eric would not need to cause such a bloody mess could be valid, or perhaps he'd just been as cruel as possible in eliminating his tormentor.

Eric? Cruel? Never.

She did what she could to repair the ravages of emotional upheaval with a coat of makeup, then went to the church in downtown Byram and sat in the front pew for a brief, pat sermon. It was, she figured, an all-purpose sermon they kept on hand for people whose names remained on the rolls but who'd given up attending services long ago.

When it was over she sat with a plastic smile firmly in place, and accepted condolences of all in attendance. Mostly co-workers, she noted. Daniel's work had been his life. It would have been more appropriate to hold the service in his office, or his basement lab.

When it was over, Curt came to her, took her hands and drew her to her feet. She'd been aware of him sitting a few seats away and watching her pensively all through the service. "Going home?" he asked.

She nodded. "I'm exhausted. I don't think any of this has sunk in yet."

"How's the hunt for the kid progressing?"

She sighed. "It isn't. I'm going to ask Kromwell to get the FBI involved. He has friends there."

"So do I," Curt said quickly. "Why don't you let me do that for you?"

Her eyes narrowed briefly. His smile seemed false, somehow. Then again, hers probably did, too. Hers *was* false. "Okay. I'll take any help I can get." She swallowed as the uneasiness she felt niggled harder. "It was sweet of you to stay with me last night, Curt. But if you don't mind, I'd kind of like to be alone tonight. I need...to sort things out. Do you understand?"

He nodded. "Call if you need me." He leaned over, pressed a brief kiss on her lips and squeezed her shoulders. She watched him leave, and pulled on her jacket. She was headed for the door herself when a soft hand on her arm stopped her. She turned, and at the sympathetic look on Hilary's face she instantly burst into tears.

Hilary hugged her hard and they stood that way until Tamara had cried herself out. She felt cleansed, and was grateful for a friend she could cry with. Hilary dabbed at her own damp eyes. "You know if you need anything..."

"I know." Tamara nodded, and swiped her wet face with an impatient hand.

"Is there any word on the little boy?"

Tamara met Hilary's doe eyes and felt another good cry coming on. She sniffed, and fought the fresh tears. "No, nothing yet. I found a piece of gauze with traces of chloroform on it near the spot where he was last seen. There was a trace of blood, too, and I'll be able to confirm it was his as soon as I check with his mother about his type."

"Why would you have to do that?"

Tamara only frowned.

"You're telling me you don't know Jameson Bryant's blood type?"

"No, I don't. I suppose it's in his records, but—"

"I *guess* it's in his record. It was one of the first things put in his records. It's the same as yours, Tamara. That Belladonna thing. I can't believe you didn't know."

"Belladonna?" Tamara couldn't believe what she was hearing. "Hilary, how do you know this?"

"I was the one who got the order to enter all of his medical records into DPI computers under level one. I remember thinking that was pretty high for simple medical records, but—''

"Who gave the order?''

Hilary frowned. "I don't know, it came down through channels. Look, I probably shouldn't be discussing any of this with you, Tam. I mean, it is filed under level one, and your security clearance—''

"Isn't high enough," Tamara said slowly. Tamara left then, with Hilary frowning after her. She got into the car and drove away from the church, barely paying attention to traffic. "He has the antigen," she mumbled to herself. "Does he have the lineage, too?''

"Of course he does. That's why his psychic link with me is stronger than with anyone else.''

Whoever ordered those records at level one deliberately classified them beyond her security clearance, she realized slowly. They didn't want her to know.

"But they knew. They knew we were close and they knew that if Jamey was in trouble, I'd go after him.'' She blinked fast. "Jamey was taken to get me out of the house...and then Daniel was murdered.''

Eric could never harm a little boy. Besides, Jamey had been taken in broad daylight. Eric hadn't killed Daniel. But someone had...someone with access to level one data. Someone who wanted it to look like the work of a vampire.

"And someone who knew about the meeting between Daniel and Eric," she whispered. She bit her lip. "Curtis?''

She almost missed the driveway. She hit the brake and jerked the wheel. She killed the engine near the front door, got out to run inside, and locked the door behind her. "My God, is it true? Was Curt angry enough to murder Daniel?'' She pressed her fingertips to her temples. "What on earth has he done with Jamey?''

She swallowed a sob and ran up the stairs to Daniel's room. She found his keys in a matter of minutes and hurried back down with them, jangling in the silent house like alarm bells. She didn't hesitate at the basement door. If she did, she'd never go down. She inserted a key, turned it and shoved the door open.

It was still only late afternoon. Outside, the sunlight glinted off the surface of the snow so brightly it was painful to see. Here a dark chasm opened up at her feet. She couldn't even see the stairs. Yet the answers to all her questions were likely a few steps below her. She had no choice but to go down.

CHAPTER SIXTEEN

Jamey shook his head to clear it, but it only brought excruciating pain. He'd been out cold...he knew he had, but had no idea how long. He was on his back and his arms, still tied behind him, had gone completely numb. He tried to sit up, and the pain that knifed through his chest was like nothing he'd ever felt. He thought it would tear him in half. He stopped with his body half sitting up and half lying down. But remaining like that hurt still more so he drew a breath to brace himself, and that sent more pain through him.

Grating his teeth, he shoved himself farther up, relieved when he felt a wall to his right. He leaned against it, then sat still and let the pain slowly recede. It didn't go far. As the blood rushed into his arms, they throbbed and tingled and prickled unbearably. He'd have yelled if he could, but the tape remained over his mouth. His eyes were still covered, and his ankles still bound. His lungs felt funny, and it was more than just the stabbing pain that hurt every time he inhaled. They felt the way they feel after you go swimming and get a little bit of water in them. He kept having the urge to cough, but he was terrified to give in to it. If he coughed, with this tape over his mouth, he'd probably choke to death—especially if that weird feeling in his lungs was what he thought it was. He thought it felt as if something were sticking right into his chest. A blade, a sharp-edged board he'd hit on the way down, something like that. And he thought that whatever kept trying to choke up into his throat might be blood. If it was, he knew he was in a lot of trouble.

She flung the file to the floor in disgust, and turned to leave the small office she'd discovered. She hadn't even made it to the lab itself, which she suspected lay beyond the padlocked door to her right. She needed no more of the revelations she'd found here. In Daniel's files she'd found what he'd termed "case studies." In truth these were detailed accounts of the capture and subsequent torture of three vampires.

Two had been taken in 1959, by Daniel and his then partner, William Reinholt. The pair were described as "young and therefore not as powerful as we'd first assumed." They were "relieved of a good deal of blood to weaken them, thus assuring the safety of my partner and myself. However, they were unable to sustain the loss, and expired during the night." Another study noted was of a woman who called herself only Rhiannon, and who was "entirely uncooperative, hurling insults and abuse constantly." Due to their last efforts, they took less blood from her, leaving her too strong to deal with.

Daniel returned to the lab after hours of "tests and study" to find his partner dead, his neck broken, the bars torn from the window and the "subject" gone.

Tamara felt like cheering for the mysterious Rhiannon. She felt like crying for the man Daniel had been. A monster, just as he'd told her. She hadn't realized just how accurate that confession had been.

She stopped herself from leaving, as appalling as she found the notes. She had to continue scouring the files if she wanted to find a clue as to where Jamey had been taken. She hoped to God there was one to find. She was beginning to think this her last chance. She had a terrible certainty in the pit of her stomach that if she didn't find Jamey soon, it would too late.

She returned to the file cabinet and pawed through more files. There was none with Jamey's name on it, but she halted, her blood going cold, when her fingers touched one with her own. Slowly she withdrew the file. It was thicker than any of the others. Something inside her warned her not to open it and look inside, but she knew she had to.

Moments later she wished she hadn't. Thumbing through the pages, she'd paused when she'd seen her parents' names on one, her eyes traversing a single passage before they became too blurred to read farther.

It has been decided that I should seek to gain custody of this child. She will act as a magnet for Marquand and possibly others of the undead species. The parents, as expected, refuse to cooperate. They are, however, expendable, and of less value than the countless lives which will be saved if this experiment bears fruit. A rare viral strain has been chosen. Their exposure will be carefully contained. Death will occur within twenty-four hours.

"No," she whispered. "Oh, God, no..." The file fell from her nerveless fingers and sheets spread over the floor. Tamara gripped the edge of the open file drawer, her head bowed over it. Daniel had killed her parents. For a moment she conjured their images in her mind, ashamed that they were blurred and indistinct. She barely remembered them. Her memories of them, too, had been stolen from her. Daniel's refusal to discuss them...to allow her to keep mementos of them...his constant advice that her mind didn't want her to remember, that she was better off forgetting.

She drew several short, panting breaths, and forced her eyes open. She blinked the tears away and glimpsed the polished grips of a handgun, protruding from beneath the files in the drawer. Just as she reached for it a hand closed on her shoulder and pulled her backward.

She whirled. "Curtis!"

His narrow gaze raked her, then the open drawers and scattered files. "Been doing a little exploring, Tammy?"

Why had she doubted Eric, even for a second, she wondered silently. Why hadn't she gone straight to his home when she realized it must have been Curt who killed Daniel? He'd have helped her find Jamey. But it was too late for hindsight now. There was still an hour before full dark. And she still had to know where the boy was. "What have you done with Jamey, Curt?"

His brows shot up. "You have been busy. What makes you think I took the kid?"

She shook her head. "I don't think, I know. Where is he?"

"He's safe. Don't worry, I wouldn't hurt the kid...right away. I'd like to study him a little. Later. When I've finished with you and Marquand. Does that reassure you?"

She shook her head so hard her hair billowed around her like a dark cloud. "If you hurt him, Curtis, I swear to God—"

"You'd be better off worrying about yourself, Tammy." He took a step nearer her and she backed up. He took another. So did she. In a moment she realized he'd backed her up to the padlocked door. She stiffened. He pulled a key from his pocket, held it out to her. "Open it."

She shook her head again. "No."

"You want to see the kid, don't you?"

"Jamey?" She glanced furtively over her shoulder at the door. "He's in there?"

"Where else would I put him?"

Relief washed over her and she snatched the key from him, stabbing it into the lock and twisting. When it sprang free she jiggled it loose and shoved the door open. If she could just get to Jamey, she thought, they would be all right. It would be dark soon, and Eric would come for them. She moved into the darkened room. "Jamey? It's Tam, I'm here. It's all right...Jamey?"

The door closed and her heart plummeted when she heard locks being slid home. A flick brought a flood of light so brilliant she had to squint to see. She scanned the room, certain now that Jamey was not here. There was a table in the room's center, with straps where a person's ankles and wrists would rest, another at the head. Beside the table a chrome tray lined with gleaming instruments. Above it, a dome-shaped surgical lamp. She swallowed hard against the panic that rose within her. Beside it was the sickening realization that this was the room where the two young vampires had died at Daniel's hand, and where Rhiannon had been tortured to the point of a murderous rage before she'd made her escape.

She turned to face Curtis when she heard his approach, and in an instant he gripped her upper arms mercilessly. He pushed her backward, oblivious to her feet kicking at his shins, or her thrashing shoulders. When her back hit the table she sucked in her breath. "My God, Curt, what are you doing?"

He brought her wrists together, held them in one hand and reached for a bottle with the other. He twisted the cap off with his teeth, then held it under her nose. She twisted her head away from the frighteningly familiar scent, but her mobility was limited and his reach was long.

When her head swam and her knees buckled he set the chloroform down and shoved her roughly onto the table. A moment later she found her ankles and wrists bound tight. She blinked away the dizziness, then averted her face fast when he held pungent smelling salts to her nose.

"That's a good girl. Don't go passing out on me, now. It would defeat the whole purpose." She tried to bring the whirling room into focus, relieved when it stopped tilting and spinning. "You can summon him mentally, am I right?"

She pursed her lips, and refused to look at him.

He gripped her chin and made her face him. "Don't answer me, Tammy. I'm betting that you can. We'll soon find out, won't we?" He read her expression correctly and smiled. "You think I'm afraid of him, Tammy? I want you to call him. When he gets here, I'll be ready and waiting."

She shook her head. "I won't do it."

Curtis smiled slowly and Tamara felt a cold chill race up her spine. "I think you will," he said, bending over her to fasten the strap over her forehead, leaving her virtually paralyzed. "I think you'll be screaming for him to come by the time I'm finished." He reached to the tray, and she tried to follow his movements with her eyes. He lifted a gleaming scalpel, looked at it for a long moment, then twisted his wrist to glance at his watch. "Another twenty minutes ought to do it, honey."

Eric went completely rigid in his coffin as a shock of pain shot through him. Eyes wide with sudden alacrity, he flicked the latch and flung the lid back. He was on his feet in a moment, brow furrowed in concentration. He focused on Tamara. He called to her. He waited for a response but felt none.

For a brief instant he wondered if it was possible she believed what Rogers had intended she believe—that he had murdered her beloved St. Claire. He dismissed the notion out of hand. She knew him too well. She was fully aware she need only look into his mind to know the truth. She wouldn't believe his guilt without giving him a chance to explain. Which was why he'd fully expected to find her waiting upstairs when he rose this evening. Instead, he sensed only emptiness. No doubt she was beside herself with grief, but he would not allow her to shut him out. He'd help her through, whether she wanted him to or not. Again he called to her. Again he received no response.

Roland rose with his usual grace, but when Eric glanced at his friend he saw an unfamiliar tension in Roland's face. He ceased his summoning of Tamara to ask, "What is it?"

"I am not sure." Roland visibly shook himself. "Have you had word from our Tamara?"

"She doesn't heed my call."

"Go to her, then. She may be out of sorts after last night, but I have no doubt she'll see the truth when you tell it. If you—" He stopped, cocking his head to one side as if listening. "Damnation!"

Eric cocked one brow, waiting for an explanation, but Roland only shook his head. "I'm still uncertain. I shall go out for a time, see if I can puzzle it out. Will you be able to manage this on your own?"

"Of course, but—"

"Good. Give my regards to our girl."

Roland spun on his heel and left as Eric watched him go, wondering what on earth was the matter. Shrugging, he returned his concentration to Tamara. *Why do you ignore me, my love?*

He felt no reply, then suddenly another spasm of pain shot through him, stiffening his spine. He blinked rapidly, realizing the pain must be hers in order to make itself so completely known to him. *Tamara! If you refuse to answer, I will come to you. I must know what—*

No!

Her answer rang loudly in his head, and he frowned. *You are in pain, love. What has happened to you?*

Nothing. Stay away, Eric. If you love me at all, stay away. Again, intense, jarring pain hit, nearly sending him to his knees, and he knew someone was deliberately hurting her. *Rogers?*

"I should have killed the bastard the first time I set eyes on him." He fairly ripped the door from its hinges in his haste to get to her. He gained the stairs, and then the frigid night air. His preternatural strength gave him the speed of a cheetah, and beyond. He raced toward her, and would have gone right through the front door had not a quavering train of thought pierced his mind. *It's a trap, Eric. Stay away. Please, stay away.*

He paused, his heart thudding, not with exertion but with rage and fear for Tamara. A trap, she'd said. He used his mind to track her down, then moved slowly around the house, seeking another way in. He finally knelt beside a barred window, obscured from view by shrubbery.

Tamara lay strapped to a table beneath a blinding light. Her blouse had been sliced up the center, as had her brassiere. She still wore a dark skirt. Her feet were bare. Hot pink patches of tissue oozed blood the way a sponge oozed water, in various spots over her torso. One was on the breast from which Eric himself had tasted her blood. Another, at the same spot on her throat. Rogers had amused himself by taking tissue samples, Eric realized. He now stood aside, laying a prodlike instrument down and picking up what looked like a drill.

"Even that baby didn't make you call him, huh, Tam? Well, I have other tricks in my bag. I could really use a bone marrow sample." He depressed the trigger, and the drill whirred. He release it, held it poised over her lower leg. "What do you say, Tammy? Do you call or do I drill?"

Tamara's face was deathly white. Her jaw quivered, but she looked Rogers in the eye. "Drop dead," she rasped.

Shrugging, Rogers lowered a pair of plastic goggles over his eyes and lowered the drill. With a feral growl Eric smashed the glass and ripped the first bar he gripped free of the window. In a second he was inside.

"Eric, no! Go away, hurry!" Her voice was unrecognizable. The stringy bark of an ancient cherry tree, the voice of sandpaper.

Eric lunged for Curtis, who dropped the drill and lifted something that looked like an odd sort of gun. Too fast, the dart plunged into his chest. He jerked backward, gaping like a fish out of water, and fell to his knees. He gripped the dart, pulled it from his flesh and held it up, looking first at it, and then beyond it, at Rogers's triumphant leer. The drug. He'd been expecting a syringe, not a gun. He forced himself to his feet and took an unsteady step toward Rogers. "You...will...die for this," he gasped. He took another step, then sank into a bottomless pool of black mists.

Roland moved in the night like a shadow, speeding over darkened streets, then stopping, listening and moving on. Ever closer to the boy. The faint sense of the boy had niggled at him since he'd arrived on Eric's doorstep. But it had been *so* faint he'd barely been aware of it, much less able to pinpoint the source. Naturally, he understood that the Chosen usually "connect" only with a single vampire. He was the only one who'd sensed Eric as a child. Others would have recognized him, had they encountered him, of course. But no others heard him calling.

They didn't feel the pull. Just as with Tamara, Eric had been the one drawn. Roland felt her only through Eric.

This boy called out to someone...not to Roland. If he'd been summoning Roland the entire matter would have been so much simpler. As it was, with the faintest trace of a signal to go by, and the boy not even aware of transmitting it, he'd be lucky to find him in time.

That was the hell of it, Roland thought as he paused again to try to feel the signals the child was sending. They grew weaker with each passing moment. The knowledge that the child's life was ebbing overlapped the pull of him like an alarm sounding in Roland's head—like one of Eric's security contraptions. If only his sense of the boy was clearer! If only the boy was reaching those invisible fingers out to him instead of someone else—someone who apparently wasn't listening. Roland hadn't known it was possible for one of his kind to ignore the desperate cries of a child, a child likely to expire before this night's end.

Eric opened his eyes and found himself strapped to the same table Tamara had previously occupied. His hands, feet and head were bound just as hers had been. Unlike her, he was still fully clothed. No doubt the bastard had been uncertain how long his drug would be effective, and was unwilling to risk personal injury. He hadn't wanted Eric waking until he was fully restrained...as if these measly straps would make a difference. Eric pulled against them, shocked when the effort left him limp and even dizzy.

He's drawn vials of blood from you, Eric. It's why you're so weak.

The explanation came to his mind from Tamara's, and with it a lingering pain, a weak, shaken feeling and utter desolation. He wanted to see her, but couldn't turn his head. He tried to attune his groggy senses to hers and they finally began to sharpen. He knew Curtis was still in the room. It was why she hadn't spoken aloud.

What has the bastard done to you?

Nothing so terrible, came the weak reply. *I'll be all right.*

I feel your pain, Tamara. I cannot see you, and keeping things from me only frightens me further. Tell me. Tell me all of it.

He felt her shudder, as if it had passed through his own body. *He...took little patches of skin. It burns, but the scrapes aren't deep. He drew blood from me, too.*

Eric sensed her pain, certain there was more. The jolts of pain he'd felt earlier hadn't been caused by superficial abrasions. *He had an instrument when I arrived—a rod-shaped device he brandished over you. What was it?*

She hesitated for a long moment. *It is...charged...with electricity.*

Rage flooded through Eric. He would kill Curt Rogers for this, he vowed silently, even as Tamara continued. *He killed Daniel. He wanted me to believe it was you, but I could never believe that. He's taken Jamey, Eric. I don't know what he's done with him—*

Her thoughts ceased abruptly with Curtis's approaching footsteps. He leaned over Eric. "Finally awake? Drug didn't last quite as long as I'd hoped, but then, it's still experimental."

"You push me too far, Rogers."

"Not a hell of a lot you can do about it at the moment, is there? I am going to need some samples from you, too, you know. A little bone marrow, some cerebral fluid. Then we'll see just how much sunlight is bearable."

Eric felt the terror Tamara experienced as Rogers described his plans in explicit detail. He also felt the weakening effects of the drug waning. His strength began to seep back into his limbs.

"Curt, you can't do this to him. Please, for God's sake, if you ever cared about me, let him go."

Rogers stepped away from the table. Eric couldn't turn to look, but he knew the bastard was touching her. He felt her shiver of revulsion, and he heard the chilling words. "You haven't figured it out yet? I never did care about you...except as a research subject. A half-breed vampire, Tam. That's what you are. The only thing you're good for is scientific study. Oh, maybe you're good for a few other things, too. I intend to find out before I'm finished with you."

She sobbed involuntarily, and Eric jerked against his restraints. The movement brought Rogers back quickly. "Hmm, you're still a little too lively for my tastes," he drawled, rattling instruments on a tray. A moment later Eric flinched as a needle was driven into his arm. He felt the life force slowly leaving his body with every pulse of blood that rushed into the waiting receptacle. In moments he was sickeningly dizzy, and too weak even to flex his fingers. He felt himself slipping from consciousness. His heavy lids fell, and vaguely he heard Tamara crying, "Stop it, Curtis, please. My God, you're killing him...."

Tamara struggled against the straps he'd tied around her, but it was useless. Her hands were bound behind the chair, her ankles tied to the chair legs. Her entire body pulsed with pain, due to the dozens of scrapings he'd taken from her skin. She was dizzy from the loss of the blood he'd drawn, and weak and shaken from the jolts of electricity he'd sent through her to try to force her to summon Eric. She'd refused, but it had done no good. Eric had felt her pain and rushed to her side. She should have known he would. He'd come to help her, and now all she could do was sit and watch while Curt drained the blood from him. Eric grew whiter and perfectly limp. Finally Curt removed the needle. He lifted Eric's eyelids and flicked a penlight at them, then nodded, satisfied.

She was surprised when Curt glanced at his watch, and then moved to close the shutters. "I think it will be safer to work on him during the day, don't you, Tam?" He brushed away the broken glass, seemingly unconcerned about the bar Eric had wrenched free. He turned to a cupboard, pulled out a fresh bottle and syringe, and Tamara flinched automatically. "Easy, now," he said softly. "I want to get a few hours' sleep. I know he isn't going anywhere, but I have to make sure you stay put, too, don't I?" He gripped her arm and sank the needle, far more deeply than was necessary, into her flesh. She stiffened, trying to resist the drowsiness that began creeping up on her. Curt let his hand move over her breasts before he drew away. She would have pulled her tattered blouse together if she'd been able to move her arms. His touch made her want to vomit.

"I hate you...for this," she managed, before she was unable to resist the lure of sleep any longer. Her head fell forward.

She had no idea how much time had passed when she lifted it again. The dark spaces between the shutters showed gray now, rather than black as before, so she feared dawn was approaching. Her arms ached from being pulled behind her, and her head throbbed so forcefully she could barely focus her vision.

When she did, she saw Eric lying exactly as he had been earlier, as pale and still as... No. She wouldn't complete the thought. He was all right. He had to be. She mustered all of her strength and hopped her chair toward him. "Eric. Wake up, Eric, we have to get out of here." That he didn't respond in the slightest did not deter her. She reached the table, and turned so her back was at his side. She bent almost double and strained her legs until she managed to lift the chair on her back. She groped with her fingers, felt his at last and gripped them. "Do you feel me touching you? Wake up, Eric. Untie me. Come on, I know you can do it. You wake enough to push your damned hidden button, you can wake enough to loosen a simple knot. Our lives depend on it, Eric. Please." She sucked in a breath when she felt his fingers flex. "Good. That's it." She angled her hand so the knot touched his fingertips, and continued speaking to him softly as she felt his fingers move. She knew it was a terrible effort. She felt the energy he forced into just moving his fingers. And then she felt the strap fall away from her hands, and she heard him exhale.

Instantly she bent and freed her feet. She stood, turned to Eric and reached down to release the straps that bound his ankles, then his wrists. When she bent over his head, releasing the final strap, she stroked his cool face with her palm. "Tell me what to do, Eric." She wanted to help him, but wasn't certain how. Hot tears rolled down her face to drop onto his.

His eyes fluttered, then remained open. "Go," he whispered.

"Leave me..." The lids fell closed again. "Too late," he finished.

"No, it isn't. It can't be. Don't do this, Eric, don't leave me."

She caught her breath as a memory surged like a flash flood in her mind. In her imagination it wasn't Eric lying on the table. It was Tamara, a very young Tamara, small and pale and afraid. Her wrists were bandaged and she knew that the bandages wouldn't help. She was going to die. She felt it.

Until the tall, dark man had appeared beside her bed. She knew his face, even then. She didn't know his name, but it didn't matter. He was her friend...she'd seen him before, even though she'd pretended she hadn't. She sensed he didn't want to be seen, and she didn't want to frighten him away. He used to come and look in on her at night. He made her feel safe, protected. She knew that he loved her. She felt it, the way you can feel heat from a candle if you hold your hand near the flame.

She was so glad to see him there with her. But sad, too, because he was crying. He stayed beside the bed for a long time, stroking her hair and feeling very sad. She wanted to talk to him, but she was so weak she could barely open her eyes. After a while he did something. He hurt himself. There was a cut on his wrist, and he pushed it to her lips.

At first she thought he wanted her to kiss it better, the way her mommy used to kiss her hurts sometimes. But as soon as the blood touched her tongue she felt something zap through her...just like when she'd touched the frayed wire on the lamp once. Except this didn't hurt and it didn't scare her the way that had. It zapped just the same, though, and all at once she knew he was giving her the medicine that would make her better, and she swallowed it.

She felt herself get stronger with every sip. A long time later he pulled it away, and wrapped a clean white handkerchief around his wrist. He slumped in the chair near the bed, and he was almost as white as the hanky. He felt weak and tired, and she felt strong and better. She knew she would be okay. And when she looked at him again, she knew his name. In fact she knew all about him, somehow. She sat up in bed, and listened as he told stories and sang lullabies. He was her hero and she adored him. It broke her heart when he finally had to go.

Tamara shook herself, and brushed at the tears. "I remember," she told him. "Oh, Eric, I remember."

His only response was a slight flicker of his eyes. His lips formed the word *Go.*

"Not without you," she told him.

"Too...weak." It cost him terribly just to utter the words. His face showed the strain. "Go on."

"Never," she whispered. "Not if I have to carry you on my back, not if I have to crawl, Eric. I'd sooner slit my own wrists than leave you here with—" She broke off there.

He forced his eyes open once more, and met her gaze. "No. You...too weak...could lose too...much." Ignoring him, Tamara brought her gaze to the tray, and snatched up a scalpel. "No..." He put as much force as he had behind the word. "Could...die—"

She grated her teeth and pulled the blade over her forearm. She forced the small cut to his mouth. Too weak to fight her, Eric had no choice but to swallow. Her blood flowed into him slowly, but with the samples Curt had already taken, she soon felt weak and dizzy. Her head swirled and the room slowly began to spin. Eric shoved her away from him, snatching up the strap that had bound her before, and jerking it tight around her arm, above the cut.

She vaguely heard the door open, just before she was jerked away from Eric. Curt spun her around and slammed a fist into her temple, sending her to her knees. Blinking slowly as the ceiling rotated above, she tried to see what was happening. Eric was on his feet. Curt was snatching a hypodermic from a shelf. He stood crouched and ready. Eric fell into a similar stance and they circled one another, wary, each ready for the other to spring.

She had to help Eric, she thought through a haze. He didn't stand a chance against Curt's new drug, and if Curt got the best of him this time, she didn't doubt he'd kill him. She couldn't just sit here and watch to see which of them was still breathing after this battle. Eric could not lose. It was that simple. If he did, they would both die here, in this chamber of horrors. And what would become of Jamey?

Unnoticed by either man, she slid backward across the floor toward the door Curtis had left wide. When she reached it she gripped the knob and hauled herself to her feet. Dizziness swamped her and she staggered, but with a desperate lunge she made it to the file cabinet, praying it was still unlocked. She heard something crash to the floor in the laboratory. She heard shattering glass and clanging metal. She yanked on the top drawer and it slid open. She reached inside, groping blindly as she looked over her shoulder, certain Curt would emerge at any second. Her hand closed on the smooth walnut grips and she slowly withdrew the handgun. Stumbling, she made her way back to the doorway. Curt's back was toward her. He stood between her and Eric, who was backed to the far wall, facing her. She thumbed the hammer back.

"That's enough, Curtis. Put the syringe down or— Curtis!" He lunged at Eric, making a sweeping attack with the syringe. Tamara's finger clenched on the trigger, and before she was aware of it, she'd shot twice.

Curt jerked like a marionette whose strings are tugged suddenly, then slumped slowly to the floor and lay still.

Eric slammed flat against the wall as if he'd been punched. Tamara saw the blood spreading across his chest, and then he, too, slumped to the floor.

"Eric!" she shrieked, and dropped the weapon. "My God, Eric!"

Outside an abandoned, crumbling building Roland paused. The boy's signal had been stronger than ever only a second ago. Now it had faded completely. Had the child died? In desperation Roland went inside, his night vision showing him the small form lying weakly against a wall.

He knelt beside the boy, a flick of his fingers snapping the ropes that bound his wrists and ankles. He took the blindfold away, and gently peeled the tape from pale lips. He gathered the child up in his arms and strode from the building, even as his senses sharpened to ascertain the problem.

The child was slipping into what modern medical people call shock, his blood pressure dangerously low, his skin cold and clammy. He was bleeding internally from a lung, punctured by a broken rib. He had a bruise on his brain—a concussion, that is—but Roland didn't believe that injury to be serious.

Cradling the child in one arm, he removed his cloak with the other, and quickly wrapped the boy in it. Warmth was vital. As was speed. He raced with the child to the nearest hospital. As they sped through the night the boy opened his eyes. "Who are you?" was all he said, and that softly.

"I'm Roland, child. Don't worry. You'll be fine."

"Eric's friend?"

Roland frowned. "You're Tamara's Jamey, aren't you?"

He nodded and settled a bit, then his eyes flew wide. "Is she okay?"

"Eric is with her," Roland replied.

They sped into the emergency room, and were immediately surrounded by nurses, with forms to be filled out and endless questions. One took the boy from him and placed him on a table. "Call my mom," Jamey said softly. Roland nodded, searching his memory for the child's last name. Bryant, he recalled Tamara saying. He went to the desk and asked for a telephone.

As he waited, he realized that Tamara must be the missing link. It was she the boy had been unconsciously summoning. She hadn't heard. She wasn't even one of them. Perhaps, though, she was meant to be.

CHAPTER SEVENTEEN

Tamara fell to her knees beside Eric and pulled his head up. She thought he'd be dead. Her weakness and dizziness, as well as her sore arm, were ignored, beaten into submission by her grief. She was amazed when he spoke through clenched teeth. "It isn't the bullets, Tamara. It's...the bleeding."

"Bleeding." She frowned. "The bleeding!" Of course. She remembered now that he'd told her how easily he might bleed to death. She shoved him flat and tore his shirt open with her right hand, then struggled to her feet. Weaving and dizzy, she made her way to the row of cupboards, ripping open three doors before she found rolls of bandages, gauze and adhesive tape. With her arms full, the left one still throbbing, she staggered back to him. Clumsily, one-handed, she wadded bunches of gauze to pack into the two small wounds. He grunted as she worked. He felt pain more keenly than a human would, so she knew this must be excruciating. Still, she made herself continue until it seemed the bleeding had stopped. She wrapped long strips around him to hold the gauze in place. She pulled them tight and taped them there.

Dizziness hit her anew, but Eric sat up and gripped her shoulders when she would have fallen. He made her sit beside him, and carefully he bandaged the small wound on her forearm, padding it thickly and then removing the strap he'd tied around her arm.

They helped each other to stand and slowly made their way out of the lab, around Curtis's still body and up the stairs. When they emerged outside into the paling light of the early predawn sky, Roland appeared in the driveway, and came toward them.

"I had a feeling you might need me. I can see I was mistaken." He eyed them both. "Rogers?"

"Dead," Eric said bleakly.

"I shot him." Tamara made herself say the words. "And my only regret is that he won't be able to tell me what he did with...with Jamey." Her voice broke, and she felt tears stinging her eyes.

"The boy is being attended now. I took him to the emergency room."

Tamara's head went up fast, and Eric's arm tightened around her. "Go to him, love. You need your arm stitched, anyway."

"I'm not leaving you until I know you're all right." She glanced up at the sky and frowned. "We'd better hurry or both of you will be in trouble."

Roland put a hand on her shoulder. "I give you my promise, child, that Eric will be as good as new by nightfall. We can make it to the house in less time than you could drive in your car. Go, see to the boy."

She looked up at Eric, and his arms closed around her. His lips, though pale and cool, captured hers and left them with a promise. "Go, love. Until tonight."

She nodded, and hurried to her car. She found a jacket in the back seat and zipped it on to cover her torn blouse before she left. There was nothing that could persuade her to go back inside that house. She noticed that Eric and Roland remained, watching until she drove out of sight, before they went their own way.

Hours later, her arm stitched and bandaged, the police's questions temporarily answered, her head mercifully clear, Tamara knelt before the fire in Eric's living-room hearth and added logs to the glowing embers. She felt safe here, knowing he was nearby. She hadn't felt this safe, she realized, since she'd been a child of six, in a hospital bed, clinging to the hand of a tall, handsome stranger, who wasn't a stranger at all.

When she'd absorbed enough heat to remove the chill from her body, she wandered to the stereo and slipped a CD into the player. Mozart's music filled the entire house, and Tamara moved from room to room, lighting every lamp. The day was beginning to wane. Night approached and she was too filled with anticipation to sit still and await it. She took her time in the downstairs bathroom, luxuriating in a hot scented tub. When she finished, she didn't resist the impulse that sent her to the bedroom upstairs for the dress he had given her. She put it on carefully, located a brush and stroked her hair to gleaming onyx. When she returned to her seat by the fire the sun rested on the horizon, about to dip below it.

In the hidden room beyond the cellar Eric looked down at his torn, bloodied shirt and grimaced.

"Not much time to clean up before retiring, was there, Eric?" Roland's grin irritated him still further.

"I suppose you find this amusing?"

"Not at all. In fact, I took it upon myself to make a few preparations after I dropped you into your coffin this morning." Roland waved a hand to indicate the fresh suit of clothes that hung nearby, and the basin of water on the stand near the fire.

Eric's temper dissolved. "Only a true friend would think of such trivial necessities."

"No doubt I will ask that you return the favor one day." Eric washed quickly, knowing she waited upstairs. He donned the clothes in haste, and hurried up the stairs to join her. Roland tactfully took his time in following.

She waited by the fire. She was wearing the gown, and Eric felt a lump in his throat. She stood quickly when she heard him, and eyed him with obvious concern. "Eric. Are you—"

"Fully recovered, love. I told you the sleep is regenerative, didn't I? You haven't been worrying about me, I hope."

"I've been worrying about a lot of things," she admitted, but relaxed into his arms, resting her head on his shoulder.

He held her hard for a long moment, eyes closed, relishing her nearness, her scent and the feel of her body so close to his. Then he straightened, took her hand in his and examined her wounded arm. "It's been stitched?" She nodded, and Eric tilted her chin in his hand and searched her face. "And the other injuries? Are you still in pain?"

Her smile was his answer. "I'm fine."

"Looks a good deal better than fine to these eyes," Roland boomed as he joined them in the parlor. "A sight to take a man's breath away, if ever there was one."

Tamara smiled at Roland and lowered her lashes. "Are all you eighteenth-century men so gifted at idle flattery?"

"I am a good deal older than that, my dear, so my flattery can be nothing but genuine." Just when Eric felt the slightest twinge of jealousy, Roland went on. "I can see you two have important matters to discuss, and I have an appointment of my own to keep, so I'll be on my way."

"I know about your appointment," Tamara said. Eric glanced down at her as she stepped out of his embrace, walked over to Roland and linked her arm through his.

"What's this?" Eric kept his tone jovial. "You two have been sharing secrets?"

"None that I know of, Eric." Roland looked at Tamara as she led him to the settee and pushed him to sit down. "Have you begun reading my mind, as well, little one?"

"No, but I spoke to Jamey's mother today." Roland nodded as if he understood. Eric, however, was still completely in the dark. Tamara returned to him, pulled him to the settee, as well, and joined him upon it. "Roland saved Jamey's life last night. Curtis had kidnapped him because he's like me, one of what you call the Chosen. That's why we've always been so connected, Jamey and I. I've been going nuts wondering what I could do to be sure Jamey would be safe...that some lunatic like Daniel wouldn't decide to further science by murdering his mother and adopting him. That's what Daniel did, you know. My parents' deaths were not accidental."

Eric nodded. For some time he'd had a lingering suspicion that had been the case. She eyed Roland. "Kathy says you've

asked her to travel to one of your estates in France. That you
need a live-in, full-time manager there and that you would like
her to do it. She says you offered her more money than she
could turn down." Tamara shook her head. "She would have
done it for nothing after you brought Jamey back safe and
sound."

"He was hardly that when I last saw him," Roland com-
mented. "How is the boy?"

"He's going to be fine."

Eric frowned hard. "I'm not following all of this. If the boy
is one of the Chosen, then where was his protector when he was
in all of this trouble?"

Roland sent Eric a meaningful glance. "I wondered the same,
until I realized the truth. The boy is fortunate to have a guardian
such as Tamara, Eric."

"What are you saying?"

Tamara seemed unaware of the currents running between the
two. She reached for Roland's hand and gripped it. "Thank you,
Roland. Jamey means so much to me. You'll make sure they
leave right away, won't you? Before anyone sees a connection
between Jamey and Curtis, and starts poking around."

"You have my word, young one. And now, I'd best take my
leave before my best friend becomes my executioner." He sent
Eric a wink. "Do not think to oppose the fates, Eric. These cards
were drawn long ago, I think." He left them without another
word.

Tamara stood abruptly, and paced restlessly toward the fire.
"We'll have to leave right away, as well, Eric. When Curt's
body is found I'll be a suspect because I lived there and didn't
report it. You'll be one, too, because of the break-in. We should
go away from here." She stopped in front of the glowing hearth,
and turned to face him. The fire made a halo of light around her,
so she seemed ethereal, truly a vision. "But first there is something else, and I think you know it as well as I do."

Eric rose, went to her and gazed down into her face. She was more beautiful, more precious to him than the most flawless diamond could be. God, but he loved her beyond reason. More than anything, he wanted to keep her with him, always. He swallowed. "It is an endless, lonely existence, Tamara. An existence of endless night. A world without the sun."

"How could it be lonely if we were together?" She gripped his lapels in her fists. "If it's a choice between you and the sun, Eric, I choose you without a moment's hesitation. Don't you feel the same about me?"

His throat tried to close off. He forced words. "You know I do. But, Tamara, immortality is not a gift. It is a curse. You will live to see all those you love return to the dust—"

"Everyone I've ever loved is gone, except for two. You and Jamey. And as much as I adore him, he's not a part of my life. He has his mother, his own life to live." She blinked as her eyes began to moisten. "Please, if you deny me, I'll truly be alone. What must be done, Eric?"

Her tears caused his own eyes to burn. "You need time to consider."

"What have I had for the past twenty years if not time?" A waver crept into her voice. "I've been wandering aimlessly in a world where I never belonged. I was never meant to be there, Eric, I was meant to be with you. To be *like you.* Roland knows it. You heard what he said, the decision isn't ours to make. My fate—" she lifted a trembling hand to the side of his face, tears streaming now down her own "—is right here in front of me."

The glow of the firelight made the satin gown seem like a soft green blaze. Her hair glistened, and even her skin seemed aglow. Her scent caressed him as truly as her hand did. She cleared her throat, and he knew she was forcing herself to go on. "I know...you have to drink from me," she whispered. "But that's only part of it, is that right? That you have to drink from me, Eric?"

He could not prevent his eyes from fixing themselves on her exposed throat, or his tongue from darting over his lips.

"And...and you from me," he answered. Just saying the words had the blood lust coursing through him, singing in his veins, gaining intensity until it throbbed both in his temples and in his loins.

She stood on tiptoes, encircled his neck with her arms and offered up her parted lips. He obliged her, and his desire for her became all consuming, just as his love for her had long since become. Her nimble fingers worked loose his shirt buttons and her hands spread themselves wide upon his chest, then slipped around it, so her lips could pay him homage.

"All my life," she whispered, her lips moving against his skin, her breath hot and moist upon it. "All my life has been spent for this moment...for you. Don't deny me, Eric. I'm already more of you than I am of this world."

"Tamara," he moaned. She tilted her head up and he captured her lips again, feeding from the sweetness of her mouth. He gathered her skirts in his fists and lifted them, his hands then running eagerly over her naked thighs and buttocks. "My God, how I want you. You are a fire in my heart, and each time the flame burns hotter, not cooler. I fear it will never cool. You are an unquenchable thirst in my soul."

Her hand slid between them to the fastenings of his trousers. In seconds she'd freed him, and she caressed his shaft with worshiping hands. "I'd like to have eternity to quench that unquenchable thirst, Eric. Say you'll give it to me."

The heat she stirred in him raged to an inferno. His hands slipped down the backs of her legs to the hollows behind her knees and he lifted her off her feet. She linked her ankles at his back, clung to his shoulders and closed her eyes as he sheathed himself inside her. So deeply he plunged that a small cry was forced from her wet lips, and even then he knew it would not be enough. Not this time.

She rode him, not flinching from his most powerful thrusts, and he held her to him, his hands tight on her soft derriere. She threw her head backward, arching the pale, satin skin of her throat toward him, a hairsbreadth from his lips. He kissed her there, unable to do otherwise. Her jugular thudded just beneath the skin. Her fingers tangled in his hair, pulling him nearer. His tongue flicked out, tasting the salt of her skin, and as he drew that skin between his teeth she moaned very softly. When he closed his teeth on her skin she shuddered, and her hands pressed harder.

"Make me your own, Eric. Make me yours forever, please."

He groaned his surrender, opening his mouth wider, taking more of her throat into his hungry mouth. The anticipation brought a new flood of desire and he tried to plunge more deeply, though he was already inside her as far as he could go. He withdrew and sank himself into her, again and again. His fever seemed mirrored in her, because her responses were just as ardent. Her legs tightening around him, she pressed down to meet his every upward thrust, arching toward him to take him further.

She arched in unspeakable ecstasy. His thrusts inside her matched the pulse of her heart pumping the very essence of herself into his body. The feel of him suckling at her throat sent tingles racing through her.

She felt herself begin to fade, to weaken. She was vanishing like mist under a searing sun, until she no longer existed apart from this feeling...this ecstasy.

Only vaguely did she notice when he raised a hand to his own throat, and then, while his mouth was still clamped to her, he pushed her face to his neck. Vibrations seemed to reach the core of her soul. A hunger such as she'd never known enveloped her and she closed her mouth over his neck and she drank.

They were locked together; he moved deep within her, while his teeth and lips demanded all she could give. His hands held her hips to his groin and her head to his throat. His movements became more powerful, and she knew hers did, as well. The approaching climax was like a steaming locomotive, about to hit them both. She moaned, then screamed against his throat again and again as she felt herself turn into the brew in a bubbling cauldron, and slowly boil over. Eric shook violently, groaning and sinking to his knees, still holding her to him.

They remained as they were as the waves of sensation slowly receded, leaving them warm and complete. She knew they'd exchanged ounce for ounce, drop for drop. They were sated...and they were one.

Carefully Eric unfolded his legs and lay back, keeping her on top of him, cradling her like something precious. She relaxed there, only moving enough so her feet were not behind him when he lay down. The strangest sensations were zipping through her. Her skin tingled as if tiny electrical charges were jolting from nerve ending to nerve ending. Her head reeled with sensory perceptions. Everything seemed suddenly more acute. The firelight, brighter and more beautiful than ever before. She'd never realized how many different colors there actually were in a flame, or how she could smell the essence of the wood as it burned.

"Eric, I feel so strange...like I'm more alive than I've ever been and yet...so sleepy." Her eyes widened. Even her own voice sounded different.

He laughed softly, stroking her hair. She swore she could feel every line of his palm as it moved over her tresses. "Thank you for convincing me, my love. I couldn't have gone on without you, you know."

"Is it done?" She struggled to stay awake.

"It is nearly done. You must sleep. I've waited two centuries to find you, Tamara. Only you, I know that now. I can wait now, through one more night, one more day. When you wake again, it will be done."

She burrowed her head into his chest. "Tell me...."

"You'll be stronger than ten humans." His hands stroked her hair, her back, and his hypnotic voice carried her like a magic carpet. "You'll get stronger as you grow older, but that will be the only sign of aging you'll see. Your senses will be altered, heightened, more so than they already are. And there are psychic abilities, too. I will teach you to control them, to use them. I'll teach you so many things, my Tamara. You will live forever.''

''With you,'' she muttered, barely able to move her lips now.

''With me. Always with me, love.''

* * * * *

TWILIGHT
MEMORIES

For Melissa and Leslie,
who recognized Rhiannon's potential
even before I did

INTRODUCTION

It's because I'm not good enough. Or, so he thinks. It isn't that he doesn't desire me, because we both know he does. And why wouldn't he? Mortal men fall at my feet like simpering fools begging for a crumb of attention. Immortals, as well, those few I've known. Why then, does the only man I desire reject me? Why does he feign indifference when I can see the lust in his eyes? Why has he asked me to remain away from him, to cease distracting him with my periodic visits? It isn't as if I bother him so often. Once every fifty years or so, when my fantasies of him no longer suffice—when my longing for him becomes too strong to resist.

My visits, though, do little to ease my discomfort. He only reaffirms his decision, each time, and pleads with me to stay away. He'd send me away himself, were he able. He'd banish me from his very sight, were it in his power to do so.

Just as my father did.

I know, I am not what most males expect a female to be. I am outspoken. I am strong. I fear very little in this world, nor would I, I suspect, in any other. But it is not my oddness that makes me so unloved by the males. Or should I say, unlovable? It can't be that, for my father rejected me before I'd had opportunity to display any of my strange tendencies. He rejected me simply for being his firstborn.

A great Pharaoh of Egypt, a god-king of the Nile, he fully expected the gods to bless him with a son as firstborn. When he was given me, instead, he saw me as some sort of punishment for whatever sins he imagined himself guilty of. I was allowed to remain with my mother only until I saw my fifth year. It would have been more merciful to have tossed me at birth from the gilded halls of his palace, and left me as bait for the jackals.

Yet he did not. At five, I was banished, sent to live among the priestesses of Isis at the temple. My brothers, when they came later, were treated as I should have been. They were welcomed as princes. Their arrivals were celebrated for months on end. Yet I, the one truly destined for immortality, was ignored.

I vowed then never again to care for the affections of any male, but I find I do now. Not that my emotions are involved. I am far too wise to fall prey to silly romanticism. I am not a simpleminded, gullible mortal, after all. No, it is not romance I want. It is only him. My desire for him is a palpable thing, as I know his for me to be, as well. It angers me that he denies it, that he sees me as unworthy.

This time, though, I will manage it. I will prove to him that I am the bravest, the strongest, the most cunning individual he's ever known.

I've come upon some information, you see. A while back, Roland had some serious trouble, along with two other immortals, back in the States. The details are not important. The gist is that the most precious being to Roland, right now, is a boy by the name of Jamison Bryant. He is one of The Chosen—that is, one of those rare humans who share the same ancestry and blood antigen as we immortals. One who can be transformed. He shares a special link with Roland, a closeness of which, I freely admit, I am envious. And the boy is in grave danger. So might Roland be. I am on my way not only to warn them, but to protect them both, in any way necessary.

Please, do not misinterpret my motive. I do not rush to his side because of any overblown emotional attachments. I've already made clear that my feelings for Roland are only physical in nature. It hurts enough to be rejected on that basis. Think how stupid one would have to be to open oneself up to more pain! No, I do this only to prove my worth. He will see, once and for all, that Rhiannon is not a bit of dust to be swept away at a whim. Not a mere limpid female, to be ignored as so much chattel. I am worthy of his affection, just as I was my father's. They are the ones who are wrong, to cast me aside.

They are the ones who are wrong.

Although...

There are times, when even I begin to doubt it. There are times when I hear my father's voice, echoing in those vaulted corridors, his condemnation of me. And I wonder. Could he have been right? Am I, truly, his curse? Nothing more than a pawn of the gods, to be used to mete out punishment to a sinful king? How could my father have been wrong, after all? He was pharaoh! Only a step below a god himself. Might he have been right?

Just as Roland might now be right in avoiding my touch? Perhaps he sees something that I have not. Perhaps he knows how unworthy I—

No!

I am Rhiannon—born Rhianikki, princess of Egypt, firstborn of Pharaoh. I am immortal, a goddess among humans, envied by women and worshipped by men. I could kill them all as easily as I could wish them good-night.

I could!

I *am* worthy...and I intend to prove it.

I am Rhiannon. And this is my story.

CHAPTER ONE

He moved as one of the shadows beneath the overhung roofs, along the twisting, narrow streets. He detested the fact that he was here, walking among *them*. Some passed so near he could have touched them, simply by raising a hand. He felt the heat of their bodies, saw the steam of their warm breaths in the chill night air. He felt the blood pulsing beneath their skin, and heard the rapid, healthy patter of their hearts. He felt like a wolf slinking silently among timid rabbits. With his preternatural strength he could kill any of them without taxing himself. It frightened him to know he was capable of doing just that, if pushed.

For an instant, murky images of the distant past clouded his vision. Air heavy with dust and the scents of sweat and blood. Fallen men, like autumn leaves upon the damp, brown earth. Hooves thundering as the riderless horses fled in a hundred directions. One man, a boy, in truth, remained breathing. The lowly squire in ill-fitting armor sat high upon a magnificent, sooty destrier. The horse pawed the ground with a forefoot and blew, eager for more. Only silence came in answer. The silence of death, for it surrounded them.

The young Roland saw the blood-coated broadsword, the crimson tears, dripping slowly from its tip. As the red haze of fury began to fade, he let the weapon fall from his grasp. Stomach lurching, he tugged the steel helmet from his head, then the mail coif, and tossed both to the ground. Aghast, he stared at the carnage, too sickened just then to be thankful their faces were hidden by helmets, their wounds covered by their armor.

The boy felt no elation at what he'd done. No, not even later, when he was personally knighted by King Louis VII, for heroism and valor. He felt nothing but a grim and disgusting new self-knowledge.

For he had enjoyed the killing.

Roland shook himself. Now was no time for remembrances, or regrets. He reminded himself that despite his likening of them to rabbits, some humans were capable of ultimate deceit and treachery. Past experience had taught him that. And if the report he'd just had from the States were true, one of those humans, more treacherous than any, might even be a few yards from him. It was that possibility that had drawn Roland into the village tonight, in spite of his self-imposed solitude.

His plan was simple. He would slip unnoticed through the medieval-style streets of L'Ombre, and into the inn called Le Requin. He would listen, and he would watch. He'd scan their thinly veiled minds and he'd find the interloper, if, indeed, there was one to be found. And then he'd deal with it.

The night wind stiffened, bringing with it the scents of late-blooming roses, and dying ones, of freshly clipped grass and of the liquor and smoke just beyond the door he now approached. He paused as the door swung wide, and the odor sharpened. A cluster of inebriated tourists stumbled out and passed him. Roland drew back, averting his face, but it was an unnecessary precaution. They paid him no mind.

Roland squared his shoulders. He did not fear humans, nor did many of his kind. More that he feared *for* them, should he be forced into an unwanted encounter. Besides that, it made good sense to avoid contact. Should humans ever learn that the existence of vampires was more than just the stuff of legends and folklore, the damage done would be irreversible. There would be no peace. It was best to remain apart, to remain forever a myth to those endlessly prying mortals.

As the door swung once more, Roland caught it and slipped quickly through. He stepped to one side and took a moment to survey his surroundings. Low, round tables were scattered without order. People clustered around them, sitting, or standing, leaning over and speaking of nothing in particular. The smoke-laden air hung at face level, stinging his eyes and causing his nostrils to burn. The voices were a drone, punctuated often by the splashing of liquor and the clinking sounds of ice against glass.

Her laughter rose then, above all else. Low, husky and completely without reserve, it rode the smoky air to surround him, and caress his eardrums. His gaze shot toward the source of the sound, but he saw only a huddle of men vying for position near the bar. He could only guess *she* must be at the center of that huddle.

To push his way through the throng of admirers was out of the question. Roland had no desire to draw undue attention. No, nor indeed, any desire to renew his timeless acquaintance with her. To resume the slow torture. He ignored the surge of anger he felt at the idea that any of the humans might be close enough to touch her. He would not wish to witness the clumsy gropings of some drunken mortal. He didn't really believe he might break the fool's neck for such an offense, but there was no need pressing his temper to its limits.

He could learn as much by listening, and he did so now, attuning his mind as well as his hearing, and wondering what she was calling herself these days. For although he sought confirmation, he had no doubt about the identity of that seductive laugh's owner. No doubt at all.

"Do another one, Rhiannon!"

"*Oui, cherié*. 'Ow about zome rock and roll?"

A chorus of pleas followed, as the willowy, dark form extricated herself from the mass. She shook her head, not quite smiling in that way she had. She moved with such grace that she seemed to float over the hardwood rather than walk on it. The slightly flared hemline of black velvet swaying a fraction of an inch above the floor added to the illusion. Roland had no clue how she managed to move her legs at all, given the way the full-length skirt clung to them from midshin on up. She might as well have paraded naked before her gaping admirers for what the garment hid. The velvet seemed to have melded itself to her form, curving as her hips did, nipping inward at the waist, cupping her small, high breasts like possessive hands. Her long, slender arms were bare, save the bangles and bracelets adorning them. Her fingers were beringed, and tipped in lengthy, dagger-sharp nails of blood red.

Roland's gaze continued upward as she moved across the room, apparently unaware of his presence. The neckline of the ridiculous dress consisted only of two strips of velvet forming a halter around her throat. Between the swatches, the pale expanse of her skin glowed with ethereal smoothness. His sharp eyes missed nothing, from the gentle swell of her breasts, to the delicate outline of her collarbone at the base of her throat. Around her neck she wore an onyx pendant in the shape of a cradle moon. It rested flat on the surface of her chest, its lowest point just touching the uppermost curve of her breasts.

That swan's neck, creamy in color, satiny in texture, gracefully long and narrow, was partially covered by her hair. It hung as straight and perfectly jet as the velvet dress, yet glossy, more satin than velvet, in truth. She'd pulled it all to one side, and it hung down covering the right side of her neck, and most of the dress. It's shining length only ended at midthigh.

On her left ear she'd hung a cluster of diamonds and onyx that dangled so long they touched her shoulder. He couldn't tell whether the earring had a mate on her right ear, due to her abundance of hair.

She paused, and bent over the man on the piano bench, whispering in his ear, her narrow hand resting on his shoulder. Roland felt himself stiffen as the beast buried deep within him stirred for the first time in decades. He willed it away. The man nodded, and struck a chord. She turned, facing the crowd, one forearm resting upon the top of the piano. With the first rich, flawless note she sung, the entire room went silent. Her voice, so deep and smooth that were it given form it could only become honey, filled the room, coating everything and everyone within.

Her expression gave the lyrics more meaning than they'd ever before had.

She sang as if her heart were breaking with each note, yet her voice never wavered or weakened in intensity.

She held the mortals in the palm of her hand, and she was loving every minute of it, Roland thought in silence. He ought to turn and leave her to make a spectacle of herself in this insane manner. But as she sung on, of heartache and unbearable loneliness, she looked toward him. She caught his gaze and she refused to let go. In spite of himself, Roland heard the pure beauty of her voice. And though he'd had no intention of doing so, he let his eyes take in every aspect of her face.

A perfect oval, with bone structure as exquisite and flawless as if she were a sculpture done by a master. Small, almost pointed chin and angling, defined jawline. The slight hollows beneath her cheeks and the high, wide-set cheekbones. Her eyes were almond-shaped and slanted slightly upward at the outer corners. The kohl that lined them only accentuated that exotic slant, and her lashes were as impenetrably dark as the irises they surrounded.

Against his will he focused on her full, always pouting lips as they formed each word of the song. Their color was deep, dark red, like that of wine. How many years had he hungered for those lips?

He shook himself. The fruit of those lips was one he must never sample. His gaze moved upward to her eyes again. Still, they focused solely upon him, as if the words she sung were meant for his ears alone. Gradually he realized the patrons were growing curious. Heads turned toward him to see who had caught the attention of the elusive Rhiannon. He'd fallen under her spell as surely as any of these simpering humans had, and as a result, he'd been unaware of the growing risk of discovery. Let her behave recklessly, if it pleased her to do so. He wouldn't risk his existence to warn her. More likely than not, his remaining here would result in trouble. Her nearness never failed to stir the beast to life, to bring out his baser instincts. That she did so deliberately was without doubt. Though if she knew the whole of it, she might change her mind.

He gripped the door, his eyes still on her, and jerked it open. He made himself step out into the bracing chill of the autumn night even as she held the hauntingly low, final note, drawing it out so long it ought to be obvious she was no ordinary woman. Yet, a second later, Roland heard no one questioning her. He only heard thunderous applause.

Rhiannon felt the sting of the slap she'd just been issued. Her anger rose quickly, but not quite quickly enough to prevent her feeling the hurt that came along with it. So Roland could look her over so thoroughly and simply walk away, could he? He could ignore the dress she'd chosen simply to entice him. He could pretend not to hear the emotion with which she'd sung or even to notice the song she'd chosen. Well, she supposed she'd need more drastic measures to get his attention.

She stepped away from the piano, quickly muttering that she had a headache and needed to slip away without her male attendants surrounding her. The piano player, Franςis, tilted his head toward a door in the back, and Rhiannon made her way toward it. She paused only long enough to grip the upper arm of the drunkest male in the room. She pulled him, stumbling in her wake, out the door.

She could only just make out the dark shape of Roland's retreating figure, farther along the narrow street. She didn't call out to him. She wouldn't beg him for something so simple as a hello, after decades of separation. She had a better idea.

She pulled the drunken man with her a few yards farther, then turned him, her hands supporting his weight mostly by clenching his shirt front. She shoved his back against a building.

For a moment, she studied him. He wasn't bad-looking, really. Red hair, and freckles, but a rather nice face, except for the crooked, inebriated grin.

She hooked a finger beneath his chin, and stared into his green, liquor-clouded eyes for a long moment. She focused her mental energies on calming him, and gaining his utter cooperation. By the time she lowered her head to his throat, the man would have gladly given her everything he owned, had she asked it. She sensed no evil in him. In fact, he seemed a perfectly nice fellow, except for his heavy drinking. She supposed everyone was entitled to one vice, though. She was about to indulge in hers.

She parted her lips and settled her mouth over the place where his jugular pulsed beneath the skin. She wished the man no harm. She only needed to get a rise out of Roland. Her willing victim moaned softly, and let his head fall to the side. She nearly choked on her laughter. She was glad one of them was getting some pleasure out of this. The act had lost its luster for her long ago.

"Dammit Rhianikki, let him go!"

Roland's hand closed on her shoulder, and he jerked her roughly away from the drunk's throat. The man sank to the ground, barely conscious, but from her entrancement of him, not from blood loss. "You could have killed him," Roland whispered harshly.

Rhiannon allowed the corners of her lips to pull ever so slightly upward. "Always so eager to think the worst of me, aren't you, darling? And it's Rhiannon, now. Rhianikki is too—" she waved a hand "—Egyptian." She gave the man on the ground a cursory glance. "It's all right, Paul. You may go now." With her mind, she released him, and he rose unsteadily. His puzzled expression moved from Rhiannon, to Roland, and back again.

"What happened?"

"You've had a little too much Chablis, *mon cher*. Go on, now. Be on your way."

Still frowning, he stumbled back into the tavern, and Rhiannon turned to Roland. "You see?"

"Why are you here?"

She lifted her hands, palms up. "Not even a hello? A how are you? A glad to see you're still drawing a breath? Nothing? How rude you've become, Roland."

"Why are you here?" His voice remained impassive as he repeated the question.

She shrugged. "Well, if you must know, I heard about a certain DPI agent, rather nasty one, too, who'd traced you here. They say he's already in the village. I was worried about you, Roland. I came to warn you."

He looked at the ground and slowly shook his head. "So, knowing an agent of the Division of Paranormal Investigations is in the village, you naturally flaunt your own presence here to the utmost possible degree."

"What better way to flush him out? You know how keen they are on vampire research."

"You might've been killed, Rhiannon."

"Then you'd have been rid of me at last."

He was silent for a moment, scanning her face. "I would find no joy in that, reckless one."

From beneath her lashes, she looked up at him. "You do have an odd way of showing it."

He placed a hand on her shoulder. She slipped one around his waist, and they moved together along the winding road, toward his castle. "You need to take more care," he went on, his tone fatherly…and utterly maddening. "You've no idea what DPI is capable of. They've developed a tranquilizer that renders us helpless."

"I know. And I know about your scrape with them in Connecticut, when they nearly took Eric and his fledgling, Tamara."

Roland's brows shot upward. "And how do you know all of that?"

"I keep track of you, darling." She smiled. "And for years I kept track of that scientist, St. Claire. He held me for a time in that laboratory of his, you know."

He sucked in a sharp breath, gripped her shoulders and turned her to face him. She could have laughed aloud. At last, some emotion!

"My God, I had no idea. When...how..." He broke off and shook his head. "Did he hurt you?"

Warmth surged within her. "Terribly," she confessed with a small pout. "But only for a short time. I had to break his partner's neck, I'm afraid, when I made my escape."

Roland shook his head, and closed his eyes. "You could have summoned me. I would've come—"

"Oh, posh, Roland. By the time you could have arrived, I was free again. No human can hope to get the best of Rhianikki, princess of the Nile, daughter of Pharaoh, immortal vampiress of time immemorial—"

His laughter burst from him involuntarily, she knew, and she drank in the beauty of his smile, wishing she could elicit its appearance more often. There was a darkness in Roland's eyes at times. Some secret that troubled him, one he'd never shared.

When his laughter died, he turned and began walking once more. "Tell me how you know about the DPI agent in L'Ombre?"

"Since St. Claire came so close to having me, I've kept a close watch on the organization. I have spies inside. They keep me informed."

He nodded. "Then you are a bit more sensible than I gave you credit for being. You know, of course, St. Claire is dead."

She nodded. "But his protégé, Curtis Rogers, is not."

Roland stopped walking again. "That can't be. Tamara shot him when he was trying his damnedest to kill Eric."

"Yes, shot him. And left him for dead, only he wasn't. He was found a short time later, and he survived. It is he who has come to France looking for you, Roland. He wants vengeance."

"On me?"

"You, Eric, Tamara...and the boy, I'm afraid."

She saw the pale coloring drain from Roland's face. She'd

known already of his attachment to the child he'd rescued two years ago. The boy was one of The Chosen, a human with an unseen bond to immortals. DPI knew it, and attempted to use him as bait in their trap. No doubt, they would not hesitate to do so again. Rhiannon knew all of this, but seeing firsthand his obvious reaction to a whisper of a threat to the lad, brought home to her the intensity of his caring. She felt the rush of turmoil that coursed through him, and she placed a calming hand on his arm.

"Jamey," he whispered. "The bastard had him once. Nearly killed him."

"And so you know why I've come."

His brows rose inquiringly, and she rushed on. "To offer my help in protecting the boy."

"Noble of you, but unnecessary. I can protect Jamey. I won't have you putting yourself in harm's way for my sake. It would be far better if you left France at once."

"For your peace of mind, you mean?"

She searched his face and she knew when his gaze fell before hers that she'd hit on the truth. "Then you are not so indifferent to me as you pretend?"

"When have I ever been indifferent to you, oh goddess among women?"

She almost smiled. "Well, your peace of mind is of no concern to me. In fact, I find a certain pleasure in keeping you off balance. And I am staying, whether you like it or not. If you won't let me help you watch over the boy, I'll simply seek out this Rogers character, and drain him dry. That should solve the problem."

"Rhianik—Rhiannon, surely you are aware that the murder of a DPI agent would only serve to instigate further trouble." He drew an unsteady breath. "Killing rarely solves anything."

She shrugged, keeping him always in her sight with sidelong, lash-veiled glances. How she delighted in baiting him! "They'll never learn what became of him. I'll grind him up and feed him to my cat.''

Roland grimaced and shook his head.

"Perhaps I'll torture him first. What do you think? Bamboo shoots under the nails? Usually effective. We could learn all DPI's secrets, and—"

"For God's sake, woman!" He gripped her shoulders hard as he shouted, but his horrified expression faded when she burst into helpless laughter.

He sighed, shook his head and eased his grip on her shoulders. Before he took his hands away, though, she caught his forearms. "No, Roland, don't."

He stood motionless, his face devoid of expression, as she slipped her arms around his waist, and drew herself to him. She rested her head upon his sturdy shoulder. With a sigh of reluctant compliance, Roland's arms tightened around her shoulders and he held her to him.

Rhiannon closed her eyes and simply allowed herself to feel him. The contained strength in him, the rapid thud of his heart, the way his breaths stirred her hair.

"I have missed you, Roland," she whispered. She turned her face slightly, and feathered his neck with her lips. "And you have missed me, though you are loath to admit it."

She felt the shudder she drew from him. He nodded. "I admit it, I've missed you."

"And you desire me," she went on, lifting her head enough so she could study his eyes as she spoke. "As you have no other…nor ever will. You disapprove of everything I am, and everything I do, but you want me, Roland. I feel it even now, in this simple embrace."

"Subtlety has never been your strong suit, Rhiannon." He took her arms from around him, and stepped away, resuming the walk without touching her.

"You deny it?"

He smiled slowly. "I want to walk in the sunshine, Rhiannon, yet to do so would mean my end. What one wants is not necessarily what one should have.''

She frowned and tilted her head. ''I hate when you speak in metaphors or parables or whatever you call those silly words you use.''

He shook his head. ''How long will you alight here this time, little bird?''

''Changing the subject won't make you feel better, you know.''

''It was a simple question. If you cannot answer it—''

''Answer mine, and I'll answer yours. Do you want me?''

He scowled. ''She is a fool who asks a question when she already knows the answer.''

''I want to hear you say it.'' She stopped, and looked into his eyes. ''Say you want me.''

Roland's glance moved slowly down her body and she felt his gaze burn wherever it touched her. Finally, he nodded. ''I want you, Rhiannon. But I will not—''

She held up her hands. ''No more. Don't ruin it.''

He chewed his inner cheek, and she felt his anger begin to boil up. ''Now my question, temptress. How long will you stay?''

''Well, I've come to help protect the boy. I suppose I will stay until the threat is gone, and...''

''And?'' His brows drew close and he scanned her face.

She tried not to smile as she answered him. ''And until I've given you exactly what you want, Roland.''

CHAPTER TWO

Roland felt as if he were the Bastille, and she the revolutionaries. For a single instant, he was certain he'd never stand a chance. He attempted to remind himself of all of her faults. She was impulsive, impetuous, and as unpredictable as the weather. She acted without first thinking through the consequences of her actions. And sooner or later it was going to cost her. Hell, it already had cost her, and dearly. He sensed she was glossing over the details of her time in St. Claire's hands. Yet he knew better than to press her for more. He'd have killed the bastard years ago, had he known. He'd kill him now, if the scientist were alive.

Studying her faults did little good. Already, the beast inside was wakening. Already, her presence had him thinking in terms of murder and retribution, had him fighting to control the violent side to his nature. He studied her and shook his head slowly. She was so much the way he'd been once, in his mortal lifetime. All the things he'd fought for years to suppress.

Perhaps he'd not succeed in dampening his desire for her by counting her faults. Perhaps instead, he ought to count his own. Even better, he should remind himself what had become of the other woman he'd lusted after.

"You're guarding your thoughts, Roland. Are they so unflattering?"

"I guard my thoughts out of habit. Do not take it personally."

"I think you lie. You don't wish me to see something."

He shrugged noncommittally. If she was determined to stay and taunt him, he'd resist her as best he could. For her sake, as well as his own. He would keep his distance. Never would the beast he held within be unleashed upon her. She'd done nothing to deserve that.

And perhaps while she was here, he'd teach her to act maturely and sensibly. He'd show her the differences between a true lady, and the untamed child she was now. Like changing a cactus flower to a rose, he thought. He refused to acknowledge that the results would benefit him, as well. For he could never be as inflamed with longing for the rose, as he'd always been for the prickly flower.

No, he told himself the lesson would be for her, to get her to exercise some caution from time to time. He liked Rhiannon, sometimes in spite of himself. He'd truly hate to see her come to grief because of her nature...the way he once had.

He frowned, and wondered briefly how long her visit would be. She hadn't told him. Her habit was to flit in and out of his life at will. She never remained long enough to do more than stir up a whirlwind, to pummel his senses—as well as his sense—with her vivacious nature, and then she would vanish. She was a desert sandstorm...a whirlpool from the Nile.

"Roland, darling, you are ignoring me."

He had been doing anything but that, though he would never admit it. Instead, he glanced down from the corners of his eyes, and gave her a sharp nod. "Precisely."

She sighed in exasperation. "I suppose if you refuse to discuss our relationship—"

"We have no relationship, Rhiannon."

"We'll simply have to discuss the boy." She kept on speaking as if she'd never been interrupted. It was another of her maddening habits. When speaking to Rhiannon, you either say what she wants to hear, or you are ignored. Maddening!

"What about the boy?"

"Where is he, Roland? Is he safe?"

He felt his spine relax a bit, now that they were on a neutral subject. "At first, he and his mother lived in the castle."

"That ruin?"

Roland stiffened. "The east wing, Rhiannon. It's perfectly habitable."

"For a monk, perhaps. Do go on."

He scowled, but kept on speaking. He had no desire to engage in verbal skirmishes. "Then Kathryn took ill."

"No wonder, in that drafty place."

Roland ignored the taunt this time. "It was cancer, Rhiannon. She died eight months ago."

Rhiannon's hand flew to her throat and she drew a quick, little breath. "Then, the boy is alone?"

"Not entirely. He has me, and there is Frederick, of course."

"Frederick?" She tilted her head slightly. "That bear of a man you found sleeping on the streets in New York? Roland, can he be trusted with the boy?"

Roland nodded without reservation. Frederick was slightly slow-witted, but he had a heart of pure gold. And he adored Jamey. "Yes. If I didn't trust him, he wouldn't be in my household. Jamey needs someone with him in those hours between school dismissal and sunset."

Still walking beside him, she stroked her long fingers across her forehead as would a Gypsy fortune-teller preparing to do a reading. "Mmm, you enrolled him in a private school, no doubt."

"He refused a private school. Said he was not a snob and had no intention of becoming one." Roland shook his head. "He does have a strong will. At any rate, he's known as James O'Brien. It's the closest I could come to Jamey Bryant."

"And where is this boy of yours, now? Tucked safely into his bed at your château?"

"He had a soccer match tonight. Ought to be arriving any time now." He glanced ahead of them, to the tall, gray stone wall that surrounded Castle Courtemanche, and the portcullis at its center.

"You provided Frederick with a car, as well? Can he maneuver one?"

He frowned, and turned to follow the direction of her gaze.

"Damn it to hell." He gripped Rhiannon's arm and drew her nearer the cover of the brush along the narrow road's edge.

"Whatever are you doing?"

"Hush, Rhiannon." Roland moved slowly, silently, approaching the gate, and gazing toward the Cadillac that sat just outside it. "That car should not be here."

"It isn't…" She bit her lip, and her eyes narrowed as she stared hard at the dark colored vehicle. "There's a man behind the wheel."

Roland nodded. Already his mind scanned the intruder's but he found it closed to him. Most humans were so easily read it was child's play to scan their thoughts. This one had deliberately closed his mind off. Roland was certain of it. In the darkness, even with his preternatural vision, Roland couldn't see clearly enough to make a positive identification. The hard knot in his stomach was the only indication Curtis Rogers occupied the car, and that he was watching, waiting…for Jamey.

Rhiannon whispered. "But I get no sense of the boy." She shook her head in frustration. "Is that Rogers?"

"I don't know, but if it is, and it's truly vengeance he wants, then Jamison is in danger."

Rhiannon sucked in a breath. "You believe this Rogers would kill the boy simply to hurt you?"

Roland shook his head. "More likely kidnap him, and wait for me to come to his rescue. But while he had the boy, Rogers wouldn't hesitate to perform tests on him, experiments to discover more about the link between The Chosen, and the undead."

"I know about DPI and their love of…experiments."

Roland slanted a glance toward Rhiannon, sickened anew by the knowledge of what had befallen her while in DPI's hands. Truly, he felt an urge to protect her from them, just as he was forced to protect Jamison. Foolish notion, he knew. Rhiannon would never stand for being protected, not by anyone. Moreover, were she with him constantly, stirring his mind to such turmoil, she would need protecting not by him, but *from* him.

"Where is the boy? It's late."

Roland shook his head, freeing his mind of its distractions, focusing again on the matter at hand. "When they win, they usually stop for a meal on the way back. They are sometimes quite late." Even as he spoke, Roland searched for Jamey with his mind. It came as a blow when he found him, and realized he was ambling along the road from the opposite direction, completely oblivious to the threat that awaited him.

The man in the car saw the boy, too, for the door opened and he stepped out. Jamey drew nearer, and before Roland could decide on a course of action, Rhiannon shot to her feet and ran toward the man.

"Oh, thank goodness, I've finally found someone!"

He turned to face her, wary-eyed and suspicious. Roland had a perfect view now, of the man's face. Curtis Rogers had changed little in the past two years. His blond hair still hung untrimmed and too long in the front. His pale brows and light eyes gave him the look of a weakling, and Roland knew that was precisely what he was. Yet with the resources of DPI and their constantly innovative arsenal of weapons and drugs, he was an enemy not to be taken lightly.

And right now, Rhiannon was standing within his reach.

"Who the hell are you?"

"Just a woman in need of assistance. My car went off the road a few miles back. I've been walking forever, and..." She continued moving forward, affecting a rather convincing little limp as she went. "You simply must offer me a ride."

Get into that car with him, Rhiannon, and I'll remove you bodily! Roland made his thoughts clear to her, and his anger with them. Had the woman no sense? If she got herself killed, he'd...

Posh, Roland, you can be such a stick in the mud.

She smiled up at Curtis as she stepped closer. "You wouldn't dream of leaving me out here on my own, would you? I'd never forgive you if you did.''

Her voice was a virtual purr now, and Roland felt his hackles rise. Rogers's gaze moved slowly, thoroughly down her body, not missing a curve, and lingering too long on the enticing expanse of cleavage her dress exposed.

"I'd like to help you, lady, but I have some business to take care of.''

Roland began to step out of hiding. Enough was enough. If he let it go on much longer—if Rogers laid one finger on her—

No, darling! Her mind reached out to his with silent fingers. *Your Jamey is getting too near. Slip around us and intercept the boy. I'll keep this one distracted.*

If he realizes you're an immortal—Roland began to warn her.

Her low, husky laugh floated to him, and caused Rogers's brows to raise. *Look at him, Roland. He's far too busy noticing I'm a woman.* As if to prove her point, she stepped still nearer the man. Her hand floated upward and she traced the edge of his lapel with her nails. Rogers's attention was riveted. Roland thought he could have danced a jig around the fool and not gained his notice. Jealousy rose like bile into his throat to replace the fear for her that had been there before. He slipped into the trees along the roadside, and quickly emerged again when he'd passed them. Jamey approached him now, only a few yards distant.

"Jamison...it's Roland. Come here at once.''

Without a moment's hesitation, Jamey ducked into the trees where Roland waited. "What's up?''

Roland frowned, noting the soon-to-form bruise under Jamey's left eye, and the slightly swollen lower lip. "What in God's name happened to you?''

Jamey shrugged in the carefree way only a fourteen-year-old can manage. "Soccer's a rough sport.'' He glanced farther along the road and the carefree demeanor left his face. "Who is that?''

He had a maturity that at times went far beyond his years,

and he'd grown as protective of Roland as he had once been of
Tamara. "I hate to upset you, Jamison, but the man in the car
is—"

"Rogers!" Jamey recognized Curtis when the man moved
into a more advantageous stance, and the boy lunged.

Roland caught his shoulders and held him easily. "What do
you think you're doing?"

"That bastard almost killed me! When I get my hands on him,
I—"

"You will watch your language, Jamison, and you will stay
quiet and do as I tell you. You can't instigate a physical alter-
cation with a grown man."

"I'm a lot bigger than I was two years ago," Jamey said, his
voice dangerously low. "And you know he has it coming. I owe
him." His milk-chocolate-colored eyes glowed with absolute
fierceness.

Roland felt a shudder run up his spine. God, but Jamison was
familiar. His rage, his anger—Roland had known all of it, at that
age. It had nearly destroyed him. It had destroyed others. Far
too many others.

"That he does, Jamison. But—"

Jamey's struggles suddenly ceased. "Who is *that?*" His eyes
widened, and Roland followed his gaze to see Rhiannon, playfully tousling Curt Rogers's hair.

Roland felt anger prickle his nape. "A friend of mine. Her
name's Rhiannon and I believe she thinks she's distracting Rogers so you can slip into the castle unnoticed."

Jamey swallowed. "She's gorgeous."

Roland just stared at her for an elongated moment. The moonlight played upon the satin skin of her shoulders like a caress.
"Yes," he said softly. Then he shook himself. "Yes, and apparently Rogers thinks so, too."

Rogers's hand settled on one of Rhiannon's naked shoulders,
and proceeded to stroke a slow path down her arm. Roland felt
the fury leap to life in his veins in a way it seldom had. For just

an instant, his palms itched to clutch the chilled hilt of a broad-sword. Then he reminded himself he no longer needed one.

"Come, Jamey, before she decides to—" He stopped himself before he finished the comment.

Jamey looked up at him, then glanced toward Rhiannon again, a sudden understanding lighting his eyes. He said nothing, only nodded, and followed Roland into the woods and up to the tall stone wall. He put an arm around Roland's shoulders. Roland did likewise, then leapt, easily clearing the wall and landing with a thud on the opposite side. Jamey hit the ground and tumbled forward. He shook his head sheepishly, got to his feet and brushed the dust from his jeans. "One of these days, I'll get the hang of that."

Roland heard Rhiannon's deep laughter filling the night air.

"Is she...like you?" Jamey had never used the word vampire, but Roland thought he knew. The boy was too insightful not to make his own assumptions, and his assumptions were usually right. Roland looked at him, and simply nodded.

"She shouldn't be out there with Curt Rogers," Jamey said.

"You're right about that. Go on inside, and wait for me in the great hall." Roland spoke while gazing toward the portcullis. When Jamey didn't reply or move to obey, Roland sent him a sharp glance.

Jamey shook his head. "No. I'm not a little kid anymore and I'm tired of other people fighting my battles for me."

Roland very nearly barked at him, then closed his eyes and gave his head a shake. For an instant, he could have sworn he was looking at the image of himself, arguing with his father on the day before he'd left home for good. Fourteen. Yes, he'd been just that. And a mere two years later...

He blocked out the memory of that bloody battlefield.

"There is no battle to be fought," he said calmly. "Please, just go inside so I can fetch Rhiannon. God knows what kind of trouble she'll get into on her own."

Jamey kicked at a stray pebble with undue force, and shoved a hand through his hair. "Why can't he just leave us alone?"

"Because he's still breathing." Rhiannon's voice startled Jamey. He jerked his head up in surprise. Roland only turned slowly and watched her approach. He'd heard her land when she'd vaulted the wall.

Apparently someone else had, too. A tall, beefy form lumbered forward from the shadows, placing himself directly between Rhiannon and Jamey. She stopped, her brows lifting.

"It's all right, Frederick. She's a friend."

Rhiannon's imperious gaze clashed with Frederick's untrusting one. Rhiannon took another step forward. "Don't you remember me, Freddy?"

He frowned, and tilted his head to one side. Then he nodded, smiling. "Rhia...Rhian—"

"Rhiannon," she supplied.

Frederick frowned, obviously remembering a slightly different version of her ever-changing name. Roland stepped forward, closing the gap between them, with Jamey at his side. He hoped the relief he felt at seeing her sound and without injury didn't show on his face.

"What have you done with Rogers?"

Rhiannon ignored Roland's question, and let her dark gaze linger on Jamey, who stared at her in turn as if she were made of chocolate.

"Hello, Jamison. I've heard a lot about you." She lifted her hand as she spoke, and Jamey took it at once, then looked down at it as if he wasn't sure what to do.

"Nice to, um, meet you." He let her hand go, after giving it a brief squeeze.

"Rhiannon..."

She met Roland's eyes. "Are you afraid I've killed him? Wouldn't we all be far better off, if I had?"

"I know we would," Jamey said softly.

Roland shook his head. "Killing is never justified, Jamison.

It never makes anything better. It can destroy the killer just as surely as it does the victim. More so. At least the victim still has claim to his soul. The killer's is eaten away slowly.''

Rhiannon rolled her eyes, and Jamey came close to smiling at her. She noticed, and bestowed upon him her devastating half smile, before turning back to Roland. ''Well, if you're too kind-hearted to kill the man, what do you suggest? He's obviously discovered Jamey's whereabouts. We can't simply sit here and wait for him to come and take the boy.''

''I'm no boy,'' Jamey said.

''I think Jamison should go to the States for a while, spend some time with Eric and Tamara. It will be safer.'' Roland glanced at the boy to see what he thought of the idea.

Jamey widened his stance and lifted his chin. ''I'm not running away from him.''

Rhiannon's warm gaze bathed Jamey with approval. He felt it, and stood a little taller. Roland was beginning to feel outnumbered. ''What have you done with Rogers?'' he asked again.

Her gaze dropped before his. ''I tired of his sloppy advances. The fool tried to put his tongue into my ear.''

Jamey chuckled hard, shaking his head, so his longish black curls moved with his laughter. Rhiannon smiled at him, while Roland scowled at her.

''Rhiannon, you have not answered the question.''

She shrugged delicately. ''Monsieur Rogers is having a nap. I think he's been overworking himself of late.''

''Rhiannon…'' Roland's voice held a warning, but it seemed she was too busy exchanging secretive glances with Jamey, to take heed.

''Oh, Roland, I merely tapped him on the head. Honestly, he won't even bear a scar.''

''Wonderful!'' Roland threw his hands in the air. ''Now he'll know you're in league with us. He'll hound your steps in search of retribution just as he does mine.'' It infuriated him that she constantly did things to put herself at risk. Then he realized how his concern for her would sound to her ears. If she knew of his true feelings, she would never let up on her attempts at seduction. And he would only hurt her in the end.

"And you've conveniently left him lying at the front gate, blocking our exit," Roland added, to give more severity to his complaints.

Rhiannon caught Jamey's eye and winked.

"All right, little bird, out with it. You haven't left him lying at the front gate, have you?"

"Well of course I haven't. I'm not an idiot." She placed a hand on Jamey's shoulder. "Come now, and pack yourself a bag or two. That lovely Cadillac is just sitting out there, all warmed up and ready to go."

"Go where?"

"My place. I have a little house just beyond the village. Rogers won't bother you there."

"No, Rhiannon. Jamey will be far safer here, with Frederick and I to watch over him."

She studied him for a long moment, and seemed deep in thought. "All right, then. I'll be back soon."

"Rhiannon, where are you—" Before Roland could finish the question, she was gone. He heard the sound of Curtis Rogers's car roaring to life a second later. Then it squealed away into the night.

CHAPTER THREE

She took the fine car. Not that she couldn't move much faster on her own. She drove for a long time, speeding past the tiny village of L'Ombre and over its twisting roads, taking sharp curves at excessive rates of speed, and laughing as she did so until gradually, the pavements broadened and traffic increased.

When she finally came to a grinding halt at the airport at Paris, she removed the keys and walked to the rear to open the trunk.

Rogers moaned, holding his head in two hands as he sat up. His narrow, angry eyes raked her but he didn't attempt to move.

"You carry a syringe in your breast pocket," she said softly. "Take it out."

He straightened, one hand slipping beneath his jacket toward the pocket. She watched him, and when that hand tensed, hers shot forward entraping it at the wrist before he'd had the chance to move it. He probably hadn't even seen her movement.

"Now, I'll stand for none of that. Roland tells me this drug of yours actually works." She pulled his hand from beneath the jacket, his resistance so puny in comparison to her strength that it was almost laughable. When the syringe was in the open, she took it with her free hand. "Perfectly awful, this little needle. Still, I suppose it's better than St. Claire's former methods. Draining our blood until we become too weak to fight him, leaving him free to perform his sadistic little experiments."

Curtis looked up suddenly, still rubbing the wrist she'd just released. "You're the one, aren't you?"

"Which one would that be, darling? Certainly not one of the two fledglings he held. The ones from whom he drained a bit too much blood? The ones he murdered? No, I'm not one of those. Not at all, as you can see."

"You're…Rhiannon. You escaped. You killed one of the finest scientists DPI has ever—"

She waved a hand. "Scientist? I say he was a twisted little pervert. He enjoyed the pain he inflicted." She tilted her head to one side and fought not to let her face reveal what the memory of that pain did to her insides. She'd been tortured to the point of near madness. To an immortal as old as she, pain was magnified incredibly. It was felt thousands of times more keenly than by a human, hundreds of times more keenly than by younger vampires.

"Then again, that night I must say I understood. I did enjoy what I did to him." She kept her voice cold, her tone without inflection. "Tell me now, Curtis Rogers, has this drug been tested on human subjects? What, I wonder, would be the effect should I inject it into you, for example?"

His face lost all color and she felt his rush of fear. "The drug has absolutely no noticeable effect on human beings."

She tilted her head back and laughed, the sound bubbling up from deep in her throat. "Oh, how you amuse me. You know I can read your thoughts. You're far too frightened right now to mask them, and yet you lie determinedly. The drug would kill you, would it not?"

He shook his head in denial.

Rhiannon held the needle skyward and depressed the plunger, sending a small spurt of silvery liquid into the air. Curtis lunged, landing on his feet on the concrete of the parking lot and immediately ready to flee. Rhiannon closed her hand over his nape and squeezed.

"It's no use, you know. I'm as strong as twenty grown men, and you with all your research of my kind, are aware of it. I'm older and more powerful than any of us you've encountered. I could kill you now without breaking a sweat, Rogers, my pet."

Still holding his nape in an unshakable grip, she dragged one nail lightly over the short hairs there. "How do you want it, I wonder? Would you like me to simply snap this neck of yours?

It would be the quickest, the most merciful way. Or I could, indeed, inject you with your own creation. Any drug powerful enough to tranquilize a vampire would probably kill an elephant in its tracks, to say nothing of a puny mortal such as yourself.''

She turned him to face her and she saw his fear. She could feel it, and she could smell it. She shook her head slowly. "No, I think those methods are not nearly poetic enough to suit me, Curtis, dear.'' She depressed the plunger farther, squirting the contents of the syringe down the front of his shirt, splattering his jacket. She tossed the empty needle to the floor. "I think, perhaps, for you—'' she gripped his necktie and jerked him nearer "—the old-fashioned methods are the best."

"No,'' he whispered. "For God's sake, no!''

She went so far as to actually rake her teeth across the tight skin of his throat, even drawing a bit of blood, which tasted so delightfully wonderful she nearly forgot to behave herself. But then she took a firm grip on her thirst, and she lifted her head from his throat.

"Oh, *mon cher,* you are delicious. But Roland has warned me I mustn't kill you. Only delay you until their flight—'' She bit her lips, as if she'd let some important bit of secrecy slip through them. "No matter. They are far from your reach now.'' She released her hold on him and he staggered backward. One hand lifted, palm pressing to his throat. When he saw the blood it came away with, he nearly fainted, such was his distress. She could have seen it even with mortal eyes, but in her vampiric state, she felt and sensed his every thought.

"Bother the boy again, *monsieur,* and I will delight in finishing you. And I assure you, despite your protests to the contrary, you shall delight in it, too. Right unto the moment of your death."

His eyes shifted frantically right and left as he sought assistance. None was to be had. "You'll pay for this,'' he shouted when he felt safer, farther from her. He edged toward an approaching vehicle. "I'll make sure you pay. All of you.''

"Yes, I know you will try. One final word, my dear, and then I must go. The taste of you on my lips has left me with a powerful appetite."

"You're an animal!"

She smiled slowly. "Quite right. A predator, to be precise. And if you go near Roland again, you will become my prey. Believe me, if it is Roland I avenge, your experience will not be a pleasant one. I will hurt you, Curtis Rogers. I will make you writhe!"

With a single burst of speed, she left him there, knowing to his human eyes, it must have seemed she'd simply vanished. He wouldn't go to the castle. Not right away, at least. She thought she'd convinced him that Roland and the boy had boarded a jet bound for parts unknown. He'd fallen so easily. He would search elsewhere first. They'd be safe during the approaching dawn. Yet, there were still precautions to be taken. Rhiannon sped toward the small rental house outside L'Ombre, to accomplish these, and of course, to fetch her cat.

Roland had no idea where she'd gone, or when she'd return. That was the thing about her. Flighty. Volatile. Unstoppable. Damn near irresistible. He groaned under his breath. He couldn't forget his desire even in his anger.

When she'd looked at Jamey earlier, Roland could have sworn he'd seen the stirrings of genuine affection. Of course, she would have to feel something for the boy. He was one of The Chosen. A human with the same two rare traits all vampires had as humans, the single combination that allowed them to be transformed. The line of descent, including, but surpassing, Prince Vlad the Impaler—yes, despite all of Eric Marquand's theories, it went back farther than that. And the blood antigen known as belladonna. A human with these traits, though he may never be aware of it, becomes the ward of the undead. Vampires watch over such ones, especially the children. They cannot do otherwise. And all preternatural beings can sense the presence of such ones, or the hint of a threat to them. Yet rarely are these Chosen ones transformed, or even contacted. Mostly, they simply go through their lives never knowing of their psychic link to a society they would believe a myth.

The situation with Jamey was unique. In order to protect him, Roland had been left with little choice but to arrange things as they now stood. DPI knew of Jamey's traits. They knew of his connection, not to one, but to three—now four—vampires. They placed a great value on the boy, his worth to them greater than would be his weight in gold. They would stop at nothing to possess him, to hold him in one of their diabolical laboratories, to run countless, torturous experiments upon his fragile young body while they awaited the inevitable arrival of his protectors.

And with all of this on the line, Rhiannon had played another of her vanishing acts.

But he knew better than that, didn't he? Unpredictable, she was, but not disloyal. Her carelessness only applied to matters of her own safety. Not to that of others. He wanted to be angry with her, but instead, found himself worried. She was gone, yes, but where was Rogers? With her? She'd been captured by a man like him once. Would she be reckless enough to end up in their hands again?

As soon as Jamey was safely installed in his modernized apartment in the east wing with Frederick at his side, Roland made the decision to search for her. She'd resent it, no doubt. She liked to do as she pleased without interference. But he felt she might be at risk, and he couldn't ignore that possibility.

Before he made it to the door, he sensed her presence. He realized a moment later that he'd felt an overwhelming sense of relief along with it. But that was ridiculous. He hadn't been *that* worried about her.

She entered the great hall through the tall, arching door of ancient hardwood, which was banded with black iron straps. At her side lumbered a panther, sleek and black as the velvet gown she still wore. The beast's green eyes glittered like emeralds, and as it gazed steadily at Roland, it stilled utterly, and emitted a deep-throated growl.

"What in God's name is that?"

"My cat. Her name is Pandora, and I would appreciate it if you would treat her with the respect she deserves."

"Rhiannon, for God's sake—" Roland took a single step forward, and froze when the cat crouched, snarling, teeth bared, about to spring.

"Pandora, hush!" At her stern command the animal relaxed, straightening rather lazily, still watching Roland's every move. "Roland is a friend," Rhiannon said softly, stroking the cat's big head with her long, dagger-tipped fingers. "Come, Roland, stroke her head, so she'll know you mean no harm."

Roland swore under his breath, but knew Rhiannon adored the beast, simply by the light in her eyes. He would indulge her, this once. It wasn't as if the cat could harm him. He moved nearer the animal, and stretched out one hand.

In a lightning-fast move, Pandora batted his hand away with claws extended, and a short angry snarl.

"Pandora!" Rhiannon smacked the cat on the nose, and reached out, gripping Roland's hand and frowning at the single scratch the cat had managed to inflict. A tiny, narrow path of beaded red droplets.

"I'm sorry, Roland. She is so protective of me, you see, and you did raise your voice." Then she lifted his hand, brought it to her lips, and, very catlike, herself, ran her damp tongue over the mark, from knuckles to wrist. She closed her eyes at the erotic impact of the act. Roland knew, because it rocked him, too.

Tongues of flame licked at his groin, and Roland winced at the force of it.

"Come, darling," she whispered. "Show Pandora how close we are. That will work to calm her. I know it will. Come, take me in your arms. Just this once. Just to calm the cat."

"Rhiannon, I don't think—"

"Why must I work so hard to earn each little touch you bestow?" She shook her head, glancing at the cat, who again, began to snarl menacingly. "Surely you won't die from my kisses, Roland, toxic though they may be. Our embrace will reassure Pandora. She will keep Rogers out of the castle while we rest, by day. She is well trained, I assure you. Now, please, just take me in your arms. Hold me to you. Kiss my lips. It will be all the evidence she requires, I promise you."

Without quite meaning to, Roland stepped closer. He slipped his arms around Rhiannon's slender waist, and she immediately pressed her hips against him. Waves of desire raced through his veins. Her deceptively fragile-looking arms linked around his neck. Her scent was unlike anything human. An exotic mingling of the preternatural blood flowing beneath her skin and the spiced juices of her arousal dampening her interior, the henna she insisted on rinsing through her hair and the mysterious incense she burned regularly.

A mortal man would notice none of it. Nor would he see the subtle change in the light refracted in her black eyes, and know it signaled the onset of the powerful lust only immortals can feel or understand. It borders on violence, this lust. It mingles with the thirst for blood until the two entwine and become inseparable.

His arms tightened around her, until her proud breasts pressed hard against his chest. Their stiff little nipples—twenty times more sensitive than a mortal woman's might be—poked into his skin, even through the dress she wore, and the shirt covering him.

He looked down into her face, his eyes feasting for a moment on her parted lips. He could still catch the faint trace of his own blood on her tongue. Slowly, he sunk into the madness only she could create within him. He lowered his head until his face, his lips, moved over her smooth cheek. He traced the high cheekbone, and then the shape of her finely arched brow. His lips nibbled a path down the straight, narrow bridge of her nose, then danced over the bit of flesh between nose and upper lip.

She made a tiny sound, like a purr, in her throat, and tipped her head back slightly, to lift her lips to his. Driven beyond restraint, Roland took her mouth the way a man dying of slow starvation takes his first crumb of food. His hands twisted themselves into her hair and his tongue swept inside her. Her taste was intoxicating, an aphrodisiac, certainly, for he throbbed with wanting her.

She felt his arousal, pressed her hips closer, and murmured his name into his mouth on a low, husky exhalation.

Roland put her from him, stepping back, though it took more effort than lifting this castle above his head could have taken. The lust in him roared loudly in his ears, but he dared not give in to it. No. He could too easily lose his sanity in Rhiannon. He could be swept completely away on a mindless journey of passion. He could forget what was important.

The boy, in the east wing preparing once again to face a fight not even a grown man should have to endure. The tiny *cimetière* in the forest beyond the castle's outer walls. The five graves, so old now they would be invisible had he not kept them up, replacing the headstones every few years, and always with more ornate and expensive pieces. His mother lay there, beneath the cold earth. His father, and his three hearty brothers who had once scoffed at his desire to become a knight. Truly, he knew, they'd only been afraid to see their youngest sibling thrown into bloody battle. They'd loved him. And he'd returned their love with hatred, and betrayal, and finally, with abandonment. No, he could never forgive himself that.

Most important of all was that he never forget the beast that lived within him. It had lurked in the depths of his black soul even when he'd been a mere mortal. It must be contained, for were it loosed now, the destruction it might wreak would be irreparable.

Rhiannon made him careless. She brought out the impulsive,

irresponsible lad he'd once been. The one foolish enough to let that beast escape. She made him, at times, long to free the animal inside. To allow it to take over. She filled him with such hunger that all else seemed unimportant.

"Roland, darling? What is it?" Rhiannon stood alone now, a yard of space between him and her. She appeared composed, but he felt the confusion, the thwarted passion frustrating her. "Don't stop now," she whispered. "We must convince Pandora…"

Roland shook himself. What he felt for her was nothing but lust. He wanted no companion at all, let alone one as uncontrollable and explosive as she. Her very presence was a danger to his sanity.

He felt the huge cat's heavy, silken body pressing to his leg, first the head, then a long, slow stroke of its neck and side over Roland's calf.

"I believe the cat is convinced, Rhiannon." Roland lowered his hand and scratched the feline's head. It arched to his touch and purred like a motorcar.

"Pandora, you traitor! I told you to wait until later to be friendly!"

Roland's brows shot up. "You mean she didn't need convincing at all, only your command?"

Rhiannon's lower lip protruded ever so slightly farther than her upper one, looking as plump and moist as a ripe plum. "I have to go to great lengths, sometimes, to get any cooperation from you, you stubborn man."

"And the cat?"

Rhiannon shrugged. "I haven't figured her out yet. Only that she can read me, and I her. We connect on a psychic level neither of us can understand. I don't need to speak to her, only to send her mental messages. Not words, mind you. Images. And she obeys me without question."

"So she snarled at me because you told her to do so?"

She shrugged, trying for a look of innocence and failing. "Just as I shall tell her to guard Jamey as we rest. No mortal shall set foot inside these walls with Pandora about. Not and live, at least.''

"Suppose she makes the boy into a light snack?"

"She would no more do so than you would, love."

The remark stung, but Roland ignored the barb. "You're certain?"

"Do you think I would risk the child you adore so blatantly?"

He pursed his lips, then shook his head. "No. I suppose you would not."

"You suppose." She tossed her hair over her shoulder and strode away, toward the crumbling, curving stone stairs that spiraled upward along the circular keep's wall. "Come, Pandora. I'll introduce you to your new friends."

As she moved up the stairs, the huge cat leaping to catch up with her, Roland scanned her mind. He saw her envisioning Jamey and Frederick, envisioning herself embracing them, and the cat being lovingly stroked by their mortal hands. He wondered at it, but he didn't question it.

He had enough on his mind at the moment. He wouldn't waste time worrying about her true motives in wishing to help the boy. She was sincere, he knew. Yet still, it baffled him; for in all the time he'd known Rhiannon, he'd never thought her capable of feeling much for any mortal. Her thirst for adventure, and constant excitement came above all else. He'd never understood her, the risks she took.

No. He'd do better to assess his own ridiculous responses to her. Naturally, she excited him. What man, mortal or immortal, could remain indifferent to her touch, her scent, her vibrancy? He didn't constantly resist her advances because he didn't want her. Quite the opposite, in fact. He wanted her too much... physically. To copulate simply for lust's sake was to lower oneself to the level of an animal.

Moreover, she would only flit out of his life when it was over. Not that he cared.

And there was the constant fear of losing control. Rhiannon inspired that tendency in him like nothing else could.

Roland composed himself after several moments of pondering, and went to the worn stone stairs. He slipped along the darkened corridor, and paused outside the vaulted door to the apartment. He opened it only slightly, and nearly cried out at what he saw.

Jamey lay on his back upon the floor, with that black beast over him, front paws pressed to Jamey's chest. The boy's hands cupped the panther's huge head, shoving it left and right roughly. The cat made deep, threatening sounds, its tail swishing in agitation. Roland tensed, about to launch himself upon the cat, but he stopped in his tracks as he realized that Jamey wasn't crying out for assistance. He was laughing!

Before Roland's stunned eyes, Jamey threw the cat over, onto its side, then Pandora rolled herself onto her back and lay still, head turned, watching the boy. He got to his feet and rubbed the animal's glossy underbelly vigorously, while the cat arched her neck and closed her eyes, emitting a loud purr.

Roland forced his gaze beyond the spectacle, to where Rhiannon stood with Frederick. She gave him a half smile. "She's just an overgrown kitten, you see?" She crossed the room to Roland's side. "It's odd, I thought I would have to introduce them...give them time to become acquainted. Yet, it's as if she recognized Jamey the moment she saw him." Her dark gaze reached out to Frederick with intensity. "You must take care with her, Freddy. She may not be as receptive to you."

Frederick licked his thick lips and moved slowly forward, his limp more pronounced now than earlier. "Pandora," he called in his baritone voice. He moved slowly toward the two on the carpeted floor. "Pandora, come here, kitty."

The cat looked up, then slowly rolled onto her stomach. She lay with paws extended, head up, still as a sphinx, eyeing Frederick. He glanced up at Rhiannon. "Can I pet her?"

Rhiannon nodded, her own gaze fixed on the panther, sending silent messages. Frederick reached out, gently touched Pandora's head, and stroked it slowly. He continued until, finally, the cat's deep purr came once more. The glittering eyes closed, and the big head pressed upward against Frederick's hand.

Frederick laughed, tipping back his big, blond head as he did. "Thank you for bringing her."

"Thank you for trusting her," Rhiannon replied. "Rogers likely won't bother us here today. I led him to believe you'd all left the country. Still, she will keep him out should he attempt anything."

"I bet she will," Frederick said softly.

"And tomorrow evening, we'll see about getting Jamey somewhere safe."

"No." Jamey stood, and faced both Rhiannon and Roland.

Roland sighed. "I know this is difficult for you, Jamison, but—"

"No. It's impossible. I'm not going anywhere tomorrow. I have one more practice, and then the big match." He faced Rhiannon. "It's the championship, Rhiannon. We can't leave until after that."

Roland opened his mouth, but Rhiannon held up her hand. "This game of yours...soccer, isn't it?"

Jamey nodded. "I've worked all season for this. I'm not letting Curt Rogers cheat me out of it. He's taken enough from me. We're playing in the dome stadium, under the lights. It's the biggest match of the year."

Rhiannon nodded. "The game, what time—"

"Seven tomorrow night." Jamey's eyes lit with hope.

Rhiannon seemed deep in thought. "It is dark by seven, is it not?"

Roland was unable to hold his silence any longer. "Rhiannon, we cannot protect the boy in a stadium crowded with spectators. Do not even suggest—"

"It is important to him, Roland. Surely you can see that."

"I have to make the practice after school tomorrow. If I miss it, I can't play in the match. Coach's rule."

"No. That I cannot arrange," Rhiannon said softly. "This practice session is by day, Jamey. We could not protect you there."

"I can protect myself."

"It is simple, really," Rhiannon went on as if he hadn't spoken. "I will simply pen a note to this coach, telling him you've twisted your ankle, and must rest it for the entire day or else not be capable of playing in the game. If he requires a note from a doctor, I will, of course write one. I will deliver this note, along with a check, a donation, if you will, to the athletic department. I'll make it a hefty enough sum that the man will be only too happy to excuse you from practice. There, you see how simple?"

Jamey smiled slightly. Then frowned. "I shouldn't take your money—"

"Posh," Rhiannon said with a wave of her hand. "I have more than you can imagine." She looked at Jamey, her eyes glowing with affection. "Besides, I can't remember the last time I watched a soccer match. So, it is decided."

She strode out the door, the picture of elegance in her black velvet gown.

Roland dogged her steps.

She stopped on the stairway and turned to face him, daring him to argue with her.

"I do not have any intention of attending this soccer match."

She shrugged delicately. "Well, we'll miss you, of course, but if that's your decision—"

"Jamison isn't going either. It's too great a risk."

She rolled her eyes. "What is life without risk?"

"I forbid this, Rhiannon."

"Forbid all you like. Jamey and I are attending the match. And believe me, darling, no mere mortal is going to harm that boy while I am near. You forget who I am."

He shook his head. "There will be, perhaps, over a hundred mortals in attendance. We'd be spotted immediately. Recognized for what we are. Have you no sense?"

She only turned and resumed walking down the stairs. "Just as I was recognized the other night at Le Requin? Roland, there are ways to disguise ourselves. A bit of flesh-toned makeup on our pale skin, a pair of shaded lenses if you fear the glow in your eyes will be seen. A bit of powder to those blood-red lips. It is so obscenely simple to fool them, you see. Besides, they are modern humans. They wouldn't believe what we are, even if we walked up to them and announced it."

"This is utter foolishness," he muttered as he watched her proceed down the stairs. How could one disguise one's nature, one's violence? How could Roland allow the two people he most wanted to protect to place themselves in such a vulnerable position?

She reached the bottom step, and waited for him to join her there. "You've lived as a hermit far too long, Roland. You deny yourself the simplest luxuries."

"I have all I require."

"Nonsense. If you could see some of the places I've lived. Mansions in the countryside, penthouse suites in the finest hotels. I have a delicious condo in New York. When I choose to drive, I only travel in the height of luxury. I attend the opera, the ballet, the theater. Roland, there is no danger. Not to us. Who could hope to harm us?"

"DPI, as you well know."

"Ah. I make one mistake in all my centuries of existence, and you cling to it like Pandora with a steak."

"They nearly had Eric, too. It can happen."

"Eric is young...a mere two centuries old, Roland. You have triple his strength and powers. Besides, what is the use of endless life if one lives it like this?" Her hands moved to encompass the great hall.

He sighed. Arguing with her was an exhausting venture. "I live here because I want to do so."

"No. I think you cling to the past. I think you fail to embrace your immortality, to relish it, as I do, out of some misguided sense of family loyalty, or something.''

"And I think you seek out danger deliberately, as if daring death to claim you. Why do you do it, Rhiannon?''

Her face quickly became shuttered, showing not a trace of emotion. Even her mind closed to him, a heavy veil dropping instantly over it. He knew he'd hit on something, but had no idea what.

"Even if that were true, you must believe I wouldn't include your Jamey in my challenge. I would not risk him, Roland.''

"Why not? What is he to you?''

"It is what he is to you that matters.'' Her ebony gaze fell to the floor, and for an instant, Roland glimpsed stark agony in her eyes. "I know how he feels. I know just the kind of pain there is in his young heart. The loss of his mother—'' She blinked rapidly, and stopped speaking as her voice grew hoarse. She whirled away from him, and headed across the stone floor toward the heavy doors.

"Where are you going?'' His mind reached out to hers. He felt as if he'd been shown a part of Rhiannon no one had ever before seen. He wanted to know more, wanted to identify the source of the pain he'd just glimpsed. Wanted to end it.

"To my lair, of course. It's nearly dawn.''

He found himself at a loss. He hadn't expected her to leave the castle today. "I...I thought you'd stay here.''

"And sleep where? I suppose you have some spare box of polished hardwood I could use, stored in those dank dungeons of yours?'' The cynicism returned to her voice.

He didn't answer.

"I prefer a soft bed, Roland. I prefer satin sheets to shrouds. A fluffy down comforter and a plump soft pillow beneath my head. I prefer fresh air, rife with the fragrance of incense.''

"Sounds very lovely. But where is your protection?''

"Come to me some dawn, darling, and I will show you.'' With a swish of her velvet dress, she turned, strode to the door and was gone.

CHAPTER FOUR

Roland woke at full dark, feeling the rush of tingling awareness sizzling in his every nerve ending. He quickly unfastened the complex locks on the inner lid, using his mind to scan the immediate area, before throwing it wide. He leapt to the floor with ease, landing soundlessly on the cold stone.

His rest had not been peaceful. Often he'd found himself hovering on the verge of consciousness, while images flitted to and fro in his mind. He was troubled, and not just on Jamey's behalf. The images had been of Rhiannon, more often than not. Beautiful, desirable, reckless Rhiannon. Had he no more sense than a rutting mortal? Could he not distinguish common, vulgar lust from true feelings of affection? Could he not banish the temptress from his mind?

He moved slowly through the crumbling passages of the dungeons in utter darkness, his extraordinary vision showing him the way. Blind, he'd have known the way. It was embedded in him. Every niche of this castle was. It had been his home in boyhood, his curse in adolescence, his prison as a young man. It had become the purgatory of the immortal, the place in which he would serve the sentence for the sin he'd committed against the family he'd adored. Yes, adored, but adored too late.

And what earthly good was done by dwelling on it now?

He tugged at an iron ring mounted in what appeared to be an immobile stone wall, using a great deal of his vampiric strength to move it. No mortal could hope to achieve the same feat without the help of some explosive or other. He slipped into the passage, and mounted the perpendicular spiral stairs of rusting iron. His every step echoed a thousand times in the darkness. There had once been a ladder here as the sole entrance to the dungeon's lowest level from the castle keep. When the ladder had needed replacing, the set of spiral stairs had seemed more apropos.

At the entrance to his chambers on the castle's ground level, he opened the door and emerged into his wardrobe, shoving hangers and suits of clothes aside. These, of course, he carefully rearranged to cover the entrance. Then he chose a fresh suit, and emerged into his chambers in the west wing.

He moved directly to the antique desk and took a long wooden match from the holder there to light the oil lamp. He repeated the ritual, lighting several more until the room glowed with a soft, golden hue. Looking around him now, he supposed Rhiannon would scoff at the place he called his home. The draperies that covered the tall, arched windows were heavy and faded with time. They smelled of dust and age. Their color was green, once brilliant as emeralds, but now dull, as if one were seeing them through a heavy fog. The windows themselves, a concession to modern times and added long after the deaths of the castle's rightful barons, were streaked and dirty. Looking through them was like looking through the filmy eyes of an old man. But wasn't that what this castle was, after all? An old, old man, whose every beloved friend had left him to wither and die alone?

The brocade upholstery on the antique settee had lost its luster long ago. The fireplace was a cold, dark cavity, holding the ashes of a fire long forgotten. The hardwood chairs, once thronelike and imposing, sat like sad witnesses to the end of an era, their wood grain and hand-tooled designs barely discernible through the years of neglect, their embroidered cushions worn and faded. High above, the chandelier, with its tier upon tier of candles, hung dark and brooding like a ghost of the past. Draped with cobwebs and shrouded with dust, it watched in silence as Roland served his eternal death sentence in the rooms below.

Rhiannon would hate these rooms.

And what did he care what Rhiannon thought of anything?

She's here, now.

The realization came to him with sudden clarity. She was here, on the grounds. He felt the vivid colors of her aura, and sensed the mad vibrations in the air, the snapping electricity that always announced her presence. In spite of himself, Roland hurried through his nightly bathing and dressing. Not because he was eager to see her again, he told himself. Not that at all. He only wished to be present to keep her in check. God only knew what she might do left to her own devices.

He followed his sense of her, moving soundlessly and quickly through the echoing corridors and finally into the great hall. Still she was not in sight. He sensed Jamey's presence now, as well, and Frederick's...and the cat's. Not within the keep, but without, in the courtyard.

Beyond the heavy plank door, he saw her in the darkness. Surprising him was something she did well and often. Why had he not grown used to it by now?

She raced over the grassless brown earth, her path illuminated by silvery moonlight, keeping a spotted ball moving along between her feet. She was clad in a pair of black denims, which had been cut off midway up her shapely thighs. Small white socks barely covered her ankles and her feet were encased in black, lacing shoes with garish red stripes and mean-looking cleats protruding from their soles.

As Roland stood, transfixed, Jamey raced toward Rhiannon thrusting one foot between her two and snatching the ball away. Rhiannon tripped and tumbled head over heels in the dirt, rolling to a stop with a cloud of brown dust rising around her. Roland lunged, but stopped himself when he heard her deep laughter. She stood and brushed the dirt from her derriere.

"Very good, Jamey." Again she laughed. She pushed the ebony hair from her face, leaving a dirt smear on her cheek. "Show me again, I want to learn this."

Roland cleared his throat, and Rhiannon turned, spotting him. "Don't look that way, love," she cooed. "I'm not going to hurt him."

For a shocking instant, Roland realized he'd been more concerned about her hurting herself. Imagine! He'd been afraid the most powerful immortal he knew might hurt herself playing soccer with a young boy. Damn strange. True enough, immortals felt pain more keenly than mortals did, and Rhiannon would be especially sensitive. But any injuries Rhiannon might sustain would heal as she rested by day. Still, it stunned him that the thought of seeing her in pain should shake him so.

"See to it you don't," he told her, unwilling to admit the true path of his thoughts. "He does have that match tomorrow night."

"Does this mean you've decided to stop arguing the point?"

He nodded, but reluctantly. Rhiannon strode baldly up to him and threw her arms around his neck. Her embrace resulted in his starched white shirt and tailored jacket becoming as dirty as she was. Yet he withstood it well enough, even though her body pressed tightly to his that way sent his pulse racing and caused his eyes to water.

"There are conditions, Rhiannon."

She gazed up at him, for though she was tall for a woman, he was still a good deal taller. "Conditions?" Her eyebrows furrowed, showing her displeasure.

He cleared his throat. He was about to anger her. Seemed to him everything he said angered her. Still, he had to speak his mind. A ball of foreboding about this excursion had lodged somewhere in his stomach and he couldn't shake the feeling that she was about to put herself at risk...yet again. "At this match, you will behave with a modicum of decorum."

"Oh, will I?"

"You will try, for once in your existence, not to draw undue attention. You will be polite, soft-spoken and unobtrusive."

Her eyes glittered. "And just why will I transform myself this way?"

Roland sighed. He only wanted to keep her from being discovered by Rogers or another one like him. Why did she have to be so defensive? "Because I have asked you to, Rhiannon.

And because it is the wisest course to take. Rogers isn't stupid, nor is he the only agent in the area. Anyone who's learned Jamey's identity will know enough to look for him at that match.''

For once, her chin dropped rather than thrusting upward into his face. She gave an almost imperceptible nod, and Roland felt a mingling of surprise and relief. He'd been certain she would argue. Protecting Rhiannon was going to be as much a challenge as protecting Jamey, he thought grimly.

''Ready?'' Roland asked the following evening, an hour before the match was to begin. He stood near the huge, empty hearth in the great hall. Rhiannon closed the heavy door, causing its hinges to groan in protest, and crossed the cold, dusty stone floor to join him.

She chewed her lower lip. ''I'm not sure. I don't have the benefit of a reflection by which to judge my appearance.''

He fought the urge to smile. ''Must be a damned nuisance to a woman of your vanity.''

She met his gaze, her own flashing. ''Quite right. You ought to paint my portrait, so I can see what I look like when I wish it.''

''You know I don't paint anymore.''

''Perhaps it's time you started.'' She glanced around her, and he knew she was noting the absence of any decoration adorning the gray stone walls. There were only torches mounted in brackets, and here and there the mounted antlers of one of his brothers' kills. ''This place could use it. Whatever became of the portraits you'd done of your family?''

He shook his head. The subject was not open to discussion. Having the faces of those he'd failed looking down at him would be too much agony to bear. ''In answer to your initial question, Rhiannon, you look fine.''

''That, my dear Roland, is no answer at all.'' She stood before him, hands at her sides. ''Look at me, darling. Describe to me what you see. I am so tired of going out and about wondering

if everything is in place.'' She waited a moment. Roland's gaze
moved over her, and he found himself unable to form a coherent
thought. ''I'll help,'' she offered. ''Begin with my hair. Is it all
right?''

She turned slowly and Roland nodded. ''It gleams like satin,
as you well know.'' His eyes traveled the length of it. She wore
it long, and unencumbered by barrettes or dressings of any kind.
She'd combed it all to one side, as she was prone to do, thus
leaving the bare length of her swan's neck visible to the point
of distraction. She had braided a tiny, silken lock on the left side
of her face, from the crown of her head all the way to her waist.
It had a petite charm that lured one to touch it.

Rhiannon, catching his gaze, lifted the braid in two fingers.
''You like it?''

''Yes.'' He licked his lips, then caught himself. ''Yes, it's just
fine. Are you ready to go now?''

''But you haven't finished.'' Her pout was utterly false. She
leaned forward. ''What about the blouse? Does it show too much
cleavage?''

Against his will, his eyes were drawn downward to the plunging neckline of the satiny, emerald-colored garment. The swell
of her creamy breasts filled the lowest part of the V, and Roland
felt a twisting sensation in his stomach. ''When do you not show
too much,'' he asked, trying for a sarcastic tone.

She shrugged, straightened and struck yet another pose, this
time hands on her hips. ''And the skirt? Do you think it's too
short?''

It was tight, molded to her hips like cling wrap, black and
made of suede. It buttoned down the front, and as if the garment
had not already been daring enough, Rhiannon had left the bottom two buttons agape. Her thighs, shimmering beneath silk
stockings, extended from the skirt's edge. As she stood there,
turning first to one side, then the other, Roland's gaze affixed
itself to her legs. ''Perhaps it's simply that your legs are too

long,'' he suggested. But instead of sounding dry and uninterested, his voice came out hoarse and none too loudly.

"These stockings are wonderful, don't you think?" She stepped nearer and bent one knee, propping her foot on a low stool. "So soft against my skin. Touch them, Roland, and you'll see what I mean." She caught his hand in hers and pressed his palm to the front of her thigh, then rubbed it up and down over the smooth, cinnamon-tinted silk.

He swallowed. "As I've mentioned before, you lack a certain degree of subtlety. Why do you not simply tear my clothes off and attempt a forced seduction?" He snatched his hand away, more angry with his own responses than with her childish attempts to lure him.

He saw the hurt in her eyes before she covered it, and he regretted his words at once. She truly couldn't help herself, he supposed. She was simply being Rhiannon. He'd allowed his anger at himself to spill out onto her. "I'm sorry, Rhiannon. I didn't mean—"

She tossed her hair. "Of course you did. You'd prefer me to become what you consider a true lady, to sit on an embroidered cushion and bat my eyes until you take the initiative, and ask me to dance. Hah! I'd be coated in more cobwebs than this great hall by the time you made up your mind."

She turned her back to him. "I was going to the match with you, but now I believe I will ride in the car with Frederick and Jamey. Enjoy your walk, Roland. And for God's sake, change into the clothes I brought for you before you leave. If you think attending a school-boy's soccer match in such formal attire is inconspicuous, you'd better think again."

He glanced down at the bag she'd dropped near the door as she whirled and walked through it.

He did not enjoy his walk. It turned out that he wasn't quite hard-hearted enough to hurt Rhiannon and take any sort of pleasure from it. He hadn't meant to insult her, but she was getting to him, dammit. Any man would be less than cheerful and charming when feeling as frustrated as he'd been. To resist her overt sexual overtures took every bit of will he possessed. But to give in to them would be foolhardy, to say the least. Not only would she never let him forget that she'd won this particular battle of wills, but she'd probably flit away like a summer breeze when the act was done. He might not see her again for years. And in the process, she'd have loosed the beast he'd battled for so long.

No. This…thing that sizzled between them was purely physical in nature. It's overwhelming potency…well, he could attribute that to the vampiric state. Every sensation was felt more keenly by immortals. Desire was simply magnified by his nature.

That explanation firmly established in his mind, he used his preternatural speed to arrive at the stadium before the little car he'd purchased for Frederick. He much preferred travel by his own power or by horse, to being helplessly hurtled through space by three thousand pounds of man-made scrap metal.

At the stadium, he felt more conspicuous in the attire Rhiannon had chosen for him than ever he had in his own overly formal clothing. The blue denim hugged his backside and clung with unaccustomed tightness to his groin. The sweatshirt was black. That part did not disturb him. But the blaze of neon paint across his chest, proclaiming him a fan of something called the Grateful Dead, had him at the end of his patience. He was not amused by the skull and crossbones, or by the not so subtle irony in her choice. At least he blended in with the crowd.

In contrast, Rhiannon, seated just to his left, was anything but unnoticeable. She shouted encouragement, not to mention a few obscenities when the opposing team made progress. She was in constant motion, wriggling in her seat, leaning forward or standing or both, when she wanted a better view, much to the delight of the males in the seats near her, Roland noted with a rush of inexplicable anger.

Still, in the seats below, near the team's bench, he saw that Frederick was nearly as animated.

Jamey, looking fierce in his uniform and with black smudges under his eyes to fight glare from the overhead lights, raced across the artificial turf with the ball. Rhiannon shouted encouragement, getting to her feet as he neared the goal.

Roland scowled. Was this supposed to be unobtrusive behavior? My God, he couldn't take his eyes off her, nor could several other men in the immediate area.

Roland forced his gaze back to the field of play, just as another lad thrust a leg in Jamey's path, tripping him so he tumbled head over heels, hitting hard. Roland caught his breath. Jamey got to his feet, though, and charged after the brat. When Jamey regained possession of the ball, Roland stood. He had no idea he'd done so, but there he was, upright. When the bully approached, Jamey skillfully passed the ball to a teammate, and when the teammate was similarly accosted, he passed back to Jamey.

A moment later, Jamey planted one foot and slammed the ball with the other, driving it into the goal with impressive speed. Roland applauded as loudly as anyone. Rhiannon released a piercing whistle that probably damaged some human ears. He touched her arm. She looked at him, her half smile a full-blown one for a change.

"You're forgetting yourself." He nearly didn't remind her. He didn't want to see her brilliant smile die.

"So are you," she told him. But she did sit down again.

Jamey's team won by a slim margin. Rhiannon felt drained from the excitement of the match. She and Frederick walked to the parking lot, while Roland waited outside the locker room to escort Jamey out. Rhiannon was certain no DPI operatives had been in the stadium. She'd kept her mind attuned throughout the match, and had caught not the faintest sense of a threat. Still, she remained watchful, and she scanned the minds of everyone who passed, in search of belligerent thoughts.

Frederick got into the car and started the engine, letting it idle as they waited for Roland and Jamey. Rhiannon stood near the driver's door, one arm propped on the car's roof. Others began to leave, a few at a time.

Within a short time, the lot was deserted. The moon's light this evening was more often than not obliterated by inky clouds. The concrete field became eerily silent, save the occasional sounds of vehicles passing on the street nearby. Time passed with leaden feet.

"The game was wonderful, wasn't it, Freddy?"

He nodded enthusiastically. "I practice with Jamey sometimes. But I'm not much good at running."

Rhiannon frowned slightly. "Your leg?"

Again, he nodded.

"Do you mind if I ask what happened to it?"

"No, it's all right. It happened when I was in the city, when I didn't have anyplace to live. It was wintertime, and I guess it just got too cold."

Rhiannon suppressed a shudder at the thought of gentle Freddy, freezing his limbs on a frigid winter's night. "Does it hurt you very much?"

"Oh, no. It hardly bothers me at all, anymore."

"I'm glad." She looked toward the rapidly darkening building. "They're taking too long."

"Maybe we better go back and check on them."

A warning prickle of danger danced over Rhiannon's nape. She sent the probing fingers of her mind in search of the source, but there was nothing tangible. "I think you should wait here, in the car." Rhiannon shook her head, still unable to pinpoint the source of her precognition. "Lock the doors," she added.

"Rhiannon, is somethin' wrong with Jamey?" Fear made Freddy's voice hoarse. "'Cause if there is, I'm going with you."

"I don't know," she said truthfully. "But it really will be better if you wait here. In case Jamey comes out and I miss him. Okay?" She tried to sound unconcerned, and for a moment it surprised her that she should care to ease the mind of a mortal.

Then again, Freddy was no ordinary human. When she saw the car doors were locked, she gave him an encouraging nod and hurried across the blacktop toward the entrance.

The thrill of foreboding grew stronger and her fear for Roland and the boy grew with it. Her quickened steps snapped loudly over the lot, and then the sidewalk. She rounded a corner and reached for the doors.

A heavy arm came around her from behind, jerking her off balance and into the shadows.

Fool! Did this human think he could hope to do battle with her and win?

She prepared to pull free, turn around and wring the idiot's neck, when pain split through her consciousness like a piercing cry. The blade tore the flesh at her waist, only a small cut, surely. Yet the scalding pain paralyzed her. And when she felt she could move again, his voice gave her pause.

"I know your weaknesses, Rhiannon. Loss of blood, exposure to sunlight, direct contact between your flesh and an open fire…and pain." The blade pressed to her rib cage, but didn't cut. "Pain," he went on, his voice a rasping serpent in her ear. "The more severe, the more it weakens you. Isn't that right?" The blade's point pressed into her sensitive skin. "And the older the vampire, the more keenly she feels it." More pressure on the blade. A trickle of blood ran beneath her satin blouse, over her abdomen. She sucked breath through her teeth. "So this must be just about maddening, isn't it?"

Teeth grated, she forced words through her lips. "What do you want?"

Again the blade poked, twisting this time. She cried out, then bit her lip. She wouldn't summon Roland, not until she knew what he would be facing. "What do you think?" he rasped.

He was not Curtis Rogers. He was not anyone she'd ever encountered before. He was strong for a human, and unstintingly cruel. The first wound, the one in her side, still pulsed hot spasms of pain as well as blood. She felt herself weakening. A vampire as old as Rhiannon need lose very little to meet her demise. She needed help. Damn, but she hated to admit that. She'd never found herself less than able to deal with adversity. It infuriated her that this human had identified her few weaknesses, and used them so skillfully against her.

Her knees began to tremble and she forced them rigid once more. "Who are you," she growled, "and why do you court death so eagerly?"

"Not death, Rhiannon. Life. Eternal life. Immortality. You have it. I want it."

The man was insane! "You have no idea what you're talking about. You're not..." She paused, dizziness swamping her brain. She blinked it away. "Release me. I must...sit." She pressed her free hand against the hole in her side, hoping to slow the flow of her life from her body.

"If I release you, lady, you might just find enough strength to kill me. That is not my goal."

"If I die, so does your chance of getting what you want."

"Not really. There are others." His grip on her tightened. His pinpoint blade pressed harder, and the end twisted slowly. She was breathing hard now, in broken, ragged gasps. A response to the pain. Tears blurred her vision. "Give me what I want and I will let you go."

"And if I refuse, you'll let me die?" The words came slowly, and her speech was slurred. "I choose death, then."

"Not death, Rhiannon. Something far worse. There are DPI agents all over this place tonight, waiting for that boy of yours. But they'd consider you a greater prize, don't you think? The vampiress who murdered one of their most highly valued researchers all those years ago? I'll just give a shout and bring them running. You're too weak to fight them. Getting weaker all the time."

She closed her eyes and focused her thoughts on Roland. *Take Jamey out of here. Be careful. They're watching, and...* Before she completed the thought, the bastard twisted his blade again, and Rhiannon couldn't stop the gasp of pain that escaped her. "Well? Are you going to give me what I want?"

Her legs gave out. The loss of blood combined with the pain was simply too much. She went to her knees, causing the man's blade to rake up over her rib cage, and nick her throat.

At that moment, the man flew backward for no apparent cause, landing with a heavy thud on the ground. "You've just ended your life, human." It was Roland's voice, and it was quivering with a rage she'd never heard in him before. He reached for the man, who lay on his back, staring defiantly up at him.

"Here!" the mortal yelled at the top of his lungs. "They're here! Hurry!"

"That won't save you." Roland lifted the man by the front of his shirt, and Rhiannon knew he was about to crush his larynx. She'd never seen Roland so angry. He'd forgotten his well-schooled caution, his carefully cultivated calm. She felt it in his every thought, saw it in every line of his face. He would kill the man, and anyone who tried to stop him. The force of his anger shook her to the core. She hadn't known he was capable of such explosive violence.

"Roland, they're coming," she managed to say. "We must go. Think...of Jamey."

He pummeled the man's face with his fist, and slowly lifted him again. "Let them come. They'll soon wish they'd kept their distance."

She put every ounce of strength she had into her voice. "Roland, please! I'm bleeding—"

All at once, it seemed, his fury dissipated. Roland dropped the limp form to the ground. Then he whirled, bending over Rhiannon and lifting her easily into his arms. He searched her face, his eyes wide with fear now, rather than narrow with a barely suppressed rage. She felt him stiffen as he realized the extent of her blood loss and the weakness of her body. In a burst of preternatural speed, he left the parking lot and the sounds of running feet behind.

"Where…is Jamey?"

"We had to sneak out a window and duck through the brush. There were DPI agents watching all the exits. I put him in the car with Frederick and saw them safely off. They're fine."

She sighed, but it was broken by pain. "Good."

"You're still losing blood." He stopped, and settled her on the ground. She glanced upward, seeing only the black outline of gnarled tree limbs against the paler gray of the night. They were in a wooded area.

She heard the tear of fabric as Roland hurriedly opened her blouse. Then there was more pain, even at his gentle touch, as he pressed a handkerchief firmly to the wound. "Hold it there," he instructed. "Hold it tightly. Ignore the pain."

She did, but cried out. "Easy for you to say. You're less than ten centuries old. I'm more than twice that."

"With age comes strength," he replied in a hoarse voice as his fingers touched the smaller wound. She winced.

"And weakness." She drew a shaky breath. "You well know that I'm far more vulnerable to pain and blood loss, sunlight and fire, than you are." Her head fell backward, her neck suddenly incapable of supporting it. "I'm not certain I'll make it to dawn, Roland."

Again, he slipped his arms beneath her, lifted her. This time, he pressed her face to the crook of his neck. "You will, Rhiannon. I won't allow it to be otherwise. You only need to drink."

She stiffened, unsure of his meaning. His hand at the back of her head pressed her nearer, his fingers moving softly through her hair as his palm held her to him. Her lips touched the skin of his throat, tasted its salt.

"Drink," he said again.

And she did.

CHAPTER FIVE

Roland closed his eyes as her lips moved against his throat. The blood lust came alive at her touch. The sexual desire pummeled him until he felt too weak to fight it. God, but he wanted her. And what she was doing now only trebled the already powerful longing. Slowly the restraint he'd been struggling to hold in place shuddered beneath the assault of desire. Roland drew a strangled breath.

"Enough!"

He hadn't meant the single command to sound so harsh. She immediately lifted her head, blinking. Roland saw the passion in her eyes, even through the pain clouding them.

"Any more and I'll not have the strength to carry you home, Rhiannon," he lied in a much softer tone. He still feared for her well-being, but in truth if she didn't stop right then, he'd have dropped her into the tangy scented leaves at their feet, and made frantic love to her, pain or no pain.

"Put me down, then. I can walk."

He only shook his head and began again, in the direction of the castle.

"I said put me down. I've never needed any man to help me, and I never will. I can manage on my own."

"You needed the help of a man tonight, Rhiannon. No doubt if you continue in your reckless life-style, you'll need it again. And you need it now, whether you'll admit it or not, so rest in my arms and be quiet."

She did settle more comfortably against him, but the set of her lips told him the argument was far from over. "I will, but only because I know the truth. You're carrying me because you like it. You like the way my body feels so close to yours. As for my needing the help of a male, you are completely wrong. I was only waiting for the right moment to rip that fool's head from his shoulders. I'm as capable as any male, mortal or immortal, young or old, and you ought not forget it.''

Roland rolled his eyes. "I thought at least to get a word of thanks for saving your life. Instead, I get scolded for daring to assume you were in need of assistance.''

She was silent for a moment, considering his words, he thought. "All right, I suppose I owe you my thanks, then. Only don't dare think of me as inferior.''

"I never have, Rhiannon.''

"That is purely a lie.''

Roland frowned, searching her upturned face as he continued carrying her through the thickening forest. Crisp leaves and fallen twigs crackled beneath his hurried steps. "Why do you say so?''

"Foolish question.''

Roland focused on the bite in her tone, rather than on the weight of her hip, or the way it slid over his abdomen with his every step. He forcibly ignored the feel of her head nestled upon his shoulder, and the softness of the rounded breast that pressed to his chest. "I believe being assaulted by DPI operatives makes you decidedly cranky.''

He saw her part her lips to reply, then she stopped herself, frowning. "I'm not sure he was DPI. At least, if he was, he was more concerned with his own interests than theirs.''

"What do you mean?''

"Roland, the man was uncommonly knowledgeable about our kind. He listed our weaknesses. He called me by name.''

Roland stopped walking, glancing ahead to the dark stone wall that completely surrounded the Castle Courtemanche. He could hear the violence of the River Tordu to his left as it splashed and roiled its way to fuse with the older, calmer waters of the River Loire. To his right, past the edge of the woods, a cool, green meadow rolled like a carpet from the outer wall to the winding dirt road. But the aromas of the grasses, of the rivers, of the very night, faded beside the scent of Rhiannon's hair and skin.

Roland shook himself and honed his senses, searching for the presence of others. They'd made excellent time, but he feared DPI forces would be on their way.

"Roland, you aren't listening. I scanned, and found no sign of this man, though he was lying in ambush. He can mask his presence, block us out."

Roland nodded. "It was only a matter of time before they learned that simple trick, Rhiannon. It shouldn't alarm you."

"He ordered me to transform him."

Roland froze, a chill of precognition tiptoeing up his spine. "That's ridiculous. He couldn't be transformed unless he was one of The Chosen. Anyone working for DPI would know that—"

"Which can only mean he *is* one of The Chosen. Roland, we should have felt his presence. He has somehow sharpened his psychic abilities. The man is dangerous."

Roland recalled again the shock of pain that had lanced through him when he'd felt Rhiannon's mind reaching out to him back at the stadium. He recalled the rage he'd felt when he'd seen the bastard holding her, that knife piercing her sensitive skin, the blade twisting as she gasped in pain, the tears shimmering over her eyes.

"You ought to have let me kill him."

She stilled utterly, searching his face. "You very nearly did, Roland. I've never seen you like that."

"With good reason." He glanced down at her. He wished to God she hadn't witnessed the ugliness inside him. But now that she had, there was little use in denying it. "I'm a man capable of great violence, Rhiannon. There lurks within me a demon, one who thrives on bloodshed."

She frowned, sable eyebrows bunching over her small, narrow nose. "I've known you from the first moment of your preternatural existence, Roland. I've never seen a sign of this demon."

"I keep it in check, or I have, until now." He gazed at her beautiful, flawless face. Why was control so much more difficult when she was near? She was like a magnet, drawing the beast from its hidden lair, stirring it to life by her very presence. "It was in me before, Rhiannon, when I was yet a mortal."

"You were a knight! One known far and wide for courage and valor and—"

"All pretty words for bloodlust. I was talented in the art of battle. A skillful killer. No more."

She stiffened in his arms. "You're wrong about yourself. This demon you claim possesses you is no more than the will to live. Those times were violent, and only the violent survived. In battle, a man must kill or be killed. You did what was necessary..." She winced all at once, and clung more tightly to his neck.

His knowledge of her discomfort was as acute as if the pain were his own. "Press the handkerchief more tightly, Rhiannon. The bleeding is beginning again." He strengthened his hold on her and ran the last few steps to the wall, leaping easily over it. Now was no time for recriminations or confessions. Not while her very life was slowly seeping from her body. Oddly enough, Roland felt as if his vitality were draining away, as well, keeping perfect pace with hers.

He carried her over the barren courtyard, past the crumbling fountain that marked its center and through the huge, groaning door. He set her on her feet to pull the door closed.

The cat lunged gracefully from the lowest stair, stopped in front of her mistress and seemed almost to study her, eyes intent and intelligent. Pandora lifted her head, and sniffed delicately at Rhiannon's blood-soaked blouse, and the sound she emitted from deep in her throat could have been a snort of alarm.

"There, kitty. It's not the end of me." Rhiannon stroked the cat's head with one hand, still holding the hanky to her waist with the other.

Jamey came bounding down the stairs with Frederick on his heels. The boy stopped a yard from Rhiannon, his face setting into a granite mask no child of his age had any business wearing.

Frederick came forward, dropped to one knee in front of her and moved the handkerchief aside briefly before pressing it tight again. "It's bad. You need stitches."

"Not necessary," Roland stated, hoping to hide the effect of those words on his equilibrium. Stitches. It brought to mind the image of a sharp object piercing her sensitive skin, an object held by his hand. The pain would be incredible.

Frederick looked again and shook his head. "It isn't gonna stop bleeding."

Roland swallowed hard. Frederick had been a medic in the army before he'd succumbed to the mental illness that kept him so childlike. The man knew a bit about injuries. Still, the thought of the pain... "She needs only rest."

"Nonsense," Rhiannon said softly. "I can rest, but the regenerative sleep will only come with the dawn. I doubt I can keep from bleeding to death until then."

At her words, Roland felt a fist in his stomach. Reckless and irritating though she was, he could not see her die. Even the thought was too much to bear. He glanced once more at Frederick. "Can you do it?"

Frederick's blue eyes widened and he shook his head. It was obvious the very idea scared him to death.

"You'll have to stitch it up, Roland." Rhiannon's voice was steady and firm, but he heard the underlying weakness. "There must be a needle somewhere in this place. You can use the silk thread from my blouse. It's ruined, anyway."

He met her slowly clouding gaze and knew she was right. The specterlike image of the needle, wielded by his own hands, inflicting what would be agonizing pain on her sickened him. He stiffened his resolve. He would do what must be done.

"I'll bring a needle," Frederick said softly. He turned and lumbered up the curving stone stairs, hugging the wall as if afraid of falling should he walk too near the open side.

Roland swept Rhiannon up once again. He turned toward the vaulted corridor to the west wing. Jamey's voice, low and trembling, stopped him. "It was Rogers, wasn't it?"

Rhiannon's head rose from his shoulder as Roland turned to face the angry boy. "No, Jamison," she told him. "It was not. It was a man I've never seen before."

"Was he DPI?"

She sighed. "I can't be certain."

Jamey's gaze met Roland's then. "Did you kill him?"

"No."

"He would have, though," Rhiannon put in quickly, as if defending him. "I had to insist he drop the man and leave before the others discovered us there."

"Killing him would have solved nothing, Jamison. It would only have brought more trouble."

Jamey shook his head slowly. "Not good enough." His gaze again met Roland's and there was an intensity burning in the young eyes that gave him cause to shudder. Like looking into a mirror and seeing his own youth. "Doesn't matter," Jamey said. He glanced back at Pandora, and simply tilted his head. Then he walked ahead of them down the corridor, with the cat leaping to keep up with him.

Roland frowned. "Did you see that?"

Rhiannon, still staring down the dim corridor after the two, shook her head. "He is communicating with my kitten."

She sounded as if she disliked the idea.

Rhiannon grated her teeth and squeezed her eyes tightly. Roland's hands trembled as he poked the needle into her skin, and pulled another tight knot in the thread. He snipped the thread with tiny scissors, and bent over her to begin again.

She wore a cream-colored camisole, stained with her own blood. Roland had deftly removed her ruined blouse and her skirt. She lay on her back on Roland's bed. Of course, it wasn't really his bed. He only kept one in his chamber for appearance's sake. She'd had a brief moment to be grateful he kept it made up with fresh linens and a fluffy down comforter, before this torture had begun.

Roland sat upon the bed's edge, grim-faced. Jamey stood at the opposite side. After the first stitch and Rhiannon's breathless reaction to it, the boy had gripped her hand. She squeezed it harder with each jolt of pain, then reminded herself not to crush his mortal bones to dust.

"This is my fault. I shouldn't have made you take me to that game."

Rhiannon shook her head quickly. "I was the one who insisted you go, and I don't regret it a bit." Her teeth clamped down on her lower lip as the needle was plied once more. She felt beads of icy sweat upon her forehead. "You played wonderfully, Jamey. I thoroughly enjoyed myself."

"You could have been killed."

"No danger of that with Roland around." Again a jab, and again she sucked in a sharp breath. "Of course, protecting helpless women is old hat to him."

"You are hardly helpless, Rhiannon," Roland stated, but his lips were set in a thin line as he worked.

"He was a knight. Did you know that?" She had to say something, anything to distract Jamey from the bitter fury she sensed overwhelming him, and to distract herself from her own suffering. It was unfair for one to be so strong and yet so weak. And though she tried to disguise her agony from both of them, she knew she was failing utterly. Roland's face grew more pale and the hatred in Jamison's eyes increased with every gasp she drew.

Her effort to distract the boy seemed to work, for Jamey's eyes widened. For once, he lost the look of a haunted young man, and looked like a boy, filled with wonder. "A knight? With armor and swords, and all that?"

"Yes. He was knighted by King Louis VII, for heroism. But he's never told me the entire story." She squeezed her eyes tightly against hot tears as the needle poked again. She wanted to hear the tale, she realized. It would alleviate some of the pain. More over, she sensed Roland needed to tell it.

He shot her a look meant to quell her, but she responded with a quick shake of her head.

"Will you tell us now, Roland?"

Roland glanced quickly at Jamey.

"Yes, I wish you would," a deep voice boomed from beyond the open door. Rhiannon looked up quickly to see a large, handsome man, and a petite woman with a head of long, dark curls and perfectly round, doe's eyes. Immortals, both of them.

"Eric." Roland stood at once, dropping his implement of torture to the bedside stand. The two men met in the center of the room and embraced as if they were brothers. Jamey ran to the woman, who wrapped her arms around him and began sniffling like some simpering human.

From the corner of her eye, Rhiannon saw Pandora crouch. The cat's teeth became visible as her lip curled away from them in a menacing snarl. Her claws extended to a dangerous length, and her haunches tensed as she prepared to spring upon the woman holding Jamey.

There was no time to shout a warning. Rhiannon lunged from the bed, landing awkwardly upon the cat, clinging tightly to her neck. The stitches Roland had painstakingly administered tore free, and she cried out in excruciating pain.

The soft-looking female flung herself away from Jamey, and fell to her knees beside Rhiannon. Pandora struggled free of Rhiannon's weakened grasp, but was firmly caught again by Jamey. Then Roland was scooping her back into the bed, swearing under his breath.

"Mind telling us what the hell is going on, old friend?"

Roland didn't look at Eric. His tortured gaze remained on Rhiannon's face. He swept her hair out of her eyes and smoothed it back. "We had a little run-in with DPI. I'll fill you in later." Roland searched for his needle, and tried to thread it without success. Through the burning tears, Rhiannon saw the violence with which his hands trembled.

The small woman touched his shoulder. "Let me."

Sighing in unmistakable relief, Roland surrendered the implements, and got to his feet. The woman took his place on the bed at her side. "I'm Tamara."

"Rhiannon," she said through grated teeth. "And I'll have no more of that needle."

Tamara frowned and glanced down at the wound, bending to push the camisole up, out of the way. "Doesn't look like you have a choice." Her head swung around sharply when the cat stepped up and sniffed at her hand. Jamey still held the panther by the diamond-studded collar.

"Pandora, my cat," Rhiannon supplied, her voice weakening by the second.

"What are you doing here?" Roland's voice was clipped as he addressed Eric. "The village is swarming with DPI agents."

"Yes, that's why we've come. We thought you might need reinforcements."

"But how did you know?"

Tamara bit her lip as she applied the needle. "I have a friend, Hilary Garner, who still works for them. She's kept us informed. DPI knows you're in the area, but not about the castle. Not yet, anyway."

Rhiannon shook her head. The woman worked swiftly, and steadily. It would soon be over, at least she could be certain of that much. "Curtis Rogers knows. He was at the front gate only last night."

"Curt is here?" Tamara's skin paled, and her hand stilled briefly.

"Not at the moment. I sent him on a wild-goose chase."

"If Rogers knows, he's keeping it to himself," Eric said, his voice low and dangerous. "No doubt he wants to exact his revenge single-handedly."

Tamara looked up suddenly, her gaze meeting Jamey's across the room. Her eyes took on a troubled expression. "Enough talk about Curt and DPI. I, for one, am dying to hear this medieval tale. Roland, a knight? No wonder you ooze such chivalrous charm."

Rhiannon shot a narrow look toward Tamara. She disliked this fledgling's open flirting.

"I was a knight. There is little else to tell." Roland's expression was guarded.

"I doubt that is the case, Roland," Eric said.

"Doubt all you like. There is little else I care to tell, then. Leave it."

His clipped tone left no question as to his stand on the topic. Eric's brows rose, but he nodded. "If that's what you wish."

Tamara put one final stitch into Rhiannon's side, tied the knot and set the needle aside. Rhiannon sighed loudly. "Thank God that is over."

"Lie still until dawn, Rhiannon. If you tear them out before then, I'll have to do it all over again."

Rhiannon was stunned. Was this mere fledgling threatening her? Her? Rhiannon? Princess of Egypt?

Then the slip of a thing glanced down at her and winked. "It's late. Jamey, you ought to be getting to bed."

To Rhiannon's surprise, Jamey didn't argue with Tamara. He nodded, and glanced toward a chair in a corner, where Freddy already slumped, snoring.

Eric had a crackling fire blazing in the hearth, behind the protective screen. Rhiannon lay still in the oversize bed, and Roland thought even she looked small in its billowing folds and covers. He hadn't seen Tamara since the death of Jamey's mother, eight months ago. Tamara and Kathryn Bryant had been friends before Tamara's transformation, so the young one had taken it hard. He still saw that pain lingering in her eyes. Along with it, he saw her worry for Jamey.

"He's so different. So...full of anger."

"Most of it aimed at DPI, and Curtis Rogers in particular," Roland told her. "It troubles me. And it troubles me still further to leave the boy unguarded by day. Except for Frederick, there is no one to watch over him."

"Well, we can solve that problem, for the moment at least."

Roland frowned at Eric's statement. "What on earth do you mean?"

"I've been experimenting with a new drug, a sort of a super-charged amphetamine. By using it, I can remain awake and alert by day."

"In sunlight?" Roland was amazed. True, he'd known of Eric's passion for test tubes and chemicals, but he'd never dreamed of results such as this.

"No, I need to remain shielded from the sun."

Rhiannon sat up slightly only to have Tamara, ever attentive, sit beside her and help her into an upright position. As she bent to tuck more pillows behind her, the young one said, "There are side effects, Roland. Without the benefit of the regenerative sleep, he gets weak, tired, not to mention damned irritable."

"Never mind that," Roland said quickly. "You'll give me this drug, and I'll be able to guard Jamey by day."

"I'll guard him myself, Roland. Until we think of a better solution."

Roland shook his head quickly. "No. It is my responsibility—"

"You can both do it," Tamara interrupted. "Take turns, for heaven's sake."

Rhiannon sighed hard and shook her head. "A fine solution, but a temporary one. I believe you are all overlooking the obvious."

Roland moved nearer the bedside. Her face still twisted with pain whenever she moved, but besides that, she seemed to be holding her own. "What is it, Rhiannon?"

"Somewhere on the planet, the boy has a father, does he not?"

Her words were a blade in his heart. "A...father?" He shot a questioning glance at Tamara.

"Kathryn's husband left her before Jamey was born. He might not even know he has a son. His name was James. James Adam Knudson." She shook her head. "I wouldn't know where to begin searching for him."

"Not that it matters. A man who would abandon a wife and child has no right to reclaim either one of them." Roland stalked away from Rhiannon. She didn't argue the point. And no one again suggested that Jamey might be better off with his natural parent.

Roland filled his friends in on what had happened at the stadium, and Rhiannon told them of the strange man who'd attacked her, and his demands.

* * *

Toward dawn, Eric took Tamara down to the dungeons, to one of the hidden resting places Roland had at the ready. After hours of discussion, Eric had finally agreed to allow Roland to take the drug, and remain awake through the daylight hours to watch over Jamey. He'd given Roland three vials of fluid, to be taken at four-hour intervals, beginning well before the lethargy began to steal over him.

Roland swallowed the first of them, grimacing at the bitter taste. He tucked the empty vial into a pocket, and climbed the stairs to check in on Jamey and Frederick. Pandora lay at the foot of Jamey's bed. Jamey slept peacefully.

He returned to his chambers. There was still an hour before dawn. He found Rhiannon still in his bed, though she'd obviously been up briefly. Long enough to "borrow" one of his white shirts, and shed the bloodstained camisole, along with every other scrap of clothing she'd worn. She lay on her side, giving him an optimum view of the long, slender leg exposed beneath the shirt's hem.

"When dawn approaches, I'll take you below."

She rolled onto her back, wincing slightly with the action, and bending one knee. "I've no desire to rest my bones in a dungeon."

"Rhiannon, it isn't safe here." He turned to pace away from her. "Hasn't this incident taught you a thing about caution?"

"Posh, Roland, this is a perfectly secure place to rest. Draw those musty old drapes of yours, bolt the door, and there you are. Indulge me just this once. I promise I won't make a habit of napping here and disturbing your precious solitude."

"With everyone milling about the castle, my solitude has long since been shot to hell, as the expression goes. Here, my dear, is the only place you'll be napping in the foreseeable future. I want you where I can be sure you're safe."

She bit her lower lip as if to think it over. He knew the tone of command in his voice would rankle her. Still, he wouldn't have her in some insecure little house so near a village overrun with DPI operatives.

"It's true that my main source of security is Pandora. With her guarding Jamey, I might be vulnerable in my usual place. I might consider staying here…"

"There is nothing to consider. You're staying."

"There are conditions, Roland."

He lifted his brows. "Conditions?"

"For one, I will sleep here, in the bed. If you're so worried about my well-being, you can simply climb in beside me. Should anyone attack me as I rest, I have no doubt one of us would rouse enough to summon Pandora, who would make them into catnip. Besides, if this new drug of Eric's works, one of you will be awake, anyway."

Roland shook his head slowly. "I will concede to that request, so long as you will give it up should there be an added threat, or reason to believe DPI can reach us here."

She nodded once. "I'm not finished. I simply cannot rest in a place that looks like this. So, you will allow me to spruce it up a bit."

Frowning, he moved nearer, and sat on the edge of the bed. "Your conditions are piling high. Surely you do not envision yourself a chatelaine."

"I envision myself comfortable, Roland. Nothing more." She lifted an arm in a sweeping gesture. "Surely you cannot mind if I wish to remove a few cobwebs and a bit of dust."

His eyes narrowed. "I know you too well to believe that is all you will do."

She shrugged, lowering her lashes over downcast eyes. "Well, I was thinking new drapes might be of use. After all, I want to be sure the sun can't penetrate by day."

He gave her a curt nod. "Drapes and dusting, then. That is the extent of it. Agreed?"

"And I wish to keep the fire." She met his gaze again, and the look in her eyes should have warned him. "It gives me that warm, cozy feeling I had when you carried me through the forest in your arms.''

"You press your advantage, Rhiannon." His voice had little force behind it. He, too, was remembering the feel of her in his arms, and of her lips upon his throat.

"Oh, but I'm not finished yet." She sat up carefully, and took his hand in two of hers, tracing invisible patterns on his palm with her nails until he shuddered. "I want you to tell me about your life before I met you. I want to know how you became a knight.''

"That is not a subject I wish to discuss."

She stared so intently he felt her tugging at the curtains that veiled his mind. "Roland, you've kept your past inside you for a very long time, and a great deal of pain along with it, I believe. You've twisted events until you've branded yourself a devil. Don't you think you might benefit from an objective opinion?''

He felt, oddly enough, an urge to tell her everything. But he feared even that Rhiannon might be repulsed if she knew the entire tale. Then he asked himself if that wouldn't be a good thing. Let her see the blackness in his soul for herself, and perhaps she would finally understand why he kept himself from her. She might even decide she no longer wanted him.

Some time later, he wondered how he had capitulated so easily. What was there about her that usurped his will?

Still, he found himself sitting with his back against the headboard, his legs stretched out over the mattress. Rhiannon snuggled down, her head resting on his thighs. He absently stroked her hair as he spoke.

"I was the youngest of four sons. It was my parents' fondest wish that I enter the monastery. In those times, there was little else for a younger son to do. My becoming a monk would bring prestige and influence to the family name.''

Her hand stroked his thigh. Her silken fingers left a fiery path. "You, a monk?" She said it as if it were laughable.

"I felt the same. So, at fourteen, I ran off, determined to make my own way. I wanted nothing more in the world than to be-

come a knight. After two weeks of scrounging myself enough
to eat, I came upon a small babe, not yet a full year of age. He
sat upon a blanket on the grass, while his mother and her ladies
gathered berries nearby. None of them saw the wolf. But I did.''

"A wolf?" Rhiannon's eyes widened and her hand stilled
upon his thigh. "Stalking the child? What did you do?"

"Froze with fear, at first. Then the babe looked toward me
and smiled. He made this gurgling, cooing sound and waved his
chubby hands in the air." Roland shook his head. "I don't know
what possessed me, but I drew my knife, the only weapon I had,
and I leapt on the wolf as it went for the child. It was a fool's
errand. I was nearly torn to shreds."

She sat up slowly, facing him. It surprised him to see her blink
fast against a moisture building in her eyes. Her face was so
near to his he could feel the quickening of her breaths. "Did
you kill this wolf, Roland?"

"Yes, apparently so. I don't remember much after the first
few bites." She closed her eyes and shuddered visibly. Her hair
fell over one eye, and without thinking, Roland reached out, and
moved it aside. His fingers lingered on her face, so soft. He
thought he might be absorbed in her eyes, those huge, exotically
slanted, jet orbs. "When next I woke, I was in a fine bed, being
tended by servants. The child was the grandson of a great baron,
and the son of a knight. Sir Gareth of Le Blanc. He took me as
his squire when I was healed. For two years, he treated me
almost as a son. He taught me all he knew, and allowed me to
train with the knights in his outer bailey."

"And you, with your stubborn determination, which I know
so well, took to that training with a vengeance. You grew
stronger and more skilled with each passing day."

He shrugged. "I did pick up some basic skills."

"Tell me the rest." She was like a child asking for a story,
he thought idly, his fingers still stroking her hair.

"I was traveling with Sir Gareth one day. There was a tour-
nament he was to attend. Of course, there were others along,
knights and their squires who rode with us. A band of knights

loyal to a sworn enemy of Gareth's father were waiting in ambush.''

She said nothing. But she lifted her hand to touch his face, almost as if she could see the pain of the memory there. "Gareth and the others fought fiercely, and killed several of them, but they were outnumbered." He shook his head slowly, and the past resurfaced as if it were yesterday. The clang of steel upon steel. The shouts and groans of the fallen men. The frantic shrieks of the horses. The pounding hooves.

"When Gareth fell...something happened to me. I don't know what. I found myself dragging him off the battlefield, into the brush, and pulling the helmet and mail coif from his head. With his last breath, he pushed his sword into my hands, and bade me fight on."

"But you were just a boy!"

He shook his head. "Sixteen was near enough to manhood in those times, Rhiannon. You know that. I demanded the other squires assist me as I removed Gareth's breastplate and hauberk, and put them on. It seemed to take forever, but we accomplished the task in minutes. I donned his coif and helmet, and pulled Gareth's gauntlets onto my hands. With his sword in my grip, and a layer of ice coating my heart, I marched straight into the melee. I was driven by a force I didn't know. It was the demon I've since discovered in my soul.

"I found my master's horse, a massive destrier with a taste for battle, and mounted him."

"And you fought in his place," she breathed.

"More than fought. I was enraged. I remember little, other than the endless swinging of the broadsword, and the shattering impact of it when it hit home. I remember the sounds, the screams of the fallen, and my own battle cry. I was a man possessed, Rhiannon. When the battle ended, I alone remained. Dead men surrounded me."

He shook himself of the memory, and gazed into Rhiannon's eyes. He was shocked to see a single tear roll slowly over her face. He leaned forward, for some inexplicable reason, and pressed his lips to it, absorbing its salty taste.

"I've never told this story to another living soul, Rhiannon." His lips moved against her dampened cheek as he whispered the words, and her fingers threaded in his hair.

"Nor will I," she promised. "Not on pain of death." She lowered her head to his shoulder. "What happened next?"

"The squires had scattered, but not far enough that they hadn't witnessed the battle. When we returned to the castle of Gareth's father, they told of what they'd seen. I was treated as some sort of hero. It wasn't long before I was summoned to the court of King Louis, who was a second cousin to Gareth's father, the baron. I was knighted as a reward for what they called valor. I had my wish. But I no longer wanted it. I wanted only to return to my family, and never experience such violence again."

"And did you?"

He forced a smile for her. Her eyelids were drooping. Apparently, Eric's potion was working, for he felt no hint of tiredness. "I'll save the rest of the tale for another night, Rhiannon. You need to sleep now. And heal."

She shook her head as she lifted it from his shoulder. "You loved this Gareth. It is no wonder you fought as you did. Your grief gave you this rage, not some demon."

He closed his eyes, and wished he could believe it were the truth. "Rest, Rhiannon. We'll talk more when you wake."

She lowered herself into the bed until her head again lay in his lap, and her arms encircled his waist. It was exceedingly strange, he thought, that he felt comfortable with her there so close, rather than disturbed. Moreover, the weight on his heart seemed somehow lighter than it had before.

CHAPTER SIX

As she felt herself falling steadily into the leaden, replenishing sleep, Rhiannon felt the hard length of his thigh beneath her head. For once, she had no desire to seduce him. In fact, she felt closer to Roland than she ever had, and he hadn't so much as kissed her.

A strange turn of events, since she knew full well her feelings for him were only physical in nature.

Still, it was nice, this closeness, this sharing. It felt right, in some way.

It also troubled her. She'd been determined to demonstrate to him that she was as worthy as any male on the planet. She'd been ready to show him she could be just as brave, just as fierce, just as strong. She'd wanted to be certain he could no longer reject her on grounds similar to those her father had used. That she was not good enough.

Now, knowing of his unstinting courage and ferocity in battle, even as a boy, she would have to try harder than ever. A man of such valor would not be easily impressed. A man who, as a mere boy, had thrown himself upon a wolf to save a babe...this was pure heroism, whatever he chose to call it. This would require some thinking.

Before the cloak of blackness settled completely over her mind, she felt the wonderful sensation of his hand cupping her face, his fingers tracing its shape. She smiled...and then she slept.

Roland studied her as she rested, but he couldn't see well enough from his present position. He slid himself from beneath her, and rose. Standing beside the bed, he could gaze down at her face to his heart's content. God, but she was a beauty. Every delicate bone beneath her satin skin delineated and shaped her face to sheer perfection.

He was suddenly, overwhelmingly, besieged with the urge to paint her portrait. He longed all at once for a brush in his hand, and the smooth feel of oils as he spread them over canvas.

Ah, but that was foolish thinking. Painting was a mortal pursuit. Something best done beneath the sun's golden rays and caressing warmth. It was not the pastime of undead, restless souls.

What was it about her that brought out such urges? By the gods, he'd actually stood in a crowded stadium and cheered on a school soccer team last night! He'd dressed in denims and a sweatshirt, and he'd placed himself into a crowd with countless DPI agents milling about. When was the last time he'd participated in anything so foolish?

He shook his head. She did have a way of reducing a man to the role of willing servant. Even him.

He knew it beyond any doubt, when, a few seconds later, he gripped her shoulders and rolled her from her side onto her back. She was so perfect. He had to see her, just see her. Though he had no intention of indulging himself in the luxury of reproducing her image on canvas, he could at least appreciate what was here before him.

He reached for the shirtfront, and hesitated. Was it wrong to look at her this way, as she rested, helpless to object?

He closed his eyes. No. Rhiannon wouldn't object in the least.

He released the buttons, the few she'd bothered to fasten. Slowly, very slowly, he parted the garment until her body was revealed to him. His sigh was involuntary, and indicative of how much he'd longed to look at her this way.

His gaze traced her arching, graceful neck to the delicately etched collarbones. Lower, to her small, proud breasts, perfectly round and lily-white. Their centers were the subtle color of the meat of a sweet melon. Their nipples pouted. He wouldn't paint her that way, though. If he were intending to capture her image, he'd tease them taut first, so they thrust outward, tempting a man's lips to touch them.

The way he was tempted now. Just to capture one soft bud between his lips, to suckle it until it became hard, until it throbbed against his tongue.

He swallowed hard against the onslaught of desire, and resumed his perusal of her form, letting his gaze move lower, over the gentle swell of her belly, the dark hollow of her navel, the narrow curve of her waist with the painful wound on one side, the soft flare of her hips. The triangle of sable curls. God, it gleamed like satin. He wanted to touch it, to see if it could truly be as soft as it looked.

Before he could tell himself not to, he was doing just that. His fingers settled themselves into the silken nest. Yes. It was as soft as it appeared. Softer. And though he knew he should not, he moved his fingers lower, parting her secret lips, delving into her. When he felt the answering moistness coat his fingers, he closed his eyes and groaned aloud. He sunk onto the bed, leaning nearer. Her subtle scent reached him and he shuddered. He moved his fingers deeper, then slowly drew them back. Her body trembled, and he looked up quickly.

She lay exactly as she had, perfectly still. But her nipples stood stiff and aroused now. He brought his fingers to his lips, his eyes closing involuntarily as he sucked the taste of her from their tips. He wanted her. More than wanted her, he had to have her. If not physically, then at least...

Roland stepped away from the bed, but his gaze remained. He had to capture her on canvas. There was no other way to rid himself of this all-consuming lust. True, he hadn't painted in a very long time. He'd lost the desire, or perhaps the ability to pour his soul onto a rectangle of canvas. Suddenly, now, that desire returned. He'd never thought to feel it again.

Today, this once, he would put brush to canvas. And when his little bird took wing, he'd have a bit of her here, with him.

In the hours of earliest dawn, behind the tightly drawn draperies and beneath a cobweb-draped ceiling, Roland worked with materials that had long ago been packed away in trunks. The oils were newer. He'd been unable to resist buying the new, modern paints whenever he'd seen them. It had become a ritual of self-torment, knowing they were at hand, and wondering if he'd ever feel moved to use them. Now, the smell of the paints in his nostrils was like a drug, and his brush flew over the canvas as an extension of his soul.

He didn't sketch her first. He didn't need to do so. He needed only to look at her, stretched upon the bed like an offering to the gods, and allow his image of her to transfer itself from his eyes to his mind to his hands.

He worked feverishly, losing himself utterly in the act of creation in a way he had not done in years. His hands moved the brush with a touch as gentle as if he were caressing her skin.

And then, almost before he'd been aware a minute had passed, he sensed movement in the castle. Jamey was awake, and Frederick. Even now they were making their way down to the great hall, and then off to the lower east wing, where the kitchens awaited them.

He sighed, saddened at having to give up so soon. He'd forgotten the delight he could feel in such a simple act. He'd accomplished so little. The shapes and colors on the canvas were not recognizable. But he knew they'd take form, gradually, over the next several days.

He reluctantly cleaned his brushes and put his paints away. The canvas, he left, to allow it to dry. He'd be sure it was stored safely long before Rhiannon stirred tonight. Not that he thought she would mind him so closely studying her nude form as she rested. He rather thought the idea would please her.

Lastly, he went to the bed, gazing once more at her nakedness. The length and firmness of her legs enticed him, with flickering images of those shapely limbs wrapped around his body, those curving hips pumping against him.

He was aroused. Painfully so. He realized that he had been the entire time he'd been painting. He closed his eyes and tried not to think that he could strip off his clothing and slip into the bed with her. He could fondle her, touch her, taste her to his heart's content, and she would never know. He could bury himself inside her. He could find release in her succulent moistness, and she'd never be the wiser.

He bent over, blowing a cool breath of air across her breasts, to see the nipples stand hard once more. Her response was immediate. Perhaps he could even bring her to climax without her being aware of it.

The thought was enticing—no, maddening. To elicit the ultimate response from her body without the awareness of her mind. By night, he could remain as resistant to her charms as he wished. By day, she could be his to pleasure.

The temptation was great, nearly too great. He took a firm grip on his mind, realizing that once again the beast inside was trying to take over. To use Rhiannon in such a way would be rape. Whether he knew she wouldn't object or not was not the issue. To take her without her consent would be unforgivable. Was this the way he would repay her for the sheer joy she'd given him?

Joy?

Roland blinked, replaying his own thoughts. Yes. Joy was what he'd felt for those brief hours this morning while he'd been painting. And earlier, when he'd watched Jamey fight his way to victory in the soccer match. He'd felt joy then, too. Absolute pleasure. Delight.

He hadn't thought himself capable of feeling any of those things anymore.

He looked at her face, and shook his head. Who'd have thought a reckless, out of control, renegade vampiress like Rhiannon could instigate the return of pleasure in his life?

He pulled the shirt together, and fastened the buttons. He tugged the comforter over her, then bent low, and pressed his lips to hers. They were moist and pliant and sweet, even in sleep. He slipped his tongue inside her mouth, tasting every part of it, only stopping when he felt madness trying to engulf him.

"Thank you, Rhianikki, princess of the Nile."

* * *

Roland was nowhere about when she rose. But she wrinkled her nose at the very slight scent in the air. She sniffed again, and frowned. It smelled a little like paint.

Unable to positively identify the lingering odor, she rolled out of the bed before she gave the wound at her waist a thought. She stiffened as she remembered it, half expecting to be pummeled by pain at any second. She wasn't, though, and when she parted the shirt she wore, she saw that the wound was gone without a trace. Only the tiny stitches remained. The area wasn't even sore.

She got to her feet and strolled about the chambers, whipping open wardrobes and peering into closets in search of something to wear. She didn't find anything, but decided not to let it dampen her spirits. She felt good this evening.

After hearing him talk last night, she'd come to the conclusion that Roland was suffering from a ridiculously prolonged state of depression and a severe guilt complex. But since he'd opened up that painful wound and allowed her to see a little of what caused it, he might be better able to heal. And that thought brought her pleasure. She hated to see him tormenting himself over things long past. It was a waste of his time and his energies. Besides, he ought to be spending both on her. It would be a far more exciting exercise.

The door opened and he entered then, bringing with him a heavy decanter made of lead crystal and filled with crimson liquid. He placed it on a stand, and a glass beside it.

She frowned. "What is this?"

"Nourishment. You need it, after last night."

"What I need is warm, and drawn straight from some innocent throat, Roland."

"Rhiannon, that is murder."

"Still perfectly willing to believe the worst of me, I see." She strode toward him, the shirt gaping in a way he could not fail to notice. "I never murder them. I only taste. A sip here, a sip there. It isn't missed.'' She was teasing him, and delighting in it as she always did.

His gaze seemed drawn to the swell of her breasts the shirt revealed, so she stepped closer, and bent low to reach for the decanter.

"But if they remember—"

"I take from men as they sleep, Roland. Most of them recall it as an erotic dream.'' She filled the glass, straightened again, and brought it to her lips.

"And the marks you leave on their throats?''

"It isn't necessary to mark the throats. Blood can be taken from any number of places, some that are difficult to examine too closely.'' She drained the glass and set it down, licking her lips. "Would you like me to show you?''

He averted his gaze, she hoped, to hide a sudden surge of passion. "No, Rhiannon, I wouldn't. And I would strongly suggest that you feed as we do, from our own supply here. It will not do to rouse undue suspicion with so many DPI operatives in L'Ombre.''

She stepped closer, and ran her fingernails up the column of his throat. "Or is it that you dislike the thought of my lips touching another man's flesh?''

He met her gaze and held it for a moment.

She licked her lips. "I had the most interesting dream as I rested.''

He quickly looked away. "Did you?''

"Mmm. It isn't often I dream, you know. The sleep is too deep. But this time...I felt things.''

"What sort of things?''

She shrugged. "It was very brief. A touch, an incredibly intimate touch. And later, a delicious kiss.''

He turned from her, and she knew he was guarding his thoughts. "Very strange, indeed.''

"Perhaps it is only that I so long for such things.'' She walked up behind him, so when she spoke, her breath would fan the back of his neck. "If only you would oblige me, I might sleep more soundly, Roland."

His back went rigid. "I'm sorry, Rhiannon. I don't think it would be wise."

She sniffed. He still wasn't impressed enough with her. He still thought her unworthy of his attention. She stepped around in front of him. "My wound needs attending. Will you at least assist me with that?"

His brows bunched with immediate worry, and when she strode away, toward the bed, he followed on her heels. "What is it, Rhiannon? Hasn't it healed yet?"

She sat on the bed's edge, then leaned back, flipping the shirt open to reveal her waist, her hip, and the lower edge of one breast. "It's healed, but I wish you would snip away the threads. They itch."

Roland closed his eyes briefly. When he opened them again, he seemed to have become a mannequin. No emotion showed in his eyes. "Of course." He located the scissors on the nightstand, and pulled up a stool, sitting so his head was more or less level with the mattress. His hand touched the spot on her waist, and stilled. Slowly, he stroked his fingers over the area.

She closed her eyes. "It feels so good when you touch me."

He drew his hand away, and brought the tiny scissors to her flesh. Carefully, he snipped the threads.

"Even when I was asleep, it felt good. You did touch me, Roland, didn't you? It wasn't a dream."

He finished the job, set the scissors aside, and got to his feet. "I'm going out to check the grounds." She felt waves of frustration emanating from him. Why was he so determined to resist her?

"I'll come with you."

"I'll go alone. Jamison is with Eric and Tamara in the great hall. You might ask him for something to wear. Eric and I will fetch some of your own things for you, later on."

She was immediately angry. "I am capable of fetching my own things, Roland. Furthermore, I'm not about to stay where I am so obviously not wanted. Perhaps I'll rest in my own bed tomorrow.''

He said nothing, only walked out of the room. Rhiannon picked up the glass from the stand and hurled it against the wall, where it smashed to bits.

She heard a small laugh and then Tamara appeared in the doorway Roland had just exited. ''You find my anger amusing, fledgling? You wouldn't, were it directed at you.''

Tamara shook her head and stepped inside. ''I'm not laughing at you, Rhiannon. Don't be so defensive. It's just that Eric has made me feel like throwing things a time or two.''

Rhiannon tossed her head. ''He could never have been as purely maddening as Roland is.'' She strode to the hearth and bent to toss a log onto the barely glowing sparks.

''He wouldn't make love to me when we both wanted it so badly we were going slowly insane,'' Tamara confided.

Rhiannon straightened, but didn't turn. ''What was *his* reason?''

''He thought I would be repulsed when I learned what he was.''

''And were you?''

''I loved him. It took a while, but I finally convinced him of it. Be patient with Roland. Don't give up.''

Rhiannon whirled to face the little thing. ''You don't think I'm in love with him, do you? My God, Tamara, I am not nearly so foolish as to allow that to happen.''

Tamara smiled. ''Of course not. Then, you're only interested in a fling?''

Rhiannon's gaze fell. ''I want him. There is nothing wrong in that.'' She frowned. ''Except for his exceeding stubbornness.''

''Does he give you some well thought-out reason for abstaining?''

Rhiannon shook her head. ''Only some nonsense about what one wants not always being what is good for one. I know the true reason. He thinks I'm not good enough. He'll soon learn better." Rhiannon searched the room for her skirt, and shed Roland's shirt, only to reach for a fresh one.

"Why on earth do you say that?"

"Because it is true." She found the skirt and stepped into it, fastening a few of the buttons, and then tucking the shirttails into it.

"That's crazy. You're the most attractive woman I've ever seen."

Rhiannon turned to face her. Perhaps the little fledgling wasn't as bad as she had first thought. "And you are indomitably cheerful."

She smiled. "Why shouldn't I be? I get to spend eternity with the man I love."

Rhiannon rolled her eyes. "Must you be so human?" She hunted for her shoes, found them and slipped them on. "Tell Roland I'll return before dawn."

She felt Tamara's rush of alarm at her announcement. "Rhiannon, where are you going?"

"To my house, to fetch some clothing."

"You shouldn't. It isn't safe, there are DPI—"

"Too bad for them if they get in my way. I'm in no mood for it tonight."

She moved toward the door, but the bold little thing grabbed her arm. "Rhiannon, please wait. There's something I need to say to you."

Rhiannon tilted her head to one side. "Say it, then. I'm in a hurry."

"It's about…the man who held you prisoner, in his lab in Connecticut."

"Daniel St. Claire?"

Tamara nodded. "Yes. He…he was my guardian. He adopted me after my parents were killed." Tamara swallowed hard as Rhiannon frowned. "I learned later that their deaths were planned. He only wanted custody of me to try to lure Eric in for live research. I know what happened to you—I read about it in his files, after he died. And, those other two he held, as well. I'm...I'm sorry.''

Compelled by Tamara's honesty, Rhiannon reached out one hand to ruffle the young one's curls. ''You have nothing to be sorry for, Tamara. These things happened before you were born. You're lucky you survived.''

''I don't know if I would've, if it hadn't been for Eric.'' She licked her lips. ''I loved Daniel like a parent for a long time, even after Eric tried to tell me the truth about him. I hope—''

''That I do not hate you for it,'' Rhiannon finished, reading the young one's thoughts. ''Rest assured, I do not.''

Tamara smiled, her eyes slightly damp. ''I'd like to be your friend.''

Rhiannon blinked fast, angry at the ridiculous lump that came into her throat. ''I don't believe I've ever had one of those.''

''Not even Roland?''

Rhiannon laughed. ''No, most especially not him. He doesn't even like me.''

''I think you're wrong about that. When we came in last night, it looked as if his seeing you in pain was killing him.''

''Really?'' Rhiannon's brows lifted and she felt something silly warm her insides. She caught herself. ''Listen to us, gibbering about males like a pair of giggling teenage mortals. We are above it, Tamara. Goddesses among women.''

''But women, all the same,'' Tamara replied.

Rhiannon frowned, considering that. Then she shook her head. ''I must go. I have much to do tonight. Some shopping, even.''

''Shopping? But, Rhiannon, the DPI—''

''Posh, let them chase me through the stores if they think they can keep up. I extracted permission from Roland to clean these chambers up a bit, and hang new drapes. I further intend to purchase enough candles to keep that chandelier glowing nightly for a year. It's like resting in a graveyard this way.''

Tamara chewed her lower lip. ''I don't blame you for wanting to spruce things up. This is like something out of an old horror movie.''

"Precisely. Besides that, my efforts will drive Roland to the point of murdering me. And I do love to torment him. Unless I hurry, the stores will close. So, farewell."

Rhiannon hurried out a rear door, leapt the wall without an effort and raced to her rental house outside L'Ombre. She wasn't a complete fool. Though she saw no sign of anyone watching the house, she took the precaution of slipping around the back. She scaled a wall, and entered through a second-story window.

She turned on no lights at all, only lit a few candles. Her night vision was excellent. She picked through her clothing until she found a short little skirt that flared when she moved, and a blouse to go with it. She packed other items into a suitcase, to take back to the castle when her errands were finished. Then she ran a hot bath until the tub was brimming, and spent a heavenly, albeit all too brief time soaking. She would have loved to linger, to burn some incense and relax, but with Roland's warnings still echoing in her mind, she didn't dare.

She'd return later for her suitcase. For now, she went over to the hidden safe and took out some of the credit cards she kept on hand. She had one more errand, an important one. She would show Roland how worthy she was before this night ended. She lifted the receiver and dialed a number she knew well.

Her agent in France, Jacques Renot, was highly paid, and utterly trustworthy. He also was an ex-DPI operative who knew how to break into their computers.

He recognized her voice at once, and she could almost hear him smiling through the phone lines. Whenever she woke him at night, it always meant a large bonus in his next check. He was worth every penny she paid him. How many others could keep track of her many aliases, her countless bank accounts? Her need for anonymity was making Jacques a very rich man.

"I need to know the name of the hotel where Curtis Rogers is staying, in L'Ombre," she said simply. "Can you get it?"

"*Oui.* It might take awhile, but—"

"I'll call you back in twenty minutes." She hung up.

It wouldn't take long to do the shopping. After all, she knew exactly what she wanted, and price was no object, so why waste time? She had important things to do.

CHAPTER SEVEN

"**S**he said she was going shopping."

Roland felt as if he would explode. Shopping! By God, Rhiannon was more than reckless. She was utterly insane! "Why the hell didn't someone come and let me know?"

Eric pulled Tamara aside and stepped in front of her, as if to guard her from Roland's anger. "I've been looking for you for two hours, Roland. I had no idea where to find you, and you ignored my summons. What more could we do?"

Roland pushed one hand through his hair, and let his eyes fall closed. "We have to find her. There are DPI operatives all over the village. And if Curtis hasn't told them about the castle, you can bet he's told them about her. They'll spot her in a second. She stands out from other women like a swan among crows."

He ignored the meaningful glance Tamara shot Eric. "Might be nice if *she* could hear you say so." Roland only shook his head. "Honestly, Roland, I don't know why you're so worried. She isn't going to do anything risky," Tamara said.

"Hah! She likes nothing better than to risk her pretty neck at every opportunity. If you knew her at all, you would be worried, too." He was racked with worry. Why on earth had he let her out of his sight after she'd been nearly killed? Why in the name of God had he thought she'd exercise some caution after that incident? Didn't he know her better? He ought to have been watching her every move. Instead, he'd deliberately closed off his mind so she wouldn't be able to track him down while he visited the little *cimetière* in the small woodlot near the castle. He'd felt a sudden need to be there, to remind himself what he'd done to his family, and to the only other woman who'd ever stirred him to this kind of madness. He'd come close to letting those sins slip his mind yesterday, and doing that would only doom him to repeat them.

As he started for the door, Eric gripped his shoulder. "I'll come with you."

He glanced through the window where Frederick and Jamey frolicked with Pandora in the safety of the courtyard.

"And leave only Tamara to watch over Jamey?"

"What do you suppose Rogers would do if he found her here with only gentle Freddy and a cat for protection?"

Tamara tossed her head, flipping her hair behind her shoulders in exactly the way Rhiannon always did. "I'm no helpless mortal," she declared. "I can take care of myself."

Eric bit his inner cheek to keep from smiling, Roland noted. "You've been around Rhiannon too much, fledgling," Roland said.

"And you haven't been around her enough," she snapped. "Either that, or you're a blind fool. She thinks you dislike her. She thinks you believe she's not good enough for you. If she does do something crazy, it will probably only be her way of trying to show you how wrong you are."

"Where on earth do you get these notions? Rhiannon believes herself good enough for God himself, to say nothing about me."

"It's not what *she* thinks that matters, it's what she believes *you* think." When he only frowned and shook his head, she fumed. "I could just shake you!"

Eric caught her shoulders and drew her back against him. "Easy, my love. You might hurt him." He glanced up at Roland. "Go on, go find your rebel. I'll keep things secure here."

Roland left the castle, but he couldn't help wondering about Tamara's words. Was there the slightest chance that Rhiannon felt she had to prove herself to him? It was utterly ridiculous, of course. But then, Rhiannon had made that remark about his seeing her as inferior. Perhaps there was some truth to Tamara's theory.

Now, though, he had no time to worry about theories or motivations. Rhiannon was out on her own, and there were at least two potentially lethal enemies lurking in the village. He needed to find her right away.

He began at the house she'd told him she was renting, just outside the village. That she'd been there was without question. The bloodstained skirt and his white shirt lay on the floor, and the tub's interior was coated in droplets announcing its recent use. The room still smelled of the scented candles she'd burned. The candle wax was still warm.

A suitcase lay on the bed, laden with clothing. He assumed she was planning to bring it back to the castle with her on the return trip, but wondered if he was assuming too much. She'd been fairly angry when he'd last seen her.

He shook his head, and checked the room thoroughly. He saw the notepad and pencil near the phone and he hurried to it. She'd written something on the top sheet, obviously. But she'd torn it off. He licked his lips, lifting the pad to the light to try to make out the indentations of the pencil. No luck. Angry, he turned to fling the thing at the wastebasket...and he saw the small bit of yellow paper, crumpled and resting atop some other rubbish. He picked it up, and smoothed it out.

There was an address, and a room number. Beneath those, underlined, one word: "Rogers."

Rhiannon saw the two men silhouetted by the lamplight. They sat in the hotel suite's front room. She clung to the windowsill, fifteen stories up, peering in at them as the sounds of traffic and mortal activity filled the night. She was at the window of a bedroom, but she could see them both clearly through the open door. For once, she wished she were older, more powerful. She longed for the power to transmute herself into a mouse, and crawl about the room that way. She'd heard there were a few who could achieve such a thing, the very ancient ones. She'd tried it herself a few times, but always only managed to give herself a walloping headache for her trouble.

She did have the ability to entrance humans. She could, possibly, lull them into a state of catatonia, and then dance through the rooms at will without arousing a response from them. But there was a chance her efforts would only result in alerting them of her presence. For the man with Curtis Rogers was the one who'd attacked her at the soccer match. And she already knew he could guard his mind from hers.

A little shiver raced over her spine as she studied his face. He was mean-looking, with a wide, pugnacious nose and a thick coating of dark stubble. He was heavy, his arms big, but not fat. He looked like one of the professional wrestlers she'd seen on cable TV a time or two. He wore his dark hair cut close to his head, in short bristles. His lips were too thick.

She listened intently, and heard little other than their voices, speaking low. She sniffed the air, and smelled the big one's sweat, and Curtis's cologne, and expensive whiskey.

Silently, she hauled herself over the edge.

"We understand each other, then?"

Curtis shrugged. Rhiannon slipped to one side, out of their range of vision should they look this way. "I don't need to understand you. If you can help me capture one of them, you can name your price."

The man shook his head. "Not just *any* one of them. Her. She's the oldest, the most powerful. It's her I want." He slugged back the whiskey in his glass and licked his lips with a fat tongue. "I want you to tranquilize her, and leave me alone with her, for as long as I need."

Curtis shook his head. He got to his feet, crossed to the bar and gripped the amber-filled bottle by its neck. "You want to screw her. You're not fooling me. Hell, I can't blame you. She's a hot one."

The other man pursed his lips and said nothing. He held his glass up when Curtis approached, and whiskey splashed into it. "Maybe I will, but that isn't my main goal. You're certain she'll be absolutely helpless?"

"Absolutely. This drug has been tested. It works." Curtis filled his own glass and paced away. "You mind if I ask why you think you can capture her when the rest of us have failed?"

"I have certain abilities. And I know their weaknesses."

"So do we."

"I know how to use them."

"Yeah, well, I can't say I have much confidence in your chances. But if you can do it, you can have her as helpless and as often as you want her."

Rhiannon shuddered at the image. She recalled too well the last time she'd been helpless at the hands of a DPI operative. Weakened from the blood they'd drained away, she could only lie there, hands and feet restrained, as they tortured and touched her.

"Then you'll tell me where they are."

She stiffened, listening.

Curtis hesitated. "There are others that interest me, besides her. They're mine. Mine alone, you understand?"

"Perfectly." He chuckled and the sound made her shiver. "You have special plans for them, no doubt. I wouldn't dream of interfering."

"And you can tell no one else. If their locale gets out, the entire DPI body will be staked out around the place. I'll never get my hands on them," Curtis said.

The man nodded. "Agreed."

Curtis sighed long and hard. "They're at a castle called Le Château de Courtemanche, south of L'Ombre."

His accent was terrible. The name of the village had sounded like "lumber." Rhiannon wished she could simply kill the both of them. God knew it would be justified. Unfortunately, Roland would never forgive her. He and his noble, knightly ideas about honor. And he thought he had a demon in him. Ha! If he had a demon, then *she* must be one.

"It might be of help if I were to take a sample of the drug—"

"Forget it, pal. That formula is top secret. No one has it but me, and that's the way it's going to stay."

So you think, Curtis, dear, Rhiannon thought.

"All right. I don't need it." The man rose and turned toward the door. Curtis turned to a table, out of Rhiannon's sight. She moved to a more advantageous angle and peered at him. He snapped the lid on a briefcase, and she glimpsed rows of test tubes, with rubber stoppers, inside.

The drug.

"Aren't you going to tell me how to reach you? I don't even know your name."

The man opened the door and paused. "I'll contact you, when it's necessary. As for my name, you may call me Lucien, for now."

He left the room, leaving the door wide. Curtis hurried to close it, shaking his head. He carefully fastened the lock, and then came toward the room she was in. She flung herself beneath the bed, and peered out to watch him. He kept going, right through the door that led to the bathroom. She pulled herself out, and hurried to grab the briefcase. In seconds she was out the window once more, and clambering carefully down.

She reached jumping distance and leapt elegantly to the ground, landing with a little bounce, and fighting to stave off laughter. She was nearly giddy with her success.

Arms came around her from behind and pulled her into a darkened alley. She struggled, but the strength in them was unbelievable, and for just an instant, she fully expected to feel the jab of Lucien's blade in her side once more.

"What the hell do you think you're doing?"

"Roland!" She turned in his grip, and went nearly limp with relief. "You frightened me half to death. I thought you were that hunk of beef who tried to knife me before."

"I could very well have been. You take less care than a whirling dervish."

"I daresay, I've known more dervishes than you have Roland, and I take a good deal more care than they." His arms still imprisoned hers, and she shook free. She lifted the briefcase, and thrust it at him. "Maybe you'll stop being so angry when you see what I have."

"I don't care what you have, you could have been killed or captured trying to get it. When are you going to listen to me, Rhiannon?"

"Just look at it, Roland. I know you'll be pleased."

He thrust the case back into her hands. "Not here." He gripped her arm and began striding away, down the alley.

She tugged free once again, sorely hurt that he didn't even care to see what she'd accomplished. "I have a car waiting. A rental."

"Leave it," he barked.

"Go to hell, Roland. My packages are inside."

She raced away from him before he could grab her again. In seconds, she'd settled herself behind the steering wheel. She was surprised when the passenger door jerked open and he slid in beside her.

"You detest automobiles."

"I'll put up with one tonight."

A little of her anger faded. "Just to be with me?"

"Yes."

She very nearly grinned.

"Because if I let you out of my sight, there is no telling what kind of foolish thing you'll do next."

He could have slapped her and hurt her less. She refused to let him see it, though. She started the engine and pulled away from the hotel. The case rested on the seat between them. He didn't make a move to look inside and she wouldn't ask again.

She pulled to a stop right in front of her rental house, and Roland scowled. "Keep going, Rhiannon."

"I only want to fetch my suitcase."

"Then park somewhere else and we'll walk back for it. No sense announcing our presence."

"Stop telling me what to do."

"Someone has to. You haven't sense enough to act responsibly on your own."

She got out and slammed the door. "That's enough. I am staying right here. I wouldn't go back to that musty old castle of yours if there were twenty DPI men waiting for me right now."

She dragged the briefcase out of the car as Roland jumped out the opposite door. She threw it at him, putting a good deal of force into it. The case hit him squarely in the chest, and he staggered backward. "Give it to Eric. It's the tranquilizer. I thought he might like to examine it, see if he can come up with an antidote, or something."

"Rhiannon, don't be ridiculous." He tossed the case back into the car and came around it. He caught up with her, gripped her upper arms and made her face him. Then his eyes widened, and he looked at her in disbelief. "You're crying."

She ripped one arm free of him, even though doing so hurt considerably, and dashed the tears from her face with her hand. "No, I'm not."

He shook his head slowly. "Rhiannon, I didn't mean to hurt you—"

"You? Hurt me?" She released a bark of laughter. "I am the daughter of a Pharaoh, a princess of Egypt. Men fall at my feet if I wish it. Mortals and immortals alike. Do you really think I can be hurt by the likes of you?" Her throat burned. "I hate you, Roland de Courtemanche. I detest you, and you will not have the opportunity to reject me ever again."

Roland returned to the castle alone. He drove the car, for the simple reason that he didn't want DPI to see it outside Rhiannon's house and realize she was inside. He wasn't even certain they knew it was her house, but it would seem likely. Her description would have been bandied about L'Ombre, and questions asked. Someone would know the elusive Rhiannon had rented the cottage.

He entered through the front door, and found no one about. He stalked to his chambers and stopped in the doorway, unable for a moment, to draw a breath.

Frederick glanced down from the ladder where he stood, polishing the silver chandelier that winked and sparkled. Tamara stopped swiping the bare windows with the wet cloth. Eric glanced up from the hearth where he knelt with a wire brush, scrubbing the stones. Jamey lowered the broom with which he'd been attacking cobwebs.

"Where's Rhiannon?" the boy asked.

Roland looked at the floor, rather than into Jamey's eyes. The cat came toward him, tail swishing, a similar question in her feline eyes. "She's at the house she rented. She wanted to stay there."

"Roland..." Tamara's voice carried a warning, but Eric stopped her with a glance and came forward.

"What's in the briefcase, my friend?"

He looked down, having nearly forgotten what he carried. "It's the drug, the tranquilizer Rogers used against you before."

Eric lifted one eyebrow. "How did you—"

"Not me. Rhiannon. She slipped into Rogers's hotel suite and stole it."

Eric's jaw dropped for just a moment.

Jamey smiled and shook his head. "Man, she's got guts."

"Guts?" Roland scowled at the boy. "It was an idiotic thing to do. Rogers was in the room at the time, not to mention that other fellow. The one who nearly killed her."

"And she went in there, anyway," Jamey insisted. "That took guts."

"She is reckless and self-destructive."

Tamara threw the washrag she'd been using onto the floor and stomped across the room. "She is brave, and cunning, and absolutely beautiful. I wish I were more like her."

Eric looked at her, a hint of alarm on his face. "I like you the way you are, Tamara."

"Rhiannon is far too sure of herself. She should be more careful." Roland slung the briefcase onto a stand and sunk into a chair.

"She's not at all sure of herself. Roland, you hurt her again, didn't you?"

"What on earth do you mean, 'again'?"

"Tamara, leave him alone. Roland is right about this. Rhiannon takes far too many risks." Eric touched her shoulder and she whirled on him, glaring in a way Roland had rarely seen her do. "If one of you had done what she did tonight, you'd be congratulating yourselves until dawn. Why on earth can't you give the woman some credit?''

"Did Rhiannon get the new drapes?'' Frederick called down from the ladder.

Roland lifted his head. He felt a heavy burden of guilt lowering itself upon his shoulders, and Tamara was only adding to it. He'd wanted to protect Rhiannon. Instead, he'd somehow hurt her. "Out in the car, I believe." He looked once again at the rooms around him, and shook his head. "You've all been working nonstop all night, haven't you?''

"Don't thank us,'' Tamara snapped. "We did it for her, not you." She hurried out of the room with Jamey on her heels. Frederick limped down from the ladder and went after them.

Eric sat in a chair opposite Roland. "A car? Care to tell me how that came about?''

Roland did, beginning with the luggage in the cottage, and ending with the scene outside it. As he spoke, Jamey carried in a package containing the new drapes, and took his place on the ladder to hang them. Frederick came in to help, setting a box containing no less than a hundred candles, on the floor.

Roland and Eric largely ignored the two, and soon they trooped out again to return with more packages. It was a full thirty minutes before Eric frowned hard and looked up. "Where is Tamara?''

Frederick only shrugged and limped out once more.

Jamey went to follow, but Eric gripped his arm. "Jamison, tell me where she is.''

Jamey licked his lips. "She went to Rhiannon's. Don't be mad, Eric. She made me promise not to say a word.''

Eric grimaced and whirled to go out the door. He nearly collided with Tamara and Rhiannon. Roland swallowed hard, relief welling up that she was here, safe. She looked around the room with ill-concealed surprise. Roland thought she deliberately avoided his eyes.

"Your drapes are perfect, Rhiannon. The color of sunshine,

and still heavy enough to keep it out. They look wonderful.'' Tamara's hand rested gently upon Rhiannon's arm.

"Tamara, you scared me half to death.'' Eric pulled her into his arms and squeezed her hard. "Next time you get the notion to go off on your own, would you check with me, please?''

"Why should I?'' She thrust her chin up at him, but slanted a glance toward Roland.

"Because I love you, Tamara. If anything should happen to you...'' He closed his eyes and shook his head. "It would kill me. You know that.''

Again she looked at Roland, her glare as piercing as a blade. When she faced Eric again, her expression softened. "I know. I'm sorry I worried you.'' She kissed him lingeringly, and Roland averted his gaze. He noticed Rhiannon had turned away, too.

Frederick had mounted the ladder and was fitting candles into the holders. Tamara turned to him. "It's late, Frederick. Why don't we leave the rest for another time?''

He nodded, fit one last candle into place, and climbed slowly down. Rhiannon picked up her case and walked through the double doors into the bedroom. She put it on the bed, and began unpacking.

Eric went in behind her. "Getting those vials was quite a coup, Rhiannon. I might be able to find a way to nullify the drug's effects, given time.''

"I was hoping that would be the case.'' She cleared her throat. "I learned a bit while I was in the hotel room. The man who attacked me is not with DPI. He calls himself Lucien.''

Roland's attention was caught. As Tamara hustled Jamey and Frederick toward the door, shooing Pandora out with them, Roland moved into the bedroom.

She didn't look at him, only kept removing things from her case, sorting them into neat stacks on the bed. "No one in DPI knows about this castle. Only Curtis Rogers and this Lucien. He convinced Curtis to tell him while I was listening in. He offered to help capture me, in exchange for certain...privileges.''

"What sort of privileges?" Roland couldn't keep quiet any longer.

Rhiannon barely spared him a glance. "He asked if Curtis would tranquilize me to the point of absolute helplessness, and then let him have me alone for as long as he needed."

Tamara gasped from the doorway. Roland swore fluently.

Rhiannon shook her head. "He wants to be transformed. I imagine that is the only thing he would force me to do. Not that I intend to give him the chance."

Roland paced toward her. "Why you? Why doesn't he target one of us?"

"He said because I was the oldest. He wants high-proof blood, Roland." It was the first time she'd addressed him directly. Her eyes still looked like those of a wounded animal, and he realized all over again how deeply he had hurt her.

Eric put a hand on Rhiannon's shoulder. "We all care about you, Rhiannon. For that reason, we hope you won't take any more unnecessary risks."

She faced him head-on. "I will not cower in a corner and wait for them to come for me. They will be the ones cowering before I finish. They will wish they'd never heard my name."

Tamara touched Eric's arm, and tilted her head toward the door. He sent Roland a sympathetic glance before they left. Alone with Rhiannon, Roland had no idea what to say.

"I, um...I'm glad you came back."

"I am only here because of Tamara. She is frightened for Jamey and she asked me to stay, and help protect him."

He nodded. She opened the drawer of an empty dresser. "They might be rather stale-smelling. Haven't been used in a while," he said.

She drew a small package from her case. "I brought some cedar chips." She sprinkled some of them into the drawer. "You haven't said anything about the drapes. How much do you hate them?"

He drew a deep breath. "Actually, I'm beginning to feel glad you convinced me to allow it. The entire place feels...warmer."

"Then you won't mind that I bought a bedspread and some throw pillows to match."

He shook his head slowly. "No. I don't mind." He felt his eyelids growing heavy, his body slowing gradually. He reached inside his jacket and removed a vial of Eric's revivifying potion.

Rhiannon frowned. "Perhaps you shouldn't. You look tired."

He only shook his head. "Rhiannon, do you feel as if you need to prove something to me?"

Her gaze lowered all at once. "No, Roland. Not anymore."

There was a finality in her tone that hit him with staggering force. Was she giving up on her relentless pursuit of him, then? Why on earth should that make him feel so utterly miserable?

He shook off the feeling of desolation, and downed the potion. "Good. Because you never did, you know." She said nothing, only continued piling clothes into drawers. "I've never doubted your abilities, Rhiannon. Your strength, your courage, your utter boldness in facing danger."

She stopped in the act of sorting nightgowns, holding a sheer black peignoir out before her. She frowned over it. "For a woman, you mean?"

"That is not what I mean. I wouldn't have wished to face you in battle as a human. I still wouldn't."

She draped the gown over the back of a chair, and Roland's mouth went dry when he realized she probably intended to wear it. He couldn't help envisioning her pale, smooth limbs beneath the translucent gauze. She scooped up a handful of clothing and moved toward the wardrobe, to begin hanging them.

Standing with her back to him, she shook her head. "I don't understand you at all, Roland. If you don't think of me as inferior, then why do you dislike me so?"

"I do not dislike you. I dislike the things you do."

She finished hanging clothes, and turned, tilting her head. "Which things?"

"Outrageous things, Rhiannon. Things that put you at risk. Like…like singing in that tavern, for example."

She smiled fully, and her eyes sparkled. "Ah, but Roland, it was such great fun. And you have to admit, I'm not bad." She frowned then. "Was that it, you think I sing horribly?"

He closed his eyes. Truly, she was exasperating. "You have the voice of an angel."

She seemed to glow with his praise. "Really?"

He nodded. "It's that you were drawing so much attention to yourself. I only want you to be careful."

"The only attention I wished to draw was yours."

"Then you ought to have come here, and sung to me in private." She opened her mouth to reply, but he continued speaking. "It's not only the singing. It's all the other risks you take. Flirting with Rogers that first night. Slipping into his hotel room tonight." He lifted his hands in a helpless gesture. "Can't you see that my anger at you was because I was afraid for you?"

She studied him so intently that he had a brief surge of hope she might actually be listening. Then, "If I had come to the castle, to sing to you in private, would you really have listened?"

He clapped a hand to his forehead. "You haven't heard a word I've said, have you?"

She waved a hand. "Of course, I have. You dislike my risky adventures. You dislike my every behavior. No doubt, you dislike the way I dress, as well."

"In public, Rhiannon, it wouldn't hurt to try a bit harder to blend in, for your own protection."

"I knew it. Well, Roland, where shall I begin? Shall I fashion a dress from a feed sack?" Her voice grew louder, her words tumbling out in a rush of anger. "Would that please you? Shall I slouch when I walk, so my height isn't so noticeable? Or maybe I should begin by hacking off my hair. It's probably my most conspicuous feature, wouldn't you say?" She strode away from him, and began a frantic search of the chambers, opening every drawer and cupboard and chest.

Roland gripped her shoulders and turned her to face him. "Stop it."

"No. There are scissors here, somewhere. I know there are. I'll even let you do the honors, Roland. Just—"

He shook her. "Stop it! You know that isn't what I meant."

"No, I don't. I don't understand you at all. If I dress and behave as a widow in mourning, will that make you want me, Roland? If I suddenly become a blushing wallflower, will you find me desirable then?"

"You want to know how desirable I find you?" He glared at her, his rage blending with his passion to overwhelm his common sense. He knew he should release her, leave the chamber this instant before she drove him too far. The beast within, taunted to wakefulness by his anger, his fear for her, and his desire, was on the rampage.

But her scent twined through his brain, eliciting the memory of her the previous day, lying all but naked before him. The taste of her seemed to come to life upon his lips. The way her breasts had looked, and how they'd responded to his touch. His lips had been so close to them. His hunger for her whipped the beast to a frenzy and he shuddered with the force of it.

"You want to know how much I desire you?" he repeated. He looked down into her blazing eyes, and knew it was too late to battle the beast inside.

CHAPTER EIGHT

There was something in his eyes, something that should have warned her. But she couldn't curb her anger. "I already know. You don't desire me at all. You want someone who looks like me, but who is timid and quiet and withdrawn. You touched me while I rested, Roland. While my body could respond but my mind could not." She shook her head in frustration. "It isn't me you want."

Roland's grip on her shoulders eased, and his hands slipped slowly down her arms. His gaze stabbing into her eyes, he reached her wrists, encircled them and drew her hands forward. Then he pressed her palms flat to his groin, and moved them slowly up and down over the solid, throbbing length of him. "You're wrong." His words were nearly a growl.

Rhiannon felt a shudder of absolute longing move through her. She closed her eyes at the force of it. Then his mouth was crushing hers, his arms were around her, pinning hers immobile. He pressed her lips open and thrust his tongue into her mouth, licking its roof, and her teeth and her tongue.

She wanted to put her arms around him, but his crushing embrace prevented that. Her hands worked, all the same, at the button of his trousers. In moments, she was able to close them around the silken, rigid evidence of how very much he did want her. She squeezed, and stroked, and ran the pad of her thumb over the tip.

He moaned into her mouth, and suddenly gripped the front of her blouse and tore it open. He was frantic, a man possessed, she thought, as he ripped the bra away, and bent her backward, bowing to suckle her breast. Ruthlessly he tugged and bit, ravaging her sensitive nipple until her knees quivered and her hands buried in his hair to urge him on.

He fell to his knees then, and yanked the skirt until its seam gave way. He pressed his lips to the front of her panties, hands gripping her buttocks, and she felt his breath and the moistness of his kiss right through them. A second later he ripped them aside, and kissed her there again.

She couldn't stand up much longer. Her legs were jelly. Her knees had dissolved.

Then his tongue parted her folds, and lapped a hot path inside. She fell to the floor, but he came right with her. Growling deep in his throat, he pressed his palms to her inner thighs, and shoved them apart. He buried his face between them.

It was torture, sweet, succulent torture, and he applied it like an attack. His mouth devoured, his tongue assaulted. His hands fought to widen the gate of her fortress, and he mercilessly deepened his invasion.

She screamed aloud when his conquest was complete, and still the siege continued, rendering her no more than a quivering, panting captive. When her hands tried to push his head away, he caught her wrists in a grip of iron, and plundered on, until every bastion of sanity had been rendered useless.

Then he was moving upward, over her body. Her newly freed, trembling hands shoved his trousers lower, and he plunged himself inside her without a second's hesitation.

His size and the force of his thrusts made her gasp. His mouth covered hers again, and the sweep of his tongue into her throat matched the rhythm of his body, pounding into hers. She pressed at his shoulders once, as a signal he should slow down. This wasn't as she had envisioned it. This wasn't the lovemaking she craved from him. But his hands only caught hers, and pinned them to the floor at her sides. His pace, if anything, became more demanding.

And in moments, her hips arched in response to that demand, and her tongue swirled around his in a savory dance. Harder and harder he rode her, until his lips left her mouth to slide down to her throat. She tipped her head back as he drew her skin into his mouth. She was approaching a second, shattering climax, and she reached for it, eagerly.

She knew he was there as well when he reared inside her, and she felt the hot pulse of his seed. Then his teeth sank into her throat, and he growled once again. She moaned in a hoarse voice as the climax held her endlessly in its grip, then shook all over as it released her.

Her muscles slowly untwined, and relaxed. His mouth was still fastened to her throat. She felt the movements of his lips and knew he still drank. Her essence flowed into him, and her body began to weaken. The lethargy that crept around her senses was tempting her, calling her to embrace it. But it would be brief, she knew. He would stop at any moment, and her head would clear.

But he didn't. On and on, he took from her, and the ecstasy she felt became tinged with fear.

She pushed at his shoulders. "Roland…"

He lifted his head with some reluctance. His eyes still glowing with passion, he stared into hers. "You're delicious," he whispered. "All of you."

She felt a sudden confusion inside her. She thought she ought to smile up at him, but instead she felt like crying. Why? For God's sake, why? Wasn't this what she'd wanted?

He rolled off her, stood and righted his trousers. He reached a hand down to her. "Come, it's nearly dawn. You're feeling it already, aren't you?"

She swallowed the lump in her throat. He hadn't even taken off his clothes. His eyes were hot with lust, but devoid of feeling. "Yes, I suppose I am." She allowed him to take her hand, and pull her to her feet. But her knees refused to support her, and she swayed away from him. She caught herself on the arm of the settee, leaning over it like a drunkard. Her head fell forward. Her hair veiled her face like a dark curtain, through which she could not see. Rather, she heard his ragged breathing slowly take on a normal rhythm. She felt the gradual ebb of his mindless lust.

Roland caught her shoulders, tugging her upright, turning her to face him. "What is it?"

She lifted her chin to see confusion in his expression. My God, he wasn't even aware...

His eyes narrowed, then focused on the fresh wound at her throat. The heightened color left his face all at once. She heard him curse roughly, and that was all. She felt herself falling, but oddly, there was no sense of landing at his feet. Instead, it was as if she simply continued a downward spiral into utter blackness.

The knowledge of what he'd done was like a blade thrust through the mists of passion to plunge into his heart as he caught her in his arms, and lifted her. Her head fell backward, her endless satin hair trailing down his legs as he carried her to the bedroom, and laid her down. He smoothed the ebony locks away from her face and pulled the covers over her pale body. He had to close his eyes tightly for the burning that assailed them. Certainly not tears. He had none. Hadn't had for centuries. What use were tears to a beast?

God, that he'd thought he might someday conquer the blood-thirsty demon within him was a joke. But to have found the proof of it like this...

Mentally, he called to Eric. She wouldn't die. As he recalled the way he'd ravaged her, second by second, he knew he hadn't taken enough to kill her. But he might have, had she not stopped him when she had. There'd been no logic in his brain at that moment. Only sensation. The feel of his body possessing hers, of her climax milking the seed from him, of her blood filling him, had chased every vestige of morality from his mind, and given free rein to the monster that lurked inside.

He heard the door creak open, but didn't turn. Instead he clasped her limp, slender hand in both of his, and brought it to his lips. "I'm sorry, Rhiannon. God, I'm sorry."

"Roland, what..." Eric's steps approached from behind, then stopped. Roland released her hand and turned to face his friend. Eric wasn't looking at him, however. His gaze fixed upon Rhiannon's white face, and then upon the two tiny wounds at her throat. "What the hell have you done?"

Roland parted his lips but found himself unable to speak. Then he was shoved roughly aside as Eric went to the bed, leaned over it and touched Rhiannon's face. Roland turned his back. Shame engulfed him. Remorse filled his every pore. "I didn't mean—I lost control, Eric. I nearly—"

Eric gripped Roland's arm and drew him from the room. He closed the bedroom door. His anger struck like a fist, and Roland couldn't blame him for it. "What the hell were you thinking? How could you allow yourself to—"

"I don't know, dammit!" Roland lowered his head, pressing a palm to his forehead. "Is she all right?"

Eric sighed hard. "She'll be weak when she wakes, and more than likely, she'll feel like hell. She'll need to feed right away. All in all, I'd say she's in better shape than you right now." He shook his head. "Tell me what happened, Roland. This is so unlike you."

"Oh, but it isn't. It's exactly like me."

"That's ridiculous. You're the most controlled man I know."

"Am I?" Roland paced away, toward the fire. He stared into the glowing coals, inhaled the pungent aroma of the smoldering wood. "Have you ever wondered why I remain such a staid, quiet individual? Have you ever once considered what fiendish qualities I might be holding in check?"

"I don't know what you're talking about." Eric came nearer.

Roland faced him, pointing one outstretched finger toward the bedroom. "That is what happens when I ease the reins of control, Eric. The lust for blood, be it in battle or in passion, takes over. It's time you knew your dearest friend is no more than evil given form and substance."

Eric frowned. He touched Roland's shoulder, then gripped it hard. "I've never seen you like this."

"What you've seen of me is a veneer, my friend. Today, you've met me for the first time. Perhaps it would be best if you took your fledgling and the boy, and went as far from me as possible, before I contaminate all of you."

"Don't be ridiculous." Eric let his hand fall away. "We'll

talk more tonight. The sun is already cresting the horizon. You ought to go below.''

Roland shook his head. "No need. I availed myself of your potion.''

Eric's frown deepened. "When?''

Roland shrugged. "An hour ago. Perhaps less. What does it matter?''

"Why didn't I realize...Roland, sit down. Crawl out of this well of self-loathing and listen to me.'' Without waiting for Roland's compliance, Eric shoved him toward a chair.

Roland sat, but he wasn't concerned with what Eric had to say. No words could alter the truth.

"It wasn't you, you fool,'' Eric all but shouted. "It was the drug. If anyone is to blame for this debacle, it's me.'' He pulled a chair close to Roland's and sat down. "The drug has a tendency to increase aggressive behavior. At least it did in the animals I initially tested it on. When the same symptoms didn't occur in me, I assumed immortals were immune to that side effect. That was a grave error, obviously.''

Roland shook his head slowly. "What a genuine friend you are to try to accept blame for my true nature. It wasn't the drug, Eric. It was me.''

"No. Roland, use your brain and listen. I should have realized that older vampires would be more susceptible to adverse effects than younger ones. Just as they're more susceptible to other elements. Sunlight. Pain. Don't you see? The drug caused this.''

Roland faced Eric without blinking. "You truly do not wish to see me for what I am. If the drug did anything at all, it was only to weaken the tenuous grip of my control. The beast within is mine alone. I know it well.''

"You're a damned fool if you believe that.''

Roland stood. "This conversation is senseless. Go below and rest before the sun fries your wits any further.''

"I've been below. I took Tamara down not thirty minutes ago. But, like you, I imbibed the drug this dawn. I understood we would take turns at this day shift of ours. And this conversation is not senseless. It makes perfect sense, and if you were not so stubborn, you would know it.''

Roland could stand no more of Eric's rationalizing. He started for the great hall. But his persistent friend followed on his heels. At the foot of the worn stone stairs, Roland turned. "You want a turn guarding the castle, be my guest. But stop hounding me, Eric. I need to be by myself for a time.''

Roland hurried up the stairs. Thankfully, Eric remained at the bottom.

He moved past the second level, and the entrance to Jamey's apartment. He continued upward, beyond the third level, and the decaying chambers that hadn't been used since his time as a mortal. The stairs ended abruptly at a heavy wood door, and Roland shoved it open. He stepped into the weapons room, a huge, circular tomb, without windows. It was black as pitch, but he could see clearly.

Suits of armor stood like dust-coated specters, the darkness within them eyeing him with what felt to him like condemnation. Well deserved, Roland thought. Broadswords hung upon the stone walls, tarnished with neglect and time. Their finely detailed scabbards were barely discernible through the filth. Crossbows lined the floor in one section, likely inoperable by now. Bolts stood in a short, wooden box. Hundreds of them, bunched together like a porcupine's quills. Shields leaned against the wall, the faded remnants of the Courtemanche family crest upon their faces.

Roland felt bitter irony when he glanced at the black, rampant lion, teeth bared, upon a field of red.

The beast and the blood. How appropriate.

He tore his gaze from the grim reminders of his past, of his family, and strode toward the ladder at the far end of the room. As he neared the top, he shoved at the trapdoor above him, and climbed through it to the tower room. He found the long, wooden matches upon the table where he'd left them, and struck one against the rough stone wall. Then he lit the candles until the entire room was aglow.

Like the chamber below, this one was circular. The walls had been lined with slits, from which the archers of old could shoot at intruders if the castle came under siege. Roland had sealed the slits only recently. There were times when he rested here, by day, rather than in the dungeons beneath the earth.

He wouldn't do so again. The dungeons were fitting enough for a man such as he.

For a moment, he stood in the room's center and turned slowly. His paintings stood all around him. Those he'd done as a boy, all but ruined by the ravaging hands of time. Once they'd been fanciful images of dragons and knights and heroic dreams. Then there were the portraits, which had come much later. The faces of his mother, and father. The accusing eyes of his brothers.

Upon an easel, the unfinished portrait of Rhiannon drew him nearer.

He'd come to this room to destroy it, to destroy all of them. He intended to slice them to shreds. He was no painter, no artist. He had not the heart of a poet, but the heart of a villain. What right did he have to hold to these memories of a human with a soul? They were false. Utter lies, all of them.

He drew a dagger from a sheath at his hip, and lifted it. He strode up to the portrait.

But something stopped him. He knew not what, only that it was a force stronger than his anger. He gazed at the image, that was now only a jumble of vague shapes and outlines. In it, he saw Rhiannon, her almond eyes reaching out to him, filled with warmth, and light. With a strangled sob, he dropped the dagger to the stone floor.

He turned his back to the painting and faced instead a small table where his paints and pallets and brushes stood at the ready. Beside it, stood another ladder. He looked slowly upward, to the trapdoor at the top. Above was the top of the castle.

He used to go up there as a boy, and look out over the woods to the spot where the two rivers joined. Narrow, rapid Tordu, laughing as it bounded into the broad, calm waters of the Loire.

As one, the two rivers continued their unending journey south-ward in a glistening, glittering strand.

Beyond the trapdoor was daylight by now. The warm rays of a golden sun, with nothing overhead to prevent its touch. He started forward, placed his hands on the rungs.

Then he paused, and looked again toward the painting. He moved as a blind man, guided by unseen hands. He grabbed up the brushes, and a pallet.

Her head throbbed, and her stomach seemed alive, the way it twisted and writhed within her. She felt slightly stronger now than she had when she'd first stirred, to find Tamara in worried attendance. She'd fed, and gradually, her strength had begun to filter back into her.

"Where is he?" She saw Tamara's face tighten when she asked the question.

"I don't know. Eric said he'd holed himself up in the tower room all day. Then at dusk, he went outside. He hasn't come back." The young one searched Rhiannon's eyes. "You were hoping he'd be here when you woke."

Rhiannon shrugged, hoping to hide her disappointment. "I was only curious."

Tamara touched her hand. "Don't be too disappointed in him, Rhiannon. Eric said he was pretty distraught over what hap-pened." She frowned, her pretty face puckering. "Not that he doesn't deserve to be."

"Oh, posh, Tamara, I'm fine. And don't tell me you don't enjoy a small sip or two in the throes of passion."

Tamara blushed. "Well, yes…but—"

"I like to think he was so overwhelmed with desire for me that he took leave of his senses. It's rather flattering, actually."

Tamara shook her head. "Eric thinks the drug was to blame. He feels terrible about it."

Rhiannon tilted her head to one side. "I know little of chem-istry. Do you think he's right?"

"Oh, yes. Eric is a genius about those things." She glanced at Rhiannon, then lowered her lashes. "Was it…very nice?"

Rhiannon almost smiled. Perhaps would have, if not for the lingering pain lodged in the center of her chest, for which she had no explanation. She'd never encountered a vampiress so embarrassed to discuss sex. "My body nearly exploded at his touch," she said frankly. "I've wanted him for a very long time, you know."

Tamara faced her fully then. "So, why do I see such sadness in your eyes?"

Rhiannon blinked and turned away.

"Come on, Rhiannon. If you aren't going to talk to me, then who?"

She met the younger woman's gaze once more. She sensed only genuine caring emanating from her. "My body was sated."

"But?"

Rhiannon sighed. "It was almost as if he were alone as he plunged himself into me. Almost as if I weren't even there."

Tamara nodded sagely. "You wanted tenderness, some cuddling, some talking. I understand."

Rhiannon lifted her brows. "Cuddling? Where do you come by such ideas, fledgling? Do I honestly look to you like the type of woman who needs cuddling?"

Tamara grinned. "He'll come around. Give him time."

Exasperated with the young woman's nonsense, Rhiannon flung back her covers and got to her feet. She didn't miss the sudden widening of Tamara's eyes, before she turned her back. Imagine, being so bashful with another woman. Well, Rhiannon certainly had nothing to be embarrassed about. She went to the dresser, tugged out a pair of designer denims and slipped them on. At the wardrobe, she removed a thin silk blouse in a stunning electric blue, and poked her arms into the sleeves. As she fastened the onyx buttons, Tamara faced her again.

"You're going out, aren't you?"

Rhiannon nodded. "Yes, and it will be useless for you to tell me to stay here and rest. I'm immortal. Granted, I feel like a brisk wind could blow me away right now, but it will pass."

She knelt near the closet and searched for a suitable pair of walking shoes.

"Eric said Roland headed for the woods, just beyond the wall."

Rhiannon turned. "Reading my mind, are you?"

"I don't have to. I'm a woman."

She'd rested too long, Rhiannon told herself as she crossed the grassy meadow, its dew dampening the hem of her jeans. Cool, moist breezes bathed her face, and the full moon lit her way. She wouldn't try to summon Roland, or to track him down by honing her senses to his. She had a feeling he would only go out of his way to avoid her if he knew she sought him.

At the meadow's edge she leaped the wall, and stepped into the darkness of the woods. Twisted, dark-skinned trees and thorny bushes surrounded her, but she pushed steadily onward, determined to find him. She had no idea what she wanted to say to him, but she knew she had to say something. Tamara had been wrong about her wishing to be cuddled, but right about the talking. She needed, desperately, to talk to Roland. More important, she needed him to talk to her.

The scents of the rivers grew stronger as she neared them, and a fine, silvery mist hung at knee level. Decomposing limbs and plants made the earth beneath her feet like a sponge. It sank with her every step.

She took her time, moving slowly, inhaling deeply to experience every aroma the night had to offer. The spinning in her head eased a bit with each passing moment, and eventually she came upon a well-worn path, meandering among the trees. She followed it, stepping in and out of the abstract patterns the moon's light painted on the ground. A small gust caused the elms to sway and groan as if in agony…or in ecstasy. Their deep tenor harmonized with the soprano voice of the breeze rushing over the smaller branches high above.

She approached a wrought-iron gate, with an elaborate C twined around its bars. It creaked as she pushed it open. The wind stiffened. Huge limbs parted, bathing the tiny cemetery in moonglow. Markers stood in uneven rows, most crumbling with age. Five stood apart, large and elaborate.

Roland stood with one hand braced against an obelisk taller than he. On the face was carved a crest, with two crossed swords above it.

Without turning, he spoke. "So, you've found me."

"So I have." She stepped nearer. The crest on the stone was one she knew well. She'd seen the same rampant lion on Roland's shield when she'd found him all those years ago, lying near death on a field of battle. "A relative?" she asked softly.

"My father." He straightened and waved a hand to the man-size crucifix beside him. "And my mother."

Rhiannon came forward until she stood very close to him. He didn't look at her. She glanced at the stone, at the likeness of the Savior painstakingly chiseled into it, every detail of his face clear in the swirling white marble. "The stone is breathtaking."

"In deference to her devotion." He shook his head. "I shudder to think what she would say, could she see what I've become."

She wanted to argue, but sensed it would best be put off for another time. She moved to the three nearly identical stones in the next row. Tall blocks, arched at the tops and made of obsidian. They differed only in the scenes etched into their faces.

Roland came behind her and pressed a palm to the proud stag depicted on the first. "Albert, the hunter," he said softly.

She could feel the pain emanating from him in waves as he moved to the next marker and touched the knight, seated upon a rearing destrier. "Eustace, the warrior," he told her. He then glanced toward the third, with the warship at full sail upon a choppy sea. "Pierre, the sailor. My brothers. Meet Rhiannon, the latest victim of my cruelty."

"Roland, no—"

"Ah, but you wish to hear the rest of the story, do you not?" He faced her with bitter hurt in his eyes. "I believe I left off after the first appearance of the beast that lives in my soul. You remember, how I butchered the men who'd murdered Sir Gareth?''

"You were little more than a boy, and enraged by your grief."

He nodded. "So you said before. No doubt, after a firsthand encounter with my violent side, you've reformed that opinion."

She studied his face, noting the puffy circles beneath his eyes, the haggard features, the tight jaw. "Eric believes it was a side effect of the drug."

"Eric would rather believe anything than the truth." He turned away from her. "Can you stomach the rest of the tale, Rhiannon, or would you prefer to leave now? I've no idea why, but some demon drives me to tell it to you. All of it. Perhaps I need to see your face when you finally realize what I am."

"I know what you are. If you want to tell me, I want to hear it."

His eyes narrowed, and one hand shot out to grip her upper arm. "You'd best be certain, Rhiannon. Once I begin, you will hear it all, whether you wish to or not."

She stared up into his face, aching for the pain he felt. "Are you trying to frighten me, Roland? To drive me away so you won't have to release this pain or exorcise these demons?"

"There is no exorcising these demons. They are a part of me. And if you are not frightened of me after what I did, then you are a fool."

She jerked her arm from his grasp, and drew herself up to her full height. "Then I am a fool." She walked past him, away from the markers to a small, grassy knoll beneath a giant of a tree. She sat down there, leaning her back against the rough bark. "Tell me."

CHAPTER NINE

She was a fool. She must be, to be here with him like this. Even with the remorse flooding his mind, he was aware of her. His body ached to join with hers once more, to find that blissful release that had nearly shattered the ice coating his heart. Just looking at her hands reminded him of how they'd felt stroking his arousal; like silk and firm and strong. So strong. The sight of her lips elicited the memory of the heat and moisture he'd found beyond them, the taste of her tongue. Beneath the thin silk blouse, she wore nothing. He found himself wondering if the brush of the fabric over her breasts would arouse her nipples to the hard tautness of pebbles, and if it did, whether he could stop himself from tearing it off her, and sucking at them until she begged him to stop.

She wore tight-fitting denims, damn her. They were pressed as snugly between her silken thighs as his body had been. He wanted to put his face into her lap and inhale her bittersweet fragrance. He wanted to taste her again, to become drunk on her own potent brand of spirits.

"Roland." Her voice was but a whisper. He saw her hand reaching up to him, and he took it. She tugged until he sat beside her against the tree trunk. "Tell me," she urged again.

He nodded. "The tale is not a pleasant one, Rhiannon." Roland drew one bracing breath and prepared himself for her reactions. "After the battle of which I told you, I longed only to return home. To put aside my sword and my lust for violence forever." He paused, looking for a long moment into her fathomless eyes. She would, no doubt, detest him when he'd finished the tale. All the better. Perhaps she'd finally get some sense and leave him alone for good.

"But when I did, it was to find my father's enemies at the castle. The Baron Rosbrook and his clan had taken it." He closed his eyes at the memory. The first sight to welcome him upon returning home had been the crumbled outer wall, then the charred, blackened section of the castle that had been burned.

Rhiannon's hand touched his face. "Your family?"

"Murdered." The single word carried little emphasis. But words could not describe what he'd felt that day. Looking like a man, but with the fears and the heart of a boy, he'd crossed the barren courtyard in time to see them cut his father's limp body down from the gallows, and toss it atop the others in a rickety wagon. He'd stood motionless, unable to believe that what he saw was real as the wagon clattered past him, and beneath the raised portcullis. Like a man entranced, he'd turned and followed, until the wagon stopped near the lip of a steep embankment. And one by one, the bodies had been flung over the side.

He began to tremble again, just as he had then. He wanted to shut out the memory, as he'd wanted to turn his eyes away from the heartrending sight all those years ago. And just as before, he was unable to do so. His father, his brothers, were tossed like refuse, their bodies rolling and tumbling to the very bottom of the rocky ravine. Other knights, stripped of their armor, some with the horrendous wounds of battle marring their flesh, others with no sign of injury save the telling fluid movement of their heads on boneless necks, tossed away without a prayer or a tear shed for them. Then the women. The first charred corpse was unrecognizable, until he'd glimpsed one unburned corner of the gown. His mother's gown.

"My God, Roland." Rhiannon's voice was choked, and she clutched his shoulders in her hands. She'd been inside his mind, he realized dully. She'd relived those moments of his long ago homecoming right along with him. "I had no idea," she whispered. "I'm so sorry."

"So am I, Rhiannon. Had I been at home, where I belonged, I might have prevented it."

"How? Roland, you were a boy, a boy with no knightly training when you left home. What might you have done, other than be killed yourself?''

He looked into her upturned face, and shook his head as he battled a rush of childish tears and a fierce burning in his throat. ''I'll never know, will I?'' He managed to swallow past the lump, and blink the blurring moisture from his eyes. ''Unfortunately, I had left. I had been trained. I'd been in battle, and gained a reputation as a fierce fighter, thanks to Gareth's family. There may have been nothing I could do before the fact. But afterward—''

''If the murder of Gareth enraged you, the murder of your family and the taking of your home must have been far worse.''

He nodded, remembering, experiencing it all again as he relived it for her. ''It happened in an instant. I went from paralyzing shock, and unspeakable grief, to rage and a thirst for revenge that drove me close to madness. It took weeks, but I gathered an army. Some were friends of my father's. Most were knights in the employ of Gareth's family. They aided me as a matter of honor. I had avenged Gareth and their fellow knights, so they would help me to avenge my family.''

''And?''

He looked into her eyes, wishing he didn't have to go on. But he did. He couldn't have stopped himself from telling her all of it now, had he wanted to.

''By my command, they gave no quarter, nor did I. Some of the Rosbrooks escaped the blade, but most died by it. Until only one remained. A younger daughter, no older than I.''

He saw Rhiannon close her eyes, and assumed she was dreading what came next. ''Her name was Rebecca, and she had the face of an angel. Silvery blond curls, huge blue eyes. She was an innocent. I ordered her thrown into the dungeons.''

She released her breath all at once.

''Why are you relieved, Rhiannon? Because I didn't kill her outright? It would have been better if I had.''

She shook her head. ''I know you, Roland. After a few days,

you must have realized that her father's sins were not hers, and released her.''

"Released her?'' He almost laughed. ''No, Rhiannon. You don't know me at all. But you are partly right. In time, I regretted that she should suffer for what her father had done. I removed her from the dungeons and put her into a bedchamber on the third level. I intended to return her to her relatives, until I learned she had none left. The girl, of course, detested me for what I'd done, just as I had detested her family for the murder of mine.''

"What became of her, Roland?''

He removed Rhiannon's hands from his shoulders, folded them into her lap and covered them with one of his own. He searched her face, waiting for the condemnation he was certain would appear there soon. ''I decided the best I could do for her would be to wed her. To keep her in the castle and try to right the wrong I'd done by making her my bride, sharing with her my wealth and my name.''

Rhiannon blinked. ''Did you...did you love her?''

"Love is an emotion of which I am not capable, Rhiannon. Nor have I ever been, even then. Does an animal feel love?''

She parted her lips, then bit them. ''What did she say to your proposal?''

"It was not a proposal. It was a command. She could marry me or return to the dungeons permanently.''

She didn't flinch from his steady gaze. ''Which did she choose?''

"Neither. She flung herself from the tower.''

"Oh, God.'' Rhiannon closed her eyes, and he noted the appearance of moisture on her thick lashes.

"So, now you know.'' He let his chin fall to his chest. A second later, he felt her fingers threading through his hair. That she could bear to touch him at all now, amazed him. That she did so with such tenderness was beyond comprehension.

He lifted his head, and met her damp gaze. ''I swear, I didn't intend to hurt you, Rhiannon. I simply lost my senses. I allowed the violent nature that is truly me, to take control. I'm more sorry than you can imagine.''

''I know. As I know you were sorry after the girl's death, and more than likely, after every battle you ever fought from then on.''

He shook his head. ''I became a mercenary knight, a hired fighter. I left the castle in the hands of caretakers. I couldn't bear to be here, with the memories of my past mistakes haunting me in every hall.''

''Ah, but now you alter the tale, Roland. For I knew of you long before you knew of me. The gallant knight who fought for a price, but always on the side of the weak, and always on the side of the just. I knew you were one of The Chosen, Roland. I was fascinated by you.''

He frowned, not believing her.

''It's true,'' she said. ''It was years after your knighting, of course, and I knew nothing of what horrors had befallen you in your youth. I heard tales of your valor and I tracked you down. For some time, I followed you and your men. God, what it did to me to see you leading them, astride that magnificent black war-horse with the eyes that seemed to blaze. To witness you in battle was worse yet. The gleaming armor, the powerful way you would wield that sword, your fearlessness.''

''You saw me fight?''

She nodded. ''The battle at Lorraine, at midnight, fought to free the kidnapped Lady la Claire. And the one in Normandy, when you helped the fallen men from the field, friend and foe alike. So I know you exaggerate this battle lust you claim.''

He felt his jaw go slack. ''Rhiannon, why did you never tell me this?''

She shrugged. ''I was afraid you'd laugh at me. An immortal vampiress, smitten by a man she'd never met. But I was, you know. I wanted to come to you, even then. Never had I seen a man so strong, or so brave. I was enamored of you, Roland. Then, you heard of Bryan, Gareth's young son, that same babe you'd rescued from the wolf, a man grown by then. He was in dire need, and you rushed to his aid."

Roland nodded. "Yes. His castle was under siege and he couldn't withstand the attackers much longer. A messenger managed to slip out, and brought word to me."

"And you went there, knowing full well you were short on men, and still exhausted from the last skirmish. With little food, and weapons in need of repair, you went. By night, you went, so I was able to follow, and to watch."

He nodded. "The enemy outnumbered us ten to one," he said, recalling his shock as he'd peered at them from the cover of the forest.

"And you attacked them all the same, but only after releasing any of your men who wished to leave. Few did, as I recall. That battle was the fiercest I had ever seen, Roland. I was terrified for you. You managed to rout the invaders, but in the end, you were cut down. I found you lying in the dirt, near death. You remember?"

He nodded, recalling vividly his first glimpse of her. A mysterious, utterly beautiful lady in a flowing black gown, leaning over him, whispering that he would live, that she would not allow him to die. He remembered her tears, raining down on his face, and the way their moist warmth transcended his pain.

"Of course, I remember. I was dying. It was then you transformed me."

"Knowing full well you were worthy of the gift. More worthy than any of us, perhaps. Yet you spend eternity grieving over past mistakes and condemning yourself for a passionate nature."

Roland stood, and gazed upward at the stars. "You call it passion. I call it evil."

She was on her feet, at his side before he was aware she'd moved. She had a talent for that, moving soundlessly, as if floating. She stood before him and lifted her soft palms to cup his face. She drew it down, so he was gazing into her eyes, rather than at the starry night. Of the two, he thought, her eyes were the most lovely, the most brilliant.

"It is time for you to let the past die."

He felt his heart contract painfully in his chest. "I cannot."

"Yes, you can. There is so much for you here, in the present. So much you deny yourself. So much you could take and savor—"

"There is nothing, Rhiannon."

"There is Jamey."

He released a ragged breath, though the pain inside only grew sharper. "Yes, there is Jamey. I've been giving him a lot of thought these past days."

Her hands fell from his face, and settled upon his shoulders.

"I'm beginning to think you were right. The boy may be better off with his natural father. He needs a normal life, not one filled with danger and immortal beings. He ought to live in a suburban house, not a crumbling ruin."

She drew a thoughtful breath. "You'll still need to watch over him, even if you are able to locate his father. And there is always a chance…" She bit her lip and her eyes filled suddenly. Roland felt her wince inwardly in pain, and wondered at it. "A chance that his father will not want him," she finished. Her hands fell to her sides, and she averted her face.

"Rhiannon, what—"

"And even without the boy, you have your friends. Eric and Tamara adore you, Roland."

"They have each other." He shook his head. He couldn't tell her how terribly lonely he felt when he had to witness their happiness. It only exaggerated his own isolation.

"What about me, then?" She faced him again, gripped both his hands in hers. "Don't tell me you didn't forget all that pain when you made love to me. Don't say you didn't feel the same sheer joy of being alive, that you made me feel."

He closed his eyes. "I did not make love to you. I assaulted you."

She drew his hands toward her, pulling them around her to the small of her back. Then she left them there, to slip her arms around his neck and press her body to his. "Perhaps you will get it right the next time, then."

He didn't push her away. He couldn't. Staring down into the endless pools of her eyes, he simply couldn't. "There cannot be a next time, Rhiannon."

"There can. There will." She pressed her lips to his, parted them, swept her tongue into his mouth.

Summoning every ounce of his faltering control, he released her and turned away. "No."

"But Roland, I—"

"No, Rhiannon. You still don't comprehend it, do you?" He shoved his hands roughly through his hair. "There is so much in you that reminds me of who I once was. The impulsiveness, the passion, the way you laugh in the face of danger. Dammit, Rhiannon, it is never as hard for me to control my nature as when I am with you. Your very presence stirs in my soul the qualities I constantly fight to suppress."

She said nothing. He couldn't turn to face her. Looking at her would only tempt him anew to give in to the beast. It was ironic that the one thing he wanted most in this world was the thing that he must deny himself. It was almost as if the gods were laughing at him, dangling this prize before him just to see him pay for his sins. "Sometimes, Rhiannon, I believe you are my punishment. My curse."

He turned then, and stopped dead. The pain in her eyes was such as he'd never before seen. Yet they remained dry. Wide, and hurting, but utterly dry. Without a word, she turned and walked away, toward the wrought-iron gate. Her rapid pace was brought up short, though, when Eric appeared just beyond it, emerging from the mist like a ghost.

"Rhiannon, thank God I've found you. Is Roland—"

"Here, Eric," Roland called. He moved forward, glancing at Rhiannon's stricken face. He'd hurt her again. Severely this time. He felt it as surely as he felt the river-moistened breeze on his face, and he had no idea how, or even if, he could remedy it.

"Excuse me," she muttered, then staggered away into the densest part of the woods.

Roland took a step to go after her, but Eric's hand on his shoulder stopped him. In the distance, he heard Rhiannon retching violently. He shook Eric's hand away and again began to go after her.

"Dammit, Roland, listen to me. Jamey is gone."

Roland halted on the dark path, his lower legs swathed in mist, river-damp air filling his lungs. An icy hand closed around his chest. He turned. "Gone? What do you mean, 'gone'?"

"He's left. Run off." Eric fished in his pocket, and pressed a folded sheet of paper into Roland's hand. "We found this in his room."

Roland glanced again in the direction Rhiannon had gone. He heard nothing now. He sent the probing fingers of his mind out to hers, but found it closed to him.

"I'll go," Eric said softly. "Read the damned note and meet me back at the castle."

Roland watched him go, then smoothed the note open with hands that were not steady, and read;

Dear Tamara,

I have to leave. Please don't try to find me. I'm a man now, and I can take care of myself. But as long as I am with Roland, he'll think he has to take care of me. Now everything is happening like it did before. Curtis is back. DPI is driving everyone crazy, all because of me. It was my fault Rhiannon got knifed at the match. And I know it was my fault she got hurt again last night. I heard you and Eric talking. I don't know what happened, only that Roland hurt her somehow, and that it was because of that stupid drug he's been taking to keep him awake. He wouldn't have been taking it if it hadn't been for me. He shouldn't have. Even I know better than to mess with drugs that way.

Tell Eric to lay off on the chemicals. He's always trying to change what he is, what all of you are. Tell him I think you're about as close to perfect as you can get. Better than any of the normal people I know, except my mom.

Don't worry about the DPI guys catching up with me. I'm not stupid. I know how to be careful. I'll write to you when I figure out where I want to stay, and get my life together, just so you'll see that I'm okay.

I really love you guys. All of you, but especially you, Tam. You've been like an older sister to me. I'll miss you, but I have to do this. Try to understand.

Love,
Jamey

Roland closed his eyes slowly, and crumpled the sheet in his fist. "Damn."

She stiffened at the approaching steps, but it was only Eric. She swallowed the bitter bile in her throat and schooled her face into an emotionless mask. Not for anything in the world would Eric see that her heart had been torn to shreds. He'd only report the fact to Roland. She would die before she'd let him know how much he'd hurt her.

His curse. Perhaps he was right, at that. She'd been her father's curse, and now Roland's. Rejected by the only two men in the world from whom she'd craved acceptance. Shut out by the only two men she'd ever loved.

Loved?

Posh, she didn't love Roland. She wasn't foolish enough to have allowed her heart to become involved in what was purely a physical attraction. She'd loved once, and once only. She'd loved her father, and his disdain had taught her well never to love again.

She lifted her gaze to watch Eric's hasty approach. She waited until he reached her.

"Are you all right?"

She lifted her palms up and glanced down at her own form. "I seem to be, don't I?"

"You were ill. I heard you—"

"Dry heaves. A reaction to too much exertion after...after what happened. No more than that, I assure you."

His eyes narrowed and she knew he didn't believe her. It was to his credit that he didn't pry.

"Go on, tell me what's happened. You didn't come charging into the woods to check on my health."

"No, I didn't. Though maybe I should have." He took her arm, his eyes scanning her face with some concern. "Come with me. I'll explain as we go."

He did, and by the time they entered the great hall, Rhiannon knew the situation was grave. Jamey, determined though he was, couldn't hope to outsmart or outmaneuver DPI. Her concern for the boy acted as a buffer against the sting of Roland's condemnation. She had a focus.

Tamara paced, her face wet with tears, her eyes as red-rimmed as a drunkard's. She whirled toward the door when they entered, and it was heartbreaking to see the disappointment in her eyes when she saw that it wasn't the boy.

Frederick sat on the floor, knees drawn as close to his bulky chest as he could get them. He looked as if he'd been crying, as well.

Rhiannon went to Tamara, and folded the slight woman into her arms. "There's no need for such devastation, fledgling. We'll find the little rat in no time."

"How? We don't even know where to begin."

"Your cat's gone, too," Frederick moaned from where he sat. "I should have been watching him closer. It's all my fault. What if those bad men get Jamey? What will they do to him?"

"No bad men are going to get Jamey," Eric intoned.

Tamara sniffed and straightened. "It's not your fault, Frederick. We were all supposed to be watching him. Jamey is too smart for us, that's all."

"I'm stupid," Frederick said softly. "If I wasn't so stupid—"

Rhiannon stepped to him, bent over and pulled him to his feet. "Freddy, you are not now, nor have you ever been, stupid.

I won't hear such nonsense from you again. Jamey slipped by all of us. Do you think *we're* stupid?''

He shook his head.

"You're right. We're not. And neither are you. Now…'' She turned, slowly, addressing all of them. "Enough of this weeping and wailing. I cannot stand it. You're all forgetting one important thing.''

"And what is that?'' The voice was Roland's. He stood just inside the doorway. She hadn't heard him come in, and his eyes sought hers now, not hard with condemnation, but desperate for help.

"Who I am,'' she said, her voice so low it was only a hint above a whisper, but as clear and resonant as a bell. "Rhianikki, daughter of Pharaoh, princess of Egypt. I was a priestess of Isis, studied the words of Osiris. I felt the burning sands of Egypt beneath my feet when the pyramids were still new. Within my soul is the wisdom of the ages, young ones, and there is nothing, *nothing*, that I cannot do.''

She watched Roland's reaction to her speech, fully expecting to see the familiar skepticism on his face. Instead, she thought she saw relief.

There was no doubt it was hope that filled Tamara's round eyes. "What should we do, Rhiannon?''

"Not we, Tamara. You. You are the closest to Jamey. You and he had a psychic bond even before Eric transformed you, isn't that true?''

"Yes, but—''

"No buts. You need only concentrate on the boy. Seek him out with your mind.''

Tamara shook her head. "I can't. I only feel him when he's trying to reach me, or—or when he's in trouble.''

"You can. It takes only the power of the mind. I will show you the way, Tamara.'' Rhiannon turned to Roland. "We'll need a quiet room. One with no outside auras cluttering it up.''

Roland frowned. "No one has used the chambers on the third level in centuries.''

She nodded and turned to Frederick, who was sorely in need of something to do. "Freddy, in Roland's chambers, in the small dresser beside the bed, you'll find two special candles and a packet of incense in a silver chalice. Will you get them for me?"

Frederick limped off to do her bidding. Eric scoffed. "Incense and candles? What kind of nonsense is this? We ought to be out searching for the boy."

"Be my guest, Eric. Go and search to your heart's content. You'll only be wasting your time. We have to know where he is."

Eric shook his head. "Don't take it personally, Rhiannon. I'm a man who believes in science, not hocus-pocus."

"No doubt were you human right now, you wouldn't believe in the existence of a race of undead blood-drinkers," she retorted.

He looked at the floor.

"Eric, listen to her," Tamara said softly. She turned from him. "I trust you, Rhiannon. Just tell me what to do."

Eric threw his hands in the air and turned to Roland. "Are you going to stand still for this?"

Roland shrugged. "Unless you have a better idea, or a clue where to begin searching…"

Frederick returned with the incense and candles. Rhiannon took them and led Tamara up the stone staircase, Roland and Eric following. On the third level, she passed several rotting doors before pausing at one. She stood still a moment, then nodded. "This one."

"Why?" Roland stared at her intently.

"You object?"

She watched him for a moment as he struggled with the decision. She didn't know why, and she told herself she didn't care. He'd made his feelings for her clear enough. She wouldn't trouble herself about them any further. Her only goal now was to locate the boy. Then she would leave and never return.

Finally, Roland sighed and nodded once. "Go on."

She pushed the door open and stepped inside, Tamara behind

her. For just a moment, she paused in the darkness to examine the chamber with her preternatural vision. The outermost wall curved with the shape of the tower, but the other three were flat. Two windows had been cut through the stone on that curving wall. Narrow openings, narrower without than within, that had no glass in them to block the night wind coming through. Two benches, facing each other, and carved of castle stone, sat near the windows. Ancient rushes, dry as husks, lined the cold floor, crackling beneath her steps. The tapestries that had once been brilliant works of art, hung in straggles from the walls.

Rhiannon turned to Roland and Eric. "It would be better if you waited below."

"And leave Tamara to play sorceress games alone with you? Not quite, Rhiannon. I'm staying." Eric stepped farther into the room, leaned back against the stone wall and crossed his arms over his chest.

"Eric—"

"It's all right, Tamara," Rhiannon said. "I'm fairly used to being mistrusted by males."

"It isn't that—"

She quelled Eric's protests with a single glance. "I'll need your cooperation if you insist on staying. You must be utterly silent and still, and you must make an effort to keep your mind closed to us. Agreed?"

"Fine."

She glanced once at Roland, though even looking at him brought a stab of pain so intense she had trouble keeping it hidden. "You won't know I'm here," he told her.

Oh, but she would.

She moved into the room's center, knelt down and waited for Tamara to join her. "I want you to lie down," she told her as she placed the candles and poured some of the incense into the chalice.

"I might have some matches," Roland offered.

"Silence." Rhiannon's whispered word carried a tone of authority, and Roland said no more.

Rhiannon stretched herself out on the crisp rushes, lying on her back. At her right, near her shoulder, but far enough away to be safe, was one blood-red candle. Near her waist, the silver dish, and a small mound of dried incense. Near her hip, the second candle. Beyond those three items, Tamara lay still.

Rhiannon closed her eyes. "Relax, Tamara. Close your eyes. Put all fear and worry from your mind. Feel the stone floor beneath your back begin to soften. Inhale slowly, deeply. That's it. Hold the breath in your lungs for a moment. Drain the nourishment from the air before you release it once more. Slowly...slowly. Yes, all of it. Every bit, until your lungs are utterly emptied. Now, wait...wait...and inhale once more. Fill yourself to bursting, but slowly. Yes."

She kept her voice low, even, hypnotic. "With each breath you take the floor is becoming softer. Feel it? It's like down, now. You can feel yourself sinking into it, can't you?"

"Yes."

"Good. Now, continue just as you're doing. And I will do the same. When your mind is floating free, you will know, Tamara. Reach out to Jamey then. Think of him. Put his image in front of your eyes. Surround yourself with the memory of his scent. Concentrate on the precise curl of each lock of his hair, the sound of his laughter, the warmth of his touch. In this way, you will find him."

Rhiannon began her own ritual breathing, then. She allowed herself to relax, and began sinking into the abyss of her own psyche. She would focus on Pandora, and hope for some clue through the cat.

Roland stood beside Eric, leaning back against the wall, watching the bizarre ritual. True, he'd been willing to give Rhiannon a chance, especially since he was afraid to open his mouth to object. He seemed to wound her every time he spoke to her. Why, he wondered? Why did he hurt her the way he did? He certainly hadn't intended to. God knew, she didn't deserve it. He'd shared with Rhiannon his most terrible secret, the one he'd been sure would cause her to hate and fear him. Instead, she'd offered comfort. Dammit to hell, she'd shed tears for him! And he'd wounded her in return.

She hadn't looked him squarely in the eye for more than a second at a time since she'd left him in the *cimetière*. He regretted that he'd caused her such pain. But at least now, her feelings toward him seemed to have cooled. One of them needed to remain at a distance, or he'd end up hurting her beyond repair. And looking at her slender body, relaxed in a trancelike state on the rush-strewn floor, he knew damned well it couldn't be him.

As the minutes ticked away, though, even Roland began to doubt her. What sort of witchcraft was she working here? How could lying about in age-old rushes help Jamey?

He was eager to be out and searching for the boy, and worried in case DPI should beat him to it. Then, with a small popping sound, the candles standing between the two women burst into flame. A second later, the incense in the dish began smoldering, sending a soft gray spiral of fragrant smoke upward.

CHAPTER TEN

Nothing came. Nothing she wanted, at least. Rhiannon sat up abruptly, and pinched the candles out with her fingers. She massaged her temples and sighed.

This had been *her* room. Rebecca's room. The girl who'd thrown herself from the tower to escape marriage to Roland. Images of the young, lovely creature had flooded into Rhiannon's psyche, making it impossible to concentrate on Pandora. There was something troubled in Rebecca's spirit, something uneasy. She was not at peace.

"Rhiannon?"

She glanced up at Roland, saw the question in his eyes. "I'm sorry."

"He's in a car."

Tamara's small voice startled them all. She still lay on her back, but her eyes were open. She remained motionless, as if she feared that moving would shake the images from her mind.

"He's in a small, black car. There's a blue duffel bag in his lap, with some clothes inside, and a little money. And his cleats. His cleats are in there, too." With that sentence, her voice warbled and her eyes filled.

Eric started forward, but Rhiannon held up a hand.

"Tamara, who is driving the car?"

She frowned. "I don't know him. He's very big. Like a wrestler. His hair is cut close to his head so it sticks up in bristles. It's dark. His nose is like a bulldog's." She frowned harder. "There is a tattoo on his right forearm, a cobra."

"Lucien," Roland whispered.

"Can you tell which direction they drive, Tamara?"

She shook her head. "There are mountains, with snow at the peaks." Tamara sat up slowly, and Eric bent to help her to her feet. She met his intense gaze. "It's the same man who attacked Rhiannon, isn't it? He has Jamey now."

Eric nodded.

Never before had Rhiannon seen such an expression on the fledgling's face. Always, she'd seemed so timid, so mild. Now, her eyes glowed with the fierceness of an approaching storm. She tossed her head like a lioness, her jaw tight with what looked like rage. "If he hurts Jamey, I will kill him." She spoke in a calm, level voice, leaving no doubt she meant what she said. Stiffly, she moved past Eric and out the door. Eric hurried behind her.

"Well. I've never seen her like that."

"I have," Roland said softly. "But only when the boy was threatened."

She turned in the doorway, where she'd been standing to watch them go. She was alone with Roland, she realized all at once. She swallowed the lump that leapt into her throat. "This was *her* room, wasn't it?"

He glanced around him, and nodded. "How did you know?"

"I feel her here. She did not detest you so thoroughly as you think, you know."

He shook his head. "That, I cannot believe."

She shrugged. "It's not my concern what you believe. I only thought you might like to know." She turned to go, but he caught her shoulder from behind.

"My words, in the *cimetière* were not meant to cause you pain, Rhiannon. If they did, then I'm sorry."

She stiffened. "It takes more than words to cause me any pain. Don't worry yourself on that account."

He pulled her around to face him, and she saw the regret in his eyes. "Rhiannon, I hurt you. I know I did, and believe me, I wish I could take back the words that caused that hurt."

"Why take back the truth?" She removed his hand from her shoulder with a brush of her own. "We have the boy to find, Roland. This conversation only delays his rescue."

Roland sat in the front of the rental car, map unfolded on his lap. Of them all, he was the most familiar with the area and the terrain, having traveled much of it by horseback in times long past. True, the towns and cities and roads differed. But the lay of the land was the same. And the only snowcapped mountains near enough for Lucien to have reached within such a brief span of time, were in the direction they now traveled.

Eric drove as Roland navigated. Rhiannon remained in the back seat beside Tamara. The small vehicle seemed to reverberate with the tension it held. It was Eric who finally broke the silence.

"I believe I owe you an apology, Rhiannon."

"Whatever for?"

"I didn't take your meditation seriously. I should have."

She waved a dismissive hand. "Don't give up your skepticism so easily. We haven't found Jamey yet."

"But we're on his trail. Tamara feels it too strongly for it to be a mistake. I don't doubt that."

Roland shook his head. "Admit it, Eric. She had you hooked from the moment those candles burst to life on their own."

Eric smiled and glanced over his shoulder at Rhiannon. Roland wished he could do the same, but looking at her had traumatic effects on his mind.

"He's right," Eric said. "That was a convincing display."

By the tone of Rhiannon's voice, Roland knew the exact expression on her face. That almost smile. The look in her eyes that said she knew something you didn't. Many, many things you didn't.

"A simple parlor trick for an immortal, Eric. I could teach you to do it. To be honest, I usually light the candles in a more mundane manner, but I was angry and wanted to be sure you were suitably chastened."

Roland glanced sideways at his friend in time to see the surprise on his face.

"Well, it worked." Eric frowned and adjusted his mirror for a better view of her face. "You say you could teach me to do it?"

She must have nodded, but Roland wasn't certain. "You have

all become familiar with the physical strength that comes with immortality. But the dark gift brings with it a psychic strengthening, as well. It grows with age, as the physical powers do. Lighting the candles is simply a matter of focusing your mind's power on their wicks. Like a beam of light, it hits, and they ignite.

"As both the strengths reach full potential, we can learn to combine the psychic with the physical to achieve the two feats even I've not yet mastered. But I've heard of some who have."

Roland tilted his head. "Rhiannon, there are some things better left alone."

"Of course there are," she told him. "Cobras and active volcanoes are among them. This is not."

Eric grinned wider. "She's got you there. Tell me, Rhiannon. What two feats are you speaking of?"

"One is flight. And I'm actually very close to mastering that one. I can remain aloft for just under a minute. The trick is in maintaining the speed, and keeping the mind utterly focused."

Roland did turn now. "For God's sake, Rhiannon! I had no idea you were experimenting with such nonsense. You'll get yourself killed."

Her eyes narrowed. "If I do, that will be no one's problem but my own." She shifted her gaze back to Eric. "Actually, practicing is horrible. I can only go up once a night. Then I fall and am usually too broken and bruised to do more than crawl back to my lair and wait for the healing sleep."

Eric frowned, and Roland felt the glance he shot his way. "That *is* pushing your luck, Rhiannon. Suppose one night you're too badly injured to make it back before dawn?"

She shrugged. "Then I supposed I would roast, wouldn't I?"

She was trying to hurt him, Roland thought. Her words were filled with bitterness and pain; pain caused by his own careless words. She was only speaking this way to strike back. What in God's name had he said to hurt her this much?

"And the other feat?" Eric prompted.

"Ah, this will amaze you. There are some, I am told, who are able to alter their form."

"You mean, change shape? In what way?"

"Any way they wish, I imagine. The tales I've heard name only one immortal capable of such feats, and the forms he's said to have taken include the raven, the wolf and the infamous vampire bat."

Now, Roland noted with a twinge of gratitude, even Tamara's attention was caught. She'd done nothing throughout the entire ride but stare out the window into the passing night.

"You've got to be kidding," she said, eyes wide. "A vampire bat?"

"Well, I like to think he has a sense of humor, and did it on a lark. Honestly, if given the ability to be anything one wished, why would one choose to be a nasty little bat?"

"Who is this talented immortal?" Eric asked, and Roland could tell by the tone of his voice that he was fascinated by the possibilities.

"He is called Damien. He is said to be the oldest and most powerful of any of us. I never sought him out. I have no desire to meet the man."

"Why not? I'd be thrilled to talk to him," Eric said.

Rhiannon lowered her voice deliberately, Roland was sure. "You know the trick I did, igniting the candles with my mind?" Eric nodded. "Well, it is said Damien can perform the same feat on people, mortal and immortal alike. He just looks at them, and...*poof!* Living torches."

Tamara nudged her with an elbow. "You're trying to scare us." She looked at Roland. "None of this is true, is it, Roland?"

He sighed. "As far as I know, it's all true. Though I've never witnessed any of it firsthand."

Eric shot Roland an accusing stare. "Why have you never told me any of this?"

"As I said, there are some things best left alone. You think I want you out leaping from rooftops and breaking your neck?

Changing yourself into a baboon and then getting stuck that way? Seeking out this man who can burn you to a cinder?''

"Honestly, Roland, you are such a—" Rhiannon stopped in the middle of the sentence, her entire body going rigid. Her hand flew to her lips. "Stop the car! Stop, Eric, at once!''

Eric slammed his foot onto the brake pedal. Tires skidded in gravel as he tried to pull to the side. Rhiannon was out the door before the vehicle had come to a full stop. Like a gazelle, she leaped the ditch and bounded into the forest.

Roland raced after her, having no idea what to expect. He knew Eric and Tamara were right behind him, but his entire being was focused on Rhiannon. He'd felt the slap of her sudden shock as if it had been his own. But she'd been so closed off to him since they'd spoken in the *cimetière* that he hadn't been able to tell what was wrong.

Then he saw her. A quivering, sobbing heap on the ground, her arms around the sleek, black body. Pandora wasn't moving. The cat's eyes were closed, and there was a sickening twist to one foreleg. Blood caked to a cut near her silken ear.

Roland knelt and pulled Rhiannon away. Eric and Tamara were there, and as Eric began to examine the cat, Roland held Rhiannon in his arms. She sobbed helplessly, her entire body quaking with each spasm. Gone was the haughty, arrogant princess. In his arms, he held a devastated child, and it tore his heart out to see her so tortured.

"She's alive," Eric said softly. "But I'm not sure we can save her. She needs a veterinarian.''

"Then we'll find her one," Roland declared, his arms tightening of their own will around her shuddering body. Her tears soaked his cloak at the shoulder. "There's a town five miles east of here. It will only be a small detour." Roland lowered his head, pressed his lips to hers. "She'll be all right, Rhiannon," he whispered into her hair. "I promise you.''

She shook her head against his neck. "She…has to be." She drew a ragged breath and lifted her head to gaze into his eyes. "I'm s-sorry." Stiffening, she pulled herself from his embrace.

She bent over the cat again, carefully slipped both forearms beneath the body and lifted her. Then she turned and started for the car, her shoulders still quaking with involuntary sobs.

Roland swallowed hard. Had he so alienated her that she couldn't even accept comfort from him?

He raced ahead of her, and opened the car's rear door. Rhiannon folded herself into the vehicle, the cat still in her arms. She scooted across the back seat, cradling the huge animal's head and shoulders in her lap. Roland gently eased Pandora's hindquarters in as far as he could, and closed the door with care. Tamara squeezed into the front, between the two men.

As Eric drove, Rhiannon whispered, stroking the cat's big, still head. She spoke as if no one else were in the car, addressing the animal as if it were human. "Don't leave me now, Pandora. There is no one else, you know. Only you. If you go, I'll be alone again." Between each few words, a sob was torn from her breast.

Tamara turned in the seat, tears dampening her lashes. "You love her very much, don't you?"

Rhiannon shook her head briskly. Her hair hung over her face, still bowed to the cat's. Tears glued strands of it to her cheeks. "Don't be ridiculous." She sniffed and sobbed once more. "I'm an immortal. I don't believe in loving anything." She stroked Pandora's head. "It's just that…she has loved me. Just as I am, she has loved me. No one else ever has."

"Oh, Rhiannon—"

"I never had to prove myself to her. I was never unworthy in her huge green eyes. Never her curse."

Roland winced at her words.

"Unconditional acceptance, absolute devotion. I've never known those things in all my years of existence except from Pandora. She wouldn't dream of rejecting me as not good enough to deserve her attention."

Roland felt a stinging in the backs of his eyes, and he heard a suspicious sniff from Eric. "Rhiannon, no one could ever see you as unworthy—"

"No one but you, you mean? Ah, but you were not the first. No, that honor was reserved for the man who sired me. Don't think your indifference is so important, Roland. The greatest Pharaoh of Egypt labeled me his curse long before you did."

Eric pulled the car to a stop at an all-night service station, and as the attendant emerged, he rolled down his window and asked in French if there was a veterinarian in town. When the answer was affirmative, Roland got out and demanded a telephone and a directory. He would rouse the man from sleep, if necessary.

As he waited for the veterinarian to answer his telephone, he berated himself endlessly. He'd known nothing of Rhiannon's past. That her father had rejected her. Oh, God, and with the same words he'd used in the *cimetière*. He could not have caused her more heartache, he suspected, had he been deliberately seeking to destroy her. Could he not inhale without hurting her? How could he repair the pain he'd caused?

Rhiannon leaned over the table in the clinic that was no more than a room in the man's home. "You ought to keep her sedated until I return," Rhiannon told him. "There is no telling how she will react to strangers."

"*Oui,* I will take no chances, *mademoiselle.*" He rubbed his balding head, and adjusted the rectangular specs on his nose. "I have treated many species, but never ze pet panther." He paused, but Rhiannon offered no explanation. After a moment he shrugged and let it go. "She was struck by ze auto, *non?*"

"I don't know. I found her in the woods like this." Rhiannon glanced up into the mortal's pale blue eyes. "If you can save her, I will build you a new clinic. An entire hospital, if you wish. I will give you more money than you can make in a year. Three years."

His smile was sudden, and genuine. He took her hand and patted it. "I adore animals, *mademoiselle.* You share zat with me, *non?* I will save her eef I can, whether you promise me the moon or bushel of apples as payment." He released her hand to stroke Pandora's silken fur.

"I believe you will." She sniffed, and swiped at her eyes.

She hadn't cried so much since the guards had carried her from her father's palace, to be placed in the temple of Isis. She'd been a five-year-old child then. She was ageless now. It was ridiculous, how fond she'd grown of the cat. "I don't know when I can come for her. A few days, perhaps."

"I will care for her. Do not fear."

"Thank you." It didn't seem enough. She'd meant what she'd said. If he pulled Pandora through this, she would shower him with rewards.

Leaving the cat there felt like abandoning a babe. Rhiannon fought her tears and forced herself to go. Jamison needed her right now. She mustn't forget that.

In the car, she sat in stony silence for a time, until Tamara took her hand and held it firmly. "She'll be all right."

Rhiannon nodded. "Lucien will not."

"You think he did that to her?"

Rhiannon nodded again. "Pandora was with Jamey. Now Jamey is with Lucien, and Pandora is on a cold table. Yes, I believe he is responsible. And I believe he will wish for death long before it's granted him." She closed her eyes and sent her thoughts over the miles. *Do you hear me, Lucien? I'm coming for you, you know.*

Her eyes flew wide with surprise when she heard, echoing through her mind, the reply. *I'll be waiting.*

"It will be dawn soon. We need to seek shelter."

Tamara sighed in frustration and Roland well understood her feelings. "We'll do Jamey no good if we all sizzle in the sun, Tamara."

"True enough."

Eric continued driving, but turned onto smaller and narrower dirt tracks, in search of a safe resting spot for all of them. Finally, an abandoned barn came into view. Roland pointed to it. "We can drive around to the back, to hide the car from view. Better yet, get the door open and pull it right inside. What do you think?"

"That would be the best idea. The ground in front looks

smooth enough. Why don't you open the door, and see if there's room inside?''

Roland did, wrenching the door. It gave way and slid on its rusted tracks until there was room enough for the car to pass through. The barn was empty, save for a huge mound of musty-smelling hay and a few ancient-looking tools scattered about. Roland moved a broken pitchfork and an old milk can out of the way, and waved for Eric to bring the car in.

As soon as the engine died, Roland closed the barn door, plunging them into darkness.

''This will be safe enough,'' Tamara observed.

''Can't be certain about cracks and crevices, Tamara. We'd best burrow into that haystack before we sleep, just to be safe.''

She nodded, moving closer to Eric, who slipped his arm around her shoulders and squeezed her closer. She let her head lean onto his shoulder and closed her eyes. ''What do you suppose this Lucien person wants with Jamey? He's not DPI.''

Eric shook his head.

''He wants immortality, Tamara,'' Rhiannon told her. ''He wants me to transform him. I imagine he will use Jamey's life to bargain with.''

Tamara grimaced, and turned fully into Eric's arms. Roland felt his stomach clench and unclench in involuntary spasms. His arms ached to wrap around Rhiannon in the same manner. But he told himself the breach between them was a good thing. No matter how bad it felt. No matter how he longed to erase the hurt he'd caused her. It was better this way.

''He knows we're coming,'' Rhiannon said. ''He has incredible psychic capacity for a human. He's waiting for us.''

''At least we know Jamison will be kept alive in the meantime,'' Roland said, seeking to comfort Tamara in some small way. Unfortunately, he was about to cause her a great deal more discomfort.

''Tamara, there is something I need to tell you. About Jamey.''

She turned, frowning. ''What is it, Roland?''

Roland averted his gaze. She would likely hate him for this. "I've initiated a search for his natural father."

Her eyes widened. "You—but why? I don't understand. Jamey doesn't need him. He has us."

Roland shook his head slowly. "I am as fond of him as you are, Tamara. You know that. But we must think of what is best for Jamison."

"To leave the people he knows and loves? To go off and live with a stranger? You think that's best for him?"

Eric touched her face, turned it toward his. "Tamara, hear him out. If you were in Jamey's place, wouldn't you at least like to know your father, to find out something about him?"

She frowned harder, and shook her head. "He abandoned his son—"

"He never knew of the boy's existence," Roland said slowly. "You said it yourself. He deserves to be informed. Jamey deserves to be given the options, and to make his own decision."

"If you're sick of caring for him, Roland, then Eric and I will take him!"

Rhiannon shook her head slowly. "Tamara, as long as he is with us, DPI will hound him. They watch us too closely, we're too easily spotted. In a normal, mortal family, Jamey would blend in as just another human boy. He'd be safe."

"I can't believe you're all saying these things," Tamara said, shaking her head. "Especially you, Eric. How could you turn on me this way?"

Eric looked stricken. "No, Tamara. I only—"

"I don't want to hear any more!" She tugged free of his grip and raced out of the barn, through a smaller, side door, and into the night.

Eric put his head in his hands. Roland felt as if he'd been saying the wrong thing at the wrong time forever. "I'm sorry, Eric. I didn't realize how strongly she would react."

Eric shook his head. "Not your fault, old friend. She'll see that it's the right thing, given time." He glanced again toward the fading night beyond the door. "I'd better go after her."

He did, and Roland turned toward Rhiannon. "You think I'm doing the right thing?"

She sighed, and walked away from him, settling herself down on the hay. "Since when does the staid and honorable Roland de Courtemanche seek the opinion of the reckless and self-destructive Rhiannon of Egypt?"

"I would like for us to remain friends, Rhiannon." He crossed the barn, and sat down beside her in the sour-smelling hay. "And while I do think you reckless and self-destructive, I still value your opinion."

"Do you?" Her finely etched brows rose above her slanted, dark eyes.

"You know I do."

She sniffed, tilting her chin upward. "Then you'll be interested to hear that I think you are the biggest fool ever born."

He frowned, studying her perfect face, seeing the hint of sadness still lingering in her eyes. "Why?"

She stared at him intensely, as if trying to light the wicks of the candles in his mind. "You'll never have with another, what you could have had with me."

His throat went dry. "I know that."

"Then you're ten times the fool I thought you were." She turned away from him.

He touched her shoulder. "I didn't know about your father's rejection, Rhiannon. I chose my words poorly when I referred to you as my curse. It's little wonder you're so angry with me." She didn't turn to face him. "Rhiannon, I didn't mean it the way it seemed to you. It's that I want—"

She jerked away from his touch and faced him, eyes blazing. "I do not care *what* you want, nor am I interested in your interpretation of your own words."

"Rhiannon, if you would let me explain, you would see that—"

"It no longer matters, so stop hectoring me with it." She looked away once again, and her eyes cooled until they held a chill that reached out to him. "I am leaving, Roland. Just as soon as the boy is safe, and Pandora is well enough to travel. I am leaving, and this time, I will never darken your door again.'' She smiled very slightly, but it was a smile of bitterness and pain. ''You ought to be extremely relieved. Your *curse* will soon be removed.''

CHAPTER ELEVEN

Roland rose before the others, flinging the mildew-scented hay away from his face, and brushing it vigorously from his clothes. His sleep had been anything but restful.

He told himself of the many possible reasons for that: Tamara's anger at him, and the rift he seemed to have caused between her and Eric; worry over Jamison's physical well-being, compounded by concern for the boy's state of mind; the question of whether the cat would recover, and if not, what effect that would have on her owner.

But none of those things were truly what had kept his mind twisting and turning all day long. In truth, it was his own careless words and the pain they had caused in Rhiannon that haunted him. God, for the power to travel back in time, armed with the knowledge about her he now had. If he'd known that her own father had rejected her with the same decree, "You are my curse," he'd never have repeated the devastation. True, he needed to remain apart from Rhiannon, but not for his life would he wish to hurt her.

The truth was, he cared for her. A great deal more than he'd ever allowed himself to admit. It had been easily denied when she'd been far away, when her visits had been few and oh, so far between. Denying it had become more difficult with her return, but not impossible. Her reckless ways and boisterous nature enabled him to mask irritation as dislike and disapproval.

But when he'd seen her on the dew-wet forest floor, reduced to uncontrollable sobbing, clutching the limp cat like a babe in her arms, he'd been unable to deny it any longer. Her pain had sliced into his heart. He'd suddenly wanted nothing more than to take that pain away.

He strolled to the side door, his feet sinking in loose hay. Three birds took flight as he passed beneath the rafters on which they nested, their wings flapping noisily and echoing into the high barn. A feather drifted down past his face, and he watched it fall.

Outside, onto the drying, browning autumn grass, he moved. The air held a hint of the winter to come, but the sky was without a cloud. Stiff weeds scraped his shoes as he moved away from the barn, senses attuned for outsiders. He heard only the perfect harmony of the crickets, the occasional whir of a bat swooping and diving overhead, the unearthly whine of the wind whipping across an ancient weather vane high atop the barn.

He didn't want Rhiannon to leave.

The knowledge made itself known to him almost as soon as her decision had left her lips. He would be utterly alone if he knew he'd never see her again. True, she'd never been a steady presence in his life, but he'd always known she was there. He'd always had the absolute certainty that if he summoned her, she would come to him; that when he least expected her, she'd show up unannounced. She'd drag him into a whirlwind, whip it into a hurricane, listen to him tell her how foolish and reckless she was, and then blow away like an errant summer breeze.

He couldn't ask her to stay. Her presence played havoc with his control, made him careless. He would only hurt her, over and over, as he'd already proven.

He closed his eyes, and her face hovered in his mind. That he could ever harm her deliberately seemed absolutely impossible. For a moment, he considered the possibility that Eric had been right. That his brutish behavior with Rhiannon had been a side effect of the drug.

Then he shook his head roughly. What difference did it make? It couldn't change what he knew about himself, what he truly was. How could he ask Rhiannon to stay, knowing her presence would drive him beyond hope of recovering?

If only she would change her reckless ways, alter her wild nature, calm her impulsive mind. He could help her. She could help him. If he could convince her of it, then perhaps...

No. Rhiannon would never change. He was sorely afraid he'd

hear of her death one day. And he had no doubt it would be dramatic and horrible.

"Roland?"

He turned at the feminine voice, knowing by its lack of depth and timber that it belonged to Tamara, not Rhiannon.

She came forward, head bowed, not meeting his eyes. She stopped when her toes nearly touched his, slipped her arms around his neck and hugged him hard. "I'm sorry I said those things to you. I know how much you love Jamey."

He returned her embrace, taking comfort in the physical closeness of another living being. "It's all right, Tamara. You're on edge. We all are."

She lowered her arms and took a step backward, her gaze meeting his at last. "I'm so afraid for him."

"We won't let any harm come to him, fledgling."

She nodded fast, squeezing her eyes tight for a moment. When she opened them again, she searched his face. "What about you? I know you're hurting. I can see it in your face."

He averted his own gaze, shaking his head in the negative.

"Don't lie to me, Roland. You're in pain. But so is Rhiannon."

He looked at her once more. "Has she spoken to you about this?"

"Of course not. She can't even admit to herself that she's hurting. But she is. When this is over—"

"When this is over, Rhiannon will go her own way, and I will go mine. To do anything else has...has risks far too great to consider."

Tamara smiled very slightly. Her palm came up to cover his cheek. "Oh, Roland. How can someone as wise as you be so blind? There are no risks too great, when it comes to love."

"Love?" He shook his head as her hand fell away. "There is no love involved here. Your romantic leanings are clouding your vision."

"Your stubbornness is clouding yours."

"Everyone ready?" Eric's words accompanied the squeaky protest of the large barn door as he forced it open.

Roland looked beyond him to where Rhiannon stood, brushing bits of hay from her hair. She moved forward, yanking the car door open. Roland couldn't stop himself going to her before she got in. He reached up, as she stiffened, and took a piece of hay from the back of her head. He held it up between them. "You missed one."

Her eyes, as they fixed on his, were wide and fathomless. He scanned their ebony depths in search of some hint she would allow him to become her friend again.

Instead, he saw a glimmering tongue of flame beyond the jet, and felt an answering fire leap to life in his soul. She still wanted him. And God help him, he wanted her, too. She licked her lips, swallowed hard and finally tore her gaze away. As she tucked herself into the car, Roland closed his eyes and swore under his breath.

"You'll work it out, old friend." Eric's hand clapped to Roland's shoulder, his deep voice, with a hint of amusement, was low and near his ear. "If you don't go stark raving mad first."

Roland shot him a scowl and rounded the car's nose to slide into the front passenger seat. He wouldn't attempt to sit beside Rhiannon in the back, though his body was demanding he do that, and anything else necessary to be close to her. He needed to focus on Jamey. All of this anguished soul-searching would wait until the boy was safe and sound once more.

Rhiannon hated herself for still feeling such potent desire for a man who'd rejected her time and time again. Still, there had been something in his eyes, something new.

She closed her eyes and shook her head. She was imagining things, that was all. The thought of leaving him, of never seeing him again filled her with such utter desolation she wondered how she would bear it. Already, the idea burrowed a fresh wound into her heart. It dug in right beside the pain she felt for Pandora, and the worry of losing her, as well. Was there to be nothing left to her?

When the car ran low on petrol, Eric pulled into a service station. He and Tamara got out to stretch their legs. Roland leapt out, as well, and she saw him head for a pay phone. He'd barely said a word to her throughout the journey, but she'd felt his eyes upon her often, and looked up to see his head turned, his gaze caressing her. And he didn't look away when she met it. He faced her and allowed her to search his eyes, to try to see what drove him now. Unfortunately, all she detected was misery, regret and confusion. No help at all.

In a moment, he returned to the car, got in and twisted around in the seat, propping an elbow along the back of it. "I phoned that vet. He says Pandora is going to pull through."

Rhiannon was stunned, and the relief that rinsed her soul with his announcement overwhelmed her. "She's all right? She's really going to be all right?"

Roland nodded. "She might have a permanent limp, but she's recovering nicely and he was able to save the leg."

Rhiannon closed her eyes and released all of her breath at once. When she opened them again, she saw that self-satisfied expression on his face. "I suppose I owe you my thanks."

He shook his head quickly. "You owe me nothing. I only wanted to see some of the worry leave your eyes."

She felt a lump form in her throat. "Why?"

"Why? What do you mean, why? I care about you, Rhiannon. To see you in pain causes me pain, as well."

The hot moisture that sprung to her eyes was rapidly battered back by her fluttering lids. She bit her lip and forced her breaths to come calmly, not in broken gasps. Was he saying he cared for her? She refused to ask. She wouldn't give him yet another opportunity to reject her.

Yet, an insane and childish hope alighted in her heart, despite her best efforts to squelch it.

Tamara returned to the car with Eric and they were off yet again, headlights bounding into the night. It was nearly dawn when they entered a tiny village in the shadows of the French

Alps, and Tamara clutched Rhiannon's hand and whispered urgently, "This is it. This is what I saw."

Eric stiffened behind the wheel. "You're certain, Tamara?"

"Yes."

Rhiannon licked her lips, her pain forgotten as she began feeling the anticipation of the showdown she sensed was to come. A little shiver of unease danced over her nape, making her shudder.

"We should park the car," Roland said, his voice sure and calm. "We'll strike out on foot, and search for Lucien's automobile. We can question any villagers we meet about the black car, and describe both Jamey and Lucien to them, in case they've been seen."

"Or we might try simply asking Lucien where he is. He wants us to find him. I'm certain of it."

Roland turned to stare at Rhiannon. "But then he would be forewarned."

"He already is, Roland. He knows we're coming," she said slowly.

"But not exactly when we'll arrive."

"Not the precise moment, no. But he knows it will be by night. And he must know that tonight is the most likely possibility, simply by the distance traveled. We do not have the element of surprise in our arsenal, Roland." She licked her lips, thinking again of Pandora's twisted leg. "Nor do we need it."

"She's right," Eric said. "I think we should get this thing underway, right now, tonight. If we begin searching, we may not find them before dawn. Then we'll be forced to leave Jamey in his hands for another day."

Roland inhaled, pursed his lips and finally sighed. "All right. Since time is of the essence, go ahead, Rhiannon. Make contact if you can."

Her brows rose at his "if you can," but she settled onto the back seat and closed her eyes. *The time has come, Lucien. Where are you?*

She didn't need to try again, or to concentrate very hard at all. It was as if he'd been attuned to her already and was only awaiting her words to make the fact known.

Very good. You were faster than I'd hoped. There is a cabin, halfway up Mont Noir. I will await you there.

She frowned, disliking the confidence emanating from his mind. *Is the boy well? Is he safe? I warn you, if you've harmed him, you will pay.*

She waited. But there was no response. Focusing her being on his, she tried again. *Lucien, this conversation is not over. I wish to know of the boy.*

Again, there was no reply. Rhiannon opened her eyes, and shook her head. "A cabin, halfway up a mountain called Noir. Odd name."

"I know where it is," Roland said. "Come, we'll have to go by foot. There are no roads up that sheer face."

Eric clasped Roland's arm before he could get out of the car. "We do not wish to be trapped up there at dawn, Roland. Is there time?"

Roland nodded. "Three hours is sufficient. I'd guess we have nearer to four." Roland glanced into the rear seat, and Rhiannon bristled, sensing what he was about to suggest. "Perhaps it would be better if some of us remain behind, in case the others are somehow bested."

"Good idea," Rhiannon said quickly. "You and Eric should wait here, while Tamara and I go up and teach this foolish mortal a lesson."

Eric turned fast, then understood her motives and smiled. "I would never allow Tamara to face danger without me at her side. Unfortunately, she feels the same about me. Aggravating as all hell, but there it is." He glanced toward Roland. "You can't hate the man for wishing to protect you, Rhiannon."

"I am capable of protecting myself," she replied, her voice thin. "And him, too, if necessary. If he knows me at all, he ought to know that."

"With your recklessness and your anger over the cat, Rhiannon, I am afraid you'll charge without hesitation into whatever kind of trap the infernal bastard has waiting." Roland sent her a quelling glare that held more than just anger. "I was only hoping to keep you from an earlier than necessary demise, if possible."

She tilted her head to one side. "With you there, constantly reminding me how foolish I am, how can I help but exercise a modicum of caution? You worry for nothing."

"I worry for you!" The words burst forth on an explosion of anger as Roland jumped out of the car and slammed the door. Rhiannon got out, slamming her door, as well, and stood facing him, formulating a scathing reply.

But his hand suddenly swept a path through her hair, settling in a gentle curl around her nape. "Stay close to me, Rhiannon. And be careful. Please, for God's sake, be careful."

Again that stupid lump came into her throat, so large this time it nearly choked her. And she heard herself answer like an obedient schoolgirl. "I will, Roland."

She shook herself.

A second later, the four of them started down the narrow, twisting roads of the village, toward the mountain that loomed at its edge. A dark, hulking shape, it rose from the smaller peaks around it like an angry god among sinners. Its sheer face seemed to be barren of anything, save dark-colored granite, and its peak was swathed in dense mists.

The climb would have been difficult for mortal men. Roland winced as he thought about Jamey, being forced, perhaps brutally, to ascend the ragged-edged slope. He would have been exhausted by the time they reached the top. Cold, perhaps hungry. Frightened. Grieving for Pandora, if he knew of her fate. The poor child had no way of knowing she would recover, or even that she'd been found.

He took a moment to curse himself for not seeking out the child's father long ago, then returned his attention to the matters at hand. Rescuing Jamison. And protecting Rhiannon. He had no qualms about admitting the sudden fear for her that held him in its grip. For it was Rhiannon who seemed to be the sole focus of Lucién's obsession. She was the one he'd attacked with his nasty little blade. She was the one whose blood he seemed determined to have running in his veins. She was the one he could contact psychically, and whom he could hear in turn. The man was no ordinary human. And his interest in Rhiannon, Roland sensed, had far greater meaning than any of them yet knew.

The slope angled sharply away from the level, grassy ground. An abrupt change from the lush and fragrant area around them. The surrounding hillsides were grassy, at least at their bases, and dotted with trees and vegetation. Not Mont Noir. A fitting locale, Roland thought, for the grim battle that was to come.

In very little time, they had ascended beyond the spots where malnourished tufts of coarse grass sprouted from between the stone, and clambered their way over sheer, bare rock.

Roland's foot slid once on the surface. He caught himself, then reached behind him to grip Rhiannon's hand and help her along. The look she shot him was not one of anger, but one of puzzlement. Why should she seem so confused by his wanting to help her? Eric helped Tamara along in much the same way.

They were four dark shapes, scaling the side of a black mountain in the dead of night. To the world below, they would be invisible. Wind howled over them, buffeting them as if to send them tumbling down. Air grew thinner and crisper with every foot they gained.

Finally, they crested to a level area and in the distance, Roland saw smoke spiraling into the night. He pointed to the pale gray column, and started toward a cluster of boulders and rock outcroppings. The smoke seemed to emanate from somewhere beyond them. Though the ground was level, and much safer here, he kept his hand curled around Rhiannon's. He half expected her to pull hers free. When she didn't, he immediately wondered why.

Hurrying now, they raced over uneven, rocky terrain, rounded the cluster of stone that blocked their way and stood facing a reddish log cabin. Small windows stood on either side of a wide, plankboard door, like eyes above a toothy grin. Frilly-edged curtains, from this distance, were the lacy lashes. So cozy, this little haven on high. So innocuous in appearance. The perfect, comforting setting to disguise purest evil.

Her hand still resting in his, Rhiannon stood beside him, gazing as he did at the quaint little building. He studied the soft yellow glow of the lamplight from beyond the windows, and he felt the shudder that rippled through her.

Instinctively, he squeezed her hand. Just as instinctively, he thought, she squeezed his in return. The exchange took place in less than a second and then they were looking at each other. Eyes searching, a thousand questions in both sets. Not a single answer in either.

Roland swallowed. He released her hand and slipped his arm around her shoulders as they started for the cabin. She didn't pull away. Eric and Tamara walked abreast of them until they stood before the door.

"I'm certain he doesn't have the tranquilizer," Rhiannon said softly as she reached for the door's curving metal grip. She closed her hand around it and pushed it inward.

It swung without a sound. Glancing around apprehensively, Roland stepped in before her. A hearth on the facing wall snapped and sparked invitingly. In an overstuffed chair, the back of Lucien's head was all that was visible.

"Come in, come in," he said without turning or moving in any way. "Rhiannon is quite right. I don't have the tranquilizer. And this is no sort of a trap. It's a meeting. One I hope will be mutually beneficial."

Roland stepped farther inside, still looking about him. His senses were honed for others present, but he sensed no one. Rhiannon came in beside him, but her eyes, he noted, were only for Lucien. They were filled with hatred and anger, and he touched her arm in an effort to calm her.

She stepped forward, gripped the back of the chair and yanked it onto its back. Lucien rolled to the floor, eyes wide. But as she loomed over him, his lips curved upward slightly.

"I'm going to kill you now, you bastard," she said slowly. "I'm going to take my time about it. Are you ready?"

He shrugged. "I have nowhere to go."

She reached down for him, but Roland grabbed her arms from behind. "Wait, Rhiannon." He looked down at the man who waited expectantly for him to finish. "Lucien, where is the boy?"

A solid line of eyebrows rose. "When I tell you that, she'll be free to murder me. I'd be kind of foolish to give away my edge, now, wouldn't I?"

Rhiannon tugged, but Roland held her firm. He was surprised to see Tamara leap forward, grip Lucien by the front of his knit sweater and haul him to his feet, though she had to lift her arms above her head to do so. Seeing such a small figure exert so much brute strength was impressive, and strange. "If you don't tell us where he is, then I will kill you, anyway, so you don't have much choice."

Again, the dark brows rose. "Such tempers on you immortal women." He pulled his sweater from her grip and stepped backward, smoothing the fabric. "I have a proposal to make. The least you can do is hear it before you make a decision."

Eric had vanished. Vaguely, Roland knew he was searching the cabin to ascertain for himself the presence of anyone else, including Jamey. He emerged from a room then. "Jamison isn't here."

"No. He isn't here. If you want to know where he is, you'll listen to what I have to say."

Rhiannon glanced over her shoulder at Roland, the look in her eyes assuring him it was safe to let her go. He released her arms, giving her a slight nod, then focused on Lucien once more. "Say your piece, *monsieur*. But know that if we dislike what you have to tell us, you'll not live to finish the sentence."

Eric came to stand close to Tamara. "And you'd best begin by telling us about Jamey. Where is he? Is he safe?"

Lucien drew himself up, though he already towered above all of them and fairly bulged with muscle. "The boy is in perfect health and quite likely to remain that way…so long as you co-operate. His location, I'm afraid, is something I cannot reveal to you just yet."

Tamara drew a shaking breath. "Tell us what you want, Lucien. Let's stop playing games and get to it."

"A woman who thinks like me. I like that." Lucien walked brashly past them, bent and righted his easy chair. He circled to the front of it and sat down, waving a hand to the other seats nearby.

Rhiannon took the rocker nearest the fire and pulled it forward, directly in front of Lucien. She sat down, her gaze glued to his unshakably. "We all know what you want, Lucien. The dark gift. Immortality. But I don't believe you realize how foolish it is to ask it."

"Why foolish?" He leaned forward. "Isn't eternal life what every man longs for in the depths of his soul? Hasn't it been that way from the beginning of time?"

"Do you know how the change is accomplished?"

He nodded. "You will drink from me. Then I from you. When our blood mingles, I will be one of you."

"You will never be one of us," Tamara snapped.

Rhiannon's eyes seemed to pierce the very space between them. "What is to stop me from draining you dry once my teeth are embedded in your muscled neck, you fool?"

He smiled, his gaze unwavering. "There is a letter in the hands of my lawyer, in which the boy's location is revealed. The letter is addressed to Curtis Rogers, of DPI. My lawyer has instructions to send a facsimile to Rogers tomorrow night at midnight."

Rhiannon blinked, and Lucien's smile widened.

"On the other hand, fair Rhiannon, if you transform me without mishap, I will reveal the boy's locale to you, giving you ample time to reach him first."

For the first time, Roland saw uncertainty in Rhiannon's eyes. She broke eye contact with Lucien, and sought Roland's gaze, instead.

"Do not trust him, Rhiannon. There would be nothing to stop him draining you dry, either. You'd be weakened by the act. You know that."

"A risk you'll have to take, my dear, if you want the boy safe. On the other hand, you can refuse and see him become a subject for live study by some of the world's most unscrupulous scientists." He leaned toward her still farther. She didn't back away. "I understand you have firsthand knowledge of just how much...*discomfort* they can impose on a living being."

Tamara caught her breath. Roland closed his eyes, knowing her memories of that horrific lab must be the stuff of Rhiannon's deepest nightmares.

"Here is how generous I can be," Lucien went on. "I'll give you time to think it over. Come back at sundown tomorrow. If you agree, we'll make the switch, and you'll have the boy back before the fax goes out. Or, you can kill me, try to find him on your own, fail and regret it for the rest of eternity. The choice is yours."

Rhiannon blinked slowly. "It seems we *have* little choice."

"One thing, Rhiannon. You come to me alone, tomorrow evening. I don't trust them for a minute. You come alone, or the deal is off."

Roland felt a blade twist in his chest. "Absolutely not," he said in a low voice. "I won't allow it."

Rhiannon acted as if he hadn't spoken. "I hope there will be time, Lucien. The gift of endless night isn't given as simply as you seem to think. There is a ritual involved."

Roland frowned, wondering what on earth she was up to.

"I care nothing for your rituals. I only want the blood."

She shrugged. "Well, if you don't want the full extent of the strength, then we can dispense with the meditation. I supposed..."

Lucien frowned, licking his lips. "How long does this...ritual take?"

"Several hours."

He tilted his head. "You won't need more than thirty minutes to get to the boy before Rogers does."

Rhiannon's brows arched. Roland thought he might be the only one who saw the triumph in her eyes. "Then there *is* sufficient time."

"Rhiannon, you can't do this," Tamara cried.

"I must, fledgling," Rhiannon said softly. "Think of Jamey." She turned, and fixed Tamara with an intense stare. *"Think of Jamey."*

Tamara blinked, and averted her eyes. "I—I will."

Rhiannon tossed her hair over her shoulder as she got to her feet with fluid grace. "Until tomorrow evening, then. Of course, you know you must fast from now until then. No food, no drink. Otherwise, you won't cross the threshold. You will die upon it."

Roland frowned again. It was absolute nonsense. Not that he intended to allow her to go through with it.

"And you mustn't sleep tonight, or tomorrow, either," she went on, crossing to the door. "If the conditions are not just right, you will die. Do you understand?"

Why was she spouting such drivel?

"You seem to take great care with the life of a man you despise, Rhiannon." Lucien's voice was laced with the shadows of suspicion.

"I would kill you as soon as speak to you, Lucien. It is the boy's life I'm taking care with. If you die before you tell me his whereabouts, he'll fall into the hands of devils. That, I cannot allow."

CHAPTER TWELVE

Well before dawn, they'd taken refuge in a dilapidated house several miles outside the village. Rhiannon boldly built a fire in the ancient-looking pot-bellied stove, using bits of the rotted shutters for fuel.

"You take many chances, for a being so sensitive to flame, Rhiannon. The chimney is likely in as sad condition as the house."

Roland again, admonishing her as always. "Stop worrying. There will be no direct contact between my flesh and the flames. And I'll see it's well doused before we rest."

Eric and Tamara had gone down into the basement to seek a resting place, and, she suspected, to spend some time alone. She suppressed her jealousy of them and tried to focus on more practical matters. Frankly, she wished she'd brought a huge, fluffy comforter along to wrap herself in. Sleeping in a mound of mildewed hay had been bad enough; this pile of refuse would be worse yet.

"Rhiannon, it's time."

She fed another bit of wood to the burgeoning fire, careful to keep her hand from the flames, closed the iron door and brushed the black soot from her fingers. "Time?"

"To tell me what you have planned for Lucien."

"So you can tell me how foolish and risky it is?" She shook her head quickly, and crossed the room to gingerly examine an ancient-looking sofa. "Thank you, no. You, Eric and Tamara can spend your time looking for Jamey. I'll keep Lucien busy... alive, but busy, until you find the boy."

"Thus the talk of a lengthy ritual?"

She nodded. "He wants power. He craves it the way a drunkard craves liquor. It's a weakness to want something that badly.

I'll use that weakness against him. If he believes my *ritual* will give him more strength, he'll take part in it.''

She thumped the ratty cushions repeatedly, watching for some creature to skitter forth. When none did, she turned and sat down.

Roland came and sat beside her. ''And what of your admonition that he neither eat nor rest?''

His shoulder touched hers, he sat so close. His thigh pressed to hers, but he didn't even try to rectify matters. She wasn't sure whether she should do it herself. She knew she didn't want to.

''Deprivation of food and sleep weakens the mind. It's used by all the most successful cult leaders, you know. I only wish I could make him fast longer before I face him.''

She didn't move away. If Roland didn't mind the closeness, why should she deny herself the supreme pleasure of it?

''Face him in what way, Rhiannon? You make it sound like a battle.''

Sighing, she leaned back against the gray-colored stuffing that poked out from the ragged upholstery, her arms crossing over her chest. ''It will be a battle, of sorts. A battle of minds.'' She closed her eyes and tried to see her hastily concocted plan clearly. She wanted it to seem like a sound course of action when she explained it to Roland, not like the ravings of a careless, reckless child.

''While Lucien *meditates,* Roland, I will be working on his mind. I will entrance him, as I've done to countless humans when the need has arisen. I will bring him completely under my control.''

Roland half turned, so he faced her. She avoided his eyes, but he would have none of it. He caught her chin in two fingers and turned her face to his. ''You are well aware this man is no ordinary human. His psychic abilities are strong. He is able to conceal his mind from yours.'' His eyes sparked with emotion, but she didn't think it was anger. His jawline tightened. His full lips thinned.

''He will be weakened and tired. I will be strong and ready

for the fight. The incense and candles that distract him will help me to focus.''

His hand dropped from her chin, to settle on her shoulder. ''If this works, and you are able to get him under your power, what then?''

She resisted the impulse to tilt her head sideways, and brush her cheek over his hand on her shoulder. Barely resisted it. ''I'll scan his mind and learn where the boy is. I'll relay the information to you and the others, and you will rescue him.''

''You make it sound so simple.''

''Because it is.''

''And if you fail? If his mind is too strong?''

''That will not happen.''

''It could, Rhiannon.''

''It won't.'' She reached up with one hand to cup his face. ''Just this once, Roland, try to believe in me. Look beyond all my faults and see the strength that is mine. I can do this.''

His frown came suddenly, and left just as fast. ''I've never doubted your strength. I do believe in you, Rhiannon. That's never been a question. But I fear—''

''That I will bungle it and cost Jamison his life.'' She lowered her hand and shrugged his from her shoulder.

''No, little bird. That you will save Jamison and risk your own existence in the process.'' Roland stood abruptly, reached down and gripped both her hands to pull her to her feet. ''Lucien nearly killed you once, Rhiannon. I have an uncanny feeling that is his intent, even now.''

''The risk is not important. Getting Jamey back is.''

''I'll go with you,'' Roland said hoarsely. ''I'll stand watch over this entire exchange, and if he lifts a hand against you, I will kill him before he draws another breath.''

She shook her head. ''You can't. He wants me alone—''

''I'll go along, or you will stay away. Your choice, Rhiannon.'' Like chips of glassy coal, his eyes glittered.

She sighed and turned away. ''Why must you be so difficult?''

A hand of steel closed on her shoulder, turning her so she

collided with his chest. At the instant of impact, another arm snapped around her waist, as firmly as a padlock's hasp. His breath bathed her face as she turned it up, and then his lips caught hers in a merciless hold. His tongue fought its way through the barricades of her lips and plundered every part of her interior within reach.

In seconds, she went from shocked victim, to willing partner. Her mouth opened wide and the sensual dance began. They took turns lapping each other's mouths, suckling each other's tongues, nipping each other's lips. Rhiannon's arms twisted around his neck. Roland gripped her buttocks in his eager hands, and pressed her hips to his, moving them back and forth to rub her against his bulging arousal.

When his mouth left hers at last, she felt the shudder that rocked through him. He lowered his face to her hair, and his lips moved against it. "That's why I am so difficult, reckless one. Because this planet, without you among its inhabitants, would be as grim a place as…as this house. And as empty."

Rhiannon closed her eyes at the sweet agony those words inflicted on her soul. She could feel the thunder of his heartbeat against her chest, his breath in her hair. "But you want that emptiness. You want my disturbing presence removed from your life."

His hold on her tightened. His words came on a voice gone gravelly with feeling. "No, Rhiannon. It's not what I want, but what is necessary. It's not you I want out of my life, but the monster that lives within me. How can I make you understand?"

The breath she drew was halting and shallow. "I don't want to understand. I only want you." She lifted her head from his shoulder and looked up into his eyes. "I swore I wouldn't give you the chance to reject me again, Roland, yet here I am offering myself up for your scathing words. When Jamey is safe, and I am far away, I'll have nothing but sweet memories of your touch, your kisses. The ghost of that single time will never be enough to sustain me, I fear."

His dark eyes fell closed, and she saw his lips tremble.

"Give me one more memory to cling to, Roland. I'll ask no more of you, I promise. Make love to me now."

He opened his eyes again, and the fire in his gaze burned into her heart. She lowered her forehead to his chest, unable to face him as he pushed her away from him, yet again.

"Go on," she whispered. "Tell me to leave you alone. Remind me that no lady would say the things I've said. Let me feel your disapproval one more time. Perhaps then I will finally get it fixed in my mind that I'm not worthy of your..." She stopped herself as her throat closed off. Love. She'd been about to say love. God, what was happening to her senses?

"I'm sorry, Rhiannon."

She bit her lip, bracing herself for his rejection. He brought his hands slowly upward, his palms skimming her spine, his fingers brushing over her nape. He cupped her head, and tipped it up, staring down into her eyes.

"It is not you who are unworthy, it is I. I ought not allow myself even this embrace, after my loss of control the last time..." He lowered his face to hers, until his lips barely brushed over hers as he spoke. "But I cannot turn you away. My desire for you burns away my will."

His mouth covered hers, his palms still pressed to the sides of her head. He kissed her as he never had before. Gently, slowly. Every sweep of his tongue was a tender exploration, every shifting of his lips, a caress. His fingers dived into her hair, raking through it again and again. And then he drew himself away, as she rose from the sofa, shivering with passion.

"Undress for me, Rhiannon. Let me see you clothed in nothing but your stunning beauty."

She nodded, and lifted unsteady hands to the silk blouse she wore. His gaze held hers captive as she slowly freed the buttons. But when the blouse fell away, and her breasts stood unclothed before him, he broke contact with her eyes to stare fixedly at her chest. She didn't flinch from the intensity of that stare. She felt her nipples harden in response to it, as if reaching out to him.

He drew a sudden breath, and moved his gaze lower as she released the fastening of the denims, and drew down the zipper. Without shame or hesitation, she pushed the jeans down, and the panties with them. She stepped out of the garments and kicked them aside.

Roland came toward her, one arm reaching out. She stepped away just as quickly, and when he sent her a quizzical glance, she smiled. "Now you."

Her smile was answered with one of his, and he quickly removed his shirt, dropping it to the dusty floor.

She let her gaze roam freely over the expanse of skin revealed to her, the dark swirling mat of hair that invited the exploration of her fingers, her lips. "I've always adored your chest, you know. So broad, so..." Unable to resist, she moved nearer him, and ran her hands over the crisp hairs and firm muscled wall. She lowered her face to its center, and inhaled his scent.

When she lifted her face away, she ran her hands upward. "And your shoulders," she whispered, surprised at the hoarse quality of the words. "And your arms. One would think you a bodybuilder by the shape of you."

"The only weight I've hefted was that of a broadsword, as well you know."

She pressed her lips to his shoulder. "Then I'm glad you hefted it." She kissed a trail toward his neck and up it, savoring the taste of his skin. Her hands slipped downward, fumbling to open his trousers, then eagerly shoving them downward. "Hurry, Roland."

He chuckled low, and helped her divest him of his remaining clothes. Then they stood, bodies pressed together, flesh against flesh. The hairs of his chest rubbed over her breasts. The hard length of his arousal stood rigid against her abdomen. She ran her hands over the curve of his back, down to his buttocks, which flexed in response to her touch.

Roland's hands rested at her waist and he kissed her deeply, hungrily. As one, they sunk to the floor. Rhiannon pushed gently until Roland lay back. She stretched out atop him and lavished his neck and shoulders with kisses. She moved her lips over his chest, and ruthlessly caught one small nipple between her teeth. He gasped in pleasure or surprise. She wasn't certain which, until his hands closed on her head to hold her closer. She sucked at the hard little nub, then licked a path down his sternum, across his belly, around his navel.

His body shuddered its response to her ministrations. His breaths came faster as she continued tormenting him. When she touched the tip of his arousal with her tongue, he groaned like distant thunder. When she closed her lips around him, his hips arched upward. His fingers twined in her hair. In moments, he was panting, and his hands sought to move her away. But she persisted in worshipping the core of him with her mouth until his panting became a helpless plea, and the hands fighting her, gripped her, instead.

He cried her name in a strangled voice, and his entire body went rigid as his essence spilled into her.

Slowly, he relaxed, still shuddering with her touch. She lifted her head and slithered up over his body. She held his gaze, and licked her lips. Instantly, his hardness pressed to her thigh and she shifted, settling herself over him, poising herself to receive him.

His hands shot down to her hips and he drew her down hard, sheathing himself inside her. Her head fell backward and her eyes closed. He filled her, more than filled her, and not just physically. Being with him this way filled some barren cavern in her soul. An unexplored place no one had ever entered.

She felt his hands glide over her back, and press to her shoulders. He drew her downward, lifting his upper body, and capturing one of her breasts in his mouth. Gently, he suckled her, then harder, the pressure of his mouth increasing with the pace of his upward thrusts.

Rhiannon felt him pushing her quickly toward that place she'd just taken him. She lifted and lowered her hips, urgently racing to that place. She cradled his head to her breast as she approached it, feeling the skim of his teeth just as the world exploded around her. She shook with the force of her release, even as he continued moving inside her. He held her hips in place, and kept the pace frantic. He nipped and tugged at her nipple until she cried out, and pulled away.

Then he lay still, staring upward into her eyes, and she knew he hadn't completed the journey with her. He pulled her down to his chest, holding her there. Her face was buried in the kinky curls, and her body still trembled with the aftermath.

Clutching her tight to him, he rolled them both over until she was beneath and he was above. He tipped her head upward and kissed her long and hard. She was breathless, and somehow, still hungry for more of him. He seemed to know for he began again, in a slow, tormenting rhythm she thought would surely drive her out of her mind. Her nerve endings seemed to have been rubbed raw, for she felt every sensation as if it were magnified a thousand times. The size of him, and her own flesh stretched around him, the whisper of his crisp triangle of hair meshing with her own, softer one, the lash of his tongue inside her mouth, the friction of his chest against hers.

As the fires inside her blazed anew, she lifted her legs to encircle him, hooking her ankles behind his back. His reply was to slide his arms beneath her, cup her buttocks, lift her hips more tightly to him and spear her more deeply than before. His pace increased as her body grew taut. His tongue lapped a path from her mouth to her ear, and then his teeth closed on its lobe.

It was she, this time, who was made to pant helplessly as his body drove hers higher and higher. But it was both of them who cried out in sweet, anguished joy as their juices met and mingled. She felt the slow throb of his body and her own convulsing around him.

Gradually, the room came back into focus. Rhiannon looked around her, then into Roland's jet eyes. "We are fortunate Eric and Tamara have not walked in before now."

His smile was slow and enticing. "They won't. I have it on good authority that they are hidden away somewhere, doing the same thing we are."

She nodded with understanding, her envy of their happiness striking her anew. For her, this would be the last time. Already the pain of that knowledge began to engulf her in misery. "Perhaps we ought to find a place to rest before dawn."

"We have an hour until dawn, Rhiannon." He lifted a hand to stroke her hair. "An hour I intend to fill in some most interesting ways."

The pain faded. "What ways?"

"Let me show you."

As dawn approached, they took refuge in a darkened closet on the second floor. They lay down in the narrow space, still naked, bodies twined together.

Already, Rhiannon slept. Her head rested on Roland's shoulder, her silken hair covering his chest like a blanket. He held her close and listened to her breathing.

He hadn't lost control. He hadn't become a raging beast, not even for a moment. Instead, he'd become one with her, and found a joy beyond anything he'd ever known in the joining.

Perhaps there was hope for him yet, he thought, finally facing the idea which had nagged him from their first kiss. He was no longer sure he had the strength to let her go.

Let her go? He shook his head slightly. There was no certainty in his mind that he could convince her not to go. Always before, she'd flitted in and out of his life with all the predictability of a cyclone.

But that was before, he thought in troubled silence.

Before what? What have we shared, beyond the consummation of a long-lived mutual lust? The fevered coupling of two willing bodies?

No. There was more to it, surely. Not love, for he knew himself incapable of such a tender emotion. He'd believed himself in love once before.

Like a blade, the memory of that other time sliced through his mind. Rebecca, so young and innocent. He'd fancied himself in love with her for a time. But his actions, his need to control and command her, had resulted in her suicide. His love, or, what he'd thought of as love, had been poison to her.

Would it be the same to Rhiannon? Was he not, already, searching his brain for ways to change her, to transform her into some meek-willed creature who'd be content to live the solemn life he preferred? Would he, in time, kill her spirit the way he'd killed Rebecca's?

He looked down at her, sleeping so peacefully in his arms. No, he couldn't do that to her. It would be a crime beyond murder to try to stifle Rhiannon. Perhaps he could convince himself to let her go, after all. Perhaps he could keep his thoughts to himself until she was free of him.

He owed her her freedom, if nothing else. It was, after all, the only gift he had to give.

Just after dusk, the two of them made the trek up the side of Mont Noir, to the quaint-looking cabin that held within its cozy walls an unmeasured evil. Lucien. Who was he? Rhiannon wondered. Why had he singled her out, of all the undead who walked the night in this twentieth-century world? There were many. Few older than she, but some. The infamous Damien, for one. Why had Lucien not sought him out to demand the dark blessing?

Rhiannon nearly laughed aloud at that notion. Even among vampires, the name of Damien was whispered with wariness. Lucien would not dare to try his games with such a creature.

She stumbled on a protruding rock, and Roland's arms came around her. She leaned gratefully into his embrace. Too soon, she would leave him. Too soon. She shook her head at the thought. Never would be too soon.

"Something troubles you."

She faced him, sighing. She was rapidly growing weary of guarding her thoughts from Roland. The venture was an exhausting one, for he seemed constantly to be probing her mind with his questioning one. He'd always been the one being with whom she'd felt most able to relax. She'd always allowed him to roam her mind at will.

Sad, how things had to change.

"I was only thinking of Tamara," she lied with unease. "She is so new to these games of the mind. I hope she is able to locate the boy."

Roland nodded, still holding her close to his side as he maneuvered around a bed of loose stone. "It would be helpful if Jamison were trying to reach out to her."

"Do you think he will?"

Roland's lips thinned as he shook his head. "Not if he thinks doing so would lead her into danger. I suspect he's learned the trick of guarding his thoughts from us. Otherwise, we'd have tracked him by now. He's a stubborn one, that boy."

Rhiannon nodded, thinking again of Tamara and Eric. She'd left them sitting upon the moss-covered ground in a small clearing of a nearby wood. Candles and incense burned between them, and Tamara's eyes were closed as she sent the fingers of her mind out into the night, in search of her beloved Jamey. If anything happened to the boy, Lucien would die, there was no question of that. For if Rhiannon and Roland didn't finish him themselves, Tamara would do so.

A small smile tugged at Rhiannon's lips. "Eric's fledgling has a dark side to her."

Roland glanced sideways at her. "Don't we all?"

"I suppose we do. But with her, it's well concealed. Like the leaves of the nightshade vine, and its wine-colored berries. Beautiful, harmless-looking, but containing a deadly nectar."

"I'd hardly classify Tamara as deadly."

"We all have the capacity, Roland, given the right motivations. I believe most humans do, as well." She licked her lips and watched his face as she spoke to him. "This notion you have that you are somehow more monstrous than the rest of us is born either of ignorance or conceit. I've not yet decided which."

He halted, turning to face her, a frown digging a ditch between his brows. "Are you angry with me, Rhiannon?"

She blinked. He'd hit on it, precisely. She was angry with him. Furious, in fact. Because of his foolish notions, she would be miserable for longer than she cared to think about. But rather than voice this newfound knowledge, she only shrugged, and pointed. "The cabin is just around those rocks, as I recall. I ought to go on alone from here."

Roland set his jaw. "I'll come a bit farther."

"He'll be able to see you. Just wait here, in the shadow of these boulders. As soon as he is assured I've come alone, you can come nearer. But do take care, Roland."

His eyes seemed to scan her face for a moment. "I can barely believe what I'm seeing. You're excited about this encounter! You're looking forward to it!"

She lifted her eyebrows, and shrugged. "I've always enjoyed facing a challenge." She knew the remark would infuriate him. She also enjoyed doing that, though she'd never quite understood why.

She glanced down at her attire, gleaned from some of the tourist shops in the village below. Close to her skin, she wore tight black leggings, and a form-fitting bodysuit of that wonderful fabric called Spandex. This would enable her to move as freely as possible, should the need arise. Her shoes were flat, and shiny black, but the soles had good treads for climbing the sheer rocks.

However, she'd covered the practical, contemporary garments with a flowing kimono of deep blue satin, which, when she freed it, would cover her feet. At the moment, it was bunched up around her waist to ease her travel. Roland had added his own black cloak as a finishing touch. It was warm, and added an air of magic to her every movement as it gleamed around her like the wings of a raven. It had neither collar nor ties, only two buttons to hold it in place at her throat.

Roland nodded in approval. "Every inch the enchantress, Rhiannon. He'll shudder in fear at the sight of you."

"Don't make light of it," she chided. "Every advantage I can use is needed, and if my clothing can help to intimidate him, that's all the better."

"I know. I wasn't." He caught her shoulders, and held them

firm. "Be careful, Rhiannon." His eyes conveyed much more meaning than his words. He was truly worried for her safety. "At the first sign of skulduggery, summon me. Don't hesitate."

"I won't." Something inside her urged her to move forward, to press her body to his just once, to lift her lips to his, and wait for his parting kiss. She fought the feeling, hoping it didn't show in her eyes, averting them in case it did. "Now, let me go, before I lose my nerve."

"The gods would lose their wisdom first," he said, but his hands fell away.

She turned and hurried toward the cabin.

CHAPTER THIRTEEN

Rhiannon halted a few feet from the cabin's little door, closed her eyes and silently composed her thoughts. She could not afford to be distracted now by worry about the boy, or even by her extreme sadness over the parting that would follow this ordeal. She must concentrate only on Lucien.

Before she was prepared, the door opened, and the object of her thoughts filled the entrance. "Come in, Rhiannon. I trust you've kept your word and come alone?" As he spoke, his beady eyes swept the area around her, and she knew he searched with his mind, as well. He would find no hint of Roland there. He could guard his presence from this man without much effort. Despite his powerful mind, Lucien was only a human.

"Of course. Did you think I'd risk the boy, or that I'd be so afraid of you I would bring reinforcements?" His gaze came back to her, and altered slightly as he took in her attire. "Don't fool yourself, Lucien. I fear no mere mortal."

He stepped aside as she strode into the cabin. She made her steps broad, kept her head high. He would see no faltering in her entrance.

"No? Not even Curtis Rogers?"

Was that remark supposed to shake her? "Him least of all. He is a weakling, blinded by his hunger for vengeance. I could kill him with as little effort as you would swat a fly. But that is neither here nor there, is it?"

Lucien shrugged and closed the door. Rhiannon focused her mind on the house, finding it empty save for the two of them. She stepped nearer the hearth, allowing the fire's warmth to spread over her.

"You're dressed quite differently from the way you were last night. Is there any significance to it?"

She turned a surprised glance upon him. "I thought you knew

all about me. Can it be your research is lacking, after all? Do you not recognize the robes of an Egyptian priestess?''

He said nothing, only eyed her up and down. ''May I take your cloak, at least?''

''You may not. I've grown rather fond of it.''

''Suit yourself.''

She studied his face. His eyes appeared slightly slack-lidded. She detected darker circles beneath them. ''You have followed my instructions?''

''I have. No sleep, no food, no drink. I'm thirsty as a sand dune right now, to tell the truth.''

''It will pass,'' she told him. ''How is the boy?''

''Fine. Safe, for the moment, at least. I've no doubt your friends are out looking for him.''

She only lifted her brows. ''Think what you will.''

''It doesn't matter. They won't find him.'' He crossed the room toward a closed door, and opened it. He stood aside, and waved a hand for her to enter.

Rhiannon moved forward, the cape swaying with every step, the kimono brushing the floor. Pausing in the doorway, she saw a small room, a bedroom, perhaps, but devoid of any furnishings, save a table and a glowing kerosene lamp.

''Let's get on with it.'' Lucien stood close behind her, his voice cold on her nape.

She stepped inside, and he followed. From a pocket inside the cloak, she pulled a small sack. Lucien's gaze took in every movement.

''What's that?''

She loosened the drawstring and removed several candles, a packet of incense and a silver dish, placing them on the floor in a small circle. ''Nothing to be afraid of, Lucien. You see?''

He knelt and picked up a candle, studying it, sniffing it. Then he lifted the packet of herbs and examined that, pouring a bit into his palm.

''Incense,'' she said. ''It goes in the dish, in the center of the circle of candles.''

He shot her a wary look, then poured as she had instructed. "You want me to light them?"

He was nervous. She saw it in the way he kept licking his lips, in the constant darting movements of his eyes. "No. We'll take care of that in a moment. Douse the light, if you please."

He frowned, but stood. Cupping a hand over the far side of the glass chimney, he blew into the lamp. The room fell into inky darkness. She could see him clearly. He could see nothing, though he tried to keep her in focus. Right now, he was squinting like a mole.

"Now sit, cross-legged upon the floor."

He did as she told him. Rhiannon rounded the circle of unlit candles and lowered herself opposite him. Tentatively, she probed his mind with her own, as a test. She found it completely closed to her.

"You must concentrate, Lucien. There must be nothing on your mind except the candles. Focus upon their wicks. Think of nothing else. Envision flames, leaping to life at your command. Do it now."

She saw him staring hard at the candle just in front of him. She aimed the beam of her own thoughts there, and in a moment a small pop sounded, and the wick flared to life.

Lucien jerked as if slapped.

"Very good," Rhiannon purred. "Your mind is strong, for a human." Again, she sought his thoughts and found nothing. "But you are not concentrating hard enough. Focus your mind."

He did. His eyes picked out another candle, and she let him stare at it awhile before she caused it to light. One by one, Rhiannon lit the candles, as Lucien's guard was slowly lowered.

His eyes widened in amazement, his face now glowing in the soft light of the tiny fires. "Now the incense. It's a bit more difficult. Concentrate."

She watched him as he stared at the silver dish, but she did not ignite the herbs it held. Instead, she probed his mind, seeking knowledge of Jamey in its foggy depths.

For a moment, she saw the boy, lying upon a cot, with a wool blanket tossed over him. But the image vanished as Lucien looked up at her.

"It isn't working."

"You're not concentrating. Try again."

He did. It was laughable the way he contorted his face with the effort. The fool grated his teeth. Again, Rhiannon searched his mind, this time seeing a bit more. A room, in utter darkness. A shuttered window. Smoky cobwebs in the corners.

She glanced at the incense and it began to smolder. Fixing her mind more firmly inside his, she tried to see the locale of Jamey's prison. It was near. Very near, but not in this cabin. Ah, there. Another cabin, similar to this, but in sad disrepair. Upon the mountain? she wondered. No. Below it, but not in the village.

A wall seemed to lower itself around his mind all at once. "You're trying to trick me, aren't you?"

He knew she'd been snooping. She met his accusing glare. "Our thoughts must mingle as well as our blood, Lucien. This will not work unless you cooperate."

Give yourself over, she chanted in silence. *My will becomes yours, Lucien.*

She saw his eyes begin to cloud.

"You must relax. Breathe deeply. Like this." She demonstrated, and he mimicked her for several long moments. His lids drooped slightly. She almost smiled in triumph.

"Much better. Now focus on nothing. Try to free your mind from your body until you feel as if you are floating."

The lids drooped a little farther. His deep, regular breathing came on its own now, without her instruction.

"Imagine yourself as a spirit, if you will. Feel the chains of your physical self falling away."

Your will is mine, Lucien. You have no desire except to do my bidding. You have no thoughts, save those I will give you. Surrender to me, Lucien. Surrender.

Slowly, his eyes fell closed. His breathing deepened still further, and came in long, drawn-out turns. His head hung downward on a neck gone limp.

Where is the boy?

Roland's entire being was focused on Rhiannon inside the cabin. He waited as long as he could stand it, then started forward, toward the tiny structure. He would go around until he located a window through which he could see what was happening. She was so involved in her efforts with Lucien that he could feel no hint of her thoughts, had no clue what was happening.

His every thought on Rhiannon, Roland stepped out of his concealment beyond the rocks. The shot came out of the darkness. Something stabbed into his chest.

His hand came up to clutch the object that pierced his flesh with a burning pain. He tugged it free, but his mind was slipping away. A black haze slowly coated his consciousness as he stared down at the blood-slicked dart he'd torn from his chest.

He fell to his knees, lifting his gaze. Curtis Rogers stood only yards from him, an evil smile lurking about his lips. Damn! Roland had been so determinedly focused on Rhiannon, he'd failed to continue scanning the area for another presence. He'd failed…he'd failed Rhiannon.

His mind whispered a warning he prayed she would hear, just before he fell forward, into darkness.

Rhiannon's thoughts were interrupted by a sudden bolt of knowledge. Something had happened to Roland.

In her moment of distraction, Lucien broke the hold she'd had on his mind, and gave his head a shake. Then he glared at her, leaping to his feet. "I know what you're trying to do. I should have known I couldn't trust one of your kind."

She stood, as well. "Do not tempt me, Lucien, or you'll die here and now. Tell me where you've hidden the boy."

"You never had any intention of keeping your side of the bargain. Why should I keep mine?"

"Because you will die if you don't." She stepped around the

candles toward him, but froze when the door behind Lucien swung wide, and Curtis Rogers stood there, pointing some sort of weapon at her.

"You!"

"Ah, we meet again, Princess."

She took a single step and no more. The dart plunged into her shoulder and she cried out in sudden pain. She closed her eyes, certain the dart contained the tranquilizer, certain her time had run out. With her final moments of consciousness, she sent her thoughts to the fledgling, Tamara, conveying all she had learned, begging her to find a way to save Roland and the boy. She fell forward, catching herself on a wall, then slipping slowly downward as her legs folded beneath her.

"Her friend was outside," she heard Rogers saying, though his voice echoed as if far away.

"Will you take him, too?" That was Lucien.

"No. I've learned from my mistakes. I don't want to deal with two of them at once. One at a time, from here on. He's not going anywhere. Let the sun take care of him."

She felt her neck muscles melt as her head fell forward. It was jerked up again by a cruel hand in her hair. Lucien's twisted face hovered before her. "Before you go beddy-bye, there's something I want you to know. The scientist you killed all those years ago, Daniel St. Claire's partner, was my father. And I won't rest until I see all of your kind pay for his death."

She tried to make her lips form words. "B-but ... you ... you wanted ..."

"To become one of you? Yes. The strongest one of all, so I could eliminate the rest with ease. So I could live to see the last of you die in agony."

"You," she whispered with the last bit of strength she possessed, "are the one...who will die."

Nearly dawn.

Roland felt the approach of morning with every cell in his body, and still he could not move. He'd managed only to pry his eyes apart. Now he could watch the horizon slowly paling, from deepest black, to midnight blue, to varying and ever-lightening shades of gray.

The cabin was empty now. There was no sense of Rogers, or Lucien...or Rhiannon. He knew they must have taken her. Again, she would be subjected to their cruel torments. Because of him.

Roland grimaced in pain at the thought of Rhiannon in Rogers's hands. He had to live—if only to free her.

Summoning every muscle to do his bidding, grating his teeth with the effort, he slowly, painstakingly, clutched at the earth and dragged his body forward. He couldn't wait for Eric to come to his aid. There might not be time, or his friend, too, might be disabled or in trouble. Again, Roland dug his fingers into the dirt and stone. Again, he hauled his body a few inches forward. At this rate, he wouldn't make it to the cabin's door before noon. Still, he had to try.

Away from the shelter of the rocks, he dragged himself. Half-way into the clear, level area, with no kind of shelter from the rising sun. Halfway to the cabin. Again, he clawed and pulled his way, glancing toward the east, where he could see the pale orange glow just touching the edge of the sky. Sweat beaded on his forehead and ran, burning, into his eyes. He clutched at the ground again, and grunted with effort as he struggled onward.

From the opposite direction came the sound of padded feet, running toward him. He turned his head, and then released his breath in a rush. To his left, the sun. Now, to his right, a wolf the size of a Saint Bernard, but with muscles rippling beneath its sleek coat instead of fat. If the one didn't kill him, the other surely would. He had no strength left to fight either enemy.

Recalling his last experience with a wolf, Roland wished the sun would hasten its arrival. Then the beast was upon him, and he knew it was too late.

But what was this? Not a snarl came from the wolf, not a bared fang did the animal display. Instead, it stopped at his side, lowering its huge head, nudging its way beneath Roland's all but useless arm.

In shocked wonder, Roland could only stare as the wolf pushed and shoved at his body. It only stopped when Roland's right arm and shoulder were supported by the animal's strong back. Having no clue what was happening or why, or whether this was some dream he was having in the throes of death, Roland fought to bring his other arm around the front of the animal's neck, until he could link his hands together. The moment this was accomplished, the wolf started forward, not even straining under the tremendous burden of Roland's limp weight. Roland's upper body was carried, the rest of him dragged, but in the wrong direction.

He could have screamed in frustration. If only he could command the wolf to drag him to the cabin, the way Rhiannon could command Pandora. He tried, but found the wolf a poor listener. He forced his head up, to look ahead, his cheek brushing the soft, deep fur at the wolf's throat, his nostrils filling with the animal's scent. Then his jaw fell open. The wolf had brought him to a small cave, dug into the side of a sheer stone wall. It was barely visible with the overlapping rock above, and the outcrop jutting from the sides. He'd never have known of the cave's presence.

The beast dragged him inside, then along the cool, uneven floor, around a sharp bend and all the way to the back. The sun would never reach here, Roland suspected. He released the wolf's magnificent neck, and lowered himself to the floor.

The wolf stood over him, staring down into his eyes for just a moment. There was a wisdom in those eyes, the likes of which had no place there.

"I know not what you are, wolf—" a memory of Rhiannon's tales about ancient ones who could alter their form, about Damien, hovered in his fogged mind "—but I thank you," Roland managed to say. His eyes were heavy and he could barely form words. "Meager reward...for saving a life. I know."

He'd expected the beast to turn and lope away. Instead, it lowered itself to the stone floor a few feet from him, and its eyes fell closed. In a few seconds, Roland's did, as well. His last thoughts were of Rhiannon. Where was she as the cruel sun rose into the sky? Was she safe? Sheltered from the burning rays?

When next Roland awoke, he was alone. He glimpsed the stone walls around him, wondering whether he'd dreamed the entire incident with the wolf.

It was night again. He felt strong, and he hurried out of the cave with one thought on his mind. Rhiannon. He must find her, now, before even another minute passed.

He strode toward the cabin. He'd begin there, to search for a clue.

"Roland!"

The shout brought him up short, but he knew an instant later it came from Eric. He faced his friend, accepted the harsh embrace. "Roland, what's happened? We've been out of our minds with worry."

Roland's soul felt as empty, as hollow as he knew his words sounded. "Rogers. He got me with one of those darts of his, then left me for the dawn to find."

"And Rhiannon?"

Roland felt his throat seal itself off. He closed his eyes. "I...I don't know."

Eric grasped Roland's arm and both men approached the cabin. Eric flung the door wide, so hard it smashed into the wall, and the two went in different directions, searching the place with methods none too gentle.

In the small, empty room, Roland stopped, his heart twisting as he eyed the circle of candles and the dish of incense. It's exotic scent still tinged the air. Then he saw the bloody little dart, lying on the floor in a corner. In a voice gone hoarse with pain, he called to Eric, and pointed. "They've taken her," he whispered.

"We'll get her back."

Roland nodded, then scanned his friend's face. "Where is Tamara?"

"She's taken the boy back to the castle, Roland. They're in

no danger, now. Jamey was suddenly released last night. It was
never him they wanted, only Rhiannon. Once they had her, they
let him go. If they need bait to lure the rest of us, they'll use
her."

Roland nodded, for the explanation made perfect sense.

"I'd have been here to help you, Roland, but Jamison was
turned loose in a forest, and left to find his own way. We spent
most of the night searching for him, and I had no idea what had
occurred up here—although I think Tamara did."

Roland cocked a brow. "How?"

Eric shrugged. "She heard something from Rhiannon…it was
what led us to that particular patch of woods in the first place.
Then she heard no more. She kept saying she was certain something was wrong, but she didn't know what." He shook his head.
"I was damned afraid for you, Roland. How did you manage to
escape the sun, with that tranquilizer in your blood?"

Roland thought again of the wolf, of the knowledge in its
eyes. "I'm not certain." He shook himself. "It doesn't matter
now. We have to find Rhiannon."

As the drug's effects waned, the day sleep took over. Rhiannon roused only very briefly between the two. In a fogged, floating kind of state, she glanced around her, knowing she was in
a chilly place with no windows or doors, no light of any kind.
She sat hunched on a cold floor, with another cold surface at
her back. And when she moved her arms or legs, there was the
sound of metal clanking against metal.

Then she slept again, so she thought it must be day. When
the sleep evaporated, she knew it was night. Or was it? For with
the setting of the sun would come the rush of tingling energy,
and the zinging awareness in her every nerve ending. With night
would come strength, and power.

Why did she still feel as if her limbs were made of lead, and
her head stuffed with wet cotton?

Lucien's face loomed above her, grinning lasciviously.
"Don't fret, Rhiannon. It's only Curt Rogers's handy little drug

making you feel so weak. I gave you a half dose just before sunset. Looks as if it was enough."

Vaguely, her brain began to function. She felt the damp chill of the stale air around her, smelled the stench of stagnant water, and rodent leavings. "Rogers...told you he'd never...give you the drug."

"Rogers didn't have a choice in the matter. Did you really think I'd let him drag you off to some sterile laboratory and hold you under military guard before I had what I wanted from you?" He laughed low in his throat and shook his head. "He had no more intentions of keeping his promise to me than you did."

Her body weak, Rhiannon struggled to her feet, only to realize that iron manacles encircled her ankles, with chains that were bolted to the stone wall. Her wrists were likewise imprisoned, with longer lengths of chain. She turned her head to one side, then the other, testing the strength of the chains with an experimental tug. The cold iron bit into her flesh.

"I'll keep you weak enough so you won't be able to tear them free, Rhiannon. Don't doubt that."

She faced him, feeling her anger well up inside her. "What has become of Roland?"

"Your friend who was lingering outside the cabin? Curtis shot him with a dart, like you, and left him there for the sun. He's probably dead by now. No hope of rescue there."

His words were like the lashes of a whip across her heart. She closed her eyes against the flood of tears.

"Oh, how touching," Lucien said, gripping her chin and lifting it. "Now, unless you want to follow him, *after* you watch me kill the boy, you will transform me."

Her eyes flew open. "You still have Jamey?"

"Of course."

She studied his face, wondering if he was telling the truth. She'd awakened with the sense that Jamey was well and safe. Had it been a dream? Wishful thinking? Or had someone been attempting to reassure her?

"I can keep you here indefinitely, Rhiannon. I have plenty of the drug, and all the time in the world. If the boy's life isn't incentive enough to convince you, we can try using pain as an impetus. I know how much you dislike that.''

Her neck was so weak she had trouble holding her head up when he took his hand away from her chin. Her memories of the time this man's father, and his partner, Daniel St. Claire, had held her captive, loomed in her mind in an attempt to drive her from her senses. She pushed it away with effort. ''And if I capitulate? If I initiate you into the world of unending night, what then? Am I to suppose you will release me, when I heard you admit you live only to see me die?''

''Suppose what you will. I'll free the boy if you do as I say. If not, you both die. The choice, fair Rhiannon, is yours.''

She lowered her head until her chin rested upon her chest. It was hopeless, then. She had no need to fight the fear, for her grief overwhelmed it.

''I have things to do. I'll return for your decision in an hour.'' With that, he left her, his steps echoing in the darkened, stone dungeon.

Yes, dungeon. Where on earth had he brought her? A dungeon suggested a castle, and a castle likely meant they were still in France. Perhaps even in the Loire valley where thousands of medieval castles dotted the landscape, Roland's among them.

Roland.

Just the thought of him brought a stab of pain to her soul. She called out to him, sending her mental voice into the night like a mournful wail. Again and again she called to him, but she heard no reply.

Could he truly be dead? Gone forever before she'd managed to tell him the truth she'd kept locked away for so long?

''I love you, Roland de Courtemanche, baron, knight, immortal, man. I love all of you,'' she whispered. She lifted her head skyward, as if to cry out to the gods. ''Return him to me, and I swear I will become what he wants. No more will I seek out danger and flaunt myself in its face. No more will I live recklessly, walking an unsteady line along the very edge of sanity. I'll become the staid and quiet woman he wants, anything he needs. Never will I leave his side, if only I am given one more chance!''

Her words died on a broken, ragged cry, and she let her head fall forward once more on a neck gone limp. Her sobs racked her body, and only the lengths of chain kept her from falling. For she knew in her heart, her chances were gone. Roland had not answered her desperate cries. He'd been taken from her, torn from her heart before she'd realized he'd made his way into it.

Her grief paralyzed her, and she sobbed endlessly, wellsprings of tears pouring from her eyes.

Still, she knew that if Roland would ask anything at all of her from beyond the grave, it would be to do what was necessary to protect young Jamison. The last gift she could ever give to him would be the boy's life. She had no choice but to do as Lucien asked. He'd kill her when the deed was done, there was no longer any doubt of that. She could only hope it would be swift and clean.

Halfway down the mountainside, her cries reached him. Roland's head came up, and his stomach clenched in a tight knot at the anguish in her voice.

Eric's hand clamped down on his shoulder like a vise. ''Don't answer her.''

''Are you insane? Listen to her—''

''I am. No doubt, Lucien is, as well. If you answer, he'll be ready and waiting for us. He already has too many weapons in his arsenal, Roland. That drug, Rhiannon's life, Curt Rogers's aid. No use giving him fair warning, as well.''

Roland swallowed hard. Rhiannon's cries kept coming, and he heard her grief, her tears, her pain. God, but he'd never been aware how much she truly cared for him. No wonder his careless words had hurt her, time and again. He cursed himself now, for having to hurt her once more, and swore on the graves of his family that he would never, in all eternity, ever cause her pain again, even if it cost him his life.

He closed his mind off, for her pleas were driving him to near madness, and his rage added to that still more. He focused only on honing his mind to her location, and then pointed himself in that direction.

He and Eric sped through the night until all at once, Eric skidded to a halt, gripping Roland's arm. "I was mistaken in that list of Lucien's advantages. Look." He pointed down a steep embankment.

Far below, a smoking wreck was all that remained of Curt Rogers's Cadillac. Roland sent the fingers of his mind into the wreckage, and saw the vision of Rogers's charred body, twisted grotesquely behind the wheel.

"This was no accident," Roland said softly. "He died by Lucien's hand."

Eric nodded his agreement. "Then Lucien has no intention of turning Rhiannon over to DPI once she's transformed him."

"No." Roland's voice was grim. "He intends to kill her."

CHAPTER FOURTEEN

They circled the ruined fortress twice, in search of guards or watchmen, before leaping the crumbling wall. They crossed the barren courtyard, Roland's palms itching to feel a steel hilt, his shoulder aching for the butt of a crossbow. A moat, filled with green brackish water that appeared thick with filth and stunk to the heavens, surrounded the castle. The drawbridge was raised.

In days of old, they'd have fashioned a bridge of a freshly cut tree, a battering ram of another. Today, matters were much simpler. The two leapt the moat, side by side, and edged around the square stone shape of the keep, in search of a way to enter quietly. Both were careful to guard their thoughts, even from each other. A steel wall had been lowered around their minds. Lucien must not know of their approach.

It was difficult, for Roland knew that somewhere within these decaying stone walls, Rhiannon was imprisoned. Weakened, perhaps in pain. Were she well, she'd have torn the place apart by now, and Lucien along with it. Her patience would have found its end.

They finally came to a small opening in the stone, a window, which had never seen glass. Roland clambered through, and stood, looking around him while Eric followed. The place was in ruin, no question. The very walls were crumbling. The stone floors had spider webs of cracks, and huge gouges. It was black as pitch within the cold walls of this castle, but with his piercing night vision, he made his way slowly forward, along decrepit corridors, his mind on Rhiannon.

His heart grew heavier with every echoing step he took. Surely these weak stone walls could not hold her in her normal state. How he wished to see her, enraged, bringing Lucien to his knees with the sheer force of her anger. He closed his eyes for a moment and shook his head. That he'd ever thought to tame her spirit was a joke. It was untamable, as she was. It was what made her Rhiannon.

After trekking through endless corridors and passages, they came to the top of a set of stone stairs, crumbling as they spiraled downward into what seemed the hub of the earth. The smells of dankness and decay assaulted him as they descended. The sounds of water trickling, of rodents scratching, and of their own steps, echoed in his ears. She was here, in this hell, more than likely believing him dead.

Each step was placed with utmost care, as silently as possible. Roland scarcely dared draw a breath for fear he would alert Lucien and incite the man to harm Rhiannon. God, the very thought of her here was enough to drive him mad. Was she imprisoned in some freezing, tiny cell? Was she, even now, shivering with the cold and with her grief over his own supposed demise? Was she drugged, weakened to the point of helplessness in the face of Lucien's brutality?

Had the bastard harmed her? Had he touched her?

He'd die if he had, Roland vowed. He would die either way, he amended. The beast was loose, and Roland, for once, welcomed its presence. He'd tear Lucien limb from limb and take great pleasure in the tearing.

Eric touched his arm, and inclined his head. Only then did Roland hear the sounds of voices, echoing softly through the cavernous underworld. Like ghosts wandering aimlessly, the voices filtered toward them.

"Are you ready, then?"

"I'm ready, Lucien." Rhiannon's voice was weak, conveying the state of her body, and of her mind. The sound of it was a torment such as Roland had never known. He crept nearer.

"Remember, no tricks. If any harm comes to me, the boy will die where he is. You understand that?"

"Yes."

"Good."

"So I will bide my time, Lucien. And you will pay."

There was the sound of grim laughter. "I knew you'd be

furious about the cat. The animal gave me no choice, Rhiannon. When it bounded in front of my car, the temptation was just too great for me.'' There was a pause. "From the boy's reaction, you'd have thought I'd killed his dearest friend.''

Roland stepped closer, still unable to see them, but he could hear more clearly. He heard Rhiannon's labored breathing, and then her voice, with the barest hint of her former spirit making her words quiver with rage. "You didn't kill the cat. And when the boy is safe again, you might well become a snack for her.''

"The cat survived? Then why are you still so angry?''

"Bastard!'' Rhiannon drew a deep, ragged breath. The argument seemed to be taxing whatever strength she still possessed. "You know...the cause of my anger. What you did to Pandora pales...beside your other crimes.'' She paused, breathing deeply, brokenly. "You...you've taken from me...the only man I have ever loved.'' The final words were barely whispered, and the evidence of tears was clear in her voice.

Roland stood stock-still when those words floated toward him through the darkness. He closed his eyes as a horrible pain washed over him, and only stirred again when Eric's voice urged him on.

"Steady, my friend. You'll get used to the idea.''

He swallowed hard, and began moving silently forward. The shock of Rhiannon's admission faded as his rage, again, began to build.

"I will avenge Roland, Lucien,'' she whispered. "Make no mistake.''

"You leave me no choice but to be sure you never get the chance, Rhiannon. One would almost think you had a death wish.''

"Take care.'' Her words were weak and faint. "For I have nothing left to lose.''

There was the sound of chains rattling. Then a strangled gasp. "Feel the tip of this needle in your side, Rhiannon? If I get the slightest notion you are trying to bleed me dry, I'll depress the plunger. There's a large enough dose to kill you in seconds.''

They rounded a corner, and Roland saw the nightmarish scene laid out before him, illuminated only by the harsh, flickering light of a single torch. Rhiannon, all but limp, supported more by the chains at her wrists, than by her own power. Her eyes were hooded and moist with pain, without light of any kind. Desolate. Her hair hung over one side of her face. The hem of the deep blue kimono was dampened and dirty.

Facing her, his back to them, Lucien stood with legs planted apart, his fist gripping the hypodermic that was jabbed into her side, right through the flowing kimono she wore. He gave it an evil twist and she whimpered, too weak to cry aloud.

Roland lunged, but Eric gripped his arm. "If you attack now, he'll kill her." The words were whispered harshly into Roland's ear. "We have to get him to remove that damned needle before we touch him."

The sight of Rhiannon suffering riled him, but he knew his friend's words to be true. He glanced around, seeing in all directions in the inky blackness. Far above, more chains dangled from a towering ceiling. Roland could guess at their torturous purposes there. He nudged Eric, and pointed.

Eric nodded. "Can you get up there without a sound?"

"I'll know in a moment. Can you get Lucien's attention without costing Rhiannon's life?"

"I'd better, hadn't I?"

Roland drew a steadying breath and leapt upward, gripping a protruding stone high above, and anchoring the toe of one shoe in a chip in the wall. He glanced below, saw Eric watching, and gave him a single nod.

Eric stepped forward, out of the shadows, into the red-orange torchlight. "Pardon me, Lucien, but you forgot to tell her a few things, didn't you?"

Lucien whirled, tearing the syringe from Rhiannon's waist as he did. Her face contorted in pain. Her cry brought a convulsion to Roland's stomach.

"Marquand, isn't it? Rogers told me about you." Lucien lifted the needle like a weapon, clutched in a beefy fist, and started forward.

"Before you killed him, you mean?"

Roland waited. He needed a bit more space between Rhiannon and the point of that needle.

Lucien glanced over his shoulder at Rhiannon. She only hung, all but limp in her chains, hopelessness etched into her face like chinks beaten into old armor.

"Shut up, Marquand."

"Afraid I'll spill the beans, are you? Once she knows, she won't be so cooperative, will she?"

Roland nodded in approval. Lucien would lose if Rhiannon were to learn Jamey was safe and sound. He would be forced to silence Eric.

"Knows...what?" Rhiannon's head came up slowly. Her eyes focused on Eric.

"Why, that Jamey—" He stopped, sidestepping Lucien's charge with all the grace of a matador dodging a bull. Roland launched himself from the toehold in the wall, soaring above the stone floor, catching the dangling length of rusted chain. It swung with the force of his momentum, carrying him swiftly onward. He let go a second later, and plunged downward, onto Lucien's broad back. Both men crashed to the floor, Lucien landing facedown with Roland's weight atop him.

Lucien's hand, still gripping the hypodermic, twisted and turned, straining backward in a doomed attempt to stab Roland. Roland rose, one knee pressed into the center of the much larger man's spine. He clamped a hand on Lucien's wrist, and squeezed until he felt the subtle cracks of bone giving way. With a shriek, Lucien released his hold on the syringe. And even then, Roland didn't let the bastard up. The beast within wanted vengeance, and it was on the rampage.

A little more pressure and you can break his spine just as easily. Snap it in two. Just press the knee a bit harder...

"Roland?"

He lifted his gaze from the quivering heap of flesh beneath

him, and saw Rhiannon staring as if she were seeing a ghost. The beast within seemed to dissolve in that instant. He no longer thirsted for vengeance, only for her. For her touch, the feel of her lips beneath his, the sight of her half smile and the mischief in her eyes.

He stood, aware that Lucien rolled to his back and clutched his shattered wrist with his other hand. He paid no attention, knowing Eric would see to the bastard. His only concern was for her as he moved slowly forward. Her eyes widened. Her lips parted slowly and she mouthed his name again, though no sound emerged this time.

He reached her, then, and his arms went around her. Oh, to feel her, living, breathing, her strong heart pounding against his chest! He cradled her head to the crook of his neck, threading his fingers in her silken hair, words tumbling from his lips without thought, or even order. Here was where she belonged. In his arms, her body pressed to his. He felt he could never release her.

She lifted her head and her eyes moved over his face with such intensity he could nearly feel their touch. "I…I thought…" Her hands came then, following the path of her eyes, touching his face as if not believing it was real. The chains jangled with her movements.

"I know," he whispered. "I know. I dared not answer you, knowing that one's psychic strength." He caught one of her wrists in his hands, drew it downward, away from his face, and easily snapped the manacle. As it clattered down, slamming into the wall, he reached for the other. "Has he hurt you, Rhiannon? Has he touched you?"

"Nothing…could hurt me…more than believing…I'd lost you."

Their eyes met for a long moment, and Roland wondered how he'd failed before to see the love in hers. He must have been blind.

Unsure what to say in the face of such powerful feelings, uncertain what this meant to either of them, Roland dropped to one knee and snapped the shackles at her ankles. Her arms came to his shoulders, and then her weight when she tried to step away from the wall. He scooped her up with minimal effort. Her head fell limply to his shoulder, and he closed his eyes in exquisite agony. God, but it was sweet to hold her again.

Eric tossed the now-unconscious Lucien aside, and came to stand beside them.

"I should have killed him," Roland muttered, gazing toward the man on the floor of his own dungeon.

Eric lifted one brow, and tilted his head toward Lucien. "Go right ahead, my friend. He can't even resist, at the moment. I'm sure, beast that you claim to be, it won't bother you in the least to lean over and crush his larynx. Only take a moment. Go on. I'll take Rhiannon for you."

Roland glanced down at Lucien once more, then at the woman in his arms. He couldn't murder a man in cold blood. In battle, yes. He'd take great pleasure in fighting Lucien to the death. But not like this. He eyed Eric, and sighed. "I suppose there is a lesson in there somewhere, my friend. But all I wish now is to take Rhiannon out of this place."

He started back through the dungeon, and then up the crumbling stairs, leaving Lucien to his own devices. Likely a mistake, but there it was.

She rested in his gentle, unfaltering embrace, sometimes conscious, sometimes not. She knew little of the exact process by which they'd arrived, only that in what seemed little time at all, they were entering the great hall of the Castle Courtemanche, to the cries and embraces of Tamara, and Jamison, and Freddy.

A low snarl drew Rhiannon's gaze downward. Pandora limped through the little gathering, her foreleg wrapped in a plaster cast. She rose on hind legs, her good forepaw on Rhiannon's chest, and nuzzled her mistress's cheek with a cold nose.

Rhiannon stroked the cat's face. "Pandora, my kitty, you're home. Yes, yes, it's good to see you, too, love." She kissed the cat's muzzle, before Roland shooed her away.

"We picked her up on the way back," Tamara said softly,

crowding forward much as the cat had, to stroke Rhiannon's hair away from her forehead. "I wanted her to be here to greet you when Roland brought you home." The young one frowned, her gaze concerned. "Are you all right?"

Rhiannon smiled her assurance that she was, though she felt far from all right. She was rapidly growing weary, resenting the powerful effects of the drug. She sought out Jamey's face, and reached out to him. "Jamison. I was so afraid for you."

He looked at the floor. "I'm sorry. I almost got you killed... again."

She shook her head, but Roland turned away from them, striding down the vaulted corridor toward his chambers, with her in his arms. "We'll all have time to talk later. She needs rest now." As he spoke, he looked down at her face.

She searched his, wondering at the uncertainty, the endless questions in his eyes. He seemed almost afraid of something. A most unusual state of being for one so valiant. Moments later, he was lowering her onto the bed, tucking her beneath the brilliant yellow comforter, propping her head and shoulders with the pillows she'd purchased such a short time ago, but seemed like aeons.

"Roland." She reached up to cup his face in one unsteady palm. "I have much to tell you."

"Shh. I want you to rest. By tomorrow evening, you'll be feeling like your old self again, I promise. We can talk then."

"My old self?" She blinked slowly, recalling her promise to whatever gods might be listening. She would lose him unless she could keep her vow. She knew that beyond any doubt. "No, Roland. I'll never be—"

He hushed her with a gentle finger upon her lips. "Rest, little bird. We'll talk later."

"Yes." She let the heaviness of her eyelids pull them down, no longer wishing to fight off sleep. "Yes, we can talk later."

But she was not herself again when she rose the following evening. Nor did she return to normal in the following days. Stronger, yes, Roland observed in the great hall. There was no longer the film of drug-induced stupor covering her diamond-bright eyes. But the mischief wasn't there, either. Or the taunting, or the come-hither gaze he'd half expected to see. She was like a shadow of her former self. Quiet, exceedingly polite, refusing to argue, no matter what stupid remark he made to incite her.

Roland leaned sideways, elbowing Eric's middle. "Do you suppose there are lingering side effects to Rogers's tranquilizer?"

Eric cocked one eyebrow. "Why do you ask?"

"Look at her. She's quiet, almost…timid. She's been like this damn near a week now." As he spoke, Roland glanced again toward Rhiannon. She sat in an oversize chair Roland had hauled down from one of the storage rooms above, staring into the flames of the huge hearth, seemingly absorbing the fire's warmth in the chill room. She absently stroked the head of the cat that lay at her side.

Eric shrugged. "I suppose she might still be a bit shaken…"

"Rhiannon doesn't *get* shaken."

"Hush, she'll hear you," Tamara whispered, crossing the room with Jamey at her side. "And this is no time to upset her. Jamey's father will be here any minute. We don't want him walking in on one of her indignant speeches, do we?"

"I'd pay to hear one of her speeches, right about now," Roland muttered, but they moved as a group nearer the fire, and the various chairs situated around it.

"The great hall looks much nicer, Rhiannon. You've done wonders."

Rhiannon looked up, smiled softly and continued stroking the cat.

"Yes," Eric said, picking up where Tamara had left off. "All the candles and lamps soften the harsh stone, and the curtains and rugs are in perfect taste. Don't you agree, Roland?"

Roland only nodded, watching Rhiannon's face, a frown tightening his own.

"I still think it would have been better if you'd let her hang your paintings, Roland," Tamara said.

Roland shrugged. He did, too. He'd only refused Rhiannon when she'd asked because he'd been sure she would argue and fuss and fight with him until he conceded. He'd been looking forward to fighting with her. He missed it. Instead, she'd only nodded in acceptance and not asked again. He felt like screaming at her.

He watched her, watching him. "It's lovely, yes. And a shame we won't be able to remain here longer. But with Lucien still alive, and knowing our whereabouts, it will be better if we all move on." He studied the way her fingers tightened around the stem of her glass. At last, he thought, as her knuckles whitened in evidence of her fierce grip. "I can think of no other solution. Can you, Rhiannon?"

For an instant, the fire flared in her eyes, so brilliant he feared sparks would leap out to burn holes in her new rugs. "The solution," she said, back stiffening, chin lifting, "would be to find that sniveling worm of a man and…" She blinked rapidly, looking at each of them in turn. Then she sunk back into her chair like a balloon slowly deflating, and shook her head. "Whatever you decide to do is fine with me, Roland."

Roland pressed two fingers to his forehead, while Tamara shot Eric a concerned look. Eric only shook his head.

A heavy knock sounded throughout the room, and Rhiannon rose with her ever-present grace. Her long skirt billowed around her, touching no part of her legs or giving any clue to her shape as she moved. Its waist was cinched, but the blouson bodice drooped over the waistline. The neck was high, and buttoned all the way. Worst of all, her hair, her glorious, raven's wing hair, was twisted into a sleek knot at the back of her head.

Give her a pair of wire specs and some button-up shoes and she'd be the picture of a nineteenth-century school mistress.

She touched Jamey's arm. "You know Roland only did this for you."

"I know." Jamey touched his pocket, the one Roland knew

held the letter from his father that had been waiting here upon their return from the mountain. He hadn't expected his solicitor to find the man so easily, or that he would reply so soon. "I'm not angry. I think...I think I need to do this."

Rhiannon stroked Jamison's hair, then hugged him to her. A second later, Tamara rushed forward to do the same, while Rhiannon opened the door.

The man who stood there was six inches shorter than she. His build suggested an active life-style, but his dark hair was short, and thin, and he wore round glasses perched on his nose. His eyes were the kindest Roland thought he had ever seen, and they focused only briefly on the beauty at the door, danced once around the great hall and the people within it, then homed in on Jamey, and glowed with emotion.

For a long moment, the two only stared at each other. Several letters and phone calls had been exchanged by now, so they were not quite strangers. Roland had to respect James Knudson's easygoing methods. He hadn't tried to convince Jamey to become his son overnight. Instead, he'd invited the boy to spend a few weeks at his home in California. To get to know his stepmother, and half brother. And Jamey had agreed.

Roland felt his throat tighten when Jamey moved forward. He stopped before his father, and for a moment the two simply stared at each other. Then the man clasped the boy in a fierce hug, and they clung for a time. When they stepped apart, James Knudson removed his glasses and pressed a thumb and forefinger to his eyes.

It hurt to know he would lose the boy to his father. But it was right, and Roland had known it for some time now. The man was a junior varsity soccer coach, for God's sake. What more could a boy wish for?

Jamey turned and met Roland's gaze. "F-father, this is Roland. He's saved my life...more than once, now." Jamey bit his lip. "And this is Eric, and Tamara, and Rhiannon." He faced each of them in turn, his eyes dampening.

James cleared his throat, obviously a bit confused by the eccentric setting, and the formal clothing all but Tamara wore. But he stepped forward and shook each hand firmly. "I know how much you all mean to…to my son." He shook Roland's hand last, and longest. "I'm more grateful than I can tell you. If you hadn't searched for me, I might never have known I *had* a son."

Roland nodded. He couldn't have replied had he wished to. His throat was too tight.

Tamara stepped forward, speaking in his place. "Remember, we love him, Mr. Knudson. And that this is only a trial run. The decision to stay with you must be entirely Jamey's."

He nodded. "I would never try to force myself on him, Miss, uh, Tamara. I love him, too."

She met Jamey's gaze, then hugged him once more. "You know how to reach me if you need anything, kiddo."

"I know." Jamey hugged her in return, then released her and faced Roland. "I'm, uh, I'm gonna miss you."

Roland's heart trembled in his breast. "No, young man. I'll visit so often there will be no chance of that."

Jamey held out a hand, and Roland gripped it firmly and pumped twice.

The boy turned toward Pandora, who'd been sleeping near the hearth, and up until now hadn't made a sound. Jamey went to her, bent over and wrapped his arms around her neck. The cat's tail swished, and she rolled, pulling the boy with her. He sat up laughing, and the cat placed a paw upon his knee.

"Take care of them, Pandora."

The cat's green eyes seemed to assure him she would. Then Jamey rose and returned to his wide-eyed father. When the man could tear his eyes from the black panther, the two moved to the door, and stood in its opening.

"We'll be watching out for you, Jamey," Rhiannon said softly.

Eric nodded. "If you get into any danger, we'll know. You can count on it."

"Curt's gone now, so there will be no more harassment from him," Tamara whispered.

"And Rhiannon's computer-expert friend is going to erase all of your files from DPI's systems. It will be as if you never existed, to them." Roland stepped nearer Rhiannon as he spoke, needing someone close for this painful parting. "You can enjoy yourself the way a fourteen-year-old ought to, with no more worry about cloak-and-dagger nonsense."

Jamey opened his mouth, then closed it. Instead of words, he moved back toward Roland and hugged him hard. Then he turned, walking quickly toward the door, and his father. "I'm ready now."

His father clapped an arm around Jamey's shoulder. He glanced back at the others. "I hope you'll stay in touch."

"Rest assured, we will," Roland said.

The pair stepped out into the night, and the door swung slowly closed behind them. Eric folded Tamara into his arms. Roland wished he could do the same to Rhiannon, but he hesitated. She'd shown him no hint of encouragement since the incident with Lucien, and he knew her well enough to know she would have, if she wanted him.

Perhaps his hard heart had finally killed the love she'd once felt for him. Why now, when he wanted it so desperately?

Amid glowing candles, Roland put the finishing strokes to the canvas before him.

In a week, he hadn't seen this woman. Oh, Rhiannon was here, as he'd prayed she would be. She'd mentioned no more about leaving him forever. But she wasn't really Rhiannon. She was a dim shadow of the vivacious, slightly vain princess of the Nile. He wanted her back again, as wild and flighty and unpredictable as before. He missed her. The entire castle seemed empty, like a tomb, without her boisterous presence filling its every corridor. He wondered why he'd never noticed the emptiness before.

His eyes traveled the image of beauty before him. His brush had captured the texture of her skin, the glow of devilment in her dark eyes, the waves of her satin hair. He longed for her as much as ever, perhaps more. But she seemed almost indifferent to him now. Where before, she'd driven him to frustration with her constant flirtations, now she barely sent him a longing glance. It was maddening.

"So that's what you've been doing up here." Eric's voice came from the trapdoor in the floor's center, just before his body followed it up.

He stood, brushed himself off, then eyed the painting, arms crossing over his chest. "Roland, it's breathtaking."

"It's Rhiannon. How could it be otherwise?"

Eric smiled, giving his head a swift shake. "Have you told her yet that you're madly in love with her?"

Roland scowled. "She'd likely laugh me out of the castle. You know Rhiannon's views on silly, human emotions."

"Her views might have changed these past weeks, my friend."

"They wouldn't be the only thing to have changed, then."

Eric studied Roland's face for a long moment. "You know, you might stop to consider that she is only conceding to your requests."

"What kind of fool notion is that? I never asked her to become a piece of the furniture."

Eric shrugged, thrust his hands into his pockets and slowly paced away from Roland. "You've constantly reminded her how reckless she is, how impulsive. You've criticized her love of attention, her need to attract notice wherever she goes, her outrageous behavior. More than once, in my presence, you've asked her—no, ordered her—to behave like a lady. Now, you're complaining because she's doing as you wished."

Roland frowned hard, and looked at the floor. "Do you really think that's what she's doing?"

Eric shrugged. "It's as good a guess as I can come up with at the moment."

Roland dropped his brush into its holder, and kept his gaze focused on it. "So what do I do about it?"

Rhiannon held the sunny, yellow pillow in two fists, pulling in opposite directions until the fabric gave way with a horrible tearing sound, and fluffy white stuffing snowed down onto her feet. She gave a little growling shriek and spun in a circle.

"Ah, Rhiannon, there you are. Where've you been hiding these past few days?"

She faced the fledgling and bit her lips. She hadn't meant for anyone to witness her release of temper. "I don't know what you're talking about."

"Ha!" Tamara came into the room, bent and picked up two handfuls of stuffing, flinging it in the air. "What's this, then? You planning to restuff all the pillows to impress him?"

Rhiannon batted aside the falling fluff. "I don't need to impress anyone."

"Of course, you don't. I only wondered if you were aware of it, that's all."

With a little snarl, Pandora leapt off the bed to pounce on the wads of stuff as it landed, batting awkwardly with her plaster-encased paw.

"You make no more sense than my cat does," Rhiannon said softly, kicking more of the stuffing aside and walking into the living area.

"How long do you think you can keep this up, Rhiannon?"

She turned to Tamara, who followed on her heels. She was about to shout a denial, but saw the wisdom in the young one's eyes. "Not much longer. Oh, Tamara, I simply wasn't created to be meek. I'm ready to claw my way up the walls. What's more, it doesn't seem to be having the desired effect at all. He's barely looked at me since that night he carried me home."

"Oh, he's looking, all right."

Rhiannon frowned, but the fledgling seemed reluctant to say more. "Out with it, vampiress, or leave me in peace."

"Some peace, tearing apart innocent pillows when it's really him you'd like to rip in two."

Rhiannon sighed, her patience as thin as her temper. "Say what you've come to say, young one."

Tamara smiled. "Eric and I are leaving tonight. I only came to say goodbye."

"Leaving?"

"Oh, don't worry. We'll come back again soon. It's just that I want to be close to Jamey, in case he needs me. And you and Roland need to be alone, I think, to work this out."

Rhiannon looked at the floor and shook her head. "I fear there is nothing to work out. He knew I meant to leave as soon as the boy was safe. I've not kept my word and no doubt, he's wondering why."

"Well, before you do, take my advice and talk to him. Tell him everything. Don't hold anything back, not anything. Get things straight between you, once and for all, Rhiannon. If you don't, you'll never forgive yourself."

Rhiannon blinked. Then she tenaciously lifted her arms and put them around Tamara's shoulders. She hugged the little thing to her chest. "For one so young, you give good counsel, fledgling. I will miss you."

They gathered that night, the four of them, round the hearth in the great hall once more. Roland watched Rhiannon's eyes, noting with some satisfaction the spark that had finally returned. She wore the black velvet gown she'd worn that first night, and she toasted them all with her blood-red nails gripping the glass she lifted.

"When next we meet, it will be someplace different," Eric said softly. "I'll miss this drafty old castle."

"Oh, I don't know," Tamara said. "Roland might not have to give the place up, after all." Her eyes held a secret, and Roland almost grinned at the childish amusement she seemed to take in knowing something the others didn't.

"Go on, fledgling, say whatever it is that's on your mind."

"Yes, Tamara. You've had that look in your eyes all evening, ever since you made those phone calls to be sure it was safe for us to return to the States," Eric said. "What on earth makes you so smug?"

She shrugged. "I spoke with my friend, Hilary. The one who's still with DPI. It seems they're investigating the disappearance of a powerful psychic, suspected of murdering Curtis Rogers."

"What?" Roland's hand gripped his glass more tightly.

Tamara shot Rhiannon a knowing glance. "The last they heard of him, he was at an emergency room in Paris, having a crushed wrist set. He vanished from his hospital bed in the middle of the night, and no one's heard from him since."

Roland slanted a glance at Rhiannon, noting that Eric and Tamara were looking at her, as well. She sipped her beverage, and pretended not to notice.

"Rhiannon, what do you know about this?"

She met his gaze and shrugged delicately. "I haven't a clue what you're talking about."

"Rhiannon..."

She sent him a silencing glare. He was so relieved to see her acting haughty again that he let the matter drop. He could see she either didn't know what had become of Lucien, or had no intention of saying.

When they'd said their farewells at the front door, Roland closed it and faced Rhiannon. The time had come, he decided, to tell her the truth. He would bare his soul to her, once and for all, risk her ridicule and her ire, admit he'd been wrong all along and ask her to forgive him. True enough, he'd driven poor Rebecca to suicide, and that was a pain from which he'd never recover. But he thought Rhiannon was too strong a woman to allow him to hurt her the same way. At least, he hoped so, because there was no way in hell he could let her walk out of his life. Not ever.

What he saw in her eyes stopped him cold. The arrogant daughter of the Pharaoh was back, indeed. She glared at him for a single moment, then started up the stairs.

"Come with me, if you will, Roland. I, too, am prepared to take my leave, but there is something I must discuss with you first."

"Leave?" He hurried after her, trotting up the worn stairs. When she proceeded right up to the tower room, he thanked his stars he'd covered the painting before he'd left it. "You're leaving? Rhiannon, I—"

"No. I've given you ample time to say your piece. You haven't so much as whispered a word of it, so my turn has come." She went to the ladder at the room's center, up it and out onto the very top of the keep.

Roland followed. When he emerged on the top, she was leaning against the uneven layer of stone that created a short wall, gazing out over the rolling field, through the night, to the junction of the two rivers. The night wind whipped her hair, until strands of it came loose from the bun at the back of her head. She turned to face him, her hands going to the knot of hair, angrily tearing pins free, and tossing them over the side with an exaggerated flourish.

When her hair whipped loosely around her, she sent him a defiant stare. "So dies your wallflower."

Thank God, he thought. But he said nothing.

She turned from him once again. "I cannot leave here until you learn the truth, because I will, in all likelihood, never see you again to tell you how your beloved Rebecca really met her demise."

Roland frowned. "I thought we had come here to discuss... you, and me."

She licked her lips, and averted her gaze. "On that subject, it seems there is little to discuss. But there is much you don't know about Rebecca." She drew a breath as if to steady herself. "You told me you never loved her, but you know you cannot lie to me. I sense your feelings...most of the time. I know how very much you cared for her."

"And what it drove her to," he muttered, glancing beyond Rhiannon, to the ground, far, far below. Remembering the way he'd found Rebecca there. The pain came to life inside him, the guilt.

"The room where I took Tamara to meditate, it was Rebecca's room. I've been back there, you see."

Roland frowned. "Why?"

"Her aura has remained. She hasn't been at peace, Roland, not in all these centuries, because of your guilt. She needed you to know."

He shook his head, not wishing to hear this.

"Tonight she will rest at last, for tonight I will tell you what she made known to me in that room."

Roland closed his eyes. "I do not wish to discuss Rebecca. Not here." The image of her body plunging over the side haunted him even though he squeezed his eyes tight to shut it out. "She loved you, Roland."

He opened his eyes all at once. "She despised me."

"She wished to hate you for what you'd done, but she found herself falling in love with you, all the same. She came here, to this tower, only to try to decide what to do. She was racked with guilt at her feelings. She felt she might be betraying her father's memory by them, but she intended to accept your marriage proposal all the same.''

He released a sudden whoosh of air. ''You lie. Why are you saying these things, Rhiannon? To try to erase the burden of guilt I've carried for ages? It's no use. I know what I did to her.''

''She wore a golden crucifix, on a leather thong around her throat.''

Roland inhaled quickly, looking into Rhiannon's eyes. She didn't seem to be seeing him. Instead, it was as if she were looking beyond him. Her hand rose, in a fist, to the spot where the cross had rested upon Rebecca's throat.

''How do you know that?''

''It was fashioned for her by her father, and she cherished it.'' Her hand came away, palm opened. Her gaze searched her empty hand. ''But the thong came loose, and the gold cross fell.''

Roland frowned, unable to speak. Rhiannon turned, and leaned over the wall. ''It became caught in a crevice of the stone. She could see it, and she tried to reach for it.''

Roland gripped Rhiannon's shoulders. Her stance, the way she leaned over, was precarious at best. He turned her toward him, astonished to see tears in her eyes. ''But she was small, like Tamara. She couldn't hope to reach it, could she, Roland? And she fell. Poor, innocent, silver-haired angel. She fell, and the cross remains.'' She stepped aside, pointing one finger downward.

Stunned, Roland stepped to the wall, and leaned over it. At first, he saw nothing. Then a glimmer caught his eye. There, wedged tightly between two rough-hewn gray stones, the small crucifix glinted a reflection of the moon above. He shook his head in wonder, as an incredible burden seemed to dissolve from its longtime place upon his shoulders.

''She didn't take her own life,'' he whispered.

''No, Roland. It was an accident.'' Rhiannon returned to the trapdoor, and stepped onto the ladder. ''So now you may live your life without the guilt you've been feeling. It is my parting gift to you.''

Roland whipped himself around to face her. "Wait!"

Despite his bark, her head vanished as she stepped down the ladder. Roland leapt through the trapdoor after her, catching her shoulders, and turning her to face him before she could reach the next door.

"I said wait."

She blinked rapidly, but her gaze didn't flinch from his. "For what?"

He shook his head. "There…are still things we need to discuss, Rhiannon. You know it as well as I."

"It no longer matters, Roland. It makes no difference now."

"Why?"

"Because, you fool, there is nothing more I can do. Nothing more I *care to do* to make myself desirable to you. For years, I've sought to show you I was worthy. These past weeks have been one escapade after another. Yet all I did to show you my strength only served to anger you further. The more I endeavored to make you want me, the more averse you became to the notion."

He felt his lips pull upward in a smile, and reached out to her, but she pulled away, turning her face from his eyes. "Rhiannon, I—"

"No. Listen to me for once, Roland. I will say this now, or never feel moved to again. You might as well know all of it. When Lucien held me in that hole, he told me you were dead. And I howled my grief to the gods. I swore I would be the meek-willed creature you wanted me to be, if only they would return you to me. Can you believe it? Me, Rhiannon, bargaining for a chance to please a man."

He closed his eyes, and shook his head slowly, but she rushed on.

"I've tried to do as I promised, Roland. For days, I have whispered around these walls like a withering primrose. And what has it accomplished? You pay less attention to me now than before. And it wouldn't have mattered if you had, because I cannot convert myself to suit you, or anyone. I've learned that only recently. I am who I am. Rhiannon, born Rhianikki, daughter of Pharaoh, princess of Egypt, vampiress, immortal woman.''

She turned, and gripped his shoulders in her hands. "Look at me, Roland. Do you not see it in my eyes?''

The only thing he saw in her eyes, just then, was a sudden, glittering flood of tears.

"I love you," she whispered. "You can search the world, sift the deserts, comb the seas, and you will never find a love like mine for you. It is endless, boundless, and it will never fade. I've fought it for most of my existence, and still it remains. Yet you choose to throw such love away, just as my father did before you. You are a fool, Roland, to let me leave here. But I am equally a fool for throwing myself at your feet one last time before I go. Step on my heart and end this agony, once and for all. At least now, you can have no doubt what you will be missing.''

Roland bit his lips. He wouldn't shout at her, though the temptation was great. "Rhiannon, are you finished?''

She nodded. "Yes. I'll keep my promise and leave you now.''

"No. Not quite yet. I believe there are a few things left unsaid between us. Will you listen?''

"No.''

He searched her face, but she turned it away. "Why not?''

Her voice came hoarsely. "I don't wish to compound my humiliation by crying like a child in front of you, when you reject me this one final time.''

He sighed as she stepped away from him. "At least hear this, Rhiannon. All this time, all the risks you've taken, the recklessness you've shown, you haven't been trying to prove your worth to me.''

She turned slowly, her gaze fierce. "Haven't I?''

"No, nor to your father." He stepped nearer, and gripped her shoulders. "You've only been trying to prove it to yourself

Your father's rejection, and then mine, made you question your own worth, Rhiannon.''

She blinked, and he saw the fresh moisture that sprung to her lashes. ''Perhaps…''

''Question it no longer. Your heroism, your courage, are beyond those of any knight I've ever known, Rhiannon. You are a woman beyond any who has ever existed, nor ever will. Believe that.''

She sniffed angrily, and tugged away from him, averting her eyes. ''Let me go. I've no wish to cry in front of you.''

''Is that what telling you I love you will do, make you cry?''

She swallowed hard, and turned to him, eyes wide with disbelief.

He took her hands in his, and brought them to his lips. ''Rhiannon, just hear what I will tell you, please. I've fought my love for you from the night when you found me, nearly dead on that battlefield, and took me in your arms. Oh, I thought I had reasons. I was an animal, unworthy of such a goddess as you. I told myself my love was poison, that it would bring you only misery as it had everyone I had loved before. I resented the way you would come and go at will, leaving me longing for your return, and convinced myself I didn't care if you stayed a day or a month with each visit. But I did, and I died a little inside every time you left me alone.''

He turned toward the covered painting, and took one corner of the cloth in his hand. ''This time I swore I'd keep a small part of you with me, for always.'' He tugged the fabric away, and heard her sharp intake of breath.

He looked at her as she stared at the image of herself on the canvas. Her hand trembled as it moved from her lips, to the painting. She touched it, and tears rolled from her eyes, down her cheeks. She shook her head. ''This…isn't…can't be…me.''

''It is the very essence of you, Rhiannon. But I'm afraid I've changed my mind.'' He met her startled gaze. ''I won't let you go this time. I won't be satisfied to gaze at this painting. I want to gaze into your eyes. And I want to see them alight with life and mischief the way they've always been. Not dull with the effort of reining in your own nature. I came to love you just the way you are, Rhiannon. And I will fight with you through all eternity if ever you try to change.''

He fell to his knees at her feet, clutching her hands to his heart. ''Stay with me for always, goddess among women. Be my mate, my lover, my friend. Never leave me alone to long for you again.''

She dropped to her knees, as well, her hands threading through his hair. ''I adore you, Roland. But I'm not sure I can exist in seclusion, live this life of a hermit the way you do.''

''No, I would not ask it of you. My sentence is at an end, Rhiannon. You've given me the keys that set me free.''

She smiled, then, and it held all the mischief and devilment he'd missed these past days. ''Tell me again.''

''I love you, Rhiannon.''

He rose, and his arms crept around her waist. Hers slipped over his shoulders. He kissed her mouth deeply, thoroughly, as if he were tasting her for the first time.

''Your father was so wrong, Rhiannon. Do you know that yet? You are a treasure, one so rare, so precious...one that can be sought, and found, but never owned. Only held for a while.''

''Then hold me, Roland. Hold me for a very long while.''

* * * * *

TWILIGHT ILLUSIONS

To Jena, who gave Damien his magic.
I love you.

CHAPTER ONE

It is an old story
But one that can still be told
About a man who loved
And lost....

Shannon took copious notes, swearing at the inefficiency of a penlight for writing in the middle of a pitch-dark theater. She swore again at the narrow arms on the seats, which were no good at all for holding a notepad. Especially when the jerks on either side of her seemed to think they owned exclusive rights to them. She growled a sigh, shoved the meaty arm to her left out of the way and whispered loudly, "Hey, do you mind? I'm trying to *work* here."

Anger was good. Anger would keep her mind away from the images burned into it. Tawny, with hair and eyes that matched her name, and a porcelain-doll face, and a smile that lit up a room. Her dreams of becoming a star, her overly dramatic way of expressing herself. Her fearlessness. Her stubbornness. Shannon wanted to remember the vibrant upstart actress by day, call girl by night, best friend forever. Not the pale, naked body sprawled on the rumpled sheets, with its vacant-eyed stare. Not the twin gossamer strands of scarlet meandering over her paper-white neck. God, not that.

The guy in the next seat grumbled and shifted as far away from her as possible. Shannon wrote, only vaguely aware of the spreading applause. The gradual quieting. The sense of expectation in the crowd. The deep, melodic voice of the man at center stage announcing that he would need a volunteer from the audience. A sudden burst of movement and loudly voiced offers from the female spectators distracted her only for a moment before she adjusted the dim penlight and continued writing.

"The women here are practically drooling. It would be easy for him to lure one anywhere he wanted. Still no one who can tell me where he was last Wednesday night between..."

Her pen stopped on the pad and a cloud of frigid air seemed to envelop her. She glanced up, toward the aisle three seats away. *He* stood there, a tall, shadowy form draped in black satin. An instant later the spotlight caught up with him, illuminating his hair, until it gleamed blue, and making his ivory skin seem even paler. His arm was outstretched, his hand reaching toward her. And his eyes, huge and round like an owl's, seemingly holding the wisdom of the gods and the pain of a thousand hells, focused on her, keeping her prisoner.

"You, miss."

She wished her heart would stop racing. There was still no shred of evidence that the man was a twisted murderer. Only a matter of circumstance and her own suspicions. "Me, what?"

His lips curved upward. His gaze fell to the notepad, the penlight and the pen she'd been juggling all evening, then jumped back to hers again. "What's your name?"

"Sh-Shannon...but, I—"

"A round of applause for the lovely Shannon, our courageous volunteer."

He said it loudly, waving toward her with a flourish and a ripple of that shimmering cloak. The spotlight obeyed him, instantly dousing her in a pool of hot white brilliance that did nothing to chase away her ominous chill. She squinted as the applause swelled. His hand closed on hers, big, warm, hard. He pulled, none too gently. The notepad, penlight, purse, everything, avalanched to the floor as she was jerked to her feet.

She gave her hand a tug, but his grip was as good as any pair of handcuffs ever invented. He pulled her along at his side. Her protests went unheard beneath the noise of the crowd and the accompanying music. He dragged her up the steps far to the right and onto the stage. She could either fight him and look like an idiot, or accept this fiasco with a modicum of grace. She decided on the latter, though she thought the vain bastard could use a good kick in his oversize ego.

He looked into her eyes, and again, his lips curved. It didn't go far enough to qualify as a smile. More like an "I know what you're thinking and find it amusing" kind of a look.

She glared at him, her mind exchanging his black eyes for Tawny's light brown ones—wide open, glazed, forever blind.

His grip on her wrist eased. He frowned down at her and his hand slid down to clasp hers. They stopped center stage. Behind them, a red velvet curtain rose as silently as a ghost. Shannon glanced over her shoulder, saw a clear pane of glass balanced across the backs of two chairs.

"The lovely Shhannnon—" he drew the consonants in her name out until it sounded like an incantation "—is about to assist me in defying the very laws of nature...of Mother Earth..."

She told herself not to lose her anger to the ever-growing tide of uneasiness that could easily become fear. Killer or not, he couldn't very well hurt her right in front of thousands of onlookers. She stiffened her spine. "If you think I'm letting you saw me in half, forget it," she rasped, teeth grated, mouth barely moving. She glanced sideways at him, saw the twitch in his lips, felt his hand tighten on hers.

"Of gravity itself," he went on.

He had a way of speaking that was utterly mesmerizing, each word enunciated slowly, his mouth seeming to caress every syllable before releasing it. It made you focus on his lips as he spoke, against your own will.

"This way, Shannon." Mist shot up from the floor, encircling their legs to twist and writhe in time with the erotic music, if music could be that. Slow, sexy, with an urgent beat. He led her to the makeshift table, waved an arm over it, then took her hand and guided her up a pair of wooden steps as the silken music swelled, his every movement in perfect synchronization with the beat. "Lie down, Shannon. And prepare to be swept away."

She shivered a little, wondering if he spoke in those slow, measured tones all the time or only onstage. She lay back on the cool glass, her gaze never leaving his face. Even his breaths and the blinking of his eyes were grace epitomized, as if they, too, had been choreographed. He circled her once, one arm extended, cloak swirling as he moved. Then, with a flick of his fingers at his throat, he whipped the cloak from his shoulders, swung it outward, draped it over her. He drew it up from her feet, covering her right up to her chin.

The fabric was heaven, satin inside and out. She wanted to rub it against her cheek. The scent that invaded her mind was dusky and potent. Like nothing she'd smelled before.

His hand touched her forehead, sweeping downward. His fingertips closed her eyes. She stiffened, again thinking of Tawny.

"Relax, Shannon. Don't move. Let your muscles melt at my command. Break the bounds of earth. Free yourself from the constraints of gravity."

She sighed hard, blinking away the angry tears the image of her friend had brought to her eyes. Damien Namtar knew how to put on a show, if nothing more. Of course, he wouldn't be the hottest magician in the world if he didn't. Damien the Eternal. She'd have rolled her eyes if they'd been open. More like Damien the Master of Optical Illusion. But maybe she'd learn something about him if she paid attention. Maybe she'd manage to stop thinking about Tawny long enough to find a hint of who'd killed her.

And how? For the love of God, how?

She focused her mind, lying still as he'd instructed. She didn't want to break this contraption and get dumped on the stage.

Nothing happened. Shannon heard a collective gasp from the audience and opened one eye. Damien stood near her feet, holding a chair in one outstretched hand. She frowned a little. The chair that had been propping up that end of the glass? But her body was still horizontal.

He set the chair down and walked to her head, pausing to lay that feather-light hand over her eyes again, closing them once more. She popped them right open again, though. She'd paid to see the damned show. She certainly couldn't see it with her eyes closed, and she wasn't about to miss what might turn out to be a clue.

He was standing at the head of the makeshift bed now, looking down at her face. He pursed his lips when he saw that her eyes were open, but she didn't close them again. His gaze grew intense, probing, piercing. He bent, and she knew he was pulling the other chair from beneath the sheet of glass. When he straightened he held the chair, whirled around and threw it off stage right.

When she could see him again he had a plastic hoop in one hand. He ran it over and under her, then around her body, back and forth to demonstrate no strings held her aloft.

The hoop was tossed aside, as well. He leaned over her face. "Concentrate with me now, Shannon. There is nothing to fear."

With a look of glee, he pulled the cloak over her head. That would teach her for not keeping her eyes closed, she imagined he was thinking.

She heard him mutter words in a language she didn't recognize. Then there was a strange sort of vibration. She felt the glass under her back move. It slid to one side. She instinctively began to clutch it with her left hand, but his caught hers and held it still. Her chilled fingers, surrounded by his graceful, warm hand. She almost squeezed it, almost turned her palm to his and laced fingers with him. Weird notion. Luckily, he released her before she had time to follow through.

She felt the glass slip out from beneath her. The music faded as the beat of drums grew louder, faster. She remained where she was, lying in midair above the stage. How the hell—

The cloak was moving now, satin rasping against the denim of her jeans as it slipped down her body. Damien stood there, stark-white shirt opened at the collar to reveal a muscled column of throat. Gleaming dark curls showed on his chest. He stood a few feet behind her, arms outstretched, palms up, eyes closed as if in concentration. He had incredible lashes for a man. In fact, everything about him was pretty incredible. Shannon knew Tawny better than anyone, and she had a feeling Tawny wouldn't have left the theater that night without at least offering...

As he lifted his hands and the drums pounded frantically, Shannon seemed to rise on a cushion of air. She caught her breath. Higher and higher she floated, until she had to close her eyes to keep from getting dizzy.

Then she just stopped, far above his head. She dared a peek downward. He was staring up at her. He stepped forward. "To me, Shannon," he called loudly, firmly, in a deep voice that would be tough to argue with. Then he bent his elbows, snapped both fingers. The music stopped all at once...and she fell. It lasted an instant, the sensation of plummeting full-speed through space, the certainty that the landing was going to hurt like hell, the urge to scream out loud. She bit her lip...and landed in his arms.

She blinked in shock. He stared down at her, and his smile was just a bit fuller. His banded arms cradled her tight to his chest, and the sensation was alien to her. She thought she might be just a little closer to understanding Tawny's alley-cat morals after tonight. He lowered his head, touched her forehead with his lips. She was sure he'd burned a brand into her skin by the touch of his mouth. But that was stupid. It was the music, and the mist and the magic making her feel ripples of pleasure race up and down her spine. Not the touch of a man. Never the touch of a man.

The crowd's roar almost deafened her. He looked away from her, out toward the audience, and she followed his gaze. They were on their feet...every last one of them, and their cheers went on and on, vibrating right to the rafters.

But her attention strayed back to the man who held her. His strong profile, the elegant line of his jaw, the aquiline nose. And the light gathering brilliance somewhere deep within those jet eyes. He loved this. He absorbed the adoration of the crowd the way the desert absorbs the rain. He was in sheer ecstasy. He almost glowed.

The curtain lowered in front of them and he set her on her feet. His hands caught her shoulders, turned her to one side and pushed gently. "Offstage, Shannon. Watch from there." A stagehand hustled toward her and Damien leaned over, whispering close to her ear, "You were wonderful." Then the short redhead gripped her arm and led her offstage. He pointed to a folding chair and ran out of sight, a clipboard clutched in one hand.

Shannon glanced back to see the heavy, rippling curtain rise as if weightless. Damien stood center stage, fastening the ties that held the cloak at his throat. When the curtain stopped its spectral ascent, the crowd beyond it still stood, still cheered.

Sketching an elegant bow, he held his hands up for silence. "Thank you. Thank you all. I'm afraid the fair Shannon won't be rejoining you. I've decided to have her for dinner."

Laughter rippled through the theater.

Damien opened his arms to his sides, the edges of the cloak held in his hands. "Farewell, my friends."

A drumroll pattered across her heart. The crowd went utterly still. He lowered one arm and swept the other over his face in typical Dracula style. He whirled in a circle, once, twice, faster, three times.

Cymbals smashed. The cloak fell, a satin puddle. He'd vanished. Shannon came to her feet, squinting, searching that shimmering black mound. She saw movement and frowned harder. What the hell was that little...

The bat launched itself from its satin nest, fluttering wildly, swooping in crazy patterns before soaring out over the crowd. It dove low, eliciting shrieks of delighted horror, gasps of surprise. Then it turned and headed back to the stage. It angled left and flitted right past Shannon's face and out of sight.

The curtain fell again and the theater shook with applause.

The noise went on and on before it slowly died. She heard people in the crowd shifting, moving. The activity backstage increased. Shannon shook away the spell the magician had briefly cast over her, and looked around her. She had a mission, despite that his mystical illusions had made her lose track of it for a few minutes. She crossed her fingers and started off in what she hoped was the right direction. She wasn't finished with Damien Namtar yet. She had questions and she wasn't leaving here until she got some answers.

A tap on her shoulder made her spin around, half expecting to see the magic man himself smirking at her. Instead it was the same red-haired man who'd led her offstage. Her purse dangled from one pudgy, freckle-smattered hand. "Damien said I should give this to you. Said all your stuff's inside."

"Thanks." She took it, her gaze busy looking beyond the man. "Where is he? I need to talk to him."

"No chance of that. He's gone already."

"He's…gone?" She felt exactly like a balloon being slowly deflated.

"Long drive to that palace of his in Tigris. And it's raining."

"Palace?"

The redhead looked at the floor, shaking his head slow. "Like somethin' outta 'Life-styles of the Richer-Than-I'll-Ever-Be.' Know what I mean?"

She did. She'd seen the photos in the entertainment magazines, which couldn't get enough of the world-renowned, millionaire magician. Nor could his legion female fans. She tilted her head. "I heard he was a recluse. You'd think he would keep where he lives secret, keep the fans from hounding him."

"Everybody knows about that place, but there's no danger of him bein' hounded. He's got a security system like Fort Knox. *Nobody* could get in there."

"Nobody, huh?" She thumbed the strap of her bag over her shoulder and turned to go.

Damien,

Once again, I write you and hope for a response. And this time, I'll make an effort to explain my motives more completely, and perhaps ease your misgivings about me. I am a vampire, like you, and a scientist. I devote my time, over two centuries now, to the study of our kind, in an effort to better understand the peculiarities of our existence. Why are we here? To what purpose? And also, in the hope of easing some of the less pleasant aspects of our lives. I study the Chosen, as well, those humans with whom we share an inexplicable psychic link. Those we're drawn to, and whom we instinctively try to protect. Those who can be transformed, and who have the same elusive antigen in their blood as all of us had at one time. My studies have yielded a great deal of information. But I crave more.

You, Damien, I've been told, are the most powerful, the most ancient of us still in existence. You're said to have abilities beyond those of younger immortals, and I've no doubt your wisdom exceeds ours, as well. I wish only to meet with you, talk to you, learn from your vast aeons of immortality. Your wisdom could benefit us all, Damien. I should like, very much, to be your friend.

Yours in darkness,

Eric Marquand

Damien crumpled the letter with its formally patterned sentences that, in his opinion, made it clear to anyone who cared that the author wasn't from this time, and tossed it into the cold ashes of his modern, marble hearth. This Marquand ought to learn to sound as if he belonged here and now. Damien had always thought that was the most important part of fitting into any culture—sounding as if you belonged. No sense drawing attention to yourself.

He grimaced, remembering the last line of the note: *I should like, very much, to be your friend. Friend.* The word disgusted him. He didn't want or need to be anyone's friend. He'd lived through that debilitating pain once, and didn't have the slightest urge to repeat it.

This Eric Marquand, this infant of an immortal, this vampire who called himself a scientist, wouldn't learn much from him, anyway. Marquand had probably gained more knowledge about the undead in his mere two hundred years of existence than Damien had in almost six thousand. Damien had existed in solitude. He wanted no contact with others of his kind, and most of all, no contact with the Chosen.

The Chosen. They scared the hell out of him. This irresistible instinct he knew all vampires felt, to watch over them, to care for them—it shook him to the bone. It threatened his solitary life. He didn't want to care for anyone. Not ever again. The only way to avoid the mental tug of those rare humans was to avoid them, and that was exactly what Damien had always managed to do.

That is, until tonight.

He'd sensed her presence in the audience from the second he'd stepped onto the stage. He'd felt her there, and there'd been that pull, magnetic, powerful. Some demon inside had urged him to see her, talk to her, touch her and feel the power snap between them. He'd felt that urge before, when he'd chanced to cross paths with one of them. He'd always been able to resist it. Not this time, though. He'd wanted to touch her, and he had.

Maybe a little too much. Damien deliberately kept his mind closed, like pulling shutters tight over a window. He didn't want or need to open himself to the thoughts and feelings of others. He didn't care about them, wasn't the least bit curious. But tonight, in the brief moments of physical contact with the woman, he'd felt an avalanche of emotions pouring from her mind to his, emotions so powerful they'd shaken him. He'd felt her pain, her anger. Most of all, her grief. Anu, for a second he hadn't been sure if it was hers or his own, resurfacing to cripple him one more time. It was so similar. The ancient instinct to make things better for her had leapt to life, forced itself to the front of his mind. He'd doused that blazing urge with an act of will, and made a greater effort to shut her out. But it had been close. It had been too damned close.

He'd need to be more careful from now on. And he'd most definitely need to avoid any more contact with this particular woman, who affected him the way no one ever had.

* * *

She wore a black spandex bodysuit and leggings. A black nylon face mask, taken from a Cat Woman costume she'd bought one Halloween, covered her face. Only her eyes and mouth showed. The thin gloves that covered her hands were black, too, as were the lightweight tennis shoes on her feet. She even wore black nylons so her ankles wouldn't stand out in the darkness.

She'd given the man a chance. She'd phoned his house three times. He'd answered the first time, and as soon as she'd told him who was calling, he'd barked at her not to bother him and hung up on her. It had been busy ever since, and she suspected the hermit had taken it off the hook. Fine. He wanted to do this the hard way, then she'd oblige him. Hell, she had nothing to lose. His refusal to talk to her was a roadblock. She wanted to find out who'd killed her best friend and how. This guy was effectively stopping her in her tracks. Too much like being controlled. Too much like letting someone else pull the strings that ran her life. There wasn't much that could make her angrier, more defensive, more ready to do battle. The last time anyone had controlled her life, she'd been sixteen years old, and the results were not pretty. It hadn't happened again.

She scanned the big hulk of black that was his mansion, and wondered what was so great about this setup, anyway. No motion detector on the fence that surrounded the place. Just an alarm that would sound if the locked gate were tampered with, and a couple of surveillance cameras mounted up top. "Big, fat, hairy deal," she muttered.

She slipped the coiled rope from her shoulder, tossed the grappling hook to the tree limb that hung right over the fence—how could *Mister Security* have missed that?—and climbed up. Walking farther out on the sturdy limb, she attached the hook again, and lowered herself to the ground inside the fence. Simple. A kid could break into this place.

Two spotlights came on, aimed right at her. She hit the dirt facedown, her heart thudding in her chest like a jackhammer. Damn!

The lights remained on for several seconds before going out once more. So there were motion detectors. Anything moved within their range and those damned lights would come on again, giving her away if they hadn't already. Okay, think.

The sensor had to be aimed at the movement in order for it to work. She was assuming it wasn't aimed right at ground level or the lights would snap on with every rabbit or field mouse or stray leaf that blew past. Okay. It was worth a shot. She hadn't heard a sound from the house so far, so maybe magic man was asleep.

She slithered toward the house on her belly. She hadn't had much of a look at it yet, in this gloomy darkness. She knew only that it was huge, and utterly dark. Not a light glowing from a single window.

She'd try the door first—not that she expected to find it unlocked, but there might be a doggy door or something she could crawl through. As long as there wasn't a doggy to go with it. She crossed her fingers and humped her way up the broad flagstone steps like an overgrown inchworm.

When the door was right in front of her face, it slowly opened, and her vision was filled with a pair of calf-hugging black boots.

CHAPTER TWO

"What, exactly, are you doing here, Shannon?"

His anger vibrated in those low, measured tones, but seemed to be held in rigid control. She opened her mouth to answer, still staring straight ahead at his gleaming skintight boots. No words came out.

"Much as I might fantasize about the implications of your present position, I think you ought to get up now."

She did, quickly, and she felt her face heating beneath the mask.

That's right, the mask. How the hell did he know it was me?

She tugged it off and glared at him. "Look, I tried to talk to you at the theater, but you left. When I called, you hung up. You really didn't leave me much choice—"

"The choice I left you with was to leave me alone."

His dark eyes burned with some inner fire. Black fire. Dark light. How was that possible? She blinked and shook herself. The wind picked up a little, and it made a deep moaning sound when it passed through the branches of the big oak tree. Perfect October night wind. She faced him, and tried to ignore the shiver of apprehension. How could a man as attractive as this one make her feel so afraid? Nothing scared her. Not even death. Not that she'd admit it, anyway. She couldn't afford to, in her present condition. "I'm afraid I *can't* leave you alone."

"Why not?"

"Let me in and I'll tell you." She watched his face, and knew when he didn't refuse that he was wavering. "It's important."

"It must be." He glanced down over her attire as he said it, and his sarcasm couldn't be missed. Just when her chin rose and a few choice set-downs jumped to her lips, he nodded once and stepped aside. "Ten minutes, Shannon. Then you either leave on your own or I call animal control."

She sauntered past him, feeling triumphant, glancing back over her shoulder. "Who do you think they'd pick up? Cat Woman or Batman?"

He grimaced, as if her little joke had been so bad it was painful, but he couldn't hide the twitch at the corners of his lips. She wondered, for a second, why he'd want to. Then she turned to see where she was going, and all her thoughts stampeded from her mind like cattle from a burning barn.

The short hall she'd traversed opened into a circular room that would put the Oval Office to shame. Black marble fireplace with two arched openings. One for the fire and the other to hold the neatly stacked logs. The mantel stretched the length of it, and was littered with artsy objects encased in clear-glass cubes of varying sizes. The floor gleamed, the same swirling black marble as the hearth, accented here and there with colorful Turkish rugs. Their patterns were wild, orderless, vivid. Were those black eyes peering up at her from behind swirls of scarlet and gold? God, these things, with their braided tassels and secret meanings, could pass for Aladdin's magic carpet. One lay near the fireplace, all but invisible under a mound of pillows. Round, square, oval, satin, silk, velvet, blacks and reds and golds.

A chaise lounge the color of goldenrod, and big enough to hold a crowd, held court to one side of the fireplace. Its shimmery fabric would glow with the firelight when there was a fire. There was a couch, but it wasn't really. It had no back. The plump red cushions angled upward at either end, curving over scrolled wooden arms. Long strands of red fringe hung to the floor all the way around it. The wooden legs and trim were engraved with obscure shapes and symbols.

She blinked and gave her head a shake.

"Not what you expected?"

It was as though an icy wind had just blown over her, the way she shivered.

But it wasn't an icy wind. It was a warm breath, and four simple words spoken softly, close to her nape.

She drew a breath, closed her eyes, calmed herself. She

wouldn't let the man's mystic demeanor shake her. After all, it was only part of the act. A persona he put on and took off like the satin cloak he wore. An image. He took it further than she'd anticipated, but that wasn't proof he'd taken it to the ultimate extreme. Was it?

"Perfect setting to keep the image intact, Damien." She continued scanning. There were two wide, arched doorways, at ten o'clock and two o'clock if the fireplace was noon. Neither of them had a door. Instead they were draped with countless strings of beads that looked like onyx. "Although," she went on, trying to keep the amazement from her voice as she found one wondrous item after another, "I don't know why you bother. I was told few people ever get past the front gate. So, who are you trying to impress?"

"The room is for me. I like it this way."

The walls and high ceiling were plastered, their surfaces rough, like stucco, and slightly yellowed, as if very old, although she was sure they were new. The lights were recessed into the walls, with half circles of intricate plaster work shading them from below. The effect was a muted glow that seemed to emanate naturally from above.

She stepped closer to the mantel, eyes widening as she looked more closely at the items within the glass cubes. Small figures of bearded, almond-eyed men. What looked like a billy goat standing on its hind legs, apparently plated in gold. A chipped piece of pottery shaped like a glass, with animals and designs painted in dulling colors and perfect symmetry. An uneven, rather rectangular hunk of stone with line after line of tiny, detailed marks. Writing? "Are these things as old as they look?"

"That depends on how old they look."

She faced him, frowning. "They're artifacts, aren't they? You collect them. But where do you find things like this, in some pharaoh's tomb?"

"Nice guess. Try a bit earlier and a little farther south." She bit her lip, racking her brain, but he cut her off. "It doesn't make any difference, Shannon. I've given you ten minutes, and you've wasted the first three gawking at my living room. Are you going to tell me what it is that drove you to dress in that ridiculous outfit and break in?''

Her anger returned, and with it, her awareness of why she was here. ''You think it's some silly thing, don't you? That I'm an obsessed fan and all I want is an autograph or a souvenir of *Damien the Eternal.*''

He tilted his head to one side, crossing his arms over his chest as if waiting patiently for her to get to the point. It was infuriating. She unzipped the small fanny pack that was snapped around her hips. The manila envelope she pulled out wasn't sealed. ''How often do you do that levitation routine, using an audience member as a volunteer, Damien?''

His gaze dipped to the envelope, then met hers again. ''It's new. Tonight was only the third time I've done it. I like to keep the act varied.''

''This was the third time,'' she repeated. ''Do you happen to remember your volunteer last week?'' She pulled out the photos, not giving him time to answer. She kept her eyes on his, careful not to glance down at the pictures she held out to him. She'd seen them too many times already.

He looked at her for a long moment, brows creasing. She saw some kind of war going on in those glittering black eyes. When he took the stack, his fingertips brushed over hers and she shivered. She turned away from him, paced to the piece of furniture that looked like Cleopatra's bed and sat down.

She refused to look at him. She gazed, instead, into the cold hearth, noticed the crumpled bit of paper there, wondered what was on it and whether he'd leave the room long enough for her to get a look.

She never heard him approach, so it shocked her when his hand closed around her wrist and he jerked her to her feet. His grip was like iron, and he glared down at her with a fire in his eyes that was potent, and dangerous.

"What in hell is this garbage?" His other hand clutched the photographs.

Fear should have taken over. That it didn't wasn't on account of her unshakable courage. More that she had nothing to lose. Nothing at all. What was the worst he could do to her? Kill her? So he'd beat the disease to the punch. Big deal. It was laughable.

"Don't you recognize her, Damien? I'll admit, it's tough with her skin white as candle wax and her eyes glazed over like that. Still, her hair is the same. Tangled, but basically the same. She was an actress, you know. At least, she wanted to be."

His grip tightened. "What kind of sick prank are you trying to—"

"You *do* remember her. Good. It's no prank, Damien. Tawny Keller is dead. She died in her bed, a few hours after she performed for the last time, as your audience volunteer."

His gaze narrowed. His grip on her arm eased, then his hand fell away. He turned slightly, shook his head.

Shannon reached into the fanny pack again, pulling out several stapled-together pages. "Don't believe it, huh? Well, try this, then." She thrust the papers under his nose. "Medical examiner's report, autopsy results."

His gaze rose to hers again. Anguished. She had the brief sense that he was bleeding inside, but it vanished as fast as it came.

"How did you get these things? Are you a cop?"

She squared her shoulders. "Not a cop, a PI." He hadn't taken the papers, so she tossed them aside. They spread their pages like wings and fluttered to the floor. Silence stretched tight between Damien and her. She didn't want to live it again, didn't want to feel it again. "I found the body." The memory rushed over her, even though she fought it with everything she had. Pounding on Tawny's door. Worried because she hadn't answered the phone, and they always talked first thing in the morning. The door hadn't even been locked. God, she was careless!

Shannon felt a cold hand grip her heart as she recalled walking in, calling, hearing no answer. But she'd known, she'd felt that dread even before she'd entered the bedroom and seen what no one should ever have to see.

She turned to hide the pain from him and paced away. "They're keeping the whole thing quiet. There'd be a circus if the apparent cause of death leaked to the press. But I saw her. I knew. I traded my silence for the photos, the reports. I've worked with this ME before, and he's a stickler for the rule book. He wouldn't have let me have these things if I'd given him a choice." She stared into the darkened fireplace, battling tears and eventually winning. "They threatened to pull my license if I got involved in this, but I don't really give a damn. She was my best friend."

He cleared his throat. "I'm sorry." He'd moved closer to her, stood right behind her now. He must walk like a cat. "But I still don't see—"

She whirled on him, poking his wide chest with a forefinger. "Don't you? She bled to death, Damien. And the only injuries found on her entire body were those two little marks on her throat. You tell me how the hell anyone could do that to her, *and then* you tell me who *you'd* suspect if you were in my shoes."

He closed his eyes as if he were in some kind of physical pain and turned slowly away from her. "It's impossible. There had to be some other injury, or—"

"Read the damned autopsy report if you don't believe me. The cause of death is listed as extreme blood loss. They can't explain it. If this were an upstanding citizen instead of a hooker-slash-actress, they'd be probably call the FBI." She closed her eyes. "But it was just Tawny. Just some nobody who grew up on the streets and did what she had to do to survive. Just my best friend since I was sixteen years old. I'd have never lived to see seventeen if it hadn't been for her."

He said nothing, only stood with his back to her, one hand shielding his eyes.

"The police think I'm crazy. They say there's no evidence to point to you. But I'm *not* crazy. I'm good at what I do, and right now the only goal in my short, miserable life is to get to the bottom of this.'' She sniffed, and tried to erase the waver from her voice. ''I'm trying to track down the woman who volunteered to be your assistant the week before Tawny did. Rosalie Mason. But you know something, Damien? I'm not having much luck. And my gut tells me I'm not gonna find her, or if I do, she won't be in any shape to tell me a thing.''

She heard his slow, long sigh. ''So, you came here to accuse me of murder. You've done that. Maybe you ought to leave now.''

''Rosalie was a prostitute, too, you know.'' She paced back and forth in front of the fireplace, ignoring his words, going a little faster with every lap. ''She attended the show that night with a john. No one's reported her missing. No one wants to talk to the cops about where she might be. They're ignoring the fact that she just isn't around anymore, because no one cared. But it's different with Tawny. Someone cared about her. And I'm not letting this go.''

''Go home, Shannon.''

His form appeared in front of her, stopping her pattern. She stared up at him.

''So, which is it, Damien? Are you insane enough to believe you *really are* what you pretend to be onstage? Or is this just a publicity stunt? A few vampire killings while you're in town to entice the populace. Oughtta work wonders at the box office.'' Her brows drew closer as she studied him. ''How much did Tawny suffer before you killed her, Damien? Just how the hell did you *do that* to her?''

His anger pounded down at her like a physical force. ''What do *you think?*''

If his tone and his threatening stance were supposed to intimidate her into cowering silence, it didn't work. She thrust her chin up and held his gaze. ''*I think* this is a pattern. And if I'm right and it holds true, then I'm next in line, aren't I? I'll know for sure, then. And you know something, Damien? I almost hope you do come for me. Because I'll be waiting.''

She felt his rage. It seemed to zap and spark in the very air between them. If it did, then it must be wrestling with her own, because she was furious. He hadn't denied a thing.

"Oh, will you?"

"You're damn right I will, and you'd better take me out on the first try, because I won't hesitate. And I never miss."

"Going to shoot me, are you?"

"Blow your head right off your shoulders. I don't know how many other girls you've left lying dead in your wake, but you messed with the wrong one this time. Tawny was my best friend in this world. It ends here. So give it your best shot, magic man. It's gonna be your last one."

She turned away from him, started for the front door, but his hand shot out to grip her arm and he twisted her around to face him again.

"You're not going anywhere."

Her eyes widened, eyes the exact color of very old amber. He felt the rush of dread that passed through her. But she didn't show it, didn't cower or even lower her head. Her golden blond hair framed her face so she looked like an angel. At the moment, a fiercely angry, avenging angel. He opened his mind, deliberately opened it, for the first time in aeons. The bombardment stunned him. He released her, his hands automatically pressing to his temples at the force of all that hit him. Voices, thoughts, emotions, sensations. Thousands upon thousands, pummeling him all at once. Too much. Too many.

He closed his eyes, took a staggering step backward. The noise of countless voices pierced his eardrums. Feelings of pain, pleasure, heat, cold, sickness, exertion, trampled over his body until it vibrated as if electrified. Visions flashed in front of his eyes, blinding him. A thousand scents assailed him, a thousand tastes coated his mouth before he managed to block them out, slamming the door of his mind like the lid of a casket. Closing it, sealing it.

For the love of Inanna! It had been so long since he'd attempted to receive the sensations of others...he'd grown in power, in strength, in the ability to do the trick, and at the same time, neglected the taming of his own abilities. He'd need to work on it, relearn the ways to filtering the vibrations, to home in only on the mind in question.

Which, at the moment, was hers.

He opened his eyes, blinking the room into focus. He was alone. He turned to stare down the short hallway. The door stood wide, with only the night beyond it.

Gone. As if she'd never been there.

Damien closed the door and stood for a moment, still trembling with the aftereffects of the blow he'd just taken. He made himself move back into his comfort room. The haven he'd created for himself. The place he felt the most relaxed. The sunken eyes of the dead woman stared up at him from photos scattered over gleaming black marble floor. The marks on her lily-white throat seemed to taunt, to laugh at him.

You think yourself the enemy of death, Damien? You think wrong. I've won at last, you see? You've surrendered. I own you now.

He lunged forward, snatching the horrible pictures from the floor, falling to his knees in front of the hearth, throwing them down on top of the cold ashes. "I didn't kill her." The words came as if on their own, in a harsh whisper. The face of the once-beautiful young actress stared at him, accusation screaming from the silent depths of her sightless eyes. He focused the beam of his thoughts, and the photo burst into flames. Red-orange tongues danced and licked, spreading to the other photos in the hearth and then to the letter he'd thrown there earlier. Damien watched them burn and wondered what more he could have done to prevent this.

The thirst—the damned need—had grown stronger with every year he'd lived. It raged now like the Bull of Heaven, sent down to wreak the vengeance of the gods on mankind. It was impossible to deny, or to deprive the hunger. Animals no longer sufficed. The cold plastic liquid stolen from blood banks couldn't fill his burning need. He couldn't ignore it.

He'd tried. In fact, he'd made it a ritual of self-torment. Whenever the hunger came, he refused to feed, fought the bloodlust, resisted it until it became all powerful. He'd thought that by resisting it, he'd be the one to grow stronger. It hadn't worked out that way, though. Every time he tried, the lust raged more potent in his veins, until every cell of him screamed for the elixir, until his mind left the realm of his control and he hunted, swathed in a bloodred haze of mindless need.

And even then, he'd thought he'd kept a modicum of restraint. He'd fed only in sips, and only from those women who'd hounded his steps after a performance. The groupies. The ones who slipped uninvited into his dressing room, baring pretty necks and offering themselves to him, sometimes begging him to take them.

Fantasies, he knew. And he'd laugh off their offers, only to appear in their bedrooms—in their dreams—a few hours later. There, twined in their warm, mortal arms, he could sate his roaring lust. And by his simple command, these willing victims would remember the entire exchange as an erotic, pleasure-filled dream. As they drew their first breaths; bathed in sunlight, the marks on their throats would begin to heal. If they noticed the wounds at all, they'd remember a minor accident to explain them. One that had never happened. He thought he'd been so careful. Always leaving them asleep, looking utterly tranquil and contented, having gained as much satisfaction from the exchange as he had.

Had he gone too far? Had that desire inside him overwhelmed him to the point that he'd drained one of them and not even been aware of it? Could it?

That's right, Damien. I've won. You've not only surrendered, you've joined my army. Joined it alongside sickness and war and famine. One of my horsemen now, Damien. An instrument of death.

He moaned in agony and folded his arms around his middle. No one despised the shadow of death more than Damien. No one. Death was his enemy. His greatest foe. If he'd reached the point where feeding his own demon meant feeding death another victim, then he'd end his existence tomorrow. He'd walk naked into the sunrise. He'd...

No.

He straightened his body and stared into the blackened remains of the photos in the hearth. Red still glowed around the edges of the letter, and bits of white showed amid the charred paper. Before he did anything, he needed to learn the truth. If he'd killed, if indeed he had taken a life, then he deserved to surrender his own.

But if not, then there was someone else.

He paced the floor, deep in thought. Someone who, perhaps, wanted the world to believe Damien was guilty.

His steps stopped near the first archway. Someone who was doing it by preying on the women whose blood he'd tasted?

No, how could anyone know that? He would have been aware if anyone had seen him, wouldn't he?

Preying on the women who'd assisted him onstage, then?

His gaze flew to the spot where he'd last seen Shannon.

If he didn't go after her, watch over her, and his theory was on target, her life might very well end tonight.

If he did go after her, as his every instinct was screaming at him to do, and his greatest fears were true...her precious life might end anyway. *Anu,* how could he risk killing someone he wanted only to protect? How could he risk his need for solitude by giving in to the urge to protect her, when his mind was telling him to run in the opposite direction?

What the hell was he going to do?

CHAPTER THREE

The raven soared into the night, its glistening blue black wings spread as it rode the wind, spiraling upward, ever upward. Then, folding those gleaming wings to itself, it dove at dizzying speeds, until anyone watching would have caught his breath in alarm, fully expecting to witness the death of a once-graceful bird. Instead, though, the wings unfurled. The bird slowed, arched upward and, with gentle flapping, alighted upon the rail of a balcony on the twenty-third story.

She slammed the apartment door, turned the lock, shot the dead bolt, fastened the chain. Breathless, she leaned back against the door, closed her eyes. The courage, the defiance, had been flawless right up until he'd grabbed her and told her she wasn't leaving. At that moment, with that iron manacle of a hand gripping her arm, those cold, sure words hanging in the air and those unnaturally gleaming, jewel black eyes holding her captive, she'd felt pure, undiluted panic.

Instantly his image flashed into her mind, a snapshot of the way he'd looked at that moment. What had happened to him? He'd released her all of the sudden, his hands going to his head as if it were splitting in two. His eyes squeezed shut tight in apparent pain.

And she'd run like a rabbit.

She'd climbed over the fence to make her escape, no longer caring how many alarms she set off. Her rope and grappling hook still hung from the monster of an oak tree out front. Her Cat Woman hood probably still lay on his front step. She'd forgotten the photos of Tawny and the autopsy report. She'd forgotten everything except that she didn't want to die. When he'd grabbed her arm and told her she wasn't leaving, she'd thought she was about to.

She squeezed her eyes tighter to prevent the stupid tears that tried to leak through, and shook her head at the bitter irony. Her, running from death. Her, not wanting to die. God, what a joke! Not for the first time, she heard herself cursing fate for its idiotic mistake in choosing Tawny as the victim of this sick killer's whim. It should have been Shannon. Tawny had a future, a life waiting for her. A career. She'd have made it happen, too. Shannon knew she would have. She had a way of willing things to go the way she wanted. Shannon swore and swept a hand over her damp eyes.

It shouldn't have been Tawny. It should have been me. God, why wasn't it me? At least one of us could have gone on, lived, maybe had a family someday....

Blinking, she crawled out of the self-pitying puddle she'd stepped into. If she didn't get herself together, it *would be her.* And it would end any chance she had of bringing Tawny's killer down before her time on this planet ran out. If he was coming for her, it would probably be tonight. Tawny had died the same night she'd volunteered as his assistant. And as far as she could tell, the other woman, Rosalie, hadn't been seen since the night she'd taken her turn in the spotlight. So he would probably come tonight. Probably pretty soon.

She was tired. Damn, but she was tired.

Shannon dipped her hand into the fanny pack for the stubby .38 revolver. It had been with her the whole time she'd been at Damien's. She'd never *really* been in any danger. She could have dropped to one knee, pulled out the little black handgun and pumped all six rounds into him in under three seconds. Sure, it would've been tough to prove self-defense, when she'd broken into his house and he'd been unarmed. So, she'd have done some time.

Not a hell of a lot, though.

She took the gun into the bathroom with her, set it on the little sand-colored counter that surrounded the shell-shaped coral basin. Within easy reach. No one was going to sneak up on her. Not even someone who walked as quietly as he did.

She stripped off her clothes, quickly and not too neatly, tossing them and leaving them where they landed. Then she stepped beneath the hot, pounding spray and just let it soothe her aching muscles. God, it would be good to take a break from all of this. Relax with a good book, or a bowl of popcorn and an old Bogart movie. Jump in the car that often cost her her grocery money and head south until she hit sand and sun, and just bask for a while. But she knew she couldn't. Not now. She'd set the wheels in motion and she had to see things through to the end. There wasn't a lot of time. She was all too aware of that.

Even with Tawny's death and all its repercussions, all the questions screaming for answers, Shannon still couldn't stop her mind from wandering where she least wanted it to go.

Damien Namtar.

The image of him floated into her brain again, damn him. He was a murder suspect. Not to the police, granted. But in her mind he was. Right now he was the *only* suspect. So she shouldn't think about the odd awareness she felt around him, the prickling sensations that encompassed her, the palpable touch of those eyes. "Physical distractions," she muttered, and tipped her head back to let the hot water drench her hair. She inhaled the moist steam, hoping it would put some sense into her head. He was utterly handsome, in a dark, exotic kind of way. Add to that the fact that his performances were always loaded with sexual innuendo, and it was no wonder her libido was responding this way.

Or was it? She'd thought herself immune to sexual desire. She'd had little experience; the clumsy, drunken gropings of the man who was supposed to be her guardian, the foster parent she'd been sent to when she was sixteen. She'd had no choice about going to live there. Orphans, abandoned children didn't have a hell of a lot of choices, and God knows she'd had none to speak of up to that point in her life. Certainly no choice over what that bastard had tried to do to her.

From that day on, though, the choices had been all hers. No one had ever told her what to do again. No one ever would.

Only one good thing had come out of that time in her life, and that was that she'd met Tawny. They'd been sent to the same foster home, from different orphanages. They'd suffered the same abuse, albeit for a short time. They'd fled before the bastard's attempts could lead to the ultimate violation. They'd had little choice. Neither Shannon nor Tawny had trusted authority enough to turn him in then. Whom would they have told? The same pencil pushers who'd sent them to him? And where would they be sent next? Someplace worse?

Later, Shannon had written a letter to the social worker, recounted everything, even signed her name—but she hadn't told them where to find her. She couldn't risk losing control of her own life again.

The results of their brief stay with that man had been totally different. For Tawny, there was no more respect for her body. It became a means to an end, and she used it that way, laughing inwardly at the men foolish enough to pay her for something they could get at home free. Idiots, she'd called them. If they were dumb enough to hand over their hard-earned cash, that was their problem. She'd always said the johns didn't know it, but they were the ones being used.

For Shannon, it was different. She'd made up her mind that she would never want to be touched by a man. Never. She couldn't even think of sex without remembering the disgust, the humiliation, the stench of his breath. How could closeness with any man ever bring her pleasure? She'd shunned Tawny's methods of survival, taken a menial job cleaning hotel rooms, instead.

It had been a long time, though. And for some reason, she wasn't recalling all that revulsion when she thought of Damien. She probably should be.

She sighed and tried to put him out of her mind, but she couldn't. She remembered his performance tonight. Scantily dressed beauties running their hands up and down his body to some frantic jungle beat as he prepared to perform the next feat, seductively touching and caressing him as they fastened chains around him for an escape trick. It was little wonder he had groupies throwing themselves at him. Little wonder he seemed to exude some mystical allure to her. He probably had the same effect on most women, which surely accounted for the gossip she'd read in the fan magazines about the ones who were constantly offering to take him to bed after a show.

The question of the hour was, did he murder them after obliging them? Had Tawny been taken in by his sex appeal and offered herself as others did? It was something Tawny wouldn't have hesitated to do. Was that why he'd killed her?

Or maybe the opposite was true. It might be the ones who seemed indifferent to him that suffered the ultimate punishment. Maybe Tawny had turned him down. Maybe that was why he'd killed her.

But why do it in such a grisly way? And how? How the hell do you drain the blood out of someone, leaving only two tiny wounds in her neck? How do you do it without a drop of blood spilling on the sheets, or the pillows the person is lying on? What the hell do you do with it after you've taken it?

She lathered her body, rinsed it, washed her hair, and still felt no closer to knowing what had happened to her friend.

There had been precious few other cases demanding her attention. She'd referred them to larger investigations firms, hating to have to give away business when she'd fought so long and so hard to get established. But this took precedence, and besides, she wasn't exactly saving up for retirement. It wasn't as if she was going to be spending much money. All she needed was enough for the next few car payments, and another month or two's rent, if that. She wouldn't be taking on any new cases. She kept the office open only for her own case now. And when she found Tawny's killer, she'd close it for good.

She intended to focus solely on Tawny's murder from here on. She couldn't afford a single distraction. She would use every second of the time she had left to—

Dizziness swamped her and she reached out blindly, clutching the shower curtain to keep from falling. She let her body rest against the cool, wet tiles of the shower stall, held her head with one hand and shut the water off with the other. She waited for the vertigo to pass, but it didn't.

Damn! Why now? Why the hell now?

She groped for a towel, twisted it around her and staggered out of the shower, pausing only to clumsily pick up her gun before continuing through to the living room. She had to get to bed, had to lie down, rest until it passed. It would pass. It always did. God willing, the bastard wouldn't show up to kill her before it ran its course.

She needed the bed, and she fought to keep her balance until she got there. She had to huddle into the blankets, because the chills would come next. And then she'd shiver and shake and run a fever until they finished with her. They usually lasted only an hour or so. But they'd been coming more frequently lately. Her body's little alarm clock, reminding her every so often that time was nearly up.

She made it just to the doorway of the bedroom before she collapsed. She felt her legs melt from her ankles to her hips, and then the floor rose up to greet her. She pulled her arms under her to push herself up, but they'd become useless, heavy, nearly impossible to move.

The shaking kicked in. Her body jerked with the chills, and she could hear her own teeth chattering. God, she was so cold. She felt the goose bumps rising on her arms and legs. If she could just get to the bed. She'd always had time to make it to the bed. The damned episodes were hitting faster, harder, than before, she realized, as well as more often. She didn't want to think about what that meant.

But why the hell did it have to happen tonight?

Concentrating fiercely, she managed to tighten her hand around the gun, though the effort cost her. She broke into a cold sweat, fought to catch her breath. She couldn't lose the gun. She had to cling to it in case he came for her. He'd kill her if he found her defenseless like this. God, she hated being helpless, weak, not in control of her own body. She focused on the feel of the cold wood grips in her hand, made herself feel the trigger, kept her mind on where the barrel was pointed, even as she strained to make her arms function and struggled to pull her shuddering body across the floor. Every muscle in her throbbed and ached in protest, burned with an unseen fire. Then the damned convulsions tried to tear them from the bone.

Someone bent over her, lifted her, and a familiar scent invaded her awareness. Dusky. Subtle. Somehow erotic. The arms around her, the chest against her, felt familiar and warm and hard. She forced her eyes open, tried to focus her vision, but saw only a blurred outline. It didn't matter. She knew perfectly well who held her, who carried her across the room and lowered her to the bed. Covers were tugged over her, tucked tightly around her. The electric blanket she'd so recently purchased for just this kind of occasion was plugged in, turned on. She knew, because she felt it begin to heat her chilled skin. He gently worked the gun out of her trembling hand and set it aside. His hands, those big, hard, magic hands with their long, elegant fingers, pushed her hair away from her face.

"Do you want me to call an ambulance, Shannon?"

She heard the words, heard that soft voice, which had been harsh the last time he'd spoken to her. It was still like velvet music on her ears, but so gruff now. So hesitant.

She tried to form an answer, gave up and shook her head, instead. Even that small effort took every ounce of energy she could summon.

"Your family, then?"

"N-noo. There's…no one."

"What is it? What's wrong with you?" The low, level timbre of his voice seemed to have deserted him. He spoke quietly, as if he might hurt her ears if he used his normal tone. She felt the strength of his hands on her shoulders. The warmth of them. The pressure of each fingertip, pressing urgently into her flesh.

Fear tried to make itself heard in her mind, but there was too much else there in the way. She knew, somehow, that she ought to be afraid of him right now, but she wasn't. And it had to be because of the illness. It must be dulling her intellect, or she'd be scared to death.

The electric blanket's heat seeped a little more deeply into her body. The shaking slowed. The chills eased, just a bit, but left that aching that made her feel as if a steamroller had just mowed her down. She felt his weight leave the bed, heard his steps.

God, she was so groggy when these spells came. Why hadn't he killed her yet? Where was her gun? Why wasn't she screaming for help, or reaching for the phone or dragging herself to the door?

He returned, the bed sinking when he sat on its edge. Pills touched her lips. Then cool water. She swallowed as he held her head up, his long fingers curled around the back of her neck, threading up into her hair.

"Ibuprofen," he told her. "For the pain and the fever."

She nodded. He lowered her to the pillow again. The shaking eased further.

"Better?"

Her eyes could not stay open, no matter how she strained to look at him, to see what he was thinking, what he'd do next, whether there was murder in his jewel black eyes.

"You care to tell me how you planned to take on a crazed killer in this kind of shape?"

He sounded angry. She wondered why.

"Did-didn't...plan this."

"Is it better? Is it easing?"

She started to fall asleep, only to feel his hands tighten on her shoulders and lift her from the pillows.

"Tell me!"

Her eyes flew wide. Here it was, her fogged mind told her. The end. And they'd find her in the morning the way she'd found Tawny. Drained of her blood, lily-white, eyes staring sightlessly at the ceiling. Dying of one of these attacks didn't seem so terrible when she considered the alternative.

She had to do something. She focused her mind, the strength of every muscle, into one small act to save herself. One all but limp hand swung outward, toward the nightstand. That was where he'd put her gun, wasn't it? She connected with the lamp and heard it crash to the floor.

He stilled, then gently lowered her back down to the pillows. Her vision was clearing. She saw his black eyes search her face, saw him reach out. Then his hand was pressing something hard and cold into hers.

"This what you're after?"

She closed her fist around the cool wood grips, breathed again.

He pushed a hand through his dark hair. "Keep it, if it will ease your mind, Shannon. But I didn't come here to kill you."

She drew the handgun close to her chest, covered it with her other hand, relaxed a little. The barrel pointed in his general direction. Her finger just barely touched the trigger. Her eyelids drooped. She popped them open again.

"It is getting better, isn't it?"

She nodded. "What...why are you here?" Her voice was slurred, as if she'd been drinking. "If you d-didn't come to kill me, then why..." Her lids tried to close. She fought to keep them open. It was getting harder.

He smiled a little. "You can barely stay awake. It's all right, Shannon. Sleep a while."

"No. Not...until you...you leave..." She licked her lips, forced her gaze to fix on him, to get her message across. "Get the hell out."

Damien had seen her eyes spit golden fire at him. And for just a second she'd reminded him of his oldest friend, the only man who'd ever had the nerve to stand up to him, and he smiled.

She was afraid, but she had the courage of Inanna. She saw him as a demon, but she challenged him to battle. Much as he'd once done. She was like him. And like Enkidu.

Damien licked his lips, hearing the ragged, shallow way she breathed as her body surrendered to sleep's unstoppable invasion.

The demon he'd once sought to vanquish had been death itself. But fighting death was a sad exercise. Death always won in the end. Hadn't he searched endlessly for the key to immortality, only to find, instead, a perpetual living death?

He did not want to do it. With the will of every second of his nearly six thousand years, he did not want to do it. But he left the bedside, went to the little bathroom and dampened a cloth with cool water. He brought it back to bathe her heated face, her sweat-slick forehead, her fiery-hot neck. He'd keep an all-night vigil, not out of affection or even a passing fondness, but out of simple decency, and in a sort of remembrance.

The sight of her burning up with fever, shaking helplessly on the bed, brought back the worst moment of his existence, when he'd watched his best friend die in such a similar way. He'd felt so helpless then. Crying out to the gods for mercy, only to have them answer in vengeance.

He reminded himself that Shannon was not his friend. She was a stranger. And these were not death throes racking her slender body, but simple fever chills. Already they were easing.

"Don't..."

He glanced sharply down at her, but she wasn't talking to him. At least, he didn't think so. "It'll help the fever," he told her, and settled the cool cloth on her forehead again.

"Don't touch me." She whimpered, and twisted in the bed. "Tawny, make him stop!"

Fat tears rolled down her face, and Damien couldn't help the lump that came into his throat when he saw them, though he knew it was stupid, senseless. He didn't care about this woman.

He touched her face. "It's all right, Shannon. No one's going to hurt you."

It shocked him when her small hand shot upward to cover his where it rested on her cheek.

"Don't leave me," she whispered. "I'm so afraid..."

She wasn't talking to him. She was asleep, still burning up with a fever and half out of her head. She was dreaming. *She was not talking to him.*

Even so, he knew he'd stay with her. How could she possibly

defend herself in this kind of state? If it was true that some maniac was preying on the women who'd assisted him onstage, then she was in danger.

He did not want to believe that was possible. And yet, part of him did. Because if someone else hadn't killed that other one, it must have been him. *And it couldn't have been him.*

He barely recalled her face. There'd been so many over the centuries, so many who'd sated his eternal hunger. Young, beautiful, all too ready to sink with him into a well of ecstasy. But he'd never killed them. Never. He *hated* death.

He forced himself to remember Tawny. She'd come to his dressing room after the performance. She'd slid her warm palms slowly over his chest and stood on tiptoe to kiss him. And she'd tucked a piece of paper into the waistband of his pants before she'd slipped away. Her address. And he'd known he would visit her there. The bloodlust that night had reached the height of its power. He couldn't fight it anymore. He'd fought it through the entire evening, forcibly wrenching himself from the luscious dancers who were his assistants in the act. Dragging his gaze away from their pulsing jugulars time and time again, as the roar in his mind grew deafening, and the hunger writhed inside, and his will weakened.

So he'd gone to her. She'd been half-asleep in her bed, and he'd awakened her with a kiss, but never spoken a word. She'd stripped away her nightgown and pulled him down to her in the rumpled sheets, hidden by the darkness of midnight. And as he'd pierced her body with his, as he'd assuaged the burning hunger at her throat, as he'd reached the precipice of blinding, urgent desire, there was that instant of insanity. That single heartbeat in time when he was no longer inside his mind.

And when he'd pulled away from her he'd felt the same flood of guilt he always felt. He'd stared down at her lying still, sinking into sleep. He'd pulled blankets over her, and silently commanded she recall the experience as nothing but a dream. Then he'd fled into the night, his conscience too raw to stay there another second.

Now he paced, beside the bed of another beautiful woman, Tawny's friend and would-be avenger. And he questioned the accuracy of his own mind. She *had* been sleeping when he'd left her there, hadn't she? Or had she been dying? Was there a chance he'd taken too much, that he'd snuffed out a young life? He'd believed the spark of decency that his soul still had left wouldn't allow him to sink to that level. And he knew, beyond doubt, that he did have a modicum of decency left. If he didn't, he wouldn't be here with Shannon right now. He'd leave her to whatever fate had in store and save himself the anguish of starting to care. It was a big risk. He knew that more every time he looked at her.

He pushed the golden blond hair away from Shannon's face, felt the silken texture of it between his fingers, against his palms. He'd make sure the threat to her was eliminated, even if he himself turned out to be that threat, and then he would run to the farthest reaches of the globe and never, *never* set eyes on her again. Never so much as *think* of her again. And he'd do it without letting himself care about her. Damien Namtar cared for no one. It had been that way for centuries, and that was the way it would stay.

He could see, though, that he had little choice except to try to find out what had happened to Tawny Keller. For if he *had* become a man who could no longer exist without taking the lives of others, he knew he had to end it.

All of these things circled like a cyclone in his mind as he sat with her, watched over her, took care of her. He was doing exactly what he'd sworn he'd never do. Taking on the roll of protector to one of the Chosen. Acting on impulses that were purely physical, instinctive, like a goose flying south in autumn.

It was only as dawn approached that he realized he couldn't leave her there alone, unprotected.

Anthar watched that building and a smile curved his lips. Just before dawn, the being once called part man, part god came out, carrying the woman in his arms. Unconscious? Or asleep? Perhaps entranced? Whatever, it didn't matter. The pagan had come to care for someone...again. He rubbed his hands together in glee. It was too perfect. Too utterly perfect. Ah, the destruction of Gilgamesh—soul and body, mind and spirit—was at hand. At last, the tools to carry it out had been given. He'd awaited them long, but patiently. For it was not possible to completely demolish a man who cared for no one. The caring, that was the key...the weakness.

As long as it truly *was* caring.

Anthar dared not attempt to read the pagan's thoughts, lest he tip his hand. It was vital he remain undiscovered, unknown, unsensed, as he observed Damien's every move. He had to be sure before he could proceed.

A test, then. Or several. Whatever was necessary to be sure. And then the slow torture and ultimate destruction would begin.

CHAPTER FOUR

She awoke feeling as if she'd been in a fight with a freight train and had lost. Her head throbbed. Her body ached. Her throat had been scrubbed with steel wool. Her tongue had doubled in size and dehydrated. She squeezed her eyes tighter against the shimmer of sunlight that glowed red against her lids, and burrowed more deeply into the big downy pillow. Its satin case caressed her cheek. When she inhaled, her lungs filled with potpourri-tinged air. She hugged the luxuriant, fluffy comforter more closely around her—

Her eyes opened wide. She stilled utterly as a snowball of foreboding rolled up and down her spine. This was not her bed. She'd never owned white satin sheets or a down-filled comforter. She rolled onto her back, sitting up and blinking until her bleary eyes focused. This was not her room, either. The black lacquered headboard, the huge matching dresser with its gold trim, the little copper potpourri pot, simmering over a white candle on the stand near her head. None of this was hers.

"What in hell..." She tossed the covers aside and got up. Plush white pile hugged her bare feet, enveloped her toes. She blinked and shook off this through-the-looking-glass sensation. The room was a triangle, and the tall, gleaming black door opposite her was its point. Where on earth was she? For the briefest second she wondered if she'd died and proceeded on to some waiting room between heaven and hell. But that wasn't it. That couldn't be it. She felt too damned miserable to be dead.

She went to the door, gripped the knob, twisted. It refused to budge. She jiggled it, tugged again and pounded on the wood. "Hey, what's going on? Let me out!" Her heart pattered harder as she awaited a response that didn't come. Only silence. A heavy, smothering silence that closed in around her like a shroud. She willed her pulse to slow, pushed a hand through her hair, tried to calm herself. It wasn't a dream. She was sure she was awake. Okay. So what happened?

The memory of the night before returned slowly, but clearly. She'd had an episode. A bad one, worse than any so far. And then Damien had been there. A slow breath worked its way into her lungs. She'd been afraid he'd come to kill her. But he hadn't. He'd actually...he'd tried to help.

"Yeah, some help. As soon as I was out cold, he kidnapped me." She glanced around the room, having no doubt it was somewhere in Damien's modern-day palace. The guy must have something against plain old square rooms. She walked the perimeter, flinging open the door in one angled wall and seeing a triangular bathroom. The door in the opposite wall revealed a triangular closet. Actually, the whole thing *would* have been a square if the three rooms hadn't had walls dividing them.

The huge bed, black lacquer like every other piece of furniture here, reclined like a decadent goddess in the center of the triangle's base. Tall narrow windows stood sentry duty on either side of it, their livery, black satin, held apart by white bows. She parted the luxurious drapes and glanced outside to confirm her suspicions. The tall fence she'd scaled the night before stood watch in the distance. Sloping roofs, at varying heights, loomed at right angles, and the vine-covered brick walls were familiar.

It was his place, all right. And the window was no good as an escape route. Looked as if she was at least three stories up, with nothing but sheer wall and the grassy ground, carpeted in decaying autumn leaves, below her. The sun was low. She'd slept most of the day.

"Damn him." Shannon jerked the drape back into place, and stalked back to the bathroom in search of a way out. A hidden door. A heating duct. Anything.

Nothing. Just gleaming porcelain, glittering chrome and sinfully thick terry cloth. Spotless. Expensive. The hot tub was big enough to hold the Democratic National Convention inside. And the robe that hung from the wall was...wait a minute, that was *her robe!*

Charging back into the bedroom, she yanked open the door of the closet, only to see more of her clothes hanging neatly inside. A pair of jeans, a button-down blouse, her brown suede jacket. Her favorite running shoes stood innocently on the floor. Her purse perched on a shelf.

"That son of a—what the hell does he think he's doing?" She paced back toward the bed, and that's when she saw the picnic basket on the floor beside it. She narrowed her eyes, moved cautiously closer, flipped it open. A pile of fruit. She looked closer, lifted the other lid. A half-dozen assorted muffins. A thermos bottle. A sugar bowl. Her stomach rumbled. Part of her wondered if he'd put something into the food. Another part wondered why he'd bother. If he'd wanted to hurt her, he'd had his chance last night.

She disliked this situation. Everything in her rebelled against it, and if she'd cared to analyze herself this morning, she would know why. Her choices had been taken away. It was almost as bad as if she were a child, a ward of the state, again. She was not in control of anything at this moment. *He* was. He'd brought her here without her consent, locked her in for some insane reason, chosen the clothes she'd wear today, the food she'd eat for breakfast, the soap she'd use in the damned shower.

When she saw the bastard again, she would probably kill him.

In the meantime she was starved. The hell her body had been through last night had drained her. And while he had chosen the food, it was entirely up to her whether or not to eat it.

She threw caution to the wind and reached for a muffin, then the thermos, praying it held good, strong, ultracaffeinated coffee.

It did, piping hot. Aromatic steam rolled from the brew as she poured. It tasted even better than it smelled.

She looked around the room again, shaking her head in frustration. "I don't know what you're up to, Damien, but you aren't going to get away with it."

Damien had decided there were only three possibilities. One, that he'd lost control of his own mind, that he'd become the harbinger of death, his hated enemy. Two, that there was another vampire hunting the streets of Arista. Or, three, that an ordinary mortal with a twisted mind was responsible for the killings, and for some sick reason, wanted them to look like the work of a vampire. Though *how* any human could manage it, he still couldn't guess. The killer might be someone who wanted Damien to be blamed for *his* kills. If that was the case, then Shannon was in grave danger. And much as Damien had sworn never to do it, he was inclined to protect her. The blood ties, damn them straight to hell, were impossible to ignore. He could hate the instinct all he wanted, but he couldn't resist it. No more than a human can resist the gravitational pull of the earth, and go floating off into never-never land. He had no choice, no matter how he looked at it. And he resented the intrusion on his solitude.

"The lady's awake, sir."

Damien pulled himself from his ponderings to glance up. The deck of cards he'd been shuffling went still in his hands. Netty tilted her small head to one side and the other, like a little, curious bird. He forced a smile, and her face crinkled with her answering one. She had the frail build of a music-box dancer, and the temperament of a saint. Where else would he ever find someone to take care of the everyday needs of this place, to deal with the repairmen and the gardeners and the salesmen, to put up with his bizarre hours and strange requests, all without question or complaint? What the hell would he do when death crept up to claim Netty?

"Thank you, Netty." He pursed his lips, wondering what he'd say to Shannon when he went up the stairs.

"Been awake for quite a while, now. Pacin'. Nervouslike."

Her head tilted again, and he knew she'd like nothing better than an explanation for the unheard-of circumstance of a stranger, much less a woman, in the house. She'd never lower her proper British ways enough to pry, though, no matter how curious she was.

"You left the food for her?"

"Oh, yes. Sleepin' like the dead, she was, when I went in.

Lovely thing, don't you think? All that angel's hair spread around her—''

"You can go now, Netty. You're through for the day."

She bit her lip, bobbed her head and hurried from the room with quick little steps. Seemed wherever she went, Netty was always hurrying. He heard the back door, then the motor of her car.

He stiffened his spine and glanced toward the staircase. He didn't have to open his mind or try the trick of scanning hers to feel the fury emanating from Shannon. It was palpable. It filled every recess of the house, and all of it was directed toward him.

He sighed heavily, cut the deck one-handed, then fanned the cards facedown on the table. With exaggerated grace, he extracted four cards and flipped them over. Four aces. One more card trick to add to the repertoire. He grimaced as he rose and started for the stairs.

When he reached the door, he paused, startled to realize there was something warm surging like a South Sea tide in his belly. Anu forbid, he was looking forward to seeing her! That worried him. "She's nothing to me," he whispered, willing his mind to remember it. "Nothing."

He freed the lock with his mind and stepped inside. The first thing that hit him was the clean, moist smell of her. She'd bathed. He could feel the steam in the air, smell the water drying on her skin, almost taste it. Her hair was still damp, curling at the ends. She wore jeans and a green button-down cotton shirt. She was in the process of rolling the sleeves, when she whirled to face him. The fact that she hadn't fastened a single button didn't seem to faze her in the least. Her amber eyes flashed gold and her jaw went taut beneath the smooth skin. There were glistening droplets still clinging to her lashes.

"It's about time you showed up. Just what the hell do you think you're doing, bringing me here! Locking me in! That's unlawful imprisonment, mister, and I can tell you, you'll find yourself in a cell the minute I—"

She broke off, glancing down, apparently having finally noticed where his gaze was focused. The frilly white edges of the bra caressed the mounds of flesh they cupped like adoring fingers, and he couldn't for the life of him look away. She was beautiful. He hadn't taken the time to really appreciate feminine beauty in too long. He satisfied his needs in darkness, with hurried encounters and no words exchanged. He realized just what an oversight that had been, as he traced her flat belly, the dark well of her navel, the swollen curves of her breasts, with his eyes. He stared long and hard at the darker circles at their centers, just visible through the white material. Their peaks came alert as he stared and he felt the razor-edged blade of desire run him through.

She turned her back to him, buttoning up. "I want a phone. I'm calling a cab and then I'm getting the hell out of here, and when I get back to my apartment, I'll probably call a cop."

He said nothing, just watched her. She tucked the shirttails into the jeans before facing him again. "Well?"

Her cheeks were pink with rage and her eyes sparkled. Her breaths came a little too fast, and her fists were clenched.

"You look a lot better. How do you feel?"

She threw her hands in the air, rolled her eyes. "Fine. Perfect. Where the hell's that phone?" She walked past him, through the door and into the wide hallway. She looked up and down it, obviously not sure which way to go.

"Do those attacks come often?"

She started, as if she didn't know he'd walked along behind her. "None of your business. Which way is the phone?"

"Answer my questions and I'll take you to it."

If her eyes could shoot daggers through his heart, they would have. When she spun on him again her hair flew out around her like a wet halo, spraying his heated face. "Why did you bring me here last night?" Her eyes widened slightly for just an instant as the obvious answer occurred to her. "I was unconscious, wasn't I? Did you *do anything* to me?"

"Shannon, for God's sake, I don't go around molesting delirious women. I brought you here because I was afraid to leave you alone. You were sicker than hell. I'd have called some of your family to take care of you if I'd known where to reach them. But I didn't, so I decided to do it myself.''

"I don't have any family." Her eyes narrowed to slits as she studied him.

"It's happened before, hasn't it?"

"Once or twice." She turned her back on him, started down the hall in the wrong direction.

"How often?"

She shrugged. "What's it to you, anyway?" She stopped a few yards away, turned and came back, apparently deciding to go the other way.

When she passed him, he took her arm, walked beside her. "Nothing," he reminded himself. "Absolutely nothing. The phone is downstairs, but you don't need it. I'll drive you anywhere you want to go."

She blinked up at him, pausing in their trek toward the stairway, which was now in sight. "You will? I mean...you're not going to try to..." Her gaze fell to the floor and she shook her head.

"What did you think—that I was holding you prisoner?"

She met his gaze, her own flashing again. "You locked me in."

"There was a reason." He started down the stairs, led her through the narrower hall to the second staircase and then down that. When they finally emerged on the first level, he guided her into his oval library, waved her toward a leather sofa.

She stiffened, remaining in the doorway. "What is this? I said I wanted out."

"Shannon, when you broke in here and asked for ten minutes, I gave it to you. I'm only asking you to return the favor."

Her head tilted to one side, a wary animal sizing up its chances with a predator. She didn't trust him. She had good instincts.

"You can leave whenever you want to. I won't stop you. There's a phone on the desk over there." He pointed. She looked, licked her lips, nodded.

"All right. Okay. Ten minutes. No more."

No more. Unfortunately for both of them, there was going to be more. A lot more. And he'd keep her with him by force if he had to. But first he'd try to talk her around to his way of thinking.

And he'd pray he wasn't worthy of all her fear.

Why the hell did she agree to sit here and listen to him? The guy could talk her into buying swampland in the desert if he applied himself. There was something about him...

She walked into the library, took a look around. The room's shape came as no surprise. The curving walls were lined with books, most of them old-looking, with that wonderful, slightly musty smell that old books always have. The sofa and chairs were rich brown leather. New. Their aroma mingled with that of the books, and that more subtle scent that was distinctly Damien.

She glanced over her shoulder at him. He stood right where he'd been before, watching her intently. It was his eyes—that's what it was. They were so huge and deep and expressive. So dark. Combined with the tenor song of his mellow voice, they were compelling.

"So, talk," she said, trying to sound callous, wishing she felt that way. She didn't want to think maybe she'd been wrong about him. She didn't want to let her defenses down. And she sure as hell wasn't going to trust the man. She didn't trust anyone. She and Tawny...they'd trusted no one but each other.

"What was that?" His sable brows rose slightly, and his jet eyes probed. He came toward her, then stopped.

"What?"

"You looked..." He licked his lips, shook his head. "Nothing. Never mind. It's none of my business."

"Probably not." She turned and ran her fingers over the dusty spines, glanced at titles. *Sumerian Mythology, The Gods of the Ancients, The Epic of Gilgamesh...*

"I know you think I killed your friend. But since I know myself better than you do, I'm inclined to disagree."

He came up behind her as he spoke. Too close. She felt his nearness like static electricity, raising the fine hairs on the back of her neck. She tried to focus on the titles instead of on the physical effects of being so close to him. A newer volume about Gilgamesh. And another. He had several versions of the same story.

"That in mind, I have to assume someone else is responsible for her murder. If I'm right, then you're at risk."

"*If you're right?* Sounds like *you're* not even convinced you're innocent." She turned in time to see him blink when she said it, as if she'd poked a raw spot.

"I thought you might be in danger. That's why I followed you home last night. That's why I brought you here when I saw that you were too sick to defend yourself. I was only trying to protect you."

She met his gaze, fighting to keep her own hard, not let it soften the way her heart had begun to do at those last few words. She swallowed hard. In all her life no one had ever thought to protect her. No one had cared enough to. She'd had no shelter against the cruel realities of life. She'd had to face them all, head-on, and her only protection had been her own strength. "Yeah? Why should I believe that? You barely know me, why would you want to protect me?"

"What was the alternative, Shannon? Stay here and let you die? Read about your body being found in the headlines of tonight's paper?"

"Tonight's, tomorrow night's...what's the difference?" *Someone* would be finding her body one of these days. After this last attack, she figured it wouldn't be much longer.

He frowned, his gaze probing so deeply she had to turn away. "What do you—"

"Look, I have to go. Is there anything else you want to say before I do?"

"If you go, and there *is* a killer stalking you, you'll be defenseless."

"I've been called a lot of things, Damien. Never defenseless, though."

"Shannon—"

"If I stay here, he won't try anything." She squared her shoulders, lifted her chin. "If he doesn't try anything, I won't be able to take him out. You get it?"

He blinked twice, understanding dawning in his black eyes. His hands went to her shoulders. Strong hands. Hard and warm and urgent. The urge to lean closer whispered across her mind. Stupid. She must still be slightly off kilter from last night.

"You *want* him to attack you."

"You're damned right I do."

"That's insane. You'll get yourself killed." He appeared shaken by the idea.

"It's perfectly sane from my point of view. And so what if I do? I'll take the bastard with me."

"You're risking your life—"

"It's not so much to risk. Let go of me."

He looked down at his hands, as if he hadn't been aware of the way they'd been holding her shoulders, the way they'd begun to pull her just a little closer. The way that scared the hell out of her, because she'd been thinking about getting closer to him. Wondering what would happen if she slipped her arms around his muscled neck and leaned against his broad chest. Would he hold her closer, harder? Push her away? Murder her?

His hands fell to his sides. He lifted his ebony gaze to hers. "What do you mean by that? That it's not much to risk?"

Fears crept up on her. She battled them away. She wouldn't talk about it. She wouldn't think about it. And she damned well wouldn't cry about it. Her eyes burned, but she blinked them cool again. What was so bad about death? *Life* hadn't exactly been a walk in the park. "I'm leaving now. You said you'd let me go. So let me go."

"I'm sorry, Shannon. But I can't."

The rush of anger was a welcome relief after the other things she'd been feeling. "I *knew* I couldn't believe a word you said!"

She brought her fist into his middle clean and fast and hard, smiling smugly when he staggered backward, doubling over. She turned and ran toward the doors.

"Stay put, damn you!" The doors thundered shut as if a gale force wind had driven them. She felt her eyes bulge, the shivering up the back of her neck, the tensing of her spine.

She turned very slowly. He was just unbending himself, one hand pressed to the spot where she'd hit him. He looked angry. "How did you—"

"I'm a magician, remember?" He grunted, standing straight again.

"The—the house is rigged?"

"Something like that."

"You can't keep me here."

"I'm not going to let you get yourself killed. Believe me, Shannon, I don't like this any more than you do. But until this threat is removed, I'm your shadow. Whither thou goest and where thou lodgest and all that. I'll be there." He shook his head slowly, as if he'd just reached a decision and wasn't at all pleased about it.

"That's bull. You're up to something. You want something from me. Might as well put it on the table, Damien. I'm not buying what you're selling."

He licked his lips and the action drew her gaze, sent hot images sizzling into her mind. His kisses. God, what would they feel like? The thought seared her from the inside out.

"I need to see her body," he said at last.

She blinked, and dragged her attention away from his mouth. "You what?"

"I want to see your friend."

Shannon's stomach clenched like a fist. "For God's sake, why?"

He averted his eyes, paced back and forth in front of the bookshelves. "I have to see for myself how she died."

She blinked again, a cold foreboding settling in her heart. "What do you think you can tell by seeing her? Do you have any knowledge of forensic pathology? Have you ever studied death, Damien?''

His head came up, eyes level with hers, and she thought there couldn't have been more pain in them if she'd shot him through the heart. "All my life," he whispered.

"I must be insane." Her voice was near his ear, a harsh rasp as they crouched in the shrubbery near the rear entrance of Arista's medical examiner's office. "I've been calling every day to try and get her body released for burial. They keep putting me off, saying there are still more tests to be run. They wouldn't even let me see her." She parted a tangle of branches and peered through.

Damien snagged her waist with his arm and pulled her down beside him again. She was noisy and in constant motion. Clandestine surveillance could never have been one of her strengths as a private investigator. "Sit still," he warned. But then he had trouble following his own advice. His arm remained around her tiny waist, despite his mind's commands that it move away. Her right side pressed tight to his left one. He could feel the softness of her breast, the curve of her hip, the firmness of her thigh against his. This was insanity.

"I didn't think anyone would be here so late," she said, as if their closeness had no effect on her at all. "What are they doing?"

A shiny black hearse with a government emblem on the sides, and the letters "DPI" in bright yellow paint, backed up to the door. The driver emerged, walked around the vehicle and opened the back. Shannon stiffened beside Damien. "They're moving her!"

He tightened his hold on her. "It could be anyone, Shannon."

She shook her head hard, meeting his gaze, her own tortured. Then her head swung forward again, as the office door opened. Two men pushed a gurney out into the night, stopping behind the hearse.

"That's the ME." Shannon nodded toward the shorter, pudgy one who wore the white lab coat. The other man was taller, elegant in his movements, solidly built and darkly attractive. He wore an expensive gray suit and a long black wool coat.

"You'll rule it a suicide," he told the medical examiner. His voice carried the ring of authority.

"There's still the PI that found that body—"

"We'll be in touch with her. Don't worry. We've dealt with situations like this before." The driver and the ME collapsed the gurney and lifted the vinyl-encased body up into the hearse, while the tall man stood with his hands thrust into his coat pockets, watching. His breath made little steam clouds that hid his face. He exuded confidence.

The ME walked back inside, shaking his head and muttering, as the driver slammed the doors. Then the two got into the front seat and the vehicle moved away.

Shannon was shaking all over. "Where are they taking her? They can't just take her away like this. Dammit, Damien, let go of me!"

He held her tighter. She kept struggling until the hearse rolled out of sight, and then it was as if the fight went out of her. She felt limp. Her head lowered to his chest and her hot tears dampened his skin. She clung to him with one hand and rained painless blows on his shoulder with the other. "You should have let me stop them."

He threaded his fingers in her hair, moved his palms over it again and again. He knew this pain. He knew just what she felt right now, what she'd felt since her friend's death. Too well. Maybe that was another reason for this closeness he had to keep fighting. The grief. The shared pain.

He held her for a long time while she cried. He hadn't had a chance to look at the body, but he'd been close enough. He'd lowered the walls around his mind for an instant, just long enough to focus on the dead woman. He needed to practice more, to hone his mind better. But he had managed to understand one thing. Tawny Keller's death had been brought about by a vampire.

Damien still wasn't certain if that vampire was him.

Shannon straightened, swiped her eyes so hard it must have hurt her. "Something's going on, Damien. Those men were feds or something—the ME wouldn't lie about a cause of death unless he had no choice. I know that. He's a suit, but an honest one."

Damien nodded his agreement, but was as baffled as Shannon. "I don't understand this any more than you do...unless..."

Her head came up sharply. "Unless what?"

He shook his head. "I was going to say, unless they actually believe in the existence of vampires, but that's unlikely, isn't it?"

She shrugged and looked away. But Damien wondered. If he hadn't kept himself so closed off from others of his kind, he might know more. Was the federal government aware of their existence? What in hell was this DPI?

Shannon touched his arm. "I want to go home. Take me home now."

He saw her clearly in the darkness, her red, swollen eyes, the track of each and every tear she'd shed, burned into her pale ivory flesh. "You'd be safer at my house, I think."

She shook her head so hard her hair flew. "I can take care of myself. Take me to my place or I'll go somewhere and call a cab. It's up to you." She sniffed loudly.

He helped her to her feet, encircled her shoulders with his arm and walked with her around the building to the sidewalk, toward where he'd parked his car. The chilly October breeze whisked over them, and he hoped it cooled her burning cheeks.

"If you insist, I'll take you to your apartment. But you still might be in danger, Shannon. I'll just have to park myself outside the building and try to watch over you from there."

"Sure you will. And pigs will fly, too." She went to the passenger door of his gleaming black car. One of his indulgences. A Jaguar. He liked it, liked driving it fast, liked the new smell of it. When that smell wore off, he'd immediately buy another. He had few enough pleasures in this life.

She opened the door and stood there, staring over the car at him. "So are you gonna drive me, or not?"

"I'm gonna drive you."

CHAPTER FIVE

Damien sat in the car near the front of her apartment building. It wasn't much of a building. Tall, narrow. Too few windows, and fire escapes with huge sections missing. The ugly red bricks looked ready to crumble. The security was nonexistent. It wasn't a slum, but he didn't like the idea of her living here.

She came onto the balcony twice, glancing down at his black car. He shivered a little when she leaned on the iron rail. The damned thing probably wasn't in any better shape than the rest of the place. After that he saw her part the curtains a few times, and he knew she was looking, checking to see if he was still there. Almost as if she expected him to leave.

Maybe she'd be better off if he did.

Damien couldn't bring himself to believe he'd killed those other women, but he couldn't ignore the possibility, either. He didn't know whether this change in his hunger was normal, something every immortal felt with age. He didn't know if others had killed without even being aware of it. Was something like that possible?

He thumped his fist on the steering wheel as the questions tormented him. Traffic and people passed by. Lights in buildings blinked off one by one as this less-than-elite section of Arista went to sleep.

He wished now that he hadn't avoided all contact with others of his kind, wished there were someone he could ask about these things, and about this DPI, whatever it was, and the murder of Tawny Keller. *Damien* ought to know. As far as he was aware, he was the oldest of any of them. He ought to have the answers, but dammit he didn't.

He thought of the letters he'd received from the one who called himself a scientist, Eric Marquand. If anyone could shed some light on all of this it might very well be that young, curious man. Damien grimaced at the idea of asking for help. The very thought of contacting Marquand made him squirm with unease. He'd existed alone, in a vacuum for so long now. His only emotional ties were the safe ones he felt with his crowds of fans. When they stood and cheered for him it was almost as if time melted away, almost as if he were an adored ruler again, a beloved king, basking in the unconditional love and loyalty of his people. It was the adoration of those crowds that had driven him to perform all these years. A man could only do without love, connections, for so long. The audiences gave him enough to sustain him. It was the only love allowed into his solitary life, and it was enough. It had to be enough.

He shook his head slowly. No, he'd try to solve this thing on his own. He'd only use Eric Marquand and his studies of the undead as a last resort. And in the meantime he'd watch over Shannon, keep any harm from coming to her.

A job that would be a lot easier if only he could listen to her mind. The idea of trying it again sent a bolt of phantom pain throbbing through his temples. Still, it was one of the benefits of being who he was. He ought to use every tool he had to solve this puzzle, to keep her safe.

He braced himself, and very slowly, began to lower his defenses to allow the myriad vibrations outside to filter into his mind. He consciously kept a thin veil in place and focused all his energy on her, putting her image firmly in his mind's eye. He tried to attune his senses to hers, to feel what she felt.

For an instant the rush of sensations surrounded him, but he forced himself to bear it. He grated his teeth against the bombardment and concentrated harder. Gradually, the intensity eased, quieted, lightened. He sifted, searched, sent his mind out in search of hers.

She wasn't in the apartment.

He stiffened in his seat as he felt her thoughts. Anger. Alarm. Urgency. Something about her car. She was running...a rear exit. A parking lot.

Damien was out of his car like a shot and speeding around

the building. He saw her there, her feet and legs bare and cold in the autumn chill. She wore a short blue nightgown that shimmered like silk, but wasn't, and her hair was pulled up into a bushy blond ponytail that bounced wildly as she ran over the pavement.

He looked in the direction she ran, and saw two young men crouched at the door of a primer brown Corvette that had to be as old as Shannon was. One of the men turned as Shannon approached, and he laughed. She never slowed her pace. The thief started toward her and lifted his hand. Damien saw the tire iron he held. He lunged forward, knowing as he did that he couldn't reach her in time. Already the two stood close, and the man's hand swung down, no doubt about to crush her skull.

But Shannon's small hand shot up and gripped the man's wrist, stopping the tire iron's descent. Her knee jammed hard into his groin, and the man grunted loud, doubled over. The tire iron clanked to the broken pavement. Damien froze for a shocked instant as Shannon spun backward, smacking her heel across the man's chin and laying him flat on his back. It happened in two clicks of a second hand.

The second man turned toward her, pulling a gun from his tattered jeans. Before he leveled its sights on her, she kicked it out of his hand, sending it sailing in an arc and then skittering across the pavement. He swung a fist at her, but she ducked, and when she straightened, she brandished the tire iron the other one had dropped.

He held his hands up in front of him, backing away. "Okay, lady. Okay, you win." As Damien hurried forward, the thug helped his partner to his feet, and the two ran into the darkness. He heard their rubber soles slapping. They didn't go far, though.

He gripped Shannon's arm, still dazed by what he'd seen. "Are you all right?"

She nodded, but didn't say anything, still trying to catch her breath. Damien turned to look at the unpainted car and shook his head. He was going to blast her for risking her life over a hunk of scrap metal, when he heard the unmistakable click of a hammer being pulled back. His head went up, and his piercing night vision showed him one of the two thugs, holding the gun, pointing it at Shannon.

Damien whirled toward her, propelling himself forward just as the blast shattered the night. He felt Shannon hit the ground hard underneath him. And he felt a searing pain burn through him.

Anthar watched as he always watched—witness to every breath the pagan drew—and smiled slowly to himself. The bastard. The insolent, blasphemous bastard. Damien the Eternal. Whatever he called himself now, it didn't matter. He'd be gone, vanquished, destroyed by his own hand. Conquered by his own emotions. And soon.

The thugs whose small minds Anthar had implanted with the notion of stealing the woman's car were bumbling fools, yes. But at least one of them had fired his weapon at her. And the heathen had thrown himself in front of the bullet.

Finally, after endless millennia, the bastard cared for another living soul. Anthar had waited so long, tried so often to hurt him this way. But Damien kept to himself, cared for no one. Not even the women he took on occasion, while Anthar watched from the shadows, his presence so carefully cloaked even Damien couldn't sense him there. Damien drank from those women so gently, so careful not to harm them. Sickening, gutless worm! So tenderly he would use them that Anthar would become convinced there must be some feeling there. But alas, none ever came. When those women had died, Damien the Eternal hadn't even been aware of their passing.

Damn him to everlasting torment!

Ah, but this time would be different. This time there *was* something more. Just the something Anthar needed to hurt him in the most devastating way possible.

But he must proceed with caution.

Damn, but it wouldn't do to take the bitch too soon. He had to test Damien's feelings yet again. He had to be sure the oldest

immortal alive would feel the ultimate pain, shame, remorse....
He had to be sure.

Another test was in order.

They were gone. He heard them run and then nothing. Damien's body lay heavily on top of Shannon's. She was on her back. He was angled across her chest, his head near her left shoulder.

"They're gone," she said, and shoved at him. "You can get off me now, Damien. I don't know why you came rushing out here like some knight on a charger, anyway. I can take care of my—" She'd pressed her hands to his shoulders to move him off her, and touched the warm dampness seeping through his shirt. He felt the shock that passed through her body. She sucked in a coarse breath. "Damien?"

He moved, but slowly. It hurt to do it. He sat up, and she jumped to her feet, bending over him. His white shirt was stained crimson. He pressed one hand to the front of his shoulder and tried to stand.

Shannon bent to help him, sliding an arm around his waist and holding him firm. "Damn you straight to hell, Damien, you've gone and got yourself shot. What's the matter with you, jumping on me like that?" She walked toward the building's back entrance, pulling him along with her.

He glanced down at her, almost giddy with relief that he'd knocked her out of the way in time. "That gun was pointing toward your head. Was I supposed to stand there and let them shoot you?"

"Yes!" She reached out to open the door, then held it with her hip while she helped him through. "Dammit, you're probably going to bleed to death."

He was not going to bleed to death. Actually, the wound was minor except for the excruciating pain it caused. Debilitating, momentarily paralyzing pain. His shoulder still screamed with it. But he'd expected that. One of the few things he did know about his kind was that sensitivity to pain—to any physical stimulus—increased with age, just as the strength and psychic powers did. As for the tendency to bleed dry, it didn't concern him too much. He could keep pressure on the wound until dawn. It wasn't bleeding all that badly. It would heal with the regenerative sleep. Any injury would.

What did concern him, besides the pain in his shoulder, was the feel of her small arm anchored around his waist. The way she held him tight to her side as they entered the elevator, the urgency in her eyes when she looked up at him. Her smell. Her warmth.

"You're pale. Did it bleed much?"

"I'm always pale. And no, it's nothing."

She narrowed her eyes and stared at the spot where he pressed his hand to the wound. "It's not nothing—it's a bullet. We'll call an ambulance from the apartment."

He shook his head, but studied her determined face, noting the strength in it. "Why did you rush out there in your nightgown, Shannon? Why risk your life, when calling the police would have been just as good?"

"What're you, kidding me? My car would have been long gone by the time the cops got here. Do you know how long and hard I work just to keep up the payments on that car?"

"Corvettes don't come cheap." Not even primer-coated ones whose rust spots had been sanded off, he supposed.

The doors slid open. She tightened her grip on him and started into the hall. "Not just a Corvette. A 1962 Stingray, mag wheels, four barrel carb and an engine that would blow your black Jag's doors off."

He smiled. He couldn't help it, and the pain didn't stop it. "Your dream car?"

"Abso-freaking-lutely. *Nobody* messes with my car."

"I'll keep that in mind."

She stopped outside her apartment door and pushed it open. She hadn't locked it and that bothered him almost as much as the hole in his shoulder, but he refrained from commenting on it. He'd seen firsthand why she kept insisting she could take care of herself. She hadn't done half-badly at it.

She pulled him inside, kicked the door closed, and didn't let go of him until she'd eased him onto the sofa. And when she did, he felt the absence of her touch like another wound in his flesh. She hurried back to the door, locked it. So she wasn't completely careless with her own well-being. Then she knelt in front of him and reached up to tear the sleeve away from his shirt. She tried to push his hand aside so she could look at the wound.

"It's barely a scratch." He kept his hand where it was.

"That's a lot of blood for a scratch, Damien."

"I'm a heavy bleeder. I'll be fine."

She scowled at him. "Hey, you jumped in front of a bullet for me. The least I can do is take a look at it." She reached for the shoulder again.

He ducked her hand. "Oh? Then you're admitting that I probably just saved your life?"

She straightened, propping her fists on her hips. "Yeah, for what it's worth, you probably did."

"At no small risk to my own?" He prompted. She said nothing, but tilted her head to one side. "Well?"

"All right. Okay, I'll give you that much. So what's your point?"

"That I'm not planning your murder, for starters." He got to his feet, not waiting for her reply, and walked to the bathroom. He was a bit weaker than usual, a response to the amount of blood he'd lost. Good thing he'd had the presence of mind to put the pressure on right away. It wouldn't take much to incapacitate an immortal as old as he was.

He closed the door behind him. One place he did not want to spar with Shannon Mallory was in her bathroom, where mirrors abounded. But he felt her presence there, even though he'd locked her out. It was in the still-damp towel slung over the shower-curtain rod. And in the clothes she'd been wearing earlier, in a little heap on the floor. And in the scent she favored. Subtle. Not floral or fruity. More enticing than that. Herbal. Like exotic incense or some rare spice. It clung to everything, even the air was tinged with it.

He opened the cabinet and tried to put her out of his mind and focus on the matter at hand, namely applying something to the wound to staunch the blood flow until dawn. He'd sit with his hand on it for the next few hours if necessary, but he'd prefer not to.

There. A roll of gauze. Some adhesive tape. A hairbrush with a few honey gold strands catching the light and glowing at him. It was like a halo around her, that hair of hers. Like something unreal. "Angel hair," Netty had called it.

Dammit, stop thinking about her!

He peeled the shirt away from his chest, tearing it so he didn't have to ease the pressure on the wound. He tossed the ragged, blood-spattered white garment into her wastebasket. One-handed, he wrestled the little cardboard box open and dumped a pile of gauze pads into the sink.

She thumped the door. "Are you all right?"

"Fine, Shannon. Relax."

"Let me in. I want to help."

"I'll be out in a minute."

"Damn you, Damien—"

"You're repeating yourself, Shannon." He didn't think the gauze pads would be enough, and glanced around for something more substantial to pack the wound. "Tell me something, will you? Why didn't you bring your gun out there with you?"

"Because I'd have killed the little bastards if I had." She pounded on the door again, jarring it. "Open the damn door."

"No."

"Fine, see to yourself. There's a little brown tin in the cabinet. Pine tar. It's made from the sap of pine trees. An old folk remedy. If you're too pigheaded to see a doctor, then at least use some of it. It'll stop the bleeding better than Super Glue."

He frowned. There was a slight trembling in her voice, one that belied the careless way she tried to throw her words at him.

He spotted the tin, flipped the top off and sniffed suspiciously at the dark brown goop it held. Piny. Okay, it was worth a try.

"Did you find it?"

He thought she'd walked away, left him to fend for himself. She was still standing on the other side of the door, waiting. "Yes. It looks disgusting."

"Smear it on."

He nodded, dipping two fingers into the stuff, then removing his hand from the wound just a little. The bleeding began again immediately, but he was able to spot the edges of the graze, and pinched them together. Then he smeared the thick, tarlike substance over the wound.

It was almost instant. The blood flow stopped. Cautiously, he eased the pressure of his fingers. But the flesh didn't pull apart. The tar held it sealed tight. He shook his head in wonder.

"Damien? You okay?"

For such an obstinate thing, she was certainly worried about his health. "I'm okay. Your concoction works wonders." He pressed a gauze pad to the wound, wrapped a strip around it and taped it in place. Then he ran a little water in the basin and washed the blood from his chest, his arm, his shoulder, his hands. Only when he'd rinsed every trace of the pinkened water down the drain did he open the door. And when he did, she was still standing there. He couldn't have missed the way her stiff stance relaxed slightly when he stepped out.

Her gaze flew over his face, to his shoulder, back to his face again. He saw her worry, her fear for him, and it touched him in spite of himself. Then her eyes moved downward, over his unclothed chest, lower, to the snap of his pants. Her cheeks colored, and he smiled a little, wishing he had the energy to try to read her thoughts again right now.

"Stupid jerk."

Damien blinked. "Excuse me?"

"You're a jerk, locking yourself in like that. What if you'd passed out in there? Huh? What am I going to do—kick the door in?"

He laughed. She got angrier, so he forced himself not to laugh anymore. "You have a very strange way of showing gratitude, Shannon."

"*Gratitude?* You think I'm *grateful* to you for almost getting yourself killed on my behalf? What're you—dense? You pull any more crap like that and I'll—" She blinked fast, and turned her back on him. Not before he'd seen the moisture gathering in her eyes, though.

Something in his throat expanded, cutting off his airway. He lifted one hand, and without intending to, settled it on her shoulder. Her hair brushed his knuckles and he shivered. "Shannon—"

She stepped away from his touch, paced to the center of the room, turned, her face expressionless. "I don't think the attempt on my car was related to this other business. Do you?"

He stared at her, wishing he knew why it bothered her so much that he'd helped her. Why it was so hard for her to accept that he wanted to protect her. "I'm inclined to think not" was all he said. "They only shot at you because you charged at them like the cavalry."

"Yeah, well, if I hadn't they'd have had my wheels."

"How did you know?" She'd turned again, walked to the sofa, sank onto it as if she were exhausted.

"I have a remote car alarm. Someone tries to get into the 'Vette, this little device in my purse sounds a warning." She pushed her hair away from her face with one hand, then paused in the act. "How did *you* know?"

"I..." He glanced away from her narrow, piercing gaze. "I was walking around the building, just checking for anything unusual. I heard them, but by the time I realized what was happening, you were..." He turned to her again, trying to see more than just what her delicate face revealed. "You were kicking the hell out of them. Where did you learn to fight like that?"

"Trial and error, mostly." She looked past him, and he wondered what she was seeing. "Tawny and I used to practice on each other. Usually ended up a pair of walking wounded, but you have to be able to take care of yourself when you're a kid on the streets. She's as good as I am...I mean, she was. That's why I can't understand why—''

She broke off, met his gaze again, licked her lips. Damien knew what she would have said. Why didn't Tawny fight off her attacker? Why did she submit? The answer was all too simple, really. A vampire doesn't have to attack his victims or struggle with them. He seduces them. They offer themselves, willingly, even eagerly, to his promise of ecstasy.

Guilt reared up inside him, and he couldn't hold her stare. Some immortal had rewarded that willingness, that childlike trust, with murder. Some immortal. But who?

Not me. It wasn't me...

"It *wasn't* you, was it?"

He shook himself free of the instant notion that she'd read his mind, or that he'd spoken the thought aloud. Coincidence. She rose and stepped closer to him, staring up into his face, her eyes narrow, darkening to the color of cinnamon.

"You wouldn't risk your life to save a stranger if you were cold-blooded enough to kill another one. Would you?"

"Of course not."

But what if I did? What if I killed that innocent girl, and what if this one is next in line? The next time the thirst becomes unbearable, the next time it overpowers my will...Inanna, save me, but already the scent of her, the warmth of her skin, the pinkness of it, is getting to me. I can hear the sweet river of blood running in her veins. I can smell it. And she's so soft, so beautiful... I want her. I want all of her....

"You stayed. I really didn't think you would."

"What?" He shook free of the voices in his mind.

"When you said you'd come here, watch out for me, I didn't believe you. You surprised me." She frowned, and paced slowly away from him, head tilting to one side as she walked. She stopped a few yards away, turned toward him once more. "So if you're not going to kill me, then what *are* you after?"

He looked at the floor, shook his head deliberately. "I should go."

"Why?"

He was turning toward the door, when she asked the question. He stood where he was, his back to her. When her body heat warmed his bare flesh as she moved to stand behind him, he went rigid.

"You agreed with me that the car thieves were probably not related to the murder. So the killer might still try, right? I mean, I'm in as much danger now as I was earlier, right?"

He closed his eyes as her scent assaulted him. "At least. Maybe more."

"Then stay."

Oh, but this wasn't right, this roar inside him, urging him to turn around and crush her to his chest. To take her mouth until she gasped for breath and to— It just wasn't right. It hadn't been long enough for the thirst to bring on this need. And it wasn't thirst alone this time, burning through him. It was desire, too. Not the desire that coupled with the hunger, but one born of itself. Or born of her.

Her hand touched his uninjured shoulder. Her small fingers squeezed his flesh. "Look, Damien, you saved my life. Much as I hate to owe anything to anyone, I can't overlook something this big. Last night, when I was sick, you took care of me. I just want to return the favor."

He shook his head, tore the door open. "You'll be safe by day."

"*By day?* What—"

"I'll keep watch until then, but not here. From the car. And if you come down there, Shannon, I can't guarantee anything. So stay put."

"But I—"

"Good night." He stepped into the hall, closed the door behind him, and with a burst of speed, managed to be halfway down the stairs before she'd yanked the door open again.

Okay, so she'd misjudged the guy. Badly. All right, she'd flat out accused him of murder. He'd pretty much convinced her she'd been wrong. Twice he'd appeared out of nowhere right at the moment she'd needed help. So far he hadn't asked a thing in return.

Of course, she wasn't stupid. He wanted something; he just hadn't gotten around to asking for it yet. Nobody helped anybody without a damn good reason. She'd learned that the hard way. Oh, the lovely foster family that had taken her in had seemed hunky-dory at first. All that bull about how they loved children, couldn't have any of their own, wanted to help a down-on-her-luck teenage orphan who had just about run out of hope of ever being adopted.

Right.

Tawny had been with them a month before Shannon moved in. She'd come from another institution, but Shannon had been in most of them by then. They'd never met—a small miracle, since their paths must have crossed a hundred times as they both went through the system. They'd hated each other's guts at first. At first. But then the insanity began. Mr. Grayson had some pretty sick ideas. And his wife knew all about it, but was too much of a mouse to let him know she knew.

Anyone who thought two sixteen-year-old girls couldn't fend for themselves on the mean streets ought to try living with that kind of threat looming for a while. The streets are a breeze after that.

God, to think she and Tawny had toughed it out through hell and high water, only to come to this. Tawny dead. Shannon not far behind her. Why the hell had they bothered surviving at all?

But that thinking was borderline self-pity, so she swiped her mind clean like a blackboard under a damp sponge and started over. Damien. Yes, she'd been thinking about Damien, and whatever it was he wanted from her.

For a second there, she could have sworn it was sex. Something about the way his body went all tight when she touched his bare skin.

But she dismissed that idea almost as soon as she thought it. The guy was an idol. He could have any woman he wanted, just by snapping his magic fingers. Why the hell would he be interested in her?

So there had to be something else. And it would be only a matter of time until she found out what.

Meanwhile, she needed to concentrate on something else. What in God's name had he meant when he said she'd be safe in the daytime?

CHAPTER SIX

She stopped in at the office for the first time in three days. The legwork had kept her out, tracing Tawny's steps in the week before she'd died, trying to find out who'd killed her, why and how on earth they'd done it in such a macabre manner.

The only lead she'd found was Damien, and she was no longer sure the guy was anything other than an eccentric, world-renowned magician who valued his privacy and went to great lengths to preserve the mystique of his alter ego. She'd tried her damnedest to check his background, but had come up empty. Before exploding onto the scene as the world's most beloved magician, he had, it seemed, no past at all.

"Shannon. Hey, where you been? I was starting to think you'd gone outta business."

She smiled at Sal, standing in the doorway of the pizzeria, with his clean white apron covering his rounded middle. She hadn't told him, or anyone, that Tawny's murder would be her last case. "Hey, Sal. Not out of business, just busy. What's new?"

"Rent's going up next month."

"What—again?" It didn't matter. She wouldn't be here next month.

Sal nodded, rolling his eyes. "Probably a letter waitin' for you. Got mine yesterday."

"This place isn't worth what we're paying now," she grumbled. She unlocked the door beside Sal's, swung it open, mounted the steep stairway.

Sal came to the bottom and called up to her. "You could afford the rent if you didn't drive such a fancy car, you know."

"So you keep telling me. It'll be fancier as soon as I save up enough for a paint job." She'd get that done. She promised herself she'd get that done before she went down for the count.

"That's baloney. You don't look good, Shannon. You eatin' right?"

"I will be today." She reached the top of the stairs and unlocked her office door, then paused to look down at Sal. "Two slices for lunch, with the works."

"Everything but anchovies. I know how you like it."

She smiled, swung her door open and stepped inside. The man sitting in a chair in front of her desk rose, set the file folder he'd been perusing aside, parted his lips to say something, and then thought better of it. His gaze dropped to the revolver she was pointing at his chest. She'd jerked the gun from her waistband in a split second, before he'd even turned fully. He stood very still.

"Who are you, and what the hell are you doing in my office?"

He licked his lips, a quick, nervous little dart of his tongue. And then she recognized him. He was the one who'd taken Tawny's body out of the ME's office last night.

"Take it easy with that thing. I have ID. May I?"

She nodded, a little shiver dancing up her neck. "You pull anything other than a wallet out of that fancy jacket you're wearing and it's gonna have a big hole in the front."

His hand dipped into the jacket, came out with a small leather folder. He handed it to her, and she took it, never moving her gaze from him. She flipped it open, glimpsed a photo ID from the corner of her eye. She took a quick look, her gaze darting back to him every other millisecond or so. Stephen Bachman. Then she read a little further and blinked.

"CIA?"

"One of its subdivisions."

"Which one?"

"That's not important."

She narrowed her eyes, scanning the card more carefully, trying to see whether it was genuine or a fraud. She had no way of knowing. She gazed at him again. Tall, broad-shouldered. He had an athletic build to him, and his dark hair curled a little at the ends. Gray suit, spotless white shirt. Telltale bulge beneath the left arm.

She wiggled the gun barrel. "Put your weapon on the desk, Mr. Bachman. Slowly."

He nodded, removed his gun, a shiny nickel-plated 9 mm Ruger, and set it on the desk. She stepped forward and picked it up, tucked it into the back of her jeans. "How'd you get in here?"

He smiled a little. "I told you. I'm CIA."

She held his gaze, nodding, and then took the file folder he'd been reading. It contained her notes on Tawny's death. She frowned hard. "Why is the CIA involved in a murder investigation?"

"Oh, come on, Ms. Mallory. We both know this is no ordinary murder. May I sit now, or do I have to be standing in order for you to shoot me?"

She nodded, moving behind her desk as he sat. She took her own seat. "Just what the hell is going on?"

The man stared hard at her. "You're the one who found her. Why don't you tell me?"

"What do you want from me, Bachman?"

"You're going to tell me all about Tawny Keller. And all about yourself. And everything you think you know about this case."

She smiled slowly. "Why would I do that?"

He shrugged, pursed his lips. "Because we both want the same thing. To catch her killer. And because if you don't, I'll have your private investigator's license pulled before noon."

"Sure do know how to sweet-talk a girl, don't you? Tell you what. I'll tell you everything I know, if you'll answer me one or two questions first." She *wasn't* going to tell him a damned thing. For all she knew, he could be a fraud. Then again, maybe not. He certainly had clout with the ME's office.

His eyes narrowed. "If I can. What do you want to know?"

"Why I can't get Tawny's body released to me. I want to

give her a funeral." She knew he had the answer to that question. She waited.

That tongue darted out again. "Settle for a memorial service. Buy a marker, if you want. You won't get the body."

"Why?"

"It's now the property of the federal government. That's all you need to know."

He might as well have slapped her. "What the hell have you done with her, Bachman? I know she's been moved. Where is she?"

"Good little private snoop, aren't you? How'd you know we moved her?"

She bit her lower lip. She wouldn't show weakness, turmoil, nothing. Not to this suit. "ME's been giving me the royal runaround. I had a suspicion. You just confirmed it."

He nodded. "Not bad. But I can't tell you where she is. Sorry."

He glanced at his watch. "You want to move on to the next question? I don't have all day."

She fought with her temper and won. Voice level, cold, she asked him, "How did she really die?"

"Blood loss."

"I know that. I mean…how?"

He stared hard at her. "Damned if I know."

It was such a blatant lie he might as well have been wearing a sign. He made sure she knew he was lying. So smug. The bastard.

"My turn, Ms. Mallory. You've been seeing a doctor—four times in the past month. What's the problem?"

She felt her brows lift. "There *isn't* any problem."

His head tilted sideways. "I thought you were going to cooperate."

"I am. I didn't feel well, got checked out. There was no problem."

"I can verify this more easily that you'd believe."

"Why am I not surprised?"

He studied her for a long time. He wasn't sure if she was being flippant or blatantly honest, she could tell. Good, let him wonder.

"You've seen a lot of Damien Namtar in the past couple of days."

She blinked, then stopped herself from registering her surprise in any other way. "Have I been under surveillance?"

"Not yet."

"Him, then?"

His lips thinned. "I need to know why you've been seeing him."

So the CIA was watching Damien. She wondered if he knew it. "I'm a fan," she told Bachman. "Is there something I should know about Mr. Namtar?"

"I'm not altogether sure you don't already know."

The puzzled expression she felt twist her brows was genuine. What the hell was that supposed to mean? "Do you think he had something to do with the murder?"

"Anything's possible."

Bachman was talking, but he wasn't saying a damned thing. The briefcase he held caught her gaze. "Maybe I should watch myself, then."

"Maybe you should stay away from him altogether."

Was that a warning? What did this bastard know?

"I'm already familiar with your background, and the victim's—"

"Tawny. Her name was Tawny. Use it."

He snapped open the briefcase on his lap, flipped open a notebook. "Whatever. You were wards of the state, assigned to a foster home in Flatbush. Then both ran away. It's what went on between then and now that's tough to document. She was obviously a whore. How did you survive? Same game?"

She pulled the man's own gun from the back of her jeans, worked the action and pointed it right at his nose. "Your time's up, Bachman. Get out."

"I'm not finished." He closed the notebook, then the case.

"You'll be more than finished if you don't leave—now."

He nodded. "Fine. There are other ways to find out what I need to know." He reached for the folder on her desk. She squeezed the trigger. The bullet shattered an ashtray two inches from Bachman's hand. He froze, turning to stare at her. It was anger not fear she saw in his eyes. "I could have you in jail for that."

"I could blow your brains out and say I mistook you for an intruder. Leave the file here, and go."

His eyes darkened, but his hand fell to his side. He stepped toward her. She opened the door and moved aside. In the doorway, he turned to face her. "You keep quiet about your friend's death, Ms. Mallory. It's going down as suicide and the first time you say differently, you might just disappear yourself."

"If you think I'll let it die, you're wrong."

"You have no choice in the matter. And I mean what I say. You don't know what you're dealing with here." He glanced down at the Ruger she still held and opened his hand. "My gun?"

"Not anymore." She slammed the door in his face.

It took her all of five seconds to decide to follow him when he left, and as she did, she racked her brain for answers. Bachman must be legit. The ME wouldn't have cooperated otherwise. So why was the government so interested in the murder of a prostitute? The *way* she'd died. It had to be. But *how had* Tawny died, exactly? How had someone put those marks on her throat, drained her blood? And why?

She had a feeling Bachman knew. But the son of a gun wasn't talking.

Damien pored over the pages of the newest translation, searching...always searching. But for what? No matter how many stone tablets were uncovered in the sands of Iraq, no matter how many cuneiform symbols told the story of Gilgamesh the hero, Gilgamesh the king, there would never be one recording the true end to the tale.

He slammed the book closed, tossed it to the floor. His eyes burned, but he blinked them clear again. Rereading the stories never failed to reignite the pain. Stupid. It was long gone now. Netty cleared her throat, drawing his attention.

"You have a guest."

At Netty's side in the library doorway, Shannon stood staring at him. She shifted the backpack that hung over her shoulder, glanced past him to the book he'd just thrown. "If it's a bad time—"

He shook his head quickly and got to his feet. "No. Pet peeve, that's all."

"She looks so much better tonight, doesn't she now, sir? More color to her cheeks." Netty patted Shannon's arm. "I'll bring ya a hot toddy. Just the thing for this chilly autumn night. Warm your bones."

"That's really not—" Shannon broke off. Netty was already hurrying away with those abbreviated, high-speed steps of hers. Shannon shook her head, smiling a little.

Damien couldn't take his eyes off her. But when her gaze met his again it was troubled. "What's wrong?"

She licked her lips. "Look, I don't know why the hell I'm even here. Except maybe I owe you. That and that I've got good instincts. I had to have, the way I grew up. Not so much who to trust and who not to trust. More like who'd slit your throat and who'd just rob you blind."

He frowned. She was rambling. Nervous. "You don't trust anyone."

"Right."

"You said you and Tawny learned to fight on the streets. I meant to ask—"

She shook her head, stopping him. "It doesn't matter."

"Yes, it does." He stared at her; those huge amber eyes seemed to reach out to him. "Where was your family?"

She looked at the floor. "My mother dumped me when I was a baby. I don't even remember her."

"Then you were adopted?"

Her lips twitched a little. "They tell me I was a sickly kid.

Skinny, asthmatic. I grew up a ward of the state, saw lots of institutions, a few foster homes. I met Tawny in one of them.'' She turned a little away from him, fingered the strap that was anchored over her shoulder.

"And then?'' He wanted to know. He didn't stop to tell himself that he shouldn't. It wouldn't have mattered if he had.

"Things got rough. We decided we could do better on our own. And we did.''

He considered reading her mind. "How old were you?''

"Sixteen. And that's all I'm going to say about it. I came here, Damien, despite the fact that I still don't really trust you, because right now I distrust you a little less than the other guy.''

She'd changed the subject so firmly that he knew she wouldn't reveal any more of her past to him. So he took the bait. "What other guy?''

She paced the room, shoving her hands into the deep pockets of her brown suede jacket. She moved toward the fire. Stood near it, as though she were absorbing its warmth. "On the streets, when someone does you dirty, you do them right back. But it works the same the other way. I guess I've never gotten that damned unwritten code out of my head. You helped me out, so here I am. Maybe I'm an idiot, but here I am.''

He moved closer, wishing he could see her face, read whatever was in her eyes. He understood her pain over losing Tawny a little better now. They'd been together since they were just kids. They must have been like sisters. "Shannon, I don't have a clue what you're talking about.''

She whirled around, standing so close he could feel her agitated breaths on his face. Her eyes were wide, dark gold.

"I think you're in trouble, Damien. I think maybe we both are.''

But the urgency in her eyes faded when she glanced past him. Frowning, he turned to see Netty just beyond the doorway, a steaming mug in her hand. She stepped forward, beaming a smile as she brought the toddy to Shannon.

"Thanks, Netty." Shannon sipped. "Mmm, wonderful. Aren't you having one?" Her gaze probed Damien's.

"Ah, he never eats a thing, this one. Surprised he don't waste away before my eyes."

"That's all for today, Netty. Go on home to your grandchildren."

She nodded, blew Shannon a kiss, then waved as she trotted away in search of her coat. Shannon sipped her drink and walked to the book lying on its bent pages. She set the mug down and bent to pick the heavy volume up.

"Oh. Gilgamesh again. You read about him a lot, don't you?"

"Hobby of mine."

He heard the back door close, though he knew the sound would never reach mortal ears. Soon afterward, the car started up and Netty drove away.

"Not a pleasant one," she said. "You weren't too happy with whatever you read in here."

"It's what I *didn't* read in there. But that's off the subject, isn't it?"

"Can I take it home? I'd like to read it."

He nodded. "It'll bore you to tears. Moldy old stories that don't matter anymore. You said you were in trouble, Shannon."

She set the book carefully on the desk. "I said *we*."

She shrugged the backpack off, let it thump to the floor. The thing was heavy. She knelt, unzipped it and pulled out a stack of papers. Then another. File folders, notebooks, photographs, manila envelopes. "I thought you ought to see these."

"What are they?"

She fished in the bottom of the bag, making sure she'd removed everything, then shifted her position, curling her legs beneath her for comfort. "Don't know for sure—haven't gone through it yet." She glanced up at him, her eyes slightly shiny. She was excited, maybe still afraid, but wound up, as well. "Damien, did you know the CIA had you under surveillance?"

"The CIA?" He almost laughed. Then he saw her frown, and

knew she was serious. He shook his head slowly and sat down across from her. "Shannon, what's going on?"

"This suit broke into my office today. It was the same man we saw last night, with the ME. When I got there he was going through my files. Flashed some fancy ID card and said he was CIA. 'One of its subdivisions' were his exact words. This DPI—if it's for real—must be it. He wanted to know all about Tawny and me, and then he started asking about you. Threatened to have my investigator's license pulled unless I talked."

Damien felt a slow anger begin to simmer. "He threatened you?"

"Don't worry—I didn't tell him anything. But he knew I'd been with you lately, and he more or less said you were being watched." She shook her head, glancing down at the pile of documents in front of her. "Do you have any idea why they'd be interested in you?"

He shook his head. There was only one reason he could think of, and that was impossible. No government agency would take the existence of his race seriously enough to investigate it. The murder, then. It must have to do with the murder. "You said they asked about Tawny?"

Shannon's glimmering amber eyes clouded just before her lashes lowered, hiding the emotion in their depths. "They aren't going to bring her back, Damien. He wouldn't tell me where they took her or why, just that her body belongs to the government now, and I...I can't even bury her." When she looked up her eyes swam with tears. "He knows how she died—I'm sure of it. But he won't say. I have to know, Damien. Can you understand that? I have to know what happened, who put those holes in her throat, what she went through, whether she suffered or was afraid..."

She was hurting, this pixie with the leather-tough heart. She was hurting because her best friend had died. And he knew that pain so well that he hurt, too. He reached up, cradled her head in his hands and drew it downward to rest on his chest, with the mound of papers on the floor between them. He stroked her silky hair, wishing he could do more. "I'm sorry, Shannon. I know how much it hurts to lose someone you loved. There's no other pain like it. I know." It wouldn't ease her pain to know how Tawny had died. She'd never believe it if he told her it really had been a vampire. So he didn't.

She let him hold her there a moment longer, then she straightened, blinked for a moment and stared hard into his eyes. "Who did you lose?"

Enkidu's face hovered in his mind's eye, his laughter filled Damien's ears. Just as if no time at all had passed. "A friend," he told her. "He was like a brother, like the other half of me. My weaknesses were his strengths, and his were mine. We did everything together...." Damien swallowed the lump in his throat, searched her face. What was it about her that had him talking about Enkidu this way? He hadn't voiced that old anguish in ages.

"And then he died," she whispered. "And now you're a recluse." She tipped her head to one side. "Is that why? Are you afraid to have any more friends, because they might leave you someday?"

"It isn't a question of 'might.' Death is certain, guaranteed to every mortal on the planet."

"I'm all too aware of that. But life's too short to waste it alone."

He smiled in an attempt to break the tension. "You're one to talk. I haven't seen hordes of companions beating paths to your door."

"No, but not because I avoid making friends. I don't shut myself away from the world, Damien, the way you do. I just don't make attachments easily."

She looked up as she spoke, and the fire's light glowed its reflection in her eyes, made her golden hair gleam. Did she want an attachment now? With him? The gods had better help him if she did. She really was beautiful. So fragile looking, skin as delicate as lily petals. The hardness, the calluses on her heart, didn't show.

Damien shook himself when he realized how he was staring. He looked away quickly, glancing down at the papers. "You haven't finished telling me how you got these."

"Oh." She blinked, seeming to gather her thoughts. "Well, I threw the guy out on his ear and then I followed him. Some spook. He didn't even notice. He's staying at the Hilton over on Tenth. I lurked around until he went out again, then just went to his room and helped myself."

Damien's head came up fast. "You—"

"It's kid's stuff, getting into a hotel room. I used to clean them, you know, to put myself through school and help pay the rent. I just gave the clerk the creep's room number and said I'd lost my key." One hand dipped into her jacket pocket and she pulled out a key card. "He was more than happy to give me another. Figured I'd hang on to it, in case we need it again."

"Shannon, the man's going to know these papers are missing."

"Yeah, and if he has half a brain, he'll know who took them. I imagine my license is as good as gone. Doesn't matter, though. He would've pulled it anyway. He was pretty ticked off when I shot at him with his own gun." She smiled, appearing more like a mischievous teenager than a wounded, wary adult. "Don't look like that—I was only trying to make a point. I didn't hurt the guy."

"It isn't him I'm worried about."

Her brows went up and down expressively. "Well, it oughtta be. He really ticked me off."

Damien felt his lips pull into a reluctant smile as she got to her feet and walked back toward the table where she'd left her drink. He scanned the folders while she sipped. She moved closer to the fire again, her back to him.

"I was planning to close the office soon anyway. Already quit working on everything except Tawny's murder. Sent most of my clients to other agencies."

A manila folder had her name on its tab. Frowning, Damien opened it and saw medical notes, test results. The file was thick.

He closed it, glancing up at her back, and slid it under a sofa cushion just as she turned again.

"Looks like we'll have to pull an all-nighter. You up for it?"

"If you are," he said. He was more than a little bit worried about letting her see whatever was in the reports on him. But he couldn't think of a way to get around it. He still couldn't believe this Bachman man knew... No. It was impossible. But if Bachman *wasn't* investigating the undead, then just what *was* his interest in this case and in Damien?

Shannon squeaked and jumped backward, sloshing her drink. A brown field mouse raced past her feet and stopped in a corner. Shannon set the glass on the mantel and grabbed the brass poker, turning toward the creature.

"Wait." Damien stepped forward, closed his hand around hers and took the poker away. He replaced it in the holder.

"What're you, nuts?" She certainly looked at him as if he was. "You let one in, you'll be infested before you know it."

He shook his head, pointed. "Look at it, Shannon." She turned her head, staring at the tiny, white-bellied mouse. Its brown eyes bulged and its body trembled. "Just stand still," he told her. Damien moved forward slowly, his eyes sending silent messages to the creature. When he was close enough he crouched down, cupped his hands and scooped the mouse into them.

"There. See how harmless he is? You scared him half to death." He closed one hand around the body, careful not to crush it.

"I scared him?"

With one forefinger he rubbed the tiny head. He glanced up at Shannon. "He's just looking for a few crumbs and a warm place to spend the winter. Want to pet him?"

He held the mouse out, and she backed away. "No, thanks."

He shrugged and walked toward the doorway.

"What are you going to do with it?" She trotted behind him. "Damien, if you put it outside it's just going to come back in."

"There's a rickety little woodshed out back. I'll turn him loose in there. Mice love woodsheds."

By the time she finished reading, Shannon was feeling more than a little bit uneasy. She'd found herself looking up at Damien over and over again while she'd read the notes, noticing the lack of a single gray hair. Not a wrinkle on his smooth face. Damn, the man had to be old enough to have accumulated a few crow's-feet. Then she'd laugh at herself, realizing how ridiculous it was to be thinking what she was thinking. Then she'd read some more, and feel a little uneasy all over again. Line after line of reasons to believe Damien Namtar was a vampire. A *vampire,* for crying out loud. The so-called evidence was lined up like a grocery list. Times of Damien's comings and goings, side by side with the times the sun rose and set on the day in question. Where he'd been seen, and when and with whom.

He read steadily, never glancing up. He looked puzzled, and then worried, and then angry.

Finally, she stood up and stretched the kinks out of her muscles. She forced herself to dismiss every bit of what she'd read as nothing more than the rantings of a nut. "Well, I guess that settles it. The guy's not CIA, or if he's is, he's suffering from burnout. God, he thinks he's the latest version of Kolchek."

"Who?" She glanced down and smiled, but the tension remained on Damien's face, in his black eyes.

"Kolchek. You remember, the old TV series with the vampire hunter.... Damien, don't look so devastated, the guy's insane."

He rose, head down, and paced toward the fire to toss another log onto the dwindling flames.

"Either that, or you're really a vampire."

He spun to face her, eyes wide.

"Hey, I was kidding. Take it easy, will you?"

"I can't take it easy, Shannon. The man's been recording my every move for days. I don't like it."

"Well, of course you don't. Who would?"

She returned to her spot on the floor and snatched up the last sheet he'd read, wanting to know what had upset him so much.

He lunged toward her, reaching for the paper, but she ducked away and scanned the lines.

Then the blood rushed to her feet and her breath froze in her lungs. "My God..." Her gaze shot to Damien's. He stood motionless, looking devastated. "You didn't want me to see this, did you?"

"Do you blame me?"

She licked her lips, and reread the lines. Tawny's body was the second that had been found. The first, another young woman, had died of identical wounds to the throat. And there was a note that she, too, had volunteered to be Damien's assistant onstage. Rosalie Mason. The woman Shannon had tried to find.

She shook her head, staring at Damien in disbelief.

"That's why I didn't want you to see it, Shannon. That look that's on your face right now. I know what you're thinking."

"That's bull, because right now, *I* don't even know what I'm thinking." She got up again, walked to where she'd dropped her backpack and picked it up. "I'm going now. I'm overtired, and if I don't get some sleep soon, I'll be bunking in your shed with that mouse."

"You can use the guest room—"

"No." She softened her tone. She didn't really believe any of this, did she? Of course she didn't. "No, I really can't. Not tonight."

"You're afraid of me."

She chewed her lower lip, blinked twice. "I'm not. Maybe that's what worries me." She took a single step, then turned back and picked up the new book on Gilgamesh, the one he'd been reading when she'd arrived. "You, uh, you said it was okay to borrow this, didn't you?"

Damien nodded. Shannon slipped it into her pack, then slung the bundle over her shoulder and started for the door. Damien followed, touched her shoulder, stopping her before she went out.

"I know you don't trust me, Shannon, but I have to follow you home. It's still dark, and—"

She spun around, blinking up at him. "That's right, it is. And that reminds me to ask you why it is you're so sure I'm safe during the day, but in danger at night."

"Vampires only hunt at night."

A little chill ran over her nape at those words. She ignored it. "Get real, Damien."

"I'm serious." He sighed hard, pushed a hand through his hair and stepped away from her.

"There's no such thing." But when she said it, her words were barely more than a whisper.

He turned and met her eyes. "Then let's say the killer wants it to look like a vampire. Can you buy that?"

She nodded, still wary.

"He'll hardly change his tactics now and strike by day."

She felt the tension in her spine ease. "For a minute there I thought you were going to say you believed in this stuff. Had me worried." She was still worried. She just wasn't sure what about. Not that he was a blood-sucking night stalker. Not that.

CHAPTER SEVEN

The final test. It would be definitive. After this there would be no question as to Damien's fondness for the delicate mortal woman.

Anthar had allowed himself no contact with her. He'd kept his mind utterly isolated from her, just as he knew his nemesis had wished to do. It would never do for Anthar to develop a soft spot for her. She was a pawn. Her purpose was to mete out punishment, and nothing more. Anthar felt no hint of the instinctive urge to protect her. And if he had, he'd have ignored it. The fuel that powered his actions was more powerful than anything else could be. The need for vengeance. He'd been obsessed with the downfall of this onetime king for too long to allow anything to interfere.

And the test he'd devised this time would tell him all he needed to know. He'd use an element that could spell destruction for any immortal. Damien the Eternal would have to risk more than the passing pain of a bullet to save his mortal pet. He'd risk his very existence this time, or watch her die. If he should try and fail to save her, well, that would only add to his torment. If he should not try at all, then Anthar would know he hadn't cared.

It was all so simple to arrange. But not now—dawn was too close. Tonight, with the first layer of darkness on the autumn sky. He'd begin by making her sleep...very soundly.

The story was riveting.

She hadn't wanted interruption. She'd turned on the answering machine and refused to answer the door, even when the man thumping impatiently on the other side had most likely been an angry CIA spook by the name of Bachman. She had no idea why he didn't just break in. Maybe he really believed she wasn't here.

Didn't matter. She had no time to talk to him. No. She needed to spend today trying to decide whether Damien Namtar could possibly, in her wildest dreams, be a cold-blooded murderer. Or maybe he was just completely insane. Multiple personalities, perhaps, and maybe one of those personalities was a vampire.

After he'd left, she'd tried to sleep, couldn't. Countless scenarios popped into her mind, and kept her tossing and turning well into the morning. The result being that when she finally did sleep, she hadn't awoken until noon. She was beginning to keep some pretty vampiric hours herself.

When she did finally rouse herself, he was on her mind again, from the second she opened her eyes. The only conclusion she'd reached was that she just didn't know enough about the man to make a judgment call. And she'd decided then and there to read this book, cover to cover. To try to see what was in here that moved him so deeply, and maybe find a clue to what made him tick.

And now she knew, and it moved her, too.

Sad, tragic story. All about a great king and the man who became his closest friend—more than a friend, really. Gilgamesh had been a bit of a tyrant at first. A strong man, fierce in combat, abundant in wisdom. So much so he was thought of as half man, half god. But he'd forgotten how to feel compassion for his people.

Enkidu was raised on the steppe, among the wild things. People thought of *him* as half man, half animal. But he came into the ancient city of Uruk one day and deliberately stood right in Gilgamesh's path. A public challenge. The two fought, and the description of the battle was more poetic than anything Shannon thought she'd ever read:

> They fell like wolves
> at each other's throats,
> like bulls bellowing,
> and horses gasping for breath...

crushing the gate they fell against.
The dry dust billowed in the marketplace
and people shrieked. The dogs raced
in and out between their legs.
A child screamed at their feet
that danced the dance of life
which hovers close to death.
And quiet suddenly fell on them
when Gilgamesh stood still
exhausted. He turned to Enkidu, who leaned
against his shoulder and looked into his eyes
And saw himself in the other, just as Enkidu saw
himself in Gilgamesh.
In the silence of the people they began to laugh
And clutched each other in their breathless exaltation.

A lump formed in her throat as she read on. The two had been inseparable from then on, and the book told of their adventures together, how they were two parts of a single whole. And how, finally, Enkidu had slowly died as his friend looked on, helpless to save him.

The verse narrative was moving, and that surprised her. She hadn't expected writers from something earlier than 4000 B.C. to be so expressive. She blinked back tears as she read another passage, aloud, just to savor the beauty of it as it described Gilgamesh's crippling grief.

"The word *Enkidu*
roamed through every thought
like a hungry animal through empty lairs
in search of food. The only nourishment
he knew was grief, endless in its hidden source.

Shannon stood very still, knowing exactly how the man had felt. She'd felt that kind of grief when Tawny had died. She still felt it. She had to wait a few minutes before she could read further. Her tears blurred her vision, but she had to finish.

Engrossed, she read on. Gilgamesh, no longer a great ruler but an ordinary man who'd lost his way, wandered in the desert, perhaps a little insane, in search of the secret to eternal life. He became obsessed with the idea of becoming immortal and of carrying that secret home with him, to bring Enkidu back to life. A mission that was doomed to fail.

By the time Shannon closed the book, there were small, spasmodic sobs pulling at her breastbone. She brushed her eyes dry, shook her head and tried to focus on her reason for reading this heartbreaking tale in the first place. To understand Damien.

Of course. He said he'd lost his best friend. God, he'd even described their closeness in a way that mirrored the closeness of Gilgamesh and Enkidu in the ancient tale. No wonder he identified with it. And with her. It was as though some triangle of endless mourning connected the three of them.

But what did that mean to her?

She set the book down, absently caressing the cover, and paced the length of her living room, then back again. Could Damien be a killer? A man who was moved to tears by a story thousands of years old? A man who obviously felt things more deeply than any man she'd ever met? He couldn't even let her kill a little field mouse, for God's sake.

All her life she'd been taught, over and over again, not to trust anyone. Not anyone. So why did she so stubbornly persist in wanting to trust him?

All right, maybe it was time she took a good long look at her motivations here. She did just that, over a long steamy soak in a scented bath.

She'd never been with a man, had never wanted to be.

Until lately. Lately, she'd caught herself thinking about it more than once. Wondering if there was a chance it could actually be as wonderful as Tawny used to always tell her it could be. And she had to be brutally honest and admit that it was Damien who was inspiring these kinds of thoughts. No wonder, really. He was such a sexual creature.

It was getting dark outside. He'd be here soon, to stand guard over her for the night. She really ought to get out of the water and dress. What would he do, she wondered, if she kissed him?

Didn't matter. She wasn't going to find out.

Was she?

She felt a peculiar lethargy stealing over her body as she soaked. An unnatural kind of exhaustion, as if she'd popped a sleeping pill or something. She sponged her skin and fought it.

She thought maybe she'd like to find out after all. Hell, she had nothing to lose, and why not experience everything she was curious about before her life ended?

God, she was tired. Her eyes drooped and her body sank a little lower in the water. She dragged herself out of the tub and pulled on a robe. Was it this damned illness making her so sleepy? She'd already dozed half the day. Whatever, it was irresistible. She shuffled to bed, wet hair and all.

It wasn't the smoke that woke her—it was the alarm. Shrieking at her, breaking the night with its whistling pitch. She was half-dressed before she smelled the smoke, creeping in and surrounding her senses, little by little, so she wasn't certain for a moment. It might be her imagination. The alarm might be malfunctioning, and...

She pulled on the jeans she'd left on the floor, since they were within reach. She was hopping into the living room as she tugged them up, snapped them, yanked on the zipper. She was headed for the door, but stopped in her tracks when she saw the wispy gray fingers reaching toward her from beneath it.

They grew longer, floating upward, spreading. She took another step and felt a deep terror twist to life in her soul. She pressed her palms to the door, only to suck air through her teeth and yank them away from the heat.

"God! Oh, God!" Panic beat a message across her heart. She fought it, tried to use her mind. She whirled in a circle, then dashed across the room, yanking a blanket from the back of the sofa, heading for the bathroom. She jerked at the tub's faucet and dumped the blanket in. She jumped in on top of it, stomping on it up and down until it was soaked, then hauled it out, dripping and cold, and carried it back to the door.

The smoke seeped steadily beneath it now, and she dumped the wet blanket to the floor, kicking it tight to the crack under the door. Then she watched. The smoke stopped.

A sigh of relief that she knew wasn't called for escaped her lips anyway. She ran to the phone, picked it up and jiggled the cutoff. Dead. Her throat went dry. She licked her lips, standing in the room's center, turning slowly in a full circle. What could she do? She was twenty-three stories up and her only way out was through a door she knew better than to open. What in the name of God could she possibly do?

She went to the bedroom to stare out the window. Flames lit the night. She saw their orange glow dancing upward from the stories below her. She saw the flashing lights of rescue vehicles bathing the crowd that had gathered below. She saw people in their nightclothes, wandering like bugs. God, how had she slept through all of this? And she saw the huge gap where the fire escape ought to be. She would be down there soon, being led around by those fire fighters like the bug people were. Just as soon as they put the fire out and came for her. She would. She only needed to keep her head.

She went to the closet, opened it and picked up her worn-out baseball bat. She hurried back to the bedroom, and the window shattered with the first impact. She hoped the people below were far enough away to avoid the flying glass. She imagined they were. They'd expect windows to be smashed by the ones still trapped.

Trapped.

She bit her lip, and tore her gaze away from the people below and the flame's color on the night sky. She went back to the living room and glanced longingly at the balcony. But red tongues of flame leapt up around it, attacking from the one below. She couldn't go out there. No haven there.

She returned to the bathroom, stoppered the tub and let more water rush into it. Cool water. And then she filled a dishpan, carried it into the living room and hurled the water at the hot door. The paint on the inside was blistering now. The smoke was finding its way around the blanket. The next dishpanful hit, spattered, splashed back on her face.

She threw another blanket into the water, this one to wrap herself in should she need it.

What else? What else?

Her heartbeat escalated when she realized she was sweating. The temperature of the room was increasing. The floors...God, the bottoms of her bare feet felt the heat seeping up through the floors.

Calm. Calm, don't panic. Go to the window again. Let them know you're here. A signal.

She tied several sheets together, taking her time, trying to keep her hands from shaking so hard, knowing there was nothing to do but wait. When she glanced up, she saw a layer of smoke suspended at waist level, and she got down from the bed to sit on the hot floor. She tied the end of her sheet banner to the bedpost and tossed the rest out the window.

They'd see the white flag in the night. They'd come for her.

Her eyes burned. The inside of her nose stung. Her chest hurt.

It's the smoke. The smoke is the enemy. Have to stop breathing so much of it.

She went to the bathroom again, to the overflowing tub, but she didn't turn the water off. She took a clean washcloth, wet it and held it to her face. She swiped at her burning eyes, but when she opened them again, it was dark.

The power had gone. The tub spluttered to a stop. She held the cloth over her nose and mouth to filter the air, but she choked anyway. She pawed for the tub, dragged the wet blanket from it. That thick, acrid stench coated her mouth and tongue. She dropped to her knees and crawled from the bathroom, pulling the sodden weight behind her.

The explosion came from nowhere and from everywhere. Burning brands rained on her like shrapnel, and a blinding wall of flame stood where the door used to be. She crawled faster, on knees only, coughing, clutching the washcloth to her face with one hand and pulling the soaked blanket with the other. She found her way to the bedroom door by the light of the inferno spreading like a pool through her apartment. She hurled herself through, then closed it and pushed the blanket to the bottom.

The coughing racked her now, and with each bout she spasmodically inhaled more of the smoke that was choking her. Killing her. She sat on the floor, turning herself slowly, blinking her watering eyes in pitch-darkness to get her bearings. The window—she wanted to get back to the window. She choked again, dragging in more of the acrid stench. Her finger screamed in white-hot pain, and she suddenly realized the ring she wore was burning a brand into it. She yanked it off, threw it away. Her hair was soaked in sweat, her skin sizzling with the heat.

And then she found the window. She found it by the glow of the sheets she'd hung out, which were burning now, like everything else. Flames climbed the sheet like a rope and leapt the windowsill to invade. She lurched to her feet, to the bed. She fumbled with the knot she'd made, but a fit of choking caught her, held her in a merciless grip. She had to stand long enough to undo the knot on the bedpost. When she finally got it free, and sent the sheets sailing to the ground below, she dropped to the floor again.

Only this time it wasn't volitional, and she didn't get up.

He had never intended to use the power of the psychic bond between her kind and his. But he was increasingly glad he'd begun to relearn the ways of doing it. As soon as dusk fell and he came fully awake, he homed in on Shannon. He'd go to her, take up his nightly vigil, just as soon as he'd showered and dressed. And until then he'd keep track of her with his mind.

He ignored the cravings of his body. He shouldn't feel such an urgent need yet. It hadn't been that long. And the damned hunger that kept dancing in his mind shouldn't be wearing Shannon's face. Damn, what was happening to him?

He tried distracting himself from this irrational need for her by thinking of new and amazing feats to perform for the crowds while he took a record-fast shower. He thought about escape tricks, and reminded himself to go through that book on Houdini that he'd bought last month, while he threw on his clothes. But all the time, in one corner of his mind, he was feeling her thoughts, experiencing what she did, smelling and tasting and hearing along with her. The old talent had come back to him with a little practice, more powerful than he'd remembered it.

She'd been silent, so deeply asleep she hadn't even dreamed.

Then there was an abrupt shift. Every one of her senses went rigidly alert. Damien smelled smoke, felt it, thick and stinging, clawing at his nostrils, scratching his eyes. Heat like a lead blanket tried to smother him. He felt her fear. Stark terror. All so fast, it had happened.

Fire. And he knew, dammit, that his skin would go up like gasoline if he touched the flame.

Didn't matter, though. He had to get her out. If not, he'd have to experience her death. Feel the gradual ebb of her life force, see what she saw in her mind as she battled the final enemy. Anyone but her, he thought in sudden panic, and the real possibility of it hit him. She couldn't die, not Shannon. It would kill him this time.

He'd done it, then, hadn't he? He'd let himself start caring about her.

Damien stepped out of his house, lifted his arms. Seconds later he soared, a shadow in the night sky, a streak of darkness there and gone so suddenly no mortal eye would see him. He soared toward her, and he felt her heartbeat slow.

Damn you, you won't win. Not this time!

He sped through the starry sky, piercing clouds like an arrow. He felt the cool, crisp air on his skin, and then the searing heat on Shannon's. He smelled the biting autumn air and then the stench of smoke. And then he was there. The conflagration raged like a tower of pure hell, and he dove, swooping through the broken glass of her bedroom window.

He thudded to the floor of a smoke-filled room, and even with his night vision, he could barely see. The heat was intense, and here and there tongues of vicious flame broke the inky blackness. He avoided them, focusing only on Shannon, and he found her, dropped to his knees beside her just as her labored, raspy struggles for breath stopped altogether.

She lay still, eyes closed, a limp angel. He scooped her into his arms, cupping her head with one hand and held her face to his. He blew his breath into her lungs. Once, twice, again.

She coughed, drew a strangled breath, only filling her lungs with more smoke. Her arms came weakly around his neck, and her face pressed to his throat. She choked his name before she lost consciousness again.

Cradling her to his chest, a burden so light he barely noticed the added weight, he leapt through the window again, speeding through the night too rapidly to be seen, like one more wisp of sooty smoke that appeared, then vanished in the blink of an eye.

He came down away from the lights and the crowd, in a darkened alley between the next two buildings. The street just beyond was a chaos of sirens. Red and white flashes bathed Shannon with color. Vehicles moved back and forth, horns blasting, voices shouting.

She stirred in his arms, drew a wheezing breath and then exploded in a seizure of coughing that he thought would tear her body apart. He held her to his chest until the paroxysm passed, then searched her soot-streaked face. "Shannon?"

She blinked him into focus with red eyes, frowned, then glanced beyond him to the burning hulk. Red-orange tongues of fire lapped at the night sky, as if they'd consume it, as well. "How—"

Her question was cut off by her coughing. He carried her out of the shadows, into the crowd. He shoved his way through until he reached an ambulance, then snatched the oxygen mask from its hook on a tank.

"Hold on, mister. I'll handle it." The young man turned a valve, held the mask to Shannon's face and waved an arm toward the ground. "Lay her down here."

"A stretcher." He bit the two words out and glared at the man in white.

"Sorry, but they're all in use. Just give her to me—" As the medic spoke he reached for Shannon, but a sweep of Damien's arm sent him stumbling aside. "Hey—" Damien shut him up with one glance before he looked for a soft place where she could rest. He spotted an empty police car and carried her toward it. The man swore under his breath, but came along, carrying the oxygen tank. Damien yanked open the rear door of the cruiser and lay her down across the back seat. She was coughing again, pushing the mask away, trying to sit up.

"Damien—"

"It's all right, Shannon. You'll be fine now."

"You got—" A fit of coughing took her and she was weak when it let her go. She sat up anyway, her arm along the back of the seat to brace her. She held the clear plastic mask to her face, head bowed as she sucked a few breaths of oxygen, but her eyes never left his. Her head came up, slowly, as if it weighed too much for her neck to support. "You got me out."

He nodded. "Rest. You need to—"

"How?"

He said nothing, just watched her. She turned her head to stare at the blazing building. She drew two more breaths, then moved the mask aside. "You went in there, didn't you? You walked into that..." Her brows drew together and she returned to her scrutiny of his face. She coughed again, drew herself straighter, searching his eyes.

An ambulance pulled up beside the police car. Two paramedics jumped out, yanked a gurney from the back and rolled it to a stop behind Damien. The one with the oxygen tank tapped the roof. "We've got an ambulance available now. We can transport her."

She shook her head. "No, I'm fine."

"We're taking you to a hospital, miss. You inhaled a lot of smoke—"

"I *said* I'm fine." She got her feet to the pavement again, shoving Damien aside so she could stand up, then closing a hand on his shoulder for support. She glanced just once more at the building, then met Damien's eyes, her own shooting sparks that were just a bit duller than usual. "Why?"

He wasn't sure just then that the smoke she'd inhaled hadn't damaged her brain. "You need see a doctor, Shannon. Lie down on this gurney and—"

"Stop talking to me like I'm two years old and spill it, Damien." She paused to cough, wheeze, gasp, pressing the palm of one hand to her chest, bending almost double. The young man held the mask she'd discarded to her face. She took one gulp of oxygen and pushed it aside, lifting her head with an obvious effort. "Why did you risk your neck for me like that? Again? You have a death wish or what?"

He frowned at her. "You know you and your lousy attitude are beginning to get to me. I went to a lot of trouble to snatch you, kicking and screaming as usual, from death's door. I don't expect a thank-you at this point, but you'd better believe you are going to see a doctor if I have to throw you over my shoulder and carry you there myself."

She sucked at the oxygen, eyes narrowing on his face.

He cocked his eyebrows. "Don't get that suspicious look, Shannon Mallory. This wasn't a plot to get you to stop suspecting me of heinous crimes. If that was all I wanted to accomplish I could have left you in there."

The mask moved away. "I never said—"

Her glare faltered, and she began coughing hard enough to tear her lungs to shreds, he thought.

He picked her up. "I'm tired of arguing with you, dammit." He held her hard and climbed into the back of the ambulance. He sat on a seat, with her on his lap, and sent the attendant a nod.

The youth clambered in with them, bringing the oxygen along, bending over to affix the mask once more to Shannon's face. Damien could see the medic wanted to suggest Damien follow in a car, meet them at the hospital. He even opened his mouth to do it, but he changed his mind. The other man closed the double rear doors and went around to the front. The vehicle lurched, jarring her against his chest. Her arms encircled Damien's shoulders and she let her head relax against him. He closed his eyes. In seconds they were under way, siren blasting.

They hadn't gone far, when she lifted her head, reached up to yank the mask from her face, but Damien caught her hand in his, held it, stared down into her eyes. He could will her to be still. But he found himself wanting to convince her, instead. He liked her spirit, irritating though it was.

"Shannon, there is nothing in this for me. That's what you're wondering about, isn't it? What my angle is, what I'm after? Nothing at all."

She twisted her hand from his and yanked the mask away. "I didn't ask for you to jump into the middle of my life." She drew a slow, careful breath. "I don't need a hero."

"I didn't claim to be one."

"Ha! You ran into that burning building like some kind of comic-book superstar! There was no earthly reason for you to—" Her accusatory comment was cut off by another bout of coughing, and Damien pressed the mask to her face again.

When she'd calmed and faced him again, he lifted the mask. She looked at him in silence for a long time. Her gaze fell to somewhere in the vicinity of his chin. "There was no reason for you to risk your life like that." She spoke more softly, he thought, so she wouldn't instigate a return of her choking and gasping.

"There was every reason," he told her. He pushed her hair away from her face.

Her eyes narrowed, shooting amber sparks at him. He wiped some of the soot from her face. She tried to sit up, and he let her. She slid from his lap to settle on the edge of the gurney. She didn't look him in the eye. She stared downward, and her golden hair fell over one side of her face. "I thought...I really thought it was all over, in there."

"I'm glad you were wrong."

She nodded. "I owe you, Damien...again." The ambulance turned and slowed. Then came to a stop. The rear doors opened, and she got to the ground by herself, refusing his help as well as the medics'. The young man reached out to take Shannon's arm, but she jerked it away. "I can walk perfectly well by myself. God, you'd think I was...was..." She stood, wavering slightly, glanced at Damien, blinked. She lifted one hand toward him.

He caught her when she began sinking. Stubborn woman! He carried her through the double Emergency Room doors that opened on their own at his approach. He walked into chrome-and-white chaos, the smell of Lysol, the squeak of rubber soles on spotless floor tiles and the clatter of wobbling wheels on gurneys as they were pushed along. She muttered that she was fine and didn't need to be carried. He was ushered to an examining room, where he laid her carefully down on a table that was covered in immaculate white paper. She smudged it with soot.

Damien evaporated as soon as the first nurse appeared with a stack of forms to be filled out. Shannon sat on the edge of the bed and filled in the blanks, wondering if they handed this same stack to cardiac-arrest victims before administering CPR.

A nurse came in with a soft, damp cloth and a basin of warm water and proceeded to wipe the soot from Shannon's face. Okay, she thought. They were sweethearts. She was just thinking bitchy thoughts because she was in a bitchy mood. Damn, she'd lost just about everything she had.

"The doctor will be right in, Ms...." The blond woman glanced at the forms. "Mallory. You just relax and let me get your vitals, okay?"

Shannon nodded as a thermometer was popped into her mouth.

As it turned out, that nurse spent a good half hour with her. The doc was in and out in five minutes flat, pronouncing her well enough to go home, and then the nurse was back, wondering what she was going to wear.

Shannon hadn't thought of that. And when she did, she thought of other things, things she'd never see again. Her Sting CDs, her brown suede jacket...

Her eyes flew wide, she clutched her middle and groaned in real pain.

The nurse grabbed her shoulder. Damien burst into the room. "What's wrong? What's happening?"

Shannon moaned again, louder. It *really* hurt. "My car. Oh, my car, my car, my car." She covered her face with her hands when Damien and the nurse exchanged looks. "After those thugs tried to steal it, I parked it in that damned sinkhole they call an underground garage. Oh, damn, don't you get it? My car..." She groaned. They didn't understand. They couldn't. "Just get out and leave me alone," she muttered into her hands.

She heard the door close, thought she might be by herself, looked up. Damien set a big shopping bag on the floor and came toward her. "You're crying." His magic fingers rose and wiped the tears from her cheeks.

"You think it's stupid, crying for a car." She sniffed and tried to stop, but more tears flowed. She gave up, closed her eyes and let them come.

His hands slipped over her shoulders, around to her back. He pulled her head to his chest, and he rocked her slightly back and forth. "I don't think it's stupid."

"Tawny...used to collect them."

"Cars?"

She sniffed and nodded, pushing her face closer to his chest. That white shirt of his still held the smell of smoke, but his scent was there, too, and it crept into her brain and rubbed her sore spots with a healing touch. "Matchbox cars," she told him. "The Corvette was her favorite. But it was my favorite, too. We'd always fight over that one. Little, candy-apple red Stingray with the doors that really opened and closed. She'd put it on her dresser, and I'd snatch it and put it on mine. We were too old for toys, but hell, we didn't have much to call our own in those days." She cried a little harder, ashamed of herself, but needing to do it. "And...and my birthday came, with no party or presents, just like always. And she—she wrapped that stupid little car up in a page of comics and gave it to me. It was her favorite, and she gave it to me. She swore someday we'd have a real one, and we'd ride around together...."

His arms tightened around her. "So that's why your car means so much to you, hmm?"

She nodded again.

"It might be okay, you know. They have the fire pretty much contained, according to the radio, and it didn't look to me like the lower floors were too badly damaged."

She lifted her head, gazing wide-eyed at his face. "You think?"

"It's possible. I'll check on it for you just as soon as we get you settled in."

She felt her brows draw together. "Settled i—"

"I went to a department store a few blocks away while you were being examined, picked you up a few necessities."

"You—"

"You're coming home with me, Shannon. And I don't want to hear any arguments about it." He stood in front of her, searched her face.

She was quiet for a long time, searching his right back. His dark eyes, his raven hair, the face that made her want to trace each strong feature with her fingertips. He'd saved her life...twice now. He certainly wasn't going to hurt her.

"Damien..." She hesitated, hating to voice her fears, but forcing herself to go on. "Do you think the fire—"

"They're saying it looks like arson, but they won't be certain for a day or two."

She gnawed her lips. "It's all connected, isn't it? Someone doesn't want me digging into Tawny's murder."

"There's no proof—"

"It might even have been Bachman. He said he could make me disappear." She eyed Damien, wishing she knew the truth.

"I just don't know. It might have been an attempt on your

life. It might have been a coincidence. Either way, you'll be safer with me. I don't want you alone anymore, Shannon.''

She didn't *want* to be alone anymore, either. She simply nodded. "Okay."

CHAPTER EIGHT

He scooped her up in his arms again and strode through the emergency room over the protests of the nurse, who kept talking about hospital regulations and wheelchairs. There was a part of Shannon that rebelled against the coddling. That little suspicious voice in her mind that insisted he must have a motive, whispered constant warnings in her ear: *You don't need anyone to take care of you. You can take care of yourself—you always have. Don't get used to this. It's not gonna last, and we both know it, don't we? It'll just make you weak. Yell at him. Tell him to put you down.*

But she didn't. Because there was another part, a part that seemed to be growing bigger all the time, that liked the way it felt to be cradled in his strength. The hard arms that held her, the solid chest she leaned against, were feeling less like invaders of her independence and more like her own solid fortress, her refuge. It felt *good* to be held this way, dammit. And who the hell ever said she didn't have the right to feel good once in a while?

She put her arms around his neck, mentally thumbing her nose at that cynical voice. He stepped outside, into the hospital parking lot, and she thought there had never been an autumn night that tasted as crisp and clean as this one. There was a second, as he carried her toward the black Jag that crouched like the cat it was named for, when she wondered how he'd got the car here so fast. Someone, probably a cop or a fire fighter, must have brought it over. It didn't matter, really.

He settled her on the seat, pulled the safety belt around her, fastened it. Then he looked at her, just looked at her for a long time. She could see his eyes moving minutely, as if he had to see every part of her face. Their focus shifted, from her forehead to her nose to her jaw. Her lips, her eyes.

She lifted a hand, thinking she might still have soot smeared on her skin. But he caught it, stopping it, holding it in his. She met his ebony gaze. His lips moved just a little, the barest whisper of a smile. He stepped back and closed her door, still staring at her face. After a moment she offered a small smile in return. Finally, he dragged his gaze away, went to his side of the car and got in. And then he drove.

When they reached the house, he carried her again. "You'll want to shower. Your robe is still in the bedroom you used before." This he said as they mounted the broad, curving staircase.

The cynic was getting louder. "Damien put me down. I'm not too helpless to walk up a flight of stairs."

"I'm not as sure of that as you are." He kept walking.

She didn't argue anymore, sensing it wouldn't do much good anyway. Besides, they were already heading up the second flight. He'd put her down soon. Now, why wasn't she as relieved by that thought as she'd expected to be? He held her crushingly tight, as if he were afraid he might drop her. She let her head rest on his shoulder, and then felt the oddest certainty that he'd bent his head to brush his lips over her hair.

Silly. Just her imagination overworking itself again.

He flung the bedroom door open, stepped through it and lowered her to the floor. His hand clasped her waist for longer than it had to, just to steady her. He looked so concerned that it made her uncomfortable, and she took a step away from him. "I think you're right. I want a shower. Get that damned smoky reek out of my hair before I choke on it."

He nodded, but didn't leave. He opened the closet and set the shopping bag he still carried on the top shelf, then turned to her again. "Can you manage by yourself?"

That made her smile a little. He really must think she was a wimp. "What are you gonna do, Damien, bathe me personally, just in case I'm not strong enough to lift a bar of soap?"

The worried expression in his black eyes changed. They darkened or intensified or something. For a long time, she couldn't look away. And when she finally did, she felt shaken, a little weak-kneed, and not from smoke inhalation.

"I'll be back to check on you in a few minutes." His voice wasn't even or calm, as it had been before. He turned and left her there, and she got the impression he was in a hurry.

When the door closed she stared at it, licked her lips. "Yeah," she whispered. "And then what?"

She scrubbed. She shampooed her hair again and again, and stood under the shower spray until she wondered if his supply of hot water was endless. As she lingered in the shower, she thought of Damien. The great magician. The man. What made him want to perform for a living? she wondered. And what had he done before? And...and was he thinking about her as often as she'd been thinking about him lately?

She shook her head and told herself to get a grip. When she thought she'd finally rid herself of that clinging smoky odor, she toweled dry and reached for the clothes he'd just bought for her, the ones she'd worn to leave the hospital. But she smelled the smoke again. Well, no wonder. She'd been coated in that scent when she'd put them on, and now the clothes were infected. It figured, didn't it?

She wrapped up in a towel and went in search of the robe she'd left here. She found it in the closet, pulled it on. But as she did, she glanced up at that shopping bag on the top shelf. It still bulged. He had said he'd bought the stuff for her, hadn't he? She wondered if there was anything more substantial in there to put on. She stretched out an arm, but the shelf was too high to reach that way.

Biting her lip and glancing around, she spotted a chair and quickly pulled it over to the closet. She climbed up, and the bedroom door opened, and Damien stood there, arms crossed, looking at her the way he might look at a little girl hanging upside down from a set of monkey bars.

He'd showered, changed. He wore a pair of black jeans that fit him way too well and a wine-colored button-down shirt, with the sleeves rolled up to just below his elbows, so her eyes were instantly drawn to the fine dark mist of hair on his forearms. When she met his gaze again, he was smiling.

She ignored his amused expression and reached for the bag. "Watch out!"

His yell came just as she felt the chair slide sideways and begin to tilt. She toppled. The bag flew out of her hands as she plummeted. She groped for a hold. The next thing she knew, she was slamming into his chest so hard his back smacked into the wall. Her arms automatically clung to his neck as he held her upright against him with her feet dangling a few inches above the floor. His arms were tight around her waist, crossed at the small of her back. Her face was above his, and only a fraction of an inch away. She caught her breath. He didn't let her go. He was staring. She didn't know what part of her so fascinated him, because her own gaze was fixed to his mouth.

It wasn't the first time she'd caught herself looking at those full lips of his and wondering what kind of a kisser he was. Would he be gentle, well mannered, neat? Or hard and hot and messy? Probably the latter, she figured, narrowing her eyes as she thought about it. Yes. Definitely the latter.

He closed his eyes and thumped the back of his head to the wall, as though trying to clear it or something. His arms loosened on her waist so she could slide down, but as her body moved over his, she felt the rigid arousal behind his zipper, and she knew her heart skipped a beat.

She turned him on? Good grief, she hadn't realized that. Well, all right, she'd suspected it once or twice, but...

Her toes touched the floor. She unlaced her arms from around his neck and lowered her heels until her feet were flat. He opened his eyes. She hadn't noticed before how thick and glossy his lashes were, or how the irises themselves were smooth as black satin. She took a step away from him, but her eyes remained mated to his.

His big hands rested just above her hips now, and she felt his fingers knead her flesh there, but she wasn't sure if it was a voluntary movement or something he did unconsciously. She thought about the magic in those hands, the ease with which he moved them onstage, the way things would appear in them as if from thin air, the way the very elements seemed to respond to their commands, to obey their every wave or even a snap of those long fingers. What kind of magic could hands like that work on a woman? And she thought about the hard length of him, stirred to life just by the touch of her body against his. And for just a second, she wondered what it would be like to let a man like this one make love to her. Probably beyond anything she could imagine.

He pushed her away, and he turned abruptly, as if he'd pound the front of his head against the wall this time. He didn't, but his magic hands were clenched into trembling fists at his sides and his shoulders were stiff and the muscled cords in his neck stood out.

Oh, come on. He couldn't possibly want her *that* much. Maybe, if she were some swimsuit model or cover girl, but not *her*. So what was this?

"I, uh, didn't hurt you, did I?"

His head fell until she figured his chin was touching his chest. He made a sound that was half snort, half laugh. His voice was very soft and kind of raspy when he said, "No, Shannon. You didn't hurt me."

She shrugged. "I didn't think so." She turned away from him, just in case he should look at her. She didn't want him to see how much he confused her. Sheesh, if he was that hot for her, why didn't he just say so? He couldn't possibly be afraid she'd turn him down. It wasn't as if a guy like this one probably got turned down often. Maybe not ever. He wanted her. So why didn't he do something about it?

She bit her lips hard, and waited.

"You ought to eat something," he said, and she wanted to scream in frustration. "Come downstairs."

In the circular room that was his favorite, a roaring fire awaited them. He wanted to be sure Shannon was really all right before he rested at dawn. She'd nearly died. He still couldn't quite believe she hadn't.

But she was alive, more alive than anyone he'd ever known. He watched her spoon down the chicken soup he'd warmed for her. He hadn't dared to try anything more complicated. It had been a long time since he'd worried about food, though there was always plenty in the kitchen. Netty had to eat while she was here, and bare cupboards might have made her wonder.

Shannon had finished her soup. Now she meandered around the room, examining things with the fierce curiosity of a child. She picked up the shiny black box that made things disappear onstage. She opened it, examined the mirrors inside, closed it again, turned it over. He watched her, seeing the life, the rampant vitality of her, her spirit. She'd nearly died. He couldn't get rid of that thought.

The robe was too short, and he really should have insisted she find something more to wear. There were other things in the shopping bag, but they both seemed to forget about that after she'd fallen into his arms. He'd forgotten everything for a few minutes. How to breathe. How to think. She'd wanted him to kiss her. He knew it with a certainty that made his head spin.

Yes, he really ought to go back upstairs for that shopping bag right now. Her legs were too shapely, too smooth-skinned and firm. It was too easy to envision them wrapped around him.

Why in hell had he brought her here? Was he completely insane? Did he really think he could keep her here with him, spend every waking moment this close to her, alone with her, and not lose control, not reveal himself? Maybe he *was* insane. How many centuries could sanity last, anyway? Was *it* immortal, as well? Hell, maybe he'd never *been* sane in the first place.

She approached the huge marble fireplace, whiskey-colored eyes catching its glow. Her gaze moved over the framed charcoal drawings of the ancient world. One depicted the Euphrates, cutting a path through the desert. She glanced at the artifacts in their clear glass cubes. Frowning, she bent closer to the marble figurine under the glass.

"What is it?"

"An ancient goddess of love and fertility. The Sumerians called her Inanna, the Babylonians, Ishtar. Queen of Heaven."

"She's beautiful. It looks old."

"Almost five thousand years old."

Her amber eyes widened, and she lifted the glass cube that covered the piece, then glanced at him. "May I?"

He nodded, watching as she held the small sculpture, ran her fingers delicately over it. "I can't believe I'm touching something that people thousands of years ago might have touched, something this old."

He wanted her to touch him that way. He was that old. Older.

She shook her head in wonder and replaced the glass. Then pointed to the piece beside it. "And this one? What is it, a goat?"

"Yes. It's newer, made around 2600 B.C. The blue in the horns and beard is lapis lazuli. The rest is gold."

"You collect this stuff?"

He nodded, watching her gaze move over his face as if its shape fascinated her. Then she turned to the last piece on the mantel. "This one's kind of ugly."

"It's not art."

"What *is* it?"

"A piece of a story." He moved forward to stand beside her. She squinted at the carvings that covered every inch of the stone's face.

"This is writing?"

"Man's earliest form of writing. Cuneiform script. This piece was done around 4000 B.C., in Sumer."

She studied it more closely, as if trying to absorb its meaning. "Does anyone know what it says?"

Damien nodded. "It's part of the story of Gilgamesh."

She looked up quickly, and he saw regret in her eyes.

"Gilgamesh. Oh, God, Damien, your book...the fire—"

"It's all right."

"But I—"

"Shannon, it's just a book. The latest translation. I have dozens of others with the same story in them. You've seen them yourself—"

"But it's precious to you."

It was. They all were. But how could she know that? "I can get another one."

"*I'll* get you another one. And a copy for myself while I'm at it." She sighed, her hand resting feather-light on the glass. "It was a wonderful, terrible story. I'm glad I read it before the book burned."

He frowned at her, trying not to see that in the firelight her skin resembled fine silk, trying not to hear the sincerity in her voice. "You did?"

She nodded absently, her gaze going back to the uneven chunk of stone. "Tell me what it says."

He closed his eyes. "You don't really want to hear—"

"I do. That story touched me, Damien. I think I understand the pain that drove Gilgamesh into the desert. I lost a best friend, too, you know."

"I know." And he did. "This is a recounting of Enkidu's death. Gilgamesh was at his side, clutching his hand. Enkidu looked at Gilgamesh and spoke to him. This is what he said."

Damien turned his eyes to the stone. "'You will be left alone, unable to understand in a world where nothing lives anymore...'" He tried not to feel the pain of that horrible day again. It had changed over the centuries, even altered its form, but never dulled. He still felt it like a freshly whetted blade slicing his soul. His voice thickened as he read on.

"'You'll be alone and wander, looking for that life that's gone, or some eternal life you have to find. Your eyes have changed. You are crying. You never cried before. It's not like you. Why am I to die, you to wander alone? Is that the way it is with friends?' Gilgamesh sat hushed as his friend's eyes stilled. In his silence he reached out to touch the friend whom he had lost."

Damien stopped with one hand braced against the mantel and

stared into the flames. He only brought himself up out of the well of pain when he heard her sniff. He lifted his head, glanced at her, and saw tears in her amber eyes.

"It's so sad. And you read it with such emotion." She sniffed once more and ran the back of one hand over her eyes. "You should have been an actor."

"I am."

She nodded, biting her lip, turning toward him again. "You told me that you'd lost a friend, too. That's why you feel so strongly about this epic, isn't it?" He nodded, not trusting his voice just then to speak. "You've read so much about Gilgamesh. Was there more?"

"More?"

"To the story." She looked at him with so much hope in her eyes. "It's so sad to believe that's all there was. There ought to be more. Did he ever find the secret? Did he manage to bring his friend back?"

Damien sighed, shifting his gaze back to the stone. "He found immortality, but it didn't make him a god, the way he'd thought it would. It didn't give him the power to bring Enkidu back. It made him a demon. The people who'd adored him hated him and called him a monster. They didn't even believe he was Gilgamesh anymore, but some evil imposter. Their king was dead. His foolish search for eternal life condemned him to an endless existence, where he was forced to witness over and over again the triumph of the one enemy he'd hoped to defeat. Death."

She turned again to the stone. "It *says* all that?"

"No, Shannon. That part of the story hasn't been uncovered yet. It's just my own theory."

She stared at him for a moment, her jaw slack. Then she blinked her shock away and lightly punched his shoulder. "Cheerful SOB. Aren't you? Couldn't you come up with a better theory? Something with a 'happily ever after' at the end?"

"I wish I could."

She smiled, but her lips trembled just a little. She reached down to the stack of logs, picked one up and tossed it into the fireplace. A shower of sparks rained out, and Damien jumped out of the way. He thought his heart skipped a beat. But none made contact, and he hastily replaced the glass screen in front of the flames.

Shannon didn't seem to notice. She was settling down on the floor, amid the pillows on the Turkish rug. She crossed her legs and patted a spot beside her. "I could discuss Gilgamesh all night. He fascinates me, but I'm hereby tabling the creation of a happy ending for him until another time. There's something a little more immediate we need to talk about."

"Like what?"

"Like how we're going to catch Tawny's killer. We haven't made a hell of a lot of progress so far, in case you haven't noticed."

He lifted his eyebrows. "Does that mean you've finally decided I didn't do it?"

"Do you think I'd be here if I hadn't?"

It wasn't really an answer. Actually, he thought she just might be here either way. She had a little too much courage sometimes. "You have an idea where to begin? Because I certainly don't." He crossed his legs and sat down beside her.

"As a matter of fact, I do."

His head came up quick at the tone in her voice. Why did the way she said those words, that slight lifting of her chin and that hint of stubbornness in her eyes, send a chill up the back of his neck?

"Tell me, then."

She tilted her head to one side, eyes sparkling again. "You're not going to like it."

"Why am I not surprised?"

She smiled, and he knew he'd made a mistake by sitting down here with her. She was too close, and her scent twined into his mind, tying it up in knots. His gaze moved over her face, such an exquisite face, high cheekbones, mouth like a plump bow, small turned-up nose. He'd like to see that face twisted in an ecstasy so sweet it was painful. He could give her that.

Problem was, he was afraid he might kill her in the process.

Her brows drew together, her hand lifted to touch his face. "You all right?"

Her touch on his skin was agony. He turned away, and her hand fell. "Fine. What's this idea I'm not going to like?"

She seemed a little hurt by his action, but she went on anyway. "The killer is only striking the women who've volunteered to assist you. At least, that's the way it looks so far. I thought he might try for me when I became your latest volunteer, but he didn't. So we have to rebait the trap. I'll be your one-and-only, full-time, exclusive assistant from now on."

"Absolutely—"

"Starting tomorrow night."

"Not."

"I knew you wouldn't like it." She held his gaze, and in the bright challenge shining from her eyes he could almost see her daring him to dish up his best arguments.

"You'd be risking your life."

"Moot point. I might already be on his hit list."

"And you might not."

"You can't keep using audience volunteers, Damien. It isn't fair to make them targets—"

He stood, paced away and turned to face her again. "I won't use them anymore."

"Then he's liable to start preying on your paid assistants." She rose, too, and came toward him. "At least with me, it's an informed decision. Those other women have no idea what they're letting themselves in for."

He pushed one hand through his hair, hating that she made sense. "I'd rather close the show, cancel the rest of the performances."

"You'd be sued."

"I don't care."

She lifted her chin, standing close to him and practically on tiptoe, trying to look him levelly in the eye. "We'll never catch him unless he tries again. This is important to me, Damien. The risk is nothing. I've got nothing to lose. All I care about right now is catching this bastard and making sure he pays for what he did to Tawny.''

''Shannon—''

''And I'm willing to make a concession.'' He waited. ''I'll stay here with you, make it easier for you to continue in this role you've taken on as my protector, much as I don't need one. If you say no, then I'm out the door, right now, tonight.''

''Where would you go?''

''I still have my office. I could bunk on the couch there.''

Stubborn, beautiful witch. ''I could camp on your doorstep and watch over you anyway.''

''But I'm safer here. This place is like a fort.''

He lowered his eyes, knowing defeat when it was staring up at him from a pair of honey golden eyes. ''All right. All right, I give up. You win.''

Her arms snaked around his neck, and she squeezed him hard. ''Thank you, Damien. You won't regret this.''

Oh, but he already did.

It was nearly dawn when she finally noticed the time and said good-night. And while he hated using mind control on her, he did invade her psyche just a little, instructing her to sleep the day through. He couldn't have her snooping around the mansion during the day, or taking off on her own and getting into trouble when he couldn't help her. She was just spirited enough to do either. Probably both. He was endlessly thankful that fire at her place had occurred at night. Otherwise, she'd be gone already.

Gone. The thought put a lump in his throat. He tried not to let it keep occurring to him over and over again after she'd gone up to bed, but it persisted anyway. He swallowed hard, and walked up the stairs to peer in at her. Some stupid need to see her once more, just to confirm that she really was alive and here with him.

He cracked the bedroom door. Naked longing, hunger, blood-lust welled up within him when he did. She lay there, amid the pile of covers she'd kicked away. Sound asleep. Her robe was a small soft puddle on the floor. If he were an artist, he'd paint her, just like this. Naked, relaxed, alive. Beautiful. One corner of the sheet clutched in her fist, held between her breasts. With everything in him he wanted to go to her, touch her, run his trembling hands over her flesh, explore her moist recesses with his fingers, his lips, his painfully erect arousal.

He pulled her door closed, pressed his back to the wall and drew a tormented, openmouthed breath, expanding his lungs until he thought they'd burst.

The thirst raged. The need. The hunger. And if she was going to be safe in this house, he had to find a way to assuage it. He knew, too well, that if he resisted, if he denied his savage nature too long, the craving would build and build until he was out of control. Until *it* took over.

That was the way it had been with the two dead women. He'd thought it would be all right. It had always been before. He'd only taken what they'd offered, sating his endless thirst in the process, feeding at their tender throats, quieting the monster within that demanded sustenance.

And for a few insane seconds in their arms, he might have taken leave of his senses. It was possible. Maybe he only regained his grip on sanity when he was home again, lying still, feeling their warm blood rushing through his veins.

No, dammit! He was certain he'd left them alive. He'd only sipped. He'd never be the instrument of a living being's death. Never. Anyone, a newborn baby, would be more likely to commit murder than Damien.

He tore himself away from the wall and stalked through the wide hallway, down the winding staircase. Now the hunger called again. This time, he wouldn't be stupid enough to deny its power over him. He wouldn't try to fight it or put it off. He couldn't let it grow until it reached the point of madness. Not again. Not with Shannon in the house. So near. So sweet.

She'd be succulent.

"No!"

Damien stopped in the center of the foyer, closed his eyes and focused on her mind, her soul. It took only a second to be sure she was still asleep. Before he left, he armed the security system. What he had in mind would take just a few minutes. No one could get to her in that amount of time. She'd be safe.

Damien slipped out into the night, whirled until he became only a gray blur to human eyes. And then he flew, a dark streak across the sky.

CHAPTER NINE

Shannon opened her eyes to see Damien standing at the foot of the bed, staring at her. His black eyes blazed. His jaw was tight, his stance rigid. He said nothing, just watched her.

She sat up, let the covers fall away from her body, and realized she was naked beneath them. She drew a gasp and jerked the covers up to her neck again. Then lifted her gaze to his. It hadn't wavered. She knew he'd seen her breasts for just an instant. She felt heat moving up through her face, a rush of embarrassment, and she couldn't keep looking at him. Her chin lowered until she saw only her fist, clutching the blankets to her throat.

She felt a tug. Then another. She glanced up fast. Damien held the bedclothes in his hands, just below her feet. He pulled them toward him. Slowly but steadily, the covers slipped away. She wanted to jerk them back...or at least part of her did, but she couldn't seem to move. Her arms were numb, heavy, useless.

Her breasts were visible now, and the blankets and sheets still kept slinking lower. Satin whispered over her hips, her thighs, her knees. She shivered, but it wasn't cold. Her ankles were exposed now. Her feet. Damien held the rumpled bundle of covers to one side and let it fall to the floor.

She couldn't roll away from those probing eyes, or lift her arms to cover herself. She sat still, immobilized by some force she didn't understand, as Damien's hot gaze explored every inch of her body. She saw the bulge at the juncture of his thighs beneath those tight black jeans he wore. She knew what was going to happen. She wasn't afraid. No. It was time. She wanted this. He took a single step toward the bed.

"Damien," she whispered.

"Let me love you, Shannon."

She couldn't catch her breath to answer, so she only nodded. He reached out to touch her—

Her eyes fluttered open, and she was alone in the room. Alone in the bed, under the soft weight of blankets and a comforter. She lifted the covers and peeked underneath. She'd slept in the buff for lack of a nightgown or any clothing at all except the loose-fitting robe, which tended to tangle around her legs. No wonder she'd had erotic dreams. The feel of satin sheets against her skin had been the inspiration, not the strange man of illusions. That was all it was. Just because he'd been invading her waking thoughts lately didn't mean he'd been the cause of her dream.

But she knew better than that, didn't she?

She grated her teeth and punched the pillow. She'd had a hell of a time getting to sleep. In some ridiculous part of her mind she'd been waiting for, even *expecting,* him to come to her. But he hadn't. Of course he hadn't.

She looked around for her robe, belatedly realizing it was dim in the room. Night already? She glanced at the little wind-up clock on the nightstand—7:15. Dusk. God, she never slept this long at once. Then again, she'd never had dreams like the one she'd just had, either. She sat up in bed, ran one hand across her forehead, and found it damp with sweat.

The knock came at her door and she jumped. Her gaze flew to the wood as his deep voice floated through.

''Shannon? Are you awake?''

She bit her lip. Her dreams had been accurate, if farfetched. They'd reproduced that satin touch of his voice on her senses. And the warmth of his breath, dampness of his lips as he'd whispered against her skin.

Not him, she reminded herself. My dream.

''Shannon?''

''Just a minute.'' She hopped out of bed, hugging most of the covers around her, still frantically looking for her robe or the clothes she'd taken off the night before. Nothing was to be seen.

She made it to the door, opened it a crack and peeked through at him.

He stood close to the door, as dark and mysterious as ever. Spotless white shirt, tight black pants with tapered legs. God, he was sexy.

"I brought you something to eat." He held a plate in one hand, but his gaze was fastened to her shoulders and her neck, and the fist with which she held sheets and blankets to her breastbone trembled. "Can I come in?"

She blinked. "I'm not exactly dressed—"

He shrugged and shouldered the door open, strolling in as though it were an everyday thing. "Shannon, I'm around half-dressed, beautiful women all the time. I can handle it, I promise." He sent her a smile as she clumsily adjusted her coverings under her arms. He set the plate on a nightstand.

"Yeah, maybe you can, but I can't." She crossed to the bathroom, blankets and sheets trailing behind her like Lady Di's bridal train. Tugging her tails in behind her, she closed the door. "Where are my clothes?"

"I asked Netty to get them cleaned for you. They're in the closet."

He sounded as if he stood right outside the bathroom door. She didn't hear him move away. "Well, would you kindly hand me something to put on?"

He chuckled, but a second later he knocked. She cracked the door and his hand poked through, clutching a pair of jeans and a sweatshirt, and fresh new underwear. "Those aren't mine."

"Netty did a little more shopping today. Can't have you wearing the same thing everyday, can we? Take them, Shannon. They won't bite."

She took the clothes and closed the door again, then quickly dressed.

"I don't know why you're bothering. You won't be in them long."

Shocked, she stared at the bathroom door. Finally, it seemed, he was ready to make a move. It wasn't at all what she'd envisioned. "That's the crudest proposition I've ever had." She opened the door and stood, hands on hips, facing him. Butterflies battled inside her stomach. She'd been right in reading the signs last night. He did want her. The moment of truth was here. "Can't you do any better?"

He touched her face, trailing warm fingertips over her cheek, until she fought the urge to close her eyes and lean against him. "I can do better. Don't doubt it. But that wasn't a proposition, Shannon. Just a statement of fact."

Her eyes popped open and she scowled. "You're taking this just a bit for granted, aren't you?" She hadn't even decided to say yes yet.

"You said you wanted to be my assistant until we caught the killer, didn't you?" She nodded mutely. "Well, you certainly can't do it dressed like that."

Embarrassment brought heat to her face, but she turned her head to hide it from his sharp gaze, and tried to convert the discomfort to something more constructive. "If you think I'm parading around onstage in one of those skimpy sarong skirts with a bikini top, the way your other assistants do, you're in for a surprise, Damien."

"You won't be parading. You'll be graceful, floating, dancing. And we only have about an hour to rehearse, so will you kindly eat this feast Netty cooked for you so we can get on with it?"

This was not right. He'd fed, just to be sure the hunger was assuaged, just to prevent himself from feeling this powerful lust for her. And he'd been sure he was perfectly in control when he'd come to the room. He'd marched in, with Shannon wearing nothing but a tangle of blankets, just to prove it to himself.

But all it had taken to convince him otherwise was a single glimpse of her smooth skin, bare shoulders and delicate neck, the outline of her collarbone under her skin, the shape of her jaw. The lust hit him again the second he'd set eyes on her, hit him as powerfully as it had before he'd fed. Something was wrong. This damned thirst must be getting stronger. He'd never felt the need again so soon. Never!

And it wasn't a temporary thing. The feelings grew more intense with every second he spent near her, until he was thinking of little else. He wanted to feel her warm flesh pressed to his own, to hear the sounds she made as he worked her body, drove her to madness, made her want the things he did.

But he couldn't make love to her. For all he knew he might kill her if he did. And even if he wasn't the one responsible for the deaths of those other women, he still had reason to keep a distance from Shannon. He didn't want to let his feelings for her get any stronger. It would kill him to care that much again. When she left—as she must—it would kill him.

What was wrong with him? There were so many things he ought to be focused on right now. The killer who stalked the streets of Arista, the person who might make Shannon his next target, for one. If he hadn't killed those two women himself, then he had to know who had, or the murders might go on and on. And this new power his nature seemed to be gaining. He needed to explore it, to find answers to the questions tormenting him. He should contact this Marquand. The man might have some answers.

And then there was Shannon and this mysterious illness he'd worried about since he'd first seen its effects. He had, he thought, the answers to that in his possession, in the supposed CIA man's files on her. But he hadn't had time to go over them yet, with her always so close. Or maybe it was the guilt he felt at blatantly invading her privacy that way. But he needed to do that, to find out what was wrong with her before it became worse. She'd admitted that attacks like that had happened before—

She whirled across his room, into his arms, and flipped backward in an apparent faint. He nearly dropped her, he'd been paying so little attention. Her body's jerking movements were proof she was fighting laughter, and her eyes popped open a second later.

"I don't know how I'm going to get through this without giggling, Damien. It's so dramatic. I'm not a dramatic person."

He couldn't help but smile at the sparkle in her eyes, the dimples in her face. "No, I'd call you more irreverent than dramatic." He lifted her upright again and took his arms from around her. Holding her like this was too much, even now.

Netty's clapping came from the doorway and she hustled forward. "'Course it seems absurd now, Shannon, wearing blue jeans and dancing in a living room. It'll all be different onstage, when you're in costume and the music is thrummin' in your ears and all that misty stuff is twirlin' around your legs. You'll see."

"You think so?"

Netty wiped her hands on her apron and sent Shannon a wink. "Oh, I know these things. Toured with the Somerset Theatre Troupe in London when I was in my prime. Played Eliza Doolittle. Knocked 'em dead, I did."

Damien frowned. "You never told me that, Netty."

"You never asked," she replied. "Truth be told—" she tilted her head, addressing Shannon "—he's always been such a cold fish, I was beginning to wonder if there beat a heart in that big chest of his. He's different now, though, since you been comin' round."

Damien opened his mouth to tell Netty she was overstepping, but she cut him off before he said a word.

"Got to get to it, if I'm going to get to the theater in time to see Shannon's debut. If there's nothing else...?"

Damien shook his head.

"Thank you for the clothes, and the meal, and everything else you've done for me," Shannon said as Netty turned to go.

"Nothin' of it, child. You remind me of an orphan in need of motherin'. I like coddling you just a mite."

Shannon's eyes widened, but Netty was already on her way out the door. She glanced at Damien as if dumbfounded.

"What is it?"

"What she said, I..." She blinked twice, then shook her head. "Just a coincidence, I guess. Never mind."

* * *

A short time later, she tugged at the bottom of the leopard-print bikini top and nervously adjusted the knot in the side of the matching sarong skirt. Roxy, Damien's former assistant, had not been happy about the change. In fact, she'd thrown a fit, and Damien had been tossing out one excuse after another, until, fed up and wondering who the hell had a name like "Roxy" anyway, Shannon had stepped between them. "Look, toots, I'm a PI. Repeat it and you'll wish you hadn't. I'm taking your place because Damien's assistant is liable to end up as some lunatic's target. Repeat *that* and I'll break your jaw. If you think I can't, try me. Any questions?"

Roxy, tall and elegant, stared down at Shannon for a long moment, gaping. Finally, she glanced at Damien again. "This had better be legit, Namtar. I have a contract."

"You'll still be paid for every performance."

She nodded once, spared a parting glare at Shannon, then turned on her heel and left.

Shannon sighed, shaking off the memory of the nasty little confrontation and focusing instead on Damien's every move out there onstage. She struggled to remember everything he'd told her. Keep her head up, back straight. Be graceful, confident.

That she was beautiful, and would be terrific. That was the second time he'd called her "beautiful." She could learn to like it.

When he nodded toward where she stood, she braced her hands against the prop table-on-wheels and pushed it out onto the stage. Damien introduced her as his "delectable assistant, Shannon." She waved to the crowd as he'd told her to, and was surprised when they applauded her loudly. The rock music swelled, and the show got easier as she went along, handing Damien the props from the table, adding little flourishes of her own now and then. When the trick was finished and Damien gallantly kissed the back of her hand, she fanned herself and winked at the audience. They loved it, applauding wildly as she sauntered offstage, pushing the little cart. It wasn't nearly as tough as she'd expected it to be. And it was kind of fun. She could flirt with him as much as she wanted, and he'd just consider it all part of the act.

She was incredible. So full of mischief tonight, and her sense of mayhem and devilment spilled over. It was contagious. The crowd adored her.

But when the mist swirled around his legs, and the low, driving music began for the finale, he glanced offstage where she waited and saw the twinkle had faded from those eyes. She was serious. She knew there was no comedy in this part of the act. He took a moment to be thankful she had her mirthful streak under control. He held one hand out toward her, and she swirled to him as the volume swelled. He took her hand, and she stilled, facing the audience, just as they'd rehearsed.

With one fingertip on her chin, her turned her to face him. Then, with a flick of his wrist, his fingers fanned before her eyes. The music pumped louder. She let her eyes take on an entranced, blank sort of stare. Then he slipped one arm around her waist, feeling the warmth of her flesh burn his skin. His other hand cupped the back of her head and he bent her backward. Drawing a steadying breath, he lowered his head to her throat, parted his lips, caught her skin between them.

And the lust roared to life.

It wasn't supposed to happen this way. He'd told himself that it would fade as soon as he began his performance. He'd repeated this same act, sometimes while the hunger was paining him, but he'd never been so tempted to make it real. He was sated. He'd fed last night just to kill the rampant desire. Why was it convulsing in his brain?

Her skin was like satin, and salty against his lips. He kissed her throat, and couldn't stop his tongue from stroking a slow path over it. He felt her shudder in response to that, and he heard her whisper his name, for his ears alone, a plea barely audible in her voice. Her scent twisted into his nostrils. The soft thrum of her pulse seemed amplified in his ears. He could feel the rush of blood passing just beneath the skin. His teeth closed just a little, and he heard the startled breath she drew.

Shaking himself, he realized that her hands clutched the back of his head. Her fingers clenched and relaxed in his hair, again and again, as if on their own. Her head tipped back a little farther and the pressure on his head increased. Ever so slightly, she pressed her throat to his sucking mouth. Imploring. Offering. Submitting. His body began to shake. The need engulfed him. Sweat dampened his face.

With a deep growl he hadn't meant to emit, he released her, tugged her arms from around him and lowered her, quickly and roughly, to the floor.

The crowd roared, coming to its feet as one entity. Damien faced them, blinking. For a few brief seconds he'd forgotten their existence. There'd been nothing but Shannon, the taste of her, the desire that suddenly exploded inside him. He'd even forgotten the capsule of stage blood he was supposed to break open and apply to her neck.

She was lying there, motionless except for the rise and fall of her chest as she breathed far faster than she ought to. His gaze was caught for a moment, mesmerized by the subtle lifting of her scantily covered breasts. They were large and round and soft. The valley between them seemed like a magnet to his lips, his face.

He looked away, sweeping the hair that had fallen to stick to his damp forehead with one hand. Without waiting for the curtain to fall and lift again, he swept the satin cloak over his face and whirled.

It was a raven that emerged from the fallen folds of his cloak tonight. It swooped out over the crowd before returning to the stage and then diving off stage right. The curtain came down to thunderous applause.

Ah, yes, this was going so well. Anthar watched, having only slipped into the theater in time for the finale. He was convinced Damien had been so engrossed in his pretty assistant that he hadn't even detected the presence of another ancient one. Of course, he never had. Anthar was good at veiling his presence from others. Still, he'd never been this close. Always before, he'd observed from a great distance, shadowed Damien's steps, witnessed his nights with those other two. But Damien had never sensed him there, and he didn't seem to have noticed Anthar's presence tonight, either. That was good. The fool was obviously enamored of the girl, obviously fighting with himself to keep his lust from sating itself on her. It was only a matter of time, then. Just as soon as Damien's will dissolved and he took the beauty to his bed, as soon as he ravaged her body and drank from her throat, Anthar would know. He was never far from Damien, always watching. He'd know when it happened, and then Anthar would move in.

It would be nothing to finish the job, to drain her dry. And he'd leave her in the bed where Damien had taken her, and he'd let that bastard find her there, let him believe her death belonged to him. Let him think he'd killed the one he loved.

Ah, the torment, the agony he'd feel then! It would be sheer beauty to see. And then the once-great king would take his own life. Anthar had no doubt of it at all. Gilgamesh the Great would be no more. His punishment, Anthar's vengeance, was at hand.

Anthar rubbed his hands together with glee and made his way out of the theater.

"You really are wonderful, Damien. They love you. Listen to them—they're still cheering."

Damien tried to take in her words without hearing the soft silken sounds of her voice. Erotic the way it stroked his ears, the way he could conjure it whimpering, sighing, crying out his name in the heights of pleasure.

Focus on something else, you idiot. Anything. The crowd, focus on the crowd.

He opened his mind, hoping the sensations of others would drown out his own. He'd feel their adoration, their love. It would be enough. It had always been enough. The only connection in his life, the only emotion he allowed himself. The love of the crowds. He deliberately ignored the voice of Shannon's thoughts, concentrating on those still cheering in the theater. And then his head came up sharply, and he grated his teeth.

Another, like him, was here tonight. Another vampire. God, he'd thought of this explanation for the murders, even tried to convince himself of it. But he hadn't really believed. Not fully. There'd been a big part of him that still believed he was the killer, and there wasn't another one like him for hundreds of miles. But one was here, tonight.

And the bastard was getting closer.

Damien leapt to his feet just as the door to his dressing room swung open. He gripped Shannon's arm, ignoring her questions, pulling her to stand behind him.

The man stood motionless in the doorway, staring at Damien. His eyes were black, his hair as raven as Damien's was. He smiled just a little and nodded, his gaze slipping past Damien to where Shannon stood behind him.

"I enjoyed the performance," he said slowly, carefully, and there was a slight accent to his words, maybe French. "You're talented, Miss Mallory."

"Thank—"

"Don't talk to her. Don't even look at her, or I'll tear you apart, right here." Damien was breathing too rapidly, and the rage that infused him was surprising.

One of the man's dark brows arched upward, as if he were puzzled. "There's no reason to be so hostile, Damien. I only came to talk to you."

"Then we'll talk alone."

"I assure you, I can be discreet, if that's what concerns you." He gave his head a small shake. "Perhaps this was a bad idea. Since you refused to answer my letters, I thought to see a performance, try to get a word with you in person. I ought to have respected your privacy." He took a step backward.

"What letters? What are you talking about?" Damien demanded.

Shannon wrenched herself free of his restraining hand, thanks to his momentary distraction, and stepped around him. "Don't go.'' She slanted Damien a sideways glance. "Honest to God, I've never seen you so rude. What's the matter?'' As she spoke she extended a hand, and the stranger took it, brought it to his lips. But when he lifted his head he was frowning.

Damien gripped Shannon's other arm and pulled her away from the stranger. "Who are you, and what do you want?''

But the other man's eyes remained on Shannon, and they were darker than before. "You'd best lie down, Miss Mallory. You aren't well.''

Damien glanced at her, noting for the first time the paleness in her face, the coolness of her skin where he held her wrist. He closed his fingers, and felt the rapid patter of her pulse. And she was beginning to tremble, just a bit.

"I'm fine. Just a little tired.''

The stranger's eyes sought Damien's, and the man shook his head so slightly it was barely a movement at all, as if to say, "She is not fine. Not at all.''

Shannon drew a deep breath, and Damien saw her stiffen her spine. "I would like to go home, though. This theater is cold as a meat locker. Maybe you and Damien could talk there, Mr....''

"Marquand,'' he said smoothly, his accent utterly charming and seeming to fit perfectly with his Old World way of speaking. "Eric Marquand, and I think that's a wonderful idea.''

"Marquand,'' Damien repeated. He closed his eyes, realizing his mistake, then wondering about it. How long had this Marquand been in town? Long enough to have committed two murders?

Stop being a fool, Damien, and get this woman someplace she can rest. She's on the verge of collapse. Can't you sense it?

The voice, coming into his mind so clearly it was as if the other man had spoken, took Damien by surprise. He'd never used the telepathy, always kept his mind closed and rarely spoke to others, except to command his victims to remember his visits as a dream.

He shook off the surprise and looked at Shannon again, this time attuning his mind to hers, as well. He felt the queasiness swirling in her stomach, the unbalanced feeling in her head, the cold creeping into her bones. Inanna forbid, not another attack!

"Shannon?"

"Fine... I'm fine."

But her speech was slurred, and her cold skin began to warm under his hand. He scooped her up and shouldered past the stranger. His questions could be answered later. Now all that mattered was caring for her, seeing her through this episode. Damn, why hadn't he found the time to read those files? Why?

CHAPTER TEN

By the time Damien's Jaguar sped into the driveway, she was barely conscious, shaking violently, burning with fever. He hit the brakes in front of the mansion, skidding on the gravel. He threw the door open, jumped out and ran to her side. His heart was in his throat as he bent to pick her up. It was bad. Whatever the hell this thing was, he knew it was bad. And it scared him. Maybe he shouldn't have brought her here, though she'd insisted. He ought to have called the paramedics, someone.

He started for the front door at a run...then froze when he saw the man who stood there, waiting. Enough like Damien to be his brother. Apparently, this Eric Marquand was powerful enough to travel faster than Damien could with the car.

The man nodded, grim faced, and opened the door.

Damien strode through, straight into the circular room Shannon liked so well, and lowered her to the sofa. The bold bastard came right in behind him, and Damien whirled. "Get the hell out!"

"Do you want to help her or not?"

His voice was very smooth, very calm. His accent barely noticeable. Damien tried to scan the man's thoughts with his unpracticed mind. He sensed no malice there. "*Can* you help her?"

"I'm not certain."

"If you hurt her, I'll kill you."

One dark eyebrow arched higher than the other. "For one so ancient you're very uninformed about our kind, aren't you, Damien? I could no more harm one of the Chosen than you. None of us can. None that I know of, at least." He glanced once more to the sofa where she lay trembling violently. "Blankets. Heavy ones. Stoke the fire, as well."

Damien scowled at the man. He was torn between wanting to set himself between Shannon and anyone who might be a threat to her, and his desperate need to help her. She moaned helplessly, and the sound slashed a path right across his heart, laying it open, making it bleed. He hurried to her side, sat on the sofa beside her. For all he knew this stranger could be the murderer. He wasn't about to leave Marquand alone with her. Not for a second.

"You'll find blankets in the closet at the top of the stairs." Marquand nodded, started to move away. Damien focused the power of his mind on the hearth, and the flames blew higher, roaring and snapping like a torch. The other man stiffened and sent an awed glance Damien's way before he continued up the stairs.

It was an hour this time before she calmed, and then she slept as if comatose. The young vampire had been of some help after all, feeding her some brew he'd concocted to ease her pain, lower the fever, and help her rest. Now he paced before the roaring fire, looking grim and sober.

"Why did you come here?" Damien finally asked, when he could drag his gaze away from Shannon's pale face. She'd be all right now. She had to be.

"If you've read my letters, then you know. I'm something of a scientist among our kind." He looked at Shannon and shook his head slowly. "I'd been warned against approaching you, but I have so many questions. I'm hoping you can answer them."

"Nothing more than that?"

Eric glanced at Damien, frowning. "I only came to see your performance, Damien. I've been hearing incredible things about you. My curiosity won out over my caution. Then, naturally, when I sensed this one's distress, I had no choice but to try to be of help." He tilted his head as he studied Shannon. "Never have I come across one so fair. Golden haired. Most are dark, like us." His head whipped around then, and that one irritating brow shot up again. "No need for that rush of jealousy, friend. I have a mate of my own. I've no desire to seduce yours."

"She is not my...*mate,* as you so quaintly put it."

Marquand's lips thinned. "What are you going to do?"

"What *can I* do?" Damien's stomach twisted into a knot. "You can see for yourself how sick she is. But she refuses to let me take her to a hospital. Hell, I don't even know what's wrong."

Eric searched his face in apparent disbelief. "Have you never known one of the Chosen before, Damien?"

"Of course not!" Damien spun away from Shannon, shoving a hand roughly through his hair and pacing the room's length. "Dammit, Marquand, you think I *welcome* this attachment? This fierce need to protect and watch over her? What does it come to, except pain and loss? I hate feeling anything remotely like this." With his audiences, he could accept the love and still remain distant. Somehow, it wasn't enough anymore.

Eric only stood, unbearably calm, and stared into the flames. "You have much to learn, my friend."

"Don't call me that. I have no friends. I don't want to have any."

Eric shrugged. "As you say. Still, there is much you need to know. About her, for example. How old are you, anyway?"

"Almost six thousand years." He heard the man gasp. "You can see you're just a child in comparison."

Eric came forward, gripped Damien's arm. "Were you the first?"

The light in the man's eyes was nearly blinding when he asked the question. "Why are you so curious?"

Eric's hand fell away. "I don't know. I've spent my entire existence questioning, seeking answers, experimenting."

"And I've spent mine in seclusion—except for the performances. I want no closeness at all." He glanced at Shannon. "She had to come to the theater that night. I'm afraid she might be dying. God help me, what if she's dying?"

"She may well be." Damien shook his head in instant denial, but the stranger went on. "None of the Chosen live beyond their fortieth year. None I've known of, at least, and I've tracked many through their lifetimes. This medicine I've developed is specifically to ease their discomfort at the end."

Damien's gaze was drawn inexorably back to her still, pale form on the sofa. The only color in her face were twin cherry blotches on her cheeks, from the fever. "I didn't know..."

"All right, my questions can wait. Yours are obviously more important right now. As I told you, Damien, I'm a scientist. The brutal truth is that these symptoms are what all of the Chosen ones experience near the ends of their lives. She's younger than most. Then again, her coloring is unique, as well. I'm certain that unless she is transformed, she'll die."

Damien swallowed hard and battled the bitter tears that fought to the surface of his burning eyes. He wanted to scream. To rant, to curse the gods. But he'd done all that once, long ago. It hadn't done any more good then than it would now. "How long?"

"How often do the attacks come?"

"This is the second time in under a week."

Eric nodded. "She has little time left, then. Days. Perhaps less. An attack will come, and she'll sleep, as she's doing now. Only it won't be sleep. It will be coma. And she won't wake from it. There is nothing to be done. The medication will keep her relatively comfortable." He moved forward, placing a hand on Damien's shoulder, squeezing gently. "I'm sorry, Damien. She won't suffer, I promise you."

Damien shook off the hand and walked slowly toward her. He fell to his knees beside the sofa and caught her warm hand in both of his. "I can't do this again. I can't watch her die."

"Damien, there are few mortals in this world who'd be emotionally stable enough to live as we do. It's not an option to be taken lightly—"

"The alternative is to let her die."

Marquand came forward, his steps soundless, stopping just behind Damien. "Would she want this? Does she even know it is possible?"

Damien said nothing. He only let his eyes trace the exquisite bone structure of her face. The delicate line of her jaw. The cheekbones. The satiny skin that covered them. And those lips, so full and plump, and slightly parted now as she rested. He couldn't bear to see her robbed of life. Not her, not the most vital, the most utterly alive person he'd ever known.

"She won't die this time, Damien. She'll recover. You'll have time to explain this to her, give her a choice. She'll need time to accept it as a viable alternative, time to consider the implications. It has to be her decision." He shook his head slowly. "And it will have to be made soon."

Damien felt a burning dampness flood his eyes. "Tell me something, Marquand. I think I already know, but tell me anyway."

"Anything," he said gently.

"Did you kill two women in Arista?"

He was silent for a long moment. "You're right. You know the answer to that already. I don't kill, Damien."

Damien dropped her hand, stood and faced the young one. "No, I didn't think you did. I would've known, I think. So this—" he lifted his palms up "—this curse. It's not even an option I can offer her. Not really."

Eric Marquand shook his head quickly as if trying to clear it. "Why not?"

"You've got no idea, do you? No, of course not. You're so young, so innocent. Where do you get your sustenance, Marquand? Animals?"

"Blood banks, and what difference does it make?" He scowled at Damien. "Where do you get yours?"

Damien paced from the sofa, deliberately keeping his back to them both. "Humans. The need…" His jaw felt tight. He lowered his head, covered his eyes with one hand. "Dammit, it gets stronger, more powerful with age. It becomes a living thing, impossible to resist. And only living blood appeases." He heard the words thickening in his throat, his voice becoming hoarse. "I can't see her die, but I can't condemn her to live like this." He lifted his head, found himself facing the tiny figure of Inanna. Her half smile seemed smug, knowing. He removed the glass, clutched her figure in his fist, raised his hand. "Damn you. Damn the world and everyone in it!" His trembling fist clenched tighter and the figure he held crumbled to bits beneath the pressure. He felt his face contort, and he bowed his head, pressing his fist to his brow as the dust and bits sifted through his fingers.

Marquand came forward. "Get hold of yourself, Damien. You have to explain this to me. Please, for her sake if nothing else. Are you saying…you kill?"

He didn't seem as much repulsed as he was fascinated. He stood beside Damien near the fire, studying him intently.

Damien lowered his fist, flung the remnants of the statue into the fire. "I didn't think so." He thought of the two women who'd ended up dead, and his fear that he'd been responsible. But he wouldn't divulge his deepest terror to this stranger.

"You needn't tell me, Damien. I hear you clearly."

Damien started, then twisted his head to stare at this stranger. "Damn you, stay out of my head!" He wasn't at all used to being around other beings capable of reading his thoughts. He'd mastered the art of keeping others' thoughts and feelings out of his mind, but never of guarding his own. There'd been no need.

"No matter," Eric said lightly, and Damien knew he was glad to have changed the subject. "It's easily learned. I'll help you. Tell me now, when did the need become so powerful? At what age did it become necessary to take from the living?"

Damien shook his head, devastation racking his body. Why didn't this child take his questions and leave him to suffer alone? Suffer? It wasn't a strong enough word. This was Enkidu all over again! The grief would kill him this time.

"I only ask because I want to help you."

"No one can help me."

"Dammit, Damien, don't be so…Enkidu? Is that the name you just—"

Damien whirled to face him. "Stay out of my thoughts, fledgling, or you'll go up in a ball of white-hot flames."

To his utter shock, the young man smiled. "Rhiannon said you could do it. I wasn't sure I believed her."

"Who the hell is Rhiannon?"

"Rhianikki, princess of Egypt. Only around three thousand

years younger than you. Until now she was the oldest vampire I knew. But she's never exhibited this lust you claim. I mean, she does occasionally sip from the living, but only because she so enjoys driving Roland to the edge of frustration. That's why I asked when this powerful thirst took over."

Damien looked up slowly. *Roland.* He recalled the name. He'd helped a vampire by that name a couple of years ago. Poor bastard had been drugged and left for the sun. And Damien had gone to him, despite his vow of solitude. But he'd gone in disguise.

"Damien?"

He started, recalling the question. "Certainly more than thirty centuries ago." He searched Eric's face.

"You see? If it hasn't affected her, then there must be a reason. Something she's done or been exposed to that you have not. Perhaps I can find out what it is."

Damien's eyes narrowed in suspicion. "What is it you want from me, Marquand?" Hell, he sounded like Shannon now, questioning Marquand's motives.

"I want you to talk to me. Tell me everything. How you were made, by whom, when. I want to know if it's true that you can alter your form, and that you've accomplished flight. I want to know how you do these things. I want—"

"And in return, you'll try to find the answer to my unquenchable thirst." Damien turned in a slow circle and finally sank into a chair. "It's getting worse since I met her, you know. All it takes is her scent to drive me insane."

Eric laughed. "Yes, well, that isn't exactly the same hunger, my—Damien. I feel that, as well, at a simple glance from Tamara. You know that the desire for sexual release and the bloodlust combine in us, each feeding from the other, until it's impossible to distinguish them."

Damien's brows lifted and he studied the man again. He really did have a lot of knowledge.

"It's true," Eric said. "And that kind of frenzied need is only at its worst when the object of it happens to be the woman you love.''

''I don't love her!'' Damien roared the denial, shooting to his feet. ''And I'm damned well not going to.'' He paced in a small circle, trying to contain his rage, trying not to vent all his anguish on Marquand, who was only trying to help. ''All right. I'll agree to tell you everything you want to know. But I don't believe you can find a way to solve my problem, so I want you to agree to do one other thing in return.'' He returned to his seat.

''Name it,'' Eric said quickly, settling into a chair opposite him.

Damien folded his hands to keep them from clenching into fists. ''I need help to find the truth about the deaths of those two women. I need all the help you can give me. And if it turns out…if it turns out that I killed them…'' He looked at Eric, at his honest, intense gaze. He was beginning to sense that he could trust this man. ''Then I want you to destroy me.''

He hadn't wanted to believe the things Eric Marquand, the intellectual, had told him. That she was dying. That there was nothing that could save her mortal life. But as Damien sat beside the bed where he'd moved her and scanned the files this CIA person had kept on Shannon, he found only confirmation of what Eric had said. The medical reports were inconclusive. Her red blood cells seemed to be dying, inexplicably. Transfusions hadn't helped. The new red cells died almost as soon as they were infused. And her rare blood type would have made transfusions an all-but-impossible treatment anyway.

The Belladonna antigen. Eric had explained all about it. The Chosen, as they were called by the undead, were humans with the Belladonna antigen in their blood, apparently handed down from a common ancestor. They were the only people genetically capable of being transformed. All the undead had shared the same rare blood type as mortals.

Their other traits were not so easily explained. The way they exuded something that alerted vampires of their presence. The way the undead felt compelled to watch over them, protect them. It was, Marquand theorized, a chemical reaction of some kind.

But as Damien stared at Shannon's pale face, her golden tresses spread over the pillows, he knew that what he felt for her was more than chemically induced. He had to find a way to save her.

The files were thorough, and he read them front to back. They told of her mother's abandonment. Her childhood of being pushed and shoved from one agency to another.

At sixteen, she'd arrived at the last of the foster homes, where she'd met Tawny. And a few months afterward, both girls had disappeared. There was a notation that the man who'd been her foster parent was later convicted of child molestation, diagnosed as a pedophile and institutionalized. He'd committed suicide a few months later.

The bastard. If he wasn't dead already, Damien would have hunted him down and done the job himself.

"What are you reading?"

He looked up quickly, then set the papers aside and leaned over the bed. It was no wonder she wore the crusty exterior all the time. She'd had to develop a shell to protect her from life. He held her hand in both of his, and his initial urge on seeing her eyes open and looking at him was to press his lips to her fingers, her knuckles. Instead he lowered her hand to the bed.

"How are you feeling?"

"Better. Fine, actually."

But she wasn't fine. She was lying to him about that. She was dying, and she knew it. She'd known it for some time. He felt incredible relief at seeing the color slowly returning to her skin, the sparkle to her eyes, but he didn't let that relief show. She wasn't comfortable with his relief. Or his concern. And it occurred to him that she didn't want him to care about her. She never had. Now he understood why.

He got up, fighting against an insistent lump in his throat that wanted to choke him. He couldn't let her know that he was aware of her condition. She'd probably never forgive him for prying. Besides, talking to her about it meant dealing with it himself, and he wasn't sure he could do that. Not yet.

He'd let himself care about her. He was going to lose her. It was going to hurt. At least now he knew. Maybe he could keep his feelings from growing any stronger than they already had. Maybe he could minimize the damage, keep his head. Find a way to help her.

He flung back her covers and held out a hand. "Come on, get up. You have any idea how long you've been lying around? All last night, all day today while Netty fussed over you. It's night again, and she refuses to go home until she sees you're feeling better. Come on downstairs or we'll never get rid of her."

She looked uncertain. And then she smiled and slipped her hand into his. He tightened his grip, just a little. "You strong enough, Shannon? Do you want me to carry you?"

Before she could answer, the bedroom door flung wide. Netty stood in the doorway, glanced at Shannon and screamed like a banshee. She ran across the room with staccato steps and folded Shannon in a powerful hug.

She released Shannon only long enough to turn to Damien. "Out with you. She's wantin' a bath and a change of clothes, and then some tea." She put an arm around Shannon and urged her toward the bathroom. "You're goin' to be just fine, my girl. Netty will see to that." But Shannon's eyes met Damien's and he felt the warmth in their message.

"Go on now. Your friend, Mr. Marquand, is waitin' downstairs. I'll bring her along when she's ready."

Damien gathered up the papers he'd been reading and left the room.

All the while she bathed and dressed, and sat quietly while sweet Netty pulled a brush through her hair, the knowledge was eating away at her guts. Damien ought to know the truth. He'd been so good to her, and he deserved to know the truth. If he let himself care about her, even a little bit, it would only lead to pain. And he did care, a little. Much as she'd hoped he never would, and much as he tried not to let it show, he couldn't hide the look in his eyes when she'd woken up just now.

He'd gone through the agony of losing a friend. So had she. So had the mighty Gilgamesh myriad years ago, and it had brought him to a grief that had devoured his soul. She knew now, since their conversation about the epic by the fire, that Damien's grief was a lot like Gilgamesh's. He'd survived a loss that should have crippled him. What would happen if history repeated itself? He couldn't get through it again—she was sure of that. So the only answer was to tell him now, before he let himself care too much.

Is that the way it is with friends?

Enkidu's dying words echoed in her ears. For a second she heard them, as if she'd been there when they were spoken, in a voice gone weak and gravelly with physical pain, instead of having heard them read with that same emotion by Damien, identical agony racking his voice.

Netty helped her down the stairs and left, wishing her good-night before grabbing her coat and leaving for the evening. Seemed every time she saw the woman, Netty was leaving. Of course, that was because she'd been keeping such odd hours since she'd come here. Up all night, sleeping all day while Netty bustled around the place.

Shannon moved toward the library, with her heart breaking. God, how much she would like to have one night with Damien, one night to explore this electric pull he seemed to emanate for her, to discover the secrets of passion. To let him teach her all of them. It wouldn't be fair to him, though. She couldn't allow herself to get close to him, not physically, not emotionally. She had to warn him of the grim future, and then let him go. Let him distance himself from the pain, avoid it.

She stopped near the library door, startled to see two dark heads leaning over the desk. Damien looked up, saw her and shot to his feet. In less than a second he'd crossed the room, and for an instant she was sure he would sweep her into his arms. He'd hold her tight to his chest, his trembling hands clenched in her hair, and she'd hear his ragged sigh, feel his muscles slowly relax.

He'd never held her that way before. Except by accident, when she'd fallen from the chair. Her response would be automatic and irresistible. Her arms would wind around his waist. Her face would press into the white shirt, and her eyes would fall closed. When she inhaled, his scent would fill her, and when she exhaled she'd feel the warmth of her breath spread through the material beneath her face.

The fantasy died when he reached her and stopped. He stood away from her, his hands on her shoulders as if she might fall without support. He was touching her, but it was impersonal. A matter of courtesy rather than passion. And since she was determined to keep her distance from him, she ought to be grateful for it.

"You all right?"

She swallowed hard, nodded. But she wasn't. And she had to tell him she wasn't. "Fine, now."

"You shouldn't be up, Shannon. You need to rest—"

"There'll be plenty of time to rest when I'm…later. I feel fine now, really." She glanced past Damien, noticing the man she'd met just before she'd collapsed sitting at the desk, watching the two of them. "Hello again. I'm afraid I don't remember—"

"Marquand. Eric to you. You look a good deal better than when I last saw you." He rose and came forward as he spoke in that odd, old-fashioned way of his. His trousers were knife pleated, his jacket cut short, and both were spotlessly black against his crisp white shirt. "I'm glad you're feeling better."

"Thank you." She glanced toward the desk, the papers that littered it, and frowning, hurried forward. "What's all this?" She fingered the sheets, reading the bold print. "DPI?" She looked quickly toward Damien, then back to Eric Marquand. "Then this government agency is for real?"

Eric nodded grimly. "The Division of Paranormal Investigations," he explained. "A subdivision of the CIA and, I believe, the employer of your acquaintance, Mr. Bachman."

She turned slowly, staring first at Eric and then Damien in blatant disbelief. "*Paranormal* investigations? As in ghosties and ghoulies and things that go bump in the night? Is this where my tax money is going? But I thought the guy was just burned out and—"

"It's a bunch of hogwash, Shannon." Damien came forward, scooping the outspread papers together into a neat stack and dropping them into a desk drawer.

"But why are they investigating you? And why me, for God's sake? There's nothing the least bit paranormal about me." Neither man spoke, though Shannon waited expectantly. Then she recalled the questions Bachman had asked. He'd been interested in Tawny's murder. He'd taken possession of her body. He'd...

"You're saying that what was in Bachman's files was true, not just a lunatic's ramblings. This agency really does believe in vampires. Not only that, but they think there's one on the loose in Arista."

Damien opened his mouth, but Eric beat him to the punch line. "Yes, they do."

She felt her jaw drop and her eyes widen. She turned to Damien. "They think it's you, don't they?"

"They use government funding to investigate seemingly paranormal events," Damien explained calmly, sending Eric Marquand a look that could have wilted fresh roses. The look Eric shot back was almost as bad. They obviously disagreed over how much to tell her. "I imagine their main goal is in uncovering hoaxes, Shannon. Maybe they'll be able to find out how Tawny's death was staged to appear so much like some vampire's handiwork."

She frowned, shaking her head. "Are you sure that's all it is?" Her gaze sought Eric's, but he averted his eyes, saying nothing at all. She shot Damien another, probing, stare. "Because, Damien, if this Bachman's opinion is representative of the whole agency, then these people are serious. Your image could be digging you into a bottomless pit. On the other hand, it ought to be fairly easy to humor them. I'm telling you, fanatics can be dangerous, and this crew would have to be pretty fanatical to believe..."

She turned from him, pacing the floor. "You could fix it, though. Stage a press conference in broad daylight. Offer to undergo a series of tests, blood work, whatever. Get a photo op on the arm of a priest, that type of—" She stopped midtirade, stood in one spot and gazed from one man to the other. "What? What's wrong with you two, why are you watching me like that?"

"I'm going to leave now," Eric said softly, and the look he sent Damien was filled with unspoken messages.

"Eric, why are you involved in this, anyway?"

He smiled at her. "I've had a few run-ins with DPI before. I thought I might be of some help." He turned, nodded to Damien and left.

She watched him go, frowning in bewilderment. What was going on between the two of them? They obviously knew something they hadn't let her in on. She turned back to Damien, puzzled, then saw the nervous way his eyes moved over her face, the anxiety there, and she sighed. He was still worried about her.

She licked her lips. "We, um...we need to talk."

He nodded, but didn't seem to be looking forward to a heart-to-heart.

Telling him the truth about her health could wait. There were secrets being kept and she didn't like it one bit.

Coward. You're jumping at any excuse to put it off, and you know it.

"I'd like to know what was going on down here."

He shrugged, turning his back long enough to stroll around the desk. "We were talking about the murder, just tossing ideas back and forth. Eric wants to help us get to the bottom of this thing."

She waited. He stood there and stuffed his hands into his deep pockets, as if he didn't know what else to do with them, as if he were nervous.

"And you were talking about Bachman and this DPI. How are you going to deal with him, Damien?"

"I haven't decided yet. But not by blowing an image I've worked years to perfect."

She threw her hands in the air, palms up. "Damien, if the man thinks you're a *vampire,* you have to do *something.*"

"No, I don't."

She narrowed her eyes, moving forward until she could lean over the desk and look him in the eye. "You're keeping something from me. Don't deny it. I can see it in those black eyes of yours. What is it, Damien?"

"Nothing that needs to concern you, Shannon."

She squinted, as if that would clarify whatever was hiding beneath his words. "If it concerns Tawny's murder, then it concerns me." She shook her head in anger, and paced away from him. "Don't you get it yet, Damien? I'm *living* to get this guy. There's nothing more important to me. Nothing."

When she turned to face him again, saw the intensity in his black eyes, she almost amended that. There was something as important, rapidly approaching *more important* to her. Him.

"And we will."

"How?"

"We've already put the wheels in motion by having you appear with me last night. Be patient. Give it some time."

"I can't be patient. And I don't *have* time." He closed his eyes when she said that, as though she'd poked him with a hot needle. She rushed on. "I mean, you only have one more show, Damien, and then it'll be over. If he doesn't make a move, we might never know who he is."

"We will," he insisted.

She rolled her eyes, flipped her head back and turned in a slow circle, sick to death of his vague assurances.

He caught her shoulders in his hands, stopping her. "I have a surprise for you. Why don't you forget about all of this for just little while. You've been sick. You deserve to relax."

She lowered her chin, searched his eyes. "A surprise?"

He nodded, gripped her hand and drew her out of the library, through the hall to the circular living room and then along the arched corridor to the front door. He opened it wide and waved one arm with a flourish. *"Voilà."*

The Stingray glistened beneath its freshly applied coat of candy-apple red paint. Even its tires gleamed like new. "Is that...*my* car?"

He was pulling her down the front steps, into the biting October wind. It tossed his dark hair in a way that made her want to push her fingers through it. He stopped by the car, opened the driver's door, then ran around to the passenger side and slid in. She was still standing by the open door, shaking her head.

"Come on, get in. It's freezing out there."

She couldn't speak. A brick or something equally huge and rough-edged was lodged in the back of her throat. She sat down in the driver's seat, reached for the key and paused, her eyes widening. "What is that?"

She glanced sideways at Damien. He reached forward and pushed a button. The Spin Doctors' latest hit blasted from the newly installed CD player, rattling the windows. She reached up and turned it down. When she looked at Damien again, she found herself battling tears. "Why?"

He shrugged. "You wanted it red. I had the money. Why not?"

It was so thoughtful, so sweet, that he'd remembered her story about the Matchbox car. Even down to the color. "And the CD player?"

"You seemed to like mine."

No one had done anything so nice for her, not since Tawny had given her that stupid little Matchbox car on her birthday. She didn't want him to care about her, dammit...

But, God, it felt good to know that he did. Good and sad and terrible all at once.

She reached a hand up, touched his face. His eyes darkened. She could barely see them through the veil of tears in her own. His lips trembled slightly.

And then he turned away. "It's no big deal, Shannon. Come on, start her up and get some heat in here. Let's take it for a drive." He reached up to turn the volume higher.

Shannon bit her lip. Then she started the car.

CHAPTER ELEVEN

She ejected the Doctors and slipped in the brand-new Sting CD. Damien had a boxful of CDs stashed in the glove compartment. The guy was full of surprises. She didn't know why it felt like some kind of exquisite torture having him do something so wonderful for her. She wasn't sure if it hurt or felt good. She didn't know whether to laugh or cry, to feel ecstatic or depressed. And feeling both was exhausting and confusing.

She knew only that the small car put them close to each other, and the sentimental words flowing from the speakers now in that husky voice filled what little space remained between them. She could smell Damien, feel his warmth. An odd zing of energy, one she only felt when they were close, whirred in her nerve endings. It was electricity and attraction and awareness, and something else. As they drove through the cool autumn night, with fallen leaves shooting up behind them as they passed, she found her gaze on Damien more often than the road. On his strong face, his deep, glittering onyx eyes and his sensual lips with their dramatic color. He didn't have flesh-colored lips like a lot of men. His lips looked like fruit that's ready to be picked. And she thought they'd taste the same way.

His hand shot out to jerk the wheel to the left. She swung her gaze back to the pavement, where it belonged, but knew it wouldn't remain there long. She pulled a U-turn at the first wide spot in the road and headed back toward his house.

If there was one thing she wanted before she died, it was to make love to this man. The only problem with that was that it would end up hurting him. She bit her lip, negating that thought inwardly. As deeply as Damien felt things, she might very well end up destroying him. She didn't want to do that, and it surprised her just how much the thought of causing him pain bothered her. She hadn't cared enough about anyone to give a damn if their feelings got hurt. No one but Tawny, at least.

And to think she'd believed he was a killer.

God, her feelings were all mixed up.

Okay, better to concentrate on her most important goal in life. Finding this killer. Driving around listening to *Ten Summoner's Tales* on a starry autumn night with this incredible man was wonderful, but it was getting her nowhere.

"You know, he's never going to make a move against me when I'm with you."

She glanced at him as she said it. She'd studiously avoided staring at him for the past few miles, but his eyes were on her, dark and deep and dreamy, when she met his gaze. He blinked, as though she'd distracted him from some deep thinking.

"What?"

"Our killer. He's not likely to attack me when you're at my side. You know that."

He averted his gaze. "Maybe I'm not in as big a hurry to see him try to murder you as you are."

"I'm in a hurry to catch him."

"I'm not going to let you walk around alone with a big bull's-eye painted on your forehead."

"Then you want to let him get away? Because that's what will happen, Damien."

He frowned, his wide sable brows touching. "We'll think of something."

"That's not good enough." She turned slowly into his winding driveway, and he used a remote control he had in his pocket to open the gate.

"After the next performance—"

"The *last* performance."

"Right. When it's over, we might stage something. Make it seem as if you're alone, when you really aren't. Try to trap him."

"I don't want to wait that long." Mostly because she doubted Damien would go through with it. He was way too protective

TWILIGHT ILLUSIONS

of her. It should irritate the hell out of her instead of making her want to hug him.

"Shannon, it's risky. It's using you like chum to bait a killer shark. It ought to be a last resort. With any luck he'll tip his hand before then, and we won't have to risk it."

She shut the engine off. She had her own ideas about how much they could and couldn't risk here. To her way of thinking, the biggest risk was the one that the killer would get away. Her life was no risk at all. It was all but over anyway. Where the hell was the risk in that?

"You're tired." He touched her shoulder.

"Hell, Damien, I've slept thirty-six straight hours. How can I be?" She didn't say she wasn't. She was. Drained.

"You're still pale."

She laughed a little. "Maybe this Bachman nut will think I'm a vampire next."

He didn't laugh with her. In fact, he looked pained for a second. She opened her door. "So, you won't let me try my plan tonight. I'm not up to fighting with you about it." She got out and started for the front door, knowing he was right behind her. "So how about we spend the rest of the night going over those notes Eric Marquand brought you? All that stuff about these DPI crazies." She waited at the door while Damien unlocked it, swung it wide and let her walk in before him.

"I've already gone over all that. There's nothing that can be of any help." He closed the door, locked it.

Shannon strolled nonchalantly through the short hall into the round room she was beginning to love. She let herself collapse backward onto the chaise. He didn't want her examining those papers Eric had given him. He'd locked them in the desk as soon as she'd entered the library and started looking at them. Strange.

"So, maybe tomorrow we can visit Bachman at his hotel, try to get him to answer some questions. What do you think?"

Damien blinked quickly. "I have a few appointments tomorrow. Business stuff. I'll have to be away for most of the day."

"Oh." She hoped her disappointment didn't come through in her voice. She wasn't eager to spend the day alone...

...*although,* the idea *did* present her with the perfect opportunity to take a peek at the papers in that locked desk.

He crossed to the hearth, tossed a couple of logs onto coals that never quite died down, then took a seat on the floor, amid the cushions. "Are you tired? You want to rest?"

"I'll be able to rest all I want tomorrow, while you're gone."

"That's a good idea."

She sat up, drawing her knees around underneath her. "So does that thing work?"

He followed her gaze to the wide-screen television. "Yes. I don't use it much. Can't say I'm overly fond of television. Mostly I watch the news and tapes of other magicians. Helps me spot my own flaws."

"If you have any flaws, Damien, believe me, they're invisible to the human eye."

He looked a little startled. She couldn't believe she'd actually done that. Flirted with him. She was a selfish bitch.

"I have them, Shannon."

Oh, why were his eyes drawing her to him like giant super-magnets? Why didn't she have enough character to resist? Why in the name of God was she sliding off the chaise and onto the floor beside him, curling up amid the pillows as if she just wanted to get closer to the fire. She did, and the fire was Damien.

"What are they? Your flaws."

His dark eyes were burning zigzag paths over her hair. "You'd run screaming if I told you."

She shook her head, and she read amazement in his eyes when her hair flew out around her and settled back to cover her shoulders. "It takes a lot to scare me. I'm not afraid of you."

His hand rose, floated magically upward, and his fingertips touched her hair, hesitant, unsure. "Maybe you should be."

She swayed forward, her mind no longer having any noticeable influence over her body's actions. She closed her eyes, tipped her face up and pressed her lips to his. They trembled a little, nearly pulled away. She pressed harder, parting her mouth in gentle invitation.

His sigh filled her. She drank it, and his hand slid more deeply into her hair, cupping the back of her head, holding her face to his. His lips opened and his tongue slipped between hers to lick at her mouth's interior. She opened wider, giving him all the access he could want. Her arms encircled his neck, and she kissed him with everything in her.

But he pulled away. He got to his feet, turning his back to her. He kept pushing a hand through his hair, and he bowed his head, staring into the fire. The tremors she felt racking her body were mirrored in his unsteady stance, his labored breathing.

"I'm sorry, Shannon."

She stayed where she was. If she got up, she'd go to him, throw herself at him like some desperate, love-starved wanton. She wouldn't do that, to herself or to him. "I'm not." She smoothed her hair a little and fought with her racing heart rate. "I've never been kissed like that before."

"Then the men you've known have been fools."

He still didn't look at her. She smiled at the compliment. A warm flood of pleasure rushed through her veins. "Wouldn't have mattered. I never wanted any of *them*."

She saw the way his spine stiffened. He couldn't have missed the implication. That she *did* want him. God, it was unfair of her to put him through this.

He turned slowly, looked at her. "Shannon, believe me, you don't want to waste yourself on me. Especially if you've never been with a man. That's something too precious to—"

"Be honest about it, at least." She got to her feet, frustrated and angry and hurt. She turned away.

He caught her shoulder, turned her around to face him. "Shannon, I'm sorry—"

"Don't be. I'll survive." She shook her head hard, so her hair flew over her face like a curtain. "I never thought I could ever want any man, Damien. Never believed it was possible. Ironic, isn't it, that when I finally do, it's a man who doesn't want me back?'' What was wrong with her? Why was she acting this way?

His hands on her shoulders trembled as they tightened, and suddenly she was crushed to his chest. His arms surrounded her, strong and hard, and her breasts pressed against him. His mouth covered hers, captured it, and his tongue delved and drank and stroked. Faster, rougher, deeper. She slid her arms around his neck, threaded her fingers in his raven hair and licked at his tongue with her own. God, he tasted good. She wanted him so much it was a living force inside her. She felt his hips grind against her and she arched toward him in response. His arousal pressed into her belly, rock hard and insistent.

A little tremor raced through her, along with memories she'd rarely allowed her mind to access. Memories of other hands, drunken, clumsy ones. And of fear. He seemed to sense her hesitance, because he lifted his head. ''Shannon?'' A choked whisper. Gleaming black eyes probed hers.

''Just promise you won't...hurt me.'' It was the voice of the little girl she'd been. The innocence she hadn't felt in so long.

His eyes fell closed. He levered himself away from her, just a bit, and his arms fell from around her, then rose to stroke her hair. ''I won't hurt you, Shannon. Not ever. And that's why this insanity isn't going to go any further.''

''Insanity?''

He pushed her away, turned her toward the arched doorway into the big dining room, urged her through it and beyond, past the library doors, to the wide staircase. ''Go to bed. Rest. And don't ever make the mistake of thinking that I don't want you, Shannon. I do. Too much.''

She turned, searched his face, not understanding. He'd ignited a fire in her blood and she wanted him to put it out. Here, now. She'd go up in flames if he didn't.

He averted his face, closed his eyes. ''Go on. Now.'' Cruel words. Angry tone. Or desperate.

She ran up the stairs, trying not to cry before she reached the bedroom. She didn't want him to see her cry, to hear her frustration. The door flew open at her touch, smashed into the wall behind it, marring the satiny wallpaper. Shannon slammed it closed behind her just as forcefully, and with her back pressed to the cool dark wood, she felt for the lock, turned it without looking. Her eyes squeezed tight against the pain of his rejection. Her teeth grated to hold it back, but the battle was useless. The tears came—bitter, loud, hot tears that blazed their paths into her skin.

He'd said he wanted her. He'd kissed her as if he wanted her. But if he wanted her, he could have had her tonight. She'd humiliated herself, acted like a whore, offered herself as freely as if she did it every day. He couldn't know how much it had taken for her to open herself up to him that way. He couldn't know how much it had cost her.

She sank to the floor, sobs tearing at her chest.

The vase hit the hearth and exploded into a thousand onyx shards, raining down on the marble tiles, the pillows, the Turkish rug nearest the fire. Damien clenched and unclenched his fists, fighting to resist the desire that threatened to overwhelm him. He'd never wanted anyone the way he wanted Shannon. She drove him insane with lust. Desire tore through his brain, roared in his ears like a living thing, like a dragon breathing fire to ignite his soul, to devour his mind.

Inanna herself could never inspire passion like this! Dammit, what Shannon did to him.

"Damien?"

He whirled, his face, he was certain, twisted in a fierce snarl that would frighten the life out of a god. Eric Marquand didn't seem frightened at all, though. He stood there, nodded as if in understanding. "Are you all right?"

"No, dammit, I'm not all right. Do I *look* all right to you?"

Marquand turned away, as if to warm his hands near the fire. Damien had a sneaking suspicion it was actually to keep his expression hidden. "Are you in love with her yet?"

Damien made a noise halfway between snort and sigh.

"That's the stupidest question... Of course not. You think I'm an idiot?"

"I didn't call you an idiot, Damien." Marquand still didn't look at him. It sounded as if there might be a slight smile hiding in his voice.

"It's physical desire. Nothing more. It's only because I'm spending too much time with her." Damien stalked into the entry hall, stopped near the door and snatched a coat from a peg on the wall. "I need to take a walk in the cold air."

"It isn't simple desire, Damien." Marquand stood beside him. "And walking isn't going to make it go away."

He thrust his fists into the coat, jerking it around him. "Oh, no? What is, then?" He injected enough sarcasm in his voice not to have it missed.

"Making love with Shannon."

Damien went utterly still, his back to Marquand. When he spoke, his voice came out as a rasping whisper, hoarse with pain and frustration. "I can't do that. I'm afraid..." He couldn't finish the sentence.

"Afraid you might kill her. I know. A hell of a predicament, my friend."

"I told you not to call me that."

"Keep telling me. I might listen someday." Marquand pulled his own coat on and calmly fastened the buttons, one by one. "Damien, I don't believe you killed those women, and I don't believe you could hurt Shannon even if you wanted to, but I suppose it's best to restrain yourself until we're sure." He clapped a hand to Damien's shoulder. "For now we'll walk, if you think it will help."

Damien turned slowly, searched this stranger's face, and felt, for the first time, the unseen bond between them. They were brothers. Marquand was sincere in wanting to help him through this hellish torment. That knowledge shook him to the core. For so long, he'd managed to avoid any kind of closeness, the slightest hint of caring. He couldn't imagine how to act, what to say. He swallowed hard, shook his head. It was as if, after wandering in darkness, lost, alone, without hope, someone had joined him. Someone with a candle.

I don't want this. Dammit, I don't want to care for this man...or for Shannon.

"Too late," a voice whispered from somewhere. Had it come from his mind or Marquand's? He glanced at the other man for an answer. Eric only smiled vaguely, and opened the door.

She couldn't have slept even if she'd wanted to, but she feigned sleep when she heard Damien's key in her door just before dawn. She knew he'd come in to stand over her, stare down at her. She felt his fingertips gently smoothing her tear-stained cheeks, pushing the tangled hair away from her face. She smelled him, felt his warmth, heard his breathing. She wanted to open her eyes, to reach up to him. God, she wanted to feel those strong arms around her again, crushing her so tightly against him. Making her feel he wanted to be closer, closer than any two people had ever been. She wanted to feel his heart racing in time with hers, but...

She slammed her mind tight against those thoughts, against *any* thoughts of him. She resisted the urge to move her face against his touch. She could almost imagine his thoughts trying to reach her, his mind telling her to rest today, to stay here until he came back for her, not to wake until he returned.

Strange, the things her mind conjured. She closed it to him, refused to hear the odd things she imagined he was telling her. Refused to think of him at all. A few moments later she felt the satin touch of his lips on her face. And then he was gone.

She stayed in the bed a long time, only rising when the soul of the house screamed its solitude, assuring her that she was alone. She showered, dressed and hurried down the stairs, calling out to Damien just in case. There was no answer.

She'd been a fool. She knew that now. The attraction she felt for the man had distracted her from her purpose, and she'd lost precious time. There was no chance for anything between them. God, she'd known it was wrong even to try. She ought to be glad he'd rejected her. It would save him heartache in the long run. She'd been selfish, thoughtless, to let him know she wanted him. She must have gone temporarily insane.

Not anymore, though. He was keeping things from her, things that had to do with Tawny's murder and with Bachman and this crazy organization, DPI. She had to find out what. How could she hope to track down a killer if she didn't have all the facts?

Shannon went to the library, glanced around the room once before closing the door. She circled the desk, stopping behind it to give the drawer an experimental tug. Locked, as she'd known it would be. She wasn't unprepared. It was nothing to break into a desk drawer. The letter opener on the blotter was all she needed, and the drawer slid open without any further encouragement.

The papers had been arranged neatly in a manila file folder. So he'd looked at them again. They were supposed to be nothing, a bunch of irrelevant information, so why had he felt the need to go through them one more time? And what was Eric Marquand doing with a packet of information on this strange government agency, anyway? He'd said he'd had run-ins with them in the past. What kind of run-ins? she wondered. She shook her head, grimacing. With his dark good looks and antiquated mannerisms, it wouldn't be surprising if the lunatics had accused Eric of being a vampire, too. Crazy.

She removed the folder from the drawer, closed it and carried it with her to the circular living room. It was a comfort room. Damien was right about that. There was something in its shape and the lighting, the warm colors, the odd furniture, even the artifacts lined up on the mantel, that seemed to hug you close, warm your soul.

Only red-orange coals glowed on the grate. Shannon arranged a pair of small logs on top and blew gently until flames licked to life. Resin seeped and snapped and flared, and for a second she remembered the fire in her apartment building, the feeling of being trapped, the fear. But this place was the opposite of that hell. This place was a haven from anything bad. Or maybe it was Damien she was beginning to think of as her haven.

She went to settle down amid the pillows on the floor, but a sharp glimmer reflected the firelight, stopping her. She knelt, and saw one broken piece, then several, of what had once been an onyx vase.

Frowning, she picked up the larger pieces, then gathered the tinier shards by rolling them up in the rug. Then she shook it outside the door. She checked all the pillows carefully, brushing all the glass away before she made herself comfortable on them.

She tried not to imagine how the vase had been broken. Tried not to wonder whether Damien had been angry or frustrated, or just nervous and clumsy. Either way, she had to be at least partly to blame. And she wondered for the first time if maybe he'd been telling the truth when he'd said that he wanted her. Maybe there was some other reason he'd turned her away. But what?

Enough already. She'd come to the conclusion that thinking about Damien only distracted her from her real purpose here, hadn't she? When would she get that through her head? She sank into the pillows, opened the file folder and began reading.

CHAPTER TWELVE

He awoke with the night in the lush third-floor bedroom beyond the hidden door. He opened his eyes, his senses gradually sharpening in response to the usual stimulants. The silken softness of the satin sheets caressed his naked flesh. The plump feather pillow cradled his head. The warmth from the fire in the hearth below radiated into the room through the brick chimney in its center. The beat of the music from the stereo he'd set to turn on at dusk, with the help of an automatic timer, filtered softly from the speakers. He'd chosen Elton John tonight. A song called "Mellow," with a sultry rhythm that lived up to the title. The electric air freshener spilled the scent of the ocean into the room. The lights came on, dim at first, but brightening gradually.

All of it designed to comfort him in an existence where there was little comfort. He took his pleasures where he could find them. In things instead of in people. He surrounded himself with modern technology, luxurious fabrics, pleasing scents and soothing sounds. As he came fully awake, he knew it wasn't enough. Not anymore. He wanted Shannon. Her heated skin against his, instead of the cool satin. Her erotic scent filling him, rather than the artificial aroma; her sighs of pleasure surrounding him, soothing him more than any music could.

He sat up slowly as his strength filtered into him. His mind cleared its dull haze and began to sharpen. And then he went stiff with the sense of emptiness in the house. She was gone.

He threw back the covers, leapt from the bed, tried the trick of opening his mind to hers, of homing in on her thoughts and feelings to tell where she was. But his mind refused to focus. His brain screamed for action, and he complied. He threw on his clothes and ran downstairs to search the house, already knowing she wasn't there.

Netty awaited him at the foot of the stairs. "She left you a note,'' she said, as if reading his thoughts. "In the library, on the desk.''

He shot a worried glance over her careworn face, and then moved past her into the library. Netty hurried along in his wake.

"Were you here when she left?''

"No. I've been in and out today, did some shopping for her, took care of some bills. She was still in bed sleepin' last time I checked in.''

Damien strode to the desk and snatched up the envelope with his name scrawled on the front. He removed the sheet of paper, unfolded it, and imagined he could still smell her scent in the ink, feel the warmth of her hands on the stationery.

"Damien.'' It was written at the top of the sheet in her small neat hand. He glanced over the paper at Netty, and she nodded once, then turned to leave the room, wringing her hands all the way.

When the door closed behind her, he read on.

I couldn't stay after last night. I don't know if I can face you again, with the way I acted. I'm sorry. It was wrong of me to put you in that position, and I don't want you to feel guilty or responsible, no matter what might happen down the road. You've done nothing but look out for me. You're the kindest man I've ever known, Damien. Maybe that's what made me want you.

Still, I hope you can understand now, why I need some time alone. I'm going away for a few days, somewhere warm. Going to laze in the sun and try to get my head together. Please don't come looking for me. I want to be by myself, and I hope you'll respect that.

There was nothing more, just her name scrawled across the bottom of the page. But as he'd read her words, he'd felt what lay beneath them. Her hurt. Hurt he'd caused. She was ashamed of her actions, ashamed of wanting him. Damn, that was the last thing he wanted her to feel!

And something else, there was something else. Something in

the lines about going away that rang utterly false in his mind, and sounded a warning he couldn't ignore.

She hadn't gone anywhere. He was sure of it even before Marquand arrived, breathless, agitated, waving a bit of paper in front of him.

"You have to get out of the house." He said it without preamble, after barging in. "I mean it, Damien. You're not safe here."

Damien ignored him, still trying to puzzle out the truth hidden in Shannon's lies.

"Damien, are you listening to me? Bachman knows where you rest. He'll try for you by day as you lie defenseless."

Finally Marquand's accented words penetrated the haze of pain and loss. "Impossible. No one knows where I rest."

Marquand thrust the sheet of paper into Damien's hands. Damien didn't have time for this, but he glanced down and read the brief note. "Bachman, he rests in a hidden room on the third floor. The entrance has to be through the second guest room on the right, though I don't know where exactly."

There was no signature, and the words were typed. No way to judge the handwriting. Damien shook his head in disbelief. His gaze met Marquand's. "Netty?"

Marquand shrugged. "It's possible."

"I can't believe she would—"

"I can't figure how else the bastard could have come upon this information. But worry about that later, Damien. For now you'd do well to get yourself another resting place, one well away from this house." Marquand paced the room in a small square pattern.

Damien frowned, studying the sheet of paper in his hand. "How did *you* come upon it?"

Marquand quit his pacing and turned to face Damien. "I simply checked the messages left for Bachman at the front desk of his hotel." He tilted his head to one side. "Honestly, Damien, you must begin to use your powers more efficiently. It's an elementary matter to use our mental powers to influence the actions of humans. I caused the clerk to leave his station for a moment and retrieved the messages. Simple.''

''If it's so simple, then where the hell is Shannon?''

One of Eric's dark brows quirked upward.

''I told her to rest until nightfall. Mentally. It's worked before. Only this time it didn't. She was gone when I woke up.''

''Interesting.''

''Interesting? It's dangerous.''

''It's possible she closed her mind to yours. The trick can be learned, even by humans, though I've rarely seen it happen. Then again, she'd have no reason to do it, since she has no idea what you are.'' His gaze sharpened. ''You didn't take my advice and tell her, did you?''

''Of course I didn't tell her.''

Eric shrugged. ''Then I can only assume she felt reason to close herself off from you. Have you angered her in some way?''

Damien felt like screaming at the man. He was so damned calm! ''Look, the why and how doesn't matter. She's gone and I get the feeling she's in danger. The only thing we ought to be doing right now is looking for her.''

''So, look. What's stopping you?''

Damien nodded sharply and reached for the door handle. He'd begin with the car. It would be easier to track down than the woman. A firm hand on his shoulder brought him up short in the hall. When he turned, it was to see Eric with a pained expression on his face as he rolled his eyes, shook his head.

''Sit down, Damien. Clear your mind. Open it, seek her out.''

''But if she's closed herself off from me...''

''You won't be able to influence her, but you ought to sense her presence, feel her surroundings, discern whether she's safe.''

Damien shook his head slowly. ''I'm not sure I can do it. God, Eric, you don't understand. I've never used this psychic ability. Never wanted to.'' He glanced up as a thought occurred to him. ''Why don't you do it?''

Another irritated sigh. ''The Chosen connect most thoroughly with a single vampire, Damien. In case you haven't yet realized it, you are that one for Shannon. I might sense her dimly, especially if she's in peril. But for you the knowledge will come much more easily. Try, please.''

Damien nodded, but doubted it would work. He walked back into the living room, lowered himself onto the chaise and tried to relax and let his mind go blank. He closed his eyes.

''All we need now is Rhiannon with her incense and candles,'' Eric muttered. Damien opened his eyes, lifted his brows. ''Nothing, just talking to myself. Concentrate, Damien. Focus your mind on Shannon. Put a picture of her in front of your eyes. Bring her to life inside you until you can feel her touch, smell her scent.''

Damien closed his eyes again, and found it remarkably easy to bring Shannon to mind. It only took recalling the way her mouth tasted, its warmth, its depth, its heat. He shifted uncomfortably, but kept his focus. The sense of danger increased with his every thought.

It was incredible, that's what it was. It was absolutely incredible. No sane person would take any of it seriously, because none of it could possibly be true.

But it *seemed* true. Shannon had read the notes on the organization known as DPI. The Division of Paranormal Investigations. It was a secretive organization, one whose purposes the taxpayers and most of the politicians in D.C. knew nothing about. And its sole reason for existence, according to Marquand's notes, was to seek out and destroy vampires, though they claimed it was to discover their secrets through research. Marquand held the organization responsible for murders, kidnappings, torture.

Of vampires.

He claimed his own wife—no, *mate,* that was the term he'd used—had been abducted by the ruthless scientists. That she'd been subjected to horrible experiments just because they knew of her association with him. And that was when she was still mortal. Before he'd transformed her.

Still mortal? He'd transformed her?

Shannon had been shaking all over by the time she'd finished reading and replaced the papers in the desk. Marquand must be as crazy as Bachman. He actually believed himself to be a vampire. He *actually believed* it. Shannon wondered if he really even had a wife, or if this beautiful Tamara mentioned in the file was just a figment of his obviously sick imagination.

But Damien believed it, too. He must, or he wouldn't still be associating with the man. He'd have had the guy committed by now.

She had to stop thinking about it, had to stay alert. She'd left the mansion in her car, knowing how noticeable it was, and she'd driven slowly, for a couple of hours, all over town, hoping to attract the notice of the killer. Then she proceeded to her office, driving so she could easily be followed.

Once inside, with the lights blazing an invitation to all comers, she checked to be sure the gun was loaded and ready. And she sat down to wait.

The killer, *the perfectly human* killer, would come for her. At least, she hoped he would. She couldn't have made it much easier for him. He'd come tonight or not at all, and if he did, she'd be waiting. She'd deal with Damien and Marquand and Bachman and their misguided delusions later. Right now, she only wanted to stop a killer, avenge Tawny, and she sensed her time was running out.

Death was a dark shadow that had been stalking her for a long time now. But tonight it felt closer than ever before. She could feel its clammy breath chilling her nape, feel its gnarled claws reaching out to her.

She had to get the bastard tonight.

She didn't have to wait long before footsteps sounded on the stairs outside. She stood up, lifted the gun, watched the doorknob turn.

But it wasn't the killer that quietly walked into her office. It was Stephen Bachman.

She lifted the gun anyway, pointing it squarely and steadily at the left lapel of that gray tweed jacket. He ignored it, walked up to her desk and took a seat.

"You ready to come over to my side yet, Shannon Mallory? Or are you going to wait until they make you their next victim?"

She blinked. He studied her steadily, just waiting.

"At least I know you're not one of them. You were driving your fancy car all over, right under the blazing sun."

"And you were following me."

"Smart girl. So why'd you leave him? You finally have sense enough to get scared?"

"I don't know what you're talking about."

"I'm talking about monsters, Shannon. Not the kind that lurk under a little kid's bed, but real adult monsters. Beings that live by killing. Animals that feed on fear and death. You know about Damien now, what he really is. You wouldn't be here if you didn't. Humans mean nothing to him, to any of them. We're disposable, here only to fill their twisted cravings." He leaned back in the chair and tugged on his flawless cuff. "You're damned lucky you got out when you did."

"You're crazy if you think I believe any of this."

"Any of what?"

"You know what. That Eric Marquand and Damien are... vampires. There's no such thing and you're nuts if you think there is."

"I don't think. I *know*." He tilted his head. "So the newcomer *is* Marquand. I thought it was, but I'd never seen him up close. We've been watching him longer than any of them. Almost had him once. Damien, we didn't know about. Not until the murders. I've only had him under surveillance since I got the report on that first body."

She laughed, ignoring the ball of knowledge that thudded into her stomach. "You're certifiable."

He leaned closer, his dark eyes intense.

"Have you ever seen him in the daytime, Shannon? Have you ever seen him eat? Hmm? Is there a mirror anywhere in that entire place?"

"There's food in the house. I've eaten there—"

"But he hasn't."

She shook her head. "And his schedule is only to keep up the image. It's a mystique, for the fans. That's all."

"A vampire murdered your friend, Ms. Mallory. And if you're not careful, you'll suffer the same fate…or something worse."

She frowned at him, her hand clenching reflexively on the pistol butt. She still pointed the weapon at him, too jumpy and nervous to relax her stance. "What do you mean, worse?"

He shrugged, got up and paced to the window. "I have a notion *Damien the Eternal* would have killed you by now, if that's what he wanted. I think he has other plans." Bachman shoved his hands into his perfectly fitted trousers pockets and pretended to study the view.

"Spit it out, Bachman. What are you dancing around?"

He glanced over his shoulder at her. "I think he wants to make you one of them. Keep you for his own sick pleasures. Forever. Worse than hell, if you ask me. You'd be his prisoner for eternity."

"How did you ever get so screwed up, Bachman?" She paced toward the door, then to her seat again, clutching the back of it with one hand, clutching her gun in the other. She stared at the floor, let the barrel drop along with her gaze. "Suppose I bought this line of crap? Wouldn't turning me into a vampire negate the whole plan? Wouldn't I be as strong as him then? How could he keep me prisoner?"

"You know precious little about the subject. Powers increase with age in these creatures. And he's so old we don't even have a handle on his origins yet. Marquand, we know about. Comes from France, transformed during the Revolution."

She knew her eyes widened as her head came up again, knew she gasped. It was stupid, because she didn't really believe any of it. "You're telling me Eric is over two hundred years old?"

He looked at her as if she was an idiot. "That's young for them. The oldest one we have a file on is from Ancient Egypt, daughter of a pharaoh. And we suspect your Damien is even older than her.''

"You're nuts." She strode over to where he stood, near the window. "Look, just what do you think you're getting from this visit? Why are you bothering to tell me all of this?''

His lids lowered to half-mast. "Why do you think?''

She frowned, took a single step backward. But his hands on her shoulders stopped her. "I like you, Mallory. I like your spunk. I even like the way you took my damned sidearm. Not to mention you're probably the sexiest damned female I've ever laid eyes on.''

Lies. All lies, and so obvious it was child's play to see it. He wanted something from her, and it damned well wasn't her body. She watched his eyes. "You don't even know me.''

"I know you're sick, dying maybe.''

Her eyes flew wide. Her chin went up. "How do you know that?''

"Your medical records. But you knew I had them. They were in the files you stole from my hotel room.''

Her medical records were in those files? But she hadn't seen them. Had Damien? Had he known all along about her health, and kept it from her? Why?

"You're a rare specimen, Shannon. You have a blood antigen and line of descent that makes you one of the few people in the world who can become one of them. Unfortunately, it also makes you sure to die young. They all do. But we're doing research at DPI, Shannon, research that might help you.''

Research. She'd read about their research in Marquand's notes. Tamara, strapped to a table in a hidden lab and tortured, until Eric Marquand had come to get her out. And then he'd been captured, drugged, nearly killed.

Maybe it wasn't all fiction after all.

"If you'd come with me, put yourself in my hands, we might be able to find a way to keep you alive. We might even find a cure—''

She pulled from his rough embrace. "Come with you where?"

"The facility in White Plains. It's a research center."

White Plains. It was mentioned in Eric's file. God, could it all be true?

"You'd be safe there, Shannon, under constant guard. We have the best doctors and scientists in the field—"

"So, then I'd be *your* prisoner? Hell of a choice I'm left with, isn't it?"

"You wouldn't be a prisoner. You'd be protected. There's a difference."

She was afraid of him all of a sudden. Afraid that he wouldn't take no for an answer. "Look, I'm all too aware how little time I have left. But I don't intend to spend it as someone's pet guinea pig. And I don't believe any of this farfetched crap about vampires. All I want to do is find Tawny's killer, and no matter what you say, I don't believe it was Damien."

His gaze raked her face. "I'm sorry to hear that."

There was a warning in his words. "Why? What are you going to do?"

He shook his head slowly. "You'll come with me, in the end. One way or another."

She lifted the gun's muzzle. "You planning to try and force me?"

"Not yet. Not with those two still out there. I don't aspire to end up like some of our other researchers who've tried that tack. But I would advise you to stay away from him, Shannon." He stepped past her, toward the door. "He's going down. I have no choice in the matter. He's a killer. And when it's over, I'll be seeing you again." The hardness in his face eased just a little. "And no matter what you might think, Shannon, it's for your own good."

She shook her head fast, following him to the door. "This is crazy. Bachman, he's not what you say he is. I swear—"

"You don't know. *I do.*" He opened the door. "I'm taking him out. There's no other way."

She argued, but she was talking to an empty doorway. Bachman was gone, threats and all.

She blinked slowly, feeling as if she were immersed in a strange dream. She wanted to wake up, but couldn't. She didn't want to accept that all of this was real. Bachman really believed in it, along with an entire division of the U.S. government. So did Eric Marquand. And Damien? What did Damien believe?

He found her sitting on the floor of her shabby little office, facing the door, her gun in her hand. Her eyes were perfect ovals of confusion. And damp. The lump in Damien's throat couldn't be swallowed away.

"I thought we agreed you would wait until after the next performance to tempt fate, Shannon."

He stepped inside. She stood. "I didn't think you'd find me so soon. You're too smart for me, I guess."

Frowning at the paleness of her face, he took a step forward. His heart jelled when she took a step back. "You afraid of me now?" he asked softly. "What happened?"

She shook her head in denial, but he saw the fear in her eyes. "I'm not. I just want to be alone, that's all. Can't you just go? Please?"

Holding her jittery gaze with his own, Damien shook his head slowly. "I can't leave you here alone. You know that."

She turned her back on him, and her hair flew with the abrupt motion. He wanted to touch it, bury his face in it, inhale its sweet fragrance. "I'm sick of you making all my decisions for me."

"I haven't—"

"You have!" She paced away, still not facing him. "*You* decided I should stay with you after the fire. *You* decided how we should investigate the case. *You* decided to let me perform with you, but only to put me off. And now you're deciding not to let me take what amounts to my last chance at getting this bastard. Look, I've been too independent for too long to let someone take over now." She stopped on the opposite end of the room, as far away from him as she could possibly get. "My life is my own. I say what I do and where I go. Right now, I want to be here, and I want to be alone.''

''Why?''

She shook her head and looked at the floor.

''Dammit, I'm not leaving here without an answer.'' He strode across the room, and she cringed, sending a bolt of pain through his chest. He gripped her wrists, holding them to her sides. They stood facing each other, the window their backdrop.

She refused to answer, but the fear in her eyes was all the answer he needed. When she looked away from him, that fear increased. Her eyes widened and her skin went milky white. ''My God…''

''What?'' He stopped speaking when his gaze followed hers to the perfect image of her, reflected in the darkened window as clearly as if the glass were a black mirror. Though he stood beside her, his image wasn't there.

She met his gaze again, blinking, fear making her lips turn bluish and tremble as if she were freezing to death. ''B-Bachman told me, but I…didn't believe…''

''Bachman. I should have known. He's been here, then?''

She nodded. What sense was there in lying to him? She searched his face, the same handsome face she'd found so beautiful before. ''God, Damien, tell me it isn't true. This is all crazy, isn't it? It's a fantasy. It's a fairy tale.''

He hesitated. ''Shannon…'' He tried to form words, but none left his lips. What could he say?

''You can't even deny it?'' Shock made her voice a whisper. ''I'm having a breakdown, aren't I? This is only happening in my mind. You aren't even here—I'm all alone. Maybe you don't even exist, and I—''

''That's enough, Shannon!'' He put one arm around her shoulders and turned her toward the door. ''Come on, let's get out of here.''

She stiffened, resisting him. ''I'm not going anywhere with you.''

''The hell you aren't.''

She snatched the gun from her waistband as she danced away, then leveled it at him. In a lightning-fast move, he took it from her, then crushed it to a small metal lump. He let it thud to the floor.

She shook her head too fast and stepped backward. Her pupils dilated, until the amber of her eyes was only a thin ring around them. He'd terrified her. He shouldn't have done that.

"I'd never hurt you, Shannon. You know that. You have to know that. I couldn't if I wanted to." Still she stared, wide-eyed, pale. He could see the erratic pulse thudding in her neck. "I can't just leave you here for the murderer to find. And I damned well can't leave you to Bachman so he can fill your head with nightmares or, worse yet, take you off in chains to some maximum-security lab for what those bastards call research." He saw her blink when he said that, and wondered if Bachman had suggested it already. "I only know about it because Eric warned me. Shannon, come with me. I'll try to explain—"

She lunged for the door, but he caught her around the waist and jerked her back. She ended up crushed to him, her heart pounding, her cheeks flushed. Her breaths came in short little puffs. She stared up at him, her lips trembling, and shook her head from side to side.

Having her this close to him stirred his senses to full alert. His heart raced in time with hers, and he spread his fingers over the small of her back. "Shannon...it kills me to see you so afraid of me. Don't you know that I could never hurt you? Don't you know...?" He whispered the words, and saw her eyes moisten. His head bent, and he took her mouth, took it with a frenzy that couldn't been tamed. His hands moved all over her, unable to touch enough of her at once. He traced her spine, kneaded her shoulders, sifted her hair, caressed the gentle curve of her neck.

Very slowly it dawned on him that she was not resisting. Her trembling hadn't stopped, but it had changed. Her hands rose, timidly, before locking around him. Her head tipped backward in response to the thrusting of his tongue, and she suckled him. His ardor flamed high. He pressed his hips forward, to show her, and her hand ran up over his shoulders and down again. When she arched against him, he cupped her round, firm buttocks, squeezed them, pulled her harder against him, and heard the soft moan she made.

Insane with wanting her, he moved her backward until she bumped the desk. With a sweep of his arm he cleared it, and then he lowered her onto its surface. Her breaths came fast and warm on his face. He ripped the front of her silk blouse open. Buttons flew. Her breasts hid behind the lacy fabric of a bra, but he tore that away, too, baring them to his hungry eyes. With a little growl, he bent to nurse at them, feeding a need that went beyond hunger, beyond lust. He sucked hard at one tight bud, feeling it stiffen and stand. He caught the peak between his white teeth, snapping them down on the crest again and again until she screamed his name and clutched his head in both hands. Then he repeated the torment on the other.

She was panting now, each inhale short and shallow, each exhale a whimper. He lifted his head, watching her face as his hands moved to her jeans, their button, their zipper. He shoved the denim down over her buttocks, running his palms over their smoothness as he did. He pushed them down her thighs and she kicked them from her feet.

Then he straightened, standing between her legs with an arousal so hard it was painful. He stared down at her, bared to him, and he told himself he couldn't do this. He shouldn't...

"If you stop this time, I *will* shoot you," she whispered. "I don't want to hear any more of this craziness. I just want you."

He knew it was wrong, knew she was as afraid as she was aroused. And yet he sank his fingers into the silken curls between her thighs. He parted her folds, and explored her tight, damp center. He found the tiny nub, and pinched it between his fingers. She closed her eyes and cried out.

"Shannon, I—"

"I don't care! What have I got to lose, Damien? Dammit, make love to me!"

He prayed she wouldn't regret that command, even as he unfastened his pants to free his throbbing erection. He saw her gaze fasten to that part of him; he felt the touch of her eyes burning him. Placing his palms to her inner thighs, he spread her wider, and stared at the delectable feminine morsel before him. Then her hand closed around him and pulled gently. She guided him up tight to her slick center, squeezed him hard and let him go. Her gaze held his as she lay back on the desk, hips arcing toward him, waiting.

He sank into her slowly, gradually, deeper and deeper until there was no more of him to offer. He pressed tight to her, and she sighed long and coarse. Her hands clutched his buttocks. His hands closed tight around her waist, better to hold her to him. That grip tightened as he withdrew, and this time, he was not gentle when he plunged into her. Again, he pulled back, holding her imprisoned between his strong hands as he thrust once more. Her muscles tightened around him, as if wanting to keep him there forever. She lifted her head and shoulders from the desk, reached for him with her mouth, and he responded, bending over her, kissing her. He made love to her mouth as hard and deep and as urgently as he was making love to her body.

And then she went still, her entire body stiffening, her hands clenching, her breaths stopping for an interminable moment. He felt the tightening around him. An instant later she screamed aloud, and her body spasmed its release in waves that forced him to respond in kind. He spilled his essence into her, feeling as if it were drained from his toes. And then he sank onto her beautiful body, and he held her in his arms.

Watching their frenzied coupling from the fire escape, Anthar swore viciously in Sumerian and then in Babylonian and finally in English. He'd waited, waited endlessly for Damien to give in to his lusts and take the woman. And he had; at long last, he had. But he'd failed to drink from her. Somehow he'd overcome the instinct as powerful as nature itself, and he'd refrained from even a sip. Dammit! If Damien had so much as *tasted* her nectar, Anthar might have found an opportunity to separate them, finish her off and leave her for Damien to find. He'd have believed himself the villain. He'd have gone insane with remorse and grief and self-loathing. Why the hell hadn't the bastard tasted her?

Now Anthar would have to wait for another opportunity. And judging by the girl's health there might not be one. He hadn't realized how close she was to her end. If she died, his opportunity for the perfect revenge would die with her. Damien had to be driven to suicide. It was the only way to ease the agony of Anthar's wrath.

After all, that was the way Siduri had died.

Siduri. Ah, how beautiful she'd been, and how he'd wanted her. He might have had her, too. Anthar had often visited her little cottage by the sea. But alas, the Great Gilgamesh had stopped there, half dead and half mad, filthy and exhausted and starving. He'd paused on his quest for immortality, just long enough to destroy the life of an innocent barmaid. And she'd taken him in. She'd fed him, clothed him and held him in her arms to ease his pain. And when he'd recovered, he'd left her, cold snake that he was. He'd never once looked back, never once paid heed to her pitiful begging of him to stay.

He didn't even know how much she'd loved him, never learned of how she'd died.

She'd just walked into the sea. Just kept walking until she could walk no more. Then she'd swum. And like him, she'd never looked back.

Only Anthar knew. For he had her words, engraved in the stone tablet, written in the script she'd been forbidden as a woman to learn. She'd learned anyway. She'd learned from Anthar himself. And many other things, as well.

So beautiful, so bright. Dead because of Gilgamesh, as surely as if he'd choked her life away with his own two hands.

Gilgamesh would pay. Yes, he would, by whatever means necessary. He would pay by losing what he most loved.

CHAPTER THIRTEEN

She curled into his arms, trembling and all but limp, as Damien struggled to put her clothes back into place. It wasn't easy. When he tried to rise away from her, she clamped her arms around his neck and fought not to let him go. When he gently removed them and stood back, righting his own apparel, he saw tears gliding silently down her cheeks.

"Ah, Shannon..." He gathered her up, standing her on her feet and holding her to his chest. But her legs seemed rubbery and weak. She sank once, then stiffened her knees as if by sheer will. She cupped his face between her hands, searched it through the pools in her eyes.

"It isn't true. I knew it. It's all just nonsense. Bachman's crazy." Her words tumbled over one another in their haste to break free. "You're no monster. No monster could make love to me the way you just did. Tell me, Damien. Say it." She kissed his mouth, his cheeks, his eyes. "I've never felt this way before. Not for anyone, Damien. Only you, so you have to tell me it's all a lie. A dream. Make-believe." Again she kissed him, his jaw, his neck. Desperation making her tremble. He caught her shoulders to stop the madness, but she rushed on. "Yes, make-believe. An illusion, just like in your act. That's all it is. Illusion. Say it, Damien..."

The trembling increased, and he felt her kisses heating. Not with passion, but with fever.

He caught her face, held her away from him just a little. Her skin glowed milky white, with those telltale apples beginning to shine in her cheeks. Her eyes already dulled and took on that unfocused quality.

"Dammit," he muttered. "Dammit, not again."

"Jus' hold me." Her whispered words slurred into one another. "I'll be all right...long's'you hold me." She melted against his chest.

He closed his arms around her, scooped her up into them. He stared down at her relaxed face, her hooded eyes, and he felt a pain beyond all endurance. Something cold and hot all at once, freezing and burning his heart until the organ split into a hundred bits. He couldn't stand to see this, to see her suffer this way, to watch her die.

He clenched his fists as he held her, and cried out loud in his agony, the words in the old language. One no living man could know. He cried her name, and Enkidu's, and he cursed the gods and the world and life and death and pain. And then he buried his face in her hair and he wept hot, bitter tears.

Her warm, satin palm rested softly on his cheek. "Don't cry. I didn't want this...didn't want...didn't mean to love you...."

He lifted his head, staring at her in shock. She smiled very slightly, "I wish...I didn't have to die...to leave you...like this." And then her amber eyes fell closed.

"Damien."

He turned slowly, but couldn't take his eyes from Shannon long enough to look at Eric Marquand.

"Damien, you must bring her away from here. There's danger."

"Look at her, Eric...." Damien shook his head fast, as if denying his own words. "It's different this time, darker. More insidious."

Eric stepped forward and bent close to Shannon. When he straightened again, his face was grim. "I'm sorry. Damnably sorry."

Damien looked up, brows lifted, the question he couldn't voice settling in his eyes.

"She'll slip into coma before this night is out. She won't wake, I fear. The end is close."

"No...." Damien's knees buckled. He fell onto them, clutching her limp form to him, bowing double as he held her, rocked her.

"Come, Damien. Bring her to the house I've rented. Bachman's been following you and Shannon, not me. I'm sure he knows nothing about the arrangements I've made tonight." Damien didn't move. "Come, at least we can make her comfortable, keep her warm."

Damien nodded, mute with pain, unable to speak.

Blasphemous bastard, it's less than you deserve!

He stopped in midstep, tilting his head and frowning toward Eric for silence. Pure rage filled his mind, the thoughts, bitter with hatred, rang clear in his brain. But from where, or whom?

Watch her die, you dog! Watch her die and wish for death yourself, for I'll bring it to you soon enough, Gilgamesh of Uruk.

Just as suddenly as it had come, the sensations flooding his mind vanished. Damien shook himself, then glanced at Eric. "Did you hear it?"

"Faintly. The message was directed to you."

"How many others…like us…are there here?" He hadn't believed there were any besides the two of them in Arista, until now. Now he wondered.

"None, Damien. We'd know if there were. They'd have no reason to hide their presence from us."

"But they could? If they wanted to, they could?"

One brow bunching lower than the other, Eric nodded.

"It was a vampire, Eric. I'm sure it was. One who knows me." Damien bolstered himself after being thoroughly shaken by feeling such a rush of pure hatred flashing through his consciousness. He focused instead on Shannon, and the pain overshadowed everything else. "I can't even take her home. Not with Bachman planning to raid the place in search of me."

"He won't come near until dawn. It's still early. We'll be secure enough for the night, at least. We can make other plans from there. Come."

Moments later, Damien tucked Shannon's pliable form onto the chaise in the circular room. He sensed she'd rather rest here, near the fire, than upstairs alone in the big bedroom. She liked this room. Eric bent to add logs to the fire, as Damien sat beside her and stroked her hair.

"Oh, my! What's happened to her?"

Damien glanced up, seeing Netty's worried face, forgetting her possible betrayal in his concern for Shannon. "She's sick, Netty. Very sick."

"She needs a doctor, she does." The woman hustled forward, quick steps bringing her beside the chaise. She reached for Shannon's hand and grasped it to her breast.

"There's nothing they can do for her." Damien's voice broke, and he let his head bow. His neck seemed too limp to hold it any longer.

"You mean, she's dying?"

He bit his trembling lips until he drew blood.

Eric turned away from the fire. "Netty, some blankets for her, if you will. We can only keep her warm and—"

Netty backed away slowly, her face a jumble of confused emotions. "No, sir. No, sir, this isn't right!" She shook her head fiercely. "He said she'd be all right. He said it was all on account of the spell you'd put on her—" She broke off, eyes going even wider. When Damien's head came up slowly, she searched his face. "But you didn't put this on her. I can see that now, you didn't. Oh, Lord, what have I done?"

Eric stepped forward, coming between Damien and Netty even as Damien rose to his feet. "You're talking about Bachman, aren't you?"

Netty nodded, her gaze meeting Damien's again. "He said no harm would come to you! He said it was all to save Shannon. He told me you were…you were…" She shuddered and looked at the floor. "Demon spawn. Said she'd die unless I helped him."

"And you told him about the secret room on the third floor." Damien could barely control his rage.

She bit her thick lower lip, tears coursing down her face now. "Bachman said she'd die if I didn't tell. I only wanted to help the girl!"

"I ought to tear your heart out—"

"Shut up, Damien!" Eric held one arm out to his side to keep Damien from walking past him. Not that he could have actually stopped him. "Netty, it's not too late to redeem yourself. I intercepted the note you left at the hotel—"

She groaned softly. "I phoned him later. He knows, he does."

"Tell us what Bachman is planning," Eric coaxed.

She nodded hard, still glancing every few seconds at Damien, fear mingling with the remorse in her eyes. "I was to let him in at first light. He wanted to look at the room where you sleep."

"What he *wants* is to murder me in my sleep, you foolish woman."

"I didn't know. I swear it!"

Damien glared at her, then turned again to resume his vigil over Shannon. "I can't think about this right now. I—" He broke off with a shake of his head.

"Is it true, then? What Bachman says you are?"

"Netty, what kind of idiot would believe such nonsense?" Eric asked, with a laugh in his voice. "Bachman is insane, a fan gone over the edge. Surely you've heard of this happening before, stalkers plaguing stars of all sorts." He paused, and Netty nodded, thoroughly engrossed. "So, Bachman has convinced himself that Damien's stage identity is the real thing, and cast himself in the role of vampire slayer." Eric stepped forward, touched Netty's arm. "He's *dangerous,* Netty. He really means to kill Damien."

"And I almost helped him do it!" she cried. She buried her face in her hands, sniffling loudly. "I'm sorry, Mr. Namtar."

He didn't care, didn't even acknowledge her apology. He was too enveloped in pain to feel anything else. "Just go. Go, both of you. Leave us alone."

Netty broke into tears and ran from the room.

Eric came and knelt beside him. "It won't be safe here beyond darkness. You know that."

"I'll take her out of here before then."

"And go where?"

Damien shrugged, staring hard at Shannon, thinking of the words she'd whispered to him before her eyes had closed. "I don't know. It doesn't matter, really."

"Shall I return for you—"

"No. You've done enough. Keep your distance now, Eric. I don't need an audience, let alone any help for this grief. It's an old, familiar companion."

Eric nodded once, and backed away.

So alive. He'd never known anyone to be as much alive as she'd been. The sparkle of mirth in her eyes. Her delighted laughter. Her ferocity when she felt cornered or bullied or threatened in any way.

It had been a very long time since Damien had shared laughter with anyone. He had with her, he realized dully. Over and over again, she'd made him smile. She'd filled his loneliness with her constant presence. She'd brought joy and tenderness back into his existence.

And now she was dying. Leaving him to walk alone, as Enkidu had done. Leaving him, just when it seemed their goal of finding her friend's murderer was within reach. Just when he'd learned of another, a fiercely angry, vampire in the city. One who hated him—

He blinked slowly as he realized the implication of what he'd just thought. Another vampire. One who hated Damien beyond all reason.

He'd been responsible for those deaths! And driven by his own demons had staged them to look like Damien's work. That had to be the answer.

A light flickered somewhere in the endless night of his soul. He *wasn't* a murderer. The thirst hadn't taken control of him. More proof of that lay in what had transpired between the two of them before she'd succumbed to this illness. He'd made love to her. Frenzied, passionate, obsessive love to her. But he hadn't tasted her life's blood. He'd remained in control, despite the lust for her that raged inside him.

His reason before for not transforming her had been simple.

He'd been suffering with the thought that he might be a killer, and couldn't bear to see her suffer the same someday. That reason was gone now. His other reason had been a selfish one. He hadn't wanted to let himself love her. He hadn't wanted to risk the kind of hurt he'd known before.

But it was already too late to avoid that. And if she were immortal, maybe he wouldn't have to lose her at all.

He looked at her, stretched out on the chaise like an offering to a demon god. Would she want it? Would she have accepted the dark magic if he'd offered it to her while she'd been able? Could she bear a life without daylight, without the kiss of the sun? Could she abide the notion of her eternal soul bound forever to her eternal body?

He swore viciously and turned away. He couldn't make that decision for her. He couldn't! No matter how much he loved her, how it would tear him apart to see her die. He had no right.

Tears swam in his eyes. He didn't battle them. He buried his face in his hands and felt his shoulders quake with sobs. And then her hand rose, touched his back.

He turned, sliding onto his knees on the floor. He clutched her hand, kissed it, then bent to kiss her face.

"I'm...sorry," she whispered. "I should...have warned you."

"It wouldn't have changed anything, Shannon." He'd have loved her even if he'd known all along. He was certain of that.

She stared up into his eyes, her own damp, unfocused and glittering with the firelight's reflection. She blinked at the tears, but more quickly flooded to take their place. This time she let them come and her hand clutched his tighter. "I'm so afraid."

He didn't know what to say. What could he say to comfort her?

"I've denied it, you know. Held my chin up, pretended to be this big brave person, but I'm not." Tears flowed freely, leaving angry red streaks on her skin. Her lips pulled tight, her teeth bared. "I don't want to die, Damien. I don't want to be brave anymore. I don't give a damn about dignity."

He stilled, staring down at her face. "Do you mean that, Shannon?"

Her face relaxed. Her eyelids drooped, and he knew the end was close. Her breaths came so shallowly, and so randomly. No longer regular. "I'd...I'd give anything..." she whispered. "Anything...if I could just live..."

Her eyes fell closed.

He cupped her face between his hands, shook her gently. But she was beyond reach now. Sinking into the coma Eric had predicted. She wouldn't wake again. But she didn't need to, did she? Hadn't she just given him her decision?

Not really. She's feverish, sick. She didn't know what she was saying, didn't realize I could actually do it...

All true. But did it really matter? Could he really bear to let her die? Could anyone, mortal or immortal, sit idly by and watch someone he loved slip away, knowing he had the power to save her?

No. No, that was beyond endurance. No matter how he tried to tell himself it was wrong, that she should have been given the option while she was still cognizant enough to make an informed decision, he couldn't turn away. He didn't have that much strength in him. He couldn't face the madness again, and he knew it would come. He felt it descending on him as he sensed her heartbeat slowing, her breaths becoming less and less frequent. He couldn't do it, dammit! He couldn't go on without her. He couldn't sit here and watch her die, when she'd just all but begged him to save her.

He lifted her, his palms sliding up to her shoulder blades. Her head fell backward, hair like a golden silk curtain. Sweet Sleeping Beauty. He was about to give her the kiss that would wake her from death's slumber. He was no prince. She deserved better. He lowered his head, and as his lips touched her skin, he whispered, "Inanna, forgive me. Enkidu, help me. Shannon, sweet Shannon...stay with me."

Anthar roared his rage aloud, forgetting his need for anonymity. It mattered little, for the heathen was too enamored with his precious morsel to notice. He'd noticed earlier, though. He knew there was another, one who wished him dead. He knew, and he'd be on his guard now. So much the better. The bastard would know why he suffered before he died.

But damn! To be robbed of watching Gilgamesh grieve for her death was a blow! He'd planned, waited so long. Of course, he'd wished to arrange it differently, to kill her himself and let the great one believe he'd done it. Then to watch Gilgamesh consumed by despair unto the point of taking his own worthless life.

All his plans were ruined.

Ah, but he would not give up his quest for vengeance. Siduri deserved to be avenged, and she would be. Anthar would simply have to kill Gilgamesh himself, and the woman, too. Her first, to increase the eternal one's pain. Perhaps he'd make Gilgamesh watch while he took her. Yes. She'd give little resistance, even with her newfound strength, she'd be a weakling compared with him.

And Anthar feared Gilgamesh himself, but little. He was nearly as old, the difference being a matter of minutes.

Anthar had followed Gilgamesh into the wilderness after Siduri's suicide. Followed to exact his revenge then. He'd caught up in the midst of Gilgamesh's meeting with Utnapishtim, the Enlightened One. The ancient wise man, it was said, had been made immortal by the gods in order to save him when the great flood ravaged the world. But he'd been charged not to share the gift, lest it become a curse instead.

Yet something about Gilgamesh must have touched the old man, for after great thought and much tormented arguing, he'd granted Gilgamesh's wish. They'd exchanged blood, and the act left Utnapishtim weak, and Gilgamesh strengthened.

"You will live forever now, my young friend," the old one had whispered, before sending Gilgamesh away.

Anthar slipped in right after, and took advantage of the old man's weakened state to force him to repeat the ritual he'd just witnessed. If Gilgamesh lived, so must Anthar. He must live long enough to have his revenge.

And so he had.

And so he would.

Shannon had no idea how much time had passed, when she opened her eyes. She felt a little foggy at first, as if her head were stuffed full of wet cotton. She struggled to sit up, but her bones felt heavy and uncooperative.

Strong hands helped her, eased her up, and she looked around, frowning. They were not in Damien's house. She glanced up at him, then remembered the way they'd made love, and she smiled softly. "How long have I been asleep?" Her brows drew together. Her voice sounded strange to her, somehow deeper and more resonant than before. But that was silly.

"All of last night, and all through today."

"It's night again?"

He nodded. His eyes were troubled, worried about something, and she had no idea what it could be, unless he was suffering over her sickness. Yes, that must be it. She'd had another attack right after that incredible sex on the desk in her office.

On the desk!

She lifted a hand to touch his face. She'd have to tell him the truth, prepare him for the eventuality that was unavoidable.

A low-flying bat swooped between them and shot upward once more, drawing her gaze. She gave her head a little shake and looked again. She could see every inch of its small body in perfect detail, despite the darkness. She could count the bones delineated in the thin black skin of its wings. Her eyes seemed to be working at high speed, because she could see each and every flutter of those wings, though they beat too rapidly for that to be possible. They ought to look like a blur. Then she bit her lip and her eyes widened even farther. She could *hear* each flutter, as well, and the piercing squeals, and their echoes bouncing back like sonar blips to tell the creature what lay ahead. And she could smell it. She could *smell it*. It was musky and ripe.

My God, she felt the air currents stirred by those wings, passing by her face.

She shook her head slowly. "That's not possible."

"What isn't?" Damien leaned forward, gripping her hand, and she could count the lines in his palm just by feeling them. She looked up into his face, and saw the unearthly gleam in his black eyes in a way she'd never seen it before. She saw the pale perfection of his skin, and she knew his scent, erotic and enticing though it was, could not be human. His hair was too perfectly raven, too silken, too soft, to be human.

Or maybe she'd succumbed to an overactive imagination because of a lunatic named Bachman. Maybe she was having a breakdown of some kind. She licked her lips. "Damien, why are we outside?"

"We had to leave the house. Bachman planned to come for us today, so I brought you here."

"Where, exactly, is here?"

He smiled and glanced around. "A cave I know of, deep in the woods outside the city. You remember? We passed these woods in your car the other night. No one can find us here. You're safe."

The wind blew a perfect harmony. She heard notes she'd never heard before. Every rustle of every leaf, every branch as it bowed. "This is so strange."

"Tell me."

She looked at him again, shocked once more that he appeared so different to her, so obviously different from any other man. And so afraid. What was he afraid of? She shook her head. "No. There's something more important I have to explain to you, Damien. About...about this illness of mine."

He lowered his eyes.

"I'm..." She licked her lips. "I'm dying, Damien."

Without looking at her, he replied, "No, Shannon. You are not."

She gave her head a shake. He hadn't seemed surprised at all.

No shock, no questions. Just a simple denial. He lifted his head. His black gaze stabbing into hers, he added, "Not ever."

She blinked. "What do you mean?"

...he wants to make you one of them. You'd be his prisoner, forever...

She tried to blink away her memory of Bachman's words, but they wouldn't leave. She shrank back a little. "Damien, what are you saying? What are you going to...to do to me?"

"It's done."

"What's done?"

He reached out, fanned his fingers in her hair, spread them wide, as if to feel more of it. "Do you remember last night, when death was so close you could feel its cold breath on your nape? Do you remember crying, telling me you'd give anything, if only you could live? Don't you feel it, Shannon? Don't you *know?*"

Her breath caught in her throat. She remembered very little after their lovemaking on the desk. Too little. Hadn't she decided that all of this talk of vampires was craziness? Someone's insane fantasy? It couldn't be real. Hadn't she begged Damien to confirm that for her, right after they'd made love?

And hadn't he failed to do it?

There are no such things as vampires!

She stood up, feeling an unfamiliar strength seep into her. The fogginess in her brain had gone, leaving it sharp and alert. Her senses jangled with awareness, as though a zillion electrodes were pulsing tiny currents into her nerve endings. She felt energized, healthy, strong. More alive than she ever had.

She glanced down, opening and closing her hand and studying it as she did. Why did it feel so different? At last, she pressed that same palm to her throat, driven by some wild impulse, some impossible notion. And she felt the tiny indentations, two punctures, quickly healing over.

Her gaze flew to his. She shook her head in denial.

"It's all right, Shannon. There's nothing to be afraid of." He lifted a hand, took a step toward her. "You won't be sick anymore. You won't die. You'll never die."

"My God!" Another step away, and still he advanced. "My God, it's true, you are—"

"And so are you."

"No!" But even as she shrieked the word, she knew it had to be true. Why else were her perceptions so altered? She cupped her palm over the wounds on her throat, as if covering them could make them disappear. "How could you, Damien! How could you do this to me?" Tears crept into her voice. She choked on them, fought them down.

"Shannon, I had to. You were dying. I couldn't let you die when you kept telling me how much you wanted to live."

"You can't do this, dammit!"

He lowered his hands, stood where he was. He seemed to bear some silent devastation she was beyond caring about. "It's done." Like a judge handing down an irrefutable sentence. Two words with more meaning than any she'd ever heard.

"So, now what happens? You keep me with you forever? I turn to you for everything? Is that what you expect now, Damien? Because you know I can't exist this way on my own, don't you? You know I have no idea how to survive like this, what to do, where to turn. So I'm utterly dependent—is that the idea?"

She was terrified, *terrified* of what she was now. Alive or dead? Human or some other sort of creature? Natural or a freak? Immortal or damned?

He only shook his head, obviously confused. "Of course you can depend on me to—"

"The hell I will!" She shouted it, her voice too loud to be natural, so loud it hurt her own ears. She squeezed her eyes tight and forced herself to speak more softly. "What can kill us?"

"What?"

"What can kill us? Tell me, damn you."

He blinked slowly before answering. "Sunlight. The slightest touch of a live flame. Any injury that causes severe bleeding.

We're like hemophiliacs in that way. If you can't get the bleeding stopped right away you…'' His voice trailed off. ''Shannon, why are you asking me this?''

''Because I need to know. Because I don't know if I want to live like this. Because…'' She covered her face with both hands and turned away from him. She was a liar and a coward. She *didn't* want to die, and she knew it. But God, what was this alternative he'd given her? Blindly, sobbing, she took a few steps away, toward the mouth of the cave.

''Where are you going?''

''Away. Just away.''

He followed, catching her shoulder. She jerked back from his touch. ''Shannon, you can't just go off by yourself.''

''Why the hell not?''

He stood there gripping her arm. ''Please. Just sit down, give yourself time to adjust. Let me explain what all of this means.…''

''Leave me alone!'' She pulled away, stood facing him, breathless with shock and anger. ''I swear to God, if you don't let me go I'll hate you forever. Does that even matter to you, Damien? Or was Bachman right about that, too?'' She turned again, and raced off into the forest, into the night.

Damien didn't go after her. He couldn't. His grief over what he'd done, preserved her life, transformed her into something she couldn't begin to understand, his knowledge that he'd acted for reasons purely selfish, nearly paralyzed him with pain. He hurt, he ached, for her. For what she was suffering right now. The confusion. The fear. And yet he couldn't bring himself to regret what he'd done. He couldn't be anything but glad that she was alive when he rose tonight, instead of lying cold and lifeless, forever still on the chaise. That was the alternative. That was what he could have risen to see tonight, would have, if he hadn't acted.

So he didn't regret it. He only wished he'd done it differently, explained things to her earlier, before the decision had to be made, allowed her to choose.

He started after her, only to find his way blocked by a solid form. His eyes met Eric's and found understanding, even sympathy, there. "Let her go, Damien. She needs time. She has to explore this new realm she finds herself inhabiting, grow accustomed to it."

Damien shoved Eric aside and strode on. "How can I let her go? You said yourself what kind of bastard this Bachman might be. You think I want to see her captured for live study by that animal? And what about this rogue vampire that's on the rampage? How do you know she's safe from him?"

Eric kept pace easily. "I didn't say we couldn't watch her. We'll keep her in sight, but from a distance. Damien, you have to give her a chance to accept this on her own. You've forced it down her throat and she's choking. Can't you see that?"

Damien stopped. He turned to stare at the other man. Then felt his own shoulders slump in concession. "You're insightful, Eric. I'll give you that."

"I'm glad you think it. For I have a few other notions. I haven't wished to involve my mate in this for fear of the risk."

"Risk?"

Eric nodded. "I'd no idea what sort of temper you possessed when first I approached you, Damien."

"And now?"

"No worse than most. I believe Tamara can be of help to your Shannon."

"That might be true." Damien walked on, but his pace was slower. Part of his mind remained focused on Shannon, felt her tears, her confusion. Another part listened intently to what Eric suggested. "There's still Bachman, and this rogue we've discovered."

"I wouldn't bring her here if I had a choice, Damien. But the fact is, she's coming, whether I like it or not. She'll be at the house I rented within the hour."

Damien only looked at him, brows raised in question as he waited for Eric to finish.

"She worries about me. She found out about Bachman's presence here, and nothing could stop her from joining me."

Damien blinked, wondering what that kind of devotion must feel like. "You're a lucky man, Marquand."

"That I am."

"Go on to your house, then, and wait for your fierce protector. I'm going back to the mansion to watch over Shannon." At Eric's frown he added, "From a distance."

CHAPTER FOURTEEN

She tried not to notice how fast she was walking, or that she didn't get winded, or that her heart didn't even speed up. She ignored the fact that, while she felt the cold as she never had before, felt its crisp touch on every inch of her body, she didn't *feel* cold, or uncomfortable with it. She didn't get goose bumps or shiver. She tried to pay no attention to the incredibly flavorful *taste* of every breath she drew, or the scents of every plant and animal she passed, and of the air itself.

God, but she'd never been so aware!

When she reached Damien's house, she climbed the gate with no trouble, wondering about this new agility and strength. She walked inside, resisting the astonishing differences. The colors in the Turkish rugs that she'd never seen before. The intricate patterns. The smell of the fire. The taste of the wood smoke.

It would overwhelm her if she paid attention. She felt she could sit for hours and explore her heightened senses. The flames in the hearth...

My God, the flames. Look at them!

She stared, paralyzed by the beauty of the dancing tongues of light and energy and color. She had to force herself to break away.

Not now. Not now. She wanted only to gather up her belongings, toss them into her car and drive far away from here. Far away from Damien and Eric Marquand and this entire nightmare she'd fallen into.

She started through the round room, not intending to pause at all, when something stopped her. Some inner knowledge she couldn't understand made the hair on her nape stand up. And she went still, trying to find the source. Finally she turned around. Her gaze went to the arched doorway on the other side, and Bachman stepped out from his hiding place just beyond the beads, his gun pointed right at her.

Some hysterical person inside her began to laugh. It began as a chuckle and grew, gaining strength until she was gripping her middle with both hands, tears pooling in her eyes. She could easily have let it go on until she sank to the floor and the laughter led to hysteria and the hysteria to madness. But she didn't. She caught hold of herself. She stopped the laughter and eyed the weapon. "Bachman, what are you doing? You want me to take that one away from you, too?"

"Where is he, Shannon?"

She shrugged and wiped her eyes dry. "Not here. But you must already know that. You've been searching the place all day, haven't you?"

He frowned, scanning her face, and she stiffened, wondering what he saw. She waited, her breath halted.

"You've been crying. Why?"

She blinked, nearly limp with relief. He didn't see the change, he couldn't. Mindful of the marks on her neck, she lowered her head. When she lifted it again her hair hung down the front of her shoulders, hiding the wounds. "Oh, Bachman, why didn't I listen to you?" She let a few new tears dampen her lashes. "I thought I loved him, you know. But he left me. Just walked out."

"And you don't know where he went?"

She shook her head sadly. "I hate him now." It wasn't true. She didn't know what she felt for Damien anymore, but it wasn't hatred. She didn't think it ever would be.

Bachman nodded, but didn't put the gun away. His face softened a little. "Shannon, come with me to the institute. We might be able to help you there."

It was a lie. She knew it the second the words left his lips. She wasn't even certain Bachman *knew* it was a lie, but she did. Amazing. Not the slight intuition she'd felt when he'd lied to her before, but a glaring neon sign flashing in her mind. "Are there others there, others like me?"

He nodded, and for an instant she glimpsed a frightening image. Men and women imprisoned in cell-like rooms. Strapped to tables. Desolation in their faces.

She licked her lips. "I don't know." Fear gripped her heart. He might honestly think he could help her, but she knew he couldn't. If she went with him, she'd become a prisoner, a research object, a guinea pig. She took a step away from him. "I'll think about it, though. Give me until tomorrow to—"

His eyes narrowed and the gun's muzzle lifted a fraction. He shook his head. "No, Shannon. You're coming with me now."

She felt herself go cold all over.

"I'm not leaving here without you," he said softly, dangerously. "I wanted to wait until I had him, but he's gone. My chance to get him is gone. But I'm not going back to White Plains empty-handed. And I'm damned well not leaving you here to die." He shook his head. "Besides, I'm not sure you don't know where he is. Maybe I can convince you to tell me."

"I told you—I don't know. He's gone. He's not coming back." She defended Damien instantly and without any hesitation. Yes, she was angry with him for what he'd done to her. But this was instinctive and had nothing to do with the other.

"He'll come if you're in trouble, I think. I didn't want to do it this way, Shannon, but if I were to, say, shoot you, I think he'd know. I think he'd be here in a matter of minutes. Seconds, maybe." He worked the action of the gun.

Fear rippled through her and her mind sought wildly for an answer. But the sixth sense she'd felt before seemed to have deserted her. Was he bluffing or would he really do it? She couldn't just stand there and let him shoot her. She held her hands in front of her, palms out. "No, don't. I'll go with you. I'll tell you where he is—I will."

Bachman nodded, his frown altering, softening. "I figured you'd change your mind. Don't worry about him, Shannon. He won't suffer. That's if I decide to let him live long enough to take him in. I might not. He's a murderer. Someone has to stop him. Someone has to stop them all."

Then there were others. Others like Damien, hunted and persecuted by people like Bachman, and maybe even killed. Just as Eric Marquand's notes had said. It was too horrible to believe.

She lowered her head, chin to chest, and forced a couple of sobs. She took one faltering, weak-kneed step toward him, then another. She swayed sideways, catching herself on a table. Her palm pressed to her forehead and her eyes closed.

He strode to her, gripping her forearm none too gently. It hurt, though she didn't think he meant it to. Her skin seemed more sensitive than before. When he squeezed her arm, pain shot all the way to her shoulder.

She lifted her other hand, settled it on his shoulder as if for support. Her fingers clenched hard into his flesh. Her knee rose and connected. She'd expected him to double over in pain, giving her time to escape.

Instead he launched into the air, propelled by the simple lifting motion of her knee into his groin. He screamed aloud, a hoarse, gravelly yell, and he sailed backward, hitting the floor five feet away. The gun skittered across the marble tiles to stop near the hearth, well beyond his reach. *Then* he doubled over.

Shannon's hand flew to her mouth, and she felt as if her eyes would pop out of their sockets. "Did I do that?" she whispered. "Ah, hell, this is so frigging strange."

He struggled to his feet, rage in his eyes, even as Shannon thought that those thugs who'd tried to steal her car ought to try it again now. If they thought she'd given them what for last time... She halted that speculating as Bachman stood, took one staggering step forward, lifted a shaking hand, forefinger extended.

"You...you're one of them."

"Not by choice," she muttered. "Look, Bachman, why don't you just get the hell out of here before I really hurt you, okay?"

He glanced toward the gun, took a step toward it. She leapt, easily covering the distance in a single, gazellelike move, and put herself between Bachman and the weapon. He thrust a hand into a pocket and emerged with a blade. "Come on, Shannon.

Come over here and try that again.'' He was panting, breathless, obviously in pain.

She held her hand up, telling him to stop. "Don't do this," she said softly. "Don't…"

"You think I *want* to?" He moved nearer, still brandishing the blade. She backed away, but he advanced. "I could kill you, you know," he rasped. "One little nick, honey, and then I could stand here and watch you bleed." She gasped. "Give it up, Shannon. Don't make me do it."

He lunged, and the blade swept toward her. She jumped back again and he missed—perhaps deliberately, she couldn't be sure—but now her back was against the mantel. There was no more retreat. Nowhere to go. He stood in front of her, grim-faced, and she recalled Damien's having told her how easily she could bleed to death.

Bachman lifted the blade. He pressed its pointed tip to her throat. "Say you'll come with me Shannon. Don't make me hurt you."

She'd die before she'd go with him. She had to do something. Her hand groped behind her, moving slowly, so as not to alert him. It bumped the glass cube that enclosed one of Damien's artifacts. She lifted the glass, set it aside and clenched her fist on the section of stone tablet.

And in that instant, that very instant as she felt the pressure of the cold blade increase, felt its tip press harder into her flesh, she sensed as clearly as if he'd spoken it, his intent to kill her unless she cooperated. And to kill Damien, as well. She knew only one thing. She didn't want to die. Damien had been right about that.

In a surge of strength brought on by panic, a surge she didn't try to gauge or temper, she swung the stone forward, catching him in the side of his head.

He fell sideways and his body slammed to the floor so hard she thought he'd cracked the marble. He didn't move, of course. She blinked, felt the bile rise up in her throat, wanted to retch.

She tore away from the wall and ran to the door, flinging it open, racing through it—and colliding hard with a broad chest.

"Shannon—"

His arms closed around her, and she sagged against Damien, clinging to his neck, sobbing. "I think I killed him. Oh, God, I think I killed him."

"I'm sorry, Shannon. I came as fast as I could, the second I sensed something wrong, but—"

He broke off, threading his fingers in her hair, lifting her into his arms. He carried her back through the house, holding her face to his shoulder as they passed through his comfort room. He took her up the stairs, laid her gently on the bed. "Shannon, I'm sorry. I'm sorry. I don't know what else to say."

She searched his face, his beloved, beautiful face, and she didn't know what to say, either. Her fingers clenched, and she realized she still held the stone. She drew it up to her chest, rolled slowly to her side, facing away from him, and closed her eyes.

Sighing, Damien covered her with a blanket, and left her alone.

Damien went downstairs to check on Bachman's condition, but the man was gone. Shannon hadn't killed him after all. It would be a relief to her to know that.

Eric's voice came from the doorway. "Are you all right?"

Before Damien formed an answer, his lovely young mate came forward, with all the grace of a ballerina in the midst of a dance. She drew a flask from a pocket inside her coat, and offered it to him. "Here, Damien. You're white as chalk. Drink."

"Tamara, love, that isn't—" Eric began, but he paused, searching Damien's awestruck face. "What is it, my friend?"

A burden floated away from Damien's shoulders. "The need. The thirst. By the love of Inanna, it's changed. Altered. I don't feel..." He smiled softly at Tamara and took the small flask from her hands. He drained it, and by the gods, it assuaged the emptiness inside him. It satisfied his thirst as thoroughly as it had thousands of years ago. He didn't feel that raging need to take from a living being. Not even a twinge of it.

Eric studied his face, reading all of these thoughts, Damien knew. "Amazing," he whispered.

"Not so amazing." Tamara tilted her head, sending spirals of raven curls over her shoulder. Her black eyes glittered with knowledge and Damien shot her a searching glance. "I know about your problems feeding, Damien. Eric and I don't keep secrets. But honestly, you men are so dense about some things. Every species has to procreate. Nature gives them all urges that, when followed, lead to mating and reproduction. Is it so far-fetched that we're burdened with the same urges? The need to drink from the living gets stronger, more maddening, more demanding, until you perform the ritual, the creating of another one of us. Then the need vanishes."

Eric shook his head in blatant amazement. "So, we must transform one of the Chosen once every thousand years or so, in order to preserve our sanity." He smiled, then laughed. "Makes perfect sense, Tamara."

Her brows rose in perfect arches. "Sure it does."

Damien paced to the chaise and sank into it. "One problem less to deal with. Why do I still feel like hell?"

"You ought to rest. It's nearly dawn. And your Shannon should be moved from that bedroom, with those big windows." Pretty young Tamara wrinkled her nose. "Although I don't think she's quite ready yet to wake up in a coffin."

"No. I think we'll be safe enough here today, in my usual place. I just wish I knew what happened to Bachman."

"You won't have to worry about him—for a while, at least," Eric said. "He staggered into the street and collapsed. A carload of teens found him and they sent someone for an ambulance. Even if Bachman comes to and starts talking, no one will pay much attention. A man with a head injury, raving about vampires, isn't exactly believable. It ought to be at least a day before he can contact DPI for reinforcements. You ought to be prepared to leave here then, though, Damien. They don't take these kinds of things well at all." He paced away. "What of Netty?"

"I bought her a ticket on a cruise ship that leaves at first light, paid her off enough to make her think twice about betraying me again."

"Good. Your troubles are dissipating, my friend," Eric said cheerfully. "You've whittled them down to two—Shannon's mind-set and this rogue in the city."

"And we'll deal with all that tonight." Tamara tugged on Eric's arm. "If we'd brought Rhiannon along, she'd have had that rogue for breakfast."

"Which is exactly why I asked you not to mention this either to her or Roland. Tamara, love, we have no idea of this renegade's age or strength. Rhiannon would charge in, fearless as always, and perhaps get herself killed."

Damien's mouth quirked up at one corner. "This woman sounds like someone I'd like to meet."

"Only in a good mood, believe me," Eric intoned. Tamara elbowed him and dragged him to the door. "Good rest, Damien."

"Good rest," he replied without thinking. He watched them go, then turned to tackle the problem of Shannon.

He came back, as she'd known he would. He just couldn't seem to understand that she needed time to herself. She rolled onto her back and faced him. Then she wished she hadn't. There was pain in his eyes when he looked at her.

She sniffed and sat up. "I felt strong before, but it's waning. Is it only temporary?"

"It's almost daylight." He spoke softly. "Day weakens us. We rest until dark, and wake feeling strong as ever." He approached slowly, as if waiting for her to object. When she didn't, he sat on the edge of the bed. "You must have a thousand questions."

She nodded.

"But it's almost dawn." He licked his lips, obviously nervous. "Shannon, you made it clear you don't want to spend eternity with me. Don't want to depend on me at all. There are others who can answer your questions. You don't have to bring them to me.''

She swallowed hard, lowering her head. She'd hurt him by saying those things. ''I didn't mean—''

He held up a hand. ''I want you to stay with me through today. There's no time to find you another safe place to rest. I'm not trying to force myself on you, I promise. I just want you safe. There's another vampire in the city. The one who killed Tawny and the other woman. Eric and I will find him and stop him. After that you're free to go where you want. Run to the other side of the world—''

She shook her head hard. ''I didn't mean—''

''Bachman isn't dead,'' he told her. ''But he'll be out of action for a while. Still, there are others, that organization he works for—they'd like to eradicate us. And this other vampire, an evil bastard who hates me for reasons I still don't understand. It isn't safe for you to go out alone until I find him, but I swear, it won't be long. Eric and I will leave with the sunset to hunt him down. Then you can leave with my blessing.''

She closed her eyes, knowing she'd hurt him deeply, maybe beyond repair. He held out a hand to her. She took it and rose from the bed. Without a word, he led her through the hall, up another flight of stairs and through a door on the third floor. He walked right into a closet, and she was surprised when the wall that was the closet's back slid open. He drew her inside, slid the door closed again, hit a button, and the lights came up. Music began, Sting, her favorite. An exotic incense filled the air. He touched her hair, then abruptly drew his hand away.

''You can have the bed,'' he said, his voice hoarse. ''I'll take a blanket and lie on the floor.''

''You'll be uncomfortable…''

''Not really.'' He smiled very slightly. ''I sleep like the dead.''

God, what was wrong with her? Wasn't this the same man she'd fallen in love with? Couldn't she find a way to forgive him for forcing her into an existence she wasn't sure she could bear?

She tried. She tried to judge her feelings for Damien. She'd been so sure before, just before all of this. When he'd made love to her, she'd known she was deeply in love with him. There'd been no doubt. And only the knowledge that she was dying had kept her from telling him so. She hadn't wanted to hurt him. But what about now? Could she love him now? Knowing what he was…what he'd made her?

She'd realized that she didn't want to die. But did she want to live? Like this?

"Give it a chance, Shannon," he whispered. "Don't walk out into the sunrise just yet."

"I wasn't thinking of that."

"Make sure you don't." She sat on the edge of the bed and he came to her, knelt in front of her, took her hands. "Hate me for bringing you over, if you have to. But don't hate yourself or what you are. You haven't changed, not really. You're the same beautiful, vibrant, wonderful woman you were before. You're still strong and capable, and as independent as you want to be."

"I have changed." She averted her eyes. "I thought I'd killed Bachman. I'm glad I didn't, but I could have, Damien. I don't think I can stand the thought of taking a life."

"You wouldn't have hurt him if you hadn't been forced. You don't know the extent of your strength yet, Shannon. And that wouldn't have happened if I'd been here faster. It was more my fault than yours." She didn't look at him, and he hurried on. "You hit the men who tried to steal your car. One of them could have hit his head and died. But you didn't find yourself questioning the value of your mortal life when it was over, did you?"

She blinked and met his gaze. "No."

"It was an unavoidable accident, Shannon. Self-defense. And Bachman is going to recover. You didn't kill anyone. Try to put it behind you."

"But don't you *have* to kill people…to live?" He closed his eyes as if that remark hurt him. She licked her lips. "You don't, do you?" Slowly, she shook her head. "No, you couldn't. You couldn't even bring yourself to kill that mouse...."

"I cherish life, all life. I despise death, Shannon. It took away the dearest, most beloved friend I ever had, until you. It tried to claim you, as well."

As she listened to him, her mind grew heavy and foggy as it had been when she'd first awakened. She glanced down at the stone she still clutched, and blinked.

Damien was easing her back onto the pillows. She stared up at his face in wonder, and recalled the story he'd told her, the ending to the *Epic of Gilgamesh*. The one that had never been recorded, that he called his own personal theory.

"He found the secret," she whispered. "But it didn't make him a god, and it didn't give him the power to bring Enkidu back. It only condemned him to an endless existence, to watching death win over and over again."

The greatest king ever to rule, driven to the edge of insanity by the grief of losing his closest friend. She lifted a hand and pressed her palm to his cheek. "It was you."

His eyes fell closed. He lay down beside her, wrapping his arms around her. "You felt the power of the bond between Enkidu and me from the first time you read of it. You cried for it. I remember. You know how I felt about him, don't you?"

"Enkidu?"

He squeezed his eyes, but a tear slipped through anyway. "The brother of my soul," he muttered in Sumerian. Amazingly, she knew what he said. She heard the words pass from his mind to hers and the meaning was clear. "As much as I loved him, Shannon, I love you even more. How could I watch you die? How *could I,* when I had the power to save you? It was wrong. I know that. I knew it then. But Shannon, I had to do it. I'd do it again."

His arms tightened around her, almost reflexively, she sensed, as if he were reliving that moment when he'd chosen to cling to her—to do whatever he had to—to keep her with him. Her eyes should have been wide with wonder at this new knowledge of him, this new understanding. But instead they were heavy, lids dropping, sleep claiming her. She snuggled close to him, twisting her arms around his waist, not wanting him to keep his promise and sleep on the floor. She pressed her face into the crook of his neck, and she smelled his scent and tasted the salt of his flesh on her lips as she whispered, "Gilgamesh..."

And then she fell asleep, thinking of the lines she'd read in the epic, lines that returned to haunt her. Lines about grief:

It could go on for years and years,
and has, for centuries...
It yearns and waits to be retouched,
by someone who can take away
the memory of death.

He was gone when she awoke. She sat up slowly, blinking, realizing vaguely that the lights were still dim. They brightened gradually. The music began as if by itself, and only grew louder as she came fully alert.

"Quite a setup he has here, isn't it?"

She started, eyes flying wider. A woman stood in the room near the doorway. She was small, a pixie, with a tiny waist and cascades of raven curls that reached it. She smiled and took a step forward.

"I'm Tamara."

She'd heard the name, she was sure. She frowned. Tamara. Then she *was* real. "Eric's wife?"

"Well, not 'wife' exactly. We didn't do a church wedding or anything. 'Till death us do part' would be kind of meaningless for us. But our vows are just as binding. No, more binding." She strode to the stereo system in the back of the room, started pawing through the CDs.

She wore snug-fitting jeans and a green silk button-down blouse. A pair of shiny black flats on her feet. Even makeup. Shannon stared, gaping, until the woman turned and smiled at her. "I know—I don't look like a vampire, do I? Rhiannon does. She's all tall and elegant and has this haughty attitude. But I think she was like that, even mortal. She's a princess, you know. And I'm just...just me.''

''I didn't mean to stare.''

Tamara came forward, sat on the edge of the bed. ''I've only been in darkness for a few years, Shannon. I know what you're going through.'' She lowered her dark, velvety lashes. ''Well, sort of. In my case, I had to practically beg Eric to bring me over. I can't say for sure how I'd have dealt with it if he'd just done it, without asking how I felt first.''

Shannon licked her lips. ''I still didn't believe you existed. The next thing I know, I wake up and I'm one of you.''

Tamara nodded, meeting Shannon's eyes with real concern in her own. ''It's a tough adjustment under any circumstances. But I'll help you, if you want.'' She smiled a little, and her hand rose to touch Shannon's hair. ''You're beautiful, you know. I've never heard of a fair-complected vampire before. You must be as rare as a flawless diamond.''

Shannon felt herself blush at the compliment.

''It's probably because of the lineage. I think the darkness is inherited, along with the Belladonna antigen.''

Shannon took that in, nodding. Then she glanced toward the door and gnawed on her lower lip.

''He and Eric went out to see if they could find this rogue vampire that's been raising hell around here.''

She nodded again. She wished Damien hadn't left before she'd awoken. She'd hurt him. He thought she wanted to be away from him. That wasn't at all what she wanted. She wasn't sure exactly what she wanted anymore, only that she understood now. She understood his pain, his loss. She'd been half in love with Gilgamesh since she'd read his epic. And now she knew why. And she knew why he'd made the decision he had when she'd been dying in his arms. Being who he was, he couldn't have done anything else.

''You'll have time to tell him all that. He'll be back before dawn.''

She blinked in surprise.

"We can hear each other's thoughts, Shannon."

"That's incredible."

Tamara smiled. *I'll teach you how to do it. You can surprise Damien when he gets back. For now, why don't you get up and shower and dress? There's so much I want to tell you about, show you....*

All of it, Shannon heard clearly. All of it spoken without Tamara's having uttered a sound. Her head spinning, Shannon got up and complied.

Tamara seemed so normal.

She'd been thrilled to ride in Shannon's car, more thrilled yet when Shannon let her drive it awhile. They took turns choosing CDs and they played them at ear-piercing volume, singing along until Shannon actually began to feel like herself again. Maybe Damien was right. Maybe she hadn't changed all that much.

They parked the car, then walked through the streets. As they did, Tamara urged Shannon to practice the telepathy, and soon they were conversing almost totally in silence. Shannon started attempting to read other people's thoughts as they passed. The results were often hilarious.

Then, in a trash-littered, abandoned alley, Tamara stood by Shannon's side. "Let's race to the other end."

A shiver of apprehension skittered over Shannon's nape. "This isn't a very good place to hang out, Tamara."

"Think about it," she said. "Who's gonna bother us?"

Shannon smiled. She was right.

"You've got a lot of strength now, Shannon. And speed. You won't believe it. Be careful not to hit the wall on the other side. Pain hurts more now than before."

"I'd noticed that."

"On three," Tamara said, and then counted mentally.

They were off like bullets from a gun, and Shannon would have collided with the wall if Tamara hadn't caught her arm and brought her to a skidding stop.

For hours Tamara helped Shannon to explore her new self. And as time flew past, Shannon began to think this wasn't so bad after all. She could jump from the top of a tree and land on her feet. She could see in the dark. All her senses were honed to razor sharpness. She was strong, energized. And she could read minds.

"You think that's incredible, just wait until you…you know." Tamara's pale cheeks pinkened.

"No, I don't know. Wait until I what?"

Tamara grinned and tilted her head to one side. "You and Damien…*you know*…"

"Oh." Shannon bit her lip. "Is it…different?"

"Way different."

Shannon licked her lips. "I don't know when I'll find out. Things aren't exactly…right between us."

"You love him, don't you?"

She thought about that, and found herself nodding emphatically. "I do. I really do. I lost sight of it for a while, a really short, confused while. But I never stopped."

"Well, he's nuts about you. You'll work things out."

Shannon nodded, recalling his words to her before she'd fallen asleep this morning. He'd said he loved her even more than Enkidu. It awed her that he could feel that strongly about her.

They walked back to the car, only to meet a stranger there. A vampire. Surprising that she knew it at a glance, but she did, and she stopped short. He was tall, and almost emaciated. So slender. In his long face every bone was visible. His neck was like a reed, his shoulders pointy and hard.

He approached them slowly, and Tamara caught her breath, gripping Shannon's arm.

"No use," he said, and his voice reminded Shannon of a cobra's hiss. "I'm six thousand years old. You're a toddler and a newborn. Don't bother running."

And in the blink of an eye, he had them, his bony arms anchored around their waists, capturing their arms at their sides. Shannon struggled. She knew Tamara did, as well, but couldn't see her. He'd taken off at such incredible speed that everything was a blur. She thought they were airborne, but couldn't be sure. Tamara hadn't told her anything about flight.

Don't call out to Eric and Damien. Tamara's thoughts echoed in Shannon's ears. *It could be a trap for them. I've been through it before.*

"No matter," the monster who held them rasped. "I've left a note at the house for them. It's long past time for Gilgamesh to meet his fate."

CHAPTER FIFTEEN

They'd tried for hours to pick up some sense of the rogue in the city. They'd sought a hint of his thoughts, his presence, in the places where the victims had been found, and in the theater, and in and around Shannon's office. The sense of him should be stronger where his physical self had been. But their efforts got them nothing. He was concealing himself against them, and doing it well.

They returned to the house then, and Damien braced himself to come face-to-face with Shannon again, to see the despair in her eyes, the fear of him, the anger. Maybe this time there would be hatred in her amber eyes, as well. He had no idea what he could say to her. She despised what he'd done, hated what he'd made her. So how could she not hate him? How could she even bear to see him again, let alone sleep another day under his roof? What would she say when he told her he'd failed, and asked her to stay with him for one more day, give him one more night to make it safe for her to leave him? He couldn't let her go until this threat was removed, even though he was sure the hatred he'd felt emanating from this rogue had been directed at himself alone.

Hell, he didn't want her to leave at all, to be honest. He couldn't bear the thought of living a night without her vibrance to brighten it. Irony tasted bitter. He no longer had to fear he had become a ruthless killer, that to love her would be to endanger her. And he no longer had to fear that death would tear her from him. But he'd lost her all the same, hadn't he?

He felt Eric tense beside him. And then he sensed it. The feeling of something wrong, terribly wrong, of danger. The knowledge that the rogue had been here.

He ran to the front steps, up them, and found the note, impaled on the point of a dagger as old as time, pinned to the door.

Eric tore it down, leaving the blade where it was, and struggled to read, but he shook his head. "It's not in any language I know."

Damien frowned, taking the sheet of paper from him. "It's cuneiform script." The symbols on the paper were similar to those chiseled into stone aeons ago. A cold shiver racing through him, Damien translated aloud: "'Gilgamesh, king of Uruk, lord of a people long dead, vile betrayer of the gods, immortal, demon, murderer. For your role in the death of one who loved you, for your hand in her murder, for the life of Siduri, my betrothed, you will stand trial. In the temple of Inanna, you will be judged, that the gods might witness your sentence carried out. No longer does the temple lie buried beneath the burning sands of Uruk. Still buried, yes, but not there. Never to be seen by mortal eyes. Brick by brick did I move it. I await you there. Your lover waits at my side. Ready she stands to take your sentence upon herself in case you fail to heed my summons. Long have I anticipated this reunion, man of old. Anthar.'"

Damien looked up from the note, to see the fear, the wonder, in Eric's eyes.

"Gilgamesh," he muttered, staring at Damien. "My God."

"I'm no one's god, just an immortal like you. We have to go now, fast."

Eric's brows rose. "But how? You've no idea where you're going."

Damien gripped his arm. "Your Tamara—"

"Will stubbornly erect a fortress around her mind rather than lure me into what she must know is a trap." Eric closed his eyes. "I'll try, but if she really doesn't want me to know where she is…" He shook his head and tried to concentrate.

"What the hell *is this?*" Shannon watched the huge doors slide slowly open, then jerked against the hands that tugged her into an elevator big enough to hold an elephant. God, he was strong. His bony hand gripped her arm so hard she thought he'd break it. Tears streamed down her face. Her throat closed so tightly she could barely draw a breath. Her chest spasmed with sobs she tried to stop. And still she fought him.

She was afraid, terrified of what this skeletal man planned to do to her. But more than that was the fear of what he'd already done. To Tamara. They'd been airborne, soaring through the night at a speed that seemed impossible, with the wind stinging Shannon's face, screaming in her ears. So high the ground seemed no more than a fast-moving, colorful blur. And he'd just let Tamara go. Just let her go!

She hadn't even screamed. Not a sound. Nothing. And Shannon couldn't see where she landed, because the bony bastard had still been speeding through space, still been clutching her tight. But Shannon *had* screamed. And she hadn't stopped screaming until he'd hit her with a skinny fist and knocked her close to senseless.

And now she was in this elevator, going down at a sickening speed, deep into the bowels of some kind of structure that seemed to sit in the middle of nowhere.

The doors opened almost before they'd come to a teeth-jarring stop. The hand on her upper arm closed tighter, and wincing in pain, she stepped out into a stadium-size room where every step echoed a thousand times. In the center of the room, she saw it, a towering wonder of whitewashed brick, gleaming, immaculate. Her gaze traveled over the angular ramps and steps and corners, all leading upward. A squared spiral at least forty feet high, topped by what looked like a temple.

"What the hell is this?" she asked again.

"Who is this Anthar?"

Damien shook his head. "He must be from my time to know who I am and understand the cuneiform so well. The blade is ancient. Sumerian. And he must have known me once to have heard of Siduri."

"A woman?"

Damien nodded. "I'll explain later. We have to hurry." Already a cold knot of foreboding twisted inside his heart. He wished he could blink his eyes and be at her side. But he knew better. He was as attuned to her mind as he could get, and all he felt was her fear. It overwhelmed everything else. There was a dim sense of the direction in which she'd traveled, and Damien followed that sense, felt himself getting closer.

Anthar. Who the hell was he, and why this quest for vengeance? Damien didn't know. He knew only that if the bastard hurt Shannon in any way, no matter how small, Damien would kill him a little at a time. She must be so frightened. By Inanna's mercy, she must be twice as sorry he'd brought her over by now. She probably wished he'd simply let her die. He'd wanted to do so much for her. To show her happiness, to make up for all the sorrow in her life. Instead he'd brought her into a world of darkness, and so far all she'd known had been fear.

He'd get her out of this safely. He would, if it cost him his life to do it. And then he'd give her what she craved. Her freedom. No matter how much it would hurt him, Damien knew he had to let her go.

Eric had been silent for some time, and when Damien broke out of his own thoughts long enough to glance at the man, he saw turmoil contorting Eric's face. He stopped, facing him. "Marquand, what? What is it?"

His jaw tight, eyes moist, Eric kept moving. Then faster. And a moment later, he knelt beside a still form on the ground, cradling it in his arms and quivering with silent rage.

Damien ran forward. "Tamara!" Her left leg bent at an unnatural angle, and one arm was twisted beneath her body. Obviously broken. Damien's heart turned to ice as he saw Eric's pain. But her lovely black lashes fluttered, and she stared up at the man who held her with so much love in her eyes it hurt Damien to witness it.

"I'm...glad to see you."

"Tamara." Eric's voice wavered. He bent lower, kissed her face.

"Gently, Eric. It...hurts."

"I'll kill him," Eric whispered. "I'll kill him for this."

Damien felt tears choking him. When the hell had he become

so attached to these people? "You're going to have to move her, Eric, pain or not. Find her some shelter before dawn."

Eric nodded and glanced around. "Where the hell are we?"

"Somewhere in Ohio, I think." Damien glanced around him. "There are houses. I can—"

"No." Tamara tried to lift her head, her good hand clutching Eric's arm. "Damien, you have to go on. Find Shannon before that beast hurts her." She drew a pained breath. "But be careful. It's you he wants."

"I know." Damien straightened and stared off into the distance.

"Go ahead, go after them," Eric said. "I'll take care of Tamara. We'll be fine."

"Are you sure?"

Tamara nodded. "I'll be okay after a day's rest, Damien. And we'll join you…with reinforcements."

Eric's jaw went rigid. "Tamara, you didn't—"

"I most certainly did. We have to end this bastard's killing spree, Eric. And we need all the help we can get." She relaxed a little, letting her head fall onto Eric's knees. "I pity that bastard if Rhiannon gets to him before Damien does."

Eric glanced back at Damien. "I wouldn't be too sure about that, Tamara."

"Neither would I." Damien turned, and started off again toward Shannon.

He was forced to seek shelter when the sun rose. But he resumed his search the instant it set, and he knew when he'd found her.

His best guess was that the structure dead center of a barren field had once been a missile silo. One of those sold by the government to private owners when arms-reduction deals took the place of the cold war. He approached the doors, and they opened. Then the bastard knew he'd arrived. Damien stepped inside what appeared to be an elevator, not caring if he was walking into a trap as long as he could get to Shannon. The car

swept downward, clanged to a stop and opened as if to spit him
out.

Damien stood frozen for a single moment, reeling at the sensation of having stepped back in time. The ziggurat stood as
haughty and immaculate as it had been when it was new. This
same temple had been the center of his city once. It had been
filled with his people, his gods. A man-made mountain is what
it was. A high, white monster of stairs and ramps, sharp corners
turning this way and that, a path to the heavens marching its
way to the cella at the very top. The temple proper. The chamber
of the gods, where sacrifices had been offered.

He knew the temple well, remembered the way the white
bricks had gleamed beneath a blazing desert sun. Now it stood
in darkness. Appropriate. Ironic.

Mounting the first steps, Damien went upward, following the
same path he had thousands of times so many years ago, only
faster now, his strides more powerful than ever before. And more
desperate. In seconds he stood at the entrance to the cella. He
stiffened his spine and went inside.

A figure like a walking skeleton moved from sconce to sconce
with a torch in his hand, lighting each as he came to it. The
main room, sixty feet in length and lined with sconces on both
sides, soon glowed with amber light as it had in days long past.
Shadows fled the touch of the torchlight, ducking into the darkened doorways that lined the chamber. Every few yards a smaller
chamber opened off one side or the other. But this was the room
of worship, the room of the gods, the room of sacrifice.

Damien stepped forward, marveling that the place had been
so well restored. The stone figures that depicted the worshippers
were just as he remembered them, some standing as high as his
knees, others smaller. Male and female, bearded and smooth
skinned, eyes too large, hands folded in prayer.

Damien moved past them, tearing his gaze away from the
figures that represented his people. Instead he focused on the
emaciated man who'd stopped at the opposite end of the chamber, and turned to face him.

"I'm here, Anthar. I've done as you asked. Where is Shannon?"

Anthar only smiled, an evil expression, the flickering orange torchlight making it more so. He stepped aside, waving a hand beyond him to the life-size statue of the god Anu. Anu's golden hair and beard had been polished until they gleamed, and his eyes, inlaid with lapis lazuli, danced with fierceness in the firelight. At his sandaled feet, upon the stone offering table, Shannon lay wide-eyed, trembling, her hands bound at the wrists, clenched together on her stomach. Her ankles, too, were bound together. She was dressed in a white gown, fastened with a jeweled brooch at one shoulder, leaving the other bare. Golden bands encircled her arms. Her feet were bare.

As Damien's gaze met hers, he felt her fear, her absolute misery. He tried to convey reassurance, hope, comfort. Anthar stepped forward to ignite the torches near her head and at her feet. She cringed from him, and a sound of terror came from deep in her throat. Damien lunged forward, but Anthar stepped into his path.

"Look around you, Gilgamesh. See the gods you betrayed by seeking to become one of them." He lifted the torch toward each of the deities that towered at Anu's right and his left. "The goddess Inanna, whose name you cursed from the deathbed of your friend. Ea, of the fresh springs, friend to mankind. Even him you have offended. Enlil, god of earth, wind and spirit, whom you have defiled. Ninurta, god of war, furious with you now."

Damien held his temper in check with an effort. "It seems, Anthar, the only one I've offended is you. The gods haven't acted against me in all this time. I hardly think their justice would be so slow in coming."

"Their justice is at hand," Anthar said in a deep monotone.

Damien shook his head. "If that's true, then I'm ready for it. Let's get on with this, Anthar. Release the woman now. Whatever you have in mind, it's meant for me to suffer, not her."

"Not just yet, Gilgamesh."

Damien moved forward, meaning to free Shannon himself. But Anthar reached to a small stone stand and snatched up a ritual dagger, its handle inlaid with glittering jewels—emeralds and sapphires, diamonds and rubies. The blade was honed to a razor's edge. He held it poised at Shannon's throat and she screamed, her voice echoing endlessly in the hollow room long after she'd gone utterly still. She stared at Damien, her gaze clinging to his almost desperately.

"If you move, blasphemer, I will hurt her. Badly I will hurt her. Likely she'll bleed dry before you can help her."

"I'm very old, rogue," Damien said softly, his voice oddly hoarse. "Older than any, except Utnapishtim himself, who made me. You ought to be careful about angering me."

"Utnapishtim made me, as well, great king of Uruk. Only moments after you."

Damien looked quickly at the gaunt-faced man. "He wouldn't have—"

"He had no choice. His exchange of blood with a young madman left him weak. I forced him to repeat the ritual, only so that I would live to see you die."

Eric's voice came into Damien's mind then, and he knew his friend—yes, friend—was on the way, monitoring events mentally, offering advice. *The blood was diluted then, when this Anthar was made. You're still stronger.*

Damien nodded, sensing Eric guarded his thoughts from Anthar. He tried to do the same. *Maybe.*

"What crime have I committed to anger you so much that you'd follow me into eternity just to see me pay?"

"Do you recall Siduri? My beautiful Siduri, who gave her heart to a beast?"

Damien nodded, stepping a bit closer, only to wince as Anthar pressed the tip of his blade harder into Shannon's neck. "Answer aloud, so that the gods present may know of your sins."

He licked his lips. "I was half out of my mind with grief when Enkidu, my friend, died. I went on a quest in search of immortality, thinking I could somehow bring that gift back to him and raise him up again. When I came to Siduri's cottage by the sea I was near starved, sunburned, travel-weary and all but insane. She brought me inside, washed the sand and the sweat from my skin. She fed me and clothed me, restored my health and part of my senses."

Anthar grimaced, his thin lips drawing away from his foul, uneven teeth. "Is that all she gave you, heathen?"

"She gave me comfort, Anthar. We shared a bed."

"She was my betrothed!" he screamed, nearly rattling the brick walls.

That declaration shocked Damien. But still it didn't seem reason enough for so much hatred. "I didn't know—"

"You used her as chattel and cast her aside to resume your mad quest. She begged of you to stay, but you turned a deaf ear to her tears."

"No. She knew I'd go on from the day I crossed her threshold. She knew—"

"You killed her. She thought herself in love with you, gave you all of herself as proof of it, even though she'd promised herself to me."

"And that was no crime!" Damien stepped forward once more, staring at this shell of a man. "You know as well as I do that in that time it was a king's right to take the virgin brides before their husbands did. Right or wrong, it was the law. So how can you say that I committed some crime by bedding your woman?" A flimsy argument, he knew, but all he could think of at the moment.

"Bastard, she lost her soul when you left her. But you wouldn't know, would you? You never looked back to see how she fared. You didn't know that she walked into the sea the very next dawn, walked and kept walking. Drowned herself for the love of a worthless king who would make himself a god!"

Eric's voice came again, like a solid hand clasping his shoulder. *It wasn't your fault. Don't let it distract you.*

But Damien felt the blow. He staggered a bit, then caught

himself. "I didn't know. She...she was kind to me, Anthar. I cared for her. I am sorry. More sorry than I can say."

"Your sorrow will not suffice, Gilgamesh. You must suffer as I did."

Incinerate him.

Damien shook his head quickly, responding to Eric in the silent form of communication he'd so recently mastered. *I'm not sure it would work, and it takes an unbelievable amount of energy to incinerate* anything. *If it failed, I'd be practically helpless.*

Damien had gone utterly still, watching the way the firelight played on Shannon's skin, in her hair, a terrible fear of what this bastard intended settling like ice water in his veins. "What are you going to do, Anthar?"

"I'm going to take your woman as you took mine." He glanced down at Shannon as he spoke. "And then I'm going to drain her, and let her die. And you are going to stand witness to it, Gilgamesh. For I want to see you suffer, before I kill you."

"You haven't got the strength to kill me."

"We'll soon see."

The man, blade still in his hand, bent over Shannon, and she screamed.

At the same instant there was a tremendous crash and a rain of footsteps at the entrance. Damien knew without turning that four immortals had entered the cella. A powerful female voice echoed like that of Inanna herself. For a second Damien wondered if the statue of the Queen of Heaven had come to life. "Exactly what kind of death wish do you have, you sorry excuse for an immortal!"

"You're in for it now, Anthar," Tamara stated flatly.

The rogue was distracted for a bare instant, and that was all Damien needed. He spun in a circle, becoming a blur, and an instant later, a massive wolf launched itself at the evil vampire, sending him crashing to the floor, the knife skittering away.

Shannon tried hard to cling to her sanity as the horror played out before her eyes. The wolf snapped at the man's throat, but then they rolled, and a second later the wolf backed away from a coiled king cobra, cape unfurled, poised to strike. The wolf leapt into the air, and as it hurtled earthward, it became a hawk that swooped and dove, drawing the snake away from her. She rolled her body off the stone table, pulled herself to her feet, both hands working as one, and began hopping toward the two who fought. The snake had the hawk cornered now, and would strike at any second. She had to stop this.

But a tug at her hands brought her to a stop. The woman, tall and slender, regal as a queen, with her ebony hair all swept to one side and diamonds and onyx dripping from her ears, leaned over the rope at Shannon's ankles. "You fledglings are nothing but trouble." With a flick of her scarlet-painted, dagger-tipped fingers, she freed Shannon's ankles, then her wrists. "I'm Rhiannon," she said, as if she were saying "I'm Queen Elizabeth." She pulled Shannon toward the corner where Eric and Tamara waited with another man Shannon didn't know. At their feet, a sleek black panther crouched, watching the struggling beasts with predatory eyes.

"None of them for you, Pandora." The woman stroked the cat's head lovingly, but her eyes were on the floor where the two battled.

Shannon whirled, half expecting to see Damien dead on the floor. But there was a lion now, and a jaguar, ripping at each other's throats, rolling in a tangle of claws and teeth.

"Do something!" She screamed.

Tamara touched her shoulder. "I don't know what we can—"

She broke off when Shannon jerked away from her touch. Shannon had spotted the glittering dagger on the floor, and she lunged for it, falling to her knees to snatch it up. Rising slowly, her gaze on the combatants, she started forward, lifting the blade high above her head, giving a little growl she'd never heard herself utter before.

The tall woman caught her shoulders. "Fool, you'll be killed! Come with us. Damien wants us to take you out of here, someplace safe."

Shannon turned on her, the blade between them an unspoken threat. "I'm not going anywhere. You try to force me and you'll wish you hadn't, lady."

Tamara's eyes went saucer-wide. The two men, who'd been talking urgently, went silent.

The woman eyed Shannon for a moment. "I'll forgive that fledgling. Once."

Shannon ignored her imperious words and turned once more. The forms on the floor had become men again. They stood, facing each other, panting, bleeding from various wounds. Eric and the strange man both lunged forward, but Damien held up a hand to stop them.

"Get Shannon out of here, for the love of Inanna!"

"I won't go!" she shrieked.

"Anthar, stop this at once. You're no match for all of us!" It was the stranger who shouted it.

"Care to put that theory to the test?"

Anthar whispered. He looked at the stranger, his gaze hardening, intensifying in a way Shannon had never seen. It was as if an energy pulsed from his sunken eyes.

"Roland!" Rhiannon threw herself at the stranger, sending him sprawling to the stone floor just as a ball of flame exploded in the air where he'd stood.

She rose, facing Anthar, rage in her eyes. "Oh, now you *will* pay—"

He laughed at her, and Shannon thought the woman's rage was so full-blown it made the air around them quiver.

Anthar turned away from her and lunged, shoving Damien onto his back on the floor. He yanked a blade from his boot and lifted his arm to plunge it into Damien's throat.

"Noooo!" It was a battle cry, emitted as Shannon launched herself. She landed squarely on the man's back, both hands gripping his wrist, pulling it away from Damien with every ounce of strength she possessed.

Anthar flung her from him like a dog ridding itself of a flea. She felt herself fly through the air. She landed brutally hard. Her head connected with the stone offering table, sending her senses reeling. Dizzy, her head exploding with pain, her body weakened by it, she forced her eyes open.

Damien growled his rage, flinging the man away from him, then focusing his eyes on the bastard as he struggled to get to his feet.

The man seemed to feel that heated gaze. He froze for an instant in time, and turned to face Damien. "Can you do it, do you think?" His thin brows rose, and he moved forward, menacingly. The black panther growled deep in its throat, crouching low. "Better question, can you do it fast enough?" Anthar sprang forward, arm swinging in a deadly arc, the knife he clutched on a collision coarse with Damien's neck. He'd behead him!

Damien stood his ground, staring harder, not backing away even an inch, and Shannon shrieked at him to move.

Just before he reached Damien, Anthar's body froze. It began to tremble, then vibrated head to toe. His eyes bulged and a wisp of gray smoke writhed from his hair. A tremor rocked the temple floor, and then a roar, as Anthar burst into a blinding ball of white flame. His keening came more loudly than the blast, and seemed to echo within the temple chamber even after he was silent. It died slowly, an eternal prisoner of the cella walls. And there was nothing, just nothing. Anthar was gone.

Damien sank to the floor as if the act had drained every ounce of his energy. Shannon struggled to her feet and ran to him, fell to her knees, not caring that the stone floor scraped them raw. She pulled him to her, her hands cradling his head. She couldn't speak. She only moaned softly and rocked him against her as the tears flowed. God, she loved him. She hadn't realized just how much until she'd thought he might die trying to save her. If he had, what would she have done? How could she have gone on?

His arms went around her waist, his face nestling in the white linen that covered her, nuzzling her belly. His hands stroked her back again and again. "It's over now, Shannon. It's all right.

You're safe now.'' He pulled himself up a little, pressed his lips to her wet cheeks; to her burning eyes. "Safe now," he whispered again, as her arms encircled his neck. "And free of me. You'll leave with the others. One more day, Shannon. You'll recover from all of this while you rest tomorrow, and then I want you to go. I just hope you can find some kind of contentment in this life I've condemned you to live."

She blinked, her tears ceasing abruptly.

CHAPTER SIXTEEN

"We're stuck here for the day," Tamara observed, her voice soft with relief. She sat on the cold floor, her knees drawn to her chest, and watched as Eric approached Damien. Shannon had withdrawn suddenly, going silent after Damien had told her she could leave him soon. He couldn't look at her to judge her mood, whether she was happy at the news or angry to have to wait through one more day. He couldn't stand the thought that he might see her eagerness to leave mirrored in her eyes. Eric reached out a hand and Damien clasped it, letting Eric help him to his feet. "I wasn't much help, I'm afraid," he said aloud, and silently he said more. *For God's sake, Damien, she jumped on the bastard to save you.*

"You were more help than you know." It was true, Damien thought, a little surprised. Not just the distractions their arrival had provided, breaking Anthar's concentration more than once and probably saving Damien's life. But the feeling of support. The warmth of friends. It was something he hadn't felt in centuries.

And she tried to help me because she feels she owes me, for saving her life in the past.

"Well, at least I can patch up the worst of these injuries for you." Normally, Damien would have turned away, insisted he could take care of himself. But not now. He stood still while Eric ripped a sleeve from his own shirt and began tearing bandage-size strips.

"Tamara's right, you know," Damien observed, loudly enough so everyone, including Shannon, could hear. He wanted her to understand that he wasn't deliberately prolonging her presence here. "We couldn't make it far before sunrise, and who knows what kind of shelter we could find out there? It's best to stay here, rest tomorrow and leave at dusk."

He chanced a peek at Shannon to see if she understood. But she was kneeling now in front of Tamara, and a second later, hugging her. "I thought you must be dead."

"I almost wished I was when I landed." Tamara smiled at her. "But I'm fine now."

Shannon shook her head slowly, mutely. The newcomer, Roland, stood with his back against a stone wall, while regal Rhiannon tore a strip from the hem of her floor-length satin dress and used it to make a sling for his arm. He must have injured it when she'd knocked him to the floor. He winced in pain, and Damien saw the woman wince along with him. Her eyes were dark with concern when she looked at him. Jealousy stabbed Damien. Why couldn't Shannon look at *him* like that?

She did a second ago. Eric again. The optimist.

No, she didn't.

"He should see a doctor," Shannon whispered. She glanced back at Damien, who was currently using pressure to stop the bleeding of a small cut on his forearm, while Eric wrapped a makeshift bandage around it. "And so should you, Damien."

Tamara ran a soothing hand over Shannon's hair. "Any injuries we have heal while we rest during the day. Hasn't anyone explained that to you yet?" She shot Damien a slightly accusing stare as she asked it.

He only shrugged. "Shannon has a lot to learn, and plenty of time to do it." Damien glanced at his watch. "It'll be dawn in a few hours. I think I'll move to one of the smaller chambers now. After that battle, I don't feel like doing anything but lying down." He avoided Shannon's eyes. The truth was he didn't want to see her anymore. It already hurt too much knowing she'd leave him so soon.

Rhiannon left Roland's side to approach Damien as he turned to go. She wasn't smiling. She seemed to float over the stone floor rather than walk, until she stood before him, chin lifted, eyes blazing. "Not until we've been introduced, at least."

"Rhiannon..." Roland's voice held a warning.

She ignored it. "So, you're the great Damien I've heard about."

"And you're Rhiannon, princess of Egypt." She was beautiful. Not as beautiful as Shannon, of course, but lovely just the same. Elegant. "I've heard of you, too."

"You nearly got my friends killed." It was a simple statement of fact.

"It wasn't his fault, Rhiannon." Tamara's voice didn't douse the hint of fire in her eyes. But Roland's good hand closing on her shoulder, his words, spoken low and near her ear, did.

"I don't think it's my imagination, Damien. The wolf I just saw fighting a cobra looked awfully familiar to me. We've met before, that wolf and I. Haven't we?"

Damien averted his eyes. Rhiannon frowned hard at Roland. "Wolf? You mean..."

"In France, my love, when you'd been captured by Lucien and I lay immobilized, watching the sun come up to fry me. The wolf that came to me, pulled me into a cave as I clung to its furred neck. That wolf with the wisdom in its eyes..."

Roland let his voice trail off. Damien said nothing, only nodded once, and turned to go into the nearest chamber. He'd gone against his vow of seclusion to help Roland back then. But he'd been in the area on tour and sensed the man's distress, loud and clear, though he hadn't been listening. Even when he'd decided to step in, knowing he couldn't let someone die when he had the power to save him, he'd done it in disguise. He'd wanted no one's gratitude. No one's friendship.

He'd been wrong. He had their friendship now. Even Rhiannon's. Her hand rose and cupped his face. She leaned forward and pressed her lips to his cheek. No words were needed. Damien nodded a confirmation to himself. He had their friendship, and he was better for it.

But he didn't have what he wanted most. Shannon. Not just her, but her heart. Her love. And he couldn't deal with the fact that he was about to lose her in front of them, friends or not. "You should all find a place to rest, be sure no light can penetrate.'' He turned once again and walked into the first darkened room within reach.

Roland lowered his head and disappeared into another one. The cat left Rhiannon's side to lumber toward Shannon. She stood, her back to the wall, a little thrill of alarm jingling her nerves. It sat on its haunches in front of her, lifted a forepaw and playfully batted Shannon's hand. She felt her eyes widen, but she stayed still as the cat rose and moved forward, shoving her head against Shannon's hand and pressing upward, eyes closed. She stroked the animal, blinking in shock.

''Her name is Pandora. She's...usually a very good judge of character.''

Shannon met Rhiannon's almond eyes, saw the ruby lips curve just slightly.

''Not everyone has the courage to shout defiance in my face. Barely anyone, actually.''

Shannon lowered her head. ''I'm sorry about that. I know you were only trying to help me, but I...'' She glanced toward the chamber where Damien had gone, a lump forming in her throat. ''I couldn't leave him.''

''You threw yourself onto the back of a creature that could have killed you.''

''I had to try.''

Her lips curved a little more. Her eyes glittered. She sent a meaningful glance toward the chamber doorway. ''Yes. A woman in love always has to try.'' And then, the picture of elegance, she floated into the room where Roland had gone. The cat trotted along behind her, a slight limp in her feline gait.

Shannon glanced down to the stone floor where Tamara sat, Eric now resting on her opposite side. Their hands were joined, fingers interlaced. Tamara met Shannon's eyes and nodded once.

Licking her lips, squaring her shoulders, Shannon turned and entered the dark chamber where Damien had gone.

He heard her come in, knew she was there even before he heard her. He felt her presence. He groaned inwardly, but there was another voice in him, one that was thrilled to have these few moments with her, alone, before she left him forever.

He'd brought a torch in here, mounted it in the sconce on the wall near the back of the room. He sat on the floor, back to that wall, watching the play of shadows on the small carved figures and the play of light on their eyes. They seemed alive.

She crossed the room, sat down beside him. By Anu's power, she was a goddess come to life, still dressed in the sacrificial gown, with the golden bands on her arms. She didn't look at him, so he was free to study her until it hurt. Her golden tresses tumbling over her shoulders, her satin skin, her velvet lashes.

"I've lost count now of the number of times you've saved my life."

He said nothing. She was sitting very close to him, but not touching. He longed to reach out, to run his hands through her silken hair, to bring her face to his and taste her mouth one more time. He clenched his hands into fists that trembled. She was here out of gratitude, he told himself. Nothing more.

"I've been thinking," she whispered. "About a lot of things. About you, mostly. The man I got to know, and the man I know now. And I realized that you're the same. Damien or Gilgamesh, mortal or immortal, you're the same."

Still he said nothing. Only watched her struggle for words, waited for her to continue, to tell him why she would leave him.

"I was afraid of something I didn't understand, and angry because I felt you'd taken control." She tugged at the tip of her right index finger, picked at the nail. Nervous. "I'm afraid to let other people have any authority or control in my life. It terrifies me."

"Because of your childhood," he said softly, unable to keep silent on the subject. "It's understandable, Shannon. If the man who tried to abuse you wasn't already dead, I'd kill him myself." He blinked, fighting down the rage that had risen inside him. "I knew how you felt. I had no right to act without asking you. No right at all, and I knew it."

She nodded slowly. Her tongue darted out to moisten her lips.

·"And what would my answer have been, I wonder?" She drew a deep breath, and released it slowly. "I've been thinking about that a lot, too. And you know, I think if I'd known all there was to know, if I'd had a chance to get to know these people, to accept what seemed impossible to me, I think I would have agreed. I think... No, I *know* I would have wanted this."

He turned his head sharply, staring down at her eyes, torchlight in amber.

"When you were fighting with Anthar...God, I was so afraid he'd kill you. And I started wondering what I would do, how I would go on without you."

"You don't have to be dependent on me, Shannon. I never meant to make you feel that way. Any of them can teach you all you need to know."

She shook her head, staring into his eyes, an intensity building in hers. "But I don't *want* any of them to teach me. I want you to do it, Damien."

He lowered his head. It was too painful to stare into her eyes for another second. "So you've decided you can bear to be immortal. You've decided you'd like me to teach you. But, Shannon, *I've* decided...that I just can't do it."

"No?"

"No." He met her eyes again, forced himself to. "I can't be around you and not be *with* you, Shannon. I want you too much, and I'm not strong enough to fight it anymore. I love you, Shannon." He got to his feet, frustration urging him to beat the walls down with his bare hands. But it wouldn't help.

She stood, too, facing him. Her expression so solemn that he had to look at her, had to wonder what she was working up to, here.

She lifted her hands to the brooch that held the white gown in place.

"No, Shannon..."

A second later, the garment was a soft white cloud settling around her feet. "I don't want you to fight it right now, Damien."

He wanted to close his eyes. But nothing could make him turn away. She was too beautiful, standing naked before him, torchlight flickering over her pale skin. He reached out with hesitant hands, and paused. But he couldn't stop himself, could he? Whether it was gratitude or just ordinary desire, he couldn't turn her away. Not when he knew so well it would be the last time.

He touched her arms, ran his palms slowly up and down over them. "Shannon…"

"I told you, I would have taken this option if you'd offered it before I got so sick," she said. "But you haven't asked me why."

He ran his palms over the perfect curve of her back, pulled her close to him, bent his head to kiss her neck, her jaw, her face. Ah, she tasted like ambrosia! He caught her earlobe between his teeth. She wanted to drive him insane, didn't she?

Her fingers traced invisible patterns in his hair. "Ask me why, Damien."

He took her mouth, fed on it, and she responded in kind. Dammit, but he wanted her. Even knowing it would only result in more pain when she left him. He fell to his knees to suckle her breasts, and his blood heated when her breaths quickened and her hands held him to her. He kissed a path over her belly, tongued her navel, then bent lower to taste her secret sweetness. He wanted all of her, every bit. He'd commit her to memory and never forget.

She gasped, her hands trembling on the back of his head as he worked her into a frenzy with his mouth and tongue. She whispered his name, and he used his teeth, smiling when she shuddered in response. Her knees buckled, but he followed her down, climbing up her body with his mouth as his hands worked to open his pants. He'd have her, one last time. He'd be sure she never forgot him, either, even if she lived ten thousand years, a hundred thousand!

He reached her face, parted her mouth with his tongue and made love to it, even as he urged her thighs wider and nudged into her moistness. She arched her hips to take him inside, and he went, eagerly. Her slick entrance clenched him, squeezed him as he drove deeper, filling her up and retreating. Holding back, teasing her until she bounced beneath him, before he plunged into her once more. It was heaven. It was hell. It was slow, burning torture.

He rode her hard on the path to ecstasy, and when he hovered at the brink, he felt her teeth at his throat. She took his essence into her body, as release pounded through her. His own climax was his reply, and she clung to him as if she were drowning. Then relaxed beneath him. He felt her muscles unwind, one by one. She sighed long and low and her fingers wound in his hair again.

"That was like nothing I could have imagined." A bare whisper. A new wonder in her voice.

He rolled off her to lie on his side, lifted her head to pillow it on his arm. "Your senses are heightened. You feel everything more thoroughly than before." He kissed her cheek. It had happened too fast. He should have taken more time, made it last, drawn it out. It was over. Dammit, already it was over.

"You can say that again." She opened her eyes to stare up at him, the laughter vanishing from the amber. "Ask me why I would have chosen to live, Damien."

He swallowed hard, a small candle of hope igniting in his dark soul, just from the touch of the light in her eyes. He hated that glimmer. It would only make the impending disappointment harder to take. But he asked her. He grasped at the straw she dangled. "Why would you have chosen to live, Shannon?"

"Not just because I was afraid of death. Not for eternal life and health and youth. Not for all this strength and energy, or even for the chance to avenge Tawny's murder."

She paused, her head lifting until her lips hovered a hairbreadth from his. Her eyes shot amber sparks at him, and the candle inside him flared brighter. "But because I love you."

"Shannon..." He caught her head in his hands, kissed her, tasted her, dug into her mouth with his tongue.

"I'll never leave you, Damien. Gilgamesh. I'll be with you

for always. You will never have to walk alone again. And neither will I.''

He kissed her again, deeply, and the slow healing of his oldest, deepest wound began.

> ...it yearns and waits to be retouched
> By someone who can take away
> The memory of death...

*   *   *   *   *